Seasons
Under Heaven

Showers
In Seasons

BEVERLY LAHAYE
TERRI BLACKSTOCK

TWO BOOKS IN ONE

Seasons Under Heaven

Showers In Seasons

ZONDERVAN®

ZONDERVAN.com/
AUTHORTRACKER
follow your favorite authors

ZONDERVAN

Seasons Under Heaven / Showers in Season
Copyright © 2010 by Beverly LaHaye and Terri Blackstock

Seasons Under Heaven
Copyright © 1999 by Beverly LaHaye and Terri Blackstock

Showers in Season
Copyright © 2000 by Beverly LaHaye and Terri Blackstock

Requests for information should be addressed to:
Zondervan, *Grand Rapids, Michigan 49530*

ISBN 978-0-310-32976-3

Published in association with the literary agency of Alive Communications, Inc., 7680 Goddard Street, Suite 200, Colorado Springs, CO 80920. www.alivecommunications.com

Interior design: Melissa Elenbaas

Printed in the United States of America

10 11 12 13 14 15 16 • 20 19 18 17 16 15 14 13 12 11 10 9 8 7 6 5 4 3 2 1

Dedication

This book is dedicated to Annie M., Susan B., and Mary K., plus the many other women who have shared their "seasons of life" with me, wondering if they were alone in their struggles, disappointments, and heartaches. And also to my husband, who has helped me through my own "seasons of life."

Beverly LaHaye

This book is also dedicated to my husband and children, through whom the Lord has taught me some of my greatest lessons. And, as always, to the Nazarene.

Terri Blackstock

Acknowledgments

We would like to thank Dr. Fred Rushton for taking time out of his busy surgical schedule to read our manuscript and check our facts. We couldn't have done it without you. Thanks also to Jim Gleason, whose Internet account of his illness, *A Gift of the Heart*, gave us so much information. And special heartfelt thanks to the family of Susan Hattie Steinsapir, for sharing her poignant transplant story on the Internet. Susan didn't survive, but the story she left behind will help thousands.

We'd also like to thank Greg Johnson, Dave Lambert, Sue Brower, and Lori Walburg for their vision and active interest in this book. You're all a dream to work with!

Seasons Under Heaven

There is a time for everything,

and a season for every activity under heaven:

a time to be born and a time to die,

a time to plant and a time to uproot,

a time to kill and a time to heal,

a time to tear down and a time to build,

a time to weep and a time to laugh,

a time to mourn and a time to dance,

a time to scatter stones and a time to gather them,

a time to embrace and a time to refrain,

a time to search and a time to give up,

a time to keep and a time to throw away,

a time to tear and a time to mend,

a time to be silent and a time to speak,

a time to love and a time to hate,

a time for war and a time for peace.

ECCLESIASTES 3:1–8

CHAPTER *One*

Joseph Dodd was not one of those kids who feigned illness to get attention. His ten-year-old sister Rachel might have, since she was the one among the four children who leaned toward hypochondria. Leah, her twin, had been known to fake an occasional stomachache in the interest of competition. And Daniel, their twelve-year-old brother, often used a headache excuse to escape pre-algebra.

But not Joseph. Brenda, their mother, knew that the eight-going-on-nine-year-old was the kind of kid who harbored no deceit at all. His feelings and thoughts passed across his face like the Dow prices at the stock exchange, and Brenda could read them clearly.

That's why she knew something was wrong on the day before his ninth birthday. He'd gotten up with dark circles under his eyes, and his skin was as pale as the recycled paper on which they did their schoolwork. His red hair, which he took great pains to keep combed because he had three cowlicks, was disheveled, as if he hadn't given it a thought. On the way into the kitchen, he reached for the counter to steady himself and hung his head while he tried to catch his breath.

Brenda quickly abandoned the eggs she was scrambling and bent down to look into his eyes. "Joseph, what's the matter, honey?"

"I dunno," he said.

"Are you sick?" she asked, feeling his forehead.

"Sorta dizzy."

"It's his blood sugar," Daniel commented, before slurping his cereal. He wiped a drip from his chin. "Remember, I studied about the pancreas last week? The book said you could get dizzy if your pancreas didn't work right."

"What's a pancreas?" Joseph asked, frowning.

"Daniel, don't slurp," David, their father, said. "Brenda, what are you teaching him? Endocrinology?"

Brenda grinned. "More like he's teaching me. We're touching on anatomy in science. I got him some extra books."

"What's a pancreas?" Joseph asked again. He was still breathing hard and beginning to sweat.

David pushed aside his coffee, leaned across the table, and felt Joseph's forehead. "You okay, sport?"

Joseph didn't answer. He was still waiting for an answer to his question.

"The pancreas is a gland," Daniel mumbled around a mouthful of cereal. "It's near your kidney."

"Mom, Daniel's talking with his mouth full," Leah spouted.

"It is not near the kidney," Rachel said. "It's near the heart."

"How would you know? You aren't studying the human body."

"No, but I have one," Rachel said, tossing her nose up in the air as if that won the argument.

"I'm going to get my book," Daniel said. "I'll prove it to you."

"Sit back down, young man." Brenda turned back to the scrambled eggs and took the pan off the stove. She turned to the table—only a step from the stove in the small kitchen—and began scooping eggs onto their plates. Her blonde hair waved across her forehead, but she blew it back with her bottom lip. It was already getting hot in the house, and the sun hadn't even come all the way up. Despite the cost of electricity, she was going to have to lower the thermostat today or she'd never get the kids through their lessons.

She reached Joseph's plate and scooped out some eggs.

"I don't want any," Joseph said.

"Joseph, son, you've gotta eat," David said.

"I will later."

Brenda set the pan back on the stove and put her hands on her hips, gazing down at her son. "Rachel, will you go turn the thermostat down? Maybe if it gets cooler in here Joseph will feel better." As Rachel popped up to do as she was told, Brenda said, "I hope you're not getting sick again, Joseph."

"You can't be sick on your birthday," Leah said. "Mom, if he's sick, can we still have the party tomorrow?"

"Of course not. We'd just postpone it."

"But I don't want to postpone it," Joseph said, sitting straighter. "I'm fine. I changed my mind. I'll eat some eggs."

Brenda grinned and spooned some eggs onto his plate as she heard the air conditioner cut on. "He'll be fine. Probably just needs to eat something. Sometimes I wake up like that, Joseph. If I didn't eat much the night before, I get up and feel downright shaky until I eat."

"Blood sugar," Daniel observed.

"Of course, mostly I eat too much." She patted her slightly overweight hips. "Somehow my body can always convince me I'm starving." She ran her fingers through her hair and studied her youngest. "Joseph doesn't need to be worried about his pancreas, though. I'm sure it's working just fine. But I have to say, Daniel, that I'm bursting with pride over your interest in the pancreas. David, don't you think he's doctor material? I mean, he's practically ready for medical school."

David smiled and patted his oldest son on the back. "I think you're right. I've always said that Daniel had a sharp mind."

"Me, too, Daddy," Rachel said, coming back to the table.

"All of you. There's just no telling what you'll be," Brenda said. "I'm going to be one of those mothers who can't open her mouth without bragging about her important children. People will run when they see me." She fixed herself a plate and pulled out a chair. "Okay, now, before Daddy goes out to the shop, let's talk about this party. Nine years ago tomorrow, the doctor put that precious little bundle into my arms. Nine years, Joseph! Think of it! Bet it seems like a lifetime to you, huh?"

Joseph didn't answer. He propped his chin on his hand and moved the eggs around on his plate.

"It seems like nine long years to me," Daniel said.

David snickered under his breath, and Brenda shot him an amused look.

"I've already called all of our homeschooled friends," she told Joseph. "I told them to be here at two tomorrow. We'll have it outside. We need to start making the cake this afternoon. Joseph, do you want white cake, yellow, or chocolate? You need to consider this very carefully, since you'll be licking the bowl."

He didn't answer.

Brenda's eyes met David's across the table again. "Joseph?" David asked, taking the boy's hand.

He looked up. "Sir?"

"Your mother asked you something. What kind of cake do you want?"

"Um . . . rectangle, I guess."

"What *flavor*?" Daniel prompted. "Mom, he really is sick."

Brenda frowned. "Baby, do you want to go back to bed?"

He nodded and pushed his plate away, got up, and headed back to his bedroom.

"I'm taking him to the doctor," Brenda told David, getting up and heading for the phone. "Something's not right."

"Yeah, you better."

"Tell 'em about his pancreas," Daniel said. "They might not think of it."

David laughed and messed up his son's hair as Brenda dialed the number.

They waited at the doctor's office for an hour, only to have a five-minute examination. David, who was busy in his workshop behind the house when they got home, rushed out and met them in the driveway.

"How's my boy?"

Brenda got out of the car. "The doctor says it's probably a sinus infection. He just needs antibiotics."

"I can still have my party," Joseph piped in. "The doctor said."

"You sure you're up to it?" David asked.

"Yes, sir," Joseph said. "I'm just tired. I'll go to bed early."

"How about right now?" Brenda asked. "Why don't you take a nap while we do school?"

He didn't argue, which spoke volumes about his fatigue. He fell into bed and slept for four hours, while Brenda homeschooled his siblings.

David came in frequently to check on his son. "He's all right," he told his wife. "He's just been staying up too late."

"Yeah, maybe," Brenda said. "I think his color's back, don't you?"

David grinned. "Never had much to start with. The curse of the redhead."

Brenda hugged her red-haired husband and laid her head against his chest. "Poor little thing. He doesn't want to be sick on his birthday."

"He won't be. He's tough, ole Joseph. It'll take more than a sinus infection to get him down."

Brenda tried to push the worry out of her mind, but it had begun to take root. She only hoped the doctor's diagnosis was reliable.

CHAPTER

The next morning, in the house next door to the Dodds on the little cul-de-sac called Cedar Circle, Tory Sullivan struggled between tears and rage at the sight of the strawberry Kool-Aid congealing on her computer keyboard. A plastic cup lay on its side in a crimson puddle. Two soaked tissues in the center of the puddle, and one lying across the keys, testified of a half-hearted attempt to clean up the mess.

"Brittany!" she screamed, succumbing to the rage instead of the tears. "Spencer! Get in here!"

There was no answer, but of course, she had expected none. The children were probably hiding in their toy closet, trying to blend in with their stuffed animals, or hunkering under the bed until the crisis passed.

She ran to the kitchen, grabbed a roll of paper towels, and tried to blot the mess. But it had been there too long, and the quicker-picker-upper failed her.

The tears came, after all, as she looked at the monitor. Its blackness testified that someone had turned the computer off, as if hoping to make it disappear. What had undoubtedly disappeared, instead, was the four pages she had written but not saved to the hard drive because she had meant to come right back to it after her shower. Her heart plunged further, and her freshly applied mascara dripped with the tears down her cheek. Frantically, she sat down on the sticky chair, ignoring the Kool-Aid soaking into her white shorts, and turned the computer back on. An error message accused her of turning it off without properly exiting. She tried to repair the problem and boot it up, but the computer wouldn't respond to the commands she tried to enter using the sticky keyboard. Besides the damage to the keyboard, she knew that her precious four pages had been sucked into the vortex of her personal cyberspace, never to be seen again.

"Brittany! Spencer!" She bellowed the names with less fury and more despair now, and grabbed a paper towel to blot the tears running down her nose. She headed straight for the closet in the first room she came to: Spencer's room, with clouds and alphabet letters and Ninja Turtles painted on the walls. "You can run, but you can't hide!" she bit out. "Who spilled the Kool-Aid?"

There was no answer, and no sign of her children among the stuffed animal faces on the closet floor. She went to the bed and threw up the bed skirt. No children hid underneath.

She tore out of Spencer's room and headed into Brittany's. Her five-year-old daughter sat at her little table with wet eyes, frantically coloring a picture of a flower. "I made you a picture, Mommy," she said quickly. She resembled a Cabbage Patch Doll as she looked up at her mother with those big round eyes. She held out the masterpiece like a sin offering, but her bottom lip began to tremble. "Spencer did it. I don't even like Kool-Aid."

The red mustache at the upper corners of Brittany's mouth would have belied the child's declaration, if Tory hadn't already known better. Tory set her hands on her hips as the anger drained out of her, leaving only the tears. "Britty, my computer. How could you blame your brother?"

"He's always knockin' stuff over," Brittany said as a sob thickened her voice. Her red lips puckered out. "I told him not to touch the computer, but he wouldn't come away, and when I pulled him . . ."

The truth came out on a squeaky, high-pitched wail, and Tory knew it was genuine. She sighed heavily and stooped down in front of her daughter. "Britty, I've told you a million times that we don't take food or drinks into that room. Now the computer won't work . . ." Her voice broke off, and she wiped her wet cheek. "Where's your brother?"

"I don't know," Brittany cried. "I hope he ran away. I hope he never comes back."

"Brittany!" Tory scolded. "That's an awful thing to say. Now where is he hiding?"

"He's not hiding," Brittany said. "He doesn't even care. He went outside while you were doing your hair."

"Outside? Britty, why didn't you tell me?" She sprang to her feet and headed out the back door. "Spencer Sullivan!"

She saw him in the yard next door, hanging on the fence that corralled the Bryans' horses. "Spencer! Get back!" She lit out across the yard toward her child.

The four-year-old looked back at her, saw that he was in trouble, and ducked under the fence, as if that would render him invisible. One of the horses whinnied in disapproval, and the colt backed up, startled.

"Spencer! Get out of there!"

She reached the fence and ducked under it, grabbed her child, and quickly pulled him out. When they were out of harm's way, she set him down and stooped in front of him, holding him firmly by the shoulders. "Spencer Sullivan, if you keep defying me, you may not make it to eighteen years old, and it won't be because of the horses."

"Sorry."

"You're in big trouble," Brittany chanted, just arriving on the scene. "You're not allowed to come see the horses without Mommy or Daddy. Boy, are you gonna get it." Her brown ponytails swayed with her words.

The red Kool-Aid mustache on her daughter reminded Tory of the busted computer and the lost pages of her novel, and her tears returned. "You're both in trouble," she said, getting up and grabbing one hand of each child. "You're both going to get it."

A mockingbird in a chestnut tree between the two homes chided her as she pulled them back toward their house. She would have sworn it said, "Fail-ure, fail-ure, fail-ure." Her cat, hunkering under the back porch steps, took offense and launched across the lawn and up the tree trunk.

The bird flew away, leaving the cat stranded in futility. Spencer stopped and began pulling to get away. "Get him down, Mommy. Get him down!"

"He can get down," she said, trying to grab his hand again before he could make another escape. "Spencer!"

As if in response, the neighbor's dog Buster began to bark, and bounded around the house to the foot of the tree. The cat squalled and climbed higher, the dog barked and stood threateningly on its hind legs, and the kids began to scream. "He's goin' higher, Mommy! Get him down."

If it hadn't been for the fact that the blasted cat had been stuck up in that tree so many times before, and that Barry, Tory's husband, had had to climb the tree to get it down more than once, she could have ignored the crisis and made it to the house. But this one wasn't going to pass.

It was nearing noon, and the sun was straight up in the sky, too hot for late May in eastern Tennessee. The little town of Breezewood was named for its cool temperatures in the summer, but today the sun seemed to have forgotten that and beat down on them with further malice. Already, Tory's dark brown hair, which she'd spent too much time rolling and spraying, was beading with sweat and pasting itself to her forehead. Her kids, who'd been freshly bathed not an hour ago, were beginning to glisten. Spencer already smelled like one of the steel mills in town—that metallic dirt-and-sweat kind of odor that made you want to hose him down. She eyed the little inflatable pool in the yard and thought of stripping him down and dunking him in it. But that would seem too much like fun to him.

The dog's barks turned to howls, and the cat scrabbled higher up, still making that skin-crawling noise like a wounded person with laryngitis. She looked around for something, anything, to stop the commotion. The green hose lay curled like a snake ready to strike, and she let go of Brittany, grabbed the head of it, and turned it on full blast. Adjusting the nozzle to shoot in a hard, steady stream, she blasted the dog.

He danced away from the tree, distracted as he tried to nip at the water stream to get a good gulp. She turned the hose up to the top of the tree, where the cat still clung for dear life. It whopped him without much force, but frightened him enough to make him jump to a lower branch.

The children laughed and jumped up and down as the cat began to parry the water blows with one fighting paw. He leaped to another, lower bough.

The cat was low enough now to jump to the ground, so she tried to center the water right over his torso to make him take the plunge.

In his excitement, Spencer ran to the wet German shepherd and hugged it exuberantly. Tory's heart deflated further as she realized that now her son smelled like sweat, rust, and wet dog. And *she* wasn't smelling much better.

"He's down!" Brittany squealed, and took off across the wet grass to chase the soaked, angry cat.

"Britty, come back here! Now!"

"But I have to dry him off, Mommy! He hates to be wet."

"Brittany, I said *now!*"

Brittany stopped and gave her a hangdog look that would have wilted a weaker mother, but Tory ignored it. Instead, she turned her attention to prying her reeking son's arms from around the wet dog. "Inside, Spencer! Hit the tub. Do not pass go, do not collect two hundred dollars."

"Huh?"

"The tub, Spencer."

"Why? I already took a bath."

"You need another one."

"But I'm still clean."

"*Now*, Spencer. Brittany, *inside*."

"Do I have to take a bath, too?" Brittany asked. "I didn't do nothin' bad. Besides, Joseph's party is outside, so we'll just get stinky again."

"I don't want you going to the party stinky. I want you going clean, and getting stinky while you're there. Head for the tub."

"Can I take a bath in my bathing suit?" Spencer asked. "Britty can take it with me."

"Fine," she said. "Britty, yours is hanging over the washing machine."

"But we didn't have lunch yet. I'm hungry."

She realized the child was right. The telephone rang as Spencer agreed that he, too, was hungry. Rolling her eyes, she shoved them inside and headed for the phone. She didn't see the dirty pair of sneakers strategically placed between her and the phone. She tripped over them and caught herself on the table, then swung around and drop-kicked them as far as she could. "Get your shoes out of here, Spencer!" she shouted, then snatched up the phone. "Hello!"

"Hey, hon." It was Barry, her husband, and she imagined him sitting in his nice quiet office with his organized desk and his functioning computer and all his metalworks accomplishments photographed and displayed like trophies around him. "What's up?"

"Oh, nothing," she said, her chin stiffening. "My computer has drowned in congealed Kool-Aid, I just rescued Spencer from the Bryans' corral, then I got the cat down from the tree, and we're all about to take our second bath of the morning because we're soaked in sweat and Spencer smells like Buster the dog . . . and we haven't even had lunch yet." She forced a saccharine tone. "And how is your day, honey?"

"What do you mean the computer drowned? I told you to keep the kids out of there."

"I was in the bedroom for maybe five minutes, getting ready for Joseph's party."

"Joseph's party? It's not for hours."

"That's not the point, Barry! It won't type. The keyboard is dead. And all the work I did this morning—four pages during *Sesame Street*—is gone."

"Tory, that computer cost over a thousand dollars."

"Tell it to the kids." She glanced at the pantry, where the kids had gotten too quiet, and saw that they'd gotten into a ziplock bag of gummy worms. "Put those down and head for the tub. I'm not telling you again!"

"Thank goodness," she heard Spencer whisper, and Brittany giggled.

"Barry, tell me what to do about the computer. I have to save it."

"Call the company. Ask them what they advise."

"All right. As soon as things get quiet."

"And Tory, punish them. Don't let them go to Joseph's party today. They've been looking forward to it, so make them stay home. It'll teach them."

She heard the bath water running, and the cat began scratching at the back door to get in. "Barry, if I do that, *I* have to stay home. And I was looking forward to some adult companionship. Even if it is with a dozen kids around." She sighed and realized she sounded like a shrew. "Look, I'll try to save the computer. And I've got to go bathe the kids. Please don't be late this afternoon. I'll have turned gray and lost my sanity by then."

"Uh, well . . . that's kinda why I'm calling. I mean, not about your sanity. About me being late."

"No, Barry!" she whined, collapsing into a chair. "Please, not tonight. This is not turning out to be a good day."

"I can't help it. I have to work late."

"So what are we talking about? Seven o'clock? Eight?"

"Maybe eight-thirty. A big client wants to have dinner with some of us. It's a huge account, for some great stuff we bid on. I can't say no."

"Of course not." She felt a headache coming on. "Look, I've got to go. I wish I had time to chat, but you've probably got to skedaddle off to lunch, anyway. Tip the waiter nice for me, will you?"

"Tory, come on."

"Bye, Barry." She hung up the phone and headed back to the bathroom to see if her kids had drowned each other yet.

They were both in their bathing suits, sitting in four inches of cold water that didn't have a prayer of getting them clean, and playing battleship with some plastic sailboats they kept on the tub. Taking the opportunity, she went to the living room and sank down on the couch. Barry was probably nursing his wounds, she thought miserably. It wasn't his fault that he had a job he liked and got to eat in restaurants and talk to adults all day. He believed her staying at home was a terrific blessing, and she knew it should be.

But as long as she was here, there was no hope of her ever making anything of herself. No hope at all. What had happened to the Miss University of Tennessee who'd edited the literary magazine, wowed her professors with papers they'd claimed were publishable, and been chosen "Outstanding Senior English Major" because her professors believed she was the one most likely to publish? Whatever happened to the girl who'd been "Most Beautiful" *and* "Most Likely to Succeed," all in the same year?

If they could see her now, she thought morbidly. Instead of mopping in the money, she was mopping up spills. Instead of nursing celebrity, she was nursing earaches and skinned knees. Instead of winning awards, she was winning free hamburgers from the scrape-off cards at McDonald's.

It wasn't what she'd had in mind when she'd become a mother.

If only they were older. If only they could entertain themselves and tie their own shoes and fix their own sandwiches and clean up their own messes. If only she had two hours a day—even one hour would do—of uninterrupted time to pursue her own dreams, without someone undoing it all with the flick of a Kool-Aid-stained finger.

She sat there crying for a long time, until finally she knew that she had to feed her kids lunch or surrender the bag of gummy bears—resulting in a sugar high that would be sure to make the afternoon as challenging as the morning.

CHAPTER *Three*

Sylvia teetered atop the ladder in her living room and carefully removed the white bow from its place near the ceiling. She'd hung bows all around the room, one every three feet, and draped lace between them. Even from this height, she could still smell the sweet fragrance of the white roses and orchids that sat in huge pots around the room. It had made for a beautiful wedding reception for her daughter. But the biggest hit of the party hadn't been the lace and ribbons and roses but rather Sarah's childhood pictures that Sylvia had blown up, placed in gold gilded frames, and hung in an arrangement on one wall of her living room. Jeff, her son, was in many of the pictures as well. Across the room was a similar display of photographs Sylvia had gotten from the groom's mother. She had finished taking that display down earlier this morning, but it was more difficult removing the ones of her own children.

Not for the first time that morning, reality hit her, and the vast emptiness of the house after all the madness of the past few weeks caught up with her. The silence seemed to scream mocking cruelties into her ear about her empty nest and her outlived usefulness. Tears came to her eyes, and she sat down on one of the ladder rungs and tried to get hold of herself.

Longingly, her gaze swept over the photograph of Sarah as a little girl, her brother Jeff hovering over her. Had it been in second or third grade that Sarah had played the Statue of Liberty in the school play? That picture had caused a lot of laughter among their family and friends. The costume party—had that been for Jeff's sixth or seventh birthday? Had Jeff gone to college yet when they'd taken the youth group to the Alpine Sled in Chattanooga? Half of those kids had come to the wedding, and the stories they'd told . . .

"Are you taking those down?"

She jumped at the sound of her husband's voice, making the ladder teeter. Harry rushed forward and steadied it. "Harry! I didn't hear you come in." Her voice was cracked and choked with emotion, and when he looked up at her, she knew he saw the tears. Quickly, she wiped them away.

"This is dangerous, Sylvia," he said gently, indicating the ladder. "You shouldn't do this unless I'm home. Wait till later and I'll help you."

She sighed and came down. "I wanted to get it done. The sooner the better."

"Why don't you rest? The wedding took a lot out of you. You deserve to do nothing today. You remember how, don't you? Think way back to before we had kids."

"I can't remember that far back," she whispered, looking up at those pictures again.

He gave her a tender look, then moved behind her and set his hands on her shoulders. Kissing her hair, he said, "You know, you don't have to take them down at all."

"They're not right there," she said. "I'll spread them out around the house. I'll have to patch the holes in the wall, you know, and repaint. There's so much to do." Again, those tears came, constricting her throat.

Harry turned her around and made her look up at him. Though his hair was more gray than black, his face had retained its youthful look, and his eyes still twinkled with mischief. The very sight and feel of him reminded her that she was not completely alone today, that her life's companion was still here, and that he would not forsake her. "Your children haven't fired you, you know," he said. "You're still their mother."

"I don't know how to be a long-distance mother," she said. "Why did we let them move to other states? They're both so far away. Before we know it, they'll have kids of their own, and we'll be long-distance grandparents who see them once or twice a year. The grandkids will have to be reminded who we are."

"Fat chance," Harry said. "Honey, when Sarah gets back from her honeymoon, she'll be calling you every day to find out how to make meat loaf and pumpkin pie, and to cry when she's homesick or mad at Larry, or just to talk because she misses you. Mark my word. You might just be the one who's not available."

Sylvia wiped her face again. "What do you mean?"

He started to say something, then seemed to think better of it. "Listen, I had a cancellation for my first patient after lunch, so that's why I came home. I was hoping to take you to lunch somewhere nice. When's the last time we went out? I thought maybe that little South American restaurant over on Hilliard Street. We could talk—"

"Harry, I don't want to go out. Look at me. I'm a mess. Could I take a rain check?"

"A mess? You're beautiful. Slim and young-looking. I heard at least three people at the wedding asking if you were Sarah's sister."

She couldn't help being amused. "Don't lie."

"Well, okay, just one. But it happened. Scout's honor."

"I'm fifty years old and I feel sixty-five. Forced into mandatory retirement. Totally obsolete."

Harry's grin faded and he frowned down at her. "You really are depressed, aren't you?"

"And you aren't?"

He slid his hands into his pockets and looked down at his feet. He was thinking, trying to answer honestly, she knew. Harry wasn't one to just tell her what she wanted to hear.

"The other night," he said seriously, "after Sarah and Larry drove off, and the guests started going home, I went in the bathroom and cried. It was tough. My baby, Daddy's little girl, riding off into the sunset with some guy who's going to take care of her for the rest of her life." His eyes misted up even now as he recalled those emotions.

Sylvia smiled softly. "I should have known. And there I was flitting around, laughing and smiling for the guests, ignoring you completely."

"I wanted to be ignored when I felt like that," he said. "But it passed. This morning, I started thinking differently. I started thinking of this time of our lives as a beginning instead of an ending. We can do whatever we want now. All these years, when we've wanted to do things, but couldn't because we had the kids to think of—well, now we can go anywhere, do anything, and it's just the two of us. No more excuses. No more reasons to stay in the same old place. I started getting excited, Sylvia."

Sylvia looked up at him, frowning, wondering where he was going with this. "So where is it you want to go? What is it you want to do?"

Again, he looked down at his feet, searching for honest words, and she realized this midday homecoming wasn't just a whim. He had something specific to say. She tried to brace herself. "Harry?"

"You sure you don't want to go eat?" he asked her. "Even just a burger? We could eat in the car, even."

She sighed. "This must be really big if you have to say it over food."

"I'm just hungry. It's really nothing. In fact, we can talk about it another time."

"Let me run a brush through my hair, and we can go," she said.

Harry grinned, and she knew it was what he'd really wanted. She went into the bathroom, brushed her just-permed hair, and applied some lipstick so she wouldn't look so pale. She powdered the redness over her nose and decided her eyes were hopeless. It was just as well that Harry wanted to go out, she decided. She did need a diversion today.

She followed him out to the Explorer and waited while he unlocked it for her. She looked around at the little houses on the cul-de-sac where they'd lived for so long. Near the neck of the little circle, she saw three of Brenda's kids helping their dad drag picnic tables into the empty lot between their house and the Sullivans. Today was Joseph's birthday, she remembered. They had invited her to the party, but she'd almost forgotten.

She remembered when her own were little, before the cul-de-sac called Cedar Circle had been developed around them. Their own house had been built on a huge, twenty-acre plot at the top of Survey Mountain. It had been much smaller then, until Harry's surgical practice had gotten off the ground. Almost yearly, they had added something to their house.

When she and Harry had made the decision to sell some of the land to a builder to develop into a cul-de-sac, they had done it for the kids. The children needed playmates, she'd told Harry, and he agreed. The developer had plotted out Cedar Circle, paved the streets, and three houses had gone up with wisteria and jasmine-covered picket fences, oaks, and elm trees. None of the homes was quite as large as the Bryans', and none had the stretch of land in the back that the Bryans had kept for their horses. But the neighbors had become close friends, and their children had always had playmates.

But all those children had grown up, and their families, one by one, had moved away. Now the cul-de-sac was populated with younger mothers with active children who only reminded her how she longed for the former days.

"Are you planning to get in, or just stand here all day gazing down Memory Lane?" Harry teased.

She looked up at him. "Sorry. I was just remembering the way it looked before those houses . . ." She got in, and he closed the door behind her, then slipped in on the other side. "I'm sorry, Harry," she said. "It's one of those days when you can't seem to keep your thoughts going in the right direction. It's the classic, textbook case of empty-nest syndrome. I read all about it when they went off to college. But they were close by, and I knew they'd be back for meals and laundry . . ."

"Yeah, this is different. This time they're really gone."

"I need a hobby," she said. "A project. Maybe that would get my mind off of it."

"Well," he said, drawing the word out a little too long, and hooking her attention. "Maybe I have the answer. I'll tell you while we eat."

A few minutes later he pulled into a Burger King, and they both went in and ordered food that was a cardiac surgeon's nightmare. When they'd found a table in the corner, Sylvia brought the subject up again. "Okay, Harry. Shoot. What's your project?"

He gazed out the window. "I'm torn. I don't know whether I should tell you while you're depressed because it might make you more depressed, or whether it'll be just the thing you need to shake you out of it."

"Well, you'll never know until you try." She took a bite of her hamburger.

"You know how we've always said that someday when the kids are grown, we'd go to the mission field?"

"Sure. Do you want to take some extra medical mission trips to Nicaragua this year?"

"No, not mission trips. Longer term."

She set her hamburger down and dabbed at her mouth with the napkin, keeping her eyes fixed on him. "You can't be serious."

He looked like a schoolboy trying to convince his mother to buy him a sports car. "Haven't we always said that, Sylvia? Even these last few years, every time we went on those little trips, we've talked about how great it would be if we were unencumbered and could just go and take the miracles of modern medicine to those people who can't afford it?"

She couldn't deny that they'd talked about it many times. She had agreed that it would be wonderful to be an ambassador of grace, to make sacrifices, to give of herself to people who needed what she could bring them. But what was that, exactly? Harry could take them medicine—she was mostly just there for support.

"It's a great ministry, Sylvia. I've felt called to do it most of my life, but I also felt responsible to give the kids a normal life. But now the kids are gone, and it's time for me to stop making excuses."

She looked in his eyes and saw the joy building there like a cresting tide. The emotions in her own heart felt like those same waves crashing against a bleak and rocky shore.

"Sylvia, just think about how much good we could do there."

"*You* could do so much good there," she said, that tightness returning to her voice. "But what could *I* do?"

"What could *you* do? You're the Doña. The one they all respected."

"I'd be useless there, Harry. Even in our own home, I wouldn't have a purpose. Every home there has a maidservant to clean. What would I do all day?"

"You could start a ministry with the mothers and children, Sylvia. Teach parenting skills, Bible studies, evangelism. You'd be such an example to them. A mother figure for them to look up to."

Tears erupted in her eyes again, and she shook her head. "I'm not prepared to be a mother to anybody but my own kids, Harry, and they're gone."

"They're not gone. You talk like they're dead. They're still alive, honey, they're just proving that we succeeded. They're happy and healthy and building lives of their own."

She shook her head and looked down at the burger. She couldn't eat another bite. Her stomach wouldn't accept it. "I'm not ready, Harry," she said through tight lips. "Not yet. Maybe next year, or the year after that. The kids still might need me, and I can't be out of the country."

He reached across the table and took her hand. "Honey, the kids will always need you. But God may want us somewhere else."

She couldn't believe this was so important to him. Had he been biding his time, chomping at the bit throughout the whole wedding process, counting the days until Sarah was gone, so he could fly off to Managua?

"Are . . . are you finished? Eating, I mean?"

He looked down at the half-eaten burger. "Yeah, I guess. Honey, this is upsetting you. I'm sorry. I should have waited until a better time, but I thought it might cheer you up. You said you wanted a project."

"Can we go home?" She was making a valiant effort to fight the tears, but she was losing.

"Sure."

She slid out of the booth and threw their wrappers away, then headed through the door. The drive home was quiet.

When they pulled back into the driveway, she got out and dashed inside.

Harry was behind her in an instant. "Honey, listen," he said, wrapping his arms around her, "I can see how upset this has made you. The timing is all wrong. Just forget I ever said anything."

But that wouldn't be right either, she knew. Harry rarely asked for anything for himself. For years, he'd been catering to his family's wants and needs. This once, he had some of his own. But they were just too hard for her to accept.

She looked around her. Over the years, she'd decorated their home exactly as she'd wanted it. It was a showplace—and it bore the sentimental, beloved scars of a family that had grown up here. The growth chart on the pantry wall, the mural they'd painted in Sarah's room, the little stained glass windows the kids had made one summer.

"What would we do with the house?" she asked on a whisper.

He seemed reluctant to answer. "I don't know. Whatever you want. I was thinking we could sell it."

"*Sell* it?" The words flipped out of her mouth with such disgust that he might have suggested setting it on fire. "Harry!"

His expression fell further. She was the archer shooting her arrow straight into his dreams. She hated playing that role. She tried to breathe in some courage and took his hands, strong surgeon's hands that saved lives with such skill . . . but there were many such hands here in the states, and so few overseas. Maybe these hands were meant to be used in Nicaragua.

She dropped them again. "You've got to understand, Harry, that this is a little sudden. Maybe you've been thinking about it for a long time. But I haven't."

"You're right." He found his smile again, and she saw that his twinkle was still there. "It's just that I've been thinking about it a lot over the last few days. I miss the kids just like you do, but I keep seeing it as a new beginning, not an end. I keep thinking that God has a purpose for us, that all the training and skill He's given me here could be used to take the gospel across the world, and take medicine to people who can't get it otherwise. Sylvia, I've never felt as needed as I felt when we were in Masaya last year. Remember all the people we led to Christ? Remember Carlos, the playboy with a string of mistresses? We were able to lead his wife to Christ for a very important reason: she trusted us after I did the appendectomy on their son. And then Carlos came to church with her, and his life changed—"

"There are lost people *here*, Harry. Some right in this cul-de-sac. Why do we have to go across the world?"

"Because someone has to."

With both hands, she wiped the tears forming under her eyes and tried to think logically. "Let me think about it, okay, Harry? Do we have to make a decision right away?"

"Of course not. Take all the time you need."

"Are you sure?" she asked. "I don't want to destroy your dreams."

"God wouldn't give this kind of calling to just one of us. If He's calling me, He'll call you, too."

She looked at him for a long moment, her eyes filling with tears again. "Is it your practice?" she asked. "Are you just bored with it?"

Again, he stared down at his shoes, thinking. "I could use a change," he said, meeting her eyes again. "But that's not all this is about." He opened his arms and pulled her again into a hug, held her there for a long moment as her tears soaked into his shirt. "It's not the end, honey. You'll see."

"I know," she said in a high-pitched voice. "I really do know that. I just don't feel like I have a lot to contribute, either here or there. It seems kind of pointless to me."

"Then I'll pray that God will reveal to you how important you are."

She laid her head against his chest. He was her best friend, her lover, her confidante, her provider and supporter. He'd always been so strong, so masterful. He'd also often been right.

But right or wrong, she was thankful he wasn't asking for a decision now.

After a few moments, he let her go and ate a dessert of petit fours left over from the reception. She sat with him, eating chocolate groom's cake. She supposed a few extra pounds on her hips wouldn't make much difference. Wasn't food always supposed to make you feel better?

But she didn't feel particularly well as she walked him back out to his Explorer. She leaned in and kissed him when he was in the car. She heard a "hello" shouted from the driveway next door, and she waved at Cathy Flaherty, her neighbor on the other side.

"Why don't you go visit with Cathy?" Harry asked. "She always cheers you up."

"I've got those pictures to take down, and all that misery to wallow in," she said with a smirk. "I wouldn't be very good company."

He kissed her and pulled out of the driveway. Sylvia tried to smile until he was out of the cul-de-sac, but it quickly faded. Her gaze drifted up to the hills in the distance. The mist that normally floated like angelic breath above them had been chased away by the bright sun. Everything looked so clear.

She only wished she could see her own future that clearly.

CHAPTER *Four*

Cathy Flaherty intercepted her German shepherd as he bounded from the Bryans' house. He was damp, she discovered as she bent down to pet him, and he smelled like a stray mutt. She wondered where he'd been. She slammed the door of her pickup truck and looked back at the Bryans again. She saw Harry kiss Sylvia before pulling out of the driveway. What a day it must be for them, she thought, to finally have all the kids married off and find that your marriage was still strong.

She went into the house, fighting jealousy. She wasn't naive enough to think marriage was always bliss. Heaven knew hers hadn't been. But some part of her—the largest part—wanted one more shot. It wasn't easy being a single mother of three kids from eleven to seventeen. She'd spent a lot of the past couple of years looking for a husband for herself in an attempt to start over. She had never expected to be forty and single, nor had she ever intended to raise her kids alone. That had been decided for her.

She went into the house, breathing in the silence as if it were a balm that could heal a troubled soul. Though her veterinary practice kept her busy, she tried to come home for lunch every day while the kids were at school, just to regroup and do the housekeeping chores she hadn't had time to do that morning. Soon the kids would be out of school for the summer, though, and the whole dynamic of her days would change.

She opened a can of soup and poured it into a bowl, stuck it in the microwave, punched out three minutes. While it was cooking, she went into the laundry room and began pulling blue jeans—the most common and indispensable item in the entire family's wardrobe—out of the mountain of laundry to wash. Even Cathy preferred jeans over anything else. She shoved pair after pair into the washing machine, emptying pockets of change and gum wrappers and breath mints. She tossed the garbage and kept the change. That was the deal, she'd told them. If they were careless enough to leave money in their pockets when she washed, she got to keep it. She saved it in a dill pickle jar and took them all out to eat when enough had been saved.

She stuffed six pairs into the machine, decided the load could take one more, and grabbed up a pair of Rick's long, lanky jeans. Two quarters fell out, and by rote, she reached into the pockets and grabbed hold of the rest of the contents. Her fingers came upon a small square. She pulled it out . . .

And her heart crashed.

It was a condom, in the pocket of her seventeen-year-old son.

She dropped it as if it had burned her. Her son hardly even dated. When would he have time enough to get into a relationship that would require a condom? Feeling sick, she backed to the wall, slid down it, and sat on the floor, hugging her knees. It couldn't be. Not her boy.

Slowly, her mind worked past the shock and began to evaluate options. Maybe she should go to the school, snatch him out of class, confront him face-to-face, and demand an explanation. But would that be overreacting? Shouldn't she be happy that her son was interested in safe sex?

No! her heart screamed. She didn't want Rick to be engaging in sex of any kind. Despite her liberal leanings, she hated the idea of her own children becoming sexually active.

The microwave beeped, and she got to her feet. As the shock gave way, rage seeped in to fill the void. Where had he gotten it? With whom was he planning to use it? Did his father know about this? Was it *his* idea?

Yes. Her thoughts seemed to crystallize as it all became clear. He'd been with his father this past weekend. It was just like Jerry to do something stupid like giving his son a condom. The man probably assumed that Rick had the same loose morals he had, and he wanted to protect him from any "mistakes." The microwave beeped again, and as if it had been the one to corrupt her son, she threw it open, grabbed the glass bowl of soup, and pulled it out. It sloshed over the side and burned her hand, so she flung it into the sink, breaking the bowl. That was all right; she didn't want to eat it anyway. She wasn't hungry anymore.

Instead, she jerked up the phone and punched out her ex-husband's work number in Knoxville. "Jerry Flaherty," he said innocently.

"What do you think you're doing?" she demanded.

"Cathy?" He seemed genuinely confused.

"Yeah, it's me. Who else can you get into a frothing rage without even being present?"

"What, pray tell, have I done now?"

"Did you or did you not give our son a condom?"

"A *what?* No, I didn't give him a condom!"

"Then who did? Could it have been Sandra?"

"No! My wife did not give Rick a condom. That's ludicrous. How could you even think that?"

"Oh, well, excuse me," she said sardonically. "But your past moral slipups tend to keep me from being too surprised at anything you do. Did you *talk* to him about condoms?"

"No. It never came up."

"Is there someone there that he's seeing?"

"No. Annie's the one we can't keep home. She's got that friend, Joni, who has a car, and who knows what they do or what boys they meet when they leave here?"

Newer, hotter rage flared up inside her like a Fourth of July display, and she forced herself to sit down on the stool at the breakfast bar. "Has it *ever* occurred to you to tell her she can't go?"

"For what reason? We haven't caught her at anything yet."

"Do you *know* where she goes?"

"Movies, Burger King, Blockbuster, that kind of thing. Come on, Cathy, calm down. It's not like we let her stay out all night. She's home by curfew."

"Then why did you just say she's probably meeting boys?"

"Because she's a girl. That's what they do."

"Have you checked up on her to make sure she's where she says? Do you know anything about this girl Joni? Have you met her parents?"

"No, Cathy. I have these kids every other weekend. I'm not intimately acquainted with the parents of their friends, and I don't see why that would be necessary. I just brought that up to say that Rick is not the one I'd worry about, if I worried about any of them. Now what's this about a condom?"

She let out a deflated breath and stared at the counter for a moment. "I found it in his pocket. If he doesn't have a girlfriend there, and he doesn't have one here, why did he have a condom?"

"Got me. Maybe he's just saving it for a rainy day."

The flippancy of his remark seared her. "You act like this is no big deal, Jerry. This is your son!"

"My son is seventeen, Cathy. Eventually, he is going to get involved with a girl, and frankly, if you want to know my opinion, I don't think a condom is a bad idea. He probably ought to keep one with him."

She ground her teeth together. "Spoken like the Father of the Year. I don't know why you still amaze me, Jerry."

"Cathy, relax. They're growing up. You can't stop them. Even Mark's going through puberty. Twelve years old, and his voice is starting to change."

"I'm not trying to stunt their growth," Cathy bit out. "I'm trying to raise them right."

"Maybe raising them right means getting them to adulthood without pregnancy or disease. Maybe that's the best we can hope for."

The words filtered through her like scorching water, and she dropped the phone from her ear and stared at it as if she could see her ex-husband through the little holes in the mouthpiece. Why was she even talking to him? He had the morals of a canine.

No longer enraged, she dropped the phone back on its hook on her wall, cutting off the connection. It was like the stages of grief. She had moved quickly from shock, to anger, and now into depression. All she could do was wait for the kids to get home, so she could find out where Rick had gotten the condom. She had exactly two hours to come up with a plan of action. Should she yell, lecture, punish? Or was it possible that she would be struck with a burst of wisdom on how to turn this from a crisis into a wonderful learning experience that the kids would always hold dear?

Fat chance.

It occurred to her to call the clinic and tell her receptionist to close the office for the afternoon, but she knew she had two litters of puppies coming in to be dewormed. She could put them off, she supposed, but she couldn't really afford to turn the work away. Knocking off at four every day and refusing to work Saturday afternoons left her few enough office hours as it was. No, she needed to get back.

She went back to the laundry room, started the load of jeans, and slid the condom into her own pocket. Then, trying to ignore the dismal thoughts flitting through her mind, she went back out to the pickup. Across the street, her neighbor Brenda stood in a huddle with her four kids, all with different shades of red hair. They were up to something, but that wasn't unusual. Brenda, who homeschooled her children, had the most creative mind Cathy knew when it came to stimulating them. She was probably doing some sort of nature hunt or demonstrating the food chain by collecting bugs in the yard, imparting some type of life lesson that they'd never forget.

Suddenly, Cathy felt like a terrible mother who didn't deserve the children who'd been entrusted to her.

As she backed out of the driveway, she saw David, Brenda's husband, dragging picnic tables to the lot between the houses. He was always there, an active partner in raising the children, making a living as a cabinetmaker from the workshop in the backyard. With his wavy red hair and his slight paunch, he had never been the catch of Breezewood. But given the chance, Cathy would have traded every material possession she had to have one just like him. She gave him a cursory wave, swallowing her swelling anger at her ex-husband. She deserved better than to be raising three children alone. More importantly, *they* deserved better.

CHAPTER *Five*

"*Come* on, hurry up, let's go. We've got to get the decorations up before the party." Brenda Dodd's tone was more grand marshal than drill sergeant as she looked around at the empty lot between her house and Tory's house next door. David had moved the two picnic tables he'd built to the center of the lot for Joseph's birthday party.

Though Joseph had sprung out of bed that morning and declared that he was well, he still looked weak. "But we don't have any crepe paper," he pointed out. "What are we gonna put up?"

Brenda grinned and lifted her eyebrows. "Did you grab a roll of toilet paper like I told you?"

"Yes, but I don't see why the kids can't just go in the house if they have to go to the bathroom," Daniel said.

Brenda laughed. "The toilet paper's for decoration, Kemo Sabe."

All four children looked down at the rolls of toilet paper in their hands, expressions of complete bewilderment on their faces. "We're decorating with *toilet paper?*" the birthday boy asked, his flaming red hair making him look even paler in the harsh sunlight.

"Isn't there some rule against that in Amy Vanderbilt?" Leah had found a thirty-year-old copy of Amy Vanderbilt's *Book of Etiquette* at a used book sale, and read it like a novel when she wasn't doing schoolwork. "I mean, I never saw it in the book anywhere, but it just seems kind of rude, don't you think?"

"Trust me," Brenda said. "Observe." Like a scientist attempting to demonstrate a life-changing experiment, she unrolled two yards of toilet paper from her own roll. "Follow me, troops. I'm about to show you how to do the most fabulous party decoration known to man, and all for the price of a six-pack of toilet paper."

The children all followed, doubtful.

Brenda laughed at the looks on their faces as she reached the center of the empty lot. "Oh ye of little faith." She looked up at the canopy of huge oaks and elms throughout the yard. Rearing back, she threw her toilet paper roll into the branches overhead. The paper caught on a limb, and the roll fell to the ground, unrolling a stream of paper behind it.

"Cool!" Daniel shouted. "Mom's letting us roll our own yard!"

The confused looks turned to expressions of sheer delight as the children joined in the act, squealing and laughing and flinging their rolls. When Brenda's naked cardboard roll fell to the ground, she stood back, watching her kids send long swoops of white toilet paper draping through the trees like crepe paper purposely placed.

"Brenda! For Pete's sake, what are you doing?" David called, leaning out the window of the workshop behind the house. "What have you taught them?"

"How to decorate on a shoestring, David," she called with glee. "Come help us."

He came out in a moment and stood there with his hands at his sides, a worried grin on his face. "How are we gonna get this stuff down?"

"Don't worry. It'll come down. We'll just pull it all off after the party."

"What if it rains?"

"It wouldn't dare."

The look on his face was so comical that she had to laugh out loud. "You up for blowing up balloons? We couldn't afford the helium kind, so I figured we'd just all blow until we ran out of air."

"Mama, can we have more toilet paper?" Rachel asked. "I ran out of mine."

"That's enough," Brenda said. "Look at it. Isn't it beautiful? Now, come help with the balloons. We're going to blow them up, tie them in bunches, and set them on top of the birdhouses."

Her children's faces testified that they had caught their mother's vision. She could have suggested that they grab some shovels and dig a ditch, and they would have been convinced they were having fun. They worked on the balloons until they'd blown up half of them, but it was getting hot, and she realized that by the time the party began, they would be nearing melt-down. Joseph was looking particularly peaked. He was pale, per-spiring, and breathing hard. "David, why don't you hook up the sprinkler in the backyard while we blow up the balloons?" she suggested. "That'll be one of the activities at the party. They can run through the sprinkler when they get hot."

"Good idea," David said. He was sweating himself, and his red hair had separated into wavy wet strands.

"But they'll be soaked," Leah said. "Whoever heard of going to a birthday party soaking wet?"

"Ms. Vanderbilt would have loved it," Brenda assured her as David headed to the backyard. "Come on, now. Get some more balloons and start blowing."

She watched the kids huff and puff. But when she noticed that Joseph, too, was only watching, she tousled his damp hair and said, "Joseph, are you feeling okay?"

"Yes, ma'am," he said. "I'm just hot."

"Wanna go sit in the air-conditioning for a minute? Get a drink?"

"No, ma'am, I'll just stand in the sprinkler to cool off."

"You're the birthday boy. Have at it."

She would have expected him to run at the rare treat, but instead he only walked around to the back of the house. "Joseph," she called after him, "remind Daddy to make sure the water doesn't reach the toilet paper."

"I will."

They finished blowing up balloons, and by the time two o'clock came, the yard looked festive and inviting. Two cars pulled up at the same time, and out spilled eight delighted homeschooled youngsters. Brenda sent the parents on their way for some rare time alone, assuring them that there would be plenty of supervision. She saw the front door of the Sullivan house open, and Tory came out with Spencer and Brittany.

Spencer took one look at the toilet paper draping the trees and sprinted away from his mother. Brittany began to jump into the air like a pogo toy. "Look, Mommy! Look!"

Tory, dressed in a pale blue shorts set that enhanced the color of her eyes, looked like a model about to do a photo shoot. Brenda wondered why she bothered to fix her hair and makeup when she would probably sweat it all off. Tory gave her a what-have-you-done-now grin as she reached the crowd. "Brenda . . ."

"It'll come down, I promise," Brenda said, raising her right hand in a mock vow. "The kids love it." She knew Tory didn't consider that a good enough reason to risk a potential mess in both their yards, but it was the best she could do.

Spencer and Brittany flung their presents to the center of the table, where the other gifts were piled. "Open mine first, okay, Joseph?" Spencer demanded. "Open it now!"

Joseph, who was cooler now that he was soaking wet, shook his head. "I can't, Spence. It's not time yet."

"Aw, man," Spencer said, then immediately switched gears. "How come you're wet?"

"There's a sprinkler going in the back. You can play in it if you want."

Spencer didn't wait to hear more. He leaped down from the picnic table and tore around to the back of the house.

"Spencer, no!" Tory shouted. "I've bathed him twice today, and he's on his third outfit."

"It'll dry," Brenda laughed. "Come on, Tory. It's part of the activities. David's back there supervising."

"Well, we could run back home and put on bathing suits . . ."

"Nooo!" Spencer protested. "It's more fun in clothes!"

Tory sighed and seemed to resign herself to a fourth outfit.

Brittany almost had a conniption fit. "Me, too, Mommy? Can I get wet, too?"

Brenda knew that Tory didn't see the appeal of "getting wet"—to her it represented another mess—but finally, she surrendered her second child to the water. As if to force her own mind off wet children, Tory looked around at the other kids. "These kids are all different ages. Aren't any of them in school?"

"They're all homeschooled," Brenda said. "We go on field trips together and stuff. I thought they'd enjoy a party. I sent their mothers away—they could use a break."

"Mama doesn't make us do school on birthdays," Joseph said, putting a balloon to his mouth to blow up. The balloon inflated slightly, and his face began to redden as he tried harder to blow it up.

"Here, I'll help," Tory said, taking one. She blew it up quickly, tied it in a knot, and handed it to Rachel, who was waiting with ribbon to tie around it.

Joseph was still working on his. Finally, he gave up and let the balloon go. It twirled in the air and collapsed on the table.

Brenda stopped what she was doing and gazed down at him. "You couldn't blow it up, honey?"

"I don't want to," he said.

"You want to run through the sprinkler again?" She pushed his wet hair back from his face and touched his forehead. It wasn't feverish. "Go ahead. It might pep you up a little."

"Yeah, maybe." He got up from the bench as if to do just that, but stopped and steadied himself.

Brenda bent over to meet his eyes. "Joseph?"

He didn't answer right away, just stared blindly into space, wobbled slightly, then went limp and hit the ground.

"Joseph!" Brenda fell to her knees beside her unconscious son. "Tory, go get David!"

But David was there before Tory could move. "What's wrong?"

"He passed out! Get me a cold rag or something."

Daniel, who was soaked from the sprinkler and had run up behind his father, pulled his wet T-shirt off and thrust it at his mother. She was shaking as she began to stroke Joseph's face with it. "Honey, wake up. Joseph?"

His eyes slowly opened and rested blankly on her.

"He's awake," Brenda cried. "David, we've got to get him to the doctor."

"But the party!" Leah cried. "We can't leave all the guests. Their mothers aren't here!"

Tory looked helplessly at David and Brenda. "Look, you two take him on. I'll take care of things here."

"He's okay, aren't you, sweetie?" Brenda asked, trying to calm her voice to keep from frightening Joseph. "I can take him by myself. David, you can stay and have the party. Just save Joseph some cake and all his presents. There's no need for everybody to go home, is there?"

"Okay," he said, and Brenda knew that he too was trying to keep the concern out of his voice. "Joseph'll be fine, and all this loot'll be here when you get back. Leah, go get him a change of clothes so Mama can get him out of the wet ones when they get there."

Already, she had Joseph on his feet and was walking him toward the car. She fumbled with the door, and David came to her aid. "David, I'll call you when we see the doctor, okay? Just have fun. Joseph is fine." How many times had they said that? she wondered. And were they saying it for the sake of the kids— or themselves?

David helped Joseph into the car as the children, some wet from the sprinkler and some from sweat, crowded around. Leah cut through them and handed Brenda her purse and a change of clothes for Joseph. As the car pulled out, Joseph looked sadly out the window.

"Well," Brenda said cheerfully as they left the cul-de-sac. "This will be a party to remember, won't it? For years, we'll say, 'Remember Joseph's ninth birthday when he passed out cold?'"

Joseph was still gazing out the window. "Toilet paper is better than crepe paper, isn't it?" he asked quietly. "Prettier, too. It was fun even before the people got there."

Brenda tried to blink back the tears in her eyes as she sped to the doctor's office.

CHAPTER *Six*

The pediatrician's office was packed to capacity with sick children and babies waiting for their monthly checkups. As they waited to be worked in, Brenda could only imagine the disappointment that Joseph must feel at having to miss the birthday party he'd spent weeks talking about. Her own heart was deflated, and she couldn't put aside the fright she'd experienced watching her child pass out before her eyes.

Maybe it *was* his blood sugar, as Daniel had suggested. Maybe the cinnamon rolls she'd made for breakfast had been a mistake, but she'd wanted to make something special for his birthday. Maybe he still wasn't a hundred percent after his virus a few weeks ago. Maybe it was just too hot for him.

As badly as she wanted to believe these simple and nonthreatening explanations, her heart found no comfort in them. Something was wrong with Joseph. Something was terribly wrong.

He laid his head back in the chair, his little body almost limp. His face still lacked color, and his hair was mussed from drying without being combed first.

She racked her brain trying to think of something to help him pass the time. She had promised him no school today, so she didn't want to practice his multiplication tables or drill him on his spelling words. No, she would keep her word. Today would only be for fun. Even if they did have to have it in a doctor's office.

She reached into her big purse that carried all sorts of child-occupying paraphernalia and pulled out a miniature legal pad. She got a green marker from the ziplock bag of markers and crayons in the bottom of her purse. Joseph looked as if he expected her to hand it to him, but instead she dropped the bag back into her purse and began to draw with the green marker.

"Whatcha drawing?" he asked.

"Never you mind. Just wait."

"Is it for me?"

She grinned and covered her paper so he couldn't see. "Just a minute. You'll see."

She finished drawing, then tore out the page and brandished it.

"What is it?" he asked.

She wrote a one and then six zeros in the center of the page. "It's a million dollar bill," she said proudly.

"A million dollar bill?" he asked. "They make those?"

"I wouldn't know," she said. "But I was just thinking a kid like you on his ninth birthday probably deserves nothing less than a million dollar bill. So I wanted you to have it." She handed it to him.

He grinned. "Gee, thanks, Mama."

"And now you have to spend it."

He looked skeptically up at her. "Spend it? How?"

She reached back in her purse for a pen, and handed him the legal pad. "You have to write down everything you'd spend your million dollars to buy, and you have to spend every cent."

His smile turned to a suspicious frown. "Are you tricking me into doing math?"

It would have been a good trick, but she'd had no such intentions. "No, it's just a game."

His eyebrows arched as his grin crept back.

"Let's just see if you can. A million dollars is a lot of money, you know."

He smiled down at the bill, as though he couldn't believe his good fortune. "Okay."

"What's the first thing you would buy?"

He leaned his head back on the chair and closed his eyes for a moment, thinking. When he opened them, she saw the twinkle there. The excitement. Already he was feeling better. "I know," he said. "A truckload of toilet paper so we could roll everybody's yard in our whole neighborhood, and up and down the streets, all the way down the mountain."

She gave him a disgusted look. "You've got a million bucks and you'd use it to buy toilet paper?"

"Well, it was fun."

"Okay, then. Write it down."

"How much is that?"

"Depends on where you get them. At Sam's Club, I guess it'd be about ten, fifteen bucks. What else?"

He thought for a while. "How much does a swimming pool cost?"

"Depends," she said. "One of those little inflatable jobs? Or an Olympic-sized pool with marble sides and lily pads floating on the top?"

"Yeah, one of those."

She shrugged. "I wouldn't know, but thirty thousand dollars ought to be safe. What else?"

He subtracted the thirty thousand. "I've still got a lot left over. How about a convertible?"

"A convertible what?"

"A convertible . . ." She imagined him flipping through his mind's database of minivans and used pickups.

Finally, he surprised her. "A convertible Jaguar!"

Television, she thought. There was a whole database he got from the hour a day she allowed him to watch.

"Okay, what color?"

"Red." He started to write it down, and she began to think about what a car like that might cost.

"Put a hundred thousand dollars. No telling what a car like that costs, but it's probably in the ballpark. How much left?"

"Too much," he said. "I'll never spend it all." He spent some time thinking, then looked up at her with wide eyes. "How about a big nice house for you? Like something that cost forty thousand or something like that."

She didn't want to burst his bubble with the real value of real estate, or break it to him that the house they lived in, which they scraped to pay for, was worth far more than that. "Thank you *very* much. What else?"

"The Bryans' new horse?" Joseph asked. "You know, the baby."

"You'd want to buy that horse?" she asked.

"If I had a million dollars I would."

"Okay, put it down."

She let him make up the price. "What else?"

"Rude lessons for Leah, since she's so worried about it all the time."

"You mean etiquette lessons?"

"Whatever. She's so afraid she'll do something wrong. We need to send her to good manners school so she can learn all the right things to do."

"She'd appreciate that."

"And . . . golf lessons for Daddy and Daniel. And clubs. Daddy works too hard."

"Good idea. I agree."

"And for Rachel," he added, "some new dresses. She's obsessed with her looks."

Brenda grinned. *Obsess* had been one of this week's vocabulary words, and she was proud to see him use it. "What else?"

His eyes drifted off as he considered the possibilities. For a moment, he seemed to watch the chattering children in the waiting room running to and fro, playing with the toys in the corner, but she knew he was still thinking. "A video camera," he said more softly. "So I could tape my birthday parties when I'm not there."

The amusement left her eyes, and she gazed down at him. "I know you're disappointed."

"It's okay," he said, grinning. "It was really fun rolling the trees and all. How'd you think of that, anyway?"

"It just came to me." Necessity *was* the mother of invention. Most of her creative ideas came from being broke. "We never have money to throw around. Just toilet paper."

Joseph giggled. "Do you think Daddy'll pull the toilet paper down before we get home?"

She thought that over. It would be just like David to do that, in an effort to spare her the work. "Tell you what," she said. "Before we leave here we'll call him and ask him to leave it up."

"But what if it rains tonight? Then it'll get mushy and fall in the yard."

"Stop worrying. It was a beautiful day today and it's going to be beautiful tomorrow. Tomorrow we'll take it down. But today is your birthday for the whole day, and that toilet paper stays up."

He smiled up at her as his eyes grew distant again. "What about the cake?"

"They're saving you some," she said. "They promised. And the presents will still be there when we get back."

"Okay," he said. He went back to his list and was still trying to think of other ways to spend his million dollars when, finally, a nurse came to the door.

"Joseph Dodd?"

Brenda stood up quickly and nodded to the nurse, and Joseph handed the legal pad back to his mother, then followed the nurse into the examining room.

The doctor put on his stethoscope and listened carefully to Joseph's heart. As he listened, Brenda could see that something troubled him.

At last, he finished and pulled the boy's shirt back down. "Brenda, I think we need to have some tests run on Joseph."

"What kind of tests?"

"Oh, several things," he said evasively. "We just want to take every precaution, make sure we don't overlook anything. Can you take him over to St. Francis Hospital?" Though his voice was calm, the question conveyed urgency.

She frowned. "Right now?"

"Yeah, I'd really like to get the results of these tests. It's not normal for kids as strapping as Joseph to go around fainting on their birthdays. Is it, son?" He patted Joseph gently on the back. "I'll have my nurse call and set up the tests. You may be there a while."

She nodded silently and tried to push out of her mind the thought of the bills that would mount as a result of these tests. She wondered briefly whether they were all necessary, but then she shook off the thought. Joseph's health was at stake, and if the doctor thought Joseph needed the tests, then he would have them.

When Joseph was out in the front room picking through the reward bucket for the perfect scratch-'n'-sniff sticker, she stopped the doctor in the hall. "Doctor, could this be something serious?" she asked softly.

He had trouble looking her in the eye. "I can't say, Brenda. He's probably just fine. Just got a little too hot, a little too excited. But I'd like to be sure." He busied himself jotting on his chart as he tried to walk off.

But Brenda stopped him again. "What are you looking for?"

The doctor still didn't look at her. "Nothing specific. It's just that the tests will go a long way toward helping us diagnose him, if there's a diagnosis to be made."

Anger sparked in her heart, and she wanted to grab him by the throat and force him to look at her. But that wasn't her way. Feeling disheartened, she went to pay the bill, knowing they'd have to stretch their grocery budget a lot further now. But she was willing to give up food entirely if it meant helping her son.

She fought the tears threatening her eyes as she led Joseph back to the car.

CHAPTER
Seven

Cathy turned into Cedar Circle and saw the toilet paper draped on the trees in the lot between the Dodds' and Sullivans' houses. What on earth was that about? She thought only homes of teenagers had stunts like that pulled on them. Twelve-year-old Daniel was probably getting old enough to have prank-playing friends. But in broad daylight?

Too preoccupied to worry about it, she pulled into her driveway just as the school bus drew up to the neck of the cul-de-sac. She got out of the car and waited as her dog, who'd been heading for her, changed his direction and loped toward the bus.

Mark got off of the bus and rubbed the dog's ears before ambling up the driveway. "Hey, Mom. Check out Daniel's yard. Cool. Why are you home so early?"

"I needed to talk to your brother." She kissed him on the forehead, but he recoiled, as if afraid someone might see. She accepted the rebuff without taking offense. "How was your day?"

"Okay." He headed into the house, and she followed.

He dropped his backpack just inside the door, and she grabbed his shirt before he could get away and turned him back around. "Take it to your room, kiddo."

"But I have homework."

"You planning to do it right here on the kitchen floor?"

"Well, no, but—"

"To your room, Mark."

He moaned and jerked the backpack up. She heard a car pulling into the garage and looked out the door. Rick and Annie were obviously embroiled in some kind of argument. She sighed. She had wondered about the wisdom of letting them ride to and from school together when they barely tolerated each other at home. On the other hand, she wasn't willing to let Annie ride home with Mario Andretti wanna-bes with more tickets than miles under their belts.

Rick got out and slammed the car door.

"You're such a jerk!" Annie shrieked as she got out and slammed hers harder.

"Make her get off my case, Mom!" Rick said. "I'm sick of it!"

They both tornadoed into the house. "Okay, what's going on?" Cathy demanded.

"He's just such a jerk," Annie repeated, slapping her long brown hair off of her shoulder. "I asked him to take one of my friends home, and he said no, right to her face. It was so embarrassing."

For two teens who were so at odds, their choreography remained identical. Simultaneously, they dropped their backpacks at the door and headed for the refrigerator. "It's not my job to run your friends all over town," Rick said, shouldering her out of his way.

Annie elbowed him like a Roller Derby queen.

"She doesn't live 'all over town.' Just a mile down the mountain. It was on the way. It wouldn't have hurt you a bit."

"When you get your car, you can drive it anywhere you want. I'm not a taxi service for you and your friends."

"Well, it doesn't look like I'm getting one since you're Mom's golden boy and I'm the middle child. I'm the one who always does without."

"Maybe if your attitude changed she'd get you—"

"Hey!" Cathy shouted. "*Hey!*" On the second yell, they both swung around, as if united in their resentment of her intrusion.

Cathy picked up the two-ton backpacks. "Put them in your rooms," she ordered.

"What are you doing home, anyway?" Rick asked, as if she had no business here.

"I wanted to talk to you," she said. "Now take these backpacks out of here!"

They both grabbed them, and Rick muttered, "Great. Can't get a minute's peace around here, what with Annie screaming in one ear and you yelling in the other. I hate this place!"

Though a more fragile mother might have been hurt, Cathy took it with a grain of salt. Rick did have a flare for the dramatic, and since he spoke with equal affection of school, his job, and his father's house, she didn't take it personally. She simply determined not to let his anger distract her from her course.

All afternoon she had worked herself into a lather thinking about that condom in her pocket. Now she couldn't decide whether to confront Rick in front of the other two, or to follow him into his room. She decided to follow him.

He didn't realize she was behind him until he dropped the backpack on the pile of dirty laundry on his bedroom floor. He turned around and saw her in the doorway. "Are you following me?" he accused.

"Yes, I'm following you." She came into the room and closed the door behind her, vowing not to ask the origin of the rancid smell wafting on the air. "We've got to talk."

He kicked some of his clothes out of the way and dropped onto his bed. "I work hard at school all day, get chewed out all the way home, and now this."

She thought of reassuring him that "this" wouldn't be so bad, but then she felt that foil square in her pocket again, and decided that it would be even worse than he thought. She felt her knees shaking and decided she had to sit down, so she knocked the clothes from a chair into a new pile on the floor, and sat. "Rick, I found something when I was doing the laundry."

"Oh yeah?" he asked, unworried. "Did I leave money in my pockets again?"

She fixed her eyes on him, wondering if he was playing innocent. "No, Rick. It wasn't money."

"What then?" Suddenly, his face changed, as if it hit him what she was talking about, and he caught his breath. "Oh! You found the . . ." He let his voice trail off, as if he didn't dare say the word.

"Yeah, it was the condom," she said. She felt her face turning red and knew that she was going to launch into a high-octave sermon that would draw the other kids from their rooms and send Rick into a defensive rage. She didn't want anything so futile and destructive to happen, so she set her elbows on her jean-clad knees and tried to think. "Rick, I want you to tell me why you had it."

He stared at her, frowning as his mouth hung open, and she braced herself for his accusation that she'd invaded his privacy. "You think I got that for *myself?*"

It wasn't the response she'd expected. "Rick, I'm not stupid."

"Neither am I! I don't believe this. I'm in trouble for something I didn't even—"

"Rick, it was in *your* pocket."

"I don't care where it was. Just because I'm carrying around a condom doesn't mean I went out and bought it and planned to use it."

"Then why did you have it?"

"Every guy at school has one."

She closed her eyes, fuming, and ground her molars together. "Rick, I don't *care* if every boy in school takes a dive off the cliff at Bright Mountain. I don't want *my* son—"

"No, you don't get it!" he cut in. "Mom, they gave them to us at school. In a class."

She opened her eyes and gaped at him. She couldn't have heard right. Had he said . . . ? "They *gave* them to you?"

"Yeah. It was 'Condom Awareness Day,' if you can believe that. It's the biggest joke of the school year, every year from seventh grade on up. They get you in the room and start lecturing you about safe sex and stuff."

He said it matter-of-factly, as if she would naturally know and understand. *Oh, yes, of course. Condom Awareness Day.* But she didn't.

Her heart began to rampage, and she stood up, facing him at eye level. "Are you seriously telling me that they gave condoms out at school?"

"Yeah," he said. He was grinning now, enjoying her shock.

"Rick, I know that sometimes I can be naive, but I didn't just ride in on a hay truck."

"Mom, I'm telling you the truth. Call the school and ask them."

It was rare for him to suggest she call the school for any reason. For him to do so now clued her that he was probably telling the truth.

"When did this happen?"

"Last Friday," he said.

"Why didn't you tell me about it?"

He shrugged. "It wasn't that big a deal, Mom. Besides, it's weird talking to my mom about condoms."

"Why didn't you just throw it away?"

"I meant to, but I forgot. Besides, if you'd found it in the trash you would have gone just as ballistic. Mom, get real. Who would I use it with? I don't even have a girlfriend."

She deflated and wilted back in the chair. "I know. That's why I was so confused."

"I mean, it's not like I couldn't get a girlfriend if I wanted one. I could and everything. I've got a date to the prom."

She didn't want to know. "Oh, yeah? Who?" she forced herself to ask.

"Jeanie Bradford."

An image of the girl came to mind. She had been in Annie's dance class for years, and she had a nodding acquaintance with her mother. "Cute girl."

"Yeah, real cute." Pink blotches colored his cheeks, exposing his embarrassment. He turned away. "It's not like I'm in love or anything. This'll probably be our only date. But it is my junior year and I felt like I ought to go."

He was off on the prom, not even interested in the condom anymore, but Cathy couldn't get her mind off of it. "So I'll just throw this away. Because there's no point in your holding onto it."

"Fine. Mom, just because I'm taking some girl to the prom doesn't mean I need *that*. You brought me up right, okay?"

"Right," she said. She thought of telling him that he couldn't go to the prom, couldn't date a girl *ever*, not until he was married. But that seemed a little radical. "I can't believe you got it at school."

"Well, didn't you have sex classes when you were in school?"

She tried to think back twenty-five years. It seemed like three eternities ago. "Seems like we saw a movie called *Splendor in the Grass*, about a girl who got pregnant. But I think that was about the extent of it." She got up and stepped over the clothes on her way out of the room. The telephone rang, and before she could make it to the stairs, Annie cried, "Mom, for you!"

She went to the door of Annie's room. "Who is it, Annie?"

"Some guy," Annie said, holding her hand over the receiver. "I'm like, 'Can I tell her who's calling?' and he's like, 'Her favorite patient,' so I go, 'Oh, the rottweiler?' and he's like, 'Are you calling me a dog?' Real big flirt, whoever he is, Mom."

"Glad you could hold your own with him," Cathy muttered. She made it down the stairs and answered the extension in the living room. "Hello?"

"Cathy, hey, it's me. John. I meant that my cat is your favorite patient, and I am *not* a flirt."

She managed to laugh. "Sorry. I didn't know you could hear that."

"Forgiven. Just wanted to see what time you wanted me to pick you up tonight."

She frowned. Tonight? Had she forgotten? Her hesitation spoke volumes, and he moaned. "You said you'd let me take you out to dinner tonight, finally. Come on, Cathy, you aren't backin' out now, are you? I've been chasin' you for weeks, and it's ruinin' my self-esteem."

"John, it's just that I'm kind of having a bad day."

"Cathy, you promised."

"I know I did, but—"

"Come on, we'll have fun, you'll see. You deserve a break today."

She thought of the McDonald's jingle, and wondered if that's where he planned to take her. John, who brought his Himalayan cat in periodically, was an attractive man. She supposed she should be flattered that he was interested. And if truth be known, she did need some adult companionship. As she held the phone to her ear, she reached up and pulled her hair out of its ponytail. "Well, okay. I guess I can get away."

"Can you work up a little bit more enthusiasm?"

She smiled. "I told you. Bad day."

"Then gimme a chance to turn it around."

There was something charming about his deep cowboy drawl, she thought. She tousled her hair and wondered how long it would take for her to get ready. Too long, but she supposed it would be worth it. "Okay, pick me up at seven."

"Will do. Don't back out, okay? I've heard all the stories. Grandmothers dyin', workin' late, dog havin' puppies . . ."

She grinned and doubted that was true.

After she had cooked supper for the kids, she started to go upstairs and get ready for her date.

"See you later, Mom! I'm outa here," Rick called up.

She went halfway back down the stairs and looked over the rail. "Where are you going?"

"To work," he said. Rick worked weekdays bagging groceries at the local Kroger, when he wasn't helping at the animal clinic.

"You didn't tell me you had to work."

"It wasn't on the schedule. I had to trade with somebody so I'd have prom night off."

"Oh." She came the rest of the way down. "Well, okay, I'm going out, so I guess Annie can stay with Mark."

"No!" From upstairs, she heard her daughter protesting. Annie came bouncing down the stairs. "Mom, I've got a date tonight!"

"A date? On Tuesday night? You're not allowed to date on weeknights."

"But Mom, I'm fifteen, and Dad lets me go."

She didn't want to talk about Jerry. "You're never with him on weeknights. We have rules in this house, Annie."

"Mom, I asked you last week if I could go to the school's baseball game tonight, and you said yes."

"You didn't tell me you were going with a boy."

"I didn't think it was a big deal. Please, Mom. It's Allen Spreway. I've liked him for months and months, and he finally asked me out. I want to go!"

"Well, what am I going to do with Mark?"

"I don't know," she said. "It's not my job to raise Mark. You're the mother."

Mark came in from the kitchen, his hand buried in a bag of potato chips. "I'm not a kid, you know. I can take care of myself."

"I'm not leaving you here by yourself."

"Then cancel your date."

She thought of calling John and canceling, but she hated to put him off again. He might not give her another chance. It occurred to her that she could simply invite him in when he came, feed him here, and they could watch a movie together. But it didn't usually work well to have men around her children. It usually took only one visit for them to decide she wasn't their type.

Funny how single mothers with smart-aleck kids weren't anyone's type.

"Mark, I'd rather not cancel my date, but I don't want to leave you here alone. Is there somebody you could spend the night with?"

"On a school night?"

"No, that won't work." She moaned. "Look, I'll just call John—"

"It's okay, Mom. I can stay by myself. Really. Give me a chance."

"I'm not ready. Maybe you could go to the game with Annie and her date."

"No way!" Annie erupted. "I'll die before I'll take him with me on a date."

"I'll die before I go," Mark threw back.

Frustrated, Cathy headed back for the telephone. She called John's number, but he wasn't in his office. She left him a message to call back. He would know immediately that she was canceling, and he'd give up on her, as he probably should. But she really didn't want him to. He might, after all, be the one.

As she waited for him to call, she went ahead and got in the shower, trying to let the hot water rinse the tension from her body. She should be feeling relief, she thought, that Rick hadn't bought the condom, that he had no plans to use it with a girl, that he hadn't had any objection to her getting rid of it. Still . . .

The fact that the school had doled them out like breath mints riled her. She just didn't know what to do about it.

She was rinsing the conditioner out of her hair when she heard Annie screaming from the hallway. "Mom, telephone!"

She finished rinsing her hair, threw a towel around herself, and ran out to get the phone. "Hello, John?"

"No, Mom, it's me."

It was Mark, and she frowned. "Mark, I thought you were downstairs."

"Nope. Across the street. I came over to see why Daniel's yard got rolled, and found out they did it theirselves. Cool, huh? Mr.

Dodd said I could spend the night with Daniel tonight. Since they homeschool, it's no big thing to do it on a weeknight."

"But *you* have to go to school."

"So I'll come home first thing in the morning and get ready. What's the big deal?"

She closed her eyes. "Let me talk to Brenda." He put her on hold, and she could hear him talking to David. Finally, he came back. "She's not here. She took Joseph to the doctor."

"Well, are you sure it's all right with her?"

"Sure," he said. "What's one more? I'll come home and get my stuff."

"Come home and do your homework," she said. "Then you can go back."

She hung up and sat down on the bed, wondering if there was any wisdom in her going out tonight, after all. Didn't she want to be here when Annie got back from her date? Didn't she want to make sure that Rick didn't go out partying after he got off work? Didn't she need to supervise Mark's homework to make sure he did it all?

The door opened and Annie shot in. "Mom, does my hair look all right? Do I have on too much eyeliner?"

Cathy gave her a once-over. Her shirt flaunted too much of the figure that Cathy would have died or killed for when she was fifteen. She tried to think of a good reason why Annie needed to change, but the girl had her on a technicality. The shirt was neither low cut, nor too tight. Cathy tried to shift her thoughts to something positive. "Your hair looks gorgeous," she said. "You look like one of those soap opera stars."

"What about my eyeliner?"

"It looks fine."

"Fine?" Annie asked, stomping a foot. "I *can't* look fine. Not *that* kind of fine, anyway." She ran into Cathy's bathroom and began digging through her makeup drawer.

"Honey, I was about to go in there. I have to get ready for my date."

"But Mom, I need your lipstick. Look at me, I look awful."

"You look beautiful," Cathy said, falling in behind her. "Come on. I need for you to move aside so I can get ready."

"But *Mom!*"

Finally understanding what a crisis this was, Cathy surrendered her makeup table and sat on the side of the tub as her daughter panicked over her date. "So tell me about this boy," she said.

"Oh, he's so cute," she said. "He's got the bluest eyes, and these *luscious* lips."

Cathy didn't want to hear about his lips. She wondered if he'd been given a condom at school. "What time will you be home?"

"As soon as the game's over, unless we go get a burger or something."

"No burgers. Come straight home."

"Mom, what do you care? You won't be here."

The fact that Annie would be coming home to an empty house with no accountability and a boy who'd just seen a film about safe sex riled her. She made a decision to have a quick dinner with John and then beg off. She had to get home before Annie did.

"I'll be here," she assured her. "I want you coming straight home. It *is* a school night."

"Well, I know, but every kid in school's going to be at that game."

"I'm letting you go to the game."

"Well, why can't I go out afterward?"

"Either agree to come home after the game, or stay home and don't go at all."

"And if I stay home, are you staying home with me?"

The smart-aleck tone made Cathy want to throw something, but she refrained. "Annie, why do you talk to me like that?"

"Because you talk to *me* like *that*."

"I'm your mother."

"And I'm your daughter."

It was one of those grueling games they played. Just like when the kids were little and they would repeat every word she said until she was a raging lunatic trying to make them stop. Sighing loudly, she headed into the closet to find something to wear. She pulled out a simple dress and a sweater, and laid it on her bed.

"You're not wearing that, are you?" Annie asked.

She turned back to her daughter. "What would you prefer that I wore?"

"Something prettier." Annie went into her closet and pulled out something more colorful. "Here, wear this."

Something about her daughter helping her get ready for a date seemed unnatural, and she felt more depressed than ever. "All right, Annie, I'll wear that. Thanks."

"Sure. And if you want me to help you with your makeup, I will. You could use more blush than you usually wear."

"All right." Cathy headed for her makeup, but Annie dashed back to it. "I'm not through, Mom."

Cathy closed her eyes. She was supposed to have been a contented married woman by the time she had teenagers who dated. She was supposed to have been settling into the prime of her life. Not competing with her daughter for the mirror so they could both get ready for dates.

When Annie finally moved aside, Cathy applied the makeup that she rarely wore and slipped on the dress. Maybe it would be nice to get out, after all. She did need a break from responsibility and routine and constant needs and demands. It would be fun to have some adult male companionship for the evening. And who knew? It might turn into something.

As the possibility entered her mind, she began to get a little more hopeful. For the first time, she actually looked forward to the evening.

CHAPTER Eight

Brenda and Joseph had been at the hospital for what seemed hours, doing an echocardiogram, a MUGA scan, and other tests she had never heard of before. She wasn't clear on the purpose for any of them, but she tried to stay cheerful and keep Joseph upbeat as the grueling day wore on.

What a terrible thing to have to endure on your ninth birthday, she thought. She would make it up to him, even if she had to have another whole party and decorate the trees again.

No one at the hospital would give her any of the results, so when she finally headed back home with Joseph, she had no more answers than she'd had earlier. They had simply told her to keep him quiet and let him get plenty of rest.

They were eating a late supper of hamburgers David had cooked out on the grill when the doctor called. "I knew you'd want to know—I got the results back on some of the tests already," he told Brenda. "I'd like you to take Joseph to see Dr. Chris Robinson. He's a pediatric cardiac surgeon."

"A what?" She immediately got up from the table and took the cordless phone into the other room where the children couldn't hear. David followed her.

"You think this is his heart?" she asked quietly.

"Some of the tests showed . . . well, it's a little enlarged. It's hard to tell why."

"Enlarged?" The word seemed to scramble the thoughts in her brain, keeping them from any logical order. "What would cause that?"

"A number of things could cause it," he said. "Possibly that virus he had a few weeks ago. Or an illness years ago could have caused damage that's just now showing up. I'd really rather not speculate. I'll be calling Robinson myself first thing in the morning, but you need to make an appointment with him. Try to get in as soon as possible."

"Sure. I'll call first thing."

"I'd really like to keep up with what's going on, so remind him to keep me informed."

"Sure," she said. "What do I do in the meantime? For Joseph, I mean."

"Just keep him quiet."

"Is there medicine?"

"Oh, sure. There are lots of ways to treat problems like this. Dr. Robinson will probably have him back to a hundred percent in no time. Don't panic until you hear what he has to say."

Don't panic. The words seemed so worthless and impossible. Slowly, she hung up the phone.

"His heart?" David asked on a rush of breath.

She met his eyes, saw the terror there. She might have been looking into a mirror.

"Maybe. Maybe not," she managed to answer. "He wants us to take him to a pediatric cardiac surgeon." She covered her mouth with a trembling hand, muffling a sob. "David, he said his heart is enlarged."

"Enlarged? What does that mean?"

"I don't know." She reached for him, and he hugged her fiercely, as though the strength of their embrace could hold back whatever evil had its grip on their son.

They managed to pull themselves together for the sake of the children and didn't speak of it again until the kids were occupied in another room. Cathy's son Mark was over, and had brought a game of Monopoly that they were all engaged in.

When they were alone, David paced across the kitchen, rubbing his face with callused hands. "He needs the best care. The absolute best. Guess I need to take on some extra work," he said. "These bills could get pretty hefty."

"All those tests today," Brenda said. She sat at the kitchen table with her Bible—the source of her strength—but somehow, she couldn't seem to concentrate on the words she had opened to. "What's our deductible again?"

He closed his eyes and leaned back against the counter. "Two thousand dollars. And it doesn't cover but seventy percent after that. The joys of self-employment."

They had decided years ago that this was the best situation for their family, in spite of the tight budget, the self-employment taxes, the poor health insurance, and everything else that came with self-employment. Being a cabinetmaker at home enabled him to help in the homeschooling of their children, to be there when Brenda had to leave, to spend time apprenticing his boys. Already, Daniel helped him in the afternoons. It was a situation that worked, and they didn't want to change it. But at times like this, they both wished they had a company benefit program with health insurance.

"We'll get by, David," she said. "The Lord will provide. He always does."

David averted his eyes, the way he always did when she spoke of spiritual things. He wasn't a believer, and he considered her faith to be nothing more than shallow superstition. She tried not to let it bother her. "David, He *will* provide. You'll see."

She knew he was thinking that *he* was the one who would have to provide. "We'll get by," he finally agreed.

"Besides," she said, reaching deep into herself and finding the optimism she was known for. "I don't really think he's that sick. It's probably some fluke thing. We'll get in to see that doctor, and he'll take a look at Joseph and say there's nothing wrong with him, that I wasted my time bringing him in. And we'll find out that he just fainted because the sun was too hot and he'd had too many sweets. That his heart is enlarged because it's so full of love . . ."

David's look told her that this was another one of those times when their faith didn't match. He swallowed hard and got up from the table. "I know it's early. It's not even dark yet, but . . . I'm going to bed. It's been a long day."

"Yeah, okay. I'm going to stay up until I get the kids into bed."

She watched as David disappeared down the hall, then turned her eyes back to the Bible again. Her thoughts were in such disarray that she didn't think she could find words to take to God's throne. She wished her husband could share this with her, and that they could pray for each other when one of them had a heavy heart. But David would have none of it.

She sat back in her chair and recalled the night, almost thirteen years ago, when she had gone to a church service with a friend and had come home to tell David that something had happened. She had found Christ that night, and she'd been overcome with joy and excitement and couldn't wait to tell him how the Holy Spirit had touched her.

She had hoped that he would want the same experience, but she'd tried to prepare herself for his indifference. What she had not expected, what had come as a shock to her, was the rage that she had never seen in David before. It was as if she'd joined some evil cult . . . as if she had announced her intention to leave him and join her new friends. It was frightening and irrational. He had tried to forbid her to go back to that church, and insisted on her renouncing the faith that he found so distasteful. She had refused.

That night, she had gone to bed in confusion while David stayed up watching late-night television in the other room. She had not been able to sleep, so she had wept and prayed. Those prayers must have reached right into that other room, because sometime after midnight, David had come to bed.

With red eyes and tears on his face, he'd sat down on the side of the bed and asked her forgiveness for losing his temper. "I have reasons for hating church," he'd said.

She sat up in bed. The light coming in from the hall illuminated one side of his face, leaving the other side in darkness. In the half that was visible to her, she saw pain. "But . . . you were raised in church. I thought you, of all people, would understand."

"I understand more than you do," he said. "Those people in that church you went to . . . they're not what you think."

"How do you know?" she asked. "You've never met them."

"I've met people just like them."

Flustered and unable to find a defense, she reached for his hand. "David, it doesn't matter about the people as much as it does about Jesus."

He got up from the bed and lost himself in the shadows. "I thought I'd escaped this. When I left home, I never had to go back. And you never cared about church. Now, all of a sudden, you're all gung ho for this religion stuff, and I'm supposed to just accept it?"

"It'll make me better, David. Not worse."

"I don't think it'll make you better," he said. "I've seen what it does to people."

The conversation had ended, and he'd gone back to the television. She had decided right then and there that she would simply pray for him to change his mind, and make sure he found nothing in her faith to be bitter about. She must have succeeded, for when they began having children, he allowed her to take them to church. But he refused to go himself.

His reasons were locked up somewhere inside him, and he refused to let them out. Over the years, though, she had guessed at some of them, from things his mother said before she died. Things about David's father being a preacher—a fact that shocked her, since David had never mentioned it. Things about that same father running off with the church organist when David was a small boy. Somehow, all of that figured into his bitterness and anger at the church. But she knew there had to be more. And she prayed daily that he would someday open that cage and share its contents with her, and turn to the God who healed past hurts.

That prayer had not been answered yet, thirteen years later, but she hadn't given up.

Her heart was as heavy as it had been in a long time, and she decided to call her prayer partner. She dialed Sylvia's number, hoping she wasn't waking her.

"Hello?"

"Sylvia, it's me. Brenda."

Sylvia had always been able to detect when something was wrong. "What is it, darlin'? Is Joseph okay? I got to the party late, and Tory told me what happened."

"Um . . . I don't really know."

"Are you dressed?"

Brenda looked down at the clothes she'd had on all day, wondering why Sylvia asked. "Yes, why?"

"'Cause I'm coming over. Meet me on the front porch."

Brenda felt better already as she hung up the phone and headed outside.

CHAPTER *Nine*

John didn't take Cathy directly to the restaurant. Instead, he told her she needed to relax, and he knew just the thing. He drove to the top of Bright Mountain to park at the Point, and as the lights flickered on across Breezewood just before dusk, he tried to skip at least three of the natural dating steps.

She pushed him away and got out of the car.

"Aw, come on. What'sa matter?" he asked as he followed her.

"John, you asked me to dinner, and I said yes, that I'd love to have *dinner* with you. I didn't come out with you tonight to get groped and manhandled."

He looked wounded and misunderstood. "I thought comin' up here would help you relax. I'm tryin' to be romantic."

"I don't want to be romantic with you," she said. "I hardly even know you."

He pretended to pull a knife out of his heart. "And here I thought you liked me. You seemed so free and loose around the clinic."

"Free and loose?" she repeated. "How do you figure that?"

He shrugged. "I just mean that bouncy ponytail and those Keds, and you always have a big smile for me."

"That's free and loose? You must be kidding."

He chuckled as though he *was* kidding. "Come on, get in the car. I'll take you to dinner."

Sighing, she got back into the car, closed the door, and hooked her seat belt. He dropped in on the other side.

"Tell me something," she said, still angry as he pulled the car back onto the road. "I'm just curious. Do other women you go out with really allow you to grope them before your car engine has even warmed up?"

He chuckled under his breath. "Come to think of it, most of 'em don't. Maybe I need to change my technique." He gave her an apologetic glance. "Hey, you can't blame a guy for tryin'. So where do you want to eat?"

She found that she wasn't hungry anymore. "I don't care, John. Frankly, I'd rather just go home."

"But that's scandalous," he said. "I can't take a gal home after less than an hour!"

"Scandalous?" She shook her head in disbelief. "Come on, John, you're not going to get what you came for, so just take me on home. Consider it a dating nightmare."

"Mine or yours?"

"Mine," she shot back. "Only it's usually my nightmare for my daughter. I never dreamed *I'd* be the one to be attacked. I thought the hormones kind of leveled off when you reached middle age."

He was more offended by her assessment of his age than his behavior. "Come on, I'm not that old!"

"Just take me home."

"Man, you can hold a grudge!" he bit out. "I said I was sorry, for Pete's sake! My worst crime was bein' attracted to a good-lookin' woman. Sue me."

When he missed the turn that would have taken them to her house, she shot him a look. "Where are we going?"

"To a restaurant," he said.

"I *told* you to take me home."

"Well, I'm not gonna do it." His tone was softer, more conciliatory. "We're goin' to a restaurant, we're gonna eat, we're gonna enjoy each other's company—and you'll forgive me. I messed up, okay? I shouldn't have got so friendly so soon. It's just that you're such a knockout. I couldn't help it."

She wondered if that was meant to flatter her. "I don't *want* to have dinner with you, John."

He pulled into the restaurant parking lot and let the car idle. "Relax. It's just dinner. I can't do anything to you in front of all these people."

She couldn't believe all the arrangements she'd made, the stupid dress, the makeup. She felt like such a fool. Now she felt like some three-year-old, holding her breath until she got her way, refusing to budge—and it was John who'd put her in this awkward position. She remembered why she hated men.

"Guess I don't blame you for bein' mad," he said in a softer voice. "I really don't behave this way with every woman I go out with. In fact, I don't even date all that much. I'm a real homebody. I was just a little nervous before I picked you up, so I had a glass of wine. It must have just loosened me up a little too much."

She tried to appear disinterested, but finally she sneaked a peak at him. "You were nervous about taking me out?"

"Of course I was. You're a beautiful, classy blonde who has everything goin' for her. I figure you're the town catch. What would you possibly see in a good ole boy like me?"

Something about the vulnerability in his confession softened her attitude toward him. She sat quietly for a moment. He let the quiet pass between them. Finally, she glanced toward the restaurant. It was Alexander's, and she'd been wanting to go there. What harm could it do to let him buy her a steak?

"All right," she said with a sigh. "Let's go."

"Really?" he asked.

"Yes," she said. "But please don't drink anymore. It doesn't become you."

He nodded and they went in, and she tried to forget the first part of the date as the second rolled by.

It wasn't that John was a poor conversationalist; it was just that his choice of topics was limited. After the first half hour of talking about himself, she'd wished they could move on to another topic. But he hadn't exhausted all the possibilities yet. He had just exhausted her.

She had a headache by the time the meal was over. Though he'd had no more to drink, and she hoped the food had dulled his appetite, she found him getting familiar again as they drove home.

"Sure you don't want to go back up to the Point?"

"Positive. Take me home, John. I need to get there before my daughter does."

"How old is she, anyway?"

"Fifteen."

"She doesn't need a baby-sitter. She can take care of herself."

"Take me home, John."

With a huff that reminded her of a frustrated kid, he headed to Cedar Circle.

CHAPTER

Ten

Barry wasn't home at eight-thirty. With each moment that passed, Tory grew more and more agitated. She got the kids bathed for the third time that day and put them to bed. But instead of going to bed herself or re-creating her four pages in longhand, she decided to ride her stationary bicycle while watching the clock and stewing.

When her odometer registered ten miles, she showered and decided to read for a while. She ignored the novels on her shelf and chose instead a self-help book her mother had bought her for Christmas on fulfilling your own destiny.

By the time she heard Barry pulling into the garage, she had read a whole chapter about setting goals and prioritizing time, something that had only made her angrier about her life. The author of the book obviously didn't have two children, a congealed computer keyboard, and a husband who came home late.

As she listened to the garage door shutting, she tried to decide how to greet him. Should she meet him in anger and lambaste him for being so late, or should she force herself into the submissive role and flutter around him like he was the prodigal son?

By the time he opened the door, she had decided to do none of the above, and instead, had put on her shoes and pushed past him into the garage without a word. He looked surprised and turned around to follow her out. "Where ya goin'?"

"To talk to Brenda," she said curtly. "Joseph got sick today. I want to make sure he's all right. The kids are asleep."

"Bad day?" he asked her back.

She couldn't believe he had the nerve to ask. She turned around and gave him a disgusted look. "*Long* day. Made longer by the fact that my husband and partner in child rearing didn't make it home until after the kids were in bed."

"You could have kept them up."

"I didn't know how long you'd be since you're later than you said."

He rolled his eyes as if contemplating the wisdom of coming home at all. "Well, we got the account."

"Bully for you."

She opened the garage door and headed out. She heard the door slam behind her.

Darkness was just falling over the ridge, a little darker than twilight, but lighter than full-blown night. The sky offered a lunar half-grin much like the birds' "fail-ure" cries of this morning, and she turned her eyes to the ground. It was cool and breezy now, unlike the day that made children smell and mothers perspire and little boys faint. A foggy mist rendered the Smoky Mountains invisible even with all the lights usually dotting their sides.

As she crossed the lot next to her house, she heard voices and saw that Brenda and Sylvia were sitting on the Dodds' front porch swing, talking quietly in the darkness. As she approached, Tory wondered if she was intruding on a private moment. She thought of going back in, but then she would have to tangle with Barry. She decided to take her chances with her neighbors.

"What are you doing out here?" she asked as she approached.

"Tory!" Brenda said. "Come sit down. We were just catching up on the day."

Catching up, Tory thought. Did that ever really happen? "I came to see how Joseph is," she said, stepping onto the porch and pulling two wicker rockers close to the swing. She sat down in one and propped her feet in the other one.

"Well . . . we're not sure," Brenda said. "He may be fine."

Tory fixed her eyes on Brenda. "What do you mean, *may* be?"

Brenda looked as if she was having trouble getting the words out, and Sylvia intervened. "They're going for more tests tomorrow. They're not sure what made him faint yet."

This sounded serious, and Tory dropped her feet and leaned forward, as if that would help her to understand more clearly. "What kind of tests, Brenda?"

Brenda sighed. "His heart . . . it seems to be enlarged a little. We have to take him to a pediatric cardiac surgeon."

"They have those?" Tory asked. It had never occurred to her that there were children with heart problems.

"Yes, apparently," Brenda said. "But he's okay. As soon as the light-headedness passed, he felt fine. We've kept him quiet for the rest of the day, made him take it easy. It's probably just a virus or something. Or they misread the X-rays. That happens, you know. They make mistakes all the time."

Tory felt the pressure on her own chest, and tried to imagine having one of her children pass out at his birthday party, and then being told that it was due to an enlarged heart. "I'd be a basket case," she said quietly. "Brenda, are you okay?"

"Yeah, sure," Brenda said with that smile that seemed a permanent part of her expression. "I mean, it's a little nerve-wracking. But things will be all right."

Headlights lit up the entrance to Cedar Circle, and they all watched a strange car pull into Cathy's driveway. Their neighbor got out and headed for the door. The driver followed a little too quickly.

"Date?" Sylvia asked.

"Guess so," Tory said. She smiled as she gazed across the street. "Cathy's lucky."

"Lucky?" Brenda asked. "Why would you say that?"

"Because. She gets to go out with handsome men who take her to restaurants and shows. Barry hasn't taken me out in two months. He barely comes home."

"Oh, for heaven's sake," Sylvia said. "He's home every night. It's not like he's a traveling salesman."

"He may sleep at home," Tory insisted, "but take tonight. One of the worst days I can remember in a long time, and ten minutes ago he finally strolled in."

"Then why aren't you home with him?"

Tory looked up at Sylvia, almost amused at the point-blank question. But Sylvia wasn't smiling. "No, I'm serious," Sylvia went on. "If you're complaining about him not being home enough, why aren't you there when he is?"

Deflated, Tory started to get to her feet. "You're right. I'll go home." It reminded her of childhood when one of her friends would offend her, and biting her bottom lip she would gather her toys and leave. Hadn't she outgrown that feeling that she didn't belong in any group, and that those who included her were just politely biding their time until she left?

"We're not trying to run you off," Brenda said quickly, ever the peacemaker. "Sylvia wasn't telling you to go home, were you, Sylvia?"

"Of course not," Sylvia said, but her tone suggested that home was exactly where she thought Tory belonged. "I'm just trying to point out that he's there now."

"I know he is," Tory snapped back. "But I'm a little mad at him right now."

"Okay," Sylvia said. "I guess that's fair. Goodness knows there were nights in my younger days when I got mad at Harry for coming in so late. Until I finally grew up and realized that, in his mind, he was doing it as much for me as for his patients. He just thought he was providing, the way he was supposed to."

"Barry isn't out saving lives," Tory said. "It was just a stupid metalworks account, which could have waited, or at least taken less time."

"My point is that you seem to wish you could be like Cathy, dating again. But I don't think you want to be in her shoes. Think how much of your life you've invested in Barry. He's your partner. If all that was gone, you'd have to start over with men you don't know. It doesn't look like much fun."

Tory was skeptical. "Cathy seems to be having fun."

No sooner had those words left her mouth than Cathy's date marched back out to his car, slammed the door, and peeled out of the driveway. They all looked at each other and laughed.

The door opened again and Cathy, suddenly in blue jeans and T-shirt, bounded out. She must have shed her dress the way Spencer shed his Sunday clothes—in five seconds flat. She came across the street, pulling her hair up in a ponytail as she reached them.

"I saw you three out here gawking at me as I drove up," she said, "so I thought I'd come over and tell you every little gory detail before I get Mark to come home."

"So who was he?" Tory asked, undaunted by Cathy's sarcasm.

"Some guy who brings his Himalayan to me every time it throws up. Seemed like a nice guy in the office. Looks can be deceiving, though."

"You didn't have a good time?" Brenda asked.

Cathy took the rocker where Tory's feet had been and plopped into it. "I had a good meal. Let's leave it at that."

"You're home early," Brenda said. "Mark and Daniel are probably still up."

"Yeah, that's the real reason I came over. I figured I'd send Mark back home so I could be the one to scrape him off the sheets in the morning before school." She finished putting her hair in the ponytail and slapped her hands hard on her thighs. "Since we're all here, I might as well make it official. I'm giving up dating. It's not worth it."

"Why?" Tory asked, amazed.

Cathy braced her elbows on her knees, an unfeminine gesture that looked quite feminine when Cathy did it. Her skin looked like that of a porcelain doll, and she was so thin she looked breakable. She had long, tapered fingers that moved like those of an artist or musician, and bright blue eyes that men gravitated to. She was spirited, like the Bryans' mare, but she didn't let feminist convention dictate her behavior. Last weekend at the wedding, Cathy looked almost glamorous.

"I was getting ready tonight, and Annie was getting ready for *her* date, and it just struck me that there's something terribly unnatural about all this. She was giving me tips and telling me what I should wear, and I thought the roles were reversed. I was supposed to be doing that for her, not the other way around."

"But you can't just give it up," Tory said. "You could date on the weekends when the kids are out of town."

"Date who?" Cathy asked. "I've just about had it. This guy tonight was all over me. He seemed like a perfectly nice guy, but he turned out to be an octopus with hands everywhere."

"What a disappointment," Sylvia said.

"You said it. But I don't know where to meet nice men." She shook her head, and that ponytail slapped each side of her head. "I don't go to bars. I'm afraid I'll run into my children there . . ."

There was a moment of stunned silence. No one ever knew for sure when Cathy was serious. But after a moment, she let that deadpan face break into a smile. "Hey, I'm kidding."

They all laughed softly. "Have you tried church?" Brenda asked.

Cathy looked uncomfortable, as she always did when the subject of church came up. "No, but going to church to find a man seems a little wrong, too. On the other hand, it sure wouldn't hurt my kids to get a little spiritual training. You're not going to believe what I found in Rick's pocket today."

"What?" Tory asked.

"A condom. He got it at school. In a sex ed class."

"He didn't," Brenda said.

"Oh, yeah. Imagine the things your kids miss when you homeschool, Brenda."

Brenda didn't seem to find that funny. "So what are you going to do about it?" She had thrown down the gauntlet, and they all knew it. Brenda was big on challenges, but she issued them with such a sweet tone that no one was ever offended.

"What *can* I do? I can't homeschool, like you. I have to make a living. And I can't take them out and put them in private school—some of those are just as bad, and besides, I can't afford it." She looked around at the faces of Tory and Sylvia. "Yeah, I know, I could take on the school board and change all the policies, before they start messing with Mark's hormones. And I'm thinking about how to do that. It's just not easy, and time is not a commodity I have a lot of right now." She looked down at her watch and tried to read it in the light from the street lamp at the entrance to Cedar Circle. "Speaking of time . . . don't you think the baseball game should be over by now?"

Tory was having trouble following the thread of Cathy's rambling. "Baseball game? What's that got to do with condoms?"

"Nothing, except that every boy on the team got one, as well as every boy in the school, including the boy that Annie is out with as we speak." She leaned back hard in the chair and brushed her fingers through her bangs. "I'm sorry. I didn't mean to dominate the conversation like that. It's just been an incredibly bad day."

"We can relate," Tory said. "The kids spilled Kool-Aid on my computer. Oh, and Joseph passed out at his birthday party today." The two events seemed equally tragic to Tory.

Cathy shot Brenda a look. "Is he all right?"

"Yeah, fine, I think." Tory wasn't surprised at Brenda's lie—it wasn't like Brenda to dump her problems out for everyone to examine. Sometimes Tory wished she would. To her, Brenda was some kind of mythical supermom who did all the right things and never had a negative thought. Just once, she'd love to see Brenda fall apart, get angry, lose her cool. It certainly would help Tory relate to her better.

"Sylvia's the only one who's had a peaceful day, I bet," Tory said, smiling at the matriarch of the neighborhood.

"Not really," Sylvia said. The swing stopped, and Sylvia swept her frosted pageboy behind her ears. "See, Harry came home today for lunch and asked me if I would think about going to Nicaragua as a full-time missionary."

"A *what?*" Cathy threw her head back and laughed uproariously, as if she'd never heard anything so funny in her life. Tory found it less amusing, and Brenda wasn't smiling at all. "Has he gone off the deep end? Sylvia, what did you say?"

Sylvia seemed puzzled by Cathy's response. "Well . . . I said I'd think about it. And no, he isn't going off the deep end. It's something he's always wanted to do. We've talked about it before. Now that the kids are gone . . ."

Cathy's smile faded, and she looked at Tory, then at Brenda, and realized that no one but she was laughing. "You're serious. You're really thinking about this."

Sylvia drew in a deep breath and let it out hard. Tory didn't think she had ever heard Sylvia sigh before. "Thinking about it. That's all. I don't know if I could do it. Sell the house, the furniture, leave the country . . ."

"Why would you *do* that?" Cathy asked. "Why would *he?* You have it so good here. You're so happy. He's a prominent cardiac surgeon. He's worked all his life to be where he is. What could possibly be in Nicaragua for you?"

Sylvia thought that over for a moment. "It wouldn't be about us, Cathy." The words were not said in condemnation. They were thoughtful words, meted out carefully. "Harry feels called."

"Wow," Cathy said. "I don't mean to seem so bowled over by this, but it's kind of hard for me to imagine. Most people work all their lives to get where he is. It's just hard to grasp."

"For me, too," Sylvia said. "I understand why he wants to do it. I'm just not sure I'm that selfless."

"Give me a break," Cathy said. "You and Brenda are the most selfless people I know."

Tory couldn't help noticing that Cathy didn't mention her. But she wouldn't have expected her to. She looked down at the boards beneath her feet.

"The first year we went," Sylvia explained, "we worked in León, about an hour and a half from Managua. I lost ten pounds in two weeks. Hardly ate a thing, because it was so disgusting to go to the marketplaces to buy meat that was hanging in the open, covered with flies."

"Gross," Tory whispered.

"The second year, we went to Masaya. I thought it would be better, because it was right on the lake. I pictured a resort area, you know? Imagine my surprise when we got there and all we saw were run-down buildings badly in need of repair. No telling where we'd live if we went there indefinitely."

"Where did you stay then?" Brenda asked.

"In the home of a missionary who was already there. And in spite of my disappointment at the location, it turned out to be a fruitful trip. Harry operated on hundreds of people and treated hundreds of others. He did all types of surgery—not just heart cases. Because of Harry, the little church the missionary started has doubled. Some of those converts are starting churches of their own. There's no doubt, it's God's work."

"For two weeks, maybe," Cathy said. "But forever?"

A strong wind whipped up, dancing in their hair, as Sylvia seemed to think that over. "I'm not sure God's calling us to do this. I'm praying about it. I want to do God's will, but frankly, I'm not sure I'm up to this. I don't have a lot to contribute, you know? Harry practices medicine there, and they flock to him by the hundreds. He helps them. But I just don't think I have that much to offer."

"You have a *lot* to offer," Brenda said. "If you put everything you have experience doing on a resumé, it would never fit into an envelope."

Tory's eyes settled on Brenda for a moment as she tried to let that sink in. Brenda made being a housewife seem noble, yet

Tory couldn't think of it that way. To her, it was a detour on the way to her career goals, something that had gotten in her way.

"So what are you going to do?" Tory asked finally.

"I don't know," Sylvia said. "Harry told me he would wait until I made the decision."

"Oh, great," Tory said. "So he dumps it in your lap?"

"I already know what he wants to do. He's leaving it up to me."

"It's better than having him come home and telling her to pack her bags, that they're on their way out of the country," Brenda said. "I think it's sweet."

"He believes that if God really is calling him, He'll call me, too."

"If I were you I wouldn't answer the phone," Cathy said. Everyone laughed.

Tory looked over at her house and saw that the light in the laundry room was on. She knew Barry wasn't doing laundry. Was he working on the computer they kept there? Cursing her for being so stupid as to leave the children alone long enough to destroy the equipment he'd worked overtime to pay for?

Wearily, she got up. "I guess I'd better go home."

"Might be a good idea," Sylvia said.

She paused a moment, crossing her arms. "Sylvia, did you ever have days when Harry was working long hours, and you just really wanted him to come home?"

"I sure did. And when he finally did, I was happy to see him."

Tory nodded, wishing on one hand that she could be more like Sylvia, and on the other stubbornly holding on to her anger at Barry. "It's just so unfair, these long hours."

"He's doing his job."

"Yeah, I know." She didn't want to talk about it anymore. Sometimes Sylvia's wisdom drove her right up the wall. "Well, I'll see you all later. Brenda, let me know if you need anything."

"Thanks."

Tory tramped back across the yard and into her garage. She took a moment to collect herself before opening the door and going in. Was he stewing now as she had stewed earlier? Was he waiting at the kitchen table, poised to attack?

She made a point of closing the door loudly enough for him to hear, then went in and looked around the kitchen. He wasn't there, so she went to the laundry room. He heard her coming and glanced over his shoulder at her. He was sitting in front of the computer with a bottle of some kind of cleaner he must have brought from the office. He had taken the keyboard apart.

"I don't know if I can fix it," he mumbled.

"Yeah, that's what I figured."

He turned around in the swivel desk chair she'd gotten for Mother's Day. "Look, I'm sorry I wasn't home sooner. This account will mean a million dollars for the company, and a sure raise for me."

It was hard to be mad at him when he put it that way. "It's okay. You just wouldn't believe all that's happened today." She wanted to make a checklist of today's tragedies, so he would understand. She wanted him to be amazed at the things she put up with; she wanted him to submit her name for "Mother of the Year." "You just don't know what it's like," she said. "Staying home all day with two preschoolers. I don't have much adult companionship. And I have no time to write. I look forward to you coming home and relieving me, and then when you don't . . ."

"Tory, we agreed," he said. "When you got pregnant with Brittany, we agreed that you would raise our children, instead of letting them go to day care. Writing a book was way down on the priority list."

She bristled. "So what's wrong with my writing a book, as long as I'm getting everything else done? The house is spotless, Barry. It always is. The kids are clean, they're fed, they're loved. What's wrong with me wanting to write a book?"

"Nothing, unless it makes you miserable when you have to spend time with the kids."

She turned away from the door and went back into the kitchen. He'd left his briefcase and his car keys on the table. She picked them up and put them where they belonged.

He got up and leaned in the doorway, right where she'd been standing. "I'm just saying, Tory, that when I work overtime, it's because I have to do that to make it possible for us to live in a nice house in a nice neighborhood, and still let you stay home with the children."

She didn't want to talk about it anymore. Though the counter was clean, as it always was, she got her sponge from the sink and began wiping it again.

"Tory, do you want to go back to work? Is that it? Do you want to get a job and let me stay home with the kids?"

She knew there was about as much chance of that as there was of her running for congress. "I want to be a writer." She slammed the sponge down and spun around to face him. "I'm smarter than this, Barry. I'm smarter than getting cats out of trees and rescuing Spencer from horse corrals and reading Dr. Seuss. People used to look up to me and admire me when I was in college. I want to make an impact. That was the plan."

"You *are* making an impact. You're raising two children who are secure and happy. You're doing a great job. But if it's instant gratification you want, you're not going to get it in child rearing."

"I'm not going to get it in writing, either," she said, "so that's a low blow. You know it's not instant *anything* I'm after."

"Then what are you after?"

"I just want to write four pages in a day without losing it to a Kool-Aid spill," she said. "I just want to be able to sit by myself and think sometimes. I just want to be able to reach a goal or two."

"Well, if you didn't spend all your time cleaning this house and reading self-help books, maybe you'd get something done."

"Oh, so now you're upset because the house is clean?"

"No, I'm upset because you have to have everything perfect. That's how you are with your writing. Other people do it for a hobby. They work it in. But if you can't have everything exactly like you want it before you start writing, then forget it."

"Barry, don't you understand that I *did* write today? I wrote four pages and it's gone."

"Did it ever occur to you to try to re-create those four pages?"

"How? The computer was broken."

"You could let the kids play in the little pool and sit out there with a legal pad and a pen. You remember those, don't you?"

He was right, she thought. It could be done that way. Lots of people did it that way. It just wasn't the way she wanted to do it.

He went to the table and sat down. "Come here," he said. "Sit down and tell me everything you can remember about what you wrote. It'll come back to you, then you can take a pen and paper and write it again."

She just stood there with her arms crossed. "Barry, it doesn't work that way."

He tapped the chair. "Come on, Tory. Just try. Is this still the story you wanted to do about the nurse in France in World War II?"

"Yes."

"And she falls for a wounded soldier, but he dies . . ."

"I had him get wounded today. He was brought into triage, and she met him. It was really good."

"Great. What else?"

She kept standing where she was. "Nothing else. That's as far as I got."

"Good. Then you don't have so much to re-create. What happens next? He's going to die, right? And while she's grieving, Dr. Right comes along and rescues her from herself?"

"Yeah."

"Then start writing. It's a guaranteed best-seller."

She shook her head. "I can't turn it on just like that. I'm not in the mood."

He stared up at her, his face hardening. "Tory, I'm trying to help you. Look, if you're so miserable, then let's try something else. Plan A was to stay home and raise our kids. But if Plan A isn't working, then let's think of Plan B. Just come up with one, Tory. You could hire a baby-sitter for a few hours a day so you could write. Whatever it takes."

She felt horrible and thought of Sylvia and Brenda telling her how she should be happy to stay home with her husband when he finally came in. She rarely heard them complain. The first time she'd *ever* heard Sylvia complain was tonight when she'd spoken about Nicaragua. Tory wondered if there was something wrong with her that rendered her incapable of appreciating things that other mothers longed for. The truth was, she didn't want to go out and get a job, and she didn't want to put her kids in day care. She *did* want to stay home with them. "It's just that . . . no one puts much value in child rearing," she said, then wished she hadn't said it aloud.

He got up and leaned on the counter, forcing her to look at him. "Just tell me one thing, Tory," he said. "Who is it that you're trying to impress?"

She couldn't believe he'd asked that. "What are you talking about? I'm not trying to impress anybody."

"You said that no one puts value in child rearing. That sounds to me like you're trying to prove something or impress somebody."

She felt her face growing hot. "You'll never understand," she said, "because you can go to work and do your job and meet people and be good at what you do and get awards and recognition and pay raises. You can stand back and look at the work you've done and be proud of it and tell everyone that you did it. I can't do any of that, Barry."

"I think you're wrong," he said. "I think Brittany and Spencer are better awards than any pay raise and any job recognition."

"Great, now you're acting like I don't value them!"

"It sounds like it, Tory. Sometimes it really does."

"That's it." She squeezed out the sponge and went to throw it into the washing machine, then dropped the top loudly.

Then she went to bed angry and cold to the sound of David Letterman in the living room.

CHAPTER

Cathy paced the front room of her house, the room they called the formal dining room, though there was nothing formal about it. Jerry had gotten their antique dining-room suite in the divorce, since it had come from his family, and now he and his new wife used it at Thanksgiving and Christmas. Cathy had never had the inclination to replace it—in addition to never having the money. Shopping for furniture was something that took time, and she never had a block large enough to do it. So she had moved a garage-sale table in here, covered it with a tablecloth, and set up her computer and printer on it.

Tonight, what drew her to the room was the fact that it had a window overlooking the front yard. From here, she could see the entrance to Cedar Circle, and each time she passed the window she peered out to see whether any headlights had lit up the street. Annie was three hours later than she'd said she would be.

When she had come home from Brenda's with Mark and realized that Annie should have been home by then, she headed over to the high school's baseball field. The parking lot was empty. The game had long been over. Getting angry, she had gone by the grocery store where Rick worked, and asked if he knew where she could be.

"She doesn't tell me anything," Rick said. "The brat's probably gone to a movie or something."

"She wouldn't dare. Not after I barely let her go to the game on a school night."

"Sure, she would," he said. "Annie does whatever she wants. Usually, you just don't know about it."

Cathy's mouth had fallen open. "Rick, I hope you intend to explain that!"

"Can't, Mom. Gotta go. I'm on the clock."

Frustrated, she had gone back to the car. She'd left Mark in it with the motor running, and he had moved to the driver's seat so people would think he was old enough to drive. The radio was on a heavy metal station and turned to full volume. She was embarrassed when she opened the door and the music came blaring out. "Move over, Mark," she yelled. "And turn that thing down. Good grief!"

He moved over but didn't turn the radio down, so she got in and turned it off.

"Hey, I was listening to that!"

"And so was half the town. There are laws about disturbing the peace, Mark. And I don't want you going deaf. You already do a pretty good job of not hearing me whenever I tell you to do something."

"So did you find her?"

Cathy didn't put the car in reverse just yet. Instead, she sat there, staring out the window, trying to think. "No, Rick didn't know anything. Mark, he said something that really bothered me. He said that Annie does whatever she wants. That I just usually don't find out about it."

"He's got *that* right," Mark said, reaching for the radio again.

She slapped his hand away. "I'm talking to you. What did he mean by that? What has she done that I don't know about?"

He looked at her then, as if trying to decide whether to talk. "I can't tell you that, Mom. It's classified. If I tell on her, she'll tell on me."

Cathy's heart deflated. Was there a conspiracy among her children to dupe her into servitude without asking questions? Were there things going on after she went to bed at night? Did they have whole identities she knew nothing about?

She popped the car into reverse and pulled too abruptly out of the parking space. The tires squealed as she came to a stop and switched to "drive."

"Way to go, Mom!" Mark said. "Burning rubber. All right!"

She felt her face reddening and forced her foot to go easier on the pedal. "Mark, I'm going to make a suggestion to you right now, and I want you to pay close attention. It would be very wise of you if you didn't utter another word until we got home . . . unless you plan to tell me what your sister has done that I don't know about."

"Sorry."

"That was a word."

"Ex-*cuse* me."

"That was two words," she said through her teeth. "Why don't you stop by the bathrooms on the way to bed and clean the toilets? Burn off some of that energy."

"Mom! You're mad at Annie and taking it out on me. No fair!"

"No, Mark, right now I'm most definitely mad at you. But it's a good thing, because I'll get clean toilets out of it, and you'll learn to respect your mother. See how these things have mutual benefits? Now, if you'd like to keep talking, there are some dishes in the sink that need washing."

Mark hadn't said another word. And now she had clean toilets, and he was sound asleep in bed. Rick had even come home from work, but Annie was still nowhere to be found.

"Mom?" She turned back from the window and saw Rick in the doorway. "I called Allen Spreway's house. His mom said he still wasn't home either, so she's obviously with him. I asked her if she knew when he had to be home, and she said he didn't have a curfew."

"Terrific. My daughter is out with some condom-carrying kid with no curfew."

He grinned. "Cool. Alliteration."

"What?"

"Never mind. Mom, I could go out looking for her, if you want."

"Where would you look?" she asked, turning back to the window.

"There are places where kids go . . . You know . . . to park and stuff."

She felt nauseous. "So you think that's where your sister is?"

"She could be. Or she could be at Pizza Hut. Lots of people go there after the game. Most of them would be gone after three hours, though."

She turned back to the window. "Why is she doing this to me?"

Rick came closer and peered out over her shoulder. He'd long ago surpassed her in height, and was filling out. He wasn't the lanky, loping kid he used to be. "Mom, don't think of it as her doing anything *to* you. She probably hasn't given you a single thought."

"Maybe we're just assuming the worst," Cathy said, as if she hadn't heard him. "What if she's hurt somewhere? What if they had a wreck? Or what if this guy, this Allen Spreway, is a jerk and won't bring her home?"

"Well, don't get mad at me for saying this, Mom, but Annie's not the victim type. Wherever she is, it's exactly where she wants to be."

Headlights lit up the street, and she caught her breath as the car turned into the driveway. "There she is!" Cathy said.

"I'm outa here," Rick said, heading for the stairs. "I don't want to hear the yelling."

Cathy didn't respond, because she knew there probably would be plenty. She went into the kitchen and waited with her arms crossed as the garage door came up. She stood poised to attack the moment her daughter came in, but she didn't right away. It took several more moments before the door finally opened.

Annie stepped into the kitchen and looked surprised to see her. "Mom? You didn't have to wait up."

Cathy's mouth fell open. "Are you kidding me? You're three hours late and that's all you have to say?"

"The game went into extra innings. I can't help it if—"

"Don't you even try it," Cathy bit out. "I went to the ballpark and the game was over hours ago. Where have you been?"

"Just riding around."

Cathy glared at her, her mind desperately seeking a response. "Just riding around? Annie, how wise do you think it was to stay out three hours late when I almost didn't let you go out on a school night in the first place? How soon do you think I'll allow you to go out again?"

"Oh, Mom. Give me a break. I'm not some little kid. I'm fifteen."

"Well, you're about to be treated like 'some little kid.' You're not going anywhere for two weeks, and right now, you can march up to your room and unplug your telephone. Bring it to me. You won't get it back until I think you deserve it."

"That's ridiculous!" Annie yelled. "I didn't do anything wrong! And I *am* going out this weekend because Allen asked me out and I said yes. There's no way I'm going to tell him that my mommy won't let me go."

"Fine. Then I'll tell him when he comes to get you," Cathy said.

"I can't believe this." Annie threw her purse down on the counter. "What is it with you? Did your date turn out to be a dud again? You *always* take it out on me when you don't have fun, but I am *not* responsible for your love life, Mom."

Cathy tried to follow that thread of logic but realized her daughter was just trying to change the subject. "Go to bed, Annie. I'll deal with you tomorrow."

"Fine. But I *am* going out with Allen this weekend. I've been waiting for him to like me all year, and now that he does, I'm not going to let you blow it for me."

A thousand reactions played through Cathy's mind—from having Annie's mouth sewn shut to chaining her to her bedroom doorknob. The child needed discipline, she thought. She needed to be taught a lesson. She needed to learn respect. She needed ...

... a father in the home.

Suddenly, Cathy was incredibly tired, and she looked at the clock and saw that it was after one. "Go get the telephone, Annie, and give it to me. Then go to bed. And when I try to wake you up in the morning, I'd better not have to tell you twice, because I'm going to be in a worse mood than you are, and I could be dangerous."

Annie jerked her purse off of the counter and huffed up to her room.

Cathy sat in the den for several moments, waiting for the phone, but Annie never brought it down. Finally fed up, she stormed up the stairs and burst into Annie's room. She was in her bed with the light off, talking on the telephone.

Cathy turned the light on, and Annie cried out, "Mom!"

She stormed to the phone jack and jerked the cord out, then grabbed the phone from Annie's hands and flung it across the room. It hit the wall with a crash, then thudded to the floor. She turned back to Annie and saw that her daughter was finally taking her seriously. "I'm not a violent woman," Cathy bit out, her hands shaking with rage and her eyes blazing. "But you're pushing me too hard, young lady. If you have one shred of judgment, you know that I've reached my threshold of maternal tolerance. From here on out it gets ugly."

"Sorry," Annie said.

It was the closest Cathy was going to get to resolving this tonight, she thought. At least Annie wasn't talking back anymore. It was a small victory, but hard won.

Without another word, she picked up the pieces of Annie's phone and stormed to her bedroom. She didn't sleep a wink for the rest of the night.

CHAPTER *Twelve*

It was all Brenda could do to wait until after eight o'clock the next morning to call in for Joseph's appointment. When she was told that the next available appointment was a week away, she took it gratefully, then hung up and wondered if she should have fought for an earlier one.

Joseph was sitting at the breakfast table with the rest of the children, eating cornflakes. She'd felt guilty for waking him this morning when he looked so tired and pale. But today was a school day, and she didn't like letting the children sleep late just because they didn't have a tardy bell. He had his face propped on his hand and was picking at his cereal. He seemed slightly out of breath, but she wondered if that was just her imagination.

David came into the kitchen and caught her watching Joseph. "Did you call?" he whispered.

"Yes." She busied herself cutting up wedges of cantaloupe and putting the pieces into bowls. "It's just . . ."

"Just what?"

"Just that they couldn't get him in for a week."

David's jaw dropped. "Did you tell them it was a referral? Did you tell them about his X-ray?"

"I did," Brenda said. "But I guess all of their patients are like that."

David turned back to Joseph and stared at him for a moment. Finally, he sat down at the table. Daniel, Rachel, and Leah were just finishing up, waiting for the fruit their mom was working on, but Joseph had hardly touched his cereal.

"You feeling okay this morning, buddy?" David asked Joseph.

"Yes, sir."

David raked his hand through the child's red hair, finger-combing it into place. "You sure? You don't look like you feel that well."

Joseph met his father's eyes. "Is something the matter with my heart?"

Brenda stopped what she was doing and turned back from the counter. The other three children looked up.

"Why would you ask that?" Brenda asked.

"Because . . . Daniel said a cardac surgeon—"

"Card-*i*-ac," Daniel corrected.

"—is a guy who works on hearts, like Dr. Harry."

David looked up at her, and Brenda abandoned the cantaloupe and sat down in her own place. "Daniel's right," David said. "Your heart might need a little tune-up, like we did to that old truck of mine."

"A tune-up?" Joseph asked. "How do they do that?"

Brenda didn't trust David's analogies to help the matter, so she touched her husband's hand, silencing him. "Joseph, there may not be anything wrong at all. You probably just have some kind of virus. We just want to check to make sure."

He kept dipping his spoon in his cereal, scooping up cornflakes and letting them fall back into the milk. "I dreamed I died."

Brenda caught her breath and covered her mouth, and tears came to her eyes. "Oh, honey . . ."

"That's it," David said, getting up. He picked up the telephone book and began flipping through.

She touched the tears at the corners of her eyes, as if she could hold them back. "Who are you calling?"

"I'm calling Harry. He's a heart surgeon."

"But he's not a *children's* cardiac surgeon. That's what Dr. Gunn said we needed."

"I know, but Harry knows what to look for. If he thinks Joseph needs to be seen right away, he'll find a way to get us an earlier appointment. Doctors listen to doctors."

"But Dr. Gunn said he would call, and it didn't help. Besides, isn't that rude, to ask a neighbor to make a house call like that?" Brenda felt like Leah now, worried that she'd make some kind of social faux pas.

"Hey, if he wants me to, I'll take Joseph over to his house. He's not like that, Brenda. He won't mind."

"Well, you may not catch him. Doesn't he do surgery early in the mornings?"

He got the number, dialed, and waited. "Sylvia? This is David Dodd. Has Harry left yet?" He paused. "No, that's okay. I was just hoping . . . Well, it's just that . . . Brenda called to get Joseph's appointment and they can't get him in for a week. Yeah. That's what I thought. Sylvia, we hate to take advantage of a neighbor . . . If you're sure . . . All right. We'd really appreciate it."

He hung up the phone and turned back to the table. All four children were frozen in silence.

"What did she say?" Brenda asked.

"She said that she would call Harry right now and see if he could come check on Joseph on his lunch break."

"Thank goodness." She leaned across the table and patted Joseph's hand. "Dr. Harry will fix you up." She looked at the other kids. "You can all have some of this cantaloupe if you want it. Rachel, will you give some to Joseph? Then all three of you clean up. Joseph, you don't have to help. You just try to eat."

He nodded as his sister gave him a bowl of cantaloupe.

Brenda took David's hand and headed back to the bedroom. She burst into tears before she reached the room. She turned around, and David pulled her into his arms. "Don't be scared," he said. "It's probably something very minor. Nothing at all."

"He dreamed he died." She let the tears out all at once, as if to relieve some of the pressure on her glands, then quickly dried up. "You're right. Harry will probably just tell us it's okay to wait a week, that there's nothing wrong ..."

They clung together for a long time, neither wanting to let go. Finally, David loosened his hold on her. "I'll be out back working," he said. "Call me when Harry comes, or if you need me."

Brenda let him go and went back into the kitchen. Already, the table was cleared, and Daniel and Rachel were rinsing the bowls and loading them into the dishwasher. Leah had found a book to put on her head and was prancing around with perfect posture as she wiped the table. Joseph was laughing at her as he carried his bowl to the sink.

Brenda found herself studying his little chest, wondering what was going on inside it. Silently, she prayed that they had caught it in time, whatever it was, or that it was all a mistake and they'd find out today that the anxiety and worry had all been for nothing. She could live with that—even without anger toward those who'd made the mistaken diagnosis. She tried to believe it—that nothing was wrong with Joseph, that he would bounce back within days and be racing around the house with his sisters and brother, playing David and Goliath. But she could not shake the fear that it wasn't going to turn out that way.

Brenda saw the concern on Harry Bryan's face as he finished his examination of Joseph. Harry's face had many lines—lines of joy that webbed out from his eyes and his mouth, lines of concern that pleated his forehead. But the lines she saw now looked like fear. Would she, too, have those kinds of lines before this was over? She glanced up at David, and saw Harry's fear reflected there.

"I'm going to call Dr. Robinson," he said softly, "and I'll make sure he sees Joseph today."

Brenda didn't know whether to be relieved or startled. "What's wrong with him, Harry?"

"I can't say, Brenda. All I know is his heartbeat is slow and weak, and in my opinion, he needs to see a specialist pretty quick."

Joseph looked up at her, his big eyes searching her face for her response, so he would know how he should feel. She wouldn't let herself show the fear she felt. She smiled. "Well, then, we can get this over with today, can't we, Joseph?"

He nodded solemnly.

"I'm going home to call," he said. "I'll call you before I go back to the office and let you know what time your appointment is."

He didn't want them to hear the conversation, she realized. What would he tell Dr. Robinson that he didn't want them to hear? "Thank you, Harry," she said, and gave him a hug.

When he'd gone, Brenda looked up at David. He looked even more shaken now, and she wanted to take him into the other room and ask him to try to smile so that he wouldn't worry Joseph.

"Good grief, Joseph," she said brightly. "You'll do anything to get out of schoolwork."

He smiled. "I think I'd rather do math than go to another doctor."

"That's what you think," she said. "We were about to work on fractions today."

He wasn't amused.

Brenda finished feeding lunch to her kids, then assigned them to separate stations around the house where they worked on different levels of schoolwork. Her heart wasn't in it today. There were ways to stimulate her kids, to challenge them to go farther than they had to go to pass the state tests. Normally, she would find life lessons in everything she taught them. They would go places and experience things. The tests were just a formality. Her kids had always scored very high.

Today, however, she was tempted to tell them that school was letting out early, that they could play and watch videos and find something to occupy themselves so she could worry. She might have to do that anyway, if the appointment came early enough.

True to his word, Harry called back within twenty minutes and told her that Dr. Robinson would see Joseph at one-thirty. She would just barely have time to get him to St. Francis Medical Center. She gave the kids their assignments and put Daniel in charge. Then, acting as if they were heading out on a field trip, she plastered a joyful smile on her face, nudged David into doing the same, and they loaded Joseph into the car.

CHAPTER
Thirteen

Cathy had decided not to wear her usual jeans and tennis shoes today, or the blue lab coat that she wore over her clothes at the clinic. Instead, she had dressed in a blazer and khakis that made her look like any other middle-class mom showing up at the high school to talk about her kids.

She waited nervously outside the principal's office, pacing back and forth, back and forth, her speech playing over and over in her mind, as if one misplaced word would send her whole case tumbling down.

A side door opened and the principal stuck his head out. "Mrs. Flaherty?"

"*Ms.* Flaherty," she corrected. "I'm divorced." She didn't know why that bit of information was relevant, except as part of her argument that, as a single mom raising her kids on her own, she needed the school to be her ally, not her enemy.

"Come into my office, Ms. Flaherty," he said. She followed him in and took the seat across from his desk.

"Aren't you the vet?"

"That's right," she said.

"My wife brings our dog to you. Gussy. Big German shepherd?"

"Of course," she lied. She treated hundreds of German shepherds each year and had no recollection of one named Gussy. There were pictures of older teenagers on his desk—his own children, apparently. She wondered if anyone in school had handed *his* son a condom when he was in high school.

He sat back in his chair and pressed his fingertips together, making a steeple. She crossed her legs, trying to look relaxed, but her right foot began to vibrate, as it often did when she was nervous or upset. She willed it to stop.

"Mr. Miller, I came here to talk to you about the sex education class that my son was involved in last week. I believe you called it 'Condom Awareness Day'?"

"Yes," he said. "It's actually about human reproduction, but naming it like that kind of gives it a sense of importance. I know that some parents have a problem with it, Ms. Flaherty, but the truth is that the teen pregnancy rate in this state is sky-high. Our children are getting pregnant left and right, and the incidence of AIDS and other sexually transmitted diseases are at an all-time high. It's very important that we teach them about safe sex."

Her eyes locked into his. "I prefer that my children have no sex. Not until they're married."

He smiled and leaned back hard. "Don't we all? That's the ideal, of course. But these kids *are* having sex."

"Then wouldn't it be better for you to teach them not to, instead of instructing them on how to do it right?"

He didn't seem to like the way she put that. She hadn't meant to antagonize him, not when he was the one she needed on her side. She picked up the framed portrait of his son on his desk. "Mr. Miller, is this your son?"

"Yes." His face softened into a smile. "He's going to the University of Tennessee right now, playing on the baseball team. He's a junior."

"And your daughter?" She pointed to the portrait of the young woman.

"My daughter is still here," he said. "She's a senior."

"She's pretty," Cathy said, forcing a smile. "I'll bet she doesn't sit home much on Saturday nights."

He laughed, flattered. "No, she sure doesn't."

"And it doesn't bother you that she dates boys carrying condoms?"

Again, his face changed and he shifted uncomfortably in his chair, bracing his elbows on his desk. "I don't think that's the case. Just because they know how to use one doesn't mean they're going to."

"Why not?" she asked. "When you were a teenager, if some authority figure had handed you something like that, saving you the shame and embarrassment of having to go into a drugstore and buy it, wouldn't you have thought it was okay to use it?"

He leaned forward now and laced his fingers together, more of an igloo now than a steeple. "Actually, no."

"Well, that's where we disagree." She shifted in her seat. "Mr. Miller, if I want my son to be instructed in condom use, that's my prerogative, but I don't think you have the right to decide that for me." She sat straighter in her chair and leveled her eyes on his. "I was wondering if I could watch the video you showed them. I realize it's after the fact—the truth is, you should have given parents the right to do that before you ever showed it to the kids. But I'd still like to see it."

"We don't have it," he said. "It floats between the district high schools and middle schools, and the superintendent's office holds it until we need it." He slid his chair back and crossed an ankle over his knee. "Look, Ms. Flaherty, I didn't write this policy. The school board thought it was a good idea. If you don't agree, and if you're set on seeing the video, I suggest you take it up with them."

She pulled a pad and pen out of her purse and poised to write. "So who do I talk to?"

"Well, you could start with Mary, the superintendent's secretary. She could let you view the video, I suppose. And if you want to challenge the policy, you could try to get this put on the agenda of the next school board meeting. Or you could go straight to Dr. Jacobs, the superintendent, and take it up with him."

"And would he listen?"

"Probably not," he admitted. "You see, you're coming from the perspective of a parent with . . . how many children?"

"Three."

"And Dr. Jacobs is coming at this from the perspective of someone who oversees thousands. He's intimately acquainted with the statistics. The problem is so big that they're considering opening a day-care center here for our kids who have kids. Personally, I'm dreading it. As if I didn't have enough to take care of. A few years ago, that wouldn't have been a problem."

"A few years ago they weren't handing out condoms in schools." She slapped her forehead dramatically. "Could there be a connection, ya think?"

"Talk to the superintendent," he said, obviously annoyed at her sarcastic tone. He got up, dismissing her. "Thanks for coming by. It's good to finally meet you, especially since I've never seen you at a PTA meeting."

The observation stung, and she realized that he was accusing her of not being involved in her children's education. Even if it was true, did that mean she didn't have the right to question their policies? "Mr. Miller, I am a single mother with a full-time job trying to raise three kids alone. It's not easy to find the time to make all of the meetings."

"I understand," he said smugly. She knew he really didn't. His home was probably perfectly intact; she doubted that he knew what it was like to have a spouse rip the heart out of the family by deciding they'd rather start fresh with someone younger and more exciting.

"Thanks for your time," she said, and left his office as hurt as if he'd insulted her outright.

Next, she went to the superintendent's office. Mary, the superintendent's secretary, claimed they had misplaced the video, but that she was sure it was at one of the schools and would "turn up" before the next school year. "Perhaps you'd like to meet with Dr. Jacobs," the secretary said.

"Of course," Cathy said.

Dr. Jacobs rose to greet her when she entered his office. But the bald, overweight superintendent shifted in his chair impatiently as she explained her position.

"You could submit a written request to be put on the agenda at the next school board meeting," he suggested. His tone implied that he didn't think she'd bother.

"When is that?" Cathy asked.

"Well, the last meeting of the school year was just last week, and there won't be another one until September."

She decided that wasn't too bad. She would have time to gather resources and allies before she actually went before the school board. And there was still time to get some policies changed before they handed out condoms again next year.

"Can I get a list of all the parents in the district?" she asked.

"What for?"

"So I can communicate with them. See if I can get any support from other concerned parents."

Dr. Jacobs stared at her as if she'd just asked him if she could use all the fifth graders to clean up toxic waste. "I'm sorry, Ms. Flaherty, but we're not authorized to give out the addresses of our students. I'm sure you understand."

"Then how am I supposed to contact the other parents?"

"Maybe you're not supposed to," he said. "If and when the policy is changed, it will show up in the new policy booklet."

"But isn't the new policy booklet given out at registration? Won't it be printed *before* school starts next year?"

"Yes."

"Then wouldn't it stand to reason that we should take care of this before that comes out?"

"There's nothing in the policy booklet regarding human reproduction classes."

"Which is exactly the problem. Parents would appreciate knowing what the administration intends to do with their children. They need to know their sons are carrying school-distributed condoms around in their pockets."

"Ms. Flaherty, if you're so disenchanted with the public school system, perhaps you should send your children to private school."

She couldn't believe the anger that mushroomed inside her. "I happen to believe in the *ideal* of public school," she said. "I pay a huge tax bill every year for these schools. They're *my* schools, as much as anyone's. I'm not going to pull my kids out just because things aren't going my way. Instead, I'm going to fight things and make sure that my tax money isn't going to waste. I want to make sure that what goes on there is not detrimental and not morally corrupting. A wholesome, solid education should not only be available to kids whose parents can afford private schools."

"It isn't morally corrupting to explain sexual safety to our children. People are dying because they're not having safe sex."

"For kids, the *only* safe sex is abstinence. Passing condoms out to children doesn't come close."

"Frankly, Ms. Flaherty, we're not sure what works, so we hedge our bets."

"Sounds like nothing's working, which is why you're considering day-care centers in the high schools." She could see the fatigue lines on the man's hard face, and she realized he had the weight of the whole school district on his shoulders. She didn't imagine that was an enviable job. "Look," she said, trying to sound less confrontational. "I think we're both out for the best interests of these children. I just happen to disagree with you on what is best."

"That's allowed."

"I'm going to fight you."

"I expect you will."

"And somehow I'll get a list, and I *will* contact all the parents."

He smiled. "Somehow, I believe that you'll manage to do just that, but I'm not going to help you."

"Fine," she said. "I'll see you in September."

His smile was weary but without hostility. And as she left the office, a seed of hope began to take root in her heart.

CHAPTER
Fourteen

Dilated congestive cardiomyopathy.

The words exploded in Brenda's head with the power of dynamite. She was glad Joseph was not in the room to see the effect this diagnosis was having on his parents; he'd have been frightened to death.

"It's a condition probably caused by a viral infection," the doctor was saying in a slow, deliberate voice. "It causes the muscle of the heart to weaken, making the chambers dilate." He held up a diagram of the heart, trying to demonstrate what he was explaining. But the alarm bells wouldn't stop ringing in Brenda's mind. "As the virus damages the heart muscle, the chambers of the heart dilate and the contractions become ineffective. Right now, Joseph's heart is not able to pump enough blood to adequately maintain his circulation."

"What virus?" David asked the doctor in a voice that sounded far away. "When?"

"There's a remote chance that he's had cardiomyopathy since birth and it's just now presenting. Or somewhere along the way, another illness may have done some damage. But my guess is that it was the virus he had a few weeks ago."

"So what do we do?" Brenda choked out, fighting tears. She couldn't go out of here with a red, runny nose. Joseph would sense her despair immediately. Nine-year-old boys shouldn't have to worry about the condition of their heart.

"Well, we have three options. There's a very good possibility that, with the proper medication, the heart muscle will make a full recovery."

"Medication?" Brenda asked as the first balloon of hope inflated in her heart. "Really?"

"It's a possibility," he repeated. "The second option is that, if it doesn't heal itself with medication, we'll have to medicate Joseph for the rest of his life to keep his heart functioning."

Her hope deflated. Medication for the rest of his life?

"And the third option?" David asked.

"Well, surgery. But it all depends on the biopsy," he said. "I'd like to put Joseph in the hospital today and perform a biopsy first thing in the morning. We need to find out the full extent of the damage to his heart before we can take any action."

"And . . ." she swallowed, trying to steady her voice. "What will that entail?"

"I won't lie to you," Dr. Robinson said, leaning on his desk. "It's a pretty tedious process for a little boy, so we'll need your help. What I'll do is cut into the artery and insert a catheter. This isn't painful. He'll be semi-awake for everything, and you'll be able to watch on the monitor as the catheter goes through the arteries and into the heart's chambers. We insert dye to help us see what we need to see, and this sometimes causes discomfort. It's a warm sensation, and passes pretty quickly. If we tell Joseph what to expect, he should take it just fine."

"Is that all there is to it?" David asked.

"Well, no. He'll have to lie flat and be immobilized for several hours afterward while we keep pressure on the incision. That's where we'll really need you. This is difficult for adults, so you can imagine how hard it'll be with a little boy."

"Joseph will do fine," Brenda said.

"What will all this tell us?" David asked.

"It'll tell us how bad things are," Dr. Robinson answered. "And what we need to do to save his life."

❧

They found Joseph sitting up and playing a game of Memory with the nurse, who seemed used to entertaining children while the doctor fulfilled their parents' worst nightmares. Joseph looked up at Brenda, and she knew that she hadn't done a very good job of hiding the evidence of her tears.

"How you feeling, honey?" she asked, hugging him so tight that she feared she might break him.

"Okay, Mama," he said.

David stooped down next to him, meeting his eyes. "Doctor tells us you're sick, buddy. He wants to put you in the hospital and do some more tests."

Joseph's hazel eyes grew round. "Now?"

"That's right."

"Don't worry, honey," Brenda said. "I'll stay with you. And you won't be in long. Just a night or two."

"Will I get to eat ice cream?"

Brenda smiled. Daniel had had his tonsils out two years ago, and the other three kids had felt deprived because of all the attention and ice cream lavished upon him. "Probably. We'll see."

As they headed for the car, Brenda wished with all her heart that ice cream was all that Joseph needed.

❧

The catheterization went well the next morning, and Joseph took it all as if it was another of their field trips. Brenda patiently tried to explain everything that was happening, taking advantage of the opportunity to teach him a little anatomy.

It was late that afternoon when the doctor came with the results. David and Brenda stepped out into the hall while the nurse fussed over Joseph.

"How is he, Doctor?" David asked anxiously.

"Well, I'm really very pleased with what we found. His heart valves and his veins and arteries look pretty good. That's good news. His left ventricle is still not pumping like it should, and it's enlarged. But it's possible that he'll make a full recovery with medication."

Brenda caught her breath. Had he really said that medication was all Joseph needed?

"Medication?" David asked as if voicing her thoughts. "Not surgery?"

"Not yet," Dr. Robinson said. "We're going to start with a couple of drugs that will lower his blood pressure and reduce the force of the contraction of the heart. We'll want to keep him another day or so. I'd like to transfer him to the telemetry unit. We'll hook him up to a transmitter and monitor his heart. He'll be able to walk around the halls and get some exercise, but the nurse's station will have the heart monitor so we can watch him. After we release him, we'll give him a portable heart monitor to wear all day, and then you can bring it back in so we can analyze his cardiac activity and see how he's doing."

Brenda didn't like the sound of any of this, but she did appreciate that they were planning to watch things so closely.

"What if things don't go like you hope?" David asked.

"They may not," the doctor admitted. "Then we'll have to look at surgery. But if he's lucky, he'll be back to normal in just a few months. And he looks like a lucky kid to me."

After Joseph fell asleep that night, Brenda and David sat quietly in the darkened hospital room, watching him, saying nothing. Sylvia, who was staying with their other three children, had encouraged David to stay as long as he wanted to, and Brenda knew that if there had been enough room, he would have spent the night there, too.

She touched Joseph's forehead. He was cold, clammy. She straightened his covers, trying not to move the cords and wires attached to his chest. The *tick, tick, tick* of the heart monitor beside his bed was getting on her nerves—especially the occasional blips that broke the rhythm, startling her. But she had been impressed by the diligence with which the nurses watched him. They had ten heart monitors over their station, monitoring ten patients, and whenever Joseph's heart stumbled, they ran to check on him.

David's hand touched her shoulder and she turned around. He pulled her into a reassuring hug. She began to weep, and afraid of waking Joseph, she pulled out of his arms and walked out of the room.

David followed her into the corridor. Not knowing where else to go, she went into the stairwell next to their door, sat on the top step, and buried her face in her hands. He sat down next to her and stroked her back helplessly as she wept.

After a while, she looked up at him. "David, if Joseph is out of here by then, I want you to go to church with us Sunday."

He looked away. "Brenda, we've talked about this a million times. I don't do church."

"I know, but this is different. We've never had a child with a heart problem before."

"And how does that make things different?"

"Because we both need to believe, David." Her words were uttered urgently, tearfully.

"Honey, I know how much you want me to believe. But wanting me to won't make it happen. I just don't. I can't."

She wiped her face and tried to look stronger. "I'm going to ask them to lay hands on him Sunday," she said. "I'd like for you to be there. It's very important."

"No way." He got up and his face began to redden. "They'll lay hands on Joseph over my dead body."

His outburst stunned her, and she got to her feet. "David, why?"

"I have my reasons." He pointed a trembling finger at her. "So help me, Brenda, they're not gonna touch my son."

Her face twisted as she tried to understand. "David, this is ridiculous. I know you're bitter about church, but for heaven's sake, the Bible tells us in the book of James that we can go to the elders of the church and they can pray—"

"I've kept my mouth shut all these years, Brenda," he cut in. The rims of his eyes were beginning to redden, and the anguish on his face astonished her. "I've let you drag all four children to church with you. It didn't seem to do any harm, so I've allowed it. But I draw the line when it comes to laying hands on my boy."

"David, if you don't believe in God, then what difference would it make to you?"

"It'll make a difference to Joseph!" he bit out. "You don't know what it's like to be a little kid and have a bunch of hateful, Scripture-chanting hypocrites surrounding you with their hands all over you. It stays with you for life, Brenda. It changes the way you think! They're not going to do it to my son!"

Brenda gaped at him, desperately trying to put this new information into the context of David's background. "Stays with you for life? Changes the way you think? David, did someone lay hands on you?"

He swung around and reached for the door handle. "I'm going home. I'll be back in the morning."

"No, David. Please! We need to talk about this. How can I understand you when you won't talk to me?"

He stopped before opening the door, and turned slowly back around. He was trying to calm himself, taking deep, deliberate breaths. His voice was low when he finally spoke. "All right. Let's talk. You want rational reasons, I'll give you some. It doesn't work, for one. If it did, everybody would be doing it, and we wouldn't need hospitals. They have funerals for Christians every day, just like everybody else."

She tried to think. Somehow, this was a conversation vital to David's life. She had to answer wisely. "Because God doesn't choose to heal everyone."

"That's convenient," he said. "You're told that He'll heal you, and then if He doesn't you can say He just didn't choose to. So how does anybody ever know what to believe?"

Her tears assaulted her again as this disappointment she had grown accustomed to hurt her as if it was new. "Faith, David. It's just faith."

"What about Joseph's faith, when he expects to be healed but walks out of there still sick? And what happens when nothing changes, and your church friends start saying it must be because there's sin in your life, or in Joseph's life—or better yet, in *my* life, since I'm the one who doesn't buy into all this? What they'll be saying is that God is cursing our little boy, because otherwise their prayers would have healed him. And then they'll say it's a demon, not a heart problem, that's keeping him from getting well. How's he going to feel about having a demon in him, Brenda? What do you think that'll do to a little kid's mind?"

She wasn't angry anymore, for suddenly she understood. These weren't hypotheticals, thrown out to win an argument. This was a scene right out of David's childhood. It had happened. New tears trickled down her cheeks as she looked at him. "They told you you had a demon?" she asked.

"I was one angry kid," David whispered, as if saying it too loudly might shatter him completely. "I had reason to be. And not because of any demon. It was disappointment."

"About your father," she whispered.

He shot her a look, as if surprised she knew.

"Your mother told me before she died," she said. "You had never told me you were a preacher's kid."

He breathed a laugh and rolled his eyes, as if he couldn't believe she would call him that. "Why didn't you ever tell me you knew?"

"I wanted you to tell me yourself," she admitted. "It seemed like such a painful thing."

"Then she told you about the organist he left town with?"

"Yes."

He nodded and stood there for a moment. Was he thinking that his mother had betrayed him? Brenda hoped not. He was angry enough at his mother already.

"So I suppose she told you about the parsonage, too—how the dear church gave us a week to get out because they had to make room for their new preacher. How we had to live in a garage apartment . . ."

No, his mother hadn't told Brenda that. She listened to him carefully, gratefully. She'd been so desperate to understand. "No wonder you were angry," she whispered.

He laughed bitterly as tears misted in his eyes. "They were sure I had a demon. Tried to cast it out."

"David, those people didn't know God. They couldn't have, or they would have loved you and cared for you. They would have seen what you needed."

He shook his head. "I know you think your church is different, Brenda. On the surface, maybe it seems that way. But it's not."

"Come and see," she pleaded. "You can stand right there as they pray for him. It won't be a bunch of people yelling and pushing on him, David. Just a few of the elders, gently touching him, talking to God and asking Him for healing. Nothing angry or evil. Just people of faith taking their needs to God. Look at me."

He raised his eyes, and she saw the trepidation, the pain there.

"David, you know how much I love our children. Would I ever put them in jeopardy? Would I let anyone frighten them or hurt them in any way?"

"Not on purpose."

"It's not going to hurt Joseph to have a group of people praying for him. It'll just remind him that God is there, with him, that He won't let him down."

Anger flashed across David's face again, and she knew what he was thinking: That there was, as Brenda had admitted, no guarantee that God would heal Joseph—and if He didn't, then in David's opinion God would indeed have let Joseph down. She knew David couldn't understand. Nor was it something she could explain to him. It was something only the Holy Spirit could convince him of.

"David, you've let me take the kids to church. You've even said it was good for them. Don't start putting limits on that freedom now."

He looked down at his feet. "Brenda, this is serious, what Joseph has. I don't want anyone playing head games with him."

"What do you want me to do, David?" she asked. "Prepare him to die?"

"No," he bit out, his face reddening. "He's *not* going to die. He's going to be all right with this medication. You'll see. With or without those people praying."

She wept at the arrogance of that statement. Softening, David held her as she cried into his shirt, her eyes so raw and heavy that she knew sleep was nearby.

When David finally left, she made up the cot next to the bed and tried to sleep, but the sound of Joseph's heart beating and stumbling, beating and stumbling, kept her awake. So she passed the time praying again for her little boy's heart . . . and her beloved husband's soul.

CHAPTER

Cathy didn't really know why she decided to take Sylvia up on her invitation to go to church Sunday morning. She supposed part of it had to do with the fact that her kids were going down the tubes. They needed some spiritual instruction. She had never been much for church herself. It wasn't that she didn't believe in God. It was just that she couldn't imagine why it was necessary to get up early on her only day off, don a dress and panty hose, and force her children to put on decent clothes and come to church with her.

That part had certainly been a challenge this morning. Annie had come out of her room looking like a runaway. Cathy had sent her back twice before she'd come out wearing anything remotely presentable— which had reminded Cathy that she hadn't made it a priority to shop for dresses for Annie, except on the rare occasions when she had to wear them for a dance. And none of those dresses was appropriate for church. They'd finally settled on a skirt that was too short, and a hot pink blouse that gave Cathy a headache. But it was the least offensive outfit Annie had come up with.

Mark and Rick had fought her tooth and nail about having to wear anything other than blue jeans, but she'd finally gotten them into khakis and dress shirts. When Mark came downstairs in filthy Nikes, she told him to go back up and change his shoes.

"I can't, Mom. I don't have any other shoes."

"You have a pair of dress shoes, Mark. Now put them on."

"You bought those last year! They don't fit me anymore. What's wrong with these?"

She looked helplessly down at Mark's feet. "They're dirty, and just not right for church. Are you sure the others don't fit?"

"Positive, Mom. This is it."

"All right," she said, giving up. "Get in the car."

They had argued all the way there that they didn't know why she had to visit church on their weekend home, when she could just as easily have done it when they were with their dad.

"I want you to come," she said. "I'm doing this as much for you as I am for myself."

"Oh, so all of a sudden you think we're heathens," Annie said.

"Mom!" Mark shouted. "*I'm* not a heathen."

"I don't think any of you are heathens," she returned. "It's just that nice people go to church, and I want you to be nice people."

"We can be nice people at home," Rick complained. "Aren't we nice people?"

His sister and brother agreed. Cathy couldn't help laughing. "It's not like I'm asking you to shave your heads. I just want you to go to Sunday school."

"Sunday school? Come on, Mom!" Rick said. "We're too old for Sunday school!"

"Is that so?" she asked, giving him a sideways glance. "I didn't know there was an age limit in Sunday school."

"So what are we supposed to do? Sit at a little desk and paste Bible verses on construction paper? Sing 'Jesus Loves Me'?"

Had it been *that* long since she'd had her children in church?
"I doubt very much that they still do that in your age-group."

"Then what do they do?"

"They talk about God," she said. "Believe it or not, it's an
important subject. You do believe in God, don't you?"

He shrugged. "Yeah, I guess."

"You guess." That made her feel even more like a failure.
"Look, Rick, I know I haven't made church a priority in this
family, but that doesn't mean I can't set things right now. I think
it's important that we all go to church."

"Give me a break," Annie said from the backseat.

She looked in her rearview mirror at her daughter's scowl.
"And what is that supposed to mean?"

"It means the only reason you wanted to go to church today
is that there's a huge singles department at the Bryans' church.
You're looking for a husband."

"What?" Cathy gasped, appalled at how close to the truth
Annie's guess was. "Where do you get this stuff?"

"I hear things," she said. "I happen to know that the Bryans'
church has one of the biggest, most active singles departments
in the state, and they have it for all ages, even for older divorced
people like you. And I've heard Miss Sylvia talk to you about it,
so I know that's why you want to go."

"This may come as a huge surprise to you, my dear," Cathy
said sarcastically, "but it is not my aim in life to get tangled up
with another man."

Annie looked out the window. "I'm just saying that it's a lot
to put us through just for a date."

Cathy had to hand it to her. Annie knew how to give her a
one-two punch. "Look, we all need to go to church." Her voice
rose with each word. "So if you don't mind, I'd appreciate it if
you'd stop complaining. Who knows? You may really like it."

"Yeah, right," Mark muttered.

As she drove, Cathy realized that there was a lot about the
way she had raised her children she wished she could change.
First and foremost, she wished she had started out making them

treat her with respect. Who would have dreamed when they were adoring toddlers that they'd ever turn on her this way? It was her own fault, she thought miserably. Now it was almost too late.

They pulled into the massive parking lot at the Bryans' church, and she sat for a moment, looking at the crowded walkway that would take them across the street and into the huge building. "Look, kids, let's just do our best not to embarrass each other, okay? I promise not to act like a floozy with the single men I encounter, if you promise you won't act like little brats."

None of the children said a word.

She got out of the car, and one by one they followed her, grudgingly, none of them walking together. They were a group of people who didn't want to be seen with each other.

When they reached the visitors' booth, she glanced back at her children to make sure they were put together properly.

"I hate being the new kid," Mark said.

Personally, she didn't mind being the new person, because she liked meeting new people. She just wondered if everyone in the Sunday school department would know instantly that she had come in hopes of meeting a decent man. If they did, was that punishable by death or eternal embarrassment? Would they all turn and look, point at her and hiss, like something out of *Invasion of the Body Snatchers?*

She swallowed her anxiety and stepped up to the booth. As she did, she glanced at her watch. A little over two hours, and she could go home with her humiliated children and a clear conscience.

After a pleasant hour with other divorced men and women her age, Cathy rounded up her kids, and they sat with Sylvia and Harry during the worship service. The Bryans seemed proud that her family had agreed to join them for worship, though Cathy couldn't imagine why. Mark scribbled a note on the church bulletin and tore it off, making a loud ripping noise that caused the people in front of them to look over their shoulders. Cathy clamped Mark's leg, warning him to be quiet. Mark passed the note to Rick, who passed it on to Annie. Cathy opened her own bulletin, found a blank space, and scribbled out, "Stop writing notes!" She started to tear it off, then stopped herself. Instead, she passed the whole bulletin down. By the time it got down to Rick and Annie, they were giggling quietly at the absurdity of her writing a note to tell them to stop writing notes.

She glanced at Sylvia and saw that she'd seen. Sylvia smiled, and Cathy wished she hadn't come.

When the sermon was over and the choir director asked them to stand and sing hymn number 132, Mark muttered, "Stand up, sit down, fight-fight-fight." Cathy had to admit that the constant standing baffled her. Why did they have to keep popping up like jack-in-the-boxes, just to sing a song? Couldn't they sing it as well sitting down?

When the service was mercifully over, Cathy braced herself. She had made the mistake of raising her hand as a visitor, but she'd really had no choice, because Sylvia had been nudging her. Would she be greeted by a dozen well-meaning strangers before she could get to the door? Would they send someone to her home to talk to her about heaven and her responsibility to her children? If they did, she hoped they would call first so she could get the front room picked up.

She was on the way across the parking lot when she spotted one of the better-looking men in her Sunday school class heading toward her. She tried to look approachable.

"Hi, Cathy," he said, reaching out to shake her hand. He was tall, blonde, and had intriguing brown eyes. "I'm Bill Blackburn. I didn't get to meet you in Sunday school, but I'm glad you came. You from around here?"

"We live up on Survey Mountain," she said.

"Nice area."

"We like it. My next-door neighbor invited us to visit. Sylvia Bryan?"

He didn't show any sign that he recognized the name. "Good, good. I'm outreach chairman of the Sunday school class you visited today," he said. "Did you like it?"

"Sure, it was nice." Behind Bill, Annie leaned against the car with her arms crossed and a smug I-told-you-so smile on her face. Cathy began digging into her purse for her keys.

"I heard you were a vet," he said.

"That's right." She glanced at Mark and Rick over his shoulder, hovering behind him like judges, mentally recording the tangible proof that she had come here to meet men.

"Would you mind if I called you sometime?" he asked. "Maybe you'd like to go to the social with me this Saturday. We try to have one every weekend. I could introduce you around."

She thought of telling him no just to shoot down her kids' theories about her intentions, but she did want a life, and the kids needed to get used to it. "Maybe," she said. She jotted her phone number on the bulletin, tore off a corner, and gave it to him. "Just call sometime this week and tell me more. It sounds fun."

"Good," he said. "It was nice meeting you."

"You, too."

He turned back to the children, eyed them one by one. "Great-looking kids you got there," he said, as if they couldn't hear.

"Thank you," she said.

When he'd gone, they got into the car one by one, and she cranked the engine. "So what do you think?" she asked.

"I think you dragged us here so you could meet men," Annie said again.

Cathy pulled out of the parking lot. "I mean about your Sunday school class. Did you like it or not?"

"Not," Annie said.

"How about you, Rick?" Cathy looked across at her big, lanky son. He had already put his Walkman headphones on and was listening, no doubt, to Jimi Hendrix. She gave up on him and glanced at Mark in the rearview mirror. "So Mark, how was yours?"

"Okay," he said. "I knew a couple of people."

She took that as a ringing endorsement. "Did you really?"

"Yeah," he said.

"Who?"

"Brad Lovell. He's pretty cool."

"And he goes to church," she said. "Imagine that. So you'll want to come back?"

"No," he said. "Not unless I have to."

She looked over her shoulder at Annie. "Did you know anybody?"

"Yes." She looked out the window, uninterested in this conversation.

"Who?"

"Sharon Greer. I can't stand her."

"Why not?"

"Because she's after Allen Spreway. She used to date him, and she thinks he's still hers. And she's not a nice girl, Mom, but she sits up there in Sunday school answering all the questions with those hypocritical church answers that the teachers are looking for, and they're like, so out of it, that they don't know she's a fraud."

Cathy's hopes wilted. "Anyone else?" she asked weakly.

"No, that was plenty."

Cathy sighed and thought that maybe they were right. Maybe she needed to attend church on weekends when they were with their dad. She wasn't sure all this pain was worth it.

CHAPTER
Sixteen

Monday morning story hour at the local library was a blessing for Tory, and she never missed a session. Brittany and Spencer loved sitting at the feet of the grandma-like librarian in the children's section and hearing picture books. Tory loved it because it allowed her time to linger alone in her favorite sections. For months, she had spent this time researching her book, reading countless articles on France, World War II, and the nurses and doctors who served in the war. Her head was a smorgasbord of little-known facts, enough to fill a dozen-novel saga.

Deciding that it was not research but motivation she needed today, she floated through the self-help section, searching for the perfect book to inspire greater progress toward her goals. She lingered over a book on personal organization—then realized that if someone could return to her all the hours she'd spent reading books on organizing, she would have written three novels by now.

She moved to the self-esteem section, with books running the gamut from knowing thyself to discovering past lives. When nothing there appealed to her, she moved to the fiction section and scanned the spines for the names of her favorite authors. Someday, her name would be up here, she promised herself. Someday she would have a book that people would ask for in libraries and go into stores intending to buy. She pulled out a book, scanned the blurb on the back, decided against it, then pulled another one. When she had put that one back too, she looked up and noticed a display of brand-new novels. The name of one of her favorite authors caught her eye, so she crossed the room.

On the cover was a woman in a nurse's uniform, and behind her were flames as if something had just been bombed. Frowning, Tory grabbed the book off the shelf and turned it over to read the blurb. "World War II . . . Annabelle Hopkins serving as a nurse. France . . ."

Tory heard a chuckle and looked up—a woman down the aisle was grinning at her. With a touch of embarrassment, Tory realized she'd been reading aloud. She looked at the woman with annoyance, then turned back to the book, whispering the words with a rush of dread. "Will Annabelle's heart be forever buried with the soldier she loves—"

Her stomach plunged and her heart began to race. Her hands trembled as she bit out the rest: "—or will she find love again in the arms of Dr. Frank James?"

She thrust the book back onto the shelf and backed away as if it had burned her.

How could it be? How could this novel have the same plot she was trying to write—only this one was finished and published, and already a best-seller?

Her chest constricted into a tight fist, and a scream of rage rose up in her, though she knew she would never let it out. She grabbed the book again and began flipping through the pages. Yes, the story was similar to hers—but so much better. She turned page after page, searching for something to reassure her that she wasn't wasting her time, that no one would even suspect the similarities between the two stories. Instead, as she skimmed the pages, she became more and more convinced that this book would make hers seem like a rip-off.

Returning the book to the shelf, she backed against the bookshelf opposite it, closed her eyes, and began to cry. It wasn't fair. She hadn't had *time* to write her book, and now someone else had done it, someone with a famous name and a following of millions of devoted readers.

The door to the children's room swung open and a dozen kids burst out, chattering with excitement. Her kids' homing devices zeroed in on her immediately. Brittany looked up at her tears. "Whatsa matter, Mommy?" she asked loudly, and three mothers turned around to look.

"Nothing, honey," Tory said, still shaking. "Come on, let's go."

"But can I get a book? Please?" Spencer was holding two huge hardback books that he'd grabbed off a table. One was a coffee-table book on antique cars. The other was a picture book about merry-go-rounds.

"No, honey, put them back."

"But you said—"

"I didn't say."

"But we always—"

"Please, I've got to get out of here!" She wiped her eyes, and Brittany kept staring at her. She hated to cry in front of them. It wasn't fair.

She put the books back, then escorted them to the car. They marched like little soldiers beside her, wondering what they had done to upset their mother now. There were no computers or horses close by, no Kool-Aid disasters, no cats in the tree . . .

She got them into the car, hooked their seat belts, slid behind the wheel, and peeled out of the parking lot.

"What is it, Mommy?" Brittany asked again in a small voice.

"Just something stupid," she said.

"I like stupid things," Spencer spouted, leaning up on her seat back.

"Spencer, hook your seat belt!"

"It is hooked. See?"

"Spencer, if you can sit on the edge of your seat, it's not tight enough. And if you keep this up, I'm going to make you use the car seat again."

Spencer moaned and sat back, and she heard him pulling it tighter.

"Mommy's okay," she said finally. "I just had a little surprise. See, the book I'm trying to write? Somebody's already written it."

In the rearview mirror, she saw that both children stared at her as if trying to figure that one out. What were they picturing? A balloon floating around in the air with a book's worth of words in it, and the first one to let the air out got to publish it? She wished that was the case.

"It just makes me feel like my work is a waste of time," she told them. "All the research I've done, and all the ways I've developed the characters. Finally, I've got three whole chapters, and what do you know? Somebody else has done it! So I guess I should just give up and get real. What do you think of that?"

The children seemed to consider it for a moment. Finally, Brittany spoke. "Can we go to McDonald's?"

Tory shoved her sunglasses on, hoping to hide the tears. She thought about Brittany's innocent, selfish request. Did she really want to go home, fix them tuna sandwiches, and look at that mocking computer screen with her three pathetic little chapters? "Yes," she said. "We'll go to McDonald's."

The children cheered.

They went to the McDonald's with the playground in the front. And as the children bounced around on the balls and in the tunnels, Tory sat on a bench wondering why she'd ever thought she could be a writer in the first place.

CHAPTER
Seventeen

Because Joseph wasn't feeling up to it, Brenda didn't take him to church Sunday. They celebrated the Lord's Day at home, singing hymns and reading Scripture, while David worked out in his shop. That afternoon, as the children scattered around the house, engaged in their own activities, Brenda closed herself in her bedroom and began to read the book of James again. She found the passage she was looking for, and read it again. "Is any one of you sick? He should call the elders of the church to pray over him and anoint him with oil in the name of the Lord. And the prayer offered in faith will make the sick person well."

She closed her eyes and recalled her argument with David. Was it better to submit to her husband on this, or follow the instructions in Scripture? She began to pray, deeply, earnestly, that the Lord would show her direction.

Finally, she told herself that David didn't have to know. She could take Joseph to the elders, and they could pray over him.

She had never defied David before, and she wouldn't do it now if her son's life wasn't at stake.

But as she saw it, she really had no choice.

The next day, she convinced David not to go with her to Joseph's doctor's appointment. It might be a long wait, she told him, and he had too much work to do. Then she called her pastor and asked him to get the elders of the church together on their lunch hour.

She was torn and tearful as she pulled into the church parking lot, and Joseph frowned and looked up at her. "Why are we at church?"

"I just wanted to stop by for a minute before we go to the doctor. Pastor Mike and some of the men want to pray for you." Her eyes misted over as she reached for her son's hand. "Is that okay with you, Joseph?"

He nodded. "Sure."

She just sat there in the car for a moment, staring across at him. "The thing is, your dad can't know."

"Why not?"

She swallowed. "He had some bad experiences with church people praying over him when he was a little boy."

"Daddy went to church?"

"Yes. But it wasn't like our church, and he doesn't understand." She gazed at him for a long moment. "I've never asked you to lie to Daddy, Joseph. And I'm not asking you now. If it comes up, you can tell him. But if it doesn't, then just don't bring it up, okay?"

His eyes were wide as he considered that. "Okay."

"Okay." She got out of the car and went around to help Joseph out. The doors to the church opened, and the pastor rushed out to help her. Several of the elders came out behind him, fussing over Joseph like doting grandfathers.

Brenda knew that she had done the right thing . . . even if it meant defying David.

CHAPTER Eighteen

Cathy waited three weeks before agreeing to go to a church social with Bill, the man she'd met in the parking lot at Sylvia's church. He had called a couple times a week since she'd met him, and had piqued her interest with talk of the fellowship they had as a singles group. He had offered to take her to Thursday night volleyball, but to avoid having Annie remind her of her reason for taking them to church, she decided to wait for a weekend when the children would be at their father's.

She agreed to go to a Saturday night ice-cream social sponsored by the singles department, and she looked forward to making some new friends.

Bill's Porsche had only two seats, and she felt as if she was crawling into Spencer Sullivan's Flintstone-mobile as she folded into it. He drove like a Nascar driver with a death wish, and she wondered if her fingernails were cutting holes into his armrest whenever he slammed on the brakes. She checked to see if he had air bags. Thankfully, he did. But she worried that if they hit anything she would shoot through the bag like a torpedo.

"So . . . where do you stand on the perseverance of the saints issue?" he asked as they curved down Survey Mountain.

"The what?"

"You know. Once saved, always saved, or predestination, or foreknowledge. I'd like to hear your take on free will versus God's sovereignty."

Was this his idea of an icebreaker? "I don't think I have a take on it," she said. "Uh . . . could you slow down just a little?"

"Sure." He glanced over at her, grinning. "I attended seminary for two years. Was going to be a preacher."

She wondered if churches looked at people's driving records before hiring pastors. If so, it was clear why he wasn't preaching now. "I didn't know that," she said, trying to appear interested.

"That's right. But they were so narrow-minded there. I was obviously at the wrong school, so I dropped out and got a job in computers. But I still study. And I consider myself in ministry— priesthood of believers and all that. I help with the soup kitchen every Thanksgiving, before I have my family over. I invite a few friends, too. An occasional vagrant."

She wondered if he wanted applause. "That's very nice of you."

"You ever do anything like that? 'Cause it's real rewarding. They always need extra hands. And if you can cook, it's even better . . ."

He seemed like a nice guy, she told herself. If it wasn't for his driving, maybe she could even like him. Wasn't a man of faith, a man of principle, what she needed? Someone strong who could be a helpmeet to her? Annie would hate him instantly, but Mark and Rick would be impressed with the car.

"So have you ever been married, Bill?" she asked, half expecting him to say that he had been widowed when his wife was thrown through the windshield.

"Yes."

Suddenly, a short answer? Suspicious, she tried again.

"Divorced?"

"Yes."

"Any kids?"

"Nope."

She couldn't decide if that was a plus or minus. If he had no children, then she didn't have to worry about them liking her. On the other hand, his tolerance level for teenagers was bound to be low.

"How about you?" he asked. "Divorced or widowed?"

"Divorced," she said.

"How many times?"

The question insulted her, and she looked over at him, frowning. "Just once."

"Oh."

She hadn't thought of it before, but now she was curious. "How about you?"

He shrugged, suddenly shy.

"Bill?"

"Three," he said. "I was married and divorced three times. Three mistakes. I have bad taste in women, I guess."

"I see." He picked up his speed again, and she clung, white-knuckled, to the armrest. "I got the impression you'd been in the singles department a long time. How long since your last divorce?"

"Six months."

She gaped at him. "Months? Then how—"

"I met all three women in the singles department," he said proudly. "We have a real high success rate there."

"Success?" she asked. "You call three divorces success?"

He shot her a look. "What are you saying?"

"Just that . . . well, it sounds like the marriage ceremony is the standard by which you judge success or failure. I mean, if you get married, you've succeeded. Never mind whether it works out or not."

"Look, those divorces were not my fault. Everybody knows that."

"Well, of course. I didn't mean ..." She didn't know what she did mean, but suddenly she wished she'd never met Bill Blackburn.

"I had biblical divorces, you know. That makes a difference."

She didn't know much about the Bible, but she thought she understood what he meant. "Oh, so they cheated on you?"

"No. They were unbelievers and they left. I thought they were believers, but obviously they weren't, or they would have been better wives. Paul said that we aren't accountable if unbelieving spouses leave us, so that lets me off the hook. It's almost like the marriages didn't exist."

As unschooled as she was in theology, she felt sure that was a misinterpretation. Maybe he could make that explanation work once, but three times?

"What about yours?" he asked. "Was yours a biblical divorce?"

She looked at him, wondering how to politely tell him it was none of his business. As if he read her mind, he said, "It's pertinent, you know. I don't want to date anyone with unconfessed sin."

She almost laughed, but with great effort managed to keep a straight face. "Rest easy. I'm off the hook, too."

He seemed happy with that. So happy, that he picked his speed up from eighty to ninety.

She was worn out by the time they reached the farm where the social was to be held. "You sure are quiet," he said as they screeched into the driveway. She considered telling him it was difficult to talk when your jaw was clenched in terror.

"I hope my driving didn't scare you," he said as if reading the fear on her face.

"'Scared' isn't the word I would use," she said.

He chuckled. "I bought this car after my last divorce, and I go a little crazy when I drive it. It just handles so well."

She tried to look impressed. "Boy, it sure does."

He opened the door and got out, and she found herself struggling with her own door. Her hands were still shaking. He came around and opened it, and she unfolded from the car.

As they approached the crowd, Cathy saw the heads of all the women turn. Were they asking themselves if she knew about his marital history? Or were they his ex-wives?

Bill wasted no time greeting everyone like a politician the morning of an election, ignoring her completely.

Not one to play the shrinking violet, and desperately glad to be safely on her own again, she introduced herself to those on the fringes of the group who looked as if they were as new as she was. Before long, she had joined a circle of men and women basking in the shade of a huge tree, exchanging homemade ice-cream recipes.

As it grew dark and the party died down and the bug zappers began to pop with their prey, Bill made his way toward her. "Ready to hit the road?"

The relaxation that had fallen over her suddenly fled as she realized she'd have to get back in the car with him. She racked her brain for a way out. Another ride home, perhaps, or a taxi . . .

Then it came to her.

"Bill, let me drive. I've always wanted to drive a Porsche."

He frowned. "I don't know. I don't usually let other people drive her. She's delicate . . ."

"But you were telling me how well it—she—handles, and I'm dying to see for myself."

Finally, he grinned, and tossed her the keys. "All right, but be careful."

She almost laughed at the admonition when he'd been so close to liftoff just hours before. She hurried to the driver's seat before he could change his mind.

He seemed bored as she drove the speed limit home, and kept pointing out features of the car she might have missed. He urged her to go faster, but she declined.

By the time they reached Cedar Circle, she was quite proud of her own ingenuity. "Well, Bill, I really had a nice time. Guess I'll see you in church tomorrow."

"That's it?" he asked. "You're not inviting me in?"

"No, it's a little too late. I'm tired."

He looked disappointed. "So how about lunch after church tomorrow?"

She started to ask him why he would want to take her to lunch, when their time together had been so underwhelming. Instead, she chose to lie her way out of it. "I can't. I've already accepted an invitation from my neighbors."

"Tomorrow night, then?"

"No, my kids will be coming home."

"Next weekend?"

She was getting flustered at his refusal to take no for an answer. "Call me. I'm usually pretty busy, but . . ."

"Okay. I'll call. I think we're a good match, Cathy. I can see myself with you."

"Oh, can you?" She tried to hide her amusement. "And why is that?"

"You're my type. Classy. Professional."

Female, she thought. "Well, I appreciate that."

"No, really. People expect me to be with classy women. I like the fact that you're a vet. That's interesting. Pays well, too."

Again, she wanted to laugh. So that was it. He thought she was wealthy.

"So I can call you?"

"Sure." She realized what a blessing caller ID was. "Thanks for taking me, Bill. It was fun."

He started to get out, but she stopped him, desperately trying to avoid a kiss goodnight. "No need to walk me to the door," she said. "Really. Goodnight."

"Goodnight," he said. He leaned toward her to kiss her, but she turned her head and his lips landed on her ear.

Quickly, she got out of the car and waved through the window.

She was giving up dating, she vowed as she got inside. There wasn't a man alive worth wasting time with. Besides, she needed to put all her energy into praying for her daughter to find one decent man on this earth amidst all the losers—and making her sons into decent men instead of the psychos she had been running into lately.

She left the television off and allowed silence—which had never been her favorite sound—to minister to her like a welcome companion.

CHAPTER
Nineteen

While Cathy was giving up men, Tory was giving up writing. She had dumped her entire manuscript into her computer's recycling bin, then defiantly pushed the button to erase it all. Systematically, she went about her house collecting all the paraphernalia relating to her writing. Her legal pads, her special pens, her books on technique, her tapes of writers' conferences and seminars she hadn't been able to attend. Then she gathered all the self-help books she had bought over the years, and as she did, she realized that none of them had really done her much good. She might be organized, she might know how to manage her time, she might know how to set priorities, but she had never reached her goals, and she wasn't going to.

So she decided to choose new goals—first among them to have a house so clean it squeaked.

Barry watched her from the kitchen table where he was making a Play-Doh dinosaur with the kids. "Come sit down," he told her, pulling out a chair. "Good grief, the house is clean enough."

"It can never be clean enough," she said. "I'm about to clean out the junk drawer. I'm going to be brutal, so if there's anything in there you want to save, you might want to tell me now."

"Honey, why are you doing this?"

"Because it's Saturday," she said. "And you're home to help with the kids and I can get something done."

"But you could be writing."

"I told you, I'm never writing again."

He shook his head. "Look, why don't you just *read* that book and see what it's like? Maybe you can learn something from it. Maybe God has a reason for this."

"God does have a reason for it," she said matter-of-factly. "It's to tell me that I'm not supposed to be a writer. That's not my destiny."

"Then why have you wanted it so badly?"

"Just because you want something doesn't mean it's God's will."

"But what if it *is* God's will—but it's just something you're going to have to work harder for?"

"How can I work harder?" she asked, looking back up at him. "I can't put any more time into it than I have, so that makes me really slow. When I started it, it was because I heard an editor on one of those writers' conference tapes say they're looking for World War II stories. Now that book is out, it's a best-seller, and they'll probably move on to something else—maybe the Civil War or the Medieval age. By the time I get anything written, it'll be too late."

"Then don't write to the trends," he said. "Write what's in your heart."

She breathed a laugh. "I don't *know* what's in my heart. I make things up, Barry. Besides, I don't have the layers and layers of life experience that that author has. She's probably been to France. She probably remembers the war. She's probably had tragic affairs with passionate men. I'm just me."

"But there are things you love, things you care about. Write about them. Write about things in the neighborhood. Heaven knows, there's enough going on around here."

"I don't want to write about real stuff. I just want to make it up. Fiction, not fact."

"But there is a lot of fact in fiction. Some of the greatest truths I've ever read were in fiction. Think of Jesus' parables."

She looked at Barry for a moment, surprised that he'd made such a profound point. Maybe *he* should be the writer, she thought bitterly. "It doesn't matter. I'm still finished with it."

"Then what about the computer? What are we going to do with that? Sell it?"

"Nope. I'm going to start keeping recipes on it. And I'm cataloguing all my books so I can be as organized as a librarian. And the kids'll use it when they start school. Don't worry, I'll come up with a new goal. I was thinking of building a greenhouse onto the back of the house, so I could start growing things. And I could dig up the yard and plant some tomato plants and lady peas. Okra."

"You hate okra. And growing things is not your gift." He pointed out the fake plants decorating every table and shelf. She had never been able to keep anything alive. As hard as she worked to perfect things, she couldn't perfect nature. It had a mind of its own.

"Okay," she conceded, "but maybe if I devoted myself to it, I could learn to grow things. If I had a greenhouse I could do it."

"Tory, you don't need a greenhouse, and you don't need to plow the backyard. You have enough to do."

"All right, fine. Then I won't grow things. I'll find something else."

He looked at her as if he didn't know what more to say to her, then ambled helplessly out of the room.

Tory dropped into a chair and covered her face with both hands. This was madness, she thought. Obsessive-compulsive madness. And she should know—she'd just finished reading a book on the subject.

Barry was right. She did have plenty to do without dragging out new hobbies. Her children needed her. Her husband needed her.

She took a deep breath, got up, and straightened the chairs. Standing in the doorway between the kitchen and the den, she saw the children lying on the floor watching a movie. Barry was sitting in his recliner, staring into space at thoughts she could only imagine.

"Hey, guys," she said. "What do you say we go out tonight? It's Saturday and we haven't done anything in a while. We could go get ice cream and maybe head down to the river, stand on the footbridge, and watch the barges come through."

"Yeah!" Spencer and Brittany said, jumping to their feet and bouncing like little windup toys.

Barry gave her a puzzled look. "Who are you?"

She grinned. "Don't press your luck."

He got up tentatively. "There must be some drawers you haven't cleaned out. Some closets that need dusting."

She got a pillow from the couch and threw it at him. He flinched. "Okay, so I was being obsessive," she said. "I've been feeling sorry for myself, and I've been making everybody miserable. But look at the bright side. The house is amazingly clean."

"Passes the white glove test," he agreed.

"Come on," she said, trying to work some fun into her voice. "Let's just get out of here."

"You sure you have time for fun?"

"You're about to lose your window of opportunity."

"Come on, kids," Barry yelled. "Let's go while Mom's in the mood!"

She picked up the pillow and placed it perfectly on the couch before she followed her family out the door.

CHAPTER

Twenty

The Smoky Mountain fog had lifted early today, and the mountain range on the other side of the valley of Breezewood was green and majestic. Sylvia felt energized after riding her mare, Sunstreak, through the undeveloped back acres of their property. She trotted back to the stables, her hair mussed from the wind and her cheeks pink from the heat.

Gently, she removed the saddle, blanket, and bridle, and brushed down the horse before returning her to her colt in the corral. Then, dusting her hands off, she headed around the house to check her mail. Again, the sight of the hills took her breath away. She had been born and raised in Breezewood, and when she left for any length of time, her eyes yearned for the sight of those hills. She wondered if Sarah missed their mountains yet, or if Jeff ever thought of coming back. If they did, they hadn't mentioned it to her.

She opened the mailbox, hoping one of them had written, even though she'd talked to each of them on the phone just yesterday. She pulled out the bundle of bills and letters and advertisements, and fought disappointment when she saw that there was nothing from them.

"Sylvia!"

She looked up and saw Brenda coming. She waved and waited for her neighbor to cross the cul-de-sac.

"Time to visit?" Brenda asked.

"On a gorgeous day like this? I've been riding all morning. Just look at those mountains. Let's sit on my porch where we can see them."

Brenda followed her onto the porch and sat down on the swing. Sylvia took the rocker next to a pot of azaleas.

"So how's Joseph?" Sylvia asked her as she flipped through her mail.

"Okay, I guess."

Sylvia looked up. "You guess?"

Brenda's smile was uncharacteristically weak. "Well, Dr. Robinson isn't that sure. We've been seeing him twice a week for four weeks, and he keeps changing doses of medication. I thought Joseph would be better by now, but he always seems so tired and out of breath."

"He'll get better," Sylvia said. "Just give it time. Be patient."

"I'm trying."

She flipped through the rest of her mail. The return address from Masaya, Nicaragua, startled her. "Carlos!" she said, picturing the man they had met last year.

"Who's Carlos?" Brenda asked.

"A man in Nicaragua. Didn't I tell you about Carlos?"

"I don't think so."

Sylvia looked off toward the mountains and smiled, remembering. "Well, last year, when we were there, Carlos's wife Maria brought their son to Harry. He was having serious abdominal pain, and Harry diagnosed it as a ruptured appendix and operated on him."

"Harry saved his life, then," Brenda said.

"He sure did. And Maria was so grateful. After it was all over, Harry led her to Christ. Then she started weeping and telling us about her husband Carlos."

"She wanted Harry to witness to him?" Brenda asked.

"Well, yes, but frankly she didn't see any hope of Carlos's conversion. He's a baker, owns his own shop, and at the time, he was a real womanizer. Very handsome. Of course, Maria is very beautiful, too. But that didn't matter. Carlos kept mistresses and spent a lot of time with them."

"Poor woman."

"Yeah. Only we started praying for him with her, and I shared with her all the Scripture I could find about being a godly wife. I helped her memorize the passage in First Peter about keeping her behavior excellent so the unbelieving husband could be won without a word. She was determined to have a gentle, quiet spirit, and to be a model wife instead of the victim he used to come home to."

Brenda's eyes misted over, and Sylvia suddenly realized that Brenda could relate to Maria, even though David had never been unfaithful.

"I hope you told her it takes a long time," Brenda said. "The Holy Spirit has to do it."

"That's the thing," Sylvia told her, leaning forward with enthusiasm. "The Holy Spirit *did* do it. About ten days later, Maria convinced Carlos to come to church with her so he could thank Harry for healing their son. The missionary who preached that day delivered a sermon that shot right into Carlos's heart. He *ran* down to the altar and fell to his knees, sobbing."

Sylvia saw the emotion in Brenda's eyes as she pictured the scene, probably imagining David in Carlos's place, and she remembered why she hadn't told Brenda this story before. She had feared it would frustrate her spirit and make her question God's silence to her own prayers.

"What a beautiful story," Brenda whispered. "Did it change his life?"

"You bet it did. He's very active in the church there, and Maria has kept in touch with me to let me know what a wonderful husband he's become." She looked down at the envelope and tore it open. "Carlos has never written to us himself. Harry will be so thrilled to hear from him."

Her eyes scanned the first few lines. "Oh, Brenda! He's committed his life to full-time Christian service. His church is raising money for him to come to the States to study in a seminary, so that he can go back to Nicaragua and start his own church." She read further. "He wants to know how much money we think they'll need to raise altogether for housing and food and tuition, and anything else that might come up that he hasn't thought of. And he needs help deciding on a seminary."

Brenda grinned. "What a miracle. It gives me hope."

Sylvia dropped the letter on her lap and stared off into the breeze. "Yeah. That's the joy of mission work. That's why Harry wants to go back there."

"Think of all the fruit Carlos is going to bear," Brenda said. "All because Harry was there to save their son's life, and you were there to teach Maria how to be a godly wife."

Sylvia gazed down at the letter again.

"So have you made up your mind about the mission field?" Brenda asked.

Sylvia shook her head. "I've prayed about it. I've told the Lord that I don't want to go. But I've asked Him to change my heart if He wants me to."

"That's fair," Brenda said. "I'll pray that for you, too."

That afternoon when Harry got home, Sylvia gave him the letter. He shed a few tears of his own and started praying immediately for Carlos and Maria and the plans they were making. Then he got out his calculator and began figuring what it would cost them to come to America to study. He would be on the phone for days, Sylvia knew, trying to line up scholarships and grants and donations from people who could help put Carlos through school. They both knew that the little Nicaraguan church Carlos attended would not be able to raise the kind of money Carlos would need.

Sylvia found her own mind racing with possibilities—and she knew that God had put those thoughts into her mind. He was showing her things she needed to consider, things she needed to offer, priorities she needed to acknowledge—but she knew she wasn't ready yet. Sweetly, generously, Harry continued to give her the time she needed, and nothing more was said.

CHAPTER
Twenty-One

It had been five weeks since Joseph's birthday party, and the medicine had not helped Joseph's condition. They'd had twice-a-week visits to Dr. Robinson, and at every visit Brenda saw the strain and tension on the doctor's face as he changed the medication or juggled doses, hoping to help things along. She'd kept Joseph as quiet as possible for the past few weeks. Even though she normally didn't homeschool during the summer, she'd continued it with Joseph just to keep him still and focused on anything other than his failing heart. He slept much of the time, and during those quiet moments, she would sit on the bed and pray for him. She could see in the pallid color of his skin and the deep circles under his eyes, in his shortness of breath after any exertion at all, in the dizziness that came more often than it went, and in the swelling of his ankles, that he was only getting worse.

All this week he'd been moody and depressed, and she knew that he needed to get out, so yesterday she had made the announcement that they would be taking a field trip today to the Adventure Museum—one of her children's favorite places. Joseph's tired eyes had danced with excitement, though that seemed to be the extent of his celebration.

She had invited Tory, Brittany, and Spencer to come with them, hoping Tory could help by dropping them off at the door so that Joseph wouldn't have far to walk. She planned to borrow a wheelchair when they got there, and she would push Joseph around so he wouldn't have to exert himself as they went from one hands-on experiment to another.

But when she went into his room to see if he was ready, he was sitting on the bed with tears on his face and his sneakers in his lap.

"Joseph, what's wrong, honey?"

He rubbed the tears on his face. "I can't get my shoes on."

"Well, I'll help you, sweetie. You don't have to cry." She took the shoes and stooped down in front of him. When she lifted his foot to slide it into the shoe, she saw how swollen it was. No wonder the shoe wouldn't go on.

"Joseph, do your feet hurt?"

"No, ma'am," he said. "They're just swollen. I can't get them on. But I want to go, Mama. I can't go without shoes . . ."

"Wear your flip-flops," she said, going to his closet. "That'll be more comfortable, anyway." She got out the flip-flops and turned back to her son. He was wiping new tears as they ran down his face. "Honey, it's okay. This is nothing new; your feet have been a little swollen every day. The doctor knows about it."

"I know."

"Then why are you crying?"

He shrugged again, and hiccuped a sob. "I don't know."

But she knew. This constant sickness, all the medication, the doctor visits—they were taking their toll on her son. He needed this outing. He needed to get his mind off his problems and have a little fun.

When they arrived at the museum and Tory let them out at the door, Joseph argued weakly that he didn't want to be pushed around in a wheelchair because it was too much like a stroller and he wasn't a baby. But by the time they'd gotten through the ticket line, he'd given in without a fight.

When Tory came in from parking the car, she let go of Brittany and Spencer and they hurried to their favorite exhibits in the art section as fast as they could, as if they feared someone would reach them before they did and suck all the fun out of them. Rachel pushed Joseph's wheelchair into the art room, and Brenda and Tory followed behind.

Tory was dressed in a matching shorts outfit that complemented her trim figure, and her hair and makeup were impeccably done. Brenda had only had time to run a brush through her hair and pull on a pair of jeans and a T-shirt. She felt frumpy in comparison.

"So how's Joseph doing on his medication?" Tory asked softly.

Brenda struggled to maintain her smile for the sake of the kids. "Not well," she admitted.

"I didn't think so," Tory said. "He doesn't look like he feels well at all. So what are they going to do now?"

"I don't know," Brenda whispered. "The doctor seems to think that as long as his heart is functioning at fifty percent, that's good enough. I just keep thinking that sooner or later this has got to get better. But I'm really worried."

"You worried?" Tory asked. "I never thought that was possible."

Brenda knew Tory meant that as a compliment, but she almost resented it. Sometimes, she was just weak, and she hated for people to be shocked by it. She went to a bench against the wall and sat down. Tory followed, still searching Brenda's face.

"You know, it *is* human to worry," Tory offered.

"But what's the point?" Brenda asked. "God knows what's going to happen tomorrow, ten years from now—He knows the very day that we're going to die. What's the point of worrying when He's got it all under control?" She felt Tory's eyes still upon her as she watched Joseph in his wheelchair, having fun for the first time since they'd rolled their yard with toilet paper.

"I know you're right," Tory said, "but worrying is one of my worst faults. I'm trying to give it up, though. That, and writing."

Glad to be off the subject of her worry, Brenda shot Tory a grin. "You're not giving up writing."

"Yes, I am. Already have." She raised her right hand as if making a vow. "I've written my last word."

"Well, you can't do that," she said. "You're called."

Tory laughed sarcastically. "Yeah? Called to do *what?*"

"You have a gift. The stuff you've let me read, it was wonderful. I don't know if you have a right to give it up."

Tory's smile died, and she frowned thoughtfully at Brenda for a moment. "I'm not sure," Tory said finally, "but that might be one of the nicest things anybody's ever said to me."

Brenda laughed. "Oh, come on."

"Really," Tory said, still serious. "I hadn't thought of it that way. As an obligation, I mean."

"Well, you should. Just because it didn't work out that one time doesn't mean it's not meant to be. For heaven's sake, how is God ever going to teach you if things go perfectly well all the time?"

"Oh, I don't know. He could send books. I could read the lessons He wants to teach me." She winked, and Brenda laughed. Brittany flopped by with ponytails wagging and both shoes untied. Tory stopped her and tied them, then with a pat on her bottom, sent her on her way.

Brenda's eyes followed the comical child. "So is Brittany getting excited about starting school?"

"Oh yeah," Tory said. "We've been shopping for school clothes and supplies. I never dreamed I'd have a baby in school this soon. Seems like it's flown by. But I have to tell you, I'm looking forward to it a little. Maybe I'll have more time to think."

"And write?" Brenda asked with a smirk.

"No, not write," Tory said stubbornly. "I told you. I'm through with that."

"Yeah, well, we'll see," Brenda said. "So you're going to send them to public school?"

Tory nodded. "I feel pretty good about our school district. And by the time they get into junior high and high school, I'm counting on Cathy having worked out all the sex ed problems."

"Maybe," Brenda said, forcing herself to keep her mouth shut about the virtues of homeschooling over public education. It was something she felt passionately about, but she didn't want to sound condemning or heap guilt on Tory. They'd had this conversation before, and Brenda knew that Tory thought she was a little paranoid.

Though Brenda chose not to say anything, her silence spoke volumes, and Tory responded. "I know, I know. Homeschooling is the best way. But you have to have a certain temperament for that, and I just don't have it."

"Don't kid yourself," Brenda said. "It's not that hard. I get to stay home and do something important for the four people I love most in the entire world. I don't have to let anybody else's crazy ideas and influences get pounded into their heads. I'm guarding their hearts and teaching them what's important, and I get to learn all over again. What greater calling could there be?"

"I see your point, and I admire it," Tory said. "I really do. But if everybody took their kids out of public schools ..."

"I know the argument," Brenda said. "Then the schools would really go to pot. And you're right. I'm not suggesting that everybody take their kids out."

Tory smiled. "Just the Christians?"

"No, not even them."

"Because a few minutes ago you told me that I'm called to be a writer, something I can't do as long as I have two kids at home all the time. Plus, there are millions of women who work because they *have* to, who don't have the option to pull their kids out of school and teach them at home. Besides, I loved the school experience. I loved all the friends I had and all the functions and events ... I don't want Britty and Spencer to miss that."

"I'm just saying that if they go, you need to stay on top of things. Watch carefully what they're taught, what they're learning. Get involved. And then when they get home, spend a lot of time teaching them the important stuff."

"Like the Bible?"

"Yes, like the Bible."

Tory gave her a contemplative look, then asked, "Does that bother David? That you spend so much time teaching the kids Scripture?"

"Not really. He feels like the lessons there are good moral lessons. Of course he doesn't believe there's anything more there."

"Do the kids get confused? I mean, since they know their dad doesn't believe, do they ever question it?"

"Sometimes," she said. "It's a problem, but I'm praying for him." She paused and considered whether to confide in Tory. "David was taught the Bible as a child—but in a real distorted way. The Christians who influenced him growing up probably meant well, but they sent him running the other way. That's just a reminder to me that what my kids are taught, and who teaches them, is critical. You can be taught the right things by the wrong people, or the right things in the wrong way, and have it turn out worse than if you'd never heard it."

Tory seemed to process that as she kept her eyes on Brenda. "Do you ever regret marrying a non-Christian?"

The question almost startled her. "I wasn't a Christian, either, when we married," she said. "David's a wonderful husband and father. I just wish ..." Her words trailed off, and she averted her eyes.

"That he had your faith," Tory prompted.

"It would be really great to have that in common," Brenda said, meeting Tory's eyes again. "But it's okay. I'm praying hard, and I know the Lord will answer. After all, it is to His glory."

"If a man could love God just by being around you," Tory said, "I'm sure he would."

Tears misted in Brenda's eyes, and she hugged her neighbor. "That's sweet, Tory. Wish it was so."

"No, I mean it," Tory insisted. "You're an exemplary wife, a wonderful mother, a model Christian. If you could twirl a baton I'd have to hate you."

Brenda laughed. "Well, thank goodness I can't."

"Really," Tory went on, leaning her head back against the wall. "I wish I were more like you. If I were one of the Israelites, I'd be grumbling about the manna and quail. I'd keep complaining that the pillar of fire just kept leading us in circles. I'd probably even be one of the people to melt down my jewelry and contribute to the golden calf."

Brenda sighed. "I think there's some of that in all of us."

Spencer came running. "Mommy, they're about to start the art class. Can I go? Please, can I go?"

"Yeah, but I have to come with you." He grabbed her hand and pulled. She winked at Brenda and followed her skipping son to the art room.

Brenda went into the room where Joseph was and stood at his wheelchair. She wondered if the other kids ever resented the fact that she spent so much time with him. It was just maternal instinct to hover over the one who needed her the most. Daniel, Rachel, and Leah were so self-sufficient, and they seemed to understand that their brother was in trouble.

Joseph got out of his wheelchair and took a few steps into the photographic booth where he could make faces, freeze-frame them, and print them out. It was his favorite thing in the museum, and it produced something he could take home and put on his bedroom wall. She glanced back at the other kids. Leah and Rachel were playing with the ink and stamps, and Daniel was creating some elaborate masterpiece they would hang on the refrigerator door. Smiling, she looked back in the booth at Joseph.

He had stopped making faces at himself and was leaning against the wall in the booth.

She ducked in. "Honey, you ready to come out?"

"Just a minute," he said, breathless.

She could see that something was passing over him—dizziness, light-headedness, perhaps. She waited for it to pass, but it didn't.

"Honey, come get back in the wheelchair and we'll go get you something to drink."

He continued to sit, limply leaning against the wall, so she reached in, took his arm, and tried to coax him out. His right hand came up to cover his chest.

And her own heart seemed to stop.

"Honey, does your chest hurt?" The tremulous words came out on a rush. He nodded slightly, got up, took a step toward the wheelchair. "Come on," she said. "Just sit down. You're going to be all right."

But before he could reach the wheelchair he fell and hit the floor like a rock.

CHAPTER
Twenty-Two

As Brenda and David waited for the doctor to come, Brenda found the silence in the hospital consultation room to be smothering—but appropriate. There were no words that could adequately describe the fear she'd felt waiting for the ambulance to come get Joseph. She had wept hysterically as the paramedics barked out Joseph's vital signs and conversed with hushed, panicky concern about the need to stabilize him en route to St. Francis. Although no one had said so, she was certain that his heart had failed. Like a sixty-year-old man, her baby had lain on the floor of the Adventure Museum in full cardiac arrest.

Brenda had ridden in the ambulance with him, and Tory had called David, then taken the other kids home. The emergency room personnel had treated Joseph like a Code Blue, which had frightened her to the point of dysfunction. David had arrived just in time to hold her together, and someone had shuffled them both into this room to wait for the verdict. In her wildest dreams, she had never anticipated sitting in a room waiting to be told if her son was dead or alive.

She'd been thankful when Harry had appeared from his office, after Tory alerted him that Joseph had collapsed. He had gone to check with the doctors and promised to give them news as soon as he knew something. But so far, no one had come to tell them anything.

David got up and walked around the room, staring vacantly at the cheap oil paintings on the wall. Brenda closed her eyes and tried to pray. She wished the words she had given to Tory at the museum could filter into her heart right now. What was it she'd said about there being no point in worrying because God was in control? He knew everything that was going to happen. Why couldn't she rest in that peace now?

Panic rose in her heart, along with the overwhelming sense that there was something *she* needed to do to keep Joseph alive. She could make her heart beat for his, make her lungs expand in and out to give him oxygen—she could keep him alive, if they would just let her go to him . . .

The door opened, and they both jumped. Harry and Dr. Robinson came in, looking like weary soldiers after a crucial battle. It took every ounce of restraint she possessed to keep from attacking them with her questions. Solemnly, Dr. Robinson and Harry shook David's hand, then Brenda's. Desperately, she watched their eyes for a clue.

"I've asked Harry to come in with me to talk to you," Dr. Robinson said, taking a seat across from them at the table.

"Is he dead?" Brenda choked out.

"No, no." Harry sat down next to her and touched her shoulder. "We would have told you."

She felt a rush of gratitude followed immediately by renewed grief, and a fresh onslaught of tears ambushed her. She wilted against David.

"The news . . . it isn't good, is it?" David asked as he held her. Brenda pulled herself together and sat up, unwilling to miss a single word.

Harry and Dr. Robinson exchanged looks. Finally, Harry spoke. "The medicine isn't working. Joseph's heart is functioning at fifteen percent capacity, and what happened today was a very close call."

"*Fifteen percent?*" David threw the words back as if they were dynamite. "Why didn't we know this before?"

"He wasn't this bad at his last checkup," Dr. Robinson said. "His decline has been pretty rapid."

"What's going to happen?" David asked, getting out of his chair, red-faced, and facing off with the two men as if they were threatening him. "'Cause you can't just keep on putting a Band-Aid on it, pouring drugs down him . . ."

"No, we can't." Again, the two doctors exchanged looks, as if silently deciding which one would go on.

"There's really only one option at this point," Dr. Robinson said quietly.

"Surgery, right?" David prodded.

It was not so much what they were saying as what they were not saying that alerted Brenda. She got slowly to her feet, her tears falling freely. "Harry, what is it that we can do to save Joseph?"

"He needs a heart transplant," Harry said.

Brenda's mouth fell open, and she sank back down.

"A heart transplant?" David's words were hoarse, just above a whisper. "But he's just a little boy."

"It's the only thing that'll save him. He's in very bad shape."

"But isn't there some other less risky kind of surgery?"

Dr. Robinson shook his head. "The damage is too great. He's going to have to have a transplant, or he'll die."

Brenda and David stared at each other, horror stricken, as if they each silently urged the other to do something to stop this madness.

"Where . . . where do we have to go . . . for a transplant?" she asked.

"Until a year ago, the only place in the state was Knoxville. But since St. Francis is a teaching hospital, we started doing them here. Our transplant team is excellent. One of the best in the South. They do a wonderful job, and the survival rate is very high."

"Survival rate?" Brenda muttered. It wasn't a question really, just words she never thought would have anything to do with her children.

"So when—when do we do this?" David choked out.

"We have to wait for a heart to become available."

"And how long will that be?"

"There's no telling," Dr. Robinson said. "The wait is usually a couple of months. It could be longer, it could be less. It just depends on when a match is available. The transplant team will meet with you tomorrow, and we have a family support team that will help you tremendously. We'll have to start testing Joseph immediately to make sure he's a good candidate for transplant, but I feel sure he will be."

"But he doesn't *have* two months if his heart is only functioning at fifteen percent," David said. "And what about next week—it could be ten percent, or five. It could stop altogether."

"We're going to put him on a Left Ventricular Assist Device, otherwise known as a Heart Mate. It's a portable heart that will keep him stable until the transplant. We'll have to keep him here in the hospital," Dr. Robinson said. "But that will keep him alive until the heart is found."

"Keep him alive," Brenda repeated mechanically.

"What is this . . . this Heart Mate?"

"It's about the size of a hockey puck, and it weighs about two and a half pounds. We implant it just under the diaphragm, and then we use an air compressor outside the body to power it. It has a battery that lasts up to thirty minutes, so he'll be able to detach from the machine and walk up and down the halls a little, to get some exercise. We'll also have him doing some supervised exercise and physical therapy to build him up for the surgery."

Brenda was speechless. She couldn't find rational thoughts, much less words.

"So he's going to have to stay in the hospital for weeks? Maybe months?" David asked in a shaky voice.

"That's right," Harry said. "It's the only option."

"I don't believe this." Brenda got up and walked across the room. "How could this happen? Just a few weeks ago, he was so healthy. How could one little virus do this?"

Neither of the doctors had any answers.

"Are you prepared to stay with him while he's here?" Dr. Robinson asked gently.

Brenda shook her brain out of its reverie. "Uh . . . yes, of course."

"What about your other children?" Harry asked.

"They'll be fine. I have to stay here with him."

David nodded. "One of us will be with him at all times."

"Doctor, are you sure he'll make it?" Brenda asked. "I mean, until a heart becomes available? Could he die before it happens?"

"Eighty percent of our critical patients on Heart Mate survive the wait for the transplant."

"*Eighty* percent?" she asked, astounded. "That means *twenty* percent don't?"

Harry hesitated, then replied simply, "He's in very good hands, Brenda."

She leaned back hard in her chair, unable to drag her mind away from the odds.

"We'll need to put him in the cardiac unit, rather than the children's hospital," Dr. Robinson went on, "so it could be a challenge to keep him occupied."

"Why there?" David asked. "Wouldn't he be better off with other children?"

"Emotionally and mentally, maybe. But they're not equipped to handle this kind of thing over there. Our transplant teams are located near the cardiac unit, and we really need to have him there so he can get the best of care."

"He's just a little boy," Brenda whispered again.

"A very sick little boy," Dr. Robinson said.

Brenda went into David's arms and buried her face against his chest. He held her tightly and looked over her head to the doctors. "What now?" David asked.

"Well, now we need to admit him and get him on the Heart Mate. Then we start the series of tests that will tell us what we need to know."

"But right now, before we do anything else," Harry said, "there's something I'd like to do. If you don't mind, I'd like to pray with you."

David shot him a surprised look. Brenda knew he'd never met a doctor who prayed with his patients. He didn't argue, probably figuring that anything they tried was better than nothing. He held Brenda tightly as Harry quietly, simply, asked God to see them through this crisis.

As soon as they'd finished praying, David let her go. He got up, slid his hands into his pockets, and faced off with the doctors again. "I have to ask you a question that'll probably seem pretty callous," he said. "But it has to be considered."

"What?"

"How much is all this going to cost?"

Dr. Robinson exchanged looks with Harry again.

"Because I don't have very good health insurance," David said. "We still haven't paid what we owe from the last time Joseph was here. And I don't want somebody in the hospital credit department finding that out and cutting off Joseph's care halfway through this. I'm a self-employed cabinetmaker. We have all the insurance I can afford, but it won't pay everything."

"Most policies cover heart transplants now," Harry said.

"*If* ours does, it'll still only pay seventy percent," David said. "We've got to pay thirty, plus a two-thousand-dollar deductible. How much are we talking?" He looked from one doctor to the other, his eyes glistening with tears. "Look, I'm just saying that I need to know ahead of time so I can work my tail off to earn it. I'm going to provide what my boy needs. I'm not going to let him die because of money."

"It can cost between fifty-seven thousand and a hundred ten thousand," Harry said. "It all depends on how long he has to be here before the heart is available, what has to be done in the interim, and how well his recovery goes."

David did the math in his head. "So, including the deductible, we're talking anywhere from nineteen thousand to thirty-five thousand, out of pocket. Possibly more." He looked at his feet. "Well, we can't get a second mortgage, because we already have one. But maybe if we sold the house . . ."

"Before you consider that, you need to talk to social services. There are programs that can help," Harry said.

David shook his head. "I want any decisions about Joseph's care to be made on the basis of his medical needs—not on the basis of cost. If social services was involved, I'd be afraid of that."

"You don't need to worry about that," Harry said. "It doesn't work that way."

David wasn't convinced. "I'm willing to pay whatever it takes. I just need to be able to plan on it."

"Well, a lot depends on how long the wait is," Harry said. "Look, if I have to pay the bills myself, David, Joseph is going to get his transplant. We'll raise the money. Don't worry about that. You have enough to think about."

Brenda wiped her eyes, praying silently that Harry's open, unashamed prayer—and his willingness to act on those prayers—would affect David. That faith-in-action was something David had rarely, if ever, seen in Christendom; it was just the opposite of the abuses that had soured him to the whole institution.

She was grateful to Harry for another reason, too: His promise to see this through gave her strength, reminding her that God was working.

But she wasn't sure that her faith was much stronger than David's. Not when her child's life hung in the balance.

CHAPTER
Twenty-Three

As David watched over Joseph, who slept soundly in his hospital room, Brenda went to the chapel to have a word with God. Kneeling at the altar at the front of the room, she gave in to the heartbreak and despair closing over her. But as earnestly as she prayed, those prayers didn't feel as if they connected.

What is it, God? she asked fervently. *Is there some sin in my life that's keeping You from hearing me?* She had confessed everything she could think of—even the despair that, she feared, demonstrated a lack of faith. But she did have faith. She knew that God would do His will in her family. She just didn't think that will was going to coincide with hers. Desperately, angrily, she pleaded for mercy, for healing, for God to align His will more closely with hers.

Then she chastised herself for such a selfish prayer. Would it make God turn away and quit listening altogether?

When the door opened, Brenda turned and saw Sylvia coming toward her. She got up to give the older woman a hug, unable to hide the despair on her face.

"David said you'd be here," Sylvia said.

They sat down on the front pew, and Sylvia gave Brenda a handkerchief. Thankfully, Brenda blew her nose and wiped her face.

"Brenda, I know how hard this must be for you," Sylvia said. "You must just be a wreck."

"I am," Brenda admitted.

"Is there anything I can do?"

Brenda shrugged. "You can explain some things to me, maybe." She could see on Sylvia's face that she knew some of the questions she had. That she had struggled with the answers herself.

"The elders prayed over him at church," Brenda said, her eyes glistening with tears. "We prayed for healing, and it didn't come."

"I know," Sylvia said. She touched her shoulder, squeezed it, and wiped her own eyes with her other hand.

"I did that against David's will. He has this . . . this thing . . . against church. It goes back to his childhood. He warned me not to do it, because he thought it would traumatize Joseph. But I did it anyway, without telling him. I thought it was the right thing to do, and what David didn't know wouldn't hurt him. I think that's what messed things all up, my doing it against David's will. God didn't honor it."

"Oh, honey." Sylvia made her look up at her. "God wouldn't punish you for following his own instructions. That's not what's wrong. Brenda, God's not a genie in a bottle. He doesn't answer prayers on demand. If God chooses not to heal Joseph, it must be for some other reason than that. I'm sure you prayed about it before you asked for the elders to pray for Joseph. I'm sure you thought it was one of those times when you have to serve God before your husband."

"I did. I thought that, Sylvia."

"Our prayers aren't buttons we push to get the results we want, Brenda. It's all tied into God's will. We don't see the whole picture, but He does."

Brenda looked up at Sylvia, her eyes pleading. "Sylvia, why does the Bible say that the prayer offered in faith will make the sick person well? Why does it say that?"

"Brenda, have you ever known God's Word not to be truth?"

She didn't even have to think about that. "No, never."

"So that passage must be truth."

"Then why didn't it happen?" Brenda asked. "Why wasn't he healed?"

"Because God's timing isn't our timing, Brenda. Maybe He plans to heal him through this heart transplant. Maybe He just needs for you to trust in Him a little longer."

"I have to," she said. "He's the only one with any power to change things."

"That's true," Sylvia said. "And it would bring real glory to Him if He cured Joseph."

"But see, that's just it." Brenda got to her feet and went to the altar, then turned back to Sylvia. "What keeps going through my mind is that sometimes *death* brings glory to God. Sometimes people are won to Christ through someone else's death, and I'm so afraid that's how He's going to use Joseph." Her voice squeaked with the words, and she broke down and covered her face with both hands.

Sylvia pulled Brenda into her arms. She dropped her forehead against Brenda's neck and held her for a long time. Through her grief, Brenda gradually realized that she was breaking Sylvia's heart, too. That was the last thing she wanted to do. She stepped back and tried to pull herself together. She looked up at the stained glass window with the dove representing the Holy Spirit, flying down from heaven.

"My mother died of breast cancer years ago," Sylvia said. "What God taught me through that death is that God gives wonderful blessings to us, sometimes in the form of people we love. And we have to hold those blessings in open hands, willing to let Him take them back if He chooses. We can't hold them in clenched fists, Brenda, because they're not ours. None of what we have is ours."

Brenda tore her eyes from the window. "I know that's true," she choked out. "I have to be willing to give my blessings back, whenever He comes to take them. But I'm just not there yet."

Sylvia wiped her own tears and shook her head dolefully. "Neither am I. I've been praying that He'll teach me, with my own kids, and they're not even sick. They're happy and healthy—just not with me. I feel so ashamed."

"Don't feel ashamed. We both love our children. For me, you can pray that I'll know for sure that God is watching over Joseph. And that everything that happens, happens because God is guiding it, that there's a reason, and that it'll work for good. I know those things in my head, Sylvia, but please pray that I'll embrace them in my heart. And pray for David."

Sylvia nodded, promising that she would.

"You know, there have been days—before Joseph got sick—when I've prayed so earnestly for David that I've told God if He had to take my life to save David's soul, I was willing. But I never volunteered Joseph's life. And I didn't expect Him to take it."

"What if that is what He has to do to bring David to Christ? What if that is God's way?"

Brenda sank back down. "I know how Jesus felt in Gethsemane. 'Let this cup pass from me.'" She covered her face and sobbed quietly for a moment, then took a deep breath and looked at her friend again. "Oh, Sylvia, pray that this is not the cup I have to drink."

Sylvia hugged her fiercely again. "Can I pray for you now?"

"Yes, please," she whispered.

Sylvia began to pray.

CHAPTER
Twenty-Four

Tory fed Rachel, Leah, and Daniel at her house that night, an event Brittany and Spencer considered the highlight of their week. They thought it was a party, but the Dodd children knew better. They had seen their little brother lose consciousness on the floor of the Adventure Museum, and it hadn't been the first time. Watching the ambulance carry him away had been traumatic for all of them. Now Tory hoped she could keep their minds off his condition until they heard from their parents.

But when Sylvia came over and asked her to step out on the front porch, she knew that the news was not good. "Brenda's been really busy and preoccupied with Joseph, so she hasn't had the chance to call," Sylvia said, keeping her voice low. "But she asked me to come tell you what they found out."

Tory waited.

"They told Brenda and David that Joseph needs a heart transplant or he'll die."

Tory felt the blood draining from her face. Slowly she reached for the chain on the swing and felt her way down. "Heart transplant?"

"I'm afraid so."

"Poor Brenda." The words came on a rush of breath.

"You said it." Sylvia sat down next to her, and the swing began to creak with their forward and backward motion. "They've admitted Joseph to the hospital. He'll have to stay there until a heart's available."

"How long will that be?"

"We don't know. It could be days, weeks, months . . ."

"And Joseph will have to be there all that time?"

"That's right. His heart's only functioning at fifteen percent. They have to keep him stabilized."

"So what's she going to do? I mean, with the other kids?"

"I'll help as much as I can. But that's not the most pressing problem right now. The biggest problem, according to Harry, is the money."

"What do you mean?"

"Well, they're self-employed, so their health insurance isn't very good. They're going to have to come up with at least thirty percent. A heart transplant is very expensive."

"What will they do?"

"I'm not sure. David told Harry a second mortgage is out— they already have one. He's thinking about selling the house."

"*What?*" Tory exclaimed. "They can't! Don't they have social services or something to help people who can't pay?"

Sylvia hesitated before answering. "David refused to contact social services. He had some stubborn idea that Joseph's care would be inferior if the hospital knew of his financial condition. He's determined to raise the money himself. But I don't think he can, and I'm like you—if he has to sell the house to do it, I don't want him to. But their share of the expenses could easily be more than David makes in a year." Sylvia met Tory's eyes. "So I'm going to do my best to help raise the money, before he has to sell the house. But I'll need help."

"Of course. Barry and I will do what we can. We don't have much extra, but—"

"I'm not asking for money from you," Sylvia said, "but I need some ideas. Ways to get the community involved. People would help if they knew. My church, your church, her church . . ."

"Of course. Surely people will help."

Spencer burst through the front door. "Mommy, Britty got out the gummy bears and she won't give me some. And there ain't enough for all of us."

"Aren't enough," Tory corrected. "Spencer, go back in there and tell her I don't want her to have any sugar before bedtime."

"But it ain't sugar. It's just gummy bears!"

"Tell her not to give them out till I come back in." She got up, and Sylvia followed her to the door.

"I should take the Dodd kids home," Sylvia said. "They need to sleep in their own beds."

"Are you sure?" Tory asked. "I'd be happy to watch them."

"No, it would really make me feel better to do something." Sylvia sighed. "And heaven knows I don't have anything better to do. Harry'll come over and help out when he gets home. Besides, they're good kids. They won't be a problem."

"All right. Are you going to tell them about Joseph?"

"No," Sylvia told her. "I'll let David do that when he gets home."

Tory's pale eyes settled on the Dodds' house. "How are Brenda and David taking it?"

Sylvia struggled for words. "It's hard. Really hard. They're taking it like we would, if Joseph was ours."

"This will be tough on the whole family."

Sylvia nodded. "We'll just have to help." She glanced at the house directly across from the Dodds'. "Look, before I take the kids home, I think I'll run over to Cathy's and tell her what happened. I know she'll want to know, and maybe she'll have some ideas."

Tory nodded mutely and watched Sylvia cross the cul-de-sac.

CHAPTER
Twenty-Five

Cathy sat at her computer in the dining room, typing in addresses for every home she'd been able to find in the school district. Since the school board had refused to give her names and addresses of all the families in the district, she had spent the previous two weekends driving down every street in the area and recording the addresses. She would do a blitz mailing—send a letter to every taxpayer in the district, addressed to "Parents of School Children." It wouldn't apply to every resident, but at least she would know she was reaching nearly all the parents that way.

"So what's this for again?" Mark asked as he faced the stack of letters she wanted him to stuff into envelopes.

"For your education and your moral health," Cathy explained matter-of-factly.

Annie, who had also been enlisted, made a derisive noise of disgust.

"What?" Mark asked.

"It's about sex ed at our schools, meathead," Annie told her brother. "And the fact that Mom is trying to ruin our lives."

"How am I ruining your life?" Cathy flung back.

"Get real, Mom," Rick said, coming in from the other room. "Our friends are already calling you 'the condom lady.' They think it's a big joke that you're fighting the school on this. I may never show my face in that place again. I'll probably run away before school starts in the fall."

"He's right, Mom," Annie said, and Cathy would have marked this rare moment of sibling agreement on the calendar if she hadn't been so appalled at their attitudes. "You wouldn't believe what a hard time we're getting. Today at the Y pool, Selena Hartfield started telling everybody that our mom didn't want them talking to her kids about sex at school 'cause we don't know the facts of life yet. It embarrassed me to death. If you wind up making any more of a deal about this than you already have, I'm going to live with Dad, 'cause I don't need this."

"I'm doing this for your own good," Cathy said. "The school doesn't have the right to pour junk into your heads, and if they can't even let a mother view the video they showed you, something's wrong. If I didn't care about you, I wouldn't go to all this trouble. You think I like spending every minute of my spare time on this?"

"Yes," Annie said. "I think you do. It's given you a life, even if it means that we can't show our faces out of the house for the rest of the summer."

"Isn't that just a little dramatic?" Cathy asked her. "So far, you haven't spent two straight hours in the house, unless you're sleeping. I think your social life is fine. Too good, in fact."

Annie shrugged. "Well, maybe for now. But when you start making speeches at the school board meeting ... Besides, look at poor Rick. His social life was already bad enough, and now he's practically an outcast."

"I am not!" Rick said. "Why don't you shut up?"

"*You* shut up. Mom and I are having a conversation." She turned back to her mother and crossed her arms belligerently.

"Mom, I'm sorry, but I have to take a stand. I refuse to be a part of this. Rick and Mark can stuff envelopes if they want, but I'm standing up for my principles."

"Principles? What principles? You're standing up for the right to have condoms passed out in the school?"

Annie looked flustered, then quickly rallied. "Mom, you just don't understand. Some people need them."

Cathy couldn't believe her ears. "Annie, tell me you don't mean that."

"I *do*. Not me, Mom, but other people. They're going to do things anyway, so you might as well arm them so they don't get diseases and stuff."

"She's brainwashed," Cathy said to no one in particular. "I'm too late. They've already brainwashed her." She covered her face with her hands, then realized she couldn't just play dead. She looked up, breathing in enough energy for the fight. "Annie, it's wrong to have sex before marriage, no matter what your friends or your teachers or your boyfriends say."

"Why?" Annie demanded. "If two people really love each other, and they're not, like, sleeping around, then why shouldn't they?"

"Because!" Cathy racked her brain for a ready reason, but they all seemed to escape her. "It's not the decent thing to do. It's . . . it's bad for you. For a lot of reasons."

"Okay, it's bad because of, like, pregnancy and AIDS. But if they're protected so those things don't happen—"

"It says not to do it in the Bible!" Cathy said, suddenly relieved that the thought had come to her. "It says it clearly."

"Where?" Annie asked. "Show me. Sarah Beth says that it tells you not to have adultery, but that's because someone's getting hurt in adultery. If it's between two consenting people who aren't hurting anybody—"

"Sarah Beth is fifteen years old!" Cathy shouted. "You're going to listen to her word over mine?"

"At least she has documentation."

Cathy wanted to throw something. "Look, I don't know where it says that in the Bible, but I *know* it talks about fornication. I'll find it." She felt flustered and frustrated, and furious at herself for not knowing Scripture.

"Well, even if you do, I'm not sure I buy into the Bible, anyway. It's outdated, Mom. Those rules may have worked in the Stone Age, but things have changed."

"Yeah, things have changed," Mark agreed.

"Things have *not* changed! The Bible is still true." Her voice broke off with the last words, and a lump rose in her throat. How could she have let this happen? How could she have raised her kids without the one value system they needed? How could she explain morals to them if they didn't have anything to base them on?

"I believe it's wrong to have sex before marriage," Rick said quietly, as if he could see his mother needed help.

Cathy fought to hold back her tears. "Thank you, Rick. That gives me some comfort."

"That's just because you're afraid of girls," Annie told her brother.

"I am not!"

"He's shy, Mom. Look at him. How often does he even go on dates?"

"I'm going to homecoming, doofus. I can get a date anytime I want!"

"That's enough!" Cathy belted out. Red-faced, she stood up and grabbed a stack of envelopes. "Sit down, Annie, and don't say another word."

"What? I told you I'm not helping with this! It's propaganda, and I don't want any part of it!"

"Sit!" Cathy shouted. "Now!"

Annie didn't sit, but she jerked the envelopes out of her mother's hand. "Rick, you too," Cathy ordered. "Start stuffing. Mark, you take these."

Annie shook her head with disbelief. "Guess I'll have to run away and live with Dad."

"I'm the one who's about to run away!" Cathy shouted. She forced herself to rein her temper in, and sat back down. "Oh, and Annie?" she said in a quieter voice that simmered with fury. "Don't threaten me with your I'm-going-to-live-with-my-daddy routine anymore, because it sends me into a rage, and I've been known to take away privileges for entire months for that, haven't I, Rick?"

"Yes, ma'am," Rick muttered.

"And you want a good reason not to have sex before marriage? Try this one. Because if I think you're even *thinking* about it, I'll ground you for life. How's that?"

The doorbell rang. Angrily, Cathy shouted, "Come in!"

Sylvia pushed the front door open and came tentatively into the living room.

"Oh, hey, Sylvia," Cathy said, wilting. "Sorry I didn't get up. I figured it was one of the kids' friends. I was ready to lambaste them, too." She noticed Sylvia's somber look. "Everything okay?" she asked. "Harry isn't making you pack for Nicaragua, is he?"

"No," Sylvia said with a faint smile. "I thought you'd want to know that little Joseph's back in the hospital."

"Oh, no. Is it his heart again?"

The kids stopped stuffing and looked up at Sylvia.

"I'm afraid so."

"What's wrong with him, Sylvia? What did they say?"

"He needs a heart transplant."

Silence. Even the three children were stunned. Cathy stood slowly. "A heart transplant? Sylvia, isn't there something *else* they can do before that? I thought that was the last resort."

"This *is* the last resort," Sylvia said. "He collapsed again today, and his heart almost stopped for good. They revived him, but apparently, without a transplant, he'll die."

Stricken, Cathy turned back to her children. Shock and amazement were evident on their faces. Even Annie was speechless. Little boys weren't supposed to experience failure in major organs. They weren't supposed to have to fight for their lives.

She forced her thoughts into a logical sequence. "Sylvia, is there anything I can do?"

"Well, maybe," she said. "We need to raise money. The Dodds don't have adequate health insurance, and David just doesn't make that kind of money."

"Sure," Cathy said. "We'll think of something. Won't we, kids?"

The children all nodded. It was the quietest she'd ever seen them. Crisis always quieted them, she realized. When their father had announced his intentions to divorce her, they had been silent for days.

"So what hospital is he in?"

"St. Francis," Sylvia said. "Harry's not his doctor, but he's keeping an eye on him."

"Good. I'm sure that gives Brenda some comfort."

"I hope so. Well, I'm going to take the Dodd kids home and put them to bed. Brenda and David are both at the hospital."

Cathy nodded thoughtfully. "Annie and I can do some baby-sitting, if that will help."

Annie shot her mother an unappreciative look, then shrugged and grudgingly said, "Yeah, sure."

"And maybe Mark and Rick could help keep their yard cut."

Rick leaned forward on the table. "Whatever I can do."

"I'm sure they'd appreciate that," Sylvia said. "And they'll probably take you up on it. It could be a long haul. There's no telling when a heart could become available."

Cathy sat again. "Boy. And I thought my problem with the school board was bad."

When Sylvia was gone, Cathy stared down at the letters she'd been so feverishly addressing. Somehow, they just didn't seem that important anymore.

"Mom, how do they get a heart?" Mark asked quietly.

"What do you mean, how?"

"I mean, like if they take it out of somebody else, won't they die?"

"That's kind of the point, doofus," Annie said.

Ricky's voice was kinder. "They take it out of somebody who's going to die anyway, don't they, Mom?"

Mark still looked confused. "You mean, out of somebody who's sick and isn't gonna get better?"

"No, nothing like that," Cathy said. "It's usually an accident victim. Somebody who's technically dead, but their heart is still functioning. They'll take it out and put it in somebody who needs it. They do that with all kinds of organs." Cathy had never imagined that she would have the need to explain this concept to her children.

"So somebody's gonna have to die to cure Joseph?" Mark asked.

"Looks that way."

The kids were quiet for a moment, and finally, Annie lost her belligerent look. Her voice was softer as she asked, "What if they don't get one in time?"

"They have to," Cathy said. "That's all there is to it."

Her eyes filled with tears, and she wanted more than anything to reach out and hug each of her kids, hold them until her arms got tired, rock them as she had when they were little. But she knew they wouldn't allow it. Somehow, she'd lost her privilege to do that years ago. Now she didn't know how to get it back.

She closed her eyes and let the tears flow for a moment. When she opened them, the kids had all dispersed to their separate rooms to deal with their own thoughts. And even in their stubborn rebellion and their maddening defiance, she found that she was thankful they all had functioning hearts.

CHAPTER
Twenty-Six

The Dodd children were unusually quiet as they got ready for bed that evening.

"Mom would have called us if anything bad had happened, wouldn't she?" Leah asked.

"Of course," Sylvia said.

Daniel was watching her face, waiting for some clue to Joseph's real condition. "So how long does Joseph have to stay in the hospital?"

"No one knows, but it could be a while."

Rachel sank down on the bed and put her hand over her heart. "I think I have it, too."

"Have what, too?" Leah asked.

"Heart trouble. My heart keeps pitter-pattering."

"Everybody's heart pitter-patters," Daniel said. "It doesn't mean you have to go to the hospital."

"But if Joseph's sick, what if the rest of us get it?"

"Stop thinking about yourself," Leah exclaimed. "Joseph's the one we should think about."

Daniel was still watching Sylvia, and she felt he could read every thought as it passed across her face. "When's Dad coming home?"

Sylvia had made a valiant effort not to lie to them, but also to avoid saying too much. David and Brenda would be the ones who'd want to break the news to them. "He should be home soon," she said. "It's been a long day for both of them."

"Well, where's Mom going to sleep?"

"They have a cot in the room with Joseph."

"Did he wake up?" Rachel asked. "Is he talking?"

"Oh, sure," Sylvia said. "He's the same old Joseph, according to Dr. Harry."

She sent them all to get ready for bed, wondering whether at their ages they needed to be tucked in. She thought back to when her children were ten and twelve. Had she tucked them in? Yes—in fact, she realized, she had tucked them in, in one way or another, until the day they'd left home. At least, she had kissed them goodnight and said a prayer with them. But she didn't know how Brenda and David did things.

After a while, she found the children huddled in Rachel and Leah's room. Daniel sat on the floor, Leah and Rachel on each of the twin beds.

"You kids ready for bed?" Sylvia asked.

"We want to pray first," Leah said. "For Joseph."

"I think that's a real good idea."

Rachel and Leah got on the floor next to Daniel, and Sylvia completed the circle. "Let's hold hands," Leah suggested.

They all held hands and bowed their heads.

She was amazed at the prayers that came from those young lips, prayers that exhorted the Holy Spirit to do His work, as if they knew Him. Brenda had been doing a good job with them, she thought. They knew where to turn in times of trouble. She wondered how David could avoid being impacted by the faith of these children.

When they'd finished praying for their brother, they all wiped their eyes, and Daniel got up and headed for his own room. She tucked in the girls one by one, gave them a kiss on the forehead, then went to Daniel's room and saw him hunched on the bottom mattress of the bunk beds. She felt more awkward approaching him. He was a cross between a boy and a man—a taller version of Joseph, a smaller image of David. She tried to remember Jeff at that age. She had treated him with understanding and respect. She tried to do the same tonight.

"Good night, Daniel," she said.

"Night," he answered. "When Dad comes home, tell him I'm sleeping in Joseph's bed."

"Okay."

He looked up at her as if he wasn't quite finished. "I mean, I don't want him to come in and freak out or anything, thinking I'm not where I'm s'posed to be."

"I'm sure he'll understand."

He sat there thinking for a minute, then finally got under the covers and pulled them up to his chest. "Joseph's going to be fine. My brother's tough."

"Sure, he is. All of you are tough."

"No, but he's *really* tough," he said. "I mean his heart. It probably isn't even that bad. It's just sick. It's going to get better, isn't it?"

"He's in really good hands. Dr. Harry's taking care of him, and Dr. Robinson. They're very well trained." She knew the words didn't comfort the boy.

"You think they'll let me go see him tomorrow?"

"I don't know. There might be a problem with visitors because of germs. We'll have to see," she said.

He thought that over for a moment. "Joseph's going to have a hard time being there," he said. "Wish we could do something like make a video every day, so he can see what's going on at home. But we don't have a Camcorder."

Sylvia smiled. "I'll loan you mine. I haven't needed it since the wedding. That's a great way to keep the family together even when it's apart."

"Yeah." His voice dropped almost to a whisper. "I wish it hadn't happened to him. I wish it had happened to me, instead, 'cause I think I could take it better."

She wanted to say something about it being God's choice, but she didn't know if that particular bit of theology would comfort the child in any way.

"Thanks for coming over and taking care of us," he said.

"No problem. Good night, Daniel."

She turned off the light and headed for the kitchen. The kids, obviously well trained, had cleaned up after themselves, but still she kept herself busy, puttering around and putting things away until their father came home.

CHAPTER
Twenty-Seven

Cathy stood in the doorway to the hospital room the next day, dressed in the surgical gown and mask the nurse had made her put on for her visit. Joseph was lying still with his eyes closed, apparently asleep. Brenda, dressed the same, looked as if she hadn't slept in days. "You didn't have to come by," she said, giving Cathy a hug. "I know you need to be at the clinic."

"I always close for lunch," she said quietly. She stood over Joseph's bed, looking down at him. As if he felt her gaze, he opened his eyes and looked up. "Hey," he whispered.

"Hey," she said, leaning over him. "What do you think of this mask they made me wear in here?"

He managed a smile.

"So how you doing there, Champ?"

"Okay," he said.

"He's a little groggy still from the procedure they did this morning," Brenda said. "They put the Heart Mate in."

"D'you know I'm getting a new heart?" he asked.

"That's what I hear," Cathy said, trying to sound impressed. She reached into the bag she carried and pulled out the games she'd bought for him. "Look, I brought some things to keep you busy while you're here. When you're feeling a little better."

Joseph couldn't work up much enthusiasm, but Brenda took them. "Look at all these games, Joseph."

"Thanks," he said.

"Annie and Mark and Rick want to come see you as soon as it's okay," she said. "You think you're up to that?"

He nodded.

As she looked down at the weak little boy, attached to the console with the air compressor and the monitor that ticked off his heartbeats, she wondered how she'd be able to hold off those tears threatening her eyes.

"So how's the fight with the school board?" Brenda asked, and Cathy could see that she needed to talk about something other than Joseph's heart.

"Well, it's going. Frankly, I keep wondering if all my efforts are useless. I wonder if I should even keep trying."

Brenda looked startled. "You *have* to keep trying."

"Why? Nobody's listening."

"How do you know that?"

"Well, I don't, for sure. Last night I sent out this letter to the homes in the district, and I told them about a meeting I was calling this week so we could discuss the problem and how to address it with the school board. But I have a bad feeling. I'm going to feel really stupid if nobody shows up."

"How many letters did you send out?"

"Thousands," she said. "You wouldn't believe it. If they don't come, I guess I'll just give up. Maybe it's not even worth the fight." She looked down at Joseph, whose eyes had closed again.

"Of course it's worth it," Brenda said. "Cathy, look at me."

Cathy met Brenda's serious eyes over the mask.

"I've been thinking a lot about this," Brenda said. "School's going to start in just a few weeks. Summer's going to be over, and I'm going to be here with Joseph if he hasn't gotten a heart by then. And even if he has, he'll need a lot of care. I've been thinking a lot about my other children."

Joseph's eyes opened again and settled on his mother, listening.

"I don't think I'm going be able to homeschool this year," she said. "I've been struggling with whether to put my own kids in public school. We can't afford a Christian school, and if I'm not going to be there, I don't want them to get behind and be unsupervised all day while David works. Public school may be the only answer."

"I can understand that," Cathy said. "But I know it must be hard for you. You were really committed."

"I'm *still* committed. And as soon as Joseph is better, I'll start homeschooling again. But Cathy, for people like me, who may not have a choice, please don't give up. Parents have a right to know what they're teaching our kids. They have a right to approve what's shown to them on videos, and what's put into their hands. Now, I don't know why you're the one who has this calling, but I believe that God gave it to you so you could set things right. We can't just abandon our public schools to a value system that doesn't work."

"I know," Cathy said. "I've told myself that."

"Then please don't give up. Don't quit. We need you."

Cathy breathed in a deep sigh. "Well, I guess if you can sit up here and fight this battle, I can fight that one. It's the least I can do."

"It's a lot to do. I appreciate it. And if I didn't need to be here, I'd be at that meeting."

"Okay then. I'll give it the fight of my life. For you, and for your kids. And, whether they like it or not, for my kids, too."

But the school board meeting was not the most pressing issue that evening when the families of Cedar Circle met at Sylvia's house to discuss how to raise money to help Joseph.

Cathy insisted that Rick, Mark, and Annie come along with her, in case there was something they could do. Annie claimed she had a date, which Cathy promptly told her to cancel. She came grudgingly, silently threatening to make the meeting miserable for Cathy. Mark whined that he had an online appointment in a chat room with his friends. Cathy told him to cancel, too. Rick was the only one who came willingly, and he lectured his sister and brother all the way about giving their mom a hard time.

Before they went in, she threatened all of them. "Act like nice people," she said. "For Joseph, act like you care."

"Right, Mom," Annie spouted. "Like we really don't."

"Shut up, Annie," Rick said. "Just answer 'yes ma'am.'"

"Mom, I don't have to put up with this. Make him leave me alone. He's just being nice 'cause he's about to hit you up for money or something."

"Money?" Mark asked. "Will we get money if we cooperate?"

Cathy moaned. "No, you will not get money. You will do this because you care about Joseph, and for no other reason. And so help me, if you embarrass me—any of you—I'll make you sorry. Got it?"

Annie did the "Heil Hitler" sign and clicked her heels together. Cathy was proud of the remarkable restraint she showed as she rang the doorbell.

When they'd caught up on Joseph's condition, they all sat around Sylvia's dining-room table. "All right, I've got a few ideas," Sylvia said. "First of all, I've put Joseph on the prayer list at my church and Brenda's church, and I'm hoping that some of the families in those churches will pitch in and help out financially. But we're going to need a lot more than nickels and dimes."

"What can we do?" Tory asked.

"I have an idea for you, Tory," Sylvia said. "You're a writer. Use your writing skills."

"How?"

"Letters. Write letters to every church you can get an address for. Ask for donations. Harry and I are going tomorrow to set up a trust fund for Joseph at our bank. David will be the executor. All the money that comes in will go directly into that account. You can do it, Tory. I've read your work. Just tell them about Joseph—appeal to the hearts and minds of parents. Tell them about the family. The money will come."

Tory looked uncomfortable. "Sylvia, there must be something else—"

Sylvia leaned forward, brooking no debate. "Tory, honey, if you start that song and dance about how you've given up writing, I might just come across this table and throttle you."

Tory grinned. "Excuse me. I'll write the letters."

"I have an idea, too," Cathy said, glancing at her kids. "Actually, it was Rick's idea."

"Good," Sylvia said. "Let's hear it."

Rick spoke up. "See, we were thinking we could have, like, an animal fair. We could like give pony rides and stuff, and Mom could do heartworm checks on all the pets, and Annie and Mark could bathe and dip pets, and I could take pictures of pets with their owners, ten bucks a shot, 'cause I'm pretty good with a camera."

Sylvia's eyes lit up, and she grinned at Tory and Cathy.

Annie began to twirl her hair on a finger. "It was kind of my idea, too," she cut in. "I thought we could have a petting zoo."

"Yeah," Mark added. "We could go around and get some of Mom's customers' animals, and little kids could pet them. We could get baby chicks and puppies and kittens, and little sheep and some ostriches . . ."

"It wouldn't raise a lot," Cathy said. "But it would raise some. The biggest plus, though, is that it would get the community involved, alert people to what's needed, and maybe out of that we could get some big donations."

"I think it's a wonderful idea," Sylvia said. "When do you want to have it?"

"Well, we need time to get it organized," Cathy said. "I was thinking maybe the Fourth of July?"

"Sounds good. Let's plan on it. Where can we do it?"

"Well, that's a problem," Cathy said. "At first I thought maybe here, in the empty lot between Tory's and Brenda's houses. But I don't think that'll be big enough. And we need a place more in the center of things, so people will see it and stop by. If people have to go too far out of their way, they might not come."

"We can do it at my church," Sylvia said. "We have a huge plot of land next to the church, and it's real visible."

"Are you sure they'd let us?" Cathy asked. "I mean, I'm not even a member, and already I'm using the fellowship hall for my meeting this week. Now I'm asking for the lawn?"

"The church is there to meet people's needs," Sylvia said. "You're doing that. Why would they object?"

"Well, all right. We'd promise to clean up after it's over."

"Yeah," Mark said. "Scoop up all the poop . . ."

Sylvia started to laugh. "Oh, my. I hadn't thought of that."

"It'll just fertilize the grass," Annie said.

"We can live with it," Sylvia said. "Meanwhile, I'll go around to as many big businesses in the area as I can and talk to their executives. See if some of them want to give a donation as a tax write-off."

"That's a good idea," Tory whispered.

"All right, then we each have a task to start with," she said. "We need to get busy."

"One other thing," Tory said. "Let's talk about what we can do to help them out with the rest of their needs. We could ask Brenda's church to bring food and stuff, so David won't have to cook for the kids. The rest of us could fill in on the nights when no one's doing it."

"Great. Could you organize it?"

"Sure," Tory said. "Also, I was thinking I could take the Dodd kids to church with me Sunday. That's real important to Brenda, but since none of us go to their church, I thought at least they could go with us."

"That's a good idea. I'm sure Brenda will take you up on it, especially since David won't take them."

Cathy spoke up. "Rick and Mark will be taking care of the Dodds' yard. David doesn't need that to worry about."

Mark rolled his eyes, but Rick nodded agreement.

"And Barry offered to do any home repairs they need. I don't think they need any right now, though."

"What else is there to do?" Cathy asked.

"There is one other thing." Sylvia closed the folder with her notes, then looked around the table from one person to the next. "You could become organ donors."

"Organ donors?" Mark asked. "What's that?"

Cathy touched her son's shoulder. "It's where you sign a card saying that, if you die, they can give your organs to someone like Joseph."

"Gross!" Annie said. "Why would anybody do that?"

"To save somebody's life," Sylvia said. "Why do you think that's gross, Annie?"

"Because . . ." She looked from Sylvia to her mom. "They wouldn't even try to save you. If somebody needed your kidney or something . . ."

"No, that's not true," Sylvia cut in firmly. "The medical team that would work on you after an accident would have nothing to do with transplants. But if you die, then they consult your family about organ donation. The transplant team isn't even contacted until the family consents."

"I still wouldn't do it," Annie said.

Sylvia sighed. "What if your mother needed a liver, Annie? If she was dying, and a transplant was the only thing that could save her? Would you see it differently then?"

Annie got quiet. "I don't know."

"I'm not trying to talk you into anything," Sylvia said. "But Joseph will die if he doesn't get a heart. Every day, nine people like Joseph die, waiting for organs."

Silence hung over the room. Finally, Tory spoke up. "Barry and I talked about it when we first got married, and decided not to sign up. We thought it would be too hard on the one left behind. But I've never known anyone who needed an organ. If it was Britty or Spencer who needed one . . ." Her voice broke, and she shifted in her seat. "What do I do? Just sign the back of my driver's license?"

"That, or fill out a donor card and keep it with you all the time. But that's just a formality. It's your family that has to consent when the time comes. You have to let them know you want to be a donor."

Cathy pulled out her driver's license and flashed the back of the card. "I've already done it. See that, kids? That means that—if you're adults when I buy the farm—you sign the consent before you throw me in the tar pit."

Annie and Mark didn't find that amusing. Rick pulled out his own wallet and removed his license. "I'll do it, too, Mom."

"I'm proud of you." Cathy tried to swallow back the emotion in her voice. "Sylvia, let's offer donor cards at our animal fair, so people can sign up. Once we make people aware, they need to have a way to follow through."

Sylvia jotted that down. "Great idea. I think we're off to a good start." She looked around at Cathy and Tory, at Mark and Rick and Annie. "I sure appreciate everyone's help. It's especially nice to see how the kids are willing to help."

Cathy's three kids looked uncomfortably at each other, and Annie covered her mouth with her hand to suppress her amused grin.

"I tell you what," Sylvia said. "While we're all here, let's pray for Joseph."

"Um . . . I gotta go," Annie said. "I have, like, a date."

Cathy shot her a look.

"Me, too," Mark said. "Some people are waiting for me online."

"They can wait," Cathy said. "Bow your heads."

Huffing with resentment, the kids bowed their heads, and Sylvia began to pray. Listening to her, Cathy realized that there must be more to this prayer thing than she had thought. Some people, like Sylvia, talked to God as if He were a good friend, someone standing right in the room with them. It was an alien concept to Cathy. But now she tried to believe it as her friend and mentor appealed to God for Joseph's sake.

That night, after a talk with Barry about organ donation, Tory had trouble sleeping. She got up, went to the laundry room, and turned on the computer. She hadn't touched it since the day she'd seen the book in the library that was so much like hers, and now she fought the feeling of defeat and failure that spiraled inside her as the computer booted up and the cursor began to flicker.

There was something more important than her own goals, she reminded herself. Joseph's life was at stake, and there were people who thought she had the skill to do something about it.

She thought about what to write in her appeal to the local churches, and as her fingers began to type, she found that it was liberating to not worry about publication or fame and fortune. Tory simply began to tell the story of the little boy whose heart was failing. The little boy who needed a heart transplant and couldn't afford it. The little boy whose family was willing to do whatever was necessary to get him the help he needed. And she told them how much that family needed the financial help of anyone willing.

She finished drafting the letter at three o'clock in the morning. She printed out a hundred copies for starters, and decided to address the envelopes tomorrow.

By the time she crawled back into bed, she felt the thrill of accomplishment, the peace of knowing she'd done something no one else on their street could have done. She fell into a deep sleep next to her husband, knowing that dawn would come too soon. Her brain would be weary tomorrow, and she would move slowly, but that was all right. The knowledge that those letters were on their way to people who could help would give her all the energy she needed.

CHAPTER
Twenty-Eight

By Thursday night, Cathy had convinced herself that Sylvia's church fellowship hall would be packed with parents who'd gotten her letter and were concerned about their children's education. She had even made copies of Tory's letter about Joseph, planning to pass them out.

She got to the church thirty minutes early and tried to organize her thoughts and her notes. At quarter till, no early birds had straggled in. At five till, she looked at her watch and began to panic.

At seven, two women came to the door. "Excuse me . . . where is the meeting about the public schools being held?"

"Right here," she said, too exuberantly. "Come in."

They stepped into the room and looked nervously around. "Where is everybody?"

"I'm afraid you're the first two here."

"Really? No one else came?"

She hated to admit it. "Well, I haven't given up yet. You know people. You tell them seven and they show up at seven-fifteen.

And of course, since it's a Baptist church, they figure we'll be having food and fellowship for a while before we get down to business. We have to allow for that." Instantly, she wondered if she'd offended them, and decided to amend that statement. "Of course, I'm sure other denominations eat a lot, too. Not *too* much, but ... you know ..."

The two women nodded skeptically and looked as if they might escape through the bathroom window. An awkward silence fell over the room as they took two seats, and Cathy pretended to be busy organizing her handouts. After a moment, she heard footsteps and looked up to see a pleasant-looking man. "Hey, I'm Cathy Flaherty," she said, her voice echoing in the near-empty room. "Are you looking for the meeting about the schools?"

"That's right," he said, hesitating at the door. "Am I in the right place?"

"This is it," she said.

He crossed the room and shook her hand. "Steve Bennett," he said. "I got your letter, and I was pretty outraged. I didn't know if I should come because I only have one child and she's just in elementary school. But I figure in a few years she'll be in those classes."

"Everybody is welcome," she said. "Even people who don't have kids. We're all paying taxes for those schools. Will her mother be coming?"

He shook his head as he took a seat in the front row. His face reddened slightly. "My wife died. I've been raising Tracy alone for the last three years."

"Oh, I'm sorry." She could have kicked herself, for she could see from the look on his face that he wasn't quite over it. "Well, I'm really glad you came. I was hoping we wouldn't just have mothers here." She glanced at the two women. "Not that there's anything wrong with mothers. I'm one, myself. I just meant ..."

Her voice faded off as she realized what a mess she was making. She heard voices, and a half-dozen more people straggled in. She tried to greet them more intelligently. She was glad she'd brought finger sandwiches so that everyone had something to do as they waited for the meeting to start. Finally, at twenty after, she decided that everyone who was going to come was here. Counting her, there were ten people.

Ignoring the microphone she had set up, she sat on a chair facing the room and told them the story of how she'd found the condom in her son's pocket. She related her meeting with the principal and the indifference she had encountered from the superintendent. They each gave her their full attention.

"I'm not the most articulate person," she admitted. "I'm used to dealing with animals and teenagers. But my intention for tonight was to educate the parents of this community about what they're teaching our kids, and hopefully get us mobilized so that when school starts, we can all show up at the school board meeting in huge numbers." She looked around at them and gave a disappointed laugh. "Well, as many as we can get together, anyway. I'm hoping that we can go there and demand to be notified before they have this talk with our children. I think the least we could ask for is the opportunity to view the videos our children will be watching, review the material they'll be studying, and have approval rights as to what they give our children and what kinds of demonstrations they show them. Really, the line has to be drawn somewhere."

The other parents agreed, and Cathy felt validated. "For those things to happen, you'll need to tell everyone you know about this. I sent the letter to as many people as I could, but I know how it is. You get a lot of letters. If you don't know who something's from, sometimes you don't open it. I'm afraid some of the parents may have just thrown my letter away without reading it. But we need to get the word out somehow. We need dozens of parents there when we face the school board in September. We need to tell them that we won't stand for this, and that this issue isn't going to go away until something is done about it. We have to protect our schools."

She hadn't expected the applause she got from the tiny group. When it died down, she went on. "I know that the number of parents in this room tonight is not a fair measure of the number of parents in this community who care about their children. It's just that we live in a very busy culture, and a lot of parents opted to be with their children tonight, instead of coming here to talk about them. So I'm not blaming them. Heaven knows, I've missed plenty of meetings myself. So I'd appreciate it if you could talk it up, then meet me at the school board meeting on September 16, so we can make sure they understand our point."

She felt good about the meeting as it broke up and people began to go home. At the door, she handed out flyers about Joseph and his problem. Steve Bennett lingered to help her pick up the dirty paper plates and cups that had been left behind on chairs.

"Tell you what I'll do," he said. "My little girl plays soccer. I'll work something up to give to the soccer parents. And I'll do some talking, too, at the games. Give me a stack of those heart-transplant sheets, too, and I'll pass them out while I'm at it."

"Good idea," she said, getting two stacks to hand to him. "I hadn't thought of that."

He paused, looking down at the sheets. His hair was cut too short, and his skin looked weathered, as if he worked outdoors. But he had a kind face. "I really appreciate what you've done, calling our attention to this," he said. "If you hadn't, I might never have known. I've tried to be real protective of my daughter, and I can't stand the thought that these educators can do anything they want to with her when she's in their building."

"I know," she said. "Kind of scary, isn't it?"

"Let me help you get your stuff, and I'll walk you to your car."

A gentleman, she thought. A gentleman who cared about his child. Would wonders never cease? She looked at him from the corner of her eye as they walked outside. She wondered what was wrong with him. Something, no doubt. There was something wrong with all of them. They just didn't make them the way young women dreamed they did.

He helped her get her papers into the car, then shook her hand again. "It was nice meeting you, Cathy." There was nothing flirtatious or suggestive in his tone. It was a welcome relief.

"You, too, Steve. Thanks for coming. I really appreciate it."
She got in the car, locked it, and watched him walk to a pickup
truck that was a few years old. Not a midlife crisis sports car.
Again, a welcome relief. She wondered if he dated much, then
quickly chased away the thought, reminding herself that she had
sworn off dating. Besides, tonight was about changing school
policy, not meeting men.

She started her car, and as she drove home, she thought that
things might be looking up. Maybe there was a chance, after all,
that they could turn the school board around.

CHAPTER
Twenty-Nine

Sunday morning, Tory and Barry took the Dodd kids to church with them. Brenda had been grateful for the offer, since David wanted to be at the hospital with Joseph and Brenda—and had already announced unequivocally that he did not intend to go to church under any circumstances. That wasn't like David, Tory thought. He was normally a sweet, gentle man. His distaste of church seemed unreasonable and out of character.

Brittany and Spencer were excited as they picked the older kids up and headed for Sunday school. "I want Daniel to come to Sunday school with me," Spencer said.

"He's a little old for your class, Spence," Barry said. "They don't generally let twelve-year-olds in the four-year-old class."

Daniel's smile was forced. "I have to go to my own class, Spencer."

"What about Leah and Rachel?" Brittany asked. "Can they come to my class?"

"No, we're going to send everybody to their own age-group," Tory said. "You all okay with that?"

The three Dodd children sitting on the backseat of the Caravan nodded complacently, but she could see that they were nervous about attending a new church. She remembered being the new kid once when she was a child. She'd hated it. And she couldn't even offer them the hope that they would run into school friends, since they were homeschooled. Their circle of friends was much smaller than hers had been at that age.

She took them in and walked them each to the classroom they belonged to. "This is a big church," Leah said quietly. "Our church is a lot smaller."

Tory was proud of the size of her church. "Yeah, God has really blessed us," she said. "When we first started, it was the size of your church, but we've grown over the years. There are all kinds of things to do here now. Brittany and Spencer take art classes here on Thursday mornings, and they go to Mom's Day Out, and I take aerobics three times a week and a parenting class on Sunday nights ..."

The kids seemed to listen with polite interest. She took them each to their classrooms and watched them go in. Leah and Rachel would be fine, she thought, because they were twins and could lean on each other. But she felt sorry for Daniel. It was tough for a seventh grader to go into a roomful of kids he didn't know and try to fit in. She could see how awkward he felt, and almost considered taking him to her class with her. But she didn't know how often she and Barry would be bringing them. If it was every week, Daniel needed to get to know the kids his own age.

After Sunday school, she retrieved all five children, and they sat in a row on the pew in the sanctuary. Occasionally during the service, she glanced down the row at them. Brittany and Spencer were drawing on the program, but the three Dodd children sat silently, very still, looking miserably at the preacher. Next to her, Barry began to nod off, and she nudged him. "Wake up," she whispered. "You're setting a bad example."

After church, they took Daniel, Leah, and Rachel to the hospital to have lunch with their parents. Barry waited in the lobby with Brittany and Spencer as Tory walked Brenda's kids up. Joseph was sitting up in bed. Tory was thankful to see that the color had returned to his face, though he still seemed tired and lackluster.

Brenda threw her arms around each of her gowned and masked children as though she hadn't seen them in a week. "Leah, look at you. You're walking like a beauty queen. Have you been practicing with that book on your head?"

"Yes, ma'am."

"It's working, honey. Look how straight that backbone is. And Rachel, darlin', your hair looks just beautiful in that braid— and to think I wasn't even there to help."

"Thank you, Mama."

"Oh, Daniel, you've grown since yesterday. Look at you, you're almost as tall as I am." She tested his biceps. "Have you been pumping iron at Mark's house again?"

"Not lately."

"Good thing. If you get any bigger, I'll have to buy you a whole new wardrobe. Look at him, David. He'll be wearing your clothes soon."

With all three children beaming, Brenda finally turned to Tory. "Thanks for taking them to church, Tory. I don't know what I'd do without you."

"It was our pleasure," Tory said, staying back at the door for fear of bringing germs in, despite her own mask and gown. "How are you feeling, Joseph?" she asked.

"Good."

She doubted that was true, but it didn't surprise her that, being Brenda's son, he put the best face on things.

"He's just blossoming," Brenda said, walking to the bed and combing her fingers through Joseph's cowlicked hair. "And his disposition is unbelievable. Most kids would be whining and fussing, but he's as good as gold. I'm the lucky one, getting to spend all this time with him. So kids, how did you like Miss Tory's church?"

"It was fine," Daniel said without much enthusiasm.

"Did you make any new friends?"

"No, ma'am."

"It was kind of boring," Rachel blurted.

"Oh, I'm sure it was fine," Brenda said, shooting Tory an embarrassed look. Tory just grinned.

"Mom, can't you take us tonight?" Rachel asked. "We've been working on the musical, and I have a solo next Sunday night. I'll lose it if I don't go to practice tonight."

"And Daniel and me have speaking parts, so we—"

"Daniel and I," Brenda said, cutting into Leah's plea.

"I had one, too," Joseph interjected. "Now I have to quit. If all four of us quit, they'll have to call the whole thing off."

"We can't let everybody down," Rachel said. "Mom, please! Daddy, couldn't you just drop us off?"

"No," David said. "I need to stay here."

Tory saw the struggle on Brenda's face. She wasn't ready to leave Joseph yet.

"Look," Tory said. "If the kids want to go tonight, I'll take them. Really, I wouldn't mind."

"*Really?*" It was the most animated Tory had seen Rachel all morning.

Brenda shook her head. "Tory, you've done so much already."

"What could it hurt? I'll drop them off so they can work on the musical, and then we'll all come back for the service and we'll bring them home afterward."

"I really appreciate that, Tory."

Tory waved off the thanks. "Okay, guys, what time do you need to be there?"

"Four-thirty," Daniel said, his eyes brighter now.

"Okay, then I'll pick you up at your house at four-fifteen and run you over."

Finally, David got up. "No, that won't be necessary, Tory. I'll drop them off at the church. If you'll just go to the service and bring them home."

"Sure, that'll work out fine." She glanced at Brenda and caught her look. She knew how much Brenda wished that David would be the one to attend the service tonight.

"I'll take that time to come back and spend with Joseph," David said. "I don't get much time during the week."

Tory wondered if he would come to see the kids perform in the musical. She couldn't imagine a father as diligent as David missing something like that.

Finally, she discarded her sterile clothes and headed back down to find her family waiting patiently in the lobby. Thankful to have them all healthy and happy, she gave them each a kiss and led them back to the car.

Brenda's church was a small building with no frills. It had about fifty pews—twenty-five each in two rows—plain windows, and a simple cross at the front—so unlike their own church, which had a huge mortgage, beautiful stained glass windows, and a sanctuary that made them all proud. Tory, Barry, Brittany, and Spencer slipped in just before the service and sat near the back. Leah and Rachel found them and ran up the aisle to scoot into the pew next to them. Daniel waved from his place up front where a handful of youth were sitting.

They started the service with praise music, and the congregation clapped their hands and sang out without inhibition. Tory saw joy on the faces around her as they sang and praised God. In her church, everything was somber and reverent, and she didn't know quite how to take this new form of worship. Brittany and Spencer were on their feet singing along, instead of seated and marking up programs.

The preacher, a less-educated, less-polished man than their own pastor, began to preach. He had power and authority, and his words cut right to her heart. She saw that Barry, too, was wide awake, riveted on every word. The sermon about sharing one's faith seemed so relevant, so directly from God, so challenging and uniquely designed for her.

When the service was over, family after family introduced themselves, shook their hands, and praised them for being faithful in helping the Dodds. They left feeling uplifted and happy, instead of tired and irritable, as they often did on Sunday nights after their own church services.

They dropped the Dodd kids off at home where David waited. As they pulled into their driveway, Tory looked over at Barry and smiled. "Well, that was fun, wasn't it?"

"Yeah, it was."

"I think he wrote that sermon just for me."

"Nope. Couldn't have." Barry grinned. "He wrote it for me."

She laughed. "Seems like the Holy Spirit was really alive there. No wonder Brenda's the way she is."

"What way is that?" he asked.

"I don't know," she said. "Just real spiritual. Real in tune with God."

"It'd be hard to be a member of that church and not be."

They got out of the car and led the children in, and for a while she busied herself getting the kids bathed and put to bed.

Later, as she was preparing for bed herself, Tory paused and leaned against the bedpost. She gazed down at her husband, who was lying on the bed in a pair of gym shorts, reading a magazine. He felt her eyes on him and looked up at her. "What?"

She shrugged. "Do you ever think about changing churches?"

He shook his head. "I couldn't think about that," he said. "I'm a deacon. Deacons don't just up and leave."

"Why not?" She touched his feet. "What would be wrong with that?"

He dropped the magazine and sat up. "Tory, how can you talk like this? We've been going to that church since we were married."

"I know. It's just that I've never felt the Spirit move quite like He did tonight."

"It was nice," he agreed. "But at our church … we worship differently. It doesn't mean the Holy Spirit isn't there, too."

"How do we worship?" she asked Barry. "By falling asleep in church? By letting our kids color and draw and ignore what's going on? By mumbling through the hymns while we check our watches to see how much longer we have to sit there?"

"So maybe our worship methods aren't perfect," he said. "Maybe we need to work on taking worship more seriously."

"Maybe." She let it go and crawled into bed next to him. But in her heart, she wondered.

The next morning over breakfast, Spencer asked her if they could go back to that church again. "Well, don't you like our church?" Tory asked.

"No. Their church was fun."

"What was fun about it?" she asked.

He thought that over for a moment. Finally, Brittany came up with the answer. "I liked the songs."

"They're the same songs we sing."

"Yeah, but they sounded different when they sang 'em."

She smiled. "They did, didn't they? Maybe we will go back."

"Can we go Sunday morning?" he asked. "Their Sunday school rooms looked cool, and me and Britty would be in the same class, Leah said."

Tory knew that was true. Since the church was small, they divided the age-groups differently. "Maybe we'll do that just until Joseph gets better and their mom can take them again."

She knew that Barry would agree to go temporarily for the sake of the Dodds, but she decided not to bring up the subject of changing churches again. Barry was right. They were committed to their own church. For now, that was where they would stay.

CHAPTER *Thirty*

Sylvia had hoped that her first visit Monday morning, to her own bank, would prove fruitful. But when the bank president declined to help, claiming that bank policy prohibited them from giving to individuals, she was deflated.

Still, not one to let the word *no* stop her, she went to her bank's chief competitor and offered to move her own accounts if they would make a contribution to Joseph's fund. The bank officer told her that they would take it under advisement, but that before they could contribute, she would have to make a presentation before the board of directors, and that it could take up to six weeks for a decision to be made.

She was even less confident at her next two stops, and she supposed it showed. She couldn't get past the receptionist in the executive offices, and was told that no one had time to see her.

By the time she headed home, her feet and head ached. But it was her pride that hurt most of all. She had half expected to rake in, in one day, all the money the Dodds would need, just through sheer determination and her power of persuasion. She had not expected to arrive home empty-handed.

She fought off tears as she headed back to the bedroom. She took off her business suit and pumps and climbed into more comfortable clothes, but physical comfort didn't help her spirits any. Finally, she gave in to her tears and got down on her knees.

She prayed with all her heart, asking God to go before her and make a way—asking God to raise the money, since she wasn't able.

Finally, she headed out back to the stables to check on her horses. The teenaged boy who worked a few hours a day grooming them had already cleaned out the stables and fed the horses.

Sunstreak whinnied as she came in, and she wondered if the mare sensed and sympathized with her mood. She let her nuzzle her hand, then reached up to hug her.

"Sylvia!" She heard the voice calling from a distance and closed her eyes. She didn't want to talk. She didn't want to tell of her failures and have anyone see her tearstained face.

"Sylvia!" The voice grew closer. "Are you in there?"

She stepped out of the stables and saw Tory, her brown hair done up in a French twist and her makeup perfectly applied, despite the heat outside. She looked like a brunette Barbie doll, and Sylvia found herself envying her. Right now, in her shorts and baggy T-shirt, Sylvia felt old and useless.

"So how'd it go?" Tory asked. "I saw you come out and I couldn't wait to find out."

Sylvia looked over her shoulder between their houses and saw Brittany and Spencer, wearing helmets, riding their bikes with training wheels in the little cul-de-sac. "Well . . . let's just say it wasn't an overwhelming success."

"Didn't you get *any* donations?"

She sighed, then hated herself for it. She hadn't been a sigher before she'd married off Sarah. No wonder no one took her seriously. "I'm afraid not, Tory."

"So you'll try again tomorrow," Tory said with uncharacteristic optimism. Then she frowned and regarded Sylvia more carefully. "Sylvia, are you all right?"

"No. Not really." She headed around to her front porch so Tory could keep a closer eye on the kids. Wearily, she sat down in one of her wooden rockers. Tory sat down on the steps of the porch, looking up at her. "I should have known it wouldn't be that easy," Sylvia said. "But I was so cocky this morning. I thought I'd just prance into anyplace I tried, demand to see the president, tell him about Joseph, and voilà, he'd hand me ten grand. What arrogance."

"Don't be so hard on yourself," Tory said. "I'm the only one allowed to do that."

Sylvia gave her a weak smile. "I'm just disappointed in myself. I was starting to feel useful again. Didn't last long, did it?"

"Come on, Sylvia. It's only been one day. You'll raise money. Let's just brainstorm for a minute. Let's be creative. There must be some way to get their attention."

"Like what? I tried telling them all about Joseph; I even had pictures of him. They weren't interested."

"Well, is there some way you could find out which businessmen in town might have sick kids? Maybe Harry could get a list at the hospital or something."

Sylvia couldn't believe Tory would suggest such a thing. "That wouldn't be ethical, Tory. I would never ask him to do that."

"Why not? There must be businessmen who've had kids in Children's Hospital. If their kids are well now, they'd be able to relate to Joseph."

"Either that, or they'd resent me for asking, since no one helped them with their bills."

"Yeah, guess you're right." Tory looked around for her children, who had laid their bikes down and were crouched at a manhole on the sidewalk. Spencer was trying to open it. "Spencer, get away from that! Now!"

Spencer kept pulling at the cover. "There are fish in there, Mommy! I wanna see!"

"There are no fish in there!" Tory called. "Let go, Spencer. One . . . two . . ."

He yanked his hands away before she could reach "three," as if the manhole cover would self-destruct at the word.

Tory turned back to Sylvia. "What about heart attacks?"

"What about them?" Sylvia asked.

"Couldn't you get a list of heart attack victims? People Harry's done bypasses on? Some of them must own businesses; they might be willing to donate as a tax write-off."

Sylvia considered that for a moment. "I still couldn't get the list from Harry. That wouldn't be right."

"Okay, then walk into the lobby of a business, befriend the secretary, and ask her which executives have had heart attacks in the past. She would know. Then ask to see them. They'd be a whole lot more willing to listen than someone who's never been sick."

"Seems awfully mercenary," Sylvia said. "And dishonest, too."

"Then tell the receptionist what you're doing. Get *her* interested in Joseph. Be honest with her. She'll help you. Mark my word."

Tory glanced back at the street and saw only Brittany. Standing up, she called, "Spencer!"

"He's looking at the horses, Mommy," Brittany tattled.

Sylvia watched as Tory headed out to corral her young son. She smiled, remembering all the chases with her own children. They, too, had headed for the stables at every opportunity.

She listened as Tory shouted at Spencer, then saw the child dash back to his bike. Tory was out of breath when she rejoined her on the porch.

"Now, where were we?" Tory asked.

Sylvia grinned. "Just wondering . . . If you're so sure all this would work, why don't you try it?"

Tory stiffened. "Are you kidding? I could never do that."

Sylvia couldn't help laughing. "You know, there's a friend of ours, Ed Majors, who had a triple bypass last year. He owns a metalworks business in town. I know I could get in to see him. Maybe I could convince him . . ."

"Why didn't you start with him?" Tory asked.

"It never even crossed my mind until you mentioned the heart attack victims."

Tory arched her eyebrows. "Who's the brains of this outfit?"

"You, apparently." Sylvia laughed. "I feel better, Tory. Thank you. I think I can go out there and do it again tomorrow."

"Sure you can," Tory said. "All you needed was a plan."

🙰

The next morning, Sylvia showed up at Majors Metalworks and asked to see Ed. He came out immediately and ushered her back to his office. It took fifteen minutes, start-to-finish, for him to agree to donate five hundred dollars toward Joseph's fund. As he wrote out the check, he apologized for not giving more, but confided that his business was "in the red" and he couldn't afford more.

Sylvia expressed her gratitude with a hug, then, armed with purpose and confidence, she headed to the next business on her list. It turned out that it was time for the receptionist's coffee break, so she offered to buy her a cup of coffee in the employee cafeteria. There, she told the woman about Joseph's plight, and asked if she knew of any executives in the company who might have had heart problems themselves and would sympathize with the Dodds. The receptionist gave her the name of one of the vice presidents who'd had a mild heart attack earlier in the year. Before she sent Sylvia to his office, she gave twenty dollars herself to apply toward Joseph's fund.

The executive who'd had the heart attack wrote her a check for a hundred dollars, then walked her to the office of the president and introduced her. After hearing her pitch, the president wrote out a check for a thousand dollars.

Though the next five stops proved fruitless, Sylvia felt victorious on her way home. She had raised $1,620 in one day, and felt that if she just kept at it, they'd have what the Dodds needed for Joseph.

Harry was already home when she arrived, and she fluttered in and apologized for not having supper made.

"That's okay," he said. "We'll go out."

"Yes, let's go out," she said. "We have to celebrate."

"Celebrate what?"

"All the money I raised today for Joseph's heart transplant."

"How much did you raise?" he asked.

"One thousand six hundred twenty dollars," she said, prancing around.

"That much?"

"That's right. I know it doesn't begin to cover it, but isn't it wonderful? Yesterday I was so discouraged, but today I armed myself for battle and went at it with all I had. We're on our way. I deposited the money on the way home. The Joseph Dodd Trust Fund has something in it!"

"I *knew* you had it in you!" Laughing, he twirled her around, pulled her against him, and began to dance. "And you thought you had nothing left to contribute."

She laughed as he spun her, then launched into a jitterbug and ended with a dip that left her giggling like a teenager.

Harry grew serious at the restaurant, while they were waiting for their food. "I was thinking about a way to help little Joseph. Of sacrifices we could make to help out."

"I'm willing to give whatever we can," Sylvia said.

"Yes, but there's something we could sell, and it might help drum up some publicity to get others to contribute."

"What?"

He looked down at his iced tea and drew a line in the condensation on the glass, as if considering how this suggestion might affect Sylvia. "Before I say it, just know that if you don't want to do it, we don't have to. It's just an idea."

"Harry, what?" she asked. "You know I want to do whatever I can. Of course, with the wedding expenses and the possibility of our going to Nicaragua . . ." She halted midsentence and met Harry's eyes. It was the first time she'd brought that up since he'd first mentioned it. "I'm just saying, if we had to, somehow, we could come up with the money to help. I'm willing to do almost anything."

He looked carefully at her. "I was thinking of selling the horses."

She caught her breath. "What?"

"Just listen," he said, closing his hand over hers. "Cathy's having the animal fair at the church. That would be a good time to auction them off. It would be good advertising and draw more people to the fair. Raise public awareness."

"But Harry, I love my horses."

"I know, but hardly anyone rides them anymore. The kids aren't here—"

"They'll ride them when they come home. *I* still ride them sometimes."

"But not that often. And they're really a lot of trouble to take care of. Think how much it would mean for Joseph's heart fund. Directly and indirectly."

Tears flooded her eyes as she stared down at her silverware. She rearranged it, then set it back like it was. She wondered how he could think of giving up all the things they had loved in their lives—their home, their land, his career, and now the horses. Did he consider this the first step toward shedding all their possessions and heading for the mission field? "That's a lot to ask, Harry."

"I know." He let silence sit like a warm cat between them, and finally, he touched her chin and made her look at him. "Remember in the Bible when David wanted to buy the site of a threshing floor from Araunah, to build an altar on it and offer sacrifices to the Lord? And Araunah wanted to give it to him for free?"

"Yes, I remember," she whispered. "David said he didn't want to offer anything to the Lord that cost him nothing."

"The horses will cost us," he said. "But it won't be just an offering to Joseph. It'll be an offering to the Lord."

The struggle in her heart was almost more than she could bear, but she knew in her mind that it was the right thing to do. Finally, she brought her misty eyes back to his. "How can I say no when you put it like that?" She dabbed at the corners of her eyes. "What am I going to do around the house with no kids and no horses?"

"Maybe you'll think of something." It was his first reminder in weeks of his desire to go to Nicaragua. She chose to ignore it.

But she couldn't ignore his choice to sell the horses. She tried to find a cheerful spot in her heart from which she could make this sacrifice. "It sure will make Tory's life easier, if Spencer's not constantly trying to escape to pet the colt. She can rest a little easier if she has to turn her back on him for a minute."

He laughed softly. "That little rascal."

"Yeah," she said. "Remember when Jeff was that little? He loved those horses. We were training him for barrel races even then."

"And now he has a horse of his own in North Dakota," he said. "He'll be fine about this."

She knew he was right. It wasn't the kids who would mourn. She was the one who didn't want to let them go. "All right, Harry," she said finally. "Let's do it."

"Just tell Cathy," he said with a smile. "Then we can start preparing ourselves. It'll sure bring more people to the animal fair. Everybody wants a bargain."

She couldn't argue with that. "I just hope it makes a difference."

"It won't get him a heart any sooner," Harry said. "But it'll sure make things easier while they wait."

CHAPTER
Thirty-One

The impromptu meeting in the middle of Cedar Circle happened by accident. Tory had walked out to check her mailbox and seen Sylvia crossing the yard, headed for Cathy's. Cathy had just driven up and was getting out of her car.

Tory waved at them both, then looked down at the mail in her hand. The envelope on top was from a church—one of those she'd sent letters to the other day. Her heart began to pound as she tore it open. She pulled out the folded note, and a check fluttered to the ground. She picked it up before the wind could blow it away and saw that it was for a hundred dollars. Quickly, she read the letter.

Dear Mrs. Sullivan,

Thank you so much for your letter regarding Joseph Dodd's heart transplant. We have shared this request with our congregation and have raised a small donation toward his medical bills. We intend to keep trying to raise more money, but wanted

*to make this first installment. We also pledge to pray for him
and his family.*
*Thank you for sharing this need with us and allowing us to do
our part. We have a small congregation, but because of your
letter, we've reached deep into our pockets.*

In Christ's name,
The Fellowship of Survey Baptist Church

Reading the check again, Tory felt the thrill of accomplishment. Survey Baptist was just a little trailer church she passed on her way down the mountain. How had they raised this much so quickly? Didn't they have a building fund? Weren't there salaries to pay? Surely there were—and yet that small fellowship had found a way to contribute.

She broke into a run across the circle.

"Cathy! Sylvia! You won't believe this!"

They both turned around, and she almost assaulted them with the letter. "Read this. Look, a check for a hundred dollars! Can you believe it?"

"You got published?" Cathy asked.

"No!" Tory said. "Better! I sent letters out three days ago about Joseph, and look! I got this response already." Sylvia took the letter, and Cathy read over her shoulder.

"Wow! It must have been some letter," Cathy said.

"That's just the tip of the iceberg," Tory said. "I must have sent letters to a hundred different churches. Do you think more money will come in?"

"Well, that hundred dollars had to have been sent out the day they got your letter," Sylvia said. "If that's any indication, I'd say yes. A *lot* more will come in." She laughed out loud and hugged Tory. "Girl, don't ever tell me that you don't know how to write."

"I just told them about Joseph," she said. "It wasn't any big masterpiece."

"Well, it got through. This is wonderful. I'll take the check and deposit it. Tory, save all the letters we get for Brenda and

David. It might be nice for Brenda to see how the Lord is providing, and I think it might be vital for David."

"I will," Tory said. She flipped through the rest of the mail, but found only bills.

"Looks like we're on our way," Cathy said. "Sylvia, tell Tory what you're going to do."

Sylvia's grin faded a degree. "Harry and I have decided to sell the horses."

Tory caught her breath. "No! You've gotta be kidding!"

"We've decided that might drum up more publicity for the animal fair that Cathy's giving, and if we auction the horses off there, we might do real well. We'll donate the proceeds to Joseph."

"But what a sacrifice! You love those horses."

"We hardly ever ride anymore. And we figure it'll give you some peace of mind about Spencer."

Tory shook her head. "He's going to be heartbroken."

"He'll get over it," Sylvia said. "Especially if he knows it's to help Joseph's heart."

"I guess you're right." She looked at Cathy. "So have we got a date for the animal fair?"

"July Fourth," Cathy said. "I talked to the folks at Sylvia's church, and they're going to let us use the grounds. And I called Brenda's church, and they're going to come over and help with food and extra booths and things. We're going to make a real big deal out of it."

"What about your church, Tory?" Sylvia asked. "Have they agreed to help any?"

Tory looked down at the bills in her hand, embarrassed. "Well, I'm sure they will. They just haven't committed yet." She sighed and looked down at the Survey Baptist letter again. It was such an encouragement. More, even, than if she had gotten published. "You know, this gives me energy. I think I'll go back in there and write some more letters. I mean, I don't have to stay in the state of Tennessee. I could write every church in the country if I wanted to. I mean, the more I can reach, the better, right?"

"Right," Sylvia said. "That's why I knew you could do it. If I'd written the letter, they would have filed it in the trash can."

"I've got work to do," Tory said with a teasing grin. "I don't have time to stand out here flapping my jaws with you. I'll see you later."

She headed back into the house, more excited than she'd been in weeks.

That night, when they were getting ready for bed, Barry sat down on the edge of the bathtub and smiled up at her as she brushed her teeth. "What are you looking at?" she asked with her mouth full of toothpaste.

"You," he said. "I'm really proud of you, you know."

She rinsed her mouth out, wiped it on a towel, and turned around to peer down at him. "Why?"

"Because your writing is so strong that it's impacting the Dodds' lives," he said.

"Well, let's not get carried away. A hundred dollars won't go *that* far."

"There'll be more," he said. "I know there will. Tory, do you realize what that means?"

"What?"

"It means you *are* called to write. You *have* got a gift. Just because some woman wrote a story you intended to write, before you could get to it, it doesn't mean you're supposed to quit."

"This isn't exactly the great American novel, Barry. It was just a few letters."

"But not just anybody could have written them. At least, not in a way that would evoke sympathy and mobilize people into action."

She smiled at herself in the mirror, wondering if that was true. Had God led her through the ups and downs of her writing "career" so that she could be the one to write the letters that would help Joseph? "Wouldn't that be something?" she asked. "If we really could raise a lot of money this way?"

"It would be miraculous," he said.

"Yeah."

They headed back into the bedroom and crawled under the covers, and she curled up next to him, absorbing his warmth. "Barry, do you think our church will come through?"

"Sure they will. I'm going to bring it up at the finance committee meeting Wednesday night."

"You are? And you think it'll be approved?"

"Well, I should hope so. The thing is, there are a lot of people in our own congregation with needs, too."

"Yeah, I know." She looked up at her husband. "Barry, remember the other night when we were at Brenda's church?"

"Yeah?"

"It was pretty wonderful, wasn't it?"

"Yeah, it was."

"It's been a long time since I've visited another church, so I didn't have anything to compare it to. But it got me thinking. Maybe there's something different that we're supposed to be doing."

"Tory, I don't want to leave our church. I'm a deacon. I don't take that lightly."

"As a deacon, do you think you can get them to help us with the animal fair? They could set up a few booths, send some volunteers over, bake some cookies, anything."

"People in our church are busy already," he said. "We have a million programs and other things we always need volunteers for."

"I know," she said. "There's a lot going on—I like that. But some things should take precedence. Hurting people should be a priority over programs."

"Our programs are *designed* to help hurting people."

"I know. I just wish they'd help Joseph, too."

He slipped his arms around her and pulled her close. "Maybe our church just needs to be appealed to differently. I'll work on them Wednesday night at the finance committee meeting. Maybe they'll let you make a personal appeal at prayer meeting."

"All right," she said. "I'm counting on you. I don't want to have to bring out the big guns."

"What big guns?"

"These typing fingers," she said, flexing them as if they were lethal weapons. "I don't think they want me to get tougher with these letters."

"You might have to," he teased. "But that's okay. Paint them a picture with words, Tory. Help them to understand who Joseph is, and why they want to help him."

"I think I can do that," Tory said.

"Oh, yeah," Barry said with a grin. "You can do it. I have faith in you."

Wednesday night, Barry seemed preoccupied as he came out of the finance committee meeting. Tory met him in the church corridor. "You coming to prayer meeting?" she asked, searching his face.

He nodded.

"What's wrong, Barry?"

He shook his head and shrugged. "Oh, nothing. I'm just a little disappointed."

Her heart crashed. "They wouldn't pledge any money?"

"Not exactly." He sank onto a Chippendale chair placed fashionably next to an antique table in the hallway. "Oh, they acted real interested. Said they were glad we were helping the Dodds. But they didn't want any direct official church involvement."

"Why not?" she asked.

"They're afraid of stepping on the toes of Brenda's church."

Tory's face began to redden. "Did you tell them her church doesn't *have* toes?"

He chuckled. "I see their point, Tory. They thought it would be more powerful if her church coordinated the efforts."

"We weren't asking anyone to coordinate any efforts," she said. "We were asking for donations."

"Well, I guess that was their way of saying no. They did put him on their prayer list, though."

She sank down next to him. "At least maybe I can get some individual donations in prayer meeting."

"Well ... actually, I guess not," Barry said. "When I asked them if you could speak at prayer meeting, they said tonight wasn't a good night. There's too much on the agenda."

"On the *prayer* agenda?" she asked. "They're putting a limit on prayer?"

"I guess there are a lot of needs." He patted her knee. "I'm disappointed, too, Tory. They think they're doing the right thing, but I don't agree."

"Barry, I'm so embarrassed. Sylvia's and Brenda's churches are coming through. What are they going to think when they hear that ours has refused? I feel like marching in there and grabbing the microphone and chewing them all out."

"We can't do that." He rubbed his face roughly. "Frankly, I can't help feeling like I'm just as guilty. I've been just as disinterested in other people's needs as they've been over the years. The only difference in this case is that we know Joseph, we care about him. They've never seen him. I just keep thinking back on all those prayer meetings I've sat through, listening to all those needs—and never uttering a single prayer for those people, just because I didn't know them. I figured somebody else would be praying for them. Even now, you don't see us in there poring over the prayer list. There are a couple dozen Joseph Dodds on that list, and we're mad because they're not making a priority out of our request."

They sat in silence for several moments. Finally, Tory looked at him. "Barry, can we just go home?"

He nodded. "Yeah. Let's go get the kids out of their classes, unless they're in the middle of something important."

They headed for Brittany's room first, and as they rounded the corner, they heard the teacher leading the class in "I'm a Little Teapot." *Well*, Tory thought, *I suppose it passes the time ...*

She knocked on the door and got Brittany out, then headed for Spencer's room. Spencer's class was sitting on the floor watching *Mrs. Doubtfire*. She wondered if anyone had bleeped out the profanity.

"We're not through with the movie," Spencer protested as she pulled him out the door. "They didn't even sing 'Dude Looks Like a Lady' yet. That's my favorite song."

"'Dude Looks Like a Lady' is your favorite song?" Tory asked, horrified. "Where have you heard it?"

"In that movie," he said. "I've saw it four times at church."

She shot Barry an eloquent look.

"Why're we leavin' early?" Brittany asked.

Barry put his arm around Tory's shoulders and gave her a reassuring squeeze. "Mommy just wasn't feeling very well."

"Let's use this time to go visit Joseph," Tory suggested.

"Yay!" Spencer hollered. "Do we get to go in?"

"'Fraid not, Kemo Sabe," Barry said. "You're not allowed out of the lobby unless you're over twelve. We don't want to take any germs to Joseph, do we?"

"I don't got germs!" Spencer objected. "I had a bath."

❧

Barry waited in the hospital lobby with the kids while Tory went up to Joseph's room. He was sitting up in a chair, dressed in jeans and a Mark Lowry T-shirt, trying to put together a puzzle. Brenda hugged her and welcomed her in. Though Tory had been asked to don a gown at the nurse's station, the mask was no longer required.

"Spencer and Britty are downstairs," she told Joseph. "They're terribly offended by the policy that says they can't come up."

"I could go down and see 'em," Joseph said. "Can I, Mom? Please? I have thirty minutes on the battery. They said I needed to walk!"

"Can he do that?" Tory asked. "It's allowed?"

"Sure!" Joseph spoke up before Brenda could answer.

Brenda laughed. "I guess it'll be okay, for a few minutes. But I don't want him in the lobby. I'll get permission for them to come up to the waiting room on this floor."

Tory went downstairs and got her gang, then decked them all out in gowns. Brittany bounced up and down on the elevator as they rode up, and Spencer plopped down on his little behind, because he said it felt funnier to ride up that way. Funny was a good thing to feel, Tory supposed.

She was happy to see Joseph, masked like a bandit, walking toward the waiting room to meet them, pushing a little cart in front of him to which his Heart Mate was attached. Spencer and Brittany were as impressed with all his wiring as they would have been with Robo Cop.

Barry supervised the conversation, making sure that Spencer didn't get a wild hare and decide to swing from one of Joseph's tubes. Tory and Brenda sat just outside the waiting room, away from the kids. "So how's it going?" Tory asked.

"It's going great," Brenda said. "I'm enjoying the time I'm getting to spend with him. He's not used to one-on-one attention. It's been fun. And I'm getting some fierce homeschooling in. He's too bored to fight it."

Tory shot her a disbelieving look. "No, I mean . . . really. You don't have to put on that bright face with me. Your child is sitting here waiting for a heart transplant. Don't tell me it's been fun."

Brenda's smile faded. "Does it show?"

"What? The humanity? Yes, as a matter of fact, it does. You look like a mother who's scared to death. Just the way I would look."

The smile in Brenda's eyes vanished, and that worry returned. "I try, Tory. For Joseph's sake, and for David's sake . . . and for my sake, I try to have faith and think about the end of all this, when Joseph is healthy and back at home. But then I imagine a different ending, and I panic . . . I don't guess I hide it very well." Brenda got up and strolled to the nurse's station, where a table was set up with a coffeepot. She poured two cups. She knew how Tory liked hers; they'd visited so many times at each other's kitchen table.

Tory waited, giving her time to say everything on her heart.

"I've had a lot of time to think the last few days," Brenda said, handing Tory her cup. "A lot of time to pray. And I guess what this has taught me is that every minute is so important, with every child."

Tory's eyes were fixed on Brenda, for she wanted to take in every drop of the wisdom Brenda had to share. "But you already seem to squeeze so much life out of *every* minute."

Brenda smiled. "Well, Tory, I guess it changes you when you realize that this moment may be the only one you have with that child. It's changed the way I look at my other kids, too."

"I think I'd be hovering over them, crying and begging and bargaining with God."

"Trust me—I've done that, too," Brenda admitted. "Oh, the bargains I've made. Like God's a car dealer or something. Like if I just hit the right combination of prayer and confession and repentance and Scripture quoting and praise, He'll say, 'Finally, she's done what I've been waiting for, so now I can answer her prayers.'"

Her eyes misted as she sipped her coffee thoughtfully. "The day they admitted Joseph, I went into the chapel to pray, and Sylvia came in, bless her heart. She was a godsend. I really needed her. I was crying, upset, angry, and everything else you can imagine. And Sylvia said something to me that I've tried to remember ever since. It was that all of the blessings we have come from God. That means our children, too. We try to hold them in clenched fists, and think they're ours. But she reminded me that Joseph belongs to God, not me. I've been entrusted with him for a while." Her mouth trembled as she got the words out. "But I have to hold that blessing in an open hand, because God could take him back at any time. He has every right to. Joseph's not an object to be bargained with, and God loves him even more than I do."

Tory only looked at her, unable to comprehend that much trust in God. "I don't think I could do it, Brenda. As much as I whine and complain about my kids, that might just be the one area of my life where I can't open my hand."

"I know," Brenda agreed. "There've been times when I've read the story of Abraham and Isaac, when he was willing to offer him as a sacrifice. And I thought, how did he do it? How do you find the strength to trust God that way?" She looked at Tory with glistening eyes. "I'm afraid I might find out."

Tory's own eyes began to fill, and she wished she knew what to say. Brenda was miles above her in the areas of wisdom and spirituality. How could Tory find any words adequate to comfort her? She fought the tightening in her throat. "So how do you keep that hand open?"

"It's not easy," Brenda bit out. "Trust me."

Tory looked down at her coffee, wiping a finger along the edge of the cup. If Joseph died, what would Brenda do? Would her faith hold, or would she rail against God? "I guess we really have no *choice* but to trust God," she said, feeling the words echo with emptiness.

"Yes, we do," Brenda said. "We can choose not to, like David." She shook her head. "But the truth is, David's lack of hope gives him even fewer options than I have. If Joseph dies, David's going to feel so angry and so defeated. He'll never be able to see any good in it."

"And you really will?" Tory asked.

Brenda touched her fingertips to her mouth, as if she could stave off the tragic expression pulling at her face. "It'll be the hardest thing that ever happened to me," she whispered. "But God understands. He was there, remember? In Gethsemane, Jesus wanted to close His fist around His own life. But He didn't. He kept that hand open, and told God that if it was His will to take His life—"

"But He grieved," Tory said quietly.

"Oh, yeah," Brenda whispered. "He did that. I'll do it, too, if He takes Joseph."

Tory dabbed at the corners of her eyes. "You're stronger than I am. I think, by now, I would have broken something. Put my fist through a wall. Gone on Prozac."

"No, I don't think so." Brenda offered her a wan smile. "Look at all the money you're bringing in for Joseph. You've got a few things going for you, too."

Tory's face brightened up, and she wiped the tears away. "Yeah, we've gotten several small checks in the mail already, and it hasn't even been a week since I sent the letters out. And I'm not finished yet. I'm going to send follow-up letters to the churches who don't answer. And I've sent out thank-yous to the ones who have. I've invited them to the animal fair so they can feel even more a part of this."

"Good idea," Brenda said. "I appreciate your efforts so much. David does, too, even though he may seem ungrateful." She sipped her coffee, then blew on the steam. "He's got so much pride. Hates the idea of charity of any kind. So he's putting a 'For Sale By Owner' sign in the yard tonight."

"No!" Tory said. "Brenda, he can't. That's why we're raising the money. Selfishly, for ourselves. We don't want you to move."

"I can't talk him out of it." Brenda got up, went to the door of the waiting room, and peered in to make sure Joseph was all right. Satisfied, she turned back to Tory. "It's probably best. Even with the donations, the expenses are so high. We'll just rent an apartment for a while."

"An apartment? With four kids? And what about David's workshop?"

"He's been looking for a job," Brenda said. "Something that pays better." She couldn't meet Tory's eyes, and finally went back into the doorway. "Joseph's got to go back to the room now before his battery runs out."

Tory followed, still disturbed, as Brenda walked Joseph to his room and plugged him back into his machine. Before she left, she hugged her friend. "Brenda, God does provide."

Brenda smiled, a real, genuine, ear-to-ear smile made more profound by her wet eyes. "Sometimes He even provides a ram in the thicket. I could use a couple of them right now."

On Cedar Circle, Leah, Rachel, and Daniel sat at their front window, watching their father hammer the For Sale sign into the ground.

"I've got supper ready for you," Sylvia said, trying to distract them.

Daniel glanced back at her. "I'm not hungry."

"Me, neither," Rachel whispered.

Sylvia walked up behind them and saw that Leah was crying. She bent down to hug the girl. "Honey, don't cry."

"I like our house," Leah said. "Where are we gonna live?"

"Wherever it is, it'll be just fine." But she had no intentions of letting them move. Somehow, she would raise the money the Dodds needed before they sold the house. Then maybe she could convince David to take it off the market.

The front door opened, and he came back in. As he stood just inside, looking at the children's sad faces, Sylvia saw the raw emotion on his own. "It's gonna be okay, guys," he said. "I haven't ever let you down before, have I?"

The three children quietly shook their heads.

He glanced up at Sylvia, then went and sat down in front of the children. "Guys, I'm counting on you now. Mama's not here to keep the house clean, and people are going to be looking at it. I need for you guys to keep it clean. You already do a really good job, but without Mama it's going to take an extra effort. Just remember, we're doing it for Joseph."

"Joseph will need a place to live when he gets better," Rachel said, her mouth beginning to quiver.

"We'll have a place to live. It may be smaller, but that's okay. We can handle that."

"But what if they raise all the money we need at the animal fair?" Daniel asked. "Then can we take the sign down?"

"They're not going to raise *that* much money," David cautioned them. "It's impossible." Again, he shot Sylvia a look before she could argue. "I do appreciate what you all are doing, Sylvia. Brenda does, too. But we have to think realistically."

She nodded. "I know, David."

He turned back to the kids. "I know things are kind of topsy-turvy right now, guys. You're not getting to see Mama much, and I haven't spent much time with you, either. But things'll get better soon. We just all have to concentrate on Joseph right now. Send him good thoughts."

"Joseph doesn't need our thoughts," Daniel whispered. "He needs our prayers."

David nodded. "Prayers, then." He got up, and Sylvia realized he had aged in the last few weeks. He looked worn, weary, almost stooped with despair. "I've got to go to the hospital now," he said. He leaned over and gave each child a hug. "I love you guys."

They each returned his love, but as he left the house, they all turned back to the window and stared at the sign as if it sealed their fate.

Sylvia just hoped she could prove to them that it didn't.

CHAPTER
Thirty-Two

The animal fair on the Fourth of July was scheduled to begin at noon, but by eight A.M., dozens of people had shown up to help. Cathy spent the morning setting up corrals where the children could pet the animals. By ten, the animals began to arrive in a steady stream, as if they were headed for Noah's ark.

Just before noon, a couple dozen people from Brenda's church showed up with casseroles and hot dogs and cakes of every kind to sell to raise money for little Joseph. Sylvia's church rose to the occasion as well. Someone donated ice. Someone else donated gallons of soft drinks. Others set up game booths, complete with prizes. She hadn't even asked them, but they had supplied.

The festivities spilled over onto the parking lot, because there wasn't enough room on the lawn. A contemporary Christian group from Sylvia's church turned out for entertainment.

Around noon, Steve Bennett, the man who had come to her parent awareness meeting, showed up with his little girl, a freckle-faced, pigtailed blonde named Tracy. Cathy was happier to see him than she'd expected to be, though she tried not to show it.

The little girl, Joseph's age, was a cute little thing who stuck close to her daddy. "I thought Tracy might enjoy the fair," he said. "If there's anything I can do while I'm here, just holler. I like animals, and they like me, so if you can think of a place where you need me, I'm glad to help."

"Not yet," Cathy said. "Just go have fun with Tracy. When she starts feeling comfortable enough to let you go, come back and I'll put you to work."

He grinned and winked at Tracy. "I imagine she'll see a lot of her friends here, but so far I'm her only buddy, right?" His little girl smiled shyly and nodded her head.

"Where do you get the pictures made?" she asked.

Cathy nodded toward Rick, who had set his camera on a tripod in front of some bushes, next to a sign that said, "Pet Pictures— $10." "Rick's taking them over there," she said. "Did you bring a pet with you?"

The little girl nodded again, and she looked down at her pocket, as if she had a secret there.

"Don't tell me," Cathy said, bending over. "You have a gerbil in there."

"No, ma'am." She pulled a little turtle out of her pocket and held him up, his arms and legs flapping in the air.

"What a beautiful turtle," Cathy said. "Where did you get it?"

"Down by the creek at home," she said. "I found it this morning, and Daddy said I could get my picture made with it. Then I have to put it back in the bucket so it can swim."

"Well, if you hurry, you won't have to wait in line."

Tracy grabbed her father's hand. "Come on, Daddy. Can we do it now?"

Steve laughed and followed her over to Rick.

Less than an hour later, Cathy was at the table testing animals for heartworms when Steve returned. She was trying to examine a dog who was apparently in heat, and other dogs in line were straining at their leashes, howling and barking, trying to get away from their masters so they could get to know her a little better.

"Tracy found a friend, so they're running around checking out the booths," he said. "Anything I can help with while I'm free?"

"Yes," she said with relief. "You could help keep these animals restrained. See that one over there?" She nodded toward a German shepherd twice the size of the girl who held it. "I'd prefer putting him in the kennel if you can get him in there."

"Sure," he said. "No problem."

He hurried to the dog and offered his help. "You can stay in line and we'll just keep him locked up until it's his turn," he told the owner.

"Oh, thank you!" she said, surrendering the leash. The dog bolted forward to get to the dog in heat, but Steve reined him back in and began to scratch his ears.

"What's his name?"

"Butch."

"Come on, Butch. You gotta stay away from these women. They're nothing but trouble."

Cathy laughed under her breath.

Within seconds, Steve had the dog contained in the boxlike kennel.

"Way to go," she said. "You've done that before."

"Yeah, when I was growing up, we raised black labs."

"Really? Still have them?"

"Not here. My folks raise them in Alabama."

"Then you probably wouldn't mind locking up one more?"

He dusted off his hands. "Lady, I can lock up as many as you want."

She handed him the dog she had just examined. "Would you mind helping this lady get her into the car? She's going to run her home and then come back and enjoy the fair. She doesn't have heartworms, but she's driving all the male dogs crazy."

"No problem," he said. Expertly, he lifted the dog up and carried it to the little car the lady pointed out.

Cathy couldn't help watching him walk away. He wasn't afraid of animals, or of children, or of getting dirty, and he didn't seem to have an agenda. She liked that about him. But just as quickly as that thought danced through her brain, she chased it away. He was a man, and she had given up men.

She glanced across the lawn at Leah, Rachel, and Daniel Dodd, who were working some of the booths. Sylvia and Harry mingled with families, talking up the reason for the animal fair. Already, Sylvia had collected more money just from spontaneous donations than Tory and Barry had collected at the donor-card table.

Then her eyes fell on David, who walked around behind a video camera, looking amazed at the level of activity—all of it because of his son. He hadn't had a moment free since the fair had begun. People had been approaching him all day, offering him encouragement, asking how they could help. Cathy knew he was moved; she was moved, herself.

Cathy hoped the video would be an encouragement to Joseph. But the truth was, over the past few days he had declined noticeably. When she'd gone to see him last, he hadn't been sitting up. He'd lain in bed, struggling for breath, with dark circles under his eyes. He wasn't eating well, Brenda had said, and he'd lost weight.

Cathy only hoped all of this was not in vain. It wouldn't matter how much money they raised, if they didn't find a heart soon.

"This must be one special little boy," Steve Bennett said, and she turned around. He stood behind her, his eyes scanning the crowd.

"He *is* a special little boy," she said. "But I guess when anybody that young is threatened, you just want to help."

"Tell me about it," he said. "Boy, I don't know what I'd do if anything ever happened to Tracy."

"Joseph's her age," Cathy said.

"Yeah, that's what I hear."

The band stopped playing, and Sylvia went to the microphone and called out across the crowd. "Cathy, Dr. Cathy Flaherty? Where are you?"

Cathy waved at her and Sylvia saw her. "Come up here and tell these fine folks why we're doing this, would you?"

Cathy shot Steve a grin, then headed up to the podium. Everyone quieted down as she stepped up to the microphone. "I just want to thank you folks for coming," she said. "Especially those of you who volunteered your time, people who are here because they want to help Joseph Dodd." The crowd applauded, and she waited for it to die down. "Joseph couldn't be here today, because he's in the hospital waiting for a heart transplant. And he's not doing very well, so we'd appreciate your prayers. But as you know, we need more than that. His father, David, is one of the hardest working men I know," she said, gesturing to David, who was still videotaping. "But as most of you know, insurance often doesn't cover the complete bill for an operation like this, and the Dodd family will still have to pay thirty percent of Joseph's medical bills, and that could add up to a fortune. So we really appreciate all the sacrificial giving we've seen today." She looked down at David, Daniel, Rachel, and Leah. "You want to say anything?"

Looking woefully uncomfortable, David handed the video camera to Daniel and stepped up onto the stage. He cleared his throat and adjusted the angle of the microphone. "This is a tough time for our family, but I'm really amazed at the way the community has turned out." His voice broke off, and he wiped his eyes and reached down for the video camera. Daniel handed it to him. "I'm videotaping this so Joseph can see what a lucky little boy he is." Overcome with emotion, he stopped for a moment, fiddled with the camera, then stepped up to the mike again. "One thing I do want to say." He cleared his throat. "It's real important . . . to Joseph, and a lot of others . . . that people be organ donors. We'd really appreciate it if you'd take the time to sign your donor cards. You can just do it on the back of your driver's license." He coughed, cleared his throat, then handed the microphone to Cathy.

"I second that," Cathy said. "Sign your donor cards, please. We have a table over there where you can get cards and sign up, but the most important thing is to let your family know you did. We'd all really appreciate that. Now you all just go on and have fun," she said, "and if you feel like giving any more money than you have already, just find one of us and we'll be glad to take it."

The crowd laughed softly.

By the end of the fair, they had raised five thousand dollars for Joseph's trust fund—not counting the money from the auction of the horses, which had brought in almost that much again. Cathy could hardly believe it.

When the crowd had thinned out and only the volunteers remained, she wondered if she would be able to get the grounds cleaned up before dark. But she was amazed all over again at the number of people who stayed behind to help. Steve Bennett was one of them. He and Rick disassembled the fencing and kennels she had set up, and loaded them into her truck. Tracy, his daughter, was sitting between Rachel and Leah in the bed of Steve's truck, and they were braiding her hair, one on each side of her, while she let her turtle run for its life on the hot vinyl bed liner.

Though Annie had disappeared, Mark grudgingly walked around the lawn scooping up the evidence that the animals had been there. It was all coming down quickly, and soon there would be no trace that they had been here. She looked across the lot at the church building, and realized that God was providing through His churches. All of this was about Him as much as Joseph. These churches were demonstrating what churches were supposed to be.

Suddenly, she had a fierce yearning for her children to grow up in a congregation like this, where people cared and helped and gave. She wondered if it was too late for them to be a real part of something like this.

Her eyes drifted across to Steve Bennett as he used a wrench to disassemble some of the railing. Was he one of God's provisions? If she were looking for a man—which she definitely wasn't—he was the kind of man she would look for. He wasn't the good-looking type who knocked women dead. In fact, he would be easy to overlook in a crowd. But there was something about him that was different from the other men she'd met lately, something that made her uneasy about walking away from here and not seeing him again.

For the first time since she'd become single again, she considered asking a man for a date. Then her own lack of courage won out, and she told herself she couldn't do that. If he wanted to go out with her, he knew where he could find her. She chased the thoughts out of her mind and finished her work.

When the lawn was clear and clean and Rick had driven Mark home in the truck so they could go to the fireworks at the high school football field, Steve and his daughter still lagged behind. He helped Cathy get the last few things into her car, then looked around him. Tracy was in the bed of his pickup truck, still playing with her turtle.

"Steve, I can't tell you how I appreciate your help today," she said. "I don't think I could have done it without you."

"Oh, sure you could," he said. "You had it going pretty well when I got here."

"But you helped so much with the cleanup. I would have been here until tomorrow."

"No problem," he said. "You know, this was a great idea. Look at all the money you raised, and I think it's just the beginning. I think a lot more will come in as a result of this."

"I hope so," she said. She opened her car door, but didn't get in.

He leaned his hand on the top of the door. "Well, it was good getting to know you a little better," he said. "I still plan to see you at the school board meeting in September."

"Good. That's great." They stood staring at each other for a moment, and she thought of inviting him over for dinner. Something prevented her, and she wanted to kick herself. She could just hear Annie lecturing her. *Mom, this isn't the fifties. Grow up. Women ask men out all the time.* She held her breath, wishing he would ask her instead.

He seemed to be struggling with something, and for a moment she was sure he would ask.

But then Tracy called out, "Daddy!"

He turned around. "I'm coming, sweetie." When he faced her again, Cathy knew the moment was shattered.

"Well, guess I'll see you later."

"Yeah," she said. "Thanks again."

He watched her get into the car, then closed her door and headed back across the lot to his own truck. He pulled Tracy out of the bed and tickled her on her way into the cab. Cathy watched him wait for the little girl to hook her seat belt, then pull out of the driveway.

Some tender spot she hadn't felt in a long time swelled in her heart, and she wondered if she was crazy. Men always disappointed her. She needed to stop fantasizing that this could be any different. Steve Bennett was still a man. He had a man's desires and a man's thoughts. He couldn't be that far removed from the other men she'd known.

But then she thought of Harry . . . Barry . . . David. And she wondered if it was possible that there was one more man like them, faithful and willing to do his part, without any ulterior motives or secret agenda. Maybe Steve Bennett was real.

So why had she let him get away?

She sighed and headed back home, trying to concentrate on the successes of the day, instead of the failures.

CHAPTER
Thirty-Three

The next morning, Rick and Annie and Mark were a little less combative about getting ready to go to church. Cathy made sure they got to their classes without making detours, then headed for her own class. They had deliberately gotten there early so they wouldn't have to walk in late. She thought it would be easier on them if they were among the first ones there instead of the last.

The 8:20 singles class was just filing out, so rather than try to fight her way through the crowd, she stopped by the visitor's desk and got a name tag, then waited until the way was clear for her to get into the room for the 9:40 class.

"Cathy?"

She swung around and saw a smiling, surprised Steve Bennett, dressed in a suit and looking like a Wall Street banker.

"Steve? Do you go to church here?"

"Yeah, for the last six months. But I didn't know you did. I thought you said you were surprised the church had let you use the lawn yesterday since you weren't a member here."

She laughed. "I'm *not* a member. I've just been visiting for a few weeks."

"Really?" he asked. "I've never seen you here."

"Apparently we go to different Sunday schools and different services."

"Well, how about that?"

She felt awkward now. She hoped he didn't think this was all a clever ploy to get to see him again.

"Where are the kids?" he asked.

"They went to their classes."

"Well, good." He looked at her again, that expression of struggle on his face, just like yesterday. "Listen . . . I know you don't know me very well, but . . . how would you feel about me taking us all out to lunch today?"

"All of us? That's six people."

"I'm aware of that," he said. "Hey, I have a decent job."

She laughed. "I'm sure you do. It's just that I hate to impose like that."

"Well, if I recall, I just volunteered it."

She grinned. "We could go dutch."

"We could, but then I might be insulted, and my pride might be crushed, and—"

"Okay!" she said. "Whatever you say. We'll order the most expensive things on the menu."

"Fine with me." His smile began to fade, and his eyes grew more serious. "I hope you don't think I'm trying to hit on you the first time I see you in church."

"No, I didn't think that's what you were doing."

"Well, there are some around here who are like that."

"Yeah, I know. We've been introduced."

"I bet you have. Somebody like you? You probably get hit on all the time."

She couldn't believe she was blushing. "Actually, that's not true."

"Well, do you have a better offer, or what?"

"Not at all."

"Okay, then, I'll tell you what. I'll meet you by the elevators after the eleven o'clock service."

"Sounds great," she said.

She sat through Sunday school feeling elated that she'd run into him again and amazed that he actually went to this church. She had vowed to give up on coming with the hope of meeting a man, and now, completely unexpectedly, she'd met one. She just hoped he didn't turn out to be a frog the moment she kissed him.

After Sunday school, her kids told her one by one that they'd found friends from school with whom they intended to sit in church. It was a pleasant surprise. She found Sylvia and Harry and slipped into the pew next to them. Before the service started, Steve came to the end of her pew. "Room for two more?" he asked.

"Sure! I thought you went to the early service."

"We did," he said with a wink. "It was so good we decided to sit through it twice."

She didn't know when she had been more flattered. "Hi, Tracy. How's it goin'?" Cathy asked.

"Pretty good," the little girl said with that shy grin. "How are you?"

"Great." Cathy was impressed with the child's politeness. It spoke well of Steve's parenting skills. She only hoped her own children's manners didn't run him off.

He sat down and she introduced him once again to Sylvia and Harry. They had met the day before, but she wasn't sure they'd remember. As the service began, Cathy found she enjoyed listening to the sound of his voice as he sang the praise songs. It was as if he believed the words he sang, as though standing up and lifting his voice to God was a joy and not a chore.

Steve followed the pastor's sermon with his Bible open and a pen poised to take notes. There was something about that unpretentious, unself-conscious attitude that appealed to her. She saw Bill, the guy with the Porsche, sitting several rows away next to a size-ten blonde in a size-six dress. She kept looking into her compact mirror, and every now and then, when the mirror was turned just right, Bill stole a glimpse at himself.

Steve, in his unself-conscious plainness, was much more attractive to Cathy than the church Casanova.

As the service wound to a close, she silently prayed that having lunch with her kids would not chase him away.

CHAPTER
Thirty-Four

Across town, as Joseph watched the video his dad had made of the animal fair, Dr. Robinson stopped by to examine him. Brenda and David watched quietly as the doctor studied his chart intensely and asked Joseph questions. The boy answered in weak monosyllables.

Finally, the doctor patted Joseph's hand and asked Brenda and David to step out into the hall.

"What is it, Doctor?" David asked when they were out of the room.

Dr. Robinson looked at the floor as if carefully considering his words. "I'm sure it's no surprise to you that Joseph's getting worse, despite our best efforts," he said. "His need for a heart is getting pretty urgent." His voice faltered again, and Brenda realized that this was taking its toll on him, as well. She wondered if treating a dying child was ever routine for him.

"Is he gonna make it?" Brenda asked him on a whisper.

It took a moment for him to answer. "I don't know," he said. "Without a miracle . . ."

He didn't have to say the words. They knew as they went back into the room that Dr. Robinson didn't think Joseph would make it. With a Herculean effort, Brenda tried not to let Joseph see her despair. Instead of focusing on what might happen, she concentrated on making him more comfortable.

Joseph was watching the animal fair with interest, but not with the joy or excitement she had hoped for. Instead, his eyes seemed sad as the footage rolled on. Finally, when it was over, she sat next to him on his bed, and leaned over him. "What's the matter, Joseph?"

He kept his eyes on the blank television screen, and Brenda met David's eyes, searching for insight into the little boy's mind. David shook his head, as if he had none.

After a while, Joseph spoke up. "They all think I'm gonna die, don't they?"

Brenda caught her breath and choked back her tears.

"Die? Of course not, sweetheart. They wouldn't have gone to all that trouble to have the fair and raise all that money if they thought you were going to die."

"But they think I'll die if we can't afford the transplant, or if we don't get a heart," he said.

With a shock, she realized that that thought, so clear to all the rest of them, hadn't yet been clear in Joseph's mind—until he saw the video. Now she wished they'd never shown it to him. "Honey, you're very sick. You know that. But they're doing everything they can for you here, and soon, you will get a heart."

"But what if it doesn't come in time?"

"It will. It has to."

He looked up at his mother, his eyes pensive. "Mama, remember when the doctor first told us about my heart, and we went to church and they prayed over me?"

David sat up straighter and met Brenda's eyes. *I told you not to allow that*, his look said. *I told you it would traumatize him.*

Her eyes misted over as she looked down at her son. "Yes, I remember," she said softly.

"That was nice," he said. "It felt like the prayers would work."

"Prayers always work, sweetheart."

"I know," he said. "But, sometimes . . ."

Her throat was so full that she couldn't answer him, and tears brimmed in her eyes. Concerned, Joseph reached up and touched her face. "Don't cry, Mama. I know I'm going to heaven."

She wanted to scream out that he wasn't going anywhere, not yet. Not now. But she couldn't make the words come out.

Squeezing his mother's hand, he turned his head to his father. "Daddy?"

"Yeah, son?"

"How do they get a heart?"

David got up and came to his side. "What do you mean, how do they get it?"

"I mean, where does it come from?"

"They get it from another person."

"What person is mine coming from?" he asked.

"We don't know yet."

Joseph thought that over for a moment. "What happens to them?" he asked finally. "I mean, after I get their heart?"

David breathed a deep sigh and leaned wearily over the rail. He began to stroke his little boy's red hair with callused fingertips. Brenda struggled to choke her tears back. "Well, son, what usually happens is that somebody is in an accident. And they die. Except their organs still work, so the doctors can take them out and give them to people like you, who need them."

A troubled expression fell like a shadow over Joseph's face. "Somebody has to die so I can live?"

David's mouth twitched at the corners as he nodded. Brenda slid her hand along her husband's shoulder, hoping to comfort him.

"Kinda like Jesus, huh, Mama?"

Brenda tried to smile. "Yeah. Kinda like."

The thought didn't seem to give Joseph much pleasure. Still frowning, he looked at the television screen again, thinking that over. "Is it going to be a kid? The person that has to die, I mean."

"We don't know," Brenda whispered.

"We can't know that, buddy," David said. "They'll give you whatever heart is available when you're at the top of the list, as long as it's a match for you. It might even be an adult's heart. It depends more on the size of the heart than the age of it. But it'll be random."

"It's not *that* random," Brenda corrected. She bent over her son, making him look into her face. "Honey, God is in control. He already knows whose heart He's going to give you. And when that person is in an accident, or whatever happens, God's going to take his or her spirit out before anybody ever takes the heart."

"So they won't feel it?" Joseph asked.

"Not at all."

"But what about their parents? Won't they be sad?"

She smeared the tears across her cheek. "Sure, they will," she whispered. "But it's up to God when that person goes home."

Silence fell between them as Joseph stared into her glistening eyes, processing his thoughts. "It's up to God when I go home, too, isn't it?"

She paused, almost unable to answer. "Yes, honey. It is."

Several moments went by as he gazed at his thoughts. "I feel bad taking somebody else's heart."

She struggled to steady her voice. "But that might be how God answers our prayers," Brenda said. "To take someone's death, and turn it into life. It's just like God, isn't it?"

Joseph didn't answer.

Later, Joseph fell asleep, and David stepped out into the hallway. Brenda followed, and found him leaning against the wall. Her eyes were swollen from crying, and she felt as if she hadn't slept in years.

"I wish you wouldn't tell him those things," David said, staring at the opposite wall.

"What things?"

"Things about your spirit leaving your body and God being in control."

"I was telling him the truth, David."

He moved his gaze to her. "I don't see that as the truth, Brenda, and I have a hard time with those concepts being put into the head of a little boy who might die."

"What would you rather he believed?" she asked, growing angry. "Would you rather have him believe that it's all random and hopeless? That his life or death means nothing? Would you rather tell him he's insignificant, that life will go on with or without him?"

"You know I wouldn't," David said.

"Then what is wrong with my telling him the truth? That God is in control, that He's taking care of him, and that *if* and *when* he gets a heart, it'll be because God chose it for him."

"And what if his body rejects it?" David flung back. "Will you tell him then that God made a mistake?"

She wanted to scream that she couldn't take much more of his disbelief. But she had no choice. "David, I don't know what's going to happen. God may take Joseph out of our hands, and we may go home and have three children to tuck in at night instead of four." She began to sob but didn't let it stop her. "But if He does, David, it won't be because of any *mistake*."

Slowly, he pulled her into a hug and held her tightly against him. "I'm sorry," he whispered. "I didn't mean to hurt you."

She tried to pull herself together, but her face was still twisted in pain. "When you talk about God as if He doesn't exist, I take it real personally, David."

"Why? We have different philosophies, that's all."

"It's not a philosophy," she whispered. "He's real. He's part of me. I love Him. And He gave up His life for you and for me. Just like somebody is going to have to give up his life to save Joseph. The difference is that they won't volunteer. It won't be a choice they make. But when Jesus came down here to die for our sins, it *was* a choice He made, David. He didn't have to do it, but He did. And when you talk about Him the way you do, it hurts me, because I'm part of Him!"

David held her face against his chest and let her weep. "I'm sorry. I guess I haven't been very sensitive to that."

"Joseph knows Him, too," she cried. "You promised, David. When I became a Christian, you told me I could raise our children that way. You said it wouldn't hurt anything. Don't pull it out from under Joseph now when it's all he has left. It's a lot, David. It's a lot. It's more than most people have."

"Shhh," he whispered. "I'm sorry. You tell him what you need to get through this. I wish I could believe it."

"I wish you could, too," she cried. She spoke the words as a prayer.

CHAPTER
Thirty-Five

Cathy's lunch with Steve was fraught with tension. Her children hadn't embarrassed her yet, but she fully expected their disrespect to manifest itself at any moment.

They were halfway through the meal when Annie fulfilled that expectation. "Mom, can Rick run me home? Allen's coming to get me, and we're going out to the lake."

Cathy didn't look up as she cut her steak. "No, Annie. I'll get you home after we eat."

"But I'm finished."

"Well, I'm not," Rick said. "Besides, I'm not running you anywhere."

"Mom, make him," she whined. "Allen will be there soon. It's rude to make him wait."

"It's rude to whine at the table," Rick shot back. "So shut up, will you?"

Cathy shot Steve an apologetic look. He seemed a little embarrassed. Keeping her voice calm, Cathy leaned toward her children. "Could we refrain from the whining *and* the bicker-ing?" she asked.

"I'm not whining," Annie said through gritted teeth. "I'm just telling you that I need to go. You don't need me on your date."

Mortified, Cathy glanced at Steve again. He was busy cut-ting Tracy's meat and acting as if he hadn't heard. But judging from the sudden hush, Cathy realized that even the people at the next table had heard. "Annie, unless you change your tone and lower your voice, you won't be going anywhere today. Now close your mouth and wait until we're finished."

"Fine." Annie threw her napkin on the table and slid her chair back. "I'll just call him and tell him to pick me up here!"

Cathy stared at her as her face turned scarlet. "You can call him, all right, and tell him that you won't be leaving the house today because you couldn't control your mouth." She picked up her purse and dug for some coins. "In fact, I'll pay for the call."

"Mom! You can't do that!"

"Watch me," Cathy said.

Furiously, Annie stormed from the table.

Cathy wanted to cry. "Steve, I'm so sorry."

"No problem," he said, but she could see on his face that it was a big problem.

It grew bigger when Annie didn't come back to the table. By the time they'd finished the meal and returned to the car, she realized that Annie had left.

"Ten bucks says Allen picked her up," Rick wagered.

Cathy tried to keep her rage contained as Steve paid the bill.

As the kids got into the cars, Steve lingered behind. "You all right?" he asked.

She thought of lying, but realized he'd see right through her. "No, actually. I'm not. I've got to get a grip on her. I'm just so sorry she ruined our lunch."

"She didn't ruin it," he said. "It was still nice."

"Be honest," she said. "It was the most expensive fiasco you've ever experienced."

"Not true," he maintained. He glanced into his truck at Tracy. "Well, I'd better get Tracy home. I'll talk to you later, okay?"

She knew better than that. "Yeah. See you later."

When they had pulled out of the parking lot, Cathy looked over at Rick. "Well, that was a nightmare."

"Not my fault," Rick said. "Annie was the brat. In fact, if you don't ground her up one side and down the other, there's just no justice."

Cathy drove in silence until they got home. She hurried into the house. Annie wasn't home. Her church clothes were puddled on the floor of her room where she'd stepped out of them, so Cathy knew she hadn't been kidnapped at the restaurant.

"She went to the lake, Mom," Mark said. "She does whatever she wants to."

"Rick? Mark?" Both boys looked at her.

"Yeah?"

"Leave the parenting to me, thank you. I'll be in my room. Let me know if your sister comes home."

Then she marched to her room and slammed the door behind her. Throwing herself on the bed, she wondered where she'd gone wrong.

CHAPTER
Thirty-Six

School started the last week of August, and Brenda came home from the hospital early that first morning to get the kids ready. They were nervous and full of questions about what was going to happen. She had already done what she could to make the transition to public school easier on them, arranging for Leah and Rachel to be put in the same classroom and for Daniel to be placed in several of Mark Flaherty's classes. Knowing that none of the three would be totally alone gave her some peace of mind.

She tried to sound excited as she packed their lunches. "Won't this be great? Instead of listening to me all day, you'll get to hear other teachers. And all those new friends you'll make . . ."

The kids were quiet. "What if people make fun of us because we've never been to school before?" Rachel asked.

"They won't. And if they do, when they see how smart you are, they'll stop."

"Mom, can't we wait until Joseph comes home and you can homeschool again? We'll work hard to catch up."

"I promise, when things have settled down, we'll start back. But just in case this takes longer than I think, I want you learning. It'll be a good experience. Trust me."

As she drove her kids to their respective schools and made sure they got through the paperwork of registration, she hoped she hadn't asked them to trust her in vain.

With every day that passed, Brenda tried to assure herself that they were one day closer to getting a heart for Joseph. But it was a thin, fragile slice of hope, for Joseph was declining daily. He spent much of the time sleeping, and twice his blood pressure slipped so low that she thought they were going to lose him.

The only color left in his complexion was the sickly gray of his freckles. He didn't get up anymore, even to go to the bathroom, so they had inserted a catheter. Monitoring his urination made them aware that his kidneys were beginning to lose their function, too.

The doctors moved Joseph into cardiac intensive care but allowed Brenda to stay with him, since she was able to take some of the burden off the nurses, who had other patients to watch. At night, David would sit with Joseph while Brenda visited with her other children in the waiting room. Taking their cue from their mother, they tried to paint a happy face on their stories about school, but Brenda could see that this crisis had taken its toll.

The fact that they were close to selling the house didn't help her spirits, either. One couple had looked at it three times and had assured David that they would be back in touch soon. In all, he had shown the house at least a dozen times. The pressure that put on the kids to keep it spotless was almost cruel, but she knew there was no way around it.

In her despair, she turned to God for comfort, but found herself praying incessantly for the heart that would save her son. God seemed to be saying "no," and she couldn't understand it.

One Monday morning, Dr. Robinson came into Joseph's area and asked her to get in touch with David because he needed to meet with both of them. As she called her husband, her heart deflated.

When Harry and Sylvia came to sit with them during their meeting with Dr. Robinson, Brenda knew that this was going to be the prepare-yourselves speech. She leaned on David as they went in, and trembled as they sat down. Sylvia sat on the other side of her, holding her hand.

"Brenda, David," Dr. Robinson began in a soft, gentle, apologetic tone. "I know it doesn't surprise you to know that Joseph is declining. You saw his blood pressure this morning. You know about his kidney function. We've done as much as we can, and we're going to keep doing it. If his kidneys don't rebound by tomorrow, we're going to put him on dialysis. Even as we speak, we're adjusting his medications. We're doing everything we can to keep him alive."

"But?" David prompted, waiting for what seemed inevitable.

"But . . ." The doctor glanced at Harry, who looked very tired, as if he, too, had been losing sleep over Joseph. "But we may not succeed. We're hoping to get a heart in time. Joseph's at the top of the list. We could get a match at any time. But if we don't . . . I'm afraid there may not be much more we can do for him."

Brenda wilted against David.

"But that Heart Mate was a bridge," David insisted. "It was supposed to keep him alive . . . until . . ."

"It has its limitations," Dr. Robinson said. "Most of the time, we have good luck with it. But in Joseph's case—"

"The dialysis," Brenda cut in. "Won't it help? Won't it get the poisons out of his body and make his heart work better?"

"It will filter out some of the toxins," Harry said. "And it might make him feel better, for a time."

"Then we can keep doing it," she said. "Just as much as we need to." She looked at David, who still looked stunned. "I don't care about the cost. We're selling the house. We can sell our furniture, our cars . . . anything. If the dialysis can make him feel better, and keep him alive . . ."

"It's his heart," Dr. Robinson cut in gently. "That's the main problem. His heart may not make it."

Brenda doubled over, covering her face with both hands as she wept into them. Sylvia embraced her and began to weep with her. David sat as still as a statue, staring at the air.

"I'm sorry," Dr. Robinson said. "I don't want you to give up hope. But I've found that it makes it easier when the parents know what to expect. When they have time to prepare themselves."

"I can't prepare myself for this," David whispered in a thick, broken voice. "I'll never be prepared."

"We're still praying for a heart," Sylvia told them. "It's not over yet. God still hears. His timing is perfect."

Brenda didn't voice the questions swirling in her mind: Why was God waiting when Joseph was so sick? Why was someone so young and bright and innocent so close to death? She tried to remember the last time she'd had a prayer answered, but it seemed so long ago. All of her prayers lately had been about Joseph—or David. None of those prayers had been answered, and now her heart demanded to know why. How long would it take for God to save Joseph?

"How long?" David asked, still wooden. "If he doesn't get a heart, how long has he got?"

Brenda looked up, trying to read the exhaustion and dread on the doctor's face. "A few days at the most," he said.

"A few days?" She collapsed into Sylvia's arms again, then pulled away and turned to her husband. "Oh, David." He opened his arms to her and held her as she cried, but he was so rigid, so quiet, that she feared what might be going through his mind.

It had to be even worse than what was going through hers. Anger, confusion, despair—what were they going to do with all these feelings?

When they got back to Joseph's room in ICU, there was no change. David wanted to stay with him, so Brenda went out to the waiting room, where Sylvia was waiting.

"How is he?" Sylvia asked.

"Terrible," she said. "Asleep."

"No. I meant David."

Brenda shook her head and sat down next to her friend. "David is . . . stone cold and silent. I can see the anger brewing inside. I think that, for the first time, David *wants* to believe in God—so he can lash out at Him." She met Sylvia's eyes. "I understand that feeling, Sylvia. I've been doing a little lashing on my own. Why won't God answer this prayer? Why won't He heal my baby?"

"He will, Brenda. One way or another, He will." She breathed a deep sigh. "I've asked Him the same questions myself over the last few weeks," she said. "When I've been out trying to raise money for Joseph. I've asked, 'Why won't You send the money they need? Why does it all have to be so hard? Why can't just part of this turn out right, to encourage them?'"

"I appreciate all you've done," Brenda said, wiping her eyes. "I know that your efforts, and Cathy's and Tory's, are going to make such a difference. I'm sorry it's been so hard for you."

"Thank you, but that's not what I was getting at," Sylvia said. "Brenda, when I've prayed those things, the Lord has reminded me that things *are* working out. Let's not forget the answered prayers, the blessings . . ."

Brenda closed her eyes and tried to think of what those blessings were. "Blessings. Let's see . . ."

"How about Dr. Robinson? Hasn't he been a good doctor?"

"Yes. And Harry. He's been a huge blessing. And so have you. I don't know what I would have done without you."

"What else?"

"The time with Joseph. Every minute. When he's been awake, we've talked and played games . . . I've never *had* time alone with Joseph. He's always had three siblings competing for his time. It's been good."

"Anything else?"

Brenda thought for a moment, then a sad smile stole across her face. "You know what this reminds me of? A few months ago, the day of Joseph's birthday party, when he collapsed for the first time, we sat in the doctor's office and played a game. He had to pretend he had a million dollars and spend every cent. The things he came up with were so sweet."

Sylvia's eyes lit up. "Then pretend you can have a million blessings—anything you want. What would they be? Just think of the snapshots of those blessings."

"A heart for Joseph," she said without thinking. "One that works." She paused. "Snapshots. Joseph on his bicycle. Joseph hugging the dog. A family portrait when the kids are grown— all four of them, not just three." Her gaze lowered, and she tried to think of more. "But if he dies, those snapshots will be so different."

"What will they be?" Sylvia asked, taking her hands and making her look at her. "Not the loss, the sorrow—what's the blessing?"

Brenda paused, forcing her mind by sheer power of will to see her situation from a different angle. "Reunion," she said finally. "In heaven. When I get there, and Joseph comes running, with Jesus right behind him. And the love he's brought to our lives, that you can't put in a snapshot, but it's there, in our family. It won't ever die. That will be one of the blessings."

"And the friends who've been praying for you and loving you," Sylvia said. "Hasn't that meant something?"

"Yes," Brenda said. "It has. I just . . . I want them to see that God does still answer prayer."

"Don't you think He does?"

She wasn't sure. "It's just like I've told you before. I want this to be answered a certain way. But I know God may have another plan. And I don't want Joseph to suffer. I want to put him into God's hands. I just don't know how." She broke down, and Sylvia hugged her again. "Pray for me, Sylvia. Pray that I'll be able to lay Joseph in God's arms, and trust Him to do the perfect thing. Even if it hurts me. Even if it hurts all of us. Right now, I feel like if I lose my focus, Joseph will die. If I close my eyes and sleep, he'll slip away. If I go downstairs to eat, he won't be there when I get back." She got to her feet. "Even now, it makes me crazy sitting out here, knowing that he could breathe his last breath. I feel like his living depends on something I can do. But in my heart, I know better. Pray that I'll trust God about Joseph, Sylvia. Pray that I'll have enough faith to let go."

"I have been all along, sweetheart," Sylvia said. "And I think that prayer is being answered as we speak."

CHAPTER
Thirty-Seven

The urgency surrounding Joseph's heart transplant became more apparent to Cathy each time she visited him that week. It was clear that he was running out of time.

On Thursday, Cathy came home from the hospital more depressed than she'd been all week. Annie was sulking in front of the television, unable to leave the house or talk on the phone since the stunt she'd pulled at the restaurant. Cathy had threatened to keep her from getting her driver's permit if she was disobedient during her punishment, and that had worked. Annie hadn't made any more surprise disappearances.

The phone rang as Cathy searched the refrigerator for something quick to cook for dinner. Annie leaped for it. "Hello?" she almost shouted. Cathy gathered from her scowl that it wasn't for her. Rolling her eyes, Annie shoved the phone toward her mother.

Cathy froze for a moment. "Is it Brenda?"

"No," Annie said. "Some guy." She looked up as Cathy took the phone. "Why? Is Joseph worse?"

"He's real bad," Cathy said. She thought of getting Annie to take a message, but the thought crossed her mind that it might be Steve. She hadn't heard from him since their lunch Sunday, and didn't really expect to. Still, she didn't want to take the chance of missing his call. "Hello?" she said.

"Cathy? This is Steve."

Her spirits instantly inflated again. "Hi."

"Hi. Listen, it sounds kind of busy there . . ."

She reached for the remote control and turned down the television, then took the cordless phone into the dining room. "No, no. Not at all."

"Well, I won't keep you, right here at supper time. I just wanted to see if you'd like to have dinner tomorrow night."

She was so stunned that she almost couldn't answer. "I can't believe you'd ask me again after being around my kids."

He laughed. "I'm not inviting them."

"Still . . . I thought I'd heard the last of you."

His laughter faded, and there was a moment of silence. "I meant to call before now. I just . . . didn't."

She didn't tell him that she'd noticed, or that she'd had at least two depressing, miserable nights hoping he would. It had taken all week for her to get philosophical about it. "It's okay. I've been busy, anyway. I didn't know if you had or not."

"Sometimes . . ." His voice faded off. She frowned, wondering what he was going to say. "Sometimes dating seems too complicated," he went on. "I start to worry about Tracy's reaction, and I think about all the potential problems . . ."

She swallowed, but tried to keep her voice light. "Hey, it's not like we're walking down the aisle together. Just two friends having dinner. Without their kids."

He laughed again. "So—Tracy will be spending the night at her grandmother's tomorrow night."

"My kids'll be at their dad's."

"Then tomorrow sounds good."

But by the next evening, Cathy's spirits were lower than they'd been all week. She was looking forward to her dinner with Steve, but she had talked with Sylvia on the phone that afternoon about Joseph's plight, and the news wasn't good.

Steve arrived exactly on time, and she tried not to look too eager as she let him in. "Hi," she said.

"Hi."

There was a chemistry between them, an electric spark that she hadn't felt in years. She liked being around him. His very presence made her feel better. "I'm almost ready," she said. "Just let me get my sweater."

"Sure," he told her. "No hurry."

She ran to get her cardigan, then hurried back to the front room. He took it out of her hands and helped her put it on. "So how's Joseph?" he asked.

"Not well," she said. "I'm starting to think he may not make it until he gets a heart."

Steve's expression mirrored her own concern. "No kidding."

"Yeah, it's getting pretty bad. I don't know how Brenda does it. She reads to him, sings to him, talks and tries to play with him. But he just lies there, too weak to do anything."

"What's your friend next door saying? The doctor?"

"They don't give him much time," she said.

His expression collapsed, and he sank onto her couch. "Wow. I didn't expect that. Guess I thought that, with all the success at the fair and all the money we raised, he'd *have* to get better. Stupid thinking, I guess."

"I had the same idea. It just seemed like everything was working out." She got her purse and looked down at him. "So where are you taking me?"

He thought for a moment. "Well, I was thinking of some place where we could get some good seafood, but ..." He hesitated.

"But what?"

He got back to his feet and met her eyes. "Cathy, I don't know how you'd feel about this, but I had this idea this afternoon ..."

"What?"

"Well, I was thinking we could go to Kinko's and print up some flyers about Joseph. Get about a thousand run off, and then go to the coliseum where they're having that big gospel thing tonight, and we could go around and put the flyers on the car windows asking for prayers and donations. I mean, if they don't send any money, we need the prayers even more."

She gazed at him for a moment, moved to tears. "You're right."

"Does that sound like a good idea, or would you rather go eat steak?"

She laughed. "How can I say no? Steve, it sounds like a wonderful idea."

"The restaurant will still be open when we finish," he said. "We'll miss the movie, but I don't care about that if you don't."

She could hardly speak. As they walked out to his car, she prayed silently that God wouldn't let her fall head over heels for this man unless it was part of the plan.

CHAPTER
Thirty-Eight

The home video of the Dodd kids singing a song for Joseph played across the hospital television screen. Brenda watched Joseph staring at the screen with dull eyes. The videos weren't cheering him anymore, and she wondered if he had the energy to smile. The song ended, and the video camera began recording the supper table conversation. They had set the tripod in Joseph's place, so it would seem as if he was there, listening to the idle chitchat and the family bantering.

On the video, David looked tired, bedraggled. She knew he'd been taking in more work than he could handle and working around the clock to get it all done. He was a proud man who didn't want to depend on donations to pay for his son's medical bills, if there was any possibility of his paying them off himself. Often, his days were interrupted by real estate prospects wanting to view their house. At night, he spent as much time as he could at the hospital with Brenda and Joseph, while Sylvia sat with the kids. She saw the despair on his face as he ate, and she wished there was something she could do about it. But she was as helpless to make things better for David as she was to help Joseph.

"You want me to turn the video off, honey?" she asked her son.

For a moment, Joseph didn't answer, then finally, in a voice just above a whisper, he said, "No, I like it."

She turned on the bed so that she was facing him, and gazed down into his pale little face. "What's wrong, honey? You seem kind of sad today."

He looked up at her and tears filled his eyes. "Mama, if I die, how long before you'll come to heaven?"

A cold hand gripped her heart. In all the books she'd read on parenting and homeschooling, she'd never seen advice on answering _this_ question. "You're not going to die."

"But if I do. How long?"

She swallowed down the lump in her throat. "I can't say for sure," she whispered. "But I bet it'll just be a blink of an eye. Time passes differently in heaven, you know."

He nodded pensively and looked back at the television screen. "You think Daddy'll ever get there?"

She turned her head back to the screen so Joseph wouldn't see her tears. The video showed David piddling in the kitchen, chattering with the kids, talking to Joseph every now and then as if he was at the table with them. "Honey, I pray every day for your daddy," she said. "Something's going to get through to him one of these days. I know it is."

His silence pulled her gaze back to him. A tear rolled down his face, but he didn't seem to have the energy to wipe it away. She did it for him. "What if I never see him again?" Joseph whispered.

She looked down at him, waging a war within herself to keep from falling apart. "It could still happen, Joseph," Brenda said in a shaky voice. "You might still get a heart." It was the only answer she was capable of giving him. That stubborn faith was the only thing keeping her functioning—keeping her in this room day by day, hour by hour, minute by minute, talking to

Joseph, trying to keep him from despairing—trying to keep *herself* from despairing.

Joseph shook his head feebly. "What if I don't, Mama?"

She didn't know if her voice would make it through an answer. "We're still praying, Joseph," she said. "God's still in control. He knows about your heart. He hasn't forgotten."

"Then why hasn't He given me one?"

"It's not time yet," she said.

He stared up at her, thinking, and she wanted to tell him to stop it, that it wouldn't do any good, that he needed to spend his time thinking little boy thoughts, pretending he was a wounded cowboy, an injured soldier, a football player who'd just scored a winning touchdown. He needed to pretend he was going to get better and get up out of this bed and go home. But he wasn't having little boy thoughts. His thoughts were those of an old man who'd lived his life to its end, and now faced the death that his loved ones weren't prepared for.

"Mama?" he whispered, finally meeting her eyes.

"Yes, sweetie. What is it?"

"I want to go home. I want to sleep in my own bed."

She stroked his forehead and tried valiantly to hold back the tears. "Of course you will, when you get that new heart and the doctor releases you. We'll have a big party. The whole neighborhood."

He stared at the ceiling for a long while as his thoughts reeled by. Finally, mercifully, his eyes closed. He fell into a light sleep. Relieved that she wouldn't have to answer his questions anymore—not for a while, anyway—she tucked his blanket around him, then went to the end of the bed to make sure his feet were warm. His toes were swollen, further testimony that his heart wasn't adequately pumping his blood. She got a pair of socks and slipped them on him, then tucked the sheets and blanket around them. She stood at the window, staring out into the night. Crossing her arms across her stomach in a self-embrace, she let the tears flow harder and faster than they'd flowed yet.

After a while, she turned back to the bed and regarded her little boy with his gray face and his bluish lips, held hostage by a heart in rebellion. Soon, that heart would go on strike altogether. It might be a quiet, merciful ending. Or there could be pain that grew worse hour by hour, long past the point either mother or son should be able to endure. Only God knew.

She heard footsteps in the corridor outside, then David appeared in the doorway. It was after visiting hours, and she hadn't expected him.

He saw her crying and quietly came to her and pulled her into his arms. She clung to him with all her might. "Did you leave the kids alone?"

"No," he whispered. "Sylvia came over to spend the night so I could come back. It was good that she did." He seemed to hesitate, then added, "I felt like I should be here tonight." His voice caught on the last words, and still holding her, he looked at his sleeping son. "Any change?" he asked.

Brenda shook her head. "He's talked a lot about dying."

David closed his eyes. His throat bobbed as he swallowed.

"We talked about heaven," she said quietly, her eyes fixed on Joseph's face. "He's worried that he'll get there but never see you."

He looked down at his little boy, then back up at his wife, and shook his head drearily. "I'll tell you something, Brenda. I find it real hard to believe in a God who would let a little boy like this get sick and die at nine years old."

The angry, whispered words cut through her heart. "David, you didn't believe even when things were fine. If none of this had ever happened, it wouldn't have made any difference to you—not spiritually."

"Well, we'll never know that, will we?" Wearily, he went to Joseph's bed, leaned over, and pressed a kiss on the boy's forehead. Then he dropped his head to the sheet next to Joseph's head, and his shoulders began to shake as the sobs tore silently out of him. Brenda put her hands on his shoulders and pulled him up. He turned around and held her, his body quaking with despair.

"You know, if I could cut out my own heart, I'd give it to him."

"I know," she whispered. "I feel the same way."

"None of this should be happening. Life stinks."

She couldn't answer. They sat down together on the vinyl couch, wiping tears from their faces as they watched their little boy sleep, checking every rise and fall of his shoulders, every weak, irregular bleep of his heart on the monitor. It was nearing midnight, and except for the occasional footsteps outside the door, there hadn't been a sound. It was as quiet as death, and she wondered if Joseph would just slip away from wherever he was right now—just stop breathing quietly, without a fight, and never open his eyes again.

Hours passed, and without meaning to, she and David dozed off, their heads resting against the back of the small vinyl couch. When Brenda awoke, it was one A.M. She felt instantly guilty for falling asleep when her son was dying, and she got up and went to Joseph's bed.

Behind her, she heard David stirring. "Is he all right?" he asked softly.

Joseph hadn't moved since falling asleep last night. Studying the monitor, she was discouraged by how weak his heartbeat was. Would those little peaks flatten out altogether before morning came?

"Brenda?" David asked, getting up and joining her beside the bed.

"He's . . . I don't know." She checked the pulse in his neck. It was so weak she almost couldn't find it. "He hasn't moved. He's just lying there, on his back. He never sleeps on his back."

They turned him on his side, and began massaging his back and legs, trying to get his blood circulating. His heart rhythm changed as they did, which brought two nurses in to check on him. They seemed somber and concerned, which made Brenda worry more. The activity around him didn't waken him.

They sat back on the couch, watching their son as if he would pass from life as soon as they took their eyes off him. When the monitor began to show a weaker beep, they both stood up.

Brenda went to Joseph's bed and shook him, watching the monitor as she did. His heartbeat didn't change. "Joseph, no!" she cried.

Suddenly the line on the monitor flattened, and an alarm sounded. Nurses bolted in and pushed her aside. Doctors rushed in behind the nurses. They all began working on her son, shouting instructions to each other and calling for equipment. Someone ushered them out into the hall, and she buried her face in David's chest as she waited for them to pronounce her son dead.

CHAPTER
Thirty-Nine

Daniel Dodd couldn't sleep that night. Sylvia heard him walking down the stairs, and she rolled out of Brenda and David's bed, pulled on her robe, and followed him down. "Daniel? Is something wrong?" she asked.

He headed into the kitchen and turned on the light. His eyes were sleepy and his hair ruffled, but he didn't look like the twelve-year-old child he was. He had changed in these past few months, just as Leah and Rachel had. He was older. Sylvia could only guess at the thoughts that went through his mind. "I couldn't sleep," he said.

"Are you worried about Joseph?"

He didn't answer. For a moment, he just looked down at the floor. "I was thinking about his shoes," he said finally. "He couldn't get them on his feet when he left for the hospital because his feet were swollen. I thought maybe he could wear mine. But they're so sweaty and dirty, I thought I'd wash them. We could take them to him tomorrow. He likes my shoes."

"Then what will you wear to school?" Sylvia asked.

He shrugged. "My flip-flops, I guess. Doesn't matter."

She remembered when her children were twelve. Shoes had mattered a lot. Sarah had gone through a stage where she'd wanted black sneakers that she'd neon-painted herself. Jeff had insisted on a certain brand of high-tops that he swore enabled him to make the junior high basketball team.

Neither of them had suffered through sleepless nights over a sibling whose shoes didn't fit.

"Do you know how to wash them, Miss Sylvia?" Daniel asked. "I know how to wash jeans and underwear and stuff, but not sneakers."

"Sure," she said, taking them out of his hands and heading into the small laundry room. She dropped them into the washer, poured the soap in, and started the cycle. When she turned back around, Daniel was still staring at the floor.

"What are you thinking, Daniel?"

Again, he shrugged. "Just that I wish I could miss school tomorrow and go to the hospital. There are things I need to tell Joseph when he wakes up."

Sylvia pulled the chair out from the table and sat down. "What things?"

"Things like . . . what a cool little kid he is. I never told him that. I just called him dumb and stuff."

She watched him standing there in a baggy T-shirt and gym shorts, his feet bare. "I'm sure he knows you didn't mean it."

"I'd still like to tell him." He was struggling with the emotions pulling at his mouth.

She knew he would never allow her to do what came most naturally—pull him into her arms and hold him. She felt helpless, inadequate. "How about some warm milk?" she asked finally.

He nodded.

She warmed it up in a saucepan, then poured two glasses, praying it would help him sleep. When he'd finished, she set her elbows on the table and gazed at him. "Feel pretty helpless, don't you?"

He stared down at the empty glass and nodded.

"Me, too," she said. "I've been praying and praying. It's like my mind won't let me rest. It keeps saying that we have to keep praying."

"We do," Daniel said. "Joseph needs us to."

"That's what I was doing when I heard you on the stairs."

He gave her a half-smile. "That's what I was doing before I came down." He got up and put his glass in the sink, then slid his chair back under the table. "Thanks for the milk. Guess I'll go try to sleep."

"Okay." She watched as he padded to the kitchen doorway. "Daniel?"

He stopped and turned back around.

"Lots of others are praying, too, you know. Joseph's pretty well surrounded with prayer."

"I know," he whispered. Then he headed back into the darkness upstairs, where she knew he would pray some more.

CHAPTER Forty

Brenda was exhausted and emotionally drained as the last of the doctors filed out of the room. Joseph had been revived. He was alive, but she knew it was just a matter of time before his heart failed for the last time. He looked as if his soul had already left his body—or as if it would flee again at any moment.

It was the longest night Brenda and David had ever shared together, yet the moments seemed so short. When morning came, she realized that Joseph hadn't stirred since he'd been revived. She went to his side and found his hand under the covers. It was cold as ice. His fingers were blue. She remembered when his hands were hot and his palms were sweaty, when his cheeks would get red after running from Daniel or chasing the dog.

Hours passed. Nurses moved Joseph, gave him injections, changed his IV, checked his monitors. He never woke up. David didn't leave the hospital. He left ICU only to get them food, which neither of them could eat. Neither of them had showered, and Joseph's breakfast tray went untouched. When the lunch tray came, they took the breakfast tray, then at supper, replaced the lunch. Still, Joseph did not wake up.

When he had been asleep for twenty-four hours, Brenda bent over his bed. "Where is he?" she asked David. "Why won't he wake up?"

David, draped across the rail on the other side of the bed, looked ragged and exhausted. She was exhausted, too, but could not take the chance of resting again.

She thought of her son's questions yesterday about death and heaven, and suddenly the thought of his dying here was unbearable. Old people died in hospitals, suffering people that saints were praying home. Not children. Children needed to be in their own homes, with things that gave them comfort.

"The last thing he said to me yesterday ..." she whispered to David. "He told me he wanted to go home. Sleep in his own bed."

David closed his eyes, and tears plopped onto Joseph's sheet.

"David, Joseph's going to die, isn't he?"

He nodded, unable to speak. She covered her mouth and bent down to press her forehead against her son's. "What if we took him home?" she asked.

There was a moment of silence, and finally she looked up and saw the tragic look on David's face.

"What do you mean?" he asked painfully.

"I mean ... if he's going to die ... let's take him home, David. Let's let him die in his own bed. Not in a cold hospital room with tubes and alarms. Not here."

Again, silence. "But the children," David whispered finally. "It would be too hard on them."

She covered her face with both hands, wishing she knew what to do. "I'm thinking of them, too. They need to say goodbye to him. He's their brother."

He stared down at the boy, his face twisted as the thoughts turned in his mind. "But Brenda, as long as he's here, there's still a chance he'll survive until—"

"David, I *don't* want my son to die here."

"What difference does it make where he dies?" he whispered harshly, the corners of his mouth trembling with the words. "Here or there—what difference does it make?"

"He wanted to go home. He wanted to be in his own bed."

"But there's still a chance . . ." His voice trailed off as despair flooded up in him, rendering him unable to finish.

"We could take the machines with us," she said. "We could take him home in an ambulance. Get a private nurse. We would keep giving him what he needs. But he would be home, in his own room, with his own family. Harry would be right across the street. If they *do* find a heart, we can have him back here in just a few minutes. And if they don't—he'd be at home, David. His own home."

David stared at her for a long moment, turning the idea over in his mind. She could see the turmoil the suggestion created in him.

"What if his heart stops again?" David whispered at last. "Who would revive him?"

The words came so hard that she almost choked them out. "How many times do we want the heroics, David, if there's not a heart? Joseph may be suffering. Maybe there's a time . . . to let go."

The rims around David's eyes reddened, and he sucked in a sob and covered his face with a callused hand. He wept for a moment, as hard and as deep as she. But finally, he raised his head and met her eyes. "Okay," he whispered. "Maybe I can catch Dr. Robinson before he leaves the building. And I'll call Harry."

David left the room, and Brenda looked down at her son, wanting so much to hold him, to cradle him in her arms, to let him feel the love she had for him. So she climbed onto the bed next to him, careful not to pull any of the tubes coming out of him. Carefully, she slid her arm under his head, and held him as she wept against his face.

Joseph never moved.

After a few minutes, David came back in. "They're still waiting for Dr. Robinson to answer his page," he said softly. "I called Harry, and he tried to talk us out of it. But when I explained, he said he understood. He said he'd help all he could."

Brenda squeezed her eyes shut. "We're taking you home, Joseph. Can you hear me? You're going home."

But Joseph didn't respond.

He just lay there, limp and gray.

CHAPTER
Forty-One

Harry couldn't sleep after David's phone call, and with Sylvia at the Dodds' house, he saw no reason to stay in bed. He spent some time praying for Joseph, and for Brenda and David, then decided to go to the hospital and see if they needed help getting Joseph ready to go home.

He tapped on the glass at the side entrance and waited for the security guard to let him in. As the door opened, he heard the sound of a woman wailing.

"What's that?" he asked the guard.

"Big accident on the interstate," he said. "Some lady's losin' it over in ER."

Concerned, Harry detoured through the emergency room. Ambulance lights flashed just outside the glass doors, but the patient had already been brought inside. A woman wept loudly, uncontrollably, in her husband's arms. Her legs gave way, and he bent with her until she was on the floor, balling up as if that could assuage her grief. The man wept, too, but more quietly, in a way that was perhaps even more tragically helpless. Clearly, someone they loved had died. No matter how many times Harry had seen it, he'd never gotten used to it.

Outside the emergency room, two paramedics turned and moved slowly down the hallway, a look of defeat on their faces.

Other patients—a man with a broken arm, a woman with a cut on her foot, a teenaged boy with asthma—all quietly watched the family's anguish. Harry, too, stood watching, wishing there was something he could do. He thought of approaching the family, but he saw that someone was already there, urging them into a conference room. He wasn't needed.

Whispering a prayer for them, he started through the swinging doors that would take him to the elevators. As he pushed through, he ran into Dr. Robinson, rushing out.

"Chris! What's the rush?" Harry asked.

The man looked shaken, distracted, and his eyes sought out the weeping parents. "I'm glad you're here, Harry," he said quietly. "I may need you."

"For what?" Harry asked.

"To talk to these parents," he said. "They just lost their eight-year-old son. But, Harry—there was no injury to his heart."

Half an hour later, Harry left the room with Dr. Robinson, feeling drained of every ounce of energy. The parents were distraught to the point of needing sedation, but they had refused any.

At first, they had rejected the idea of giving up their son's heart. They hadn't yet accepted his death, and the idea of donating his organs was more than they could bear. So Harry had begun to tell them about Joseph—lying upstairs, hours, maybe moments, from death himself. He told them about Brenda and David's intentions to take Joseph home to die.

Finally, they had realized that their son's heart could spare another family the pain they were suffering. It could keep another child alive.

Reluctantly, miserably, they had agreed to sign the papers.

Drained, Harry followed Dr. Robinson to the elevators. "What now?"

"I'll contact the transplant team. We have to make sure it's a match for Joseph. If it's not, we transport it to a recipient who does match. If it's a good heart for Joseph, we'll operate within a few hours. Right now, we have to tell the Dodds."

The elevator doors opened, and they both stepped on.

"What if it doesn't match?" Harry asked. "Is there any way to keep from getting their hopes up?"

"No," Dr. Robinson said. "We have to start prepping Joseph. You might start sending up some of those prayers you're so popular for. Joseph is going to need them."

CHAPTER
Forty-Two

Brenda and David heard a flurry of activity outside Joseph's room. She looked into the hall and saw Dr. Robinson and Harry at the nurse's station. Dread constricted her throat. She was sure they had come to help them get Joseph ready for his last trip home. Then she saw that the nurses seemed to be celebrating, hugging each other and smiling. She looked back at David.

"What is it?" he asked, stepping to the doorway behind her.

"I don't know."

Harry and Dr. Robinson started toward them. Both of them seemed breathless, though they seemed less celebratory than the nurses.

"What's going on?" David asked as they reached them.

"Brenda, David, I may have good news," Dr. Robinson said. "We may have a heart. We're running some tests now, and the transplant team will determine soon whether it'll work for Joseph. If so, we'll do the surgery in the next few hours."

Brenda stepped back, trying to process what Dr. Robinson had just said. She couldn't speak. Hope flooded her—she had almost forgotten what it felt like. Stunned, she turned to David.

"Doctor, how long will it take for the heart to get here?" David asked.

Dr. Robinson hesitated a moment. "It's already here. The transplant team is on their way."

Brenda saw the beginnings of the first smile she'd seen on David's face in days. "There's hope, David," she whispered. "There's hope."

But both of them knew it could be false hope, so they settled in for a long, anxious wait as the nurses began to prep their son.

Within two hours, Dr. Robinson was back in their room. This time he was smiling. "It's a go," he said, and they sprang to their feet and threw their arms around each other. "We'll start the surgery soon."

"We've got a heart! We've got a heart!" Brenda squealed, nearly dancing.

A nurse who was painting Joseph with iodine laughed. "I'll bet you have some phone calls to make," she said.

"Yes!" Brenda said. "We've got to get everybody praying."

CHAPTER
Forty-Three

The telephone rang, waking Cathy, and she squinted at the clock. Which one of her children's friends would be rude enough to call this late, she asked herself, and picked up the phone to tell them it wouldn't be tolerated. "Hello?" she snapped.

"Cathy, this is Brenda."

She sat up straight in bed. "Brenda. What is it?"

"We've got a heart. They're taking Joseph to surgery now."

"Yes!" Cathy shouted triumphantly. "I'll be there in fifteen minutes!"

"You don't have to come. That's all right."

"Are you kidding? I'll be there." She hung up and began throwing her clothes on as fast as she could.

Annie appeared at the door, still wearing her jeans and T-shirt. She hadn't yet gone to bed. "Who was that, Mom?"

"Brenda. They've got a heart. Joseph's going into surgery."

"I wanna come!" Annie cried.

Rick stepped into the hall in a pair of shorts and a T-shirt. "What's all the noise?"

"Joseph's got a heart," Annie said. "Mom, wait, I have to get my shoes."

"Hey, I'm goin', too," Rick shouted.

"But there's nothing to do but wait. Anyway, somebody has to stay with Mark."

Mark stepped groggily into his doorway. "What's all the yelling about?"

She pulled on her shoes and headed to the stairwell. "Joseph is getting his new heart," she shouted. "I'm headed for the hospital. You three just stay here."

"Please, Mom!" Mark protested. "I wanna come with you."

She stopped and turned back on the stairwell. Annie had found her shoes and was leaning over the banister with a pleading look on her face. "Mom, we're in this, too. We helped. We want to be there."

"Please, Mom," Rick begged.

She sighed. "Everybody has five minutes to get dressed and into the car, or I'm leaving without you." She went back into her room and brushed her hair and teeth, and hoped that her gang would bring more encouragement than noise to the hospital.

Tory wasn't conscious enough to make sense out of the ringing telephone. Finally, Barry answered it. "Hello?"

She felt him sit up quickly in bed, then shake her shoulder. "Wake up, babe, it's Brenda."

Tory grabbed the phone and tried to shake the cobwebs out of her brain. She gave Barry a dreadful look. He returned it. Was Brenda calling to tell them Joseph had died?

Already feeling sick, she brought the phone to her ear. "Brenda?"

"Tory, we've got a heart," Brenda said.

Relief washed over her. "You're kidding! That's great! I'm coming to the hospital to wait with you."

"All right," Brenda said. "You might be able to catch Cathy and come with her."

Tory hung up and threw open her closet door. "Barry, they've got a heart! I'm going to the hospital. Will you stay with the kids?"

"Sure," he said. He was on his feet, too, wide awake now.

"If it goes all night, I'll try to get back in time for you to go to work."

"Don't worry about it," he said. "I'll go in late."

She pulled out the clothes she would wear, then swung around. "Oh, Barry, pray hard!"

"You got it." He slid his arms around her. "You be careful, okay? Don't drive like a maniac."

"I'm not driving if I can catch Cathy," she said. "Barry, will you call her while I get dressed and ask if I can have a ride?"

He picked up the phone.

"Oh, Barry, this could all be over soon."

As Barry punched Cathy's number, he looked up and said, "Maybe our prayers are finally being answered."

❧

At the Dodds' house, Brenda's phone call to tell Sylvia about the heart had awakened Daniel. By the time Sylvia hung up, Daniel was standing in the doorway, listening.

"What is it, Miss Sylvia?" Daniel asked.

When she saw the fear on his face, she got up and put her hands on his shoulders. "Daniel, they've found a heart for your brother. They'll be taking him into surgery soon."

Daniel stared at her, then swung around and ran back up the hall. "Leah, Rachel, wake up! Joseph's got a heart!"

Sylvia thought of trying to stop him, but it was too late. The girls sprang from their beds, dancing with joy. "Joseph's got a heart! Can we go there, Miss Sylvia? Please!"

Sylvia decided there were things more important than keeping hospital rules. "Get dressed," she said. "I'll take you."

They whooped and hollered as they pulled on their clothes. Within minutes, they were in the car, headed for the hospital.

CHAPTER
Forty-Four

Cathy, with Tory and her kids, made it to the hospital in record time. They parked near the emergency room because the lights in the parking lot were stronger there, and they felt safer cutting through the building than walking through the parking lot. They headed to CICU first to see if the Dodds were waiting there. A few reporters with television cameras were standing in the hallway, and Tory wondered if they considered Joseph's transplant newsworthy. But how would they have known about it?

"I'll go see if Brenda and David are in there," Tory said, and left Cathy and the kids in the corridor. She pushed through the press into the CICU waiting room. She didn't see the Dodds—only a scattering of strangers, most of them asleep in chairs. In the corner, a woman was crying, and her husband was holding her as a doctor in scrubs spoke softly to them. Against her chest, she clutched a pair of small, dirty tennis shoes.

Tory turned to leave, but before she reached the door, she heard the woman's voice. "Please ... can you put these on his feet? I don't want his feet to get cold."

Tory turned back to the couple and saw the doctor take the shoes as the woman crumpled painfully against her husband. Tory met the woman's eyes, saw the shattering despair, the tragedy. *There must have been a death in that family*, she thought. Compassion surged through her ... but then she remembered Joseph. A passing nurse pointed out the surgical intensive care waiting room, and Tory rushed back out, grabbed Cathy and the kids, and headed for it.

The waiting room filled up fast. By the time they had all arrived, the surgery had begun. Tory looked around at the tired, jubilant faces, so thankful that they had this chance to save Joseph. At first, the conversation was hyperactive and ecstatic, but as the hours ticked by, Brenda and David got noticeably quieter. Brenda couldn't seem to sit still. She kept crossing the room, back and forth, back and forth, going down the hall to the Coke machine and back, and constantly checking the telephone in the waiting room for a dial tone, since the doctor had promised to call the moment surgery was over.

Once, when Brenda left the room, she didn't come back for a while, and Tory decided to look for her. When she didn't find her roaming the halls or in the bathroom, she checked the chapel. Brenda was sitting on the pew at the front of the small room. Tory started to turn back and leave her alone to pray, but when Brenda turned around and saw her at the door, she said, "Come on in, Tory. It's okay."

"Go ahead," Tory said. "I don't want to interrupt."

"No, really," Brenda said. "Come on in."

Tory walked the short aisle, feeling as if she were entering holy ground. Though Brenda's eyes were red and wet, her face glowed with a beauty Tory knew no amount of makeup could achieve. It came from deep inside, nurtured and cultivated by the trials Brenda had endured. Tory sat down next to her. "It's taking a long time, isn't it?" she asked.

Brenda nodded and got to her feet. She paced in front of the altar, then stopped and stared at the stained glass. "But we knew it would. You don't swap hearts out just like that. I don't want them to rush."

Tory thought of how impossible heart transplant surgery seemed, and how miraculous that doctors had ever found a way to make it work. The thought of her own children lying on that table under oxygen masks and anesthesia, their chests open and exposed, and their very life sitting in a container waiting to be put into their bodies—the thought made her eyes well up with tears. She tried to fight it, for Brenda's sake.

Brenda turned around and settled her misty eyes on Tory. "I was just thinking," she whispered, "about the parable of the talents."

Tory looked at her, wondering how that particular parable could possibly apply to what was happening here. Had she been worrying about the money?

"I was thinking how those talents could just as well be our children," Brenda said. "God gave them to us, and we have the option of either hiding them in the ground or investing them."

Tory tried to make the analogy, but came up short. "What do you mean hide them in the ground?"

Brenda shrugged. "Oh, I don't know. Ignore them, maybe. Stay too busy to spend time with them. There are an awful lot of stray kids running around with no one to take care of them. Oh, I don't mean that they're homeless or orphaned. Their parents are meeting their physical and material needs, but that's about it. They're not loving them, teaching them, training them up in the way they should go."

Tory kept her eyes on Brenda, trying to follow where she was leading.

"In fact," Brenda went on in a shaky voice, "they're wishing they didn't even have them, because they cramp their style and interfere with their goals."

Tory felt slapped down, as if Brenda had just nailed her. But she could see in Brenda's face that she hadn't directed that at

Tory. She wasn't pointing a finger; she was just painting a picture. Maybe she didn't realize how close to home she had hit.

"So many people just keep looking to the future," Brenda went on. "They think, 'Someday my kids'll grow up and I'll be happy.' And others look back and think, 'If only my kids were home again, I'd be happy.' And some think, 'If I could just do this or be that, I'd be happy.' But it's funny how they're never very happy. Even Christians," she said, as if that surprised her. She looked down at Tory. "But you know what?"

Tory wiped her face and shook her head. "No, what?"

"I've been happy. God's given me these four children, and I've invested them. They're my life's work. I know you want to be a writer, Tory," she said, sitting back down and taking Tory's hand. "You'd love to win a Pulitzer prize and have your books on the shelves of bookstores. But you know what? To me, that's not as exciting as what you and I get to do every day. Think of it," she whispered. "We've got these little human beings in our hands, and it's our job to raise them up in the way God wants them, so that when He comes back for them, we can say we invested them wisely."

Tory stared at the altar, trying to let the words sink in. She had never thought of her children as being much of a blessing. They had come easily, just when she'd planned them, and most days, she found them to be an obstacle between her and her ambitions. That exasperation was an occupational hazard, she had told herself. All mothers felt this way. Worn out, overworked, spinning their wheels. As much as she loved them, she often resented them.

She looked up at Brenda, and saw that her eyes were brimming with tears. "God may take Joseph back today," Brenda went on. "But if He does, I'll know that I gave Joseph all I had. I invested him wisely." Her voice broke, and her lips trembled as she got the words out. "If he grows to be an adult, I've prepared him to be a godly man. And if he doesn't, I think God will be happy with what I did for him, anyway."

Silence fell like snowflakes between them.

After a while, Tory whispered, "Imagine that. Guilt-free parenting, knowing you could look God in the eye, because you did your best." It was a concept hard for her to grasp.

Finally, Brenda wiped her tears with both hands and got to her feet. "We'd better get back. The doctor might call."

Tory couldn't manage to move just yet. "I'll be there in a minute," she said. "I just want to pray a little myself."

Brenda nodded and gave her a tight, lingering hug. Then she left Tory alone.

Tory looked up at the stained glass dove, then down at the altar, letting the words her friend had just spoken seep into her heart. She began to weep harder. "Lord, forgive me," she whispered. "Forgive me for seeing my children as an inconvenience. For not investing them wisely. For not giving them everything I have." She went to the altar and knelt, her face in her hands. "Lord, little Joseph has been invested wisely, and if he's allowed to grow up, there's no telling what he can do for Your kingdom." A sob rose in her throat, and she wiped the tears away. "Oh, Lord. Please let him live. And thank You, thank You, for my children."

She felt the peace of the Holy Spirit fall over her. Bone tired and still reeling with the wisdom Brenda had planted in her mind, she headed back to the waiting room.

CHAPTER
Forty-Five

By daybreak, the tension had grown unbearable. Brenda paced back and forth, back and forth in the surgical intensive care waiting room, waiting for word. David stood in the doorway, watching for the doctor.

Cathy sat with her head back against the wall, unable to move because Annie had fallen asleep on her shoulder. It was the closest her daughter had been to her in months, so she didn't dare wake her up. Daniel and his sisters, who had been elated at first, had now grown quiet as they saw the stress mounting on their parents' faces. Mark and Rick, who'd chattered a lot earlier in the morning, had now grown quiet, too.

Sylvia and Tory sat next to each other, conversing quietly about what kind of geraniums Tory should plant on the east side of her house, and whether the Bryans should tear down the stables since the horses had been sold. But they kept their eyes on the door, waiting for someone—anyone—to bring them word.

Mark and Rick finally offered to go to the cafeteria and get everyone a breakfast roll, but before they'd reached the elevator, the doors opened. Harry, dressed in scrubs, got off. They knew he'd been assisting in the surgery, so they stopped cold. "Is it over?" Mark asked.

Harry put his arms around their shoulders. "Yeah. It's over." He led them back into the waiting room, and everyone froze.

Harry looked first at Brenda, then at David. The exhaustion on his own face matched the fear and anxiety on theirs. Neither of the Dodds could ask the question they were all waiting to have answered, and Harry seemed too drained to speak. Finally, with obvious effort, he took a deep breath and looked around.

"Joseph came through just fine," he said, and a whoop went up as Brenda and David threw themselves at each other. The Dodd kids got to their feet, cheering and embracing. Sylvia threw her arms around Harry, and he laughed as tears came to his eyes.

"Can we see him?" Brenda asked over the noise.

"He's still in recovery. It was a perfect heart, Brenda. Strong and healthy." His voice broke, and he cleared his throat. "You can see him when they get him into surgical ICU. Meanwhile, the transplant team needs to see you both downstairs. There are a lot of things they need to go over with you."

Tory was exhausted by the time she got home. Her children were still sleeping, but Barry was sitting at the kitchen table, drinking a cup of coffee and watching the news on television. He got up when she came in, and gave her a kiss.

"Is he all right?" he asked.

"The surgery was successful. Joseph has a new heart."

"And?" Barry asked. "What happens now?"

"Well, it's kind of touch and go. He's going to be in SICU for a while. They're watching him real closely. But they're saying they'll have him out of bed walking around by tomorrow, and he may be able to come home in a week or so if all goes well. The drugs suppress his immune system, so they figure he's safer at home than in a hospital full of germs. We just have to see what happens."

"You must be tired," he said. "Let me get you some breakfast."

"No, that's okay. I'm not hungry."

As she watched the news absently, a snapshot of a little boy with a buzz cut and huge brown eyes flashed on the television screen, and she glanced up as the anchor read, "Eight-year-old Tony Anderson was killed instantly when the oncoming car crossed the median and barreled into his family's Ford." The little boy's face was replaced by scenes of the wreck that had killed him—and then by footage of the grieving parents in the hospital waiting room. Tory slowly got to her feet. The camera zoomed in on a little pair of dirty tennis shoes, clutched against the heart of the grieving mother. It was the same couple Tory had seen in the waiting room before the surgery, when she'd been looking for the Dodds.

". . . pronounced dead at one thirty-five at St. Francis Hospital," the report went on.

That woman, whose eyes she had met, the woman who had been clutching her child's shoes and wailing with such horrible grief, had lost her child last night, not an hour before Tory had gotten to the hospital. Her eyes filled with tears.

Barry noticed it. "Honey, what's wrong? Are you okay? What is it?"

"The news," she said. "That little boy."

"Did you know that family?"

"No, but last night . . ." She caught her breath. "I saw them in the waiting room. They were devastated. And there were cameras in the hall. I must have seen them right after the cameras filmed them." She looked up at Barry, her eyes intense. "Do you think that could have been the heart that Joseph got?"

He looked thoughtful. "Did they say where his heart had come from?"

"No," she said. "But Brenda was surprised at how fast they had gotten it. It was already at the hospital when they told Brenda and David. That wouldn't have happened, would it, unless the child had died there?"

"Probably not," he whispered.

He held her, letting her cry against his shoulder. "Why is this upsetting you so?" he asked.

"Because I looked that mother in the eye," she said, "and I saw her pain. Then I went up to the room where everybody was celebrating that Joseph had gotten a heart. But it was *that* little boy's heart."

"Maybe," Barry said. "But if it weren't for that heart, Joseph's parents would have been the ones grieving."

"I know," she whispered. "I know. It just hit me so hard. When you see dying children, and you come home to your own, you wonder why they were spared." She pulled out of his arms and tried to catch her breath. "The kids aren't up yet?"

"No," he whispered. "They're in Britty's bed. Spencer claimed to be scared for her, so he got into bed with her."

Tory managed to smile. When something frightened their son, he always claimed he was scared for his sister. "I'll go see if they're awake."

She pulled out of his arms and headed for Brittany's room. The two children lay tangled in the covers, Spencer in his Superman pajamas, Brittany in a Tennessee Oilers T-shirt.

She started toward them—and promptly tripped on Spencer's shoes, lying in the middle of the floor. Steadying herself, she bent down and picked them up—and was immediately reminded of those shoes the bereaved mother had clutched last night, and the despair in her voice as she'd asked the doctor to put them on her son so his feet wouldn't get cold.

How irrational. How perfectly understandable.

The woman had lost her son.

Tory closed her eyes and clutched Spencer's shoes against her chest. New tears came to her eyes. Feeling Barry's hands on her shoulders, she turned around and looked intently up at her hus-

287

band. "I'm going to change, Barry. You'll see. I'm not going to whine anymore. Why did I ever think that my only goal and purpose in life is to write, when I have these wonderful children?"

He just held her tightly.

"Mommy?" It was Spencer's voice, and he yawned and stretched, then got up and reached for her. She sat on the bed and pulled him into her lap. Brittany woke up then, too, and sleepily said, "Hey, Mommy."

"Hey, darlin'. Guess what? Joseph got a new heart last night."

"Does he like it?" Spencer asked.

Tory grinned. "I'm sure he does."

"Will he come home now?" Brittany asked.

"I think so. In a few days. If everything goes well." She patted Spencer's bare little leg, then ruffled Brittany's hair. "So what do you guys want to do today?"

"Aren't you tired?" Barry asked. "Don't you need to sleep?"

"I've still got a little energy left," she said. "I want to invest it in my family."

CHAPTER
Forty-Six

Sunday morning, Barry and Tory decided to take Brenda's children to their own church again. Brenda and David wanted to stay at the hospital with Joseph, who was doing well but wasn't out of the woods. Because of the animal fair and the amount of time Tory had spent at the hospital with Brenda, she felt as if she knew a lot of the members of Brenda's church already. They welcomed her and Barry as if they were family, and the children couldn't wait to get to their Sunday school classes to tell of the miracle Joseph had received.

Instead of Sunday school that morning, the adults of the church met in the sanctuary for what they called a "power session." Barry and Tory weren't sure what they were getting into, but when they learned that it was an intense hour of prayer for Joseph's recovery, they were all for it.

They all met around the steps at the front of the small podium and prayed from the bottoms of their hearts, one at a time as they felt led. By the end of the hour, both Barry and Tory felt as if they had been touched personally by the Holy Spirit. Their hearts felt cleansed; their minds were clear and alert. When it was time for the service, and they had Spencer and Brittany and the Dodd children back with them, they sat close to the front. Barry stayed awake the whole time—in fact, Tory saw him smiling and nodding during the sermon. And at the end, when they were singing the final praise songs before closing the service, Barry surprised her with the exuberance in his voice and the tears she saw in his eyes.

When they had dropped the Dodd kids off at the hospital and were on their way home, Tory glanced at her husband. "So what do you think about that worship experience?"

He smiled. "I think I need to quit worrying about being a deacon. It's time to change churches."

The kids erupted with excitement in the backseat. Tory only smiled. "Are you sure, Barry? They depend on you a lot at our church."

"They can depend on others," he said.

"Maybe we're supposed to stay and light a fire under everybody."

Barry considered that for a moment. "I think we're the ones who needed a fire lit under us. We're not in any position to activate anyone right now. Let's go to Brenda's church for a while longer, and then decide whether we should go back to our church and get something going. But personally, I need some discipling." He paused a moment. "You know what the pastor quoted today from Second Peter, about growing in respect to your salvation? I don't think I've done that. As far as I know, I've never borne any fruit."

"Me, either," Tory agreed. "And then I see Brenda, and I think, Lord, if I can't be like You, let me be like her."

When the children were down for their naps, Barry came into the kitchen where Tory was reading the paper. He picked up his car keys.

"Where you going?" she asked.

He shrugged and looked down at the floor. "I thought I'd go up to the hospital and see David."

"Really?" They had never been close friends. The relationship between families had primarily been between Brenda and her. "Okay. I'm sure he'd appreciate that."

He nodded. "I'll be back in time to take us all back to church."

"Okay, you can bring the Dodd kids back with you."

"Good idea," he said.

As he headed to the door, Tory sat back in her chair, thinking. She wasn't sure whether Barry had ever shared his faith with anyone before, other than cursory conversations with the children—but she had no doubt that's what Barry was intending to discuss with David. That sermon must have given him a sense of urgency. She was thankful. She only hoped that David would listen—so that Barry would be encouraged to share his faith even more.

Then, maybe, she'd start doing it herself.

CHAPTER
Forty-Seven

At the hospital, Brenda was surprised when Barry arrived alone. He bantered with the kids for a while, welcome entertainment when they were all confined to the SICU waiting room—they were only allowed to visit Joseph for a few minutes every couple of hours. When Barry asked David if he'd like to go down to the cafeteria for a cup of coffee, and David agreed, Brenda was more confused than ever. She watched, perplexed, as they left the room. Then she turned back to the children, who were playing a game of Monopoly.

"Mama, I think the Sullivans really liked our church this morning," Daniel said.

"Really?"

"Yes, ma'am. Mr. Barry even had tears in his eyes."

"How about that?" Brenda said, amazed. She looked at the doorway again, wondering if that had anything to do with Barry's visit. Just in case, she breathed a silent prayer for him.

Downstairs in the cafeteria, Barry and David sat at the table across from each other, eating a piece of pie. "So how are you holding up?" Barry asked.

"Fine," David said. "I'm not going to lie to you. It hasn't been easy."

"I went to Brenda's church this morning," Barry told him, as nonchalantly as he could manage. "They had a power session for Joseph during the Sunday school hour."

"Power session? What's that?"

"It's when they all get together and pray intensely for someone. I'd never heard of it before, but it was a really good idea. And then I come here and I see how well Joseph's doing, and I'm just amazed. I really think prayer has had a lot to do with it."

David smiled and nodded his head politely, as if he didn't want to argue with Barry. "Doctors had a little something to do with it."

"Of course," Barry said. "But I believe that Joseph is doing so well because so much prayer went into it. Not that those of us who are praying should take any credit—I just mean that God answered."

"Yeah, that's what Brenda tells me. But you know me. I have trouble with that." He crossed his arms on the table and looked up at Barry. "We were about to take Joseph home that night. We didn't want him to die in the hospital. And then—there was a heart."

"And you don't think God was working all that out?"

David smiled and shook his head. "I can't believe that. I think things just have a way of working out sometimes. And other times they don't."

"So you put more faith in accidents and coincidence than you do in God?"

"Not really," David said. "I don't have faith in accidents or coincidence either. They just happen. I guess I don't have faith in much of anything, except for my wife and my kids."

Barry didn't know how to respond. He knew that Brenda had shared the gospel with David many times, and that nothing he said today was going to change David's heart. Only the Holy Spirit could do that. Silently, he prayed for words that weren't confrontational, but that would shoot through the faithlessness straight into David's heart.

"You know, Brenda said something just before we got the heart," David said. "We thought we were going to lose Joseph. I told her I couldn't believe in a God who would take our child from us. And she pointed out that, even when our children were all healthy, I didn't believe." He glanced up at Barry. "She was right. You know, if there was any way I could force myself to believe, for Brenda's sake, I'd do it. I've thought of faking it, going to church with her, sitting beside her, singing those songs loud and clear like I was one of them. But church and I have a long history together, and it's not a very pretty one. I've done enough faking in my life. For now, I'd rather be honest about my disbelief. I'm not willing to fool my wife just for the sake of peace in the family."

"I don't know about your history," Barry said. "But maybe if you went to Brenda's church once, you'd find out it's not like you remember."

David looked down at his plate, frowning deeply, as if something Barry said had triggered a flood of memories. "I don't think that would happen. I have trouble with the way they do things there. Even those power sessions or whatever you call them. I mean, they seem like name-it-and-claim-it mumbo jumbo to me."

"It wasn't anything like that," Barry said. "We prayed that God's will, whatever it might be, would be done."

"Yeah, well, I really resented the elders praying over Joseph. But then the way they've supported us through this, bringing meals to the house, donating money, coming to the hospital ..." He cleared his throat. "It wasn't that way for us—my mother and me—when I was a kid." David leaned back and stretched, and Barry knew that he'd said all he was going to say about his past.

"But that whole business about God's will—that's another area where I have trouble. There's something a little superstitious about trusting completely in God's will, no matter what happens. Whether you lose your father, your husband, your home, your friends . . ."

Barry suspected that David hadn't meant to say those last few words, but he decided it might be the opening he'd prayed for. "Are you talking about your mother?"

David looked down at his hands, folded in front of him. "It was like a mental illness with her. No matter what my father did, no matter how cruel the church was to us, even when we were out on the street, she kept saying it was God's will. But it was just her excuse not to do anything for herself, not to try to make it better . . ."

"Sounds like a real burden to have to carry around," Barry said quietly.

"What do you mean?"

"You have a lot to forgive. An awful lot, I'd say. That kind of stuff can weigh you down, control your life, until you cut it loose."

"I'm over it," David said, shrugging it off. "I'm just telling you, church and I don't go together. But I live a good life, even without believing what you believe. Brenda keeps talking about abundant life. I feel like our lives are pretty abundant. Sure, I could want more financially, that kind of thing, but other than Joseph's illness, things have gone pretty well."

"But when you have trouble, like this business with Joseph, there's an awful lot that's out of your control."

David took a skeptical breath and looked off across the room. "So you think I should believe that God's in control?"

"Sure. Because He is, whether you believe it or not."

David shook his head and finished his pie, then abruptly changed the subject to football and fishing. Finally, they made their way back up to the SICU waiting room. Brenda looked up.

"I'll take the kids with me now if you want me to," Barry said. "We'll get them back to church. Tory and I are planning to go back tonight. We're thinking about moving our membership."

Brenda caught her breath. "That's wonderful! We'll be going to church together."

"Yeah," he said. He glanced at David. "You tell Joseph to keep getting better, okay? Tell him they're really missing him back at that church."

"I will," Brenda said.

Then with a wave, he headed out of the room, praying silently that the Holy Spirit would finish what he'd started.

CHAPTER
Forty-Eight

The night of the school board meeting, Cathy dressed in her most conservative dress and prayed that people would come. For the past couple of weeks, she had used those skills she'd learned raising money for Joseph's bills. She'd gone from parking lot to parking lot, putting out flyers about the Monday night school board meeting. She'd made countless phone calls. She'd gone to baseball and soccer parks, left flyers on windshields, and chatted with parents she met there. She didn't think she could have worked any harder if she'd been running for congress. All of this was hard for her. She wasn't a confrontational person; she wasn't used to rocking the boat or making people angry. But that, she suspected, was exactly what was going to happen tonight when she got up to speak to the people making decisions about her children.

She had seen Steve only once or twice since their date and had decided that he was no more reliable or interested in commitment than any other single man she'd met. Yes, he was apparently attracted to her—but he seemed torn between that attraction and his allegiance to the wife he'd lost. And he was lukewarm, at best, about Cathy's kids.

Still, when he did call, she found her heart racing and hoped he would suggest another date. She refused to show it, and even prided herself in pretending she was so busy she hardly had a moment to talk.

She expected him to be at the school board meeting, and he didn't disappoint her. In fact, he was still sitting in his car in the parking lot when she arrived, as if he was waiting for her. She got out of the car and looked around at the other cars already filling the parking lot.

"Looks like a big turnout," he said.

"You think it's for us?" she asked.

"I don't know. Let's go in and find out."

Inside, she studied the crowd that had filled the room. There was standing room only. The school board members were scurrying around, trying to find places for everyone to sit. It was an open meeting, but it was clear that the board wasn't used to a crowd this size.

She made the rounds, shaking hands with some of the people who were still standing, and learned that they had, indeed, come to find out about sex education in the schools. Her heart leaped as she realized that her work had not been in vain. The school board would have to listen to her now!

When they had found enough chairs to seat everyone, the meeting came to order. She waited as the board covered various housekeeping items. Finally, the school board president called on her to speak. She went to the microphone at the center of the table in front, facing the school board with the audience behind her.

"As most of you know, I'm here about something that happened in the junior high and high school at the end of last year, something I've been told happens every year," she said. "I found a condom in my son's pocket. You can imagine how upset I was. I naturally assumed that he had bought it. But when I confronted him, he explained that he'd gotten it at school, and that they'd had a video about safe sex and how to use condoms. I was told that this was not the first time. I was very disturbed." There was applause behind her, as if other parents in the room were equally disturbed, and she paused and looked over her shoulder, gaining strength as she went.

"As you can see, I'm not the only concerned parent here," she said when the applause had died. "And I wanted to appeal to you as the people with the power to stop this madness. Our children don't need the school system to teach them about sex—*especially* about condom use. They have parents to do that."

Again, there was applause.

"I think with teen pregnancy at an all-time high," she said, "what we need to teach our students is abstinence, not supposedly safe sex."

"Dr. Flaherty," one of the board members said, taking the floor, "I understand your concern, but the kids are going to do this anyway. We have to teach them how to keep from getting deadly diseases. I, personally, don't want to have to bury my son because of AIDS."

"I wholeheartedly agree—not your son, or mine, or any of the other students in our district," Cathy said. "But the best way to prevent that is to teach them to control themselves."

Again, there was jubilant applause behind her, but she held up her hand to quiet them. Her eyes blazed with passion as she went on.

"A few months ago, someone told me that the best we can hope for is to raise our children to adulthood without pregnancy or disease." The memory of her ex-husband's statement reddened her face. "But for the last few weeks, I've been watching another parent fighting for the life of her child—a child that did have a disease. But that child had such character, even when we thought he might die. Character that his mother instilled in him, not from teaching him a list of do's and don'ts, and not from giving him tools that enable him to make bad choices. She taught him character by giving him a value system that never changes."

Her voice broke, and she blinked back the tears in her eyes. "If— no, when—that little boy grows up, he probably won't ask her what's wrong with sex before marriage as long as nobody gets hurt. He'll already know that everybody involved is hurt by pre- marital sex, because he'll know where his values come from." She cleared her throat, and tried to steady her voice.

"I haven't always known that myself, so my children *have* asked those questions. I'm ashamed to say that sometimes I haven't had answers. But watching my friend has shown me that we *can* teach our children better. We *can* expect more of them. We *can* demand more from ourselves. If we want to do the best for our children, we can give them a firm base of values that come from someplace specific, someplace like the Bible, instead of passing out condoms or showing titillating videos. We can show them how a moral life works, instead of giving them the means to *ruin* their lives."

Again, applause erupted, until Superintendent Jacobs began to speak. "You think they'll stop having sex just because we tell them to?" he asked. "We have to arm them, Dr. Flaherty."

Cathy leaned in to the microphone again. "It's interesting that you would use a metaphor involving weapons, what with all these recent school shootings." The room got so quiet she could have heard a pin drop. The school board members sat straighter in their chairs. "You don't give a violent kid a gun and think it'll deter him from shooting it, and you don't give a hormonal teenager a condom and think that's going to somehow keep him from having sex."

Again, there was raucous applause behind her, and she felt her face reddening and perspiration tingling on the edge of her lip. "As you can see, I'm not the only one here who feels this way." She looked from school board member to school board member and realized that some of them were smiling and nod- ding their heads, as if to encourage her. This confused her. Were some of them on *her* side? Deciding not to dwell on it, she pulled out a magazine article she had brought. "If you'll turn over the sheet I just passed out," she said, "you'll see an article that came out in a major parenting magazine recently, describing an abstinence program that has worked in many cities, bringing down the teen pregnancy and AIDS contraction rate drastically."

"I've read all about this program," Jacobs said. "But I don't think it would work well in this community."

"Why wouldn't you try it?" she demanded. "Don't you think our children are worth that?"

"I wouldn't try it because it's a waste of time."

"A waste of time? You'd rather encourage them to go to bed with each other than to teach them how *not* to act like animals?"

The crowd roared behind her, and the superintendent slammed the gavel and took control of the microphone. "Thank you, Dr. Flaherty. I think you've made your point. Does anyone else have anything to say?"

At least fifty parents stood up and raised their hands, and the members began to look at their watches as if they might be there all night. Finally, the superintendent leaned back hard in his chair. "All right, please line up at the microphone. You have three minutes each. We won't have time to hear all of you out, but we'll hear some of you before we take a vote."

Cathy left the microphone and sank down in the seat Steve had reserved for her. She felt as if a hundred pounds had floated off of her shoulders. He was grinning from ear to ear. One by one, other parents added to what she had said, conveying comments their children had made after viewing the video, and tearfully sharing incidents of teen pregnancy and abortions—in some cases, as a result of the sexual activity that began the day they'd been given condoms.

After forty-five minutes of testimony, the superintendent suggested that they take a vote. When all was done, the school board had voted six to two to allow parents to view any sexual material before it was shown to their children, and to do away with the current sex education program. To Dr. Jacobs' chagrin, the school board president assigned someone to look into the abstinence program Cathy had suggested, and set a date to vote on its use locally. When the gavel struck to adjourn the meeting, the parents all cheered.

After the meeting, Cathy was treated as a celebrity. They patted her on the back and thanked her for what she had done. Steve stood back, letting her bask in the adulation. When the room had mostly emptied except for the school board members, one of them came and set her arm around Cathy's shoulders. "Way to go," the woman whispered.

Cathy gaped at her. "You were on my side all along?"

"You got *that* right," the woman said. "I'm a parent, too. I have kids at the middle school and high school."

"Then why haven't you objected to what's going on?"

"Didn't know about it," she said. "Here I am sitting on the school board, and none of my kids ever told me what's going on. Until it came up on this agenda, I didn't have a clue. I've only been on the board a year; they implemented this program before that."

"I'm glad I came, then," Cathy said.

"Good thing you did," she said. "You know, the people on this school board are good people. They're trying to do what's best for the kids. But sometimes we need the help of parents like you to call our attention to problems and help us get things across to those of our members who don't agree. It's not easy, this education thing."

"No, I don't suppose it is."

She squeezed Cathy's shoulders, then let her go and started out the door. She stopped at the door and turned back. "Woman, you pack a wallop when you want to. Next time you've got a beef with the school board, how about giving me a call first so I can brace myself?"

Cathy laughed and followed her out.

Steve was talking to a few stragglers in the parking lot, and when she got into her car, he came to the window and leaned in. "I'm pretty proud of you, lady," he said.

She laughed. "I'm kind of proud of myself. So . . . you want to go have a milkshake and celebrate?"

He smiled apologetically. "Wish I could, but Tracy's home with a baby-sitter and I promised I'd be the one to tuck her in."

"Can't argue with that," she said. "I like a man who's a good dad."

His smile faded. "I like a woman who's a good mom."

She hadn't heard those words in a long time. There was no one to praise her mothering skills and tell her she was doing a good job. More often, she had a million reasons for self-condemnation. It almost brought tears to her eyes. "Do you really think so?" she asked, feeling a little foolish.

"I know so," he said. "How many moms would have fought this hard for their kids?"

"Well, my children wouldn't agree. They're embarrassed to death. They said their friends are calling me 'the condom lady.'"

He laughed softly. "They'll appreciate it one day."

"Yeah, maybe." She cranked her car. "Well, looks like we're the last ones here." Their eyes met, locked for a long moment. Finally, he leaned in and pressed a kiss on her cheek. Her heart jolted.

"I'll call you tonight, after I get Tracy to bed," he whispered. "And then we can relive your moment in the spotlight."

"I'll look forward to that."

As she drove home, she thanked God for helping her to pull the whole thing off, for getting the school board to vote for her instead of against her—and, most of all, for letting her still have a chance with Steve.

CHAPTER
Forty-Nine

Sylvia sat at the patio table covered with papers, and looked out at the empty corral. She had expected to be sad about the loss of the horses, as she had been after Sarah's wedding, when the house had felt so empty. But she realized now that it was a blessing and not a curse.

Harry came out drinking a glass of iced tea and sat next to her. "So whatcha doing with all these papers?" he asked.

"Counting up all the money we've raised," she said. "It looks like we've covered all of the bills they've received so far. Of course, most of the bills haven't come in yet. But I still have some pledges coming in. You know, I think we might just cover it all, if we work really hard. I think God is helping us keep the Dodds on our street. Since the couple who wanted to buy their house didn't qualify for the mortgage, we have a little more time. If we can raise enough money, I'm sure David will take the sign down."

"So how much of these donations came from your visits to corporate America?" he asked.

She smiled. "About half."

He leaned on the table. "Excuse me, but aren't you the woman who had nothing left to contribute?"

She threw her head back and laughed. "Okay, so I may still have a little life left in me."

He picked up the letter from the Nicaraguan couple who had asked for advice and help. "You know, I feel bad. All this time we've been so busy with Joseph, I haven't had time to look into much of anything for Maria and Carlos."

"It's not too late," she said. "Besides, I've done a little thinking."

He set the letter down and looked up at her. "Yeah?"

"Yeah." She fixed her eyes on him for a moment. "Harry, what would you think about our offering our house to Carlos and Maria while he's in seminary? We could also pay his way, and line up a job for him and a school for their son while they're here."

He frowned. "You wouldn't mind having them live with us?"

She held his gaze for a moment. "We're not going to be here, Harry."

He sat up straighter, and his eyes widened. "What do you mean?"

She reached out and clutched his hand. "We're going to Nicaragua."

His eyes misted over. He studied her face for a moment as if waiting for her to scream out, "Gotcha!" But she didn't. "Are you sure?" Harry asked.

"I've been praying a lot about this," she said, "asking God to change my heart. A few months ago, when all this came up, I didn't think I had much to contribute. But now I can see that I do still have talents God can use. I *can* work with the children, and I can teach the mothers. I want to go. You have so much you can take to those people, and I think I have some things I can take, too. I may not be able to cure their diseases, but I can help to cure their hearts."

"You're absolutely sure?"

"Absolutely," she said. "And if Carlos and Maria stay in our house, I'll have the peace of knowing that we'll have it to come back to. Or, after they finish seminary, we can sell it if we want."

Harry leaned back hard in his chair and let out a laugh that seemed to shake the trees. "I can't believe I'm hearing this!"

"Believe it," she said. "I asked God to change my heart if He wanted us to do this. I didn't *want* Him to, and I didn't expect Him to. But He did. Now I'm getting excited."

Harry got up and hugged his wife with all his might.

CHAPTER *Fifty*

That night after supper, Tory, Sylvia, and Cathy went to the hospital to sit with Brenda and Joseph. He had been moved to his own room and was doing well, so while he slept, they went into the small waiting room across the hall and talked softly about the best moments of the last few months.

"When they told us they'd found a heart," Brenda whispered. "That was a good one."

"Me, too, when you called to tell me," Tory agreed.

"When my kids wanted to help raise money," Cathy said.

Sylvia began to laugh. "When Ed Majors gave me that first check."

Brenda grinned. "Rolling my own yard with my kids for Joseph's party."

"The animal fair," Tory added, "when Spencer finally got to ride Sylvia's horse before she sold it."

Brenda smiled. "When they prayed over Joseph at church."

"When I met Steve Bennett," Cathy added. They all looked at her and smiled knowingly.

"When we discovered Brenda's church," Tory whispered.

"When *I* discovered Sylvia's church," Cathy echoed.

"When Harry came in and told us the surgery was a success."

"When your kids made all those videos," Sylvia said.

"When Joseph opened his eyes after the surgery."

"When you told me what you did about investing our children wisely."

"When I told Harry I wanted to go to the mission field."

They all got quiet for a long time, their thoughts centered on blessings instead of trials, on joys instead of heartaches. It was so much different than the night they'd gotten together months ago, after Joseph's first collapse—when they'd thought they had so much to complain about.

"Some of the best moments," Tory whispered finally, "have been sitting right here with you tonight, and knowing that we're all different people than we were when we started out."

"Yes," Sylvia whispered. "These are definitely some of the best moments."

Barry was asleep on the floor with the children—in front of the television—when Tory got home that night. She stood quietly over them, filled with an overwhelming love for her family. She knelt there beside them and wept for the blessing of them.

An idea came to her, and quietly she went into the laundry room, turned on her computer, and began to write her feelings down. She wrote about the little cul-de-sac of Cedar Circle, about the child who needed a heart, and how the neighbors had banded together to raise the money. She wrote about the things she'd learned about loving her own children, about the blessings she was too busy to see, about the joy she was too rushed to experience. She wrote about God changing her heart, and Sylvia's and Cathy's, and she wrote about the courageous love of

Brenda, who trusted God enough to open her hand for Him to take Joseph away from her. She talked about the lessons of investing her children wisely, and how God had taught her, through Brenda, that her children, not her writing, were her life's greatest work.

When she finished, it was five A.M., and she realized that she'd written an entire article. She would send it to her favorite magazine and see if they wanted it. If they didn't, that was okay too. After all, it wasn't the words, but rather the meaning behind them, that was most important: the changes in her heart, and the changes that would occur in her family as a result.

Quietly, she slipped outside. The sky was just surrendering its darkness to the beginnings of day. She walked down the driveway to the mailbox, slipped the envelope in, and put the flag up. Then she turned and saw the sun's rays just coming up over the mountains. She watched, breathlessly, as the sky grew brighter, brighter, until the sun burst like a fireball above the mountain peaks.

For a moment, she stood and took it all in, like an epiphany in her heart as this new morning in her life dawned. Joy and incredible gratitude washed over her like the sun's light, and suddenly she couldn't wait to see what the day would bring.

She could have stood like that for hours, just watching the miracle of God's new day, but instead, she went back into the den, where her family still slept on the floor. Instead of waking them and taking them all to bed, she lay down with them, curled up between her two children, her hand on Barry's arm. There was no place she needed to be, nothing calling her away. This was her work and her greatest joy.

This was where she belonged.

THE END

Dedication

To Stephen, Beverly's dear grandson,
who has taught the family that Down's Syndrome
can be a blessing rather than a curse

And to all those mothers and fathers of
handicapped children who thought it would be a
sacrifice to care for their handicapped child . . .
then discovered it produced some
of life's special blessings

I will bless them and the places surrounding my hill. I will send down showers in season; there will be showers of blessings.

EZEKIEL 34:26

CHAPTER *One*

As crises went, Tory Sullivan usually put nausea at the bottom of the scale. When it was her children who were sick, she dealt with it just fine. She washed their faces and rinsed out their mouths, and laid them down on the bed with towels in case another wave assaulted them. Then she would matter-of-factly clean up the mess while she thought about the lantana plants that needed watering, or how badly she needed to paint the living room.

But she didn't handle it as well when she was the patient. Queasiness seemed like an insult to her, as if her body were taking away her control and running rampant like a rebellious child. She wouldn't have it. If she stopped thinking about it, it would go away.

Tory stopped rocking and tried to concentrate on the leaves whispering in the breeze. Her friend Brenda Dodd kept moving in the matching chair on her porch, but the sound and motion made Tory close her eyes. She didn't have time to be sick, she thought. She simply didn't have room for it on her schedule.

The sound of Brenda's voice, as sweet as it usually sounded, droned on as she read the words of the article that Tory had written. Tory would have thought it was the terror of having her words read aloud that had turned her stomach, but the truth was that she was exceptionally proud of them. She had deliberately brought the article here so that Cathy and Brenda could be amazed. Cathy Flaherty, in her light blue veterinarian's lab coat, responded with dutiful admiration as she chomped on the Fritos she was having for lunch.

Tory wondered if the smell of Fritos made others want to gag.

"Cool, you got a zipper on your front!"

Tory looked down at her four-year-old son, Spencer, who sat with Joseph on the steps. Joseph, Brenda's nine-year-old, had his shirt pulled up and was showing four-year-old Spencer the scars healing on his chest. The fact that he'd gotten a heart transplant just a few weeks ago fascinated Spencer.

"It's not a zipper, Spence," Joseph said. "It's where the doctor cut—"

"No, Joseph!" Tory cut in. "Don't . . . please don't . . ." But she couldn't get the words out. It took too much concentration not to let her body have its way.

Brenda shot Tory a puzzled look and leaned down to her startled son. "Your surgery may be a little too graphic for Spencer," she explained softly.

"Just give him the broad picture," Cathy suggested with a wink.

"No." Tory didn't want them to think she was angry at Joseph for going too far. Spencer had seen much worse on television. Just the other day, she had caught him watching a face-lift on cable. "It's me." She touched her stomach and tried to turn back the wave of nausea.

Brenda and Cathy gaped at her as if waiting for the rest of a sentence. After a few seconds, Spencer lost interest in Joseph's chest and began turning cartwheels in the grass. "Look, Mommy!"

Tory couldn't look.

"Tory, are you okay?" Cathy asked. "You look as white as a couch potato."

Brenda laughed. "A couch potato?"

"Well, yeah. They never get any sun. Tory?"

Tory couldn't manage a smile. She opened her eyes and got slowly to her feet. "I don't feel so good."

Brenda looked up at her, alarmed. "Tory, you really don't look good. What's wrong?"

"Just a little . . . sick." She stood there for a second, then bolted for Brenda's front door. "Bathroom . . ."

Brenda launched out of her chair and threw open her front door, and Tory dashed into the house and made a beeline for the bathroom.

When she came out several minutes later, Cathy, Brenda, Joseph, and Spencer were all lined up in the hall, looking at her as if she'd just performed an amazing stunt.

"Tory, did you eat breakfast this morning?" Brenda asked her.

"Of course," she said, still feeling wobbly. "Wheaties. Breakfast of Champions, huh, Spence?"

"Maybe the milk was bad," Spencer suggested. "Bad milk makes me hurl."

"The milk was not bad," she said. "I've been feeling a little sick off and on for a while, but it hasn't gotten me like that before. Maybe it's a bug. Guess I'd better get out of here so Joseph doesn't get it." She realized how serious it could be for Joseph to contract a virus. Because of the high-dose steroids he was taking to keep from rejecting his heart, his immune system couldn't protect him at all. "Oh, Brenda, I'm so sorry."

"It's fine," Brenda said, though Tory knew she must be concerned. "Just passing you in the hall isn't going to make him sick. The kids are bringing home backpacks full of germs every day."

"Do you have any Lysol? I really should sanitize the toilet so Joseph won't be hurt by the germs."

"Don't worry about it. I'll do it. You go on home."

"No, I think she should do it," Cathy said with that amused look on her face. "Just pull that puppy up and go boil it for a couple of hours. David must have a vat you could use."

Joseph looked horrified, and Spencer looked fascinated. "They boil toilets?" Joseph asked.

"No." Brenda playfully shoved Cathy. "She's kidding, guys. Tory, you don't have to sanitize my toilet. Just go take care of yourself."

Tory was too distracted to laugh. She knew that Brenda was too kind to tell her that the more time she spent here apologizing, the more germs she would spread. So she took Spencer's hand and started out the door.

"Want me to walk with you?" Cathy asked, hurrying out beside her. Thankfully, she had gotten rid of the Fritos while Tory was in the bathroom.

"That's okay. I'll be fine. I have to go pick up Brittany."

"I could do that for you before I go back to the clinic."

Tory considered that, then decided that it wouldn't be necessary. "No, I think I'm over it now. Really. Boy, I hate being sick."

"Unlike the rest of us who enjoy it?" Cathy asked with a smirk. Her blonde ponytail bobbed as she walked along beside them. She wore a white T-shirt under her lab coat, jeans, and Nike tennis shoes. Tory envied Cathy for being so unselfconscious. "Spencer's probably right," Cathy said. "You probably ate something that made you sick. What'd you guys have for supper last night, Spencer?"

"Pork chops," Spencer said with a sour look. "They tasted like Daddy's shoes."

Cathy laughed and looked at Tory. "Mmm. Sounds good. He's tasted his daddy's shoes, has he?"

Tory couldn't help grinning now. "The pork chops were dry. Barry said they tasted like shoe leather. They did not make me sick. No one else in my family is nauseous."

"That's 'cause we all spit them out when you weren't looking," Spencer announced.

Cathy's mouth came open in delight. "You see there?"

"Okay, so I'm sick from the pork chops," Tory conceded. But that didn't explain the queasiness that had assaulted her for several days.

Giving up, Cathy told Spencer to take care of his mom, then bopped back across the cul-de-sac. "Call me if you need anything," she said over her shoulder. "I'll be home around four."

"I will."

As they reached their house, Spencer looked up at her with big, serious eyes. "Want me to get you a barf bag?"

She couldn't imagine where in the house they might have such a thing. "I'm okay, honey. Let's just get in the car and go get Britty."

The wave of nausea passed over her again as she drove to Brittany's school at noon to pick her up. Beside her, Spencer was chattering nonstop about the action figure he wanted for Christmas, even though it was only October.

The nausea ambushed her again as she got into the line of traffic picking up kids at the school. Quickly, she pulled out of the line and parked the car.

Spencer looked up at her, puzzled. She saw in the rearview mirror that Brittany was standing on the curb staring at her with a troubled expression, not knowing whether she should launch out in front of the stream of cars to her mother, or wait patiently as her teacher had told her. To her children, obedience was always a cause for careful consideration. It was one of the few things they thought about before doing it. "Come on, Spence. I need to run in and use the bathroom."

"Are you gonna barf again?"

The crude question made her situation even more urgent. Without answering, she got out and waited for Spencer, then grabbed his hand and crossed the busy lane of traffic.

"Mommy, what are you doing?" Brittany asked as she approached.

She kissed Brittany's forehead, then put Spencer's hand in hers. "Both of you just stand here for a minute. Mommy has to use the bathroom." She darted into the school just as she heard Spencer explaining, "She's been puking all over the place."

Wondering where he'd gotten these expressions, Tory made it to the bathroom, into the stall, and stood with her back to the door, thinking, perhaps, that the feeling would pass. She took a deep breath and tried to concentrate on something other than her stomach.

She really did not have time for this.

She had promised herself she would write this afternoon while the children were napping. She wanted to tweak her article one more time before sending it off, and she had that deadline looming over her. Nausea was an unexpected factor in this equation.

As if in answer to her mental declaration that she didn't have time, her body proceeded to show her that it could make time for whatever illness had gripped her.

She couldn't remember feeling this way since the last time she was pregnant.

She rose up slowly, trembling, as the thought seemed to settle on her consciousness like a visitor who liked the view.

No, she couldn't be pregnant. Not when she had just gotten one child in school and the other in a Mother's Day Out program three mornings a week. Not when she was finally writing and selling her work. Not when she had gotten her priorities straight and listed them so tightly that there was little room for adjustment.

The wave came over her again, and she leaned over the toilet.

She *couldn't* be pregnant!

As if in answer, that stranger settling on her consciousness seemed to say, *Of course you can.*

She went to the sink and cupped water in her hand, drank some, and splashed the rest on her face. Her makeup wasn't waterproof, so she set about trying to blot it and repair it, but it was no use. At least her hair still looked decent. The teachers at the school had never seen Tory when she looked less than her best. Beauty and control were both near the top of her priority list, and today she seemed to be losing her grip on both.

The worst part of the nausea was gone, though she still felt the queasiness lurking somewhere in the back of her mind. She forced herself to head back to her kids.

Spencer had engaged the poor, bedraggled teacher in conversation, and was telling her about his mother getting sick all over his friend's bathroom. She supposed that, in Spencer's mind, that wasn't a patent lie, for he'd probably misinterpreted the Lysol exchange. But she found it hard to look the teacher in the eye as she took her kids' hands.

"Are you all right, Tory?" the teacher asked.

"I don't know what's wrong with me," she said on a laugh. "Just not feeling my best."

"I've thought you were getting too skinny lately," the teacher said. "You've always been thin, but you're even thinner than usual. My friend started losing weight like that and found out she had stomach cancer."

Tory tried to plaster a pleasant look on her face, and fought the urge to thank the woman for her cheery optimism. "I watch my weight, that's all." She took each child by the hand. "I probably just have a stomach virus. Either that, or I'm pregnant."

She couldn't believe she had said the words out loud, and as the teacher's pointy eyebrows shot up, Tory began to laugh, as if that was the funniest thing she'd ever said. The woman joined in with as much mirth as Sarah and Abraham must have had upon hearing of Sarah's pregnancy.

Fortunately, her kids were fighting at the time, because Spencer was certain that Brittany had gotten their mother's good hand, and he wanted to trade. Brittany never did anything Spencer asked without a fight, even when she knew that one hand was as good as the other. Neither of them heard the explosive word that had rolled off her tongue like a prophecy.

She got them both to the car, belted them in, and sat with the car idling as she tried to decide if she needed to run back in for one last round with the toilet. As she did, she tried to count back to her last period. Was it late?

She had it written down, she thought. On the calendar in the kitchen, she always used little dots to indicate her cycle. She could count up the weeks.

But as she drove, she began to feel that loss of control again. Her well-planned life was tipping a little on its axis. She and Barry had planned for both Brittany and Spencer. They hadn't planned for a surprise. Tory didn't like surprises, and she didn't like disruptions to her schedule. She had her days planned down to the moment. Brittany could tie her shoes, and Spencer could make his own peanut butter sandwich. She didn't have the heart to start over with an infant.

The nausea seemed to subside as she blew the air conditioning into her face, despite the fact that Brittany and Spencer complained about being cold. Usually, she deferred to them, but today she had no choice. By the time they pulled into their driveway, she was feeling better.

She got out of the car and helped her children out, then went straight for that calendar.

She counted the weeks—one, two, three, four, five . . .

She shook her head. That couldn't be right. She would have realized it.

. . . six, seven, eight, nine . . .

She stood there for a long moment, gaping at the calendar weeks, while Brittany and Spencer began to fight over whether to watch reruns of *Full House* or *Saved by the Bell*.

How could this be? How could she have missed an entire period without realizing it?

The answer came to her suddenly. *Joseph.*

Her first missed period had been during the worst part of Joseph's illness, before they had found a heart. He had been dying, and Tory had hung on with Brenda. She and Sylvia and Cathy, her other neighbors, had been steeped in grief and worry, not to mention the stress of trying to raise money to pay the medical bills. As Joseph slipped away, Tory's period must have slipped her mind.

Now she had missed another one.

She stood there with her mouth open, counting the weeks over and over, wondering if she had just forgotten to mark the calendar. But she knew it wasn't an oversight. All the signs pointed to pregnancy.

But it couldn't be! She and Barry hadn't planned to have more kids. She was thirty-five years old, and their family was complete. Could she really be pregnant?

"Everybody back in the car!" she yelled, desperately trying to take back the reins of her life. "We have to go to the drugstore."

"Can I get a Darth Vader?" Spencer asked, seizing on his mother's obvious distraction.

"Yes."

"I want M&M's," Brittany shouted.

"Okay."

As she grabbed her purse and headed back out to the car, she checked off her list in her mind. Action figure, M&M's . . .

And the fastest pregnancy test she could find.

CHAPTER *Two*

Cathy didn't give Tory's nausea another thought as she finished up the load of laundry she had folded during her lunch hour. She tripped over Mark's backpack as she was taking a stack of folded clothes to his room. Since he was supposed to be at school, and she was quite sure that they hadn't had any kind of seventh grade holiday, she was baffled. She unzipped it and saw a couple of textbooks, several dirty, dog-eared folders, three pencils, a sharpener, and pencil shavings on the bottom of the bag, along with other filthy substances she didn't want to examine too closely. His lunch was smashed in a sack between his English and history books. He obviously hadn't changed backpacks or decided not to use it today. Everything he needed was in here.

Had those adolescent hormones so flooded his brain that he had forgotten to take it? Had he not noticed, when he got on the bus this morning, that he was empty-handed? She sighed, conceding to herself that she was about to enter the twilight zone of teenagehood with him. It was too soon. She didn't know if she could survive it with a third child. Rick and Annie had already driven her to the brink of insanity.

She picked up the backpack, wondering if they made textbooks out of cement these days, since the pack was so heavy that no normal backbone could support it. No wonder he hadn't wanted to carry it. But it was after lunch by now. Hadn't he noticed that it was missing? Why hadn't he called her and asked her to bring it to him?

She got into her pickup and dropped the backpack on the seat. Maybe all her admonitions to her children that they'd better be in serious physical jeopardy to call her at the clinic had finally gotten through. But it seemed unlikely that he would heed her warnings now. This was the same kid who had called her during his lunchtime last week and asked her to bring him a Snickers bar before fifth period because he needed it to bribe his teacher. She remembered shouting something about how Mrs. Jefferson's dying cat was more important than a stupid Snickers bar, and that if he'd done his homework he wouldn't have to worry about bribing teachers. He had slammed the phone down, as if she had done him wrong.

Now, just a few days later, he was too considerate to call her about his backpack? She didn't think so.

She got to the school, parked in front of the door, and flung the backpack over her shoulder. Trudging along like a hiker carrying a VW on her back, she made her way to the office.

The overworked office worker looked up at her as she came in. "May I help you?"

"Yeah," she said, out of breath as she slid the backpack off and dropped it onto the counter. "These things weigh a ton. They ought to put wheels on them or something. Our kids are all going to grow up bent over like ninety-year-old men." She saw that the lady was in no mood for her humor. "Uh . . . I need to send this to Mark Flaherty, seventh grade."

The woman turned to her computer to look up Mark's schedule, then lowered her glasses and peered at Cathy over the top of them. "Mark is absent today."

"No," she said, leaning across the counter to look on the screen. "He's here. He just forgot his backpack."

The woman looked at the screen again. "Sorry. He's been marked absent in every class."

Cathy's mouth fell open. Had he been kidnapped on the way to the bus stop, or had he deliberately cut school? "Would you do me a favor?" she asked. "Would you look up his friends? Andy Whitehill and Tad Norris? Are they here?"

She typed their names in, then shook her head. "No, I'm afraid they're absent, too."

Her face grew hot. She wondered if smoke was coming out of her ears. Any minute now the top of her head would blow off. "So you're telling me that my son and those two are playing hookey?"

"They're not here," the woman said, smiling now, as if she finally heard something that amused her.

"Well, don't you people call parents when kids don't show up? I mean, what if he'd been kidnapped or something? They'd have made it to Memphis by now."

"You're supposed to call us," the woman said. "If your child is going to be out, you're supposed to call by nine."

"But if he's *not* supposed to be out, and I *don't* call, what then?"

"Then he's marked unexcused."

"Well, if he's *dead*, it doesn't really *matter* if it's unexcused, does it?" she asked, raising her voice more with each word. "As some kidnapper hauls my child across the country, it's not really relevant if he gets zeroes on his assignments!"

The woman removed her glasses and gave her a disgusted look. "Mrs. Flaherty, don't you think you're overreacting a little? Your son obviously skipped school with his friends. Instead of blaming us, why don't you go look for him? I suggest you try the homes of the other two boys. They're probably there."

Flinging the backpack back over her shoulder, she trudged back out to her car. She was perspiring as she flew to the home of one of the boys. Looking up, she saw that one of the upstairs windows was open and smoke was drifting from it. Someone was home, and they were smoking enough to fill a saloon in Marlboro Country.

She went to the door and rang the bell, then banged on the door like someone with authority. She wasn't sure if that would help or not. Authority might be just the thing to keep them from answering the door.

She heard footsteps on the stairs, heard someone say, "It's your mother, man!" Then more footsteps . . .

After several moments, Andy opened the door. He was faking sickness. He squinted his eyes as if she had gotten him out of bed, and wore an expression that was a perfect counterfeit of the one Tory had worn earlier. "Oh . . . hi, Dr. Flaherty. What are you doing here?"

She crossed her arms. "You should really join the drama club, Andy. Your talents are wasted here."

"Huh?"

She sighed with disgust. "I'm looking for Mark. I know he's here."

"No," he said. "I'm sick, and nobody's here."

She was getting tired of this, so she pushed open the door and bolted past him into the house. "Mark Flaherty!" she called upstairs. "I know you're here. Get down here immediately! You *don't* want me to come after you."

Slowly, Mark emerged from the room upstairs. He came down the stairs, reeking of cigarette smoke. "Hi, Mom."

"Get in the car." She waited as her son rushed out of the house, then turned back to the boy who lived there. "Get one of your parents on the telephone, Andy. They need to know about this." She looked upstairs and raised her voice again. "And Tad, you'd better get down here and when Andy's finished, you can call yours."

"But Mrs. Flaherty . . . I really am sick," Andy whined. "It's not my fault Mark and Tad came over here."

"Just call them."

She spoke to both sets of parents—neither of whom knew their kids weren't at school—and prayed that they would do something about it, instead of just shaking their fingers at their wayward sons. Then she went back out to her car. Mark looked as if he feared for his life. As she started the car and popped it in reverse, he turned his round, innocent eyes to her.

"Mom, I'm sorry. I'll never do that again."

"Got that right." She glanced over at him. "You were smoking, too, weren't you?"

"We were just playing around. I didn't even inhale."

"Oh, now there's an original thought." She turned right at the red light.

"Where are we going?"

"Back to school," she said.

"Mom, you can't take me there. There's only forty-five minutes left till the bell rings."

"You got unexcused absences in every class, but by golly, you will not get one in your algebra class. You're going to go to that school and face that principal with what you've done, and then you're going to go to that class and learn something. Am I making myself clear?"

"Yes, ma'am."

"And then you're going to come *home* and learn something."

"What? Are you going to ground me from breathing oxygen for a month?"

"Worse. And frankly, Mark, I need time to think about it. I'll have figured it out by the time you get home."

"Well, how bad is it gonna be? Will I be better off running away from home?"

"Don't even think about it. I'll hunt you down and find you."

"You know, they'll probably suspend me for cutting school. You realize that, don't you? That you might be responsible for getting me suspended?"

"I'm not responsible, Mark, you are. And I'm willing to let you suffer whatever consequences you've brought on yourself. I don't like it, and it makes me so mad that I can hear my heart beating in my ears . . ." She swallowed and tried to calm her voice. "But that's the way it goes, and I want this to be such an unpleasant memory for you that you never want to repeat it."

"I'm already there."

"Oh, no," she said. "Not by a long shot. You have a long way to go, kiddo."

CHAPTER *Three*

Brenda Dodd went from sanitizing her bathroom to interviewing for the job she had been praying she could get, but she worried that she smelled of Lysol as she stepped into the busy room. It was a telemarketing firm, and she looked around and saw dozens of people sitting in cubicles with headsets on, talking to people who didn't want to be bothered.

She swallowed back her trepidation and, clutching her purse, looked for someone who seemed to be in charge. She saw a real office, with four walls and a ceiling, at the back corner of the room, so she cut across the floor. Everyone was talking at once. How could they hear themselves think?

She reached the door. Peering in, she saw a disheveled man sitting at a desk behind a mound of paperwork. She knocked.

"Yeah," the man said without looking up.

She stepped into the doorway. "Uh . . . I'm Brenda Dodd. I spoke to you on the phone?" When he still didn't look up, she added, "I'm here for the job interview?"

He finally looked up at her and gestured toward a chair. "Have a seat."

He turned back to the computer he'd been typing on, and got a scowl on his face. "Give me a break!" he bit out, then shot to his feet and headed to the door. Without saying a word about where he was going, he burst out into the workroom. She watched through the door as he raced to one of the cubicles and bent over to chew someone out. She couldn't hear what he was saying, but it was clear from the look on his face that he was livid.

The young woman he had verbally assaulted winced and began to clear her desk. He kept railing behind her, and finally, she abandoned the rest of her personal items and took off for the door.

Brenda's heart sank.

He came back in and took his seat, still angry. His face was red, and she wondered if he had high blood pressure and ulcers. "So . . . what did you say your name was?" he demanded.

"Brenda Dodd," she said, trying to smile.

"And why, exactly, do you think I'd want to hire you?"

She didn't know if that was a deliberate insult, or one of those psychological employer's questions designed to see what she was made of. She sat straighter, and clutched her purse more tightly. "Because I'm good with people, and I'm diligent and hard-working. I need a job I can do at night when my husband isn't working, because one of my children had a heart transplant not too long ago, and I need to be there for him during the day."

"Uh-huh," he said, looking down at something that she assumed was the application she had sent in earlier. It was clear he had little interest in her problems. "Any experience?"

She had decided on the way here that she wouldn't let her stay-at-home-mom status get in the way of this. "Yes, lots. I've been an educator, a health care provider, a bookkeeper, an administrator, an interior designer, a chef, and an executive assistant."

He frowned and looked up at her. "You must not stay at anything very long."

Her smile broadened. "Actually, I've been doing all of them at the same time for thirteen years."

She could see the struggle on his face to picture a job that encompassed all of those things. "Well, then you may be overqualified to work here," he said. "The last thing I need is some over-educated bonehead—"

"Oh, I'm not overeducated," she cut in, realizing she had made herself look *too* good. "Really. I don't even have a degree."

"Then where did you work all those years?" he asked, flipping through her application. "Says here you were a housewife . . ." His voice faded off, and he looked up at her as the light dawned. "Wait a minute. You were being cute, weren't you? Making yourself out to be some kind of genius when all you are is a lousy housewife."

Her smile crashed. She thought of defending herself, telling him that she had not overstated her qualifications, that she had homeschooled her four children until this year, that she had nursed her child when he was at death's door, that she had managed the bills and the finances in their home, that she cooked and cleaned and decorated on a shoestring, that she was her husband's biggest supporter and helpmeet. But this man would not be impressed.

She got up and smoothed out the creases on her skirt. Her voice trembled as she said, "Mr. Berkley, I don't think I want this job after all. I'm sorry I wasted your time." She started to the door, her knuckles turning white as she clutched her purse.

"Wait," he said.

She didn't know why she stopped, but she did, and slowly turned around.

"Sit down," he ordered.

She hesitated.

"Come on," he said impatiently. "If you come back in here and sit down, you've got the job."

Her eyebrows shot up. She wasn't sure if the emotion flooding through her was relief or dread. Slowly, she went back to the chair and sat down.

"I don't care if you were a housewife or a princess in Peru. Can you work seven to midnight?"

"Yes," she said. "But . . . who do we call that late? I mean, aren't people in bed?"

"We reserve our West Coast calls for the later hours, since they're three hours earlier."

"What exactly are you selling here?" she asked.

"Lots of things. We have a number of accounts. We sell everything from magazine subscriptions to diet programs. When can you start?"

"Uh . . . well, maybe tonight."

"All right," he said. "Report here at seven. I'll get you set up before I leave for the day. And don't be late. I hate people who are late."

As she headed back out to her car, Brenda tried to tell herself that she was excited about her new job. It would bring much needed income into the household, and take some of the pressure off of David, who made furniture for a living. She would be there all day for Joseph, and still get to spend three and a half hours with Leah, Rachel, and Daniel before she had to report to work. She and David could make up their time together on weekends. It would all work out.

But as she got back into her minivan, she sat there for a moment, making a valiant effort not to cry. When she was certain she had her emotions under control, she started the car and headed home. She wished Sylvia was still living in Cedar Circle. This was one of those times when she would have called her neighbor and asked her to pray. But Sylvia was in Nicaragua, working as a missionary. Noble work. Purposeful work. God-ordained work.

She wondered what Sylvia would say about Brenda reentering the work force this way. She would probably blame herself because she and Tory and Cathy hadn't raised more money to pay Joseph's hospital bills. The truth was that her friends had raised more than enough to pay for Joseph's transplant. But now the costs of the drugs he took, the frequent visits back to the doctor, and the weekly biopsies to head off his rejection of the heart were phenomenal. She had wondered more than once over the last few weeks if they had done the right thing when they took their house off the market. Maybe they should have sold it after all.

But as she began to sink into depression, she began to sing the soft, clear chorus of "I Love You, Lord." As always, her spirits rose back to bearable heights. She was blessed, she thought. Joseph was alive. Her other children were safe and healthy. David, though an unbeliever, was a wonderful father and an attentive husband. And now she had a job.

Yes, she told herself as she headed up the mountain to Cedar Circle. She was blessed, indeed.

CHAPTER
Four

The secondhand car that Harry had insisted on buying for Sylvia in León, Nicaragua, was a 1975 Fiat Berlina that sounded like a lawn mower and drove in fits and starts. The morning they had bought it, the back window had fallen out and shattered on the backseat. They had not been able to get the glass to replace it, so they had taped plastic across the hole with duct tape to keep out the rain.

She wished it wasn't the rainy season in Nicaragua. If it weren't, she might not have had so much trouble getting around. Her windshield wipers didn't work, and despite all the duct tape, there was a leak somewhere that caused a puddle to form in the backseat every time she took the car out in the rain.

She found the university, which was her main landmark in her directions to the restaurant, since the Nicaraguans weren't big on addresses. The restaurant where she was meeting another American missionary couple was a half block north. She found it with little trouble, located a place to park the car, and got out.

A child about the age of Joseph Dodd, her little nine-year-old neighbor back home, approached the car, soaking wet from the rain and carrying a dead chicken. In Spanish, he asked her if she wanted to buy it, but she shook her head and thanked him. She wished she spoke more Spanish. She missed talking to children, hearing their funny little thoughts, laughing at their antics. The children here were no different than they were in Tennessee. Except they were much more conscious about money, because they had to help their families make a living.

The child spouted out some more Spanish, then in broken English, asked, "Watch your car?"

She had been through this every time she had parked the car, so she knew what he wanted. "*Si*," she said. "You watch my car." Clutching the dead chicken, which she knew he would sell before she returned, the child leaned possessively against her car.

It was a ritual that had taken some getting used to. She had learned the hard way to allow someone to "watch her car," when her side mirror and all four hubcaps had been stolen off the car the first time she'd parked it. She learned quickly that, if someone offered to car sit, you had to let them, or they would rob you blind. Then when you returned, you had to pay them something before getting in. Sometimes the person watching the car when she returned wasn't the same person she'd started with. But she had to pay them nonetheless.

She hurried up to the La Cueva del León and saw that the young couple was already there waiting. She rushed in, and the Andersons got to their feet. "I'm so sorry I'm late," she said. "I still get so lost here. And my windshield wipers don't work."

"Don't worry about it," Julie Anderson said as they sat back down. She was a slight woman with short blonde hair and big brown eyes. Her husband, Jeb, was about five-eight and round, but had a jolly face that was always lit up in a smile. Sylvia had heard that children loved him.

She ordered *puntas de filete a la jalapena*, then settled back, trying to get comfortable with the couple she had been praying for. They had come here strictly on faith with hardly any support at all, and seemed to lack any clear direction for their ministry. Yet they had resisted joining with her and Harry, as if they were certain that God wanted them working elsewhere in the city.

"I'm sorry Harry couldn't be here. He's so busy with the clinic. You wouldn't believe the number of people he sees each day. I've been staying real busy myself, just checking up on his sickest patients. You know, if you wanted to come help out, there's tremendous ministry opportunity. We need more people to visit the patients at home, to make sure they're taking their medicine and doing all right. It really builds trust. We've seen dozens of people come to Christ already. And Pastor Jim is doing a great job with them."

Julie looked at her husband, then Jeb leaned on the table. "That's what we wanted to talk to you about," he said. "We feel like we've gotten our marching orders from God. We have a plan now."

Sylvia had visited with them a couple of other times and had been amazed at the number of things they had tried in their missionary work. Their work seemed to be constantly unsuccessful, yet they didn't lose heart. She had encouraged them to develop a ministry plan, since they seemed to be going in too many directions. "Great," she said. "What is it?"

"We're going to start a school," Julie said.

"A school?"

"Yes, a Christian school," Jeb said. "We're both teachers, and we know other Christian teachers in the States who are trying to raise their support right now so they can come join us."

"We figured it was a great way to reach the little ones," Julie said, "and then possibly reach their families through them. And we were wondering if you would be interested in teaching there with us."

Sylvia's eyes widened. "But I can hardly even speak Spanish. I couldn't communicate with them. And I don't have a teaching degree."

"You don't have to have one," Julie said. "And the kids need to learn English. You could teach them that."

"Think about it, Sylvia," Jeb said. "While you're teaching them English, you can also teach them the Bible. And we know how you love kids . . ."

She had to admit that she liked the idea. Even while she had urged Julie and Jeb to get a plan, she'd found herself lacking one. Harry's mission was clear. Hers had been a little hazier, especially since she was still learning the language.

"Well, where do you plan to have this school?"

"Here in León. We found an old building over near San Felipe Church. It used to be a warehouse of some kind, but we were able to buy it with the money our church sent us. We've finished cleaning it out, and we're about to start painting the classrooms. There won't be many at first, but we figure we'll grow."

"Well, it sounds wonderful. But didn't your church send you that money to live on?"

"They wanted us to use it for God's work," Julie said. "God will meet our needs, but we felt very clearly that the Lord wanted us to use it for the school."

Sylvia had her own thoughts on the difference between walking in faith and demanding miracles. She had learned the hard way that God could not be manipulated.

Julie leaned forward, locking eyes with Sylvia. "Do you think Dr. Harry would let us promote the school through his clinic? We need to be able to talk to the families, convince them that this would be good for their children . . ."

"Well, I don't know. Harry doesn't like to bombard his patients with too much at once. His main goal is to meet their physical needs, so that they can hear the gospel. If they're getting too many messages at the same time, it might make it harder for them to listen to his message about Jesus."

"But we're all in this together for the same purpose," Jeb said. "Whether we get them to your little church or to our little school, Jesus is lifted up."

Sylvia tried to banish her negative thoughts. These two needed encouragement, but she wasn't sure she had any to offer. "How many students do you have signed up so far?"

Jeb and Julie exchanged looks again. "Well . . . none."

"None at all?"

"Well, no. But we have faith that God is working in this. We know he told us to do this. The building practically fell into our hands, and we've had supplies like paint and the tools we've needed fall into our laps. Our church back home is collecting textbooks already . . ."

"But you don't have one child yet? And you've spent all this money on this building?"

"We're calling it The Ark," Jeb said. "We're building this school on faith. We're being obedient, even if it looks crazy. We *know* God is in this, Sylvia."

Sylvia tried not to dash their hopes with her practical wisdom. She loved seeing faith like theirs, but part of her couldn't help worrying that their dreams would be destroyed in the next few months. Things worked very slowly around here, and they could pour all of their time, money, and energy into something that was doomed to failure. If God had really told them to do this, that was one thing, but she feared it was one of those times when a missionary, so desperate to see God's results in their lives, heard his own voice and attributed it to God. They would need students, teachers, materials, lesson plans . . . Too many things would have to come together to make this work.

Still, she promised she would talk to Harry and see what they could do.

As she headed back out into the warm rain, she looked up at the hills surrounding León, lined with houses with red-tiled roofs. She missed the different kind of hills surrounding her home in Breezewood. She missed the ease of life and the things she could take for granted. She missed feeling purpose and certainty in her life, as she had as a young mother with children at home. She feared she might never know that kind of purpose again.

She wondered if Brenda and Cathy and Tory were all right. She could sure use one of their round-porch discussions right now. It would be heaven to sit on her porch with her neighbors, sipping sweet tea and talking about their children and their husbands and their churches. She longed for Brenda's vibrant optimism, for Cathy's sharp wit, for Tory's honest faith.

Oh, how she missed them.

She couldn't wait to get home and send them an e-mail, just to touch base. Maybe her latest stories would remind them how blessed they were.

CHAPTER *Five*

The pregnancy test couldn't be used until the next morning, so Tory hid it under her pillow and decided not to tell Barry until she was sure. But as Tory cooked supper and Barry helped Brittany with her homework, Spencer broadcast her secret. "Mommy's been perjecting all over the place," he said. "At Joseph's house, at Britty's school . . ."

"Perjecting?" Barry asked, mildly amused. "What do you mean, perjecting?"

"You know. Gettin' sick. Perjectine barfing."

"Projectile?" Barry asked, shooting Tory a look. "Tory, are you okay?"

She drew in a deep breath and looked wearily at her son. "Spencer, where do you get these words? He must have used six synonyms for vomiting today."

"He gets it from Nickelodeon," Brittany said.

Barry nodded agreement. "It's one of their favorite subjects."

"I told you we needed to get rid of television."

"So is it true?" Barry asked. "Have you been sick?"

She shrugged. "Must be a stomach virus. I don't know."

"I thought you looked a little pale." He got up and came to the stove. "Here, let me finish cooking. You don't need to be standing over this if you're sick."

"Yeah, I'm probably spreading germs, anyway," she said. She couldn't believe she was rooting for germs, when she spent so much time blasting Lysol on anything that could breed them.

He kissed her cheek. "Go sit down."

"I'm fine," she said as she headed out of the room. "Really. By tomorrow, I'll be as good as new." But even as she said the words, she knew it wasn't true.

Later that night, Barry read the kids a chapter of *Charlotte's Web*, while Tory cleaned the kitchen until it shined. She worried as she worked. When she was finished, she went to tuck them in, and wondered what it would be like to have a third little one demanding a glass of water, another kiss good night, a better hug, and a night-light that didn't cast shadows.

When she finally made it back to her bedroom, Barry was changing into a pair of sweatpants and a T-shirt. "How do you feel?" he asked.

"Okay, right now," she said. "It just hits me, all of a sudden."

"How long have you been doing this?"

"Just today. I've been kind of queasy for a few days," she said, downplaying it as much as she could. "It always passed."

She tried to keep her eyes averted, but he grabbed her hand and pulled her to face him. Sliding his arms around her, he looked down at her with amused eyes. "You're not pregnant, are you?"

She couldn't help grinning back. If she said yes, Barry wouldn't see it as a tragedy. "The thought has occurred to me."

He kept grinning down at her, as if trying to decide if she was serious. "Are you late?"

"Maybe a little."

His grin faded. "How late? One week? Two?"

She swallowed hard. "About ... um ... nine weeks, as far as I can tell."

He dropped his arms and stepped back. "Nine weeks? Tory!"

"I know," she said, clutching her head. "It's so stupid not to realize I'd already missed one. My last period should have been around the time Joseph was so sick. I must have been so distracted that I didn't realize I was late. And I've been really busy with the kids and the writing. I just didn't realize—"

"Okay." He grabbed his keys off of the dresser. "That's it. I'm going to buy a pregnancy test. How late is Walmart open?"

"No need, Barry," she said, stopping him. "I beat you to it." She went around the bed and got the box out from under her pillow.

The reality of it seemed to knock the wind out of him. He sank down on the bed, looking a little shell-shocked. "You really think you could be, don't you?"

"What if I am?" she asked him. "This will be the first one we didn't plan for. Can we still be happy about it?"

He seemed to think that over, and slowly a smile returned to his face. "Of course we can. I'm just so . . . stunned. You never mentioned that you were late, or that you felt bad . . . But yes, we can be happy about it. *Of course* we can be happy about it." He laughed then, a sound that filled her with relief. He reached out to pull her onto his lap. "We can be very happy about it."

"But I'll turn into a cow again, and I'll waddle like a duck . . ."

He stroked her hair behind her ear. "Tory, both times, you were the best-looking pregnant woman I'd ever seen. You *never* waddled like a duck. You gained all of twenty pounds on each baby, and lost it in the first six months. The doctor was yelling at *me* for not making you eat more."

"I would have gained more if I hadn't had such bad morning sickness." She sighed. "Barry, I don't know if I'm ready to go through all that again. And my writing is going so well. How will I ever write if there's a new baby to take care of?"

"You can make time if you really want to."

"That's the thing," she said. "If I have a new baby, I won't really *want* to write. It takes so much energy to take care of a baby." Her face flushed pink at the thought, and she gave in to a smile. "A baby . . ." she said with awe. "Barry, another little baby." Her smile faded again, and she closed her eyes. "Oh, no. A baby."

"Tory, stop worrying. It's out of your control. Either you are, or you aren't. If we have another baby, it's because God wants us to. End of story."

She couldn't help laughing softly. "You're right. And if I am, I'm sure I'll be happy."

He chuckled against her ear. "Happy? You'll be thrilled. You'll probably cry if the test is negative."

She knew that was true. There was some part of her that hoped it was positive. "What about you? How will you feel?"

"I'll feel like the luckiest guy in the world," he said. "A new baby. It's about the best thing I can think of."

"Even if we don't have an extra bedroom? Even if we don't have time?"

"We'll build on. And since when did anyone really have time for a baby? Once it comes, you laugh that you ever thought it was something you had to fit in. It just takes over."

"But Spencer and Britty have already taken over."

"So we'll have three little tyrants, instead of two. We'll love it."

Still grinning, she opened the box of the pregnancy test and read the instructions. "It says that we can do the test the first thing in the morning. The results will be ready in ten minutes."

"So just get some rest and don't worry about it until morning."

But Tory knew that she would worry all night. This wasn't the kind of thing she could shift to the back of her mind. If that test was positive, their lives would never be the same.

CHAPTER *Six*

If it turns blue, it's positive." The words seemed frightening to Tory as she stood facing her husband in the bedroom the next morning. The children were still sleeping. She had deliberately risen early with hopes of putting her fears to rest before breakfast.

Barry looked down at his watch. "Eight minutes left."

"What if we get a false answer? How do we know we can trust this test?"

"I trust it," he said. "They're pretty accurate. It was right the last couple of times."

"And what if it's clear?" she asked, frowning. "I thought about it all night. A little baby." Her eyes misted over, and she swallowed hard.

"If it's clear, you'll cry a little and go on."

"And if it's blue?"

He grinned. "You'll cry a little and go on."

"So it's a lose-lose situation."

"Win-win, is what I was thinking."

"Okay, so that vial is either half full or half empty . . . with either clear or blue liquid." She clutched her head with both hands. "Why am I so nervous?"

"Because you don't know what you want. Decide if you want it to be blue or clear."

"What do *you* want?" she asked.

He grinned. "Blue, I think."

A matching grin tiptoed across her face. "I think I do, too."

He looked at his watch again. "Five more minutes."

"If it's going to turn, do you think it would have turned a little by now?"

He got up. "I'm going to look."

"No!" she said, grabbing his arm to stop him. "No, I don't want to know."

"Well, I do!"

"I changed my mind," she said, as if her wishes could change the test's results. "I want it to be clear."

"Maybe it is."

She fell back on the bed with a bounce. "No, I want blue." She threw her hands over her face. "I don't know."

"You don't have to make up your mind," he said, laughing and bouncing down next to her. "It's either blue or clear. Simple as that." Rolling to his side, he grinned down at her. "This is kind of fun, isn't it? In the next five minutes, we could be a family of five."

"Or not."

He checked his watch. "Two more minutes."

She grinned. "One, two, three . . ."

Chuckling, he joined in, and they counted together. When they reached a hundred twenty, they both launched off the bed and headed for the bathroom, giggling and almost knocking each other down in the process.

Barry reached it first, but didn't look. "Are you ready?"

"Show me," she whispered, throwing her hands over her face.

She peaked through her fingers. He was grinning as he held up the vial. The bluest liquid she had ever seen seemed to glow from it like neon. Tears pushed into her eyes, and a gale of laughter almost blew her over. Barry started to laugh, too, and setting the vial down, pulled her into his arms. "We're pregnant," he said in a voice soft and high-pitched.

"We're pregnant," she agreed, shaking her head, unable to wipe the smile off her face.

"Will he be like Spencer, or like Britty?"

"*She'll* be altogether different," Tory said. "Not like either one of them. This baby will be one of a kind."

CHAPTER *Seven*

Several days later, Barry went with Tory for her first prenatal visit. He had been humming and grinning ever since they'd learned about the baby, but she had convinced him to keep it quiet until the doctor confirmed that the at-home test was accurate. She didn't want the kids getting all excited if it turned out to be a mistake. Still, he had gone up to the attic and gotten down the maternity clothes and all the baby clothes they had put away, and had begun drawing up plans to build an extra room onto their house. She hid all the clothes from the children, and shushed Barry over and over so he wouldn't give it away. But the blood test she took confirmed her pregnancy in a matter of minutes, and the ultrasound showed a tiny little fetus with a strong heartbeat. They couldn't have been more thrilled if it had been their first child.

Dr. Grentwell sat down and began going over the routine for prenatal care. They listened, holding hands, nodding as he spoke, for none of this was new to them. The doctor was a painfully thin man who looked as if he needed medical care himself, and he spoke like a flight attendant who'd made the same speech five thousand times. As he spoke, he jotted prescriptions for prenatal vitamins, which Tory already had, and nausea pills, which she had no intentions of taking.

"You realize, don't you, that we consider someone of your age to be at a higher risk in pregnancy than a younger woman?" he asked in a matter-of-fact monotone.

Tory bristled. "Someone of my age?"

"Well, you just turned thirty-five. The risk of chromosomal problems in the baby is higher, and we recommend that all of our obstetric patients who will be thirty-five or older at the birth of their babies have a CVS or an amniocentesis. It's a little early for an amnio, but since you're ten weeks, we could go ahead and do the CVS."

"What's a CVS?" Tory asked.

"Chorionic villi sampling is a relatively new procedure, where we get samples of tissue from the placenta. Those cells are fetal cells, so we can culture them. In a week to ten days, we can determine the chromosomal makeup of those cells."

Tory thought that over for a moment. "Do I have to have that test? What if I opt out?"

"You certainly have that option."

"No," Barry said. "We need to have it done. She's a worrier, and if we don't know, she'll worry about it the whole pregnancy, just based on what you said about women over thirty-five. I'd rather rule out that kind of problem from the start. Besides, if there's something wrong, I want to know."

"It doesn't matter," she said. "Even if something was wrong, I would never terminate a pregnancy."

"A lot of women say that," Dr. Grentwell said, tapping his pencil against his pad. "But I recommend the test, because if your baby has Down's Syndrome or another chromosomal defect, it might take you several months to prepare yourself. Not only that, it's helpful if we know there could be problems when the baby comes, so we're prepared to treat them."

He stood up, and Tory noted that the man needed a wife to tell him that his pants were pulled up too high, and that his lime-green shirt didn't quite match the army-green pants he wore under his lab coat. His brown socks made her wonder if he was color blind.

"So what do you think?" Barry asked, nudging her. "You know there's nothing wrong. But you also know that you'll obsess about it for the next six months if you don't rule it out."

She sighed. "Okay, we'll do it."

The man sat back down then, his bony elbows on his bony knees, and began his next rote speech on the minor risks involved with the procedure.

CHAPTER

Tory wasn't sure if it was intuition that something was wrong, or just her melancholy personality clinging to all of the worst possibilities, but something in the back of her mind still kept her from telling their families or friends that she was pregnant. She asked Barry to wait until the results on the CVS were back. At first, he had argued that she was borrowing trouble, that there was nothing to fear, but when he saw how serious she was, he had agreed.

Perhaps it was the fact that Barry had an autistic brother who had been totally disabled since birth that made her suspect the worst. She'd had the niggling fear of having a baby like Nathan with both of her other pregnancies, even though the doctors had assured her that autism was not genetic. But they had never considered her high risk before. The fact that they did now gave her unprecedented fears that she couldn't quite assuage.

The two weeks crept by like decades, and Tory tried to assure herself that thirty-five-year-old women had babies all the time. Women in their forties had children without problems.

Still, some distant worry in the back of her mind—as well as the nausea becoming a routine in her life—prevented her from abandoning herself entirely to the joys of pregnancy.

When the results were finally in, the doctor asked them to come in to the office. As the receptionist explained, he never gave these results over the phone. It was a game he played, Barry said. Carry the drama out as far as you can, make the couple sweat, so that when you finally found out everything was fine, you'd appreciate it all the more.

He wanted to throttle the doctor, and so did she. But they made the appointment and went in together, and sat stiffly in his office, waiting for the brittle man to come in and end the drama for them.

But the drama continued as he took his place behind his desk, frowned down at the file in front of him, clasped his skinny fingers, and brought his big, bloodshot eyes up to them. He looked as if he'd been up all night delivering a baby. She thought of offering him some eye drops.

Shoving his glasses up on his nose, he looked at the file again. "I'm afraid there's bad news."

Tory's heart crashed like a glass that had slipped from her hand. She thought for a moment that she hadn't heard him right, but then she was certain she had. She wanted to cry out that it was impossible, that there was nothing wrong with her baby. But she couldn't manage to find her voice.

"Bad news?" she heard Barry ask, as if the doctor had just uttered something so absurd that it couldn't be believed.

"Yes. The fetal cells showed an extra chromosome."

Both of them stared at him, stunned into silence, as several moments ticked by. Finally, Tory managed to swallow the lump in her throat. "What does that mean, Doctor?"

Dr. Grentwell took off his glasses and rubbed his eyes, then focused on Barry and Tory again. "It means that your baby has Down's Syndrome."

"No." The word came out unbidden, and Tory began to shake her head. She turned to Barry, her expression pleading for intervention. But it seemed that the life was slowly bleeding out of him as he focused on some invisible spot in the air.

"Are you sure this isn't a mistake?" he asked in an incredulous whisper.

The doctor opened his hands. "Unfortunately, yes. This test is conclusive."

"But . . . I've never had a history in my family," Tory said. "There's nobody in my family who's ever had a child with Down's Syndrome. And I'm still of child-bearing age." It was as if the right combination of facts could change the test's results. If the man just understood her history, her genes . . .

The doctor shook his head. "I wish I could tell you what causes this, but I can't. Sometimes it's genetic, sometimes it's age, sometimes it's completely inexplicable. All I know is that there are different degrees of illness, and some children with DS can function very well in life."

"And some of them can't." Barry's face was dull as he stared accusingly across the desk at the doctor.

"That's right," Dr. Grentwell said. "Some of them can't."

"Well, what can we do about it?" Tory demanded. "There must be something. Some kind of surgery. They do all kinds of things now. They can fix this, can't they?"

"No," he said, and she saw the compassion in his eyes, despite the fatigue and the thick glasses he had shoved back on. "There's no cure for this. No treatment in utero. Or even after birth, for that matter. We can treat any problems the baby may have, such as heart problems, eye problems, respiratory infections, gastrointestinal abnormalities. But we can't take away that extra chromosome. We can't change what the baby is."

Tears began to burn in her eyes, and rage rose to her face. "But that's not fair!" she said through her teeth. "They can do almost anything. Heart transplants, genetic mapping . . . *Cloning*, for heaven's sake! Why can't they do something about a little baby with one extra chromosome?"

"They just can't yet." She knew Dr. Grentwell, in his yellow shirt and blue seersucker pants, was unequipped to deal with choosing his wardrobe, much less handling an angry mother. They probably didn't teach emotional shock management in medical school.

"They just can't yet," she repeated through thin lips. She turned to Barry again, beginning to sob. "Barry, did you hear that?"

But Barry didn't move. He didn't look at her, didn't look at the doctor, didn't answer. With a deep crease on his pale brow, he stared straight ahead.

Dr. Grentwell shifted uncomfortably. "I know this is difficult for you."

She wanted to scream out that "difficult" was what you called your senior year of college. It was getting through thirty minutes of traffic in fifteen. It was waiting for the results of a CVS.

This wasn't difficult. It was cruel. It was agonizing. It was impossible.

He leaned forward, steepling his bony fingers. "There are some options we should discuss."

Her hope rose on delicate wings. Tory wiped her face with a trembling hand.

Barry seemed to snap out of his reverie, and looked at the doctor. "Options?" he asked. "Like what?"

"Well, families who find out they have children like this choose to do different things. Some choose to put the baby up for adoption. There are families who take these children."

"That's not a viable option," Tory said, as if he was insane.

"Another option," the doctor continued, "is putting them in a school after a few years."

"You mean to live?" she asked.

"Yes."

"That's not a school, it's an institution."

"There are some very good ones," he said. "They take excellent care of children with special needs, and they're a great relief to the families."

Those burning tears came faster. She grabbed a Kleenex from the doctor's desk and shoved it against her nose. How many grieving mothers had needed tissues from that box?

"What else?" Barry asked.

"The third option is to have the baby and make the best of it. A lot of families are enriched by a Down's Syndrome child. These children can be happy, and they bring joy into a lot of hearts. But they can be disruptive and have severe medical problems. It all depends on the family and the degree of retardation."

Barry bent forward, dropping his face into his hands. Tory knew he was thinking of his brother, sitting in a wheelchair all his life, staring out at something no one else could see.

"And then there's the fourth option," the doctor said quietly.

They both looked up at him, this time with dull, hopeless eyes, but Tory prayed that this one would be the miracle that would turn their fortune around, and change the destiny of this baby inside her.

"That fourth option, of course, is abortion."

"Abortion?" Tory spat the word out as if it had burned her mouth. "How can you even suggest such a thing? A man who delivers babies . . . I asked that before I came to you. They said you didn't do abortions—"

"I don't do them myself," he said, "but I could refer you to someone. I just thought it was important that I give you all of your options, because that is one of them."

Tory turned to Barry, horrified. "Did you *hear* that?"

Barry's eyes were still vacant. "Yeah, I heard it."

She got up and jerked her purse off of the floor. "I'm not going to abort my baby, Doctor, no matter what's wrong with it."

"That's certainly your choice."

Tory grabbed the door and started through it. Barry hesitated a moment, then slowly got up and followed her like a robot whose limbs were almost too heavy to operate.

Dr. Grentwell stopped them. "Wait. There is one more thing we didn't discuss."

Tory turned back, but Barry just stopped next to her, his hands in his pockets and his troubled eyes fixed on the wall.

"Do you want to know the sex of the baby?"

Somehow, it seemed vitally important to think of this child as a boy or a girl, and not as one of "these children." "Yes," she said, without asking Barry. "Tell me."

"It's a girl," he said.

Somehow, the announcement of that fact made the news seem more tragic. A baby girl, connected to her in the most intimate of ways. A baby girl that would be handicapped. She didn't know what to think or how to feel, so she surrendered herself to the numbness as she hurried from the building with her silent husband trudging behind her.

CHAPTER *Nine*

The numbness spread through Tory like an anesthetic going in through a vein, slowly branching out over her heart, reaching her heavy, pressured lungs, oozing into her arms and her hands and her fingers. The tears on her face dried as she walked out to their car, and she would not allow new ones to fall.

Tennessee wind whipped up from the Smokies, blowing her brown hair back from her face, but her eyes could not absorb the sight of the majestic autumn hills in the distance. She couldn't fathom the thought that there was more than pavement and metal farther down the road.

By habit, Barry opened her car door, and Tory slipped inside, quiet as he came around to the driver's side and got in beside her. They both sat for a moment, staring vacantly out at those hills, but seeing only the windshield that seemed to block their view.

"There has to be some mistake," Barry said, shattering the silence.

Tory looked over at him. "You think? Could they have gotten our lab tests mixed up with someone else's? Misread it or—"

"They must have."

"But he said it was conclusive."

He seemed stumped by that, and kept staring at the windshield. "Still, it has to be a mistake," he said. "God doesn't give you more than you can handle. But we—you and I—we're not cut out to have a child like this. You were going to write, and Brittany's just now in school."

"An hour ago I was going to put that on hold for the baby, and neither of us minded."

He swallowed hard. "But it's not like a normal, healthy baby," he said through his teeth. "We're not talking about putting things on hold for a while." His knuckles turned white on the steering wheel. "We're talking about giving them up entirely. We're talking disruptions to our family, neglect of our other children, a lifelong commitment to raise a child who will never grow up."

The numbness fled. And as the feeling began to seep back into her, tingling in her toes and her fingers, throbbing harder behind her eyes, she fought the tears threatening to drown her. She knew that Barry wasn't speaking out of ignorance. He was thinking of Nathan, the autistic skeleton in Barry's closet, who sat like a fixture in his mother's home, staring into space and ignoring holidays and birthdays, the births of nephews and nieces, the accomplishments of people who loved him.

Tory had been uncomfortable around Barry's brother since the first day he brought her home to meet his parents. She had always wondered whether to speak to him or pretend he wasn't there. Was there some part of his brain that heard and understood, even though his face never betrayed it? Did he quietly harbor annoyance and irritation at the people who talked to him like a baby, in a loud voice, as if he was hard of hearing? Or perhaps, he was. No one really knew for sure. He spent his days staring at some dimension no one else could see, moaning at discomfort, but sighing aloud at the modest pleasures, like the sun hitting his face as he sat in the prayer garden in his mother's backyard. And then there was the whistling that never ceased, except when he was asleep. Every day for years he had whistled songs over and over, whatever tune he heard last, whether it was on the radio or the television, or from his mother's fingers as she played the piano in the living room.

Tory stared at a spot on the windshield, and wondered if it was a chip hewn by a rock, or if it was a smashed bug or some debris that could be scraped off with her fingernail. Then she wondered why such a mundane thought would cross her mind at the worst hour of her life.

"At least we haven't told the kids," he said.

Again, the pain sliced through her heart. "I was so looking forward to telling them today."

He glanced over at her. "What did you think? That the doctor would tell us everything was fine? That there was nothing to worry about? You were the one who wanted to keep it secret."

"I don't know why. Part of me thought something could be wrong. The other part thought it would all be just fine. Pretty stupid, huh?"

He shrugged. "Never in a million years did I think . . ."

His voice cracked, and he let the thought hang. He started the car and pulled out of the parking lot, and they were silent as they drove home. Her mind raced through the conversation with the doctor, replaying every word, every line, reading hope and denial into every nuance of what he had said.

As they reached their own neighborhood and pulled into Cedar Circle, Tory prayed that neither Brenda nor Cathy, nor the Gonzales family who was living in Sylvia's house while she was gone, would see them coming. She couldn't talk to them now.

Suddenly, the injustice of it all overwhelmed her. Everyone else had healthy children. Everyone else could expect normalcy. In their pregnancies, they could expect nine months of joy and anticipation. They could go into labor and know that it would end well, hear that baby's cry, clutch it in their arms. They could have showers and celebrate and take the baby to grocery stores and not be plagued with the fear of someone staring or pointing, or simply not knowing what to say.

Barry pulled his car into the driveway, and Tory got out. She stood there, staring at the door, and suddenly realized that she couldn't go in and face the babysitter, or the children. Not yet.

"I need to be alone for a minute," she told him. "I'm just gonna go for a walk."

He didn't stop her. She knew that he, too, wanted some solitude to sort through his thoughts. But someone had to tend to the children, and she had asked first. As he went in, she launched out to the backyard, and crossed behind Sylvia's house. She hoped the Gonzaleses didn't come out and speak to her now. She didn't have the patience to listen through their accents and explain the customs that made so little sense to them. They were still so curious about the upcoming Halloween that they had a million questions even she couldn't answer.

She pulled her sweater more tightly around her and passed behind the empty stables where the horses used to be. Her anger increased with every step as she trod down the path through the woods that came out to a pasture on the other side. The wind was crisp as it whipped through the trees and blew up her hair around her face, cutting through her clothes and making her shiver. She walked faster as she went, each step making the anger coil up inside her like the red-hot heat in a radiator. Tears stung her eyes and burned down her face, and she wiped them away with cold hands as she kept walking.

She came out on the other side of the mountain, where she could see more of the hills that loomed behind their homes. A few thick clouds loomed over their peaks, and she looked up even farther above them, her eyes searching the sky for the God who watched over it all.

"It's not fair," she whispered between her teeth, but the words seemed to get lost on the wind. She lifted her chin, still searching the sky. "It's not fair!" she bit out, her voice undulating on the emotion that gave it wings. The wind whipped up harder, colder, against her face. She closed her hands into fists.

"Why!" she screamed louder this time, the word echoing out over the valley.

She fell to her knees in the grass and covered her face with both hands, weeping out her anguish as the wind rustled through her clothes and dried the tears as fast as they came. She was beginning to feel nauseous, just as she had this morning when she had awakened, and her head still throbbed with the pressure of her emotion. She wept and wailed, knowing that no one was nearby who could hear. No one would hear unless they lived downwind in the valley, and then they would only look up and know that someone was suffering somewhere. Maybe they would say a prayer for her.

She heard a cat squall a few feet behind her, and she turned around to see her pet scrabbling down a tree trunk with a baby bird in its mouth. She heard fluttering above her and looked up to see a small nest with baby chicks rustling around their mother, chattering and chirping about the feline that had almost done them all in.

She clapped her hands to startle the cat. "No, Babs! No!" But the cat wasn't intimidated.

The mother bird left the nest and flew down to the ground, a few feet away from the cat. Helpless, she watched as the cat dropped the chick into the grass. Tory got up and went to grab the cat, but he only darted away playfully, as if daring Tory to chase him. Tory turned back to the baby bird and saw that it wasn't moving.

All of her pain, all of her anguish, all of the wrenching anger that had gripped her heart and driven her to her knees, seemed suddenly to focus on that little wounded bird. The mother flew up to a low branch on the tree, but kept her eyes on the chick.

She picked up the little bird, cradling it in her hands, and realized it was dead. There was nothing she could do.

Tory wondered if mother birds grieved.

That inexpressible sadness sucked her under again, and she laid the chick back down and turned away from the mother. They had no control, either of them. Their children were vulnerable to terrible things, and there was absolutely nothing they could do. Of all the jobs in the world, she thought, motherhood had to be the most frightening.

Despairing that inside her a wounded baby grew, she wailed. She put her hands over her stomach. She was just as pregnant now as she had been this morning before she'd known what kind of child she was carrying, just as pregnant as she'd been two and a half weeks ago when she'd read that pregnancy test. This baby was as real as Brittany or Spencer had ever been, and just as much hers. It was as real as that dead baby bird on the ground.

But God knew about the baby bird, she realized suddenly. He knew about the mother bird, still watching hopefully, helplessly, from her perch. He knew about the baby Tory was carrying.

She sat back on the grass and looked up at those clouds again. She felt a raindrop hit her cheek, her nose, her eyelid. In seconds, it was raining on her and around her, a soft warning of the storm to come. But she had the sense that she wasn't alone.

"My baby," she whispered, weeping for the child and all the heartache that might come to her in her life, for all the things she would never have and all the things she would miss. For all the things she would never understand.

There was so much uncertainty, she thought. So much she wouldn't know until the baby came and they saw how severe the retardation was. Until then, there was only one thing that was certain. This baby would be a part of her family, the little sister of Brittany and Spencer, the third and youngest child with the Sullivan name. Somehow, God would give Tory the grace to endure. This was her child. It was God's child, too.

She breathed in a deep, cleansing breath and got back to her feet, dusted her pants off, and let the rain drizzle through her hair and wash her face. But it didn't wash the grief away. It still weighed her down, bending her and threatening to break her.

Slowly, Tory started back up the path toward Cedar Circle, knowing her "why" would not be answered now. Sometimes there was no clarity, no sense to be made. Sometimes one just had to trudge through, trusting that there would be joy again on the other side.

When the clouds passed, the rain would stop. Life would be cleansed and fed and sustained. Mothers would patch their hearts back together and move on, doing what had to be done. She would endure these rains somehow.

CHAPTER

The rains were pouring harder in León, Nicaragua, as a huge hurricane swirled up from the Pacific. Sylvia had seen Internet reports that it had already reached deadly force. Unless it turned in another direction, it was headed straight for their coast.

She stood just outside her open front door under the eaves of their house, watching the rain pound down and listening to the thunder. Because of the hard rain, business at the clinic had slacked off for the day, and Harry had been trying to update the files he kept on his patients. Sylvia had wanted to go out and visit some of his sicker patients, but there were areas of the city that were already flooding, and she feared that her car would get stalled and she wouldn't be able to get back. That sense of having no purpose assaulted her again, and she longed for the days when she had two children at home, and didn't have one moment to herself. Those moments had fled so quickly. And she longed for her friends in Cedar Circle. She remembered sitting on Brenda's porch on rainy nights, laughing and talking as Tory grew and Cathy learned and Brenda taught. Sylvia had been the mother figure of the bunch, whether she'd wanted to play that role or not. But she had been older than the others, and already had her child-rearing work behind her. That made her an expert.

Funny, she didn't feel like an expert in anything now.

She heard Harry's footsteps on the parquet floor behind her and looked over her shoulder. He began to hum a tune, one she couldn't identify, and he took her hand and swung her around with a flourish. "Rain always makes me want to dance," he said.

She laughed as he began to move across the floor with her, then dipped her, and pretended he was going to drop her. "Harry!" she cried. He pulled her up again, then crushed her against him and spun around. Harry always knew how to make her laugh. She pressed her face against his neck and listened to his deep humming. She loved his voice. It was so strong and gentle, so full of compassion and joy.

He spun her and dipped her again. Holding her frozen in that dip, he asked, "So tell me why a good-looking woman would be staring out into the rain with a sad look on her face."

The sad look was gone, and she grinned up at him. "You're going to drop me, aren't you?"

"Not until you tell me what was on your mind."

"*Then* you're going to drop me?"

He laughed and pulled her up again with an exaggerated flourish, then let her go. She slid her arms around his waist and kissed his chin. He pushed the hair back from her cheek and gave her the understanding look that had helped her through so many trials. "Come on. What's wrong?"

"Just homesick," she said. "Remembering."

He slid his arms around her and held her tight. "We have great memories, don't we? And many more to come."

"Yeah. But I'm having trouble not knowing what those future memories are going to look like. What's God going to do with me here?"

"He's going to use you to advance his kingdom. The same thing he's done with you for most of your life."

"I know, but this . . . this is so concentrated. I feel like I have to do something quickly, or it's not worth our coming. Days like today, with all the rain, I feel kind of helpless."

"Well, if that hurricane hits, we're all going to feel helpless. There'll be lots of work to do. Let's take advantage of this calm before the storm. God doesn't want us to use it feeding depression."

She smiled up at him. "Then what does he want us to do with it?"

He grinned in that amazing way he had that reminded her why she had married him. "He wants us to dance," he said.

And as he began to hum again, they danced to the sound of rain just outside their door, and thunder cracking around them.

CHAPTER  Eleven

The lights were off in Barry's office. He had come in today and tried to do his work, but it was difficult when he hadn't slept all night. The doctor's words yesterday had plagued him all night, and the wrenching despair in his heart rendered him unable to think or do anything except dwell on the inevitable. Stripes of brightness from the sun came in from the slats in the closed blinds, providing the only light in the room, for darkness had seemed more appropriate. He sat in the shadows, staring at the potted plant that his secretary kept watered, while his mind saw something else entirely.

He was ten years old, sitting on the stage of his elementary school, nervous about his first violin solo. It wasn't much, just a few bars of Beethoven's "Ode to Joy," but he never liked to do things poorly, and he wasn't sure he had practiced enough. He remembered looking out into the audience from that dusty stage with its faded curtains and seeing his parents sitting on the back row with his brother Nathan propped up in his wheelchair.

Nathan was whistling along with the strings after hearing the first chorus, and Barry remembered the sick, tight feeling that clawed at his stomach as the song ended.

But Nathan's whistling didn't.

Barry had fixed his eyes on his teacher, praying that she would quickly start them in the next song. He pretended he didn't hear his brother's loud, proud rendition of the song, shrilling out over the crowd. From the corner of his eye, he saw the heads beginning to turn, seeking out whatever rude soul was interrupting the silence between numbers. A few people chuckled, others shushed him, and he saw his teacher turn from the small orchestra and look to see who was whistling.

He decided right then and there that he would never play an instrument again, never give his parents cause to attend a concert and drag his brother with them.

Somehow, he had gotten through the song, but there was no longer joy in it, for he knew that the minute the song ended again, Nathan would be whistling it until someone distracted him with another tune. Guilt surged through him that he couldn't just smile, brag that that was his brother, and admit how funny it was that he always whistled the last tune he heard. He shouldn't be ashamed of the boy who had no choice in who he was or how he'd turned out. Barry should be happy that *he* was whole and healthy, that he could think and play violin, that he could sit up here with a solo and show his parents what it was like to have one child who could learn.

But he had been ashamed that day, the last day he'd ever played his violin.

Someone knocked on his office door, and he jumped and turned in his chair as they opened the door. Linda Holland from marketing stuck her head in. "Barry? I thought you weren't in here. It's dark."

"I had a headache," he said. "The light was hurting my eyes."

She came tentatively into the room and set a report down on his desk. Her red hair looked as if she'd combed it in the car that morning. Rumpled curls cascaded around her face, and he wondered if she'd taken the rollers out and left them on the seat while she drove. Her dress looked wrinkled as if she'd thrown it on in haste without ironing it, and she walked in stocking feet. He wondered where she'd left her shoes.

"I have some Tylenol if you want it," she said, regarding him with concern.

"That's all right. I'll be fine."

"Okay." She kept looking at him as if he had a sign on his forehead that said his life was falling apart. "Here's the report on the Hayes account." She squinted in the darkness. "Are you sure you're okay?"

"Yeah." He got up, rubbing his forehead, and looked at his watch. "I'm gonna take an early lunch. I'll read the report when I get back."

She preceded him out of the office. "If you decide you need that Tylenol . . ."

He nodded. "Thanks." He stepped into the light, squinting, and didn't meet her eyes. His secretary, in the cubicle not far from his office, looked up to see where he was going. He mouthed that he was going to lunch, and she frowned at the early hour. But he didn't care. He had to get out of here.

He drove in silence across town, then got on the highway and followed it to the next little town, where his mother lived with his brother. His father had died over two years ago, and he felt a surge of guilt that he hadn't done more to help his mother since that time. Her house needed painting and the porch steps were in need of repair.

He pulled into the driveway and saw that her car was home. He knocked on the kitchen door to warn her that he was coming, then pushed the door open and stepped inside.

"Barry!" she said, hurrying across the floor to greet him. "What are you doing here?"

He smiled and leaned down to kiss his mother's cheek. "Hey, Mama. I was in the area and thought I'd stop in and fix a sandwich."

"In the area?" she asked. "Way out here?"

When he evaded the question, she added, "We have ham and turkey slices and peanut butter and jelly." Her face glowed at the sight of him. "Help yourself. I was just feeding Nathan."

He looked through the door. "Where is he?"

"Out in the garden," she said. "It's a beautiful day, so I'm feeding him out there."

He glanced out the window, saw Nathan, taller than he but so scrawny that he looked like his bones would break if he lifted an arm, propped in his wheelchair with his head held up by a brace at the back. He supposed his brother's low weight was a blessing, enabling his strong mother to lift him. "Want me to feed him?" he asked.

"He'd like that," his mother said, handing him the bowl and the spoon she held in her hand. "I'll fix you a sandwich while you do."

He took the bowl of mashed food and went outside to his brother. Nathan was whistling the theme song to "Wheel of Fortune," and Barry knew he'd probably heard it playing on the television just inside the door. "Hey, Nathan," he said as he pulled up a lawn chair next to the wheelchair and sat down.

Nathan gave no acknowledgment that he was there, just kept whistling and staring into the flowers.

"So let's see what you got here today," he said, looking into the bowl. "Ummm. Egg, banana, milk, cereal." It was no surprise. Nathan had that for every meal, for as far back as Barry could remember. Everything else he spat out, making a mess that was unpleasant for even his mother to clean up.

He dipped out some of the food, spooned it into his brother's mouth, and the whistling stopped. As he fed him, he tried to picture Tory in his mother's place, with a thirty-five-year-old bigger than she was, who still needed his diapers changed and had to be fed. He tried to picture Spencer and Brittany feeding him, grown with children of their own, remembering back on their music recitals and the shame that they'd had to repent of time and time again.

He let his brother chew in the messy way he had, then wiped his face with the napkin tied like a bib around Nathan's neck. Nathan sat quietly, waiting for the next bite, his eyes fixed on the green azalea bushes as if waiting for them to bloom. It would be months before they would, Barry thought, but Nathan would keep staring.

As he had a million times before, Barry looked into those vacant eyes and wondered if, somewhere behind them, there was a normal man in there, trapped and waiting to be freed. He pictured his brother in heaven, laughing eyes meeting his for the first time, his arm rearing back to throw a football across a meadow that he didn't need a wheelchair to cross.

He took the wheelchair's arm, unlocked one side, and turned Nathan's chair until they were face-to-face. He leaned forward, nose to nose with his brother, staring into Nathan's eyes as he'd done every day as a boy, trying to make their eyes connect just because Nathan had nowhere else to look. He tried to imagine that Nathan saw him, knew him, that there was a flicker or a hint of intelligence in his head. "You're smarter and better looking than any of us, aren't you, buddy?" Barry asked in a low voice. "Deep down in there, you're really getting it all, aren't you?"

Nathan began to whistle "Wheel of Fortune" again, and Barry leaned back. Nathan's skin was tightly drawn over his face, but he had the same dark hair that Barry had, the same blue eyes, the same mouth. At first glance, no one would suspect the vacancy there. But upon closer scrutiny, one could see the dull stare in his eyes and the slack expression on his face. Barry wondered if the baby Tory was carrying would look like Nathan.

His eyes filled with tears. "If you'd had a choice to be here, would you?" he asked softly, wishing just once his brother would stop whistling and look into his eyes, and answer a simple yes or no. Once would be enough.

But he just kept whistling and staring through Barry's head, looking at something just on the other side . . . something that wasn't even there.

Barry remembered the bowl in his hand, and dipped out another spoonful. His mother came out with a plate that had a sandwich and a pickle, a pile of potato chips on the side. She stopped just over him and saw the red rims of his eyes. "Barry? What's wrong?"

He looked up at her and smiled. "Nothing, Mama." He got up and offered her his chair, and got another one that was folded up against the house.

"You look like something's bothering you," she said, sitting down but not taking her eyes from him. "Why did you really come by today?"

He sat down and let her trade his plate for Nathan's bowl. "I don't know. Just wanted to see you guys, I guess."

"Everything all right at home?"

He thought of telling her about the pregnancy, the news that had rocked him almost to Kentucky and back, the sick, deep, drowning feeling that kept destroying any concentration he might have had. "Yes, ma'am. Just fine."

She sighed and spooned Nathan another mouthful. "Nothing on your mind, then? Nothing at all?"

"No, ma'am." He leaned back in his chair and took a bite of his sandwich without looking to see what she'd made. When he bit into it, he noted that it was ham. It felt tasteless and rubbery in his mouth. He hadn't had an appetite since they'd left the doctor's office yesterday. He set the sandwich down and watched his mother feed his brother, watched her wipe his chin. "Mama, do you ever get tired?"

"'Course I do."

"Of taking care of Nathan, I mean."

She shot him a look that was full of words. "He's my son. Just like you. Who else would take care of him?"

"But do you get tired?" he asked again. It was suddenly very important for him to hear his mother say it straight out.

She looked down at the food in the bowl and stirred it up with the spoon. "I worry," she said. "About what will happen to him if anything happens to me." She shot him a look. "Is that what this is about? Have you been thinking what would happen if I passed on?"

The thought had never occurred to him. "No, I just wondered. Most mothers have an end to it, somewhere down the road. Their kids grow up and move out and have kids of their own. They get to go on vacations and piddle around the house and spoil their grandchildren. Your job with Nathan never ends."

She was quiet as she fed Nathan another spoonful, and Barry wondered for a moment if he'd offended her.

"I was just thinking about that," he said quietly. "Realizing how much of your life you've given to Nathan."

She smiled then and looked up at Barry with perfect peace in her eyes. "God chooses our path, honey. I'm just walkin' mine. And it's fine by me."

His eyes filled with tears again, and he nodded, suddenly unable to take another bite. He was afraid his lips would start that twitching again, that his heart would push up in his chest and into his throat, that he wouldn't be able to hide Tory's pregnancy on his face anymore. Quickly, he looked at his watch and got up. "Oops. Got to get back to the office."

"But you didn't eat."

"I'll take it with me, Mama. Thank you for making it."

She got to her feet. "I'm glad you came by, darlin'. I don't see you enough. Give Spencer and Brittany a kiss for me. Tory, too."

"I will." He kissed her cheek, then patted Nathan's knee, and darted back through the house. "Bye, Mama," he yelled behind him before she could see his eyes reddening again.

He heard her say good-bye as he rushed back out to his car.

CHAPTER *Twelve*

Brenda had never been so glad to see midnight come in her life. The noisy room was somehow lonely, full of people too busy to talk to each other, and the last few phone calls she'd had to make that evening had been excruciating. She had watched the hands on the clock constantly as she listened to people hanging up in her face, telling her they weren't interested, or yelling at her for calling so late.

Because she hadn't quite made her quota of sales for the night, the night supervisor had chewed her out and warned her that her pay would be docked if she didn't do better the following night.

She had cried all the way home.

When she pulled into her driveway, she found a tissue and wiped her eyes so David wouldn't know how upset she was. Last night, her first night on the job, she had come in with a huge smile and let him think that she'd loved it. Tonight, she feared she wouldn't be able to pull that off.

When she got inside, she saw that David was waiting up—or trying to. He had fallen asleep in his chair with the television on. She smiled and went to him, pressed a kiss on his eyelids, and gently woke him.

He looked up at her.

"I'm home," she said. "You didn't have to wait up."

"I missed you," he said. He rubbed his eyes. "How was it?"

"Good," she said. "Did the kids get to bed all right?"

"Yeah," he said. "A little late. Leah and Rachel had homework in every subject. And Daniel had to finish his project. Oh, and Joseph had one of his mood swings. I went in his room and found him crying in bed."

"Crying? What did he say?"

"He said he didn't know what was wrong. And I don't think he did. It's the medicine, you know."

"Yeah, it does that." She dropped down on the couch, feeling weary to her bones. "But he's healthy, David. A few mood swings are a small price to pay."

"You said it," David said. He got up and reached for her hand. "Come on, let's go to bed. Morning'll be here before you know it."

She hung onto that promise as she crawled into bed next to him moments later. Morning would come. She was certain of it. She could endure a little darkness until it did.

CHAPTER
Thirteen

Sylvia Bryan rubbed her aching neck as she walked through the old Nicaraguan school that Jim, their pastor, and Harry had secured to use as a storm shelter. The structure wasn't any stronger than some of these families' homes, but it stood at the center of León, away from the hills and volcano that threatened to bury them in mud slides.

Still, the tropical winds whistled and moaned against the building, warning of the hurricane that was just hours away from León. Internet news was reporting millions of dollars in damage, and hundreds of lives lost in the places already hit.

Already, dozens of families had come to spend the night, and the sound of crying babies, chattering children, and stern voices of parents echoed in the building. In one of the classrooms, Harry offered medical care to those who had been injured trying to get from their homes as flood waters rose. Other medical missionaries occupied different classrooms, but the majority of their staff had gone out to warn citizens of the coming hurricane and urge evacuation.

Despite all the activity and the worries about what they faced, Sylvia couldn't get Tory off her mind. Something was wrong. Through e-mail, Brenda had mentioned Tory's nausea. In another e-mail, Cathy expressed concern that Tory seemed to be avoiding them. According to Spencer and Brittany, whom Cathy had seen playing outside, their mother was still battling her illness.

Brenda had tried taking her a casserole, but Tory hadn't answered the door. Once, Brenda had waylaid Barry when he'd driven home from work. She had written that Barry looked tired and red-eyed, and had promised her that Tory was fine.

She hated not being there. Something was definitely wrong. The worst things had been running through her mind all day. Did Tory have cancer? Was she dying? Why would she and Barry be keeping it a secret from their closest friends?

Harry met her in the hall as she came from the gym. "Have you checked the Internet news lately? The wind is getting stronger, and a family just came in talking about a tornado that hit their street. It's getting bad out there."

"I was going to check," she said. "Was anyone injured in the tornado?"

"They don't know," Harry said. "Their house wasn't hit, but they saw the tornado knocking down houses up the hill from them. The kids are terrified. Go check the weather, and then maybe you can come help calm these little ones down."

She nodded and hurried into the classroom where they had set up the laptop, complete with extra batteries in case the electricity went out. She checked the location of the hurricane, saw that it was still headed this way. There were reports of five tornadoes down the coast of Nicaragua and Costa Rica already, and more were expected. Even here, they were not safe.

Her hands were shaking as she took them off the keyboard and covered her face. "Lord, I prayed for purpose," she whispered. "I think you're about to answer that prayer, aren't you?" She sighed and opened her eyes and went to the window to look out. She wondered if they should board this up. In just a few hours, the winds could shatter the glass.

"Help us, Lord," she whispered. "Go with us through this storm. Use it to draw these people to you." Then her mind jolted back to Tory again, and she wondered if the Holy Spirit was prompting her to pray for her friend. What kind of storm was Tory riding out?

She bowed her head and prayed for her friend, then remembered the children that needed calming in the shelter. She went to turn off the computer, but before she did, checked her e-mail one more time. There was still nothing from Tory, despite all the e-mails Sylvia had sent her asking how she was.

She hit "compose," then typed in Tory's e-mail address.

> *Okay, what gives, Tory? Something's wrong; I know it is. You can't hide it from me. Please write back and tell me if you're sick or your marriage is on the rocks or you're just too busy to answer. I'm waiting for a hurricane to hit, and there are desperate, frightened people all around me, but I can't quit thinking about you. For the sake of a nervous friend, come clean, okay?*
>
> *I'll be saying a prayer for you, honey, because whatever's wrong, God can fix it.*
>
> *Love,*
> *Sylvia*

She hit "send," then dropped her face into her hands and prayed once more for the safety of the people of León as this hurricane tore through their city, and for the spiritual protection of the families in Cedar Circle, where her heart longed to be.

CHAPTER
Fourteen

When Barry suggested they get a babysitter and go out to dinner, Tory hadn't been very enthusiastic. She didn't feel they had much to celebrate, especially since Barry had been brooding worse than she. But when he had taken it on himself to ask Cathy's daughter Annie to baby-sit, Tory felt she had to go.

She took special care with her looks that night, pulling her hair up and applying retouch to hide the red circles under her eyes. But she didn't feel pretty. Her husband's eyes were dull as he looked at her. They had been dull ever since that day they'd sat in Dr. Grentwell's office and learned how their lives were about to change.

They got to the restaurant and were seated at a quiet table, but still, he couldn't seem to meet her eyes, couldn't seem to muster a smile or reach for her hand. Her heart ached for the struggle he was having with the news of their child, and she began to wonder why he had wanted to come.

Then she remembered Cathy's story of the night her husband had asked for a divorce. She had known there were problems, had even suspected there was another woman, but he had consistently denied it. Then the night came when he had taken her out to a nice restaurant, had held her hand and danced with her. And then he had offered the punch line.

Over candlelight and to the romantic piano music, he had asked for a divorce.

Had Barry brought her here to drop some equally explosive bomb?

They ate in silence, and finally, Tory reached for his hand across the table. His eyes met hers. "Why did you bring me here, Barry?" she asked. "Neither of us is really in the mood for this."

He set his fork down and leaned back in his chair, still holding her hand. "We have to talk, Tory."

"Okay. Let's talk."

He swallowed and looked down at his food, as if drawing his words from the peas on his plate. "I've been thinking a lot the last few days," he said.

"So have I."

"I've been thinking about the things the doctor said. About the options."

She frowned, trying to chart where this was going. "There's really only one option," she said.

Again, his gaze drifted away. He was having trouble looking at her. She let go of his hand and leaned forward on the table. "Barry?"

Candlelight flickered between them, dancing on his face with wobbling uncertainty. He looked away, casting half of his face in shadow. "We have to talk about this," he said again.

"About what?" she asked. "The options? What do you mean? Giving the baby up for adoption? Institutionalizing her? Abortion?"

His mouth trembled as he tried to hold back his emotions. "I've been through it all," he said. "I've turned it all over in my mind, and I've thought a lot about Nathan."

She had known his brother would play into this somehow, so she wasn't surprised. "I knew you'd be thinking about Nathan. And you're right to. I guess it's a situation that's real similar."

"I look back sometimes and I wonder what would have been different about my family—would it have worked better, would I have been a healthier human being, would things have been different, if Nathan had never been born?"

She wanted to deny that, to tell him to stop thinking it, that Nathan *had* been born and there was no point in thinking such things, but she wanted him to talk, so she stayed quiet and listened.

"His life is one of imprisonment," he said. "He was born in a prison and he's in a prison today. He's locked in the bonds of that wheelchair, and he can't think, he can't learn, he can't communicate, he can't contribute."

She looked down at the linen tablecloth, rubbed it with the tip of her finger, and did valiant battle with the tears in her eyes.

"Yet my mother is . . . and has always been . . . a slave to him. She will be until the day she dies. And then who do you think will take over the care of Nathan?"

Her gaze came slowly up.

"Us, that's who," he said. "We'll have to care for Nathan for the rest of his life, and then we'll be the ones who are slaves to him. Or we'll put him in an institution and deal with the guilt and the grief of letting strangers care for him. One way or another, *we'll* be in bondage then."

She frowned and tried to take that in. "I hadn't ever thought of our having to take over the care of Nathan."

"That's because I try not to think of it," he said. "No one has ever asked me if I would take him. But he's family, and I'll be the one responsible."

"But your mother is young," she said. "She's healthy. She's not going anywhere."

His eyes were brimming, and he swallowed hard. "My point is that this is a lifelong commitment, not just for them, but for me, too. And I look at him and I search for something in his eyes, some awareness, something that tells me that his life has been worthwhile. But I don't think it has." His voice broke off, and he rubbed his jaw, then clenched his hand into a fist and dropped his forehead on it. She waited, giving him time to go on. After a moment, he found his voice again. "He's sat there in his own little world for all these years, never once knowing what it felt like to love, never knowing laughter, never thinking about the past or the future or even the present. Just sitting there in that chair, day after day, hour after hour, minute after minute, just staring out into space. Who knows what he sees, what he hears, what he can think?"

"He doesn't have Down's Syndrome," she cut in. "He's not like our baby."

"No, but it's similar. His brain doesn't function normally, and neither will this child's."

She still couldn't see where he was going with this. He wasn't just venting. He was leading up to something. Something she wouldn't want to hear. "So what are you saying?"

His eyelashes were wet, and he rubbed his eyes harshly. "I'm thinking that I couldn't live with myself if we institutionalized our baby."

She breathed out a sigh of relief. "Good. I'm with you so far."

"And I'm thinking that giving it up for adoption—"

"Her," she said.

"What?"

"Not it. Her."

"Oh, yeah." He seemed to struggle with the pronoun, then started again. "Giving the baby up for adoption is something else I probably couldn't live with. The shame of it, for one thing. Letting everyone in the world know that we didn't have what it took to bring up our own baby. That we would give it to perfect strangers to take into their home." He shook his head. "I just don't think I could do that."

"Neither do I," she said. "That's just not an option for me."

He nodded in agreement, then leaned on the table, meeting her eyes. "That leaves the third option."

Her eyes narrowed as she tried to understand what he meant. "Well, of course. Raising the baby ourselves."

He shook his head. "No, that's not the option I meant."

She stared at him as his words sank in. "What *did* you mean?"

He looked down at the uneaten food on his plate. She saw a tear fall into his potatoes. The realization dawned slowly over her.

"Not abortion," she whispered.

His silence spoke volumes.

She felt her face reddening, her temples throbbing, her eyes stinging. "Barry, you don't believe in abortion. Neither do I. Especially not our own child—"

"Just listen," he said. "Try to put your emotions aside and just listen . . ."

She couldn't believe he could sit there and bring up the subject of killing their own child, and tell her not to get emotional. But she grew quiet, hoping he would correct her, tell her that was not what he meant at all, that he could never consider that.

"I was thinking . . . about what I said the first day we found out about it . . . when I said it must be a mistake."

She gaped at him, her mouth slightly open.

"And I started to realize that maybe sometimes God even makes a mistake."

She couldn't believe her ears. Her face twisted as she got out the words. "God does not make mistakes, Barry. This baby I'm carrying is not a mistake."

"He gave us the technology for a reason," Barry said. "I don't think it was for convenience or so that teenaged moms wouldn't have to suffer the consequences of their actions." He leaned in, lowering his voice but intent on making his point. "Maybe he gave it to us so that people who are going to have crummy lives don't have to be born in bondage."

Somewhere, deep within her, she felt the pain of rejection and betrayal rising up inside her like a thick, smothering fluid designed to do her in. "You're really suggesting . . . we abort this baby?" she asked through stiff lips.

His eyes were filled with tears, and his mouth still trembled. "No one has to know," he said. "We can say it's a miscarriage. It happens all the time with babies who have things wrong with them. The mothers miscarry, and nobody blames anybody."

"But I haven't miscarried."

"Think of it as that," he told her. "Not an abortion. I mean, we wouldn't have to go to an abortion clinic or anything. We could just go to the hospital and take care of it . . ."

The horror of his suggestion pressed the breath out of her. "You *are* suggesting we abort our baby!" The words rang inside her ears, bounced and echoed through her brain.

"I'm suggesting that we love this child enough to save it from a life of misery."

Rage gripped her heart. "Why do you keep calling her 'it'?" she demanded. "Are you trying to convince yourself that this is a blob of tissue and not a human life?"

"No, of course not."

She breathed in a sob and clutched her head in both hands. The waiter came to the table, saw her condition, then quickly retreated. "Then how can you justify this?" she asked. "How? I've been reading about children with Down's Syndrome. They don't have lives of misery. They may not be as aware as we are of the ugliness and the stuff that goes on from day to day. Maybe a lot goes over their heads. But they're not miserable, not unless we make them that way."

"I'm speaking from experience," Barry said, getting as angry as she. "You don't know. To you, this is a challenge, and you think you're up for it, but you're not. I've been there, Tory. I've been where Brittany and Spencer are. I've been the neglected one because my brother needed more attention than I did. I've been the one who looked for my parents at ball games and they didn't show up because Nathan was having a bad day. I've been the one who was humiliated at a school play because Nathan chose that moment to start moaning in the middle of the auditorium. I never went on a family vacation because we couldn't leave Nathan with anybody, and we certainly couldn't take him with us."

"But a child with Down's Syndrome won't necessarily be confined to a wheelchair. Most of them aren't. They can walk; they can learn. But even if they couldn't, even if we had one like Nathan, I still couldn't consider the possibility—"

"You *have* to consider it," Barry said, slamming his fist into his hand. "I'm one of the parents. This is not just your decision. It's mine, too. It affects the rest of my life. You have to consider our other two children."

"And you have to consider our third one," she said through her teeth. "Our little girl, who hasn't done anything to deserve this."

"You're right," Barry cut in. "She didn't ask to be born. That's what they all say. 'I didn't ask to be born.' So she doesn't have to be."

Tory gaped at him, incredulous. "What was all that pro-life stuff about? You sent letters to Congress when they were voting on the partial birth abortion ban. You go to pro-life rallies every year. Who *are* you?"

That seemed to break him. He set his elbows on the table and covered his face with both hands. His shoulders shook with the force of his despair. Finally, he moved his hands. "This decision . . . is . . . *unspeakable* to me. It's one of the worst things I can think of doing." He covered his mouth and looked at his plate again. "But I've got to tell you, Tory, there is something worse, and that something worse is allowing another baby like Nathan to come into the world and be trapped in bondage, and never be able to contribute one thing to this world."

She thought of blowing out the candle so the diners around them wouldn't see their tears. But she couldn't move, except to shake her head.

"Tory, listen to me. I know this is hard for you. But it's just a miscarriage. Nothing but a miscarriage. We'll grieve our baby's loss, we'll be sad, we may never get over it, but it's a whole lot better than being trapped for the rest of our lives."

"God doesn't create life that isn't supposed to be here," she said again. "I believe that."

"Tory, this isn't something that can be patched up, that a mother's kiss can fix."

"I won't do it," she said through stiff lips. "I'm sorry, Barry, but I will not do it."

Angrily, he swiped the tears from his own face. "You won't even consider it? What about my wishes, Tory? What about my say in all of this?"

"If you want to kill our baby," she said, "then you don't get a say." With that, she shoved back her chair and headed out of the restaurant. She reached the parking lot and looked around for their car, not knowing whether to call a cab or get in the car and drive home without Barry.

He caught up to her in seconds. "Tory, don't you walk out on me!"

"I'm going home, Barry." The tears wouldn't stop coming.

Barry got ahead of her and opened her door.

He got in on the other side, started the car, but couldn't drive. He began to weep over the steering wheel. "We've already lost our baby, Tory," he cried. "The baby that we thought was coming, the baby we expected . . . It's gone. And instead, we have this choice."

"My baby is not a choice," she bit out. "It's not a right, and it's not a blob. This is a *child*."

"Tory, all we have is a bunch of horrible choices, and I'm just trying to choose the one that is least bad. Abortion is the least of the evils I have to choose from."

"The birth of this baby will not be an evil," she yelled. "She's a human being. She may not be as smart as you, she may not be as productive . . ." Contempt rolled off her tongue with the word. "Barry, I hate this, too! But when you can't figure things out for yourself, you don't choose between evils! You go back to God and you let him tell you what to do. If God wants us to lose this baby, then I *will* have a miscarriage, but if he doesn't, then this baby was meant to be in our family. My child . . ."

"It's my child, too," Barry said.

"No, it isn't." She slammed her hand on the dashboard. "Not if you could do this. Not if you could even suggest it. It's not a choice, Barry, it's a sin. A heinous, horrible sin. The worst one I can think of."

"There are times when we have to sin," he said. "I would steal bread to feed my children. And in a way, that's what I'm doing now."

"Stealing bread to feed your children?" she repeated, incredulous. "You can turn this into some noble thing that you're doing for our family?"

"You don't understand! You're not even trying to understand. I've been there; I know what it's like. You don't."

"So I don't," she said. "So what? Your mother had never done it before Nathan came along."

"You're not up to this, Tory. I know you."

"And I know me, too," she said. "I know that I'm selfish and resentful and I know that sometimes I put other things ahead of my family. I know that I want to be a writer. I know *all* that! But I'll have to work on this, I'll have to change, and maybe God gave us this baby so I would. Maybe he did so *you* would. Maybe there's good to be seen here somewhere. We can't just assume there's not!"

He started driving, silent as he navigated the streets home. She was silent, too, except for the sound of her crying. When they pulled into Cedar Circle and into their own driveway, they sat there for a moment before going in.

"Tory, I know what a shock it's been for you to hear me say this tonight," he said. "All I ask is that you give it a few days and consider it—"

"No," she said. "I won't."

"I'm the leader of this family," he said. "I'm responsible for it, I have to protect it, and I have to support it. You have to at least consider my wishes."

She gave a bitter laugh. "So you're using the submission card? Barry, I'll submit to you on everything except things that go against God's will. I will *not* do something that is heinous and awful. If I did this I could never live with myself. It would ruin my life, just like I believe it ruins the life of every woman who does it. I'm gonna follow God instead of you."

"How do you know that I'm not listening to God, too?" he yelled. "How do you *know* that I haven't talked to him about this, that this isn't *exactly* the answer he gave me?"

"Because the answers God gives never include sin. And if you can convince yourself that abortion is not a sin, then you're not the man I thought you were at all." With that, she got out of the car and stormed across the yard, unwilling to face Annie's teenaged chatter or the kids who might still be up. Barry would have to do that, she thought. Let him explain why their mother was distraught.

She went to the swing in the back of their yard, sat down, and doubled over, pressing her hands against her face. As softly as she could, she sobbed into them, all the injustice and crushing disappointment of her husband's answer to this crisis falling over her like an avalanche.

CHAPTER

Fifteen

The woman who had run into the school barefoot and covered with mud was hysterical, shouting and wailing out rapid-fire Spanish too fast for Sylvia to understand. Harry ran from the room he'd set up as an examining room and called across the noisy gymnasium for Jim.

The bilingual pastor broke free of the people he was attending to and hurried to the woman's side. He barked out Spanish to her, but didn't get much out before she began to rant and rave again, pointing to the door and toward the Cerro Negro volcano whose mud slides had brought hundreds of people here for help.

Jim looked weary from all the work so far. They had been taking people in and trying to feed them and find places for them to sleep, while the hurricane grew closer.

She saw Jim's face twist with emotion, and he turned back to them. "She says she sent her oldest child to get an elderly neighbor to come ride the storm out with them, but he never came back. She decided to leave her four other children and go looking for him, but . . ." His voice broke off, and the woman began chattering again. "She . . . says a mud slide buried her house while she was gone. Her four children . . ." He rubbed his mouth. "She's been trying to get to them, but some of the rescue workers pulled her away and brought her here."

Sylvia reached for the mud-covered woman and pulled her into her arms. The woman wept and wailed against her, clinging as if she knew instinctively that this was another mother who would know the pain.

"The child she went looking for?" Harry asked Jim.

Jim shook his head. "She hasn't found him, either. Harry, he was probably buried before she went looking for him. That volcano is nothing but sand. When it rains like this . . ."

"Well . . . should we go there and try to dig them out? See if there's some way they lived?"

"There's no possible way," he said. "Besides, there'll be more mud slides as the hurricane gets closer. Even after it's gone. We can't go near it."

The woman cried and groaned in agony, stomping her foot and pulling at her mud-caked hair.

Dear God, how do I comfort her? Sylvia prayed. It was too much. She couldn't do it.

She took the woman to a cot and sat down with her. She and Harry prayed over her while she wept and moaned. When they had finished, Harry gave her a sedative, and eventually, the woman lost her fight and lay back on the cot, still weeping softly. Sylvia didn't leave her until she was asleep.

She got up, feeling shell-shocked, and not even noticing the mud covering her own clothes, looked for someone else who needed her help. She could hear the wind tearing at the walls of this weak structure, pulling off pieces of the roof. Something crashed on the side of the building, and she met Harry's concerned eyes across the room. It was a tree, she thought, or a piece of someone's house. She wondered how long these walls would remain standing. What would they do if their own roof flew off?

She looked helplessly around her. Families were huddled side by side and on top of each other in the smelly gym. Children cried at the sounds around them. Some of the men stood at the doors, watching through the windows that hadn't shattered yet. Mothers tried to keep the children occupied and distracted. Spanish was spoken all around her, but even without understanding their words, she knew how to attend to their needs.

But this was only the beginning. After the hurricane, diseases would be rampant because of the corpses of animals lying around. Those who didn't have their property ravaged by flood may well be those who lost everything to the mud slides. Tornadoes would take what floods and mud slides didn't. It was as if God's wrath was beating down on this country . . . but if so, it was beating down on others, as well. There had been too many hurricanes in too many places this year. Three had already threatened the East Coast of the States. One had ravaged the Florida coast.

She couldn't believe that, just yesterday, she had felt sorry for herself because she lacked purpose.

She wished she could call the neighbors on Cedar Circle and tell them to pray without stopping. She wished she could talk to her children, Sarah and Jeff. If she could just hear those voices, maybe she could forget the anguished cries of that mother who'd lost everyone she loved in one moment. But there wasn't time to make calls, even if the phone lines worked. There was too much to do.

She prayed she would have the energy to do it.

CHAPTER
Sixteen

Brenda read the clipped e-mail Sylvia had sent during the night, and tears came to her eyes at what her friend was experiencing. She went to the television and turned on the Weather Channel to see if the hurricane showed any sign of leaving Nicaragua. But it seemed parked there, intent on ravaging the small country that wasn't equipped to endure it.

"Lord, please keep her safe," she whispered under her breath. "Protect her so she can help those people."

The door of her little computer room opened, and David stepped inside. He was a large, ruddy, red-haired man who seemed to have aged years in the last few months. "Are you finished with the computer?" he asked.

"Yeah." She sighed. "I was just checking my mail from Sylvia."

"Everything all right?"

She shook her head. "The hurricane sounds bad." She got up and offered David the computer chair.

"How's it feel to have a night off?" he asked.

She smiled. "Thank the Lord for Saturdays. David, the kids are all in bed. I'm going to walk outside for a little bit. I need to think."

"And pray?"

She breathed a laugh. "Yeah, actually. How'd you know?"

He took the seat she had occupied and pulled up his money program on the computer. "You know, you don't have to say 'think' if you mean 'pray.' I won't be offended."

"It's just that I know you don't see any value in that."

"I wouldn't say that," he said. "There must be some. We have Joseph to prove it."

Something in her heart swelled. Maybe her prayers for David were being answered. "We sure do." She leaned over and hugged him from behind.

The money program came up full-blown on the screen, and David clicked a few keys and waited for the bottom line. "How's it looking?" she asked.

He got that look on his face that he got each time he examined their finances. "Well, when you get paid, we'll almost be okay. I was thinking of taking on some extra work, doing it at night after the kids go to bed."

"No," she said. "I don't want the kids in here alone. Maybe I could find something I could do during the day. Typing or something."

"You can't take on any kind of daytime commitment when Joseph has to see the doctor so often. With the biopsies and the echocardiograms and the meetings with the transplant teams, they take half a day, at least, every week. And if anything ever even looks like it's going wrong, they'll have him back in the hospital so fast we won't know what hit us. You can't hold a daytime job and handle that. Besides, you'll be exhausted. It isn't worth it."

"To make sure we can keep paying for Joseph's medical bills, I'll do whatever I have to do," she declared.

He looked up at her. "I hate it. I hate having you out at night. I hate that the kids don't have you here when they go to bed. I hate going to bed without you."

"But look how blessed we are," she said. "I still get to have supper with the family. It's almost time for the kids to go to bed by the time I leave. They hardly even know I'm gone. And I'm able to be home with Joseph during the day . . ."

"But the kids miss homeschooling. They miss you."

"It's only for a little while." But the truth was, she didn't see an end to it. "This is really not a terrible thing," she said. "We could be going through a hurricane. Our children could be threatened. We could have tornadoes and floods and mud slides. Those poor people." She sighed. "I'm gonna go pray." She kissed his cheek, then straightened. "I'll be outside, honey."

The night wind was brisk, cool, and smelled of chimney smoke. It was often windy at night here, but tonight it was especially so, as if the winds from Nicaragua swept all the way across the world to Tennessee, offering that small connection that would remind her how seriously Sylvia needed prayer. She sat on her porch for a moment, swinging back and forth in the wind, praying to the Lord who she knew heard her, that the hurricane would pass quickly, that Sylvia would know how to do the work she needed to do, that she'd have the resources she needed, that no more people would be killed or injured, that the mud slides would cease and the flood waters would recede. As she prayed, a sound on the wind distracted her, and she looked up for a moment and listened. It sounded like weeping from somewhere nearby, but whether it came from another mountain across the valley, swept here by the wind, or somewhere right within reach, she wasn't sure.

She heard a door close and saw Cathy coming out of her home and crossing the street.

Had Cathy been crying? she wondered, getting to her feet. But when Cathy reached her she could see that her eyes were dry. "Brenda, I just called and David said you were out here," Cathy said. "Did you get Sylvia's e-mail?"

"Yeah, I was just praying for her."

"Me, too," Cathy said. "Man, I miss her. And talk about bad luck. Getting there and having a hurricane hit you before you've even had time to settle in."

But Brenda wasn't listening. She still heard that sound of weeping on the wind. It wasn't loud, not wailing at all, just the muffled, occasional sound of someone in great pain. "Listen," she whispered. "Do you hear that?"

Cathy got quiet. "Someone crying?"

Brenda shook her head. "I don't know. I'm not sure."

"It sounds like it's coming from Tory's," Cathy said. She frowned. "Have you heard anything from her?"

"No. She still won't return my calls. I'm getting worried."

"Do you think she's embarrassed about throwing up or something?"

"Of course not. Besides, it's been almost three weeks."

"Well, you know how she is. Everything has to be perfect. Her image is pretty important to her. But it's not like she did it in front of us. There's really nothing to be embarrassed about, even for Tory."

"Three weeks is a long time," Brenda said. "Almost like she's hiding out. Avoiding us."

"It's enough to give you a complex," Cathy agreed.

Again, they heard the weeping, blown up by the wind.

"Come on," Brenda said, stepping off her porch. "That's got to be her." They took off across the empty lot between Brenda's and Tory's homes, and the weeping grew clearer as they reached Tory's yard. They followed the sound into the back. Tory was sitting on the swing at the back of her yard, under a cluster of trees. She had her face in her hands and was weeping her heart out. Brenda started running before Cathy had even seen her.

"Tory!" Brenda fell to her knees in front of her neighbor. "What's the matter, honey?" Tory went into Brenda's arms. "What is it?"

Cathy sat down next to Tory and stroked her back as Tory wept onto Brenda's shoulder.

"Tory, tell us," Cathy whispered. "What is it?"

Tory managed to pull herself together enough to pull back from Brenda. She took a deep breath and tried to speak. "I'm . . . pregnant," she choked out.

"Pregnant!" Brenda whispered. "Well, Tory, that's wonderful. No wonder you were sick. But. . . why the tears?"

"Is it the writing?" Cathy asked, trying to get to the bottom of her grief. "That you'll have to slow down?"

"No!" Tory cried. "I'm not *that* shallow."

"Then what?"

Tory looked up into the star-sprinkled sky, shaking her head. "My baby . . . has Down's Syndrome."

Brenda and Cathy were both stunned to silence as they stared at Tory's wet face in the darkness. "Are you sure?" Brenda asked.

"Oh, yeah. We found out a couple of days ago." She sucked in a breath. "I know I should have called. I should have told you, but when I first knew I was pregnant, I had this . . . sense . . . that I didn't need to tell anyone until I'd been to the doctor. And then he wanted the tests, so I waited for the results. I was just so stunned, I didn't know what to do. I didn't want to say the words until I could get it out without crying, because I feel so guilty. This is my baby girl—"

Brenda and Cathy looked at each other, stricken. "You have nothing to feel guilty about," Brenda said.

"No," Cathy told her. "Why would you feel guilty for being sad that something's wrong with your baby?"

"I should be happy that a new person is coming into our family. I should be able to handle this." She wiped her eyes. "If it were you, Brenda, you could handle it. You'd look at it so positively. You'd be dancing around, and it would be almost like you'd ordered a child with Down's Syndrome."

"Tory, you give me entirely too much credit."

"Wouldn't she, Cathy?" Tory asked.

Cathy sighed. "Well, it does sometimes look like you can handle anything, Brenda. Even this job of yours. I'd be whining to anybody who'd listen. She's working nights, Tory. Seven to twelve. And does she complain? Nope."

"And she wouldn't complain if she were in my shoes, but I've just been so miserable . . ."

"You two have a lot to learn about me." Brenda reached up and stroked Tory's hair out of her eyes. "I'd be upset, too, Tory. But it's gonna be all right."

"That's not all," Tory said. "It's not just the Down's Syndrome. I mean, it's been a couple of days, and I'm over the shock. I was planning to tell both of you tomorrow, and e-mail Sylvia. Barry's been real quiet about it. We've hardly talked about it at all. And then tonight Annie baby-sat and we went out to dinner."

"Yeah," Cathy said. "I was hurt that you were talking to my daughter and not me."

"I'm sorry," she said. "I just couldn't yet."

"Did you have a nice time?" Brenda asked, her voice still sympathetic.

Tory breathed a mirthless laugh. "It wasn't exactly a romantic evening out."

"Of course not," Cathy said. "You're still getting over the shock. You don't need to expect that much of yourselves right now. It's going to take some time to get used to this."

"Barry doesn't want to get used to the idea," she said.

Brenda frowned. "What do you mean?"

"I mean, the doctor gave us *options*." Her lips curled with the words.

Brenda's face changed. She knew what those options were. Cathy seemed to understand, as well. Brenda just pulled Tory back into a hug.

After a moment, she whispered, "He's upset, Tory. He probably doesn't even know what he's thinking. Just give him some time, be patient with him. It's harder for him. He's not carrying the baby. He doesn't have all those maternal hormones pulsing through him."

"He wants me to get an abortion." Tory said the words on a rush of anguish, as if to make sure they understood.

"He may think he wants that," Brenda said, "but he'll change his mind. Like I said, just give him time."

Tory shook her head. "I don't know what disappoints me more," she said. "The knowledge that this baby isn't anything like I thought she would be, or the knowledge that my husband isn't who I thought he was."

"Who did you think he was?" Cathy asked.

Tory looked over at her. "I thought he was someone who believed in life. Every life. But he doesn't. He doesn't even believe in the life of our child. See, he has this brother—"

"Barry has a brother?" Brenda asked. "I didn't know that. I thought he was an only child."

"No," she said. "He has a brother who's autistic. He doesn't communicate with anyone, and he's in a wheelchair. The only thing he does is whistle. Whatever song he heard last, he whistles it. That whistling goes on day and night until he falls asleep. Then you know when he wakes up in the mornings, because he starts whistling again. But he's never been able to look anyone in the eye, or take care of his bodily functions, or feed himself, or anything. His parents have kept him home all his life, but his father died, and his mother is still caring for him. Barry has this fear of repeating that in our family."

"That's understandable," Cathy said. "Tory, I hope you understand that he's not some kind of monster. A lot of parents might feel the way he does."

"Not if he believes what he claims he believes," Tory bit out. "This man, who has written letters to congressmen, gone to prayer rallies to pray for legislation to prevent abortion. If he doesn't really believe it now, then what else did he claim to believe that isn't true?"

"I don't think it's not true," Brenda said. "He's just confused."

"And I'm not?" she asked. "The only thing I know for sure is that I'm carrying a baby with Down's Syndrome. But she's my baby, and God gave her to me."

"He'll come around, Tory," Cathy said. "He's a wonderful dad. I envy you all the time. And he's a strong Christian man."

"He just doesn't know what he wants right now," Brenda added. "He just needs to have your love and support while he thinks this through, and he'll make the right decision. I know he will."

Tears filled Tory's eyes again, and she slumped forward. "I'm just so disappointed in him."

"I know you are," Brenda said, rising up and sitting next to Tory on the bench. "I don't blame you. But things are not always as they seem, and they don't always end up the way they start out."

Cathy nudged Tory. "She's starting to sound like Sylvia."

"Speaking of Sylvia," Brenda said, "she's been worried about you, too. Did you get her latest e-mail?"

Tory leaned her head back on the swing. "No, I haven't been near the computer in days."

"They're going through a hurricane as we speak."

"Is it bad?"

"Terrible. A lot have already died in floods and mud slides. She's huddled in a shelter trying to ride it out."

"How did she e-mail?"

"Apparently the phone lines aren't down yet, at least where she is. But that could change."

"She's worried about you," Cathy said. "We kind of told her we couldn't get in touch with you, that you'd been sick."

Tory swallowed. "I should have told her. I should have told both of you. It was too much to carry."

"You don't have to bear these things alone."

"I know," she said. "I just didn't think I'd ever have to bear anything like this at all. Normally my life is so simple, and I find so many things to complain about, anyway."

Cathy and Brenda laughed softly.

"You'll get through this," Cathy said.

But as the wind whipped up harder from the valley and blew the hair back from Tory's face, Brenda knew that she didn't see the pain ending anytime soon.

Later, when Tory went inside, Barry was nowhere to be found. She checked on Spencer and Brittany, saw that they were sleeping soundly. Annie had long since gone home. The checkbook lay out on the counter where Barry had paid her.

She went back to their bedroom and found that Barry's pillow was gone. Further exploration revealed that the basement door was open. He had apparently opted to sleep down there tonight. She fought the urge to kick the door shut, but she didn't want to turn this crisis into a war.

The truth was, she didn't want to sleep in the same bed with him tonight, anyway, knowing what he wanted for their child. Funny thing, she thought. Two weeks ago, when she'd first learned she was pregnant, it had drawn them so close together. They had counted seconds together, waiting for the results of the test. She had enjoyed being the pregnant wife. Now they couldn't even stay in the same room together. Even being in the same house would be harder and harder as the months of her pregnancy passed by.

She touched her stomach as if silently telling her baby that one of her parents cared. Then she got ready for bed and dropped into it. Her eyes were tired from crying, and her body was weary from the tension that had worked on her today. She wondered how many more days like this she would have before the baby came. And then there would be a lifetime of crisis management.

She dropped into bed and tried to pray, but tears came instead. Quietly, she cried herself to sleep.

CHAPTER
Seventeen

The next afternoon, Cathy bent over the mangled poodle that had been hit by a car not an hour earlier. She had sedated it to keep it still and out of pain while she tried to X-ray it, but now it was obvious that the animal had several broken bones and a punctured lung, and was hemorrhaging from somewhere in its abdominal cavity.

"So if I only had twenty more dollars, I could get the shoes that I absolutely have to have," Annie was saying, following Cathy around the office as if she was doing nothing more important than dusting the wood.

"Annie, I'm a little busy right now."

"But Mom, how am I supposed to talk to you if I don't come here? You're never home."

Her children always used this tactic to get her attention. Cathy was used to it.

"I get home every day when you do," Cathy said. "This is an emergency, and you know it. There's a lady out in that waiting room crying her eyes out because this dog, who is the only family member she apparently has, is on its deathbed."

Annie absently reached out to stroke the animal's groomed ear. "I'm sorry about that, Mom. You act like I'm cold-hearted or something. I'm not. I just need shoes."

"Annie, you *have* shoes. You have shoes in every color under the rainbow in several different styles, and I'm just not real concerned that you have a new pair of hiking boots at the moment. You *have* hiking boots."

"I have those old cheesy kind. But who wants to wear those? They look like something you'd wear in the army."

"And these others don't?"

"No. These others are classy. They're in style. Everybody has them."

"They're *hiking* boots, Annie. That's all they are. You never hike anywhere. Besides, you bought the other pair, and you can live with them." She went to the door and opened it for Annie to leave. "You'll have to excuse me now. I've got to tell this dog's owner what the prognosis is."

Annie just stood there, petting the dog's ear and giving her a dreadful look. "Are you gonna put her to sleep?" she asked.

Cathy sighed. "I don't know. It'll be up to the owner."

"I'll be in your office," Annie said, lowering her voice. "Be gentle. You know how you can be."

Cathy spun around. "No, Annie. How can I be?"

"Well, abrupt, as my English teacher likes to say. You know. 'Sorry your dog got hit, but he's a goner, so let's just put him out of his misery.'"

Cathy's mouth fell open. "I would *never* say that."

"Well, okay, so sue me. I'm just saying you're a little unsympathetic sometimes. Try talking to you about shoes."

Cathy left her, shaking her head, and went into the waiting room to sit down with the crying woman. "Miss Anderson, I've X-rayed your poodle."

"Shish-kabob," the woman said, dabbing at her nose with a red bandana.

"Excuse me?" Cathy asked.

"Shish-kabob. That's what I call her." The woman patted her chest as if to keep it beating.

"Oh." Cathy cleared her throat. "I've just finished X-raying Shish-kabob, and—"

"You've got to save him!" A vein on the woman's neck stood out, punctuating the seriousness of her words. "Look at me. I can't live without him. You've *got* to save him!" She grabbed Cathy's coat. "Please!"

Cathy tried to compose herself. The woman obviously needed compassion, even if she was bordering on violent. "I don't know if I can, Mrs. Anderson. He's got multiple fractures, he's punctured a lung, and he's bleeding internally. Even if I could patch him up, this is going to be a long, excruciating recovery for him. If left alone, he would probably die."

"Then *don't* leave him alone!" the woman shouted, and for a moment she reminded Cathy of a mob leader making an offer she couldn't refuse. "I'll pay you anything! You've got to save him!"

"Miss Anderson, it would take several surgeries. I'm not sure I could get everything the first time. We'd have to insert a feeding tube, put him on a ventilator ..."

"I don't care what it costs," the woman said, clutching her heart again. "I don't care what you have to do. Please, I'll pay you anything."

Cathy didn't know what to do. She hated running up a patient's bill beyond what was reasonable to sustain a pet, but the cost of keeping this dog alive was more than she could handle with the equipment she had. Still, she understood the attachment a lonely woman might have to her pet. "Well, I guess I'd better get in there, then, and see what I can do."

As she hurried back from the waiting room, the phone began to ring. Since her receptionist had already gone home for the day, because they usually closed at three, Cathy snatched the phone up. "Flaherty Animal Clinic. May I help you?"

"Uh . . . Mom . . ." It was Mark's voice, and something about his tone made her forget the dog slipping away at the back of the clinic, or the hysterical woman out front.

"Mark? What is it?"

"Uh . . . the principal . . . sort of . . . needs to talk to you."

"The principal?" Before she had a chance to question Mark further, a man's voice came on the line.

"Dr. Flaherty?"

"Yes?"

"This is Principal Ernest Little. I'm afraid we've had a problem this afternoon."

"A problem?"

"Yes. I'm afraid we caught your son taking drugs in the bathroom."

"*Drugs?*" she shouted out, and Annie came running up the hall, as if she couldn't take the chance of missing this. "There must be some mistake!"

"No mistake," the principal said. "I caught him red-handed. He and the two friends who were with him have been put on three-day suspension, and unfortunately, while we were talking in the office, he missed his bus."

The blood rushed from her face, and she felt like that woman in her waiting room. Had she been in the principal's office, she would have climbed across the desk and grabbed him by the throat, and demanded to know what he *meant* by drugs.

"What kind of drugs?" She prayed that it would be something benign. Tums, perhaps.

"Marijuana," he told her.

"No way!" Cathy cried. "My son was *not* smoking marijuana!"

"I'm afraid he and his friends were caught red-handed."

"What friends?" she asked. "Who were they?"

"Andy Whitehill and Tad Norris."

She slapped her forehead and backed up. "I can't believe this. I told him he was not allowed to hang around with those kids. They're bad news. Mr. Little, you have to understand that Mark was probably just following the crowd. He's not the leader type."

"I'm not suggesting that he is, Dr. Flaherty. But that doesn't change the fact that he was in the bathroom smoking that stuff. I could actually call the police and have him arrested for possession, but I thought it was better this first time just to call you instead."

She closed her eyes. "Mr. Little, I appreciate your call. You can be certain that I'll take care of this from my end. You will never catch my son smoking pot again." She turned and saw Annie staring at her with her mouth wide open. "Right now, can I send my daughter to get him? I'm kind of in the middle of an emergency. A dog has been hit by a car and I need to do surgery immediately."

She knew what he was thinking already. He was probably wondering if she considered a dog's life more important than her son's. She looked through the glass at the woman still crying in the waiting room. That vein on her neck was getting bigger.

"Certainly. That'll be fine," Mr. Little said in a disapproving voice.

"All right, thank you."

She hung up and thought of throwing her receptionist's paperweight through the glass, but decided that would be too entertaining to Annie. She was going to throttle Mark. And then she was going to scream and yell at him, and then she was going to spend a few hours making him memorize Scripture. She wondered if there was anything in the Bible about smoking marijuana. She'd have to ask Brenda . . . or Steve. She was still too new at all this.

Then she realized that she couldn't tell Steve, the man she had been seeing for five months. She couldn't let him know that her child was a reprobate who took drugs and got suspended from school.

Who was she kidding? He knew her children weren't little angels. Already, they'd embarrassed her so many times that she didn't know why he was still hanging around.

"Mom, what is it?" Annie asked.

She shoved her hair back and looked at her daughter in the doorway. "Annie, I need you to go get your brother."

"My brother?" she asked. "I just heard the word *marijuana* hollered up the hall, and now you're telling me that phone call was about Rick?"

"Not Rick. Mark."

"*Mark?* So what happened?"

"He's in the principal's office. Just go right in there and tell the principal who you are—"

Annie's eyes were round and slightly amused. "Mom, you have to tell me. This is my little brother we're talking about."

"Oh, right. Suddenly you're very concerned about your little brother. It's moving, Annie."

"So did he get suspended or what?"

"For three days," Cathy bit out.

"No way!"

"Annie, go get your brother. I have a poodle to keep alive."

It was six before Cathy got home to deal with Mark. She had hesitated to leave the poodle, who had casts on three legs, wire stitches in her stomach, a feeding tube down her throat, and a ventilator tube in her lungs. The best she could tell the owner was that the dog would be sustained through the night, but she couldn't even promise that. The woman didn't threaten to attack, but went home wailing.

She pulled into the driveway and said a quiet prayer for strength before she went inside. At the back door, she stepped over the three backpacks that had been carelessly tossed down, and saw Annie, Mark, and Rick sitting together before the television in an unusual show of solidarity. Normally, they would be scattered across the house, studiously avoiding each other's company, except to fight over the telephone or the computer.

Their intense interest in the *Brady Bunch* reruns was hard to swallow. She dropped her purse on the table. The fact that they didn't turn around told her they were bracing themselves.

"Hi, Mom," Annie said, glancing back at her. "How's the poodle?"

"Alive." Cathy crossed her arms. "What have you got to say for yourself, Mark?"

He looked much younger than thirteen as he turned to face her. "Mom, I didn't do anything."

She laughed sarcastically. "I might have expected that, Mark. Of course you did something, and you got caught red-handed." She walked into the den and stood over him. "I want to know where you got the drugs."

"Mom, you can get them anywhere."

"Where did *you* get them?"

"Tad had it."

"Mark, you know better than that. You know better than to smoke cigarettes in the boy's rest room, let alone dope!"

"It wasn't dope, Mom. It's not like I was freebasing crack or something. It was just a little grass."

The fact that her baby knew the term *freebasing* brought tears to her eyes. "Mark, what has gotten into you? I knew what would happen if you hung around with those kids. I knew they would drag you down the wrong path. Do you feel better now, Mark, being thrown out of school for three days? Making zeroes on everything that happens while you're gone? Missing tests?"

"Well, it's not like I was an A student."

"Right," she said. "So now your C's and D's will drop to F's."

"You don't have to be so negative."

"*Negative!* Mark, you must be kidding me!"

Annie tried not to laugh, but the humor overcame her. "That was not the thing to say, Mark."

"Listen to her!" Cathy shouted. "She knows!"

Rick got up, unfolding to his full six feet. "Mom, don't be so hard on him. He's been punished enough."

"Punished enough?" she shouted back. "Rick, I don't need advice from you on parenting. If he'd been punished enough, then this wouldn't have happened!"

"Where's all that Christian love and forgiveness stuff you've been trying to teach us?" Mark asked.

"It doesn't give my child license to hang around in the bathrooms with kids who take drugs. Mark, Mr. Little could have called the police. You could be in jail tonight."

"Mom, they don't send thirteen-year-olds to jail."

"They send them to the detention center, Mr. Smart-mouth. Would you like me to take you there to show you?"

Mark rolled his eyes, which almost sent her over the edge of control. "You know, now that I think about it, that might be an excellent thing to do. Brenda's always taking her kids on field trips. Maybe we need to go on one. Tomorrow, while you're on vacation, I'm going to take you to the juvenile detention hall downtown, and I'm going to show you just how cool it is. And then maybe you'll think before you decide to take drugs again."

"I just wanted to see what it was like!" he shouted.

"Now you've seen, and you're going to see a little more. It's *like* getting suspended from school, it's *like* being grounded from associating with your friends for the rest of the school year. It's *like* going to the juvenile detention center, only not as a visitor. Not as a tourist with your mom."

"Boy, you've done it now," Annie told Mark.

Mark looked distraught. "Mom, I'd rather go to algebra."

"Well, you're not going to algebra, because you're suspended. You're coming with me." She stormed into the kitchen, racking her brain for what to cook for dinner. When she reached the counter, she saw the note that Rick had jotted. Steve had called. She hoped to heaven that they hadn't told him what Mark had done.

She turned back around and saw all three kids still sitting in front of the television. "Go clean up your rooms," she said. "All of you. And don't come out until all your homework is done."

"I don't have homework," Mark said. "I'm suspended."

"Do it anyway."

"Do *what?*"

"Whatever homework you would have been doing if you hadn't been suspended."

"I don't know what that would be because nobody ever gave it to me."

Annie shoved her brother. "Mark, shut up. You're making it worse!"

"Yeah," Rick said. "Go count the dirty socks in your room, before you make her turn on us, too!"

"Turn on you?" Cathy repeated. Then she stopped herself and realized this was going nowhere. "Annie? Do you have homework?"

"None. I did it all at school."

"How about you, Rick?"

Rick shrugged. "I had three tests today, so we're starting on new material."

"Good." She grabbed the Bible and flipped it open to Philippians 2. "Memorize this, then. Philippians 2 verses 14 through 16. Go upstairs and clean up your rooms, and when you get finished, since you don't have anything to study, don't come out of your rooms until you've memorized these verses."

"Mom, that's impossible!" Annie said. "That's too long!"

"I can't remember all that!" Mark moaned.

Rick took the Bible and rolled his eyes at the verses. "Oh, come on, Mom. Is this some kind of joke?"

"Read it out loud, Rick," she said. "I want to hear you read it."

He let out a laborious sigh, and began reading. "Do everything without complaining or arguing, so that you may become blameless and pure, children of God without fault in a crooked and depraved generation, in which you shine like stars in the universe as you hold out the word of life—in order that I may boast on the day of Christ that I did not run or labor for nothing." He looked up at her.

She smiled. "Good. Run along now. And if you don't memorize it, you'll be in your room all night."

"Mom, we're not gonna go into the ministry just because you forced us to memorize Scripture," Rick said.

"Maybe not. But it'll make me feel like I'm doing one positive thing in your upbringing."

"Yeah, nice positive verse to start with," Annie said. "Our crooked and depraved generation."

"Go! *Now!*"

Huffing and puffing, they all three headed up the stairs. She could hear voices in the hallway up there, and knew they were raking her over the coals, but she didn't care. The phone rang, and she snatched it up. "Hello?"

"Cathy? Steve. You sound like you're expecting someone else."

She tried to breathe out her anxiety. "No, not at all. I was just kind of in the middle of something with the kids."

"Really? What?"

"Uh . . ." She glanced toward the stairs. "Bible study."

"Really?"

"Yeah. We were going over Philippians 2."

"That's great," he said. "Did the kids understand it? Were they receptive to it?"

"They're trying to memorize it before supper," she evaded.

"No kidding." He chuckled. "I'm very impressed."

She fought the urge to burst into tears and tell him everything that had happened that day, from the pictures on the television about the aftermath of the hurricane in Nicaragua, to the poodle that she had on life support, to the marijuana in the bathroom.

"So did you have a good day today?"

She felt the anger seeping out of her, like air out of slashed tires. "I've had better."

"Want to talk about it?"

She shook her head. "Oh, Steve, I'd really like to, but I can't. Not right now."

"I was hoping you were up to a pizza. Tracy and I were thinking we might bring a couple over and eat with you and the kids."

Though it seemed tempting, she knew that one of the kids would give the disaster away. "It's just not a good idea tonight," she said. "Maybe tomorrow night. I'm really beat and I don't think I'd be very good company. Plus I have to run back to the clinic in a little while to check on a poodle who got hit by a car."

"Well, I understand." She could hear the disappointment in his voice. "I'll just call you tomorrow, and if you feel like talking anytime tonight and you get a free minute, give me a call and I'll be here."

"Thanks," she said. She hung up as a tender smile softened her lips. He always did make her feel better. She was just sorry she had misled him into thinking she was having a sweet little family Bible study with her kids. Breathing out a deep sigh, she reached for the phone book, looked up the nearest pizza restaurant, and began to dial.

CHAPTER

Outside, Joseph Dodd rode his bicycle around the little cul-de-sac as Brenda swept the driveway, fighting the urge to order him off his bike. The idea of her child taking any kind of risk, after the suffering he'd endured just weeks ago, was almost more than she could bear.

But there was something miraculous about seeing him on a bike again, though he didn't yet ride fast or far, and she didn't want to spoil it for him. He wouldn't last long, pedaling around the circle. He was still working on rebuilding his stamina, but he was getting stronger each day. The doctor assured them that by next summer, he might be able to play baseball again. Though he took dozens of pills each day to keep from rejecting the heart, and would for the rest of his life, his recovery had been remarkable.

Leah and Rachel, her eleven-year-old twins, sat at the picnic table doing their homework. Daniel had gone inside to look something up on their computer.

"Mom, this is so boring," Leah said. "You did this with us two years ago. I told Mrs. Higgins I already knew it, but she said just to do it again."

"Well, I guess we can't blame them for going slow," Brenda said. "When I was homeschooling it was just us. We could go as fast as we wanted."

"Now we go as slow as the slowest person in the class," Rachel said. "And in science we're studying atoms, and I told them we did a science project on that last year and won third place in the state, but the teacher acted like it didn't count because it was homeschool."

"Well, she just doesn't understand. Be patient with her. How could she know?"

"Mom, can't we start homeschooling again? Joseph's doing fine, and he wants us back home. We don't spend enough time with you when you work nights."

Brenda had given it a lot of thought. She missed her children and wanted to teach them, but she just didn't think she had the energy to do a good job as long as she was working nights. "I miss being here, too," she said. "But we're all doing okay." She stopped sweeping and smiled as she looked at Joseph. "Just look at him. If I have to work to keep him healthy, then none of us should complain."

"But Mom," Leah said. "I'm just stagnating in that school."

"Stagnating?" Brenda asked, amused. "Is that one of your vocabulary words this week?"

Leah shrugged. "Maybe. But I am."

"Well, that was a perfect use of it. See? You *are* learning."

"But not like we learned at home. Mom, if you let us homeschool again, I promise I'll never complain again about having to read all that historical stuff."

"Historical stuff? You don't mean the Federalist Papers, do you? You complained for weeks about that."

"Mom, they don't read that in public school until the eleventh grade honors classes, and then they only read pieces of it. You made us read *all* of them in fifth grade."

"And you understood them. That was the amazing thing."

Rachel piped in. "I'll read it all again if you'll let us come home. Mom, reading things in bits and pieces, learning theories without doing experiments . . . How can you remember any of it?"

"So what you're saying is . . ." Brenda leaned down and rubbed noses with Rachel. ". . . that there's method in my madness? Making you read entire original documents isn't equivalent to child abuse?"

"We promise, Mom. We'll never complain again."

She smiled. "I'm thinking about it," she said. "And so is your dad. But there are problems with homeschooling now. On the days when I have to take Joseph for his biopsies, you'd all be at home wasting time. And it's very possible that they might occasionally have to put him back into the hospital. I wouldn't be able to teach you then. Besides, I think going to school might be good for you. You need to see what it's like, make some new friends, find out how it is to be taught by somebody besides your mom."

"I like being taught by my mom," Leah said. "In class, I sit through a whole hour doing math, and I never get called on. We move so slowly. At home, when I'm working with you, I get to answer all of them. And I like having time to really dig into things like you make us do. Not just get the homework done and see what the grade is."

"Grades are important," Brenda said.

"I know they are, but it's not the same. When I make an A at home I know I've really done something. And Mom, on the days that you're at the hospital with Joseph, Daddy will still be here. And you can give us assignments to work on while you're gone. We won't waste time."

"Yeah, and if you have to spend the night in the hospital, we can make our schoolwork up on Saturdays," Rachel added. "I wouldn't care."

Brenda laughed at the drastic compromises they were offering, and messed up her daughter's hair. "I'll give it some serious consideration, okay?"

As the girls took their books in, Brenda sat down at the picnic table. Maybe it was time to bring the kids back home, after all. They hadn't been in public school but two months. It had been a positive experiment, but maybe it wasn't necessary anymore.

She did miss them, after all, and if she had to work nights, she could get as much out of the days as possible.

Maybe it was time.

CHAPTER
Nineteen

The baby section at Tory's favorite bookstore had way too many books on birth defects. She pulled a number of them out and carried them to a table near the stacks, hoping to choose a few before her children emerged from story hour. She could handle this pregnancy, she thought, if she only had enough information. A couple of books to read. A strategy. Information was everything.

But she knew that, no matter what she learned, it wouldn't change Barry's mind.

She made three trips with the books to the table, careful not to strain herself. She supposed a real miscarriage would be the perfect answer for Barry, and then they could move on with their lives and never look back. But the damage had been done. Barry wasn't the man she thought he was, and that was all there was to it.

It had broken her heart and made her so bitter.

She began flipping through the pages, searching for something that would ease her worries, help her to organize her thoughts. She was having trouble sleeping nights, and her nausea was coming more and more frequently. She spent the day walking around like a zombie, her mind on anything but what she was doing.

Funny, she thought, sitting back in her chair and scanning the books stacked around her. Just a couple of weeks ago, she had come in here and lingered at the fiction shelf, once again considering the thought that she might be able to tackle a novel.

Now she wondered if that day would ever come again, when she'd be able to get lost in her thoughts, bask in the silence that fed her creativity. She didn't know, but some part of her said it didn't matter, that if God had given her this child to love, then love it she would.

She put her hand over her stomach, as if silently barricading the baby that had caused such a problem in her marriage. She wasn't the heroic type, nor the stoic kind of mother who sacrificed all things for the good of her children. No, on the scale of motherhood, she supposed she was near the bottom. She loved her children, took care of them, but so often got impatient and frustrated, and selfishly begrudged every hour of time or energy that took her away from her goals. She supposed the Lord was going to have to do a powerful work on her to equip her for this baby.

Defeated, she dropped her forehead into her palm and tried not to cry.

The sound of children's laughter and chattering came from the back of the bookstore, and she knew that children's hour was over. Quickly, she made a decision and picked three of the books from the stack in front of her. Before she could put the other ones back, Spencer was at her side.

"Mommy, can I buy a book? They got one about horses."

"Not today, Spence," she said, kissing him on the forehead. "Mommy's got to buy some books today."

"Then a dog book."

Tory laughed. She knew that Spencer wouldn't give the book a thought once she got it home. She considered buying it just to appease him, then bring it back tomorrow, but she knew it wasn't good for him to get everything he thought he wanted.

"No, we're not gonna buy a dog book right now."

He saw the books spread out on the table in front of her. "Then a baby book."

She frowned. "You want a baby book?"

"Yeah, one of these," he said.

She breathed a laugh. "Well, as it happens, I was just about to buy a couple of these."

"Cool," he said, jumping up and down as Brittany reached them. "Britty, we get a baby book!"

"Me, too?" Brittany asked.

Tory pulled her daughter into a hug. "Yeah, you, too. If you want a book about babies, you got it."

As she drove home, she listened to them chattering in the backseat about the storyteller's poofy hair and glittery finger-nails, and the way she poked at the air and bared her teeth when she read the part of the monster. Her mind wandered as they went on with the grand story that she supposed bore little resemblance to reality.

She looked down at the bag of books she had bought about Down's Syndrome. What would Barry think when he saw them?

She jerked her thoughts back. She didn't care what he thought. She was going to prepare for this baby whether he liked it or not. She glanced in her rearview mirror to her children in the backseat, and wondered when she should break the news to them. Wouldn't they be thrilled to know that their mother was expecting another baby?

But Barry didn't want her to tell them, not when he was hop-ing she would terminate the pregnancy and it would all go away. As she thought that over, she realized how binding it would be to tell the children. If she did, then Barry certainly couldn't keep pressing for an abortion. He could never explain to his own chil-dren what had happened to the baby their mother was carrying.

She glanced in the mirror again. Maybe it was something she should consider. Usurping his timing, and telling the kids they had a baby sister. She wasn't sure. Maybe it was the wrong thing to do. Sylvia would know, she thought as she drove up Survey Mountain to their home. She wished Sylvia were home so she could tell her about Barry's heartbreaking rejection of this child, and find out what her mentor thought she should do.

She didn't have Sylvia here, but she did have e-mail.

When they reached home, she sent the children to play in their rooms, and hurried to the computer room. She had to e-mail the neighbor who meant so much to her but lived so far away.

CHAPTER

Twenty

Sylvia wasn't reading her e-mail these days. There wasn't time. The damage from Hurricane Norris had been much worse than she'd expected. Power lines were down all over the city of León, and several areas were completely wiped out due to the tornadoes spawned from the high winds.

Floods had killed many who lived near Lake Telica River, and had driven thousands from their homes below the Cerro Negro and Telica volcanoes and other hills around the city. Meanwhile, mud slides had buried dozens of homes. Still it rained, threatening to start more mud slides. Word was that many of the people living in high-risk areas refused to leave. They were putting the little property they owned above their very lives.

She and Harry visited the hospital in León, hoping to send some of their injured and sick to be cared for there. But already it was overcrowded. The limited staff was trying to make the best of a very difficult situation, but even their best was far below the standards Harry was used to. Every wall needed painting, and many of the ceiling tiles were missing. The fire hose cases were empty, and every clock in the building had stopped working. The rooms, the halls, and even the treatment areas were dimly lit, which made the place look even dirtier. Most of the beds were without sheets, and patients were lying on plastic-covered mattresses. Even the babies being treated had no diapers. Sanitation was obviously low on the hospital's priority list.

Harry and the other American doctors decided that they would need to make the proper request of the Nicaraguan government to set up their own makeshift hospital. They knew that they would have limited supplies and equipment, but something had to be done to try to accommodate the increasing number of patients waiting for emergency medical care. Even though it would be poorly equipped, they were determined to make it bright and sanitary, a place of hope instead of dread.

Sylvia and Harry prayed earnestly that permission would be granted quickly, even though the government of Nicaragua was not known for quick decisions. They knew God had intervened when the officials, who saw the need for quick action, granted almost immediate permission.

With the help of several local churches, Harry and the other doctors shifted into high gear and put the hospital together. White paint, scrub brushes, cots, clean sheets, bright light bulbs, and many hours around the clock began to turn the unused building into a bright and acceptable place for caring for the medical needs of these people.

Many of the first patients were sick with dengue fever, a sickness that comes from being bitten by a mosquito that is carrying infected blood. Since the floods had encouraged the breeding of mosquitoes that spread the disease, more and more people were being brought in for immediate care.

Adjacent to the hospital building was the old schoolhouse they were using as a shelter. Already, Sylvia and the other missionaries had crammed as many as they could into the makeshift shelter. They were having trouble gathering enough food to feed everyone. Even on good days in León, the supermarkets were poorly stocked.

There was an overabundance of things like vinegar and ketchup, brooms and rakes, but for Sylvia to get the food she wanted she often had to go to the outdoor markets where meat hung out in the heat with flies swarming over it. The outdoor markets had not been open during the storm, but several store-keepers had had the marketing savvy to come by with tortillas, onions, and cream, which made the *quesillos* that would sustain them until the next day. The vendors had insisted on payment in "green parrots," their name for U.S. currency. Sylvia, Harry, and Jim had given up all the cash they had to pay for the food, but didn't know how they would pay tomorrow. Until the banks opened, cash would not be available in either currency.

Sylvia had spent the night trying to make sure they each had something to sleep on, but now, in the aftermath of the hurri-cane, she saw the extent of their grief and mourning as they real-ized the degree of devastation around them. Many of their homes were gone, and the sense of despair hung heavily in the air. Even she had begun to wonder if God was covering his ears to block out their prayers.

"Sylvia!"

She turned around and saw Harry through the crowd, try-ing to get her attention over the mass of people just outside the shelter. He looked tired, and she doubted he had slept even two hours last night. He'd been patching up wounds and treating ill-nesses all night. She pushed through the crowd and made her way to her husband. "Harry, what is it?"

"Jeb Anderson's here," he said, taking her hand and pulling her along with him as he pushed through the people. "He said the rescue workers have been bringing them children. There are so many, just wandering around the streets, filthy and soaking wet. We can only assume their parents were killed or injured, but something's got to be done with them. The rescue workers heard about the school they were working on, so they brought the children to them."

"The school?" Sylvia stopped in her tracks and looked at him. "Harry, I thought they were crazy when they started working on that place. They didn't have teachers or books, but they were sure God told them to get it ready."

"Don't ever doubt God's call on people's lives again," Harry said over the noise. He started walking again, and she came beside him. "He did tell them to get it ready. It just wasn't for what they thought. They thought it was a school, but it may well turn into an orphanage. God knew it would be needed. He was providing for the children in advance."

Sylvia had trouble seeing through the tears that came to her eyes, reminding her that she had been so unfaithful that she had felt sorry for the Andersons, who were only being obedient to God. "Where is Jeb?" she asked. She owed him an apology.

"He's inside. He brought some of the kids to the clinic for me to examine. A few of them have minor injuries, and some have dengue fever from the mosquitoes. Most of those have been hospitalized. But we have to send people out to look for more survivors. The government is loaning us a helicopter so we can search. We can't leave them out there." As they reached the building that Harry was using as a clinic, she saw the group of filthy, injured children of all ages.

Her heart felt as if it had suffered a fatal blow. She suddenly wished she'd worked harder at language school so she could speak to them more fluently. As it was, her Spanish was broken and she doubted they could understand her. They came upon Contessa, a Nicaraguan woman who helped Harry translate at the clinic. She was trying to clean a child's gaping wound, and the little boy was screaming and trying to pull away.

"Have you asked each one about their parents?" Harry asked her.

Contessa nodded. "Some saw parents to hospital," she said.

Sylvia tried to follow her English. "They saw their parents taken to the hospital?"

"*Sí.* Others, they don't know."

"How could this happen?" Sylvia demanded. "How could any-one take a parent to the hospital and leave their child behind?"

"I guess if the parent was unconscious and couldn't tell them," Harry said, bending over to pick up the screaming boy. "Or if there was chaos, and they were trying to save a life." He bounced the boy and tried to calm him, then nodded to the perimeter of the group of children. "Sylvia, I want you to help with the kids. Help me get their wounds cleaned, and rank them according to the most needy first. Oh, and if you would, take that baby down there."

Sylvia's eyes scanned the hopeless, crying, filthy children, and she saw the baby he spoke of. She was in the arms of a girl who looked no more than twelve and who had a huge gash on the side of her head. She wondered if the two girls were siblings, or if the girl had just been put in charge of the infant since she was one of the oldest of the group. The girl looked weak and pale, and Sylvia wondered if she had the energy to endure the baby's crying and squirming much longer.

The baby was wearing a filthy shirt. Her diaper was the only clean thing on her, and Sylvia assumed that Julie Anderson had been able to do that much for her before sending her with Jeb.

Sylvia motioned for the girl to give her the baby. The girl surrendered her gladly. Sylvia took the baby, whose face was caked with dirt and mud, except for the places where tears had washed the dirt away. Her nose was crusty, and her long black eyelashes were webbed with tears. She looked no more than eighteen months old. Black hair strung into her face. Several cuts and bruises marked her dark skin.

Sylvia pressed the little head against her chest, and the baby seemed to relax instantly. Sylvia's heart burst. This poor child. Where had she come from? Where had any of them come from?

She tried to shake her thoughts back to the matters at hand. "Contessa," she called to the Nicaraguan woman. "Can you ask this child a question for me?"

Contessa came over and looked at the child's head wound. "*Si*. What question?"

"Ask her if she is this baby's sister."

Contessa asked, and the little girl said no and muttered some things Sylvia didn't understand. "She don't know this *bebe*," Contessa said. "She just holding her."

"Tell her I appreciate her taking care of her, especially when she's not feeling well."

Contessa spouted that off, and the little girl looked up at Sylvia. Sylvia swung around and found her husband. "Harry! This girl has a bad head wound. Can you see her first?"

Still holding the boy, who had quit crying now, Harry came to the girl. "Let's get her into the clinic."

As Harry ushered the girl inside, Sylvia spotted Jeb. She made her way to him. "Jeb, what's the story on this baby?"

Jeb was wrapping a bandage around a little boy's leg. "She was alone at the site of a house that had been flattened, probably by a tornado," he said. "No parents anywhere around. She was sitting alone in a ditch when they found her. Apparently there were quite a few casualties in that area, and they've taken a lot of them to the hospital. They've already dug out a dozen others who were dead. They found her when they came back for one last search."

"But is anyone trying to find her mother?"

"Not yet. We haven't figured out how to get the word out. Electricity is down, so we can't use the television. If we could get film and find someone to develop it, we could take pictures of them and post signs all over León. Maybe that would be a start in getting some of them back together with their families. But we have our work cut out for us, and a lot of these children are orphans now. That's just all there is to it." He blinked the tears back, as if he didn't have time for them. "But Julie and I are ready. We have the building. All we need is blankets and cots. Food . . ."

She didn't know if he realized what a tall order that was, but then she kicked herself again. God would provide. He had already proved that.

She looked down at the baby in her arms, and realized that the child had been so tired that she had drifted to sleep in

Sylvia's arms. Oh, the poor mother who was missing this child, Sylvia thought. If she was alive, she must be turned inside out with worry.

The thought of sending this little one back to the school with Jeb was more than she could bear. But she couldn't think of that now. Keeping the baby clutched next to her heart, she went from child to child, giving each one a cursory examination so she could get the most injured ones in to see Harry first. But she was having trouble concentrating with the child asleep against her breast.

Oh, Lord, she prayed. *Please don't let this baby's mother be dead.*

There were others out there, she thought. Other stray children wandering the streets, looking for hope and help. How would they find them all?

Realizing that she could solve only one problem at a time, she set about trying to get these wounds sanitized before infection and disease set in.

CHAPTER
Twenty-One

The sight of Mark on his hands and knees, cleaning out the dog cages, was immensely satisfying to Cathy. The thirteen-year-old had sported visions of three days of vacation from school, sleeping late, watching television or playing on the computer all day with no one breathing down his neck.

Cathy had other plans. She had informed him quickly that three days of suspension from school meant three days of hard labor for her at her clinic. And that had only begun *after* their field trip to the juvenile detention center. Mark had expressed deep humiliation at being taken there, even just to look around, but she had gotten the guard to show them everything from the cells to the isolation rooms. He had been very quiet as they drove home. She hoped he had resolved never again to do anything that would land him there.

Mark saw her looking in at him now. He tried to look weary, and wiped the sweat from his brow. She almost broke into a chorus of "Chain Gang" just to accompany his performance. "Why do I have to do this? You pay Joe and Carol to do it, and you're not paying me. This is child abuse," he said. "There are laws, you know."

She smiled. "You're right. I do pay employees to do this, and they are extremely thankful to have a break from it while you're here. You've made them very happy."

"Mom, haven't I been punished enough?"

"Punished enough?" she asked. "Mark, this is only the second day of your suspension. The fence around the yard needs painting. The floor in each of my examining rooms needs Lysol. All the trash cans need emptying."

"Can't I just play with the dogs you're boarding? I could take them out one at a time and walk them."

"Nope. That's what Joe and Carol are doing today. You're freeing them up to get a lot more done. I can hardly wait until the next time you get suspended."

She knew he wasn't fooled by her facetious joy over his plight. The fact that her son had gotten three days of zeroes because he had dallied in drugs in the school bathroom had been enough to make her want to lock herself in a dark room and mourn for a week. She had kept quiet about it, had not told Brenda or Tory, because she didn't want them to know how miserably she had failed as a parent. She had avoided Steve for the same reason.

She realized she was doing exactly what she had chided Tory for doing—keeping her problems secret from people who could have prayed for her. What did that say about her belief in the power of prayer, she wondered.

"Mom, I'm tired. I can't wait to go back to school so I can get some rest."

That was just where she wanted him, she thought. Wishing to go back to school. Looking forward to sitting in class.

She wished she could ensure that he would stay away from those boys who had influenced him into doing things he might never have done otherwise.

But that was the hard part, she thought. That was why this parenting thing wasn't easy. While Mark was here, cleaning out cages, she had some control. But the minute he stepped foot off of her property, he was prey for whatever vulture was out there, waiting to bite.

She didn't know if she had it in her to get through the teenage years with this one.

CHAPTER
Twenty-Two

Brenda sat with Joseph in the room where she homeschooled him, and put up a good front as she read the essay he had written on his experiences with his heart transplant. She didn't want him to see her getting all teary-eyed again, but the wounds were still fresh. She glanced up at him, saw him working on his project on the aortic system. She had used his heart transplant to teach him how the heart worked. In the process, she was learning, too. "Good job, Joseph."

"The project or the essay?" he asked.

She swallowed. "Both, but I'm not finished reading the essay yet."

He squeezed out some more glue and carefully placed a piece of construction paper on one chamber of the heart. She went back to the essay, reading about the last day before they'd found a heart, and how he had expected to die, and all the regrets he had because his father didn't believe in God, and his fear of never seeing him again.

She thought of showing David the essay, but he hated things like this. Though he was extraordinarily proud of his children—all of them—he would tell her that she was emotionally blackmailing him with Joseph's essay. Besides, she knew it wouldn't work. Nothing Joseph or Leah or Rachel or Daniel had ever said had changed him into a believer. Even the neighbors' selfless efforts to raise money to pay their hospital bills hadn't done it. He wasn't going to believe what he didn't believe, he'd told her time and again. He had believed as a child, but Christendom had all but destroyed him when his father, a preacher, ran off with his church organist, and the congregation subsequently evicted him and his mother from the parsonage. They had lived in a one-room apartment above someone's garage, and he had grown into a bitter, angry young man from whom the most zealous ones of his father's flock had tried to cast out demons.

He had never gotten over it.

If I be lifted up, I will draw all men to myself. The words of Christ railed around and around in Brenda's mind, reminding her that David's salvation was not in her hands. The Holy Spirit would convict him when it was time. She had to believe that.

She wiped her eyes and smiled up at her little boy. "That's wonderful, Joseph. Great essay."

"Any mistakes?"

"No. It's an A+. I'll bet you'll be a writer someday. You'll change the world. Already writing this well at nine years old?"

"I used all my vocabulary words," he said with a wry grin. "Did you notice?"

She looked back down at the paper and realized that he had used them so well that she hadn't even noticed. "You sure did. Would you look at that?"

He wiped his hands on the paper towel she had given him, and sat back to survey his work. His cheeks were a little more plump than they had been a few months earlier, before he'd had to go on steroids and a dozen other drugs to stay alive. She was grateful for those plump cheeks now.

"Mama, do you think you're gonna let Leah, Rachel, and Daniel quit school?"

She grinned. "Quit school? You sound like they want to drop out and get jobs."

"I want them to stay home," he said. "It's lonesome here."

She got up from the desk and went to sit by her son. He was getting stronger every day. His sutures were beginning to heal, and the weekly hospital visits had been positive in every way. She had to be careful to administer the right amount of medication at the right time, and watch the scars that were giving him some pain as he healed. But things had been going well so far.

"I know you're lonely, sweetheart, but I'm not sure it's the right thing to do."

"You think I'll get sick again," he said. "But I won't. I'm doing good."

"Well. You're doing well."

"I'm not gonna reject my heart. I promise."

She couldn't help smiling. "If you do, the doctors will know even before we do, and they'll just adjust your medication. But we have to stay flexible."

"But they could be flexible if they quit school. It could be like old times."

Old times were less than six months ago, she realized, but they must seem like an eternity to Joseph.

"I'm thinking about it."

"Think hard."

"I am," she said. "Just between you and me, I think I'm ready to go back to homeschooling, too. It'll be good to get things back to normal."

"Well," he said. "It'll be well to get things back to normal."

"No, *good*. *Well* is an adverb, and *good* is an adjective."

"See, Mom? You're a born teacher."

He was good, she thought. Well. He was good and would soon be well. Maybe it was time that she brought her children back home, after all.

She wanted to resume homeschooling for them, but she also couldn't help thinking about the financial advantage it would give the family. Even though they were in public school, there were constant needs for money. Yearbooks, class pictures, music fees, class party fees, field trip costs, book fairs ... That didn't even include the cost for clothes and shoes so they wouldn't feel out of place. The list went on and on, times three, and she was beginning to have to let her children go without. If they were back at home, maybe she could save a little money. Wouldn't God provide the energy she needed to homeschool *and* work nights?

Somewhere, there was a way. The Lord hadn't brought them this far to drop them now.

CHAPTER
Twenty-Three

Steve's calls kept coming, though Cathy avoided talking to him. Desperate to keep him from knowing the truth about her wayward child, she hid behind the injured poodle and claimed she was too busy to talk to or see him. Each time, she heard the pain in his voice, as if he thought something else was going on. But she could not reassure him without explaining about her son's tryst with drugs. If he knew, she suspected he would end things with her, anyway. What kind of future could they have together if he saw her children as discipline problems who could be a negative influence on his daughter?

She told herself that it might be better for them to slow things down, anyway. She needed to give whatever energy she had left to her family. If Steve got tired of waiting and moved on . . . well . . . at least that was one less ticking bomb in her life.

But on the last day of Mark's suspension, Steve showed up at the clinic. She heard him asking the receptionist if she was there. At the time, she was engaged in checking the vital signs of the

434

poodle that was still hanging on for dear life. She took her time, trying to organize her speech in her mind. *I haven't been avoiding you, Steve. I've just been so busy with this poodle . . .*

Before she had the speech completely planned, she heard Mark burst out into the waiting room. "How's it going, Steve?"

It was the first time in his life that Mark had addressed Steve with any kind of enthusiasm. But it didn't surprise her that he did so now. Mark must have sensed her reluctance to share his plight with Steve, so of course, he had to go wave his problems like a flag in Steve's face.

Cathy leaned her forehead against the examining room wall as she heard Steve's surprise. "Mark! What are you doing here?"

"Mom's forcing me to work for her during my suspension," Mark said. "Talk about child abuse. You should tell her there are laws. She listens to you."

"Suspension? You got suspended from school?"

Cathy groaned. It was done. The secret was out, dropped on the waiting room floor like a living thing with claws. "Well, yeah," Mark said. "She didn't tell you? I figured you were the first one she called."

Cathy adjusted the poodle's useless IV, then carried him back to his kennel. She had to go out there, she told herself. She had to face Steve and explain why she hadn't wanted him to know. She stepped slowly into the hall and listened.

"She's got me in here cleaning up dog mess and dipping animals. I've practically been clawed to death, and I probably have pneumonia from all the stink." When Steve looked less than sympathetic, he threw in, "And yesterday a Doberman bit me."

It was a real sad story, Cathy thought, and she hoped Steve would ask to see the scars. The puppy's "bite" hadn't left any.

Deciding that she'd better intervene before Mark could spill his guts about what he'd done to receive such brutal punishment, she plastered a smile on her face and stepped into the waiting room. "Steve, what are you doing here?"

The sight of him reminded her how much she had missed him. He looked nervous, standing with his hands in his pockets, and wearing a strained smile. "I thought since you were avoid-ing me I'd just pop in. Unless you ran and hid, you'd have to talk to me."

She tried to laugh, but didn't tell him that running and hid-ing had crossed her mind. "I've been talking to you," she said as if that was the silliest thing she'd ever heard. "I've talked to you every night on the phone."

"I've never had so many thirty-second calls in my life."

She sighed, realizing she had hurt him. "Okay, let's talk." She gestured for him to follow her back to her office. "Mark, take Jumbo out for a walk. He's getting a little restless in his cage."

Mark groaned. "I hate that dog. He's fat and lazy and he smells bad."

"Do it anyway."

"*Man!*"

Cathy took Steve into the office and closed the door. Before she could get around the desk, he said, "Come here."

She hesitated, so he reached for her and pulled her into a hug. All the self-defense tactics melted right out of her as he held her. "I've missed you," he said. "You're not about to cut me loose, are you?"

"No," she said. "You might cut yourself loose when you hear what's going on, though." He let her go, and she sank down in her chair. "Steve, I've been avoiding you because of Mark's sus-pension. I didn't want you to know."

He kept standing. "Why not?"

"I don't know." Dramatically, she bent over and put her face in the circle of her arms. Gently, he pulled her ponytail up.

"Cathy, why not?" he asked when their eyes met. "Tell me."

"Frankly, I was a little embarrassed. I thought the fewer people who knew, the better."

He looked crushed, and finally sat down. "Well, I can under-stand that. I mean, it's personal, and it's your family. It's nobody's business."

"No, don't do that." Cathy clutched her head as if it might split down the middle. "It's not that it's none of your business. It's just that, well, I've been a little depressed about the whole thing. It just . . ." She covered her face. "Steve, it's not *that* he was suspended. It's *why* he was suspended."

"He didn't tell me," he said. "What did he do? Get in a fight?"

"No, it's worse than that." She made herself look at him. "Steve, he got caught in the bathroom at school, smoking marijuana."

She could see that Steve was struggling not to look shocked. *"Mark?"*

"Yeah, Mark."

He looked down at his feet, as if trying to process what he'd heard. "So you've been working him in here?"

"I figured hard labor was the best punishment. But I have a real bad feeling that tomorrow when he gets back to school, he's gonna go right back into that group of friends, and there's no telling where they may lead him next."

Steve sat back hard in his chair. "Cathy, I wish you'd have talked to me about this before. There's no need for you to hold this in all by yourself."

"Why not?" she asked, throwing her hands up. "I'm a single mom. That's what we do. We take care of things by ourselves."

He was quiet for a moment. "Have you told his father?"

She breathed a laugh. "Yeah, I told him. He wasn't that concerned. Said suspension didn't mean the same thing today that it did when we were kids."

"That's *all* he said?"

"Yep, that's it. Didn't even mention the marijuana. Like every kid gets caught taking drugs in the bathroom." She touched the corners of her eyes, valiantly fighting back the tears. "You know, I do the best I can. I really do. I mean . . . well, okay, in some ways I've done a pretty sorry job. But I'm trying to teach them right. I mean, I know that there's no excuse for Mark doing what he did, but I can't help thinking that if his father was still in our home, the authority would be there, and maybe he'd be too afraid to take a step like that."

"But if his father didn't take a stand, it wouldn't matter if he *was* in the home."

"But it seems like he would take a stand if he was here every day. He'd care more. It's real easy to stand back from a hundred miles away and decide that nothing is very important."

"You're right," he said. "But if you don't mind my saying so, I think you're doing a great job."

She gave a loud, sad, skeptical laugh. "Right. That's why my child came this close to getting arrested the other day. Honestly, I'm not sure why the principal didn't call the police." She rubbed her forehead. "You know, I'll never forget when Jerry said that the most we could hope for in child-rearing is that we would get our kids to adulthood without pregnancy or disease. I guess he'd like to amend that now. Pregnancy, disease, or a prison sentence. I had visions of raising that bar, but it looks like even that is going to be a struggle." She drew in a deep breath. "You must think we're the most dysfunctional family you've ever seen."

"Cathy, your family is anything but dysfunctional. You've got Mark here paying for his crime. You didn't let him off the hook. Your family *is* functioning just fine." He reached across the desk to brush a wisp of hair out of her eyes. "Cathy, don't close me out. You don't realize how attached you are to someone until you think you're losing them."

She smiled. He was good medicine.

"So now that this is out in the open, do you think we can get together, or are you gonna keep hiding from me?"

It was as if the burden had been lifted off of her back. "We can do something tomorrow night," she said. "Sound okay?"

He got up and came around the desk, settled his hands on the arms of her chair, and bent over to kiss her on the forehead. "It's good to see you," he whispered.

"It's good to see you, too." She touched his jaw, and smiled at the fine sandpaper feel of it.

"I don't mean that in a polite sort of way. I mean it's good to see your face. Good to look into your eyes."

Her eyes misted over again, and she got up and hugged him. He held her tight as time ticked by. She could get used to this, she thought. Every morning ... every night ...

"Don't hide anymore, okay?" he whispered. "It gives me a complex."

"I won't," she promised.

She walked him out of the office and back up the hall. Mark was grumbling to himself as he was putting the leash on the St. Bernard.

"Ready to get back to school, Mark?" Steve asked.

Mark shrugged. "Anything's better than this. Even that."

Steve laughed as he left the building. And as Cathy went back to work, things didn't seem so bad anymore.

CHAPTER
Twenty-Four

The baby girl's black hair had a slight curl to it, and Sylvia brushed it gently, then pulled it back from her face with a little bow glued to a bobby pin. She had washed the clothes the baby had been found in, but hadn't been able to come up with anything new for her to wear, for the stores were still closed due to damage from the storm. Many of the families in the shelter had nothing to wear but the clothes on their backs, so she had little hope of finding the child anything in the near future.

She checked the digital camera and made sure it was hooked up to her laptop. The fact that she had gotten this was evidence of yet another provision from God. Several engineers from the Army Corps of Engineers had flown down to do geological surveys and give advice to the government on where the next mud slides might occur, and one of them, a Christian, had sought them out. When he saw all the children that were homeless and orphaned, he gave them both his digital camera and the small color printer he had brought with him for printing out the reports he needed. He told them he would buy new ones with his own money when he returned to the States.

It would take days for her to photograph the children one by one and post them to the web site that Jeb had managed to set up for them. But at the moment it was their best hope of reuniting parents with their children. Government officials had agreed to make computers available to people looking for lost loved ones. They even planned to print the pictures out and take them into the hospitals.

Carly—the name she had given to the baby she had been keeping in her own home—was the first of the children to be photographed. The rest of the children were lined up on the floor in the hallway of what had become the orphanage, and Julie went from one to the next, brushing hair and washing faces so that nothing would impede recognition by family members.

"I wish we could dress them all up in Easter clothes," Julie said as she worked. "Back home, kids wear those dresses one time, then toss them in the back of their closets. If we could just get some of those forgotten clothes."

"I know where we can get some," Sylvia said, trying to make Carly stop sucking her thumb long enough to take the picture. "We'll tell my neighbors in Breezewood. They'll help us. They're great at getting the word out. You should have seen how we raised money for my little neighbor's heart transplant." She clicked the picture, then picked Carly up. "There, I got her. Perfect." Still holding the baby, she went down the line and took pictures of each child in turn.

"Do you think you could get word to them soon?" Julie asked.

"Now that the phone lines are working again, I think I can. I think my laptop's battery still has a little charge."

"They said they'd have the electricity back up soon," Harry said.

Sylvia turned to her husband. "Really?"

"Yeah. They said they were giving special priority to our part of town because we're sheltering so many people. The Corps of

Engineers had a little to do with that, too. They told them about our work, and got the government interested." He grinned at the sight of her holding Carly. "You know, you'd get that done a lot faster if you weren't holding the baby."

She smiled and bounced the little girl she'd grown so attached to. "I'm doing just fine. I hardly even know she's here."

"Right," he said. He walked up behind her and stroked the child's hair. "I don't think you've put her down in four days." He waited while she took the next child's picture. "So how soon can we get their pictures up?"

"God willing, I plan to get them up today," Sylvia said. "If I have to stay up all night, I will. Plus, Julie and I decided that I need to e-mail the States—everybody I know there, starting with Brenda, Tory, and Cathy—and ask them to start a clothing drive for the people."

"Well, it sure is needed," he said. "Most of the people I've seen today have been wearing the same thing since the hurricane."

"The girls will come through for us," Sylvia said. "I just know they will. Won't they, Carly?" She smiled down at the little girl.

Harry had been opposed to naming her at first. It would confuse her, he said, but since they didn't know her real name and weren't any closer to finding out, Sylvia had insisted on calling her something.

He reached his hands out for the child, and she came willingly. Sylvia hated to let her go, but she used the opportunity to take some more pictures. When she'd finished the dozen or so children in the hall, she asked Jeb to send in another group. As Julie lined them up on the floor, Sylvia looked at little Carly in Harry's arms. She had her thumb in her mouth and was sucking hard. She'd been restless off and on, no doubt grieving for her mother. Occasionally, she would cry, and not even Sylvia could calm her. Constantly, she looked toward the doors and windows, as if anticipating her mother walking in to get her.

Harry tickled her ribs, and she giggled. "Is Mrs. Sylvia taking good care of you?"

The baby just put her thumb back in her mouth. Harry pressed a kiss on the dark, chubby little cheek. "We're getting too attached, aren't we?"

"Yes, we are," Sylvia said. "But I can't help it. I had a long talk with the Lord this morning, Harry, and I asked him to find her family. But I can't help being selfishly happy that God brought her to us. So my heart gets broken when her family's located. I guess I'm willing to risk it."

"And if we never find her family?"

Sylvia's eyes misted over, and her face tightened. She couldn't utter the thoughts going through her mind. They were crazy, and might frighten Harry to death. Still, she couldn't help thinking that, if that happened, she would want to keep her. "I don't know, Harry," she said.

"Let's keep praying about it." He threw Carly up in the air. She giggled with delight.

Sylvia laughed with them. "All I know is that I've missed having a baby," Sylvia said. "And I'm grateful for however long I have her."

He laughed at the child, and threw her up again as Sylvia turned back to the children waiting to be photographed.

Late that night, Sylvia came home with Carly in her arms, and found that the electricity had been turned back on. She laid Carly in the little bed they had made for her out of a big basket. She had finally finished photographing the children, and had managed to get them all loaded into the computer before the battery had run out. It had taken hours, and she had done most of it with Carly in her lap.

When Harry came in, he looked more exhausted than she had ever seen him. She made him some tea and tried to help him get comfortable in his favorite chair. "We had record numbers professing Christ today," he said, laying his head back on the chair and holding the hot mug in his big hands. "They're so hopeless. An afterlife is all some of them can even think of looking forward to."

"You're doing good work, Harry. I know God is pleased with you."

"He's pleased with you, too. Getting those kids processed was a major undertaking. But it was so needed. And as people claim their children, we can tell them about Jesus, and how he loves each of them so much that he provided ways for them to reunite. Even the ones who never will . . . He will provide for them, too."

She went to the basket and sat down on the floor, stroking Carly's back. "I can't help thinking that Carly might be part of the work God has for me here."

Harry's eyebrows came up. "Sylvia, you're not thinking . . ."

"No," she said quickly. "Of course I want to find her mother. I just mean, it feels so right to hold her. Like it's a natural fit. I love feeling like a mother again."

"You *are* a mother. We have two children, Sylvia. They still need you."

"I know. But they're so far away, and have their own lives. There's nothing like holding a tiny little body against yours."

"Just be careful. Getting attached like that doesn't seem very healthy."

She gave him a smile that said he was worrying needlessly. "I'm the healthiest person you know. I can handle this, Harry. When God gives you somebody to take care of, you don't think about how it's gonna affect you when they leave. You just do what you've got to do. And you have to agree that I can't leave her at the children's shelter. She's too young. She needs more attention."

"I know," he said with a sigh. He finished off his tea and got up. "I have to go to bed."

"Go ahead," she said. "I'm just going to stay up and e-mail Tory, Brenda, and Cathy, now that we have electricity. Then I'll come."

She kissed Harry good night, then checked her e-mail. Her notes from home were piling up, but she hadn't been able to read them in days, for she had been conserving her battery. Even tonight she didn't have time to read them—not yet. Instead, she wanted to tell them of the work she was doing here, of the devastation and the homelessness, of the injuries and the deaths. Of the need for clothing and food.

But mostly she wanted to tell them about the little girl who had come into her life to brighten it up, even in these dark post-hurricane days in Nicaragua.

CHAPTER
Twenty-Five

The silence between Tory and Barry was deafening. Tory didn't know how much longer she would be able to endure it, but she had nothing to say to him. She could tell by the way he sat at the kitchen table, after the kids were in bed, watching her wipe counters and put things away, that he was waiting for her to stop so they could talk. When the phone rang, she pounced on it as if it was her rescue.

It was Brenda, telling her that she had the night off, and she and Cathy were going to be sitting on the front porch, reading the e-mails they'd gotten from Sylvia. She had quickly agreed to meet them there.

"I'm going over to Brenda's," she said as she hung up the phone.

Barry looked wounded. "Tory, I thought we could talk."

"I don't want to talk to you," she said. "There's nothing to talk about, anyway."

"Tory, there's a *lot* to talk about. This is my baby, too."

"Then I don't know how in the world you can sleep at night," she said, scrubbing harder than she needed to. "You seem to be sleeping just fine down there in the basement."

"That's because you don't want me in the bedroom," he said. "If I weren't sleeping down there, *you* probably would be."

"Got that right," Tory threw back.

He swallowed and got to his feet. "Tory, this isn't getting us anywhere. It's not helping the baby, and it's not—"

"Helping the baby?" she cut in, swinging to face him. "How dare you?"

He got quiet and slid his hands into his pockets, looked down at his feet.

"You've got a lot of nerve acting like you care about our baby," she said.

"Tory, you've got to consider the options."

"There *aren't* any options! The only option I know of is that we're going to have a baby and there's something wrong with her. *I'm* going to take care of her. I don't know about you."

"You don't even know what you're talking about," he said. "You don't know what it's going to be like having a baby for the rest of your life, who grows and gets bigger than you, whose diaper you still have to change, who has medical problems and never leaves the house unless he's with you. Do you want that, Tory? Because I don't think you're ready for it. You like order. Perfection. Look at this house, for Pete's sake. It won't be like this if the baby comes."

"I'll do what I have to do," she said. "I'll *become* what I have to become. God wouldn't have given me this baby if he couldn't make me into what I need to be."

"What about Nathan?" he asked through his teeth. "Are you willing to devote yourself to caring for two mentally retarded people, when you've hardly even gone near Nathan since I've known you? Do you want Spencer and Brittany to be embarrassed at every school function, and finally just drop out of everything because they don't want to have to suffer the humiliation of having their sister disrupting things?"

"Those are hard things, Barry!" she cried. "But they don't change the fact that we're talking about human beings. It doesn't change the fact that I'm carrying her right now and I don't have a choice in the matter."

"You *do* have a choice," he said.

She shook her head, unable to stand the thought that he was using the word *choice* as if it was benign and safe. As if it wasn't lethal. "I'm going," she said. "I'll be at Brenda's."

He followed her out into the garage, stopping her at the outer door before she could leave. "Tory, don't think I don't care about this baby. Don't think I don't care about my brother."

"That's exactly what I think."

"Then you'd be wrong." His eyes filled with tears and he hammered his fist on the wall. "I haven't been able to think about anything else for the last couple of days. I haven't been able to accomplish anything at work. I've just been thinking and think-ing what it would be like. Considering all the options in my head." He stopped and swallowed, tried to control his voice. "It's hard for me, too," he said more softly, his voice sounding hollow in the garage. "I can't stand the thought of what I'm asking you to do. It makes me sick. I didn't think I'd ever want it for a child of mine. But I went to see Nathan a couple of days ago, and I sat there looking at him, wondering if he'd really want to be born if he had it to do over. If someone had told him, 'Nathan, you're not going to live a normal life; you're not going to grow up. You're going to be bound by your mental age, your physical problems. You'll never understand what it's like to be a father, or to accomplish anything, or to contribute something.' If he'd had the choice and someone had asked him, would he have decided to go for it anyway? To sit in his wheelchair all his life, drooling, eating mushed bananas and eggs, whistling his life away? What purpose does he have? That's what I don't understand."

"God put this baby in our family, Barry. You know all those commandments in the Bible and all those suggestions for behav-ior? They're not just there for the good times, they're there for the hard times, when it doesn't make any sense. They're there for when you don't have any place else to turn. You have to have a source, Barry. You have to have a plumb line. *You're* the one who taught me that."

"I still believe it," he said. "But these are extraordinary circumstances, Tory."

"You're telling me."

Tears came to his eyes, and she saw the muscles under his lips twitching, saw him looking at his feet and struggling for the right words. "See . . . I know that it's harder for you. You're the one throwing up all the time, watching your body change, feeling all those hormones pumping through you. Your body is screaming out 'motherhood,' and your heart is breaking over this baby."

The words melted her to tears, and she turned away, unwilling to share her emotions with him.

He came up behind her and set his hands on her shoulders, dropped his forehead into her hair. "Honey, I want to be there for you. I want to protect you, too. I want to protect Brittany and Spencer. Even the baby . . ."

She closed her eyes as tears rolled down her face. "This baby is going to need protecting all her life," she whispered. "From all kinds of people. From kids who make fun of her, from doctors who give up on her, from strangers who stare at her. I don't want to have to protect her from her dad."

"You think I want that? I love my children, Tory. All of them."

"Then don't suggest abortion for one of them."

"Maybe I love her enough to do that."

She jerked away from him. "You're *so* wrong! It's not love to kill a baby, no matter how noble you can convince yourself you are!" Her lips twisted. "Or are you buying into the belief that this isn't a baby? That it's just a blob of tissue?"

"I don't know, Tory. All I know is that she'll never reach her potential. She'll never be able to offer anything back to the world. She won't have a purpose."

"How do you know?" she screamed. "You don't know what God's purpose is for *you*, much less a baby who hasn't even been born! And whose potential are we talking about?"

"Look at Nathan, Tory!"

"*You* look at Nathan! Nobody but God knows what his potential is. It's not up to you to decide that."

"But if Nathan could be in heaven with God ... if he had the choice of walking streets of gold or sitting out decades and decades in a wheelchair, whistling and staring at nothing ... If we really believe in heaven, wouldn't we choose for him to be there?"

"We don't get to choose that, Barry," she cried. "That's God's job."

"But think about our baby!" he shouted. "About whether you want our baby being shunned by society, or in heaven in a perfect body, waiting for us."

"You could say that about any baby who was ever aborted," she said. "From the most perfect, healthy, unwanted one, to one like ours. You could say abortion is good because it sends little souls to heaven instead of bringing them into this evil world."

"It's true. God does gather up those little souls. He has them all."

"But what about the blessings they might have been on their families? What about the potential they might have had on earth? They might have cured AIDS or cancer. They might have evangelized the world. And what about the sin that eats away at the mother and father who choose to take that way out, chipping away at their lives and their hearts and souls, because even if no one else ever knows what they did, *they* know. What about the women whose lives are ruined because they have to act enlightened and liberated, like masters of their own bodies, when really they're in deeper bondage to the abortion they had than they ever would have been to the baby? Abortion is just as bad for the mother as it is for the baby, Barry. Don't you care about that? Don't you care what it would do to *me?*"

"Of course, I do," he said. "Of course." He turned away from her, wiped his face, and wilted over the hood of their car. "I don't know what to do." She watched his back rise and fall with his anguished breath. "Have you thought about this with anything other than your emotions and hormones, Tory?"

"Of course, I have," she admitted, knowing it would cost her. "I've thought how ... disappointed I am. I wanted people to stop in aisles and tell me how precious she is. But they'll be looking away, pretending they don't see." He looked up at her, and their eyes met. "We have beautiful children, Barry."

He straightened, and whispered, "They have a beautiful mother."

She shook her head. "All the work on my looks. My hair, my makeup, my weight ... I put so much into it. Perfection, it's my stock—and trade." Her voice broke off, and she looked at her reflection in the car's window. She didn't like what she saw. "Do you think this is how God's punishing me? Giving me a child who isn't perfect, so I'll learn?"

"Learn what?" Barry asked.

"Learn that it isn't what's on the outside that's important. It's what's on the inside. Maybe perfection really has to do with the heart. Maybe this baby will be the most perfect one of all our children. Inside, where we all need to learn to look."

"It's more likely that she'll be the most miserable."

The vulnerability she had begun to share fled as that rage erupted in her again. She slammed her hand on the fender. "I *don't* know that. But if I did, I'm not sure it could change anything. You shouldn't be able to choose whether to abort a baby or not based on whether you think she'll have a good life. If we did that, we'd think we'd have to go around to all the poverty-stricken families and abort all of theirs. We'd kill anyone who isn't born in America, or in an upper-middle-class family, or in a family with high IQ's and beauty awards."

He didn't seem to know what to say to that.

Weary, she leaned back against the garage wall. "I miss my mom."

"I do, too," he said. "I miss her for you." Her mother had died of breast cancer just a few months after their wedding. She had never seen her daughter pregnant with even her first child, had never been able to teach her how to change a diaper or bathe an infant. She had never been there to talk her through marital problems or adult crises. Tory needed her now.

Sylvia had done a lot to take her mother's place. She had been there, the older, more experienced woman who had already walked the ground that Tory was walking. She had been so full of wisdom and patience, had always had such good advice. Tory wished she could pick up the phone and call Sylvia in León, and have her drop everything and listen to Tory for a while. "I miss Sylvia, too," she said.

He drew in a deep breath, let it out in a rugged sigh. "Go on over there," he whispered finally. "Listen to her letters. Maybe it'll make you feel better."

She hesitated, wondering how their marriage would ever recover. "What about you?" she asked quietly. "What's going to make you feel better?"

He shrugged. "I don't know. Maybe I'll pray for a while."

"Good," she whispered. "That's good."

He crossed the garage floor, took her hands, and bent down to kiss her wet cheek. "Making everything all right is my job in this family," he whispered. "I'm trying to do that."

"If you keep trying to talk me into ending our baby's life, Barry, nothing is ever going to be all right again."

"And if I just let things go, leave it all to chance, nothing will, anyway."

"God is bigger than chance," she said through her teeth. "I thought you trusted him more than that."

"I trust him to lead me in making the right decision."

"Wait a minute." She jerked her hands away. "Did you say 'me'? Are you telling me that this is *your* decision? One of those 'spiritual leader of the family' decisions?"

"That's not what I meant," he said.

"You said, 'lead *me* into making the right decision.' Like it's your decision. Period. Think again, Barry! You can make all the decisions you want, but this is my baby, too. And if God doesn't want it born, he's going to have to decide that on his own."

With that, she slammed her hand on the button that would open the garage and darted out under it before it had the chance to rise all the way. She heard it closing behind her as she took off across the lot between hers and Brenda's homes.

CHAPTER
Twenty-Six

Brenda and Cathy were already on the porch when Tory launched across the yard. A cool breeze whipped up from the valley, teasing and ruffling her hair, but it did nothing to quell her anger. The life she had known was coming quickly to an end, and she had no power to stop it.

Both women saw the distress on Tory's face and reached out to hug her.

"How are you doing, honey?" Brenda asked.

"Fine," Tory lied.

"How's Barry?" Cathy asked.

Tory shook her head. She couldn't make herself answer the question.

"Want to talk?" Brenda whispered.

Tory shook her head and swiped at the tears on her face. "Not now. Just read me Sylvia's e-mail. I think she sent me a copy but I haven't had time to turn on my computer."

Reluctantly, Brenda began to read, and Tory welcomed the chance to think about problems other than her own. Sylvia was suffering a trial, and she had given them a way to help.

When they had finished reading, Cathy's eyes were glowing. "Well, now we know what we can do," she said, as if they'd all been looking for new endeavors. "We can have a clothing drive. Heck, everybody gives away their old clothes. All we have to do is get people to clean out their closets."

"How would we get them to Sylvia?" Brenda asked.

"I don't know," Cathy said. "But my church would love to help Sylvia, since she went there all her life, and as big as it is, I'd bet *somebody* could donate the use of a plane."

"I'll do whatever I can," Brenda said.

Cathy started rolling up her sleeves, as if she was ready to start work here and now. "It'll be fun, knowing we're helping Sylvia in some way. But Tory, you don't have to help if you don't want to."

"Why not?" Tory asked with dull eyes. "It's not like I can do anything to solve my own problems. I might as well be doing something for someone else. I was just thinking that some of Spencer's old clothes might fit the little girl with Sylvia."

"Good idea," Brenda said. "But are you sure you won't need them for the baby?"

Tory's face slackened. "No, it's a girl. I'll keep Britty's things for her."

"A little girl," Brenda whispered with awe. "I forgot you told us that. How wonderful."

Tory looked at her feet and nodded. They both stared quietly at her for a moment, neither knowing what to say. "Tory, are you sure you're all right?" Cathy asked again.

"Yeah," she said. "As all right as I can be, under the circumstances." She looked up at Cathy, seeking a way to change the subject. "So when do we get started?"

"Tomorrow," Cathy said. "I'll tell Steve tonight and get him involved, and he'll have flyers printed and distributed by morning. The man's amazing. And he has a heart as big as Survey Mountain."

Tory smiled. She loved watching Cathy's romance develop. "So, how are things with you two?"

"Pretty ... fabulous, actually. We would have gone out tonight, but I keep having to go back to the clinic to take care of the million-dollar dog."

"The what?" Brenda asked.

"This poodle that got hit by a car the other day. He had about a one-percent chance of pulling through, even with all the best technology. If there's ever been such a thing as a canine ICU, I've got one set up at my clinic now. I had to rent all this extra equipment. It's costing his owner a fortune, but she's willing to pay whatever it takes to keep him alive. And if he lives, he may never walk again ..."

Something inside Tory snapped as Cathy's words sank in. She couldn't explain the unmitigated rage that began to rise inside her. A dog was being rescued with every resource available, while Tory's own husband was lobbying for the quick, easy death of their child? "Unbelievable," she said.

"What? The cost or the effort?"

"Both." She got to her feet, trembling. "This much energy can go into saving a dog, but when it's a human who's in jeopardy, the doctors are so quick to suggest the easiest options." She touched her temple with a trembling hand. "You know, I hate that word," she bit out. "*Options*. It sounds so sterile. Did you use that word with the dog's owner, Cathy?"

Cathy's face fell, as if she'd been wrongly rebuked. "Well, I don't know. I think I told her what could be done ..."

Tory's eyes stung with tears, and her lips stretched thin across her lips. "And the poodle's owner thought it was worth it. Spend the money, utilize the resources, take the little paralyzed animal home and love him no matter what shape he's in, no matter what he can *contribute*, no matter what his potential may ever be, this ... this *poodle* who is so wanted!" Blood pumped furiously through her face, punctuating each word with her own fury.

Cathy and Brenda both stared up at her, stricken and speechless.

"It kills me," Tory went on. "I'm carrying a *human being*, and my husband thinks she's not even as valuable as that poodle in your clinic!"

Cathy swallowed. "I shouldn't have brought it up, Tory. I'm so insensitive."

"No, you're not," Tory wept. She walked down the porch steps and stood in the grass, looking furiously up at the stars. Finally, she turned around. "You're the one keeping the poodle alive. You've assigned value to that life, even if it isn't human. They fight for whales, and baby seals, and tuna, for heaven's sake. I just don't understand how people could assign *less* value to a little baby . . ."

Brenda looked heartbroken as she got out of her chair and came down the steps. She reached for Tory, and Tory went into her arms. Helplessly, Cathy got up and joined in the hug.

"What are we gonna do without Sylvia?" Tory asked.

Brenda pulled back and wiped her own face. "We're not going to do without her," she said. "She's still one of us."

"I just want to talk to her," Tory said in a high-pitched voice. "I want to tell her about the baby. I want to ask her what to do about Barry."

"Well, I'm no Sylvia," Brenda said. "But I know where she gets her wisdom. We could go to the same source tonight, Tory."

"You mean pray?"

Brenda smiled. "Yeah, we could pray. Take all these things to God. He's the only one who can help, anyway."

Together, the three neighbors spent the next hour talking to the Lord, pouring out their hearts for Tory's and Sylvia's problems.

When Tory finally went home that night, she felt calmer, and thought that she and Barry might be able to navigate their way through these decisions now. But Barry was already in the basement. She went to the steps and creaked down them, crossed the concrete floor to the couch. He was already sound asleep, fully dressed, with a blanket thrown over him.

She thought of waking him up, resuming their conversation, but she didn't know what more could be said. They would never agree on this. Never.

Defeated, she went back up the stairs and to their bedroom, and slept alone again.

CHAPTER
Twenty-Seven

The death of the poodle, Shish-kabob, made Cathy late getting home on Monday, Mark's first day back at school. The distraught owner had detained her for more than an hour as she wept on Cathy's shoulder. Cathy didn't know how to tell her that her pain needed to be cut short, because Cathy needed to be home when her son got off the bus. So she had held the woman and let her cry as the moments ticked by.

The fact that Mark was out sweeping the driveway when she drove up clued her that something was wrong. He looked up at her as she pulled her car into the garage, and she saw the trepidation on his face. She left everything sitting on her seat and braced herself as she got slowly out of the car. "Mark?"

"Hey, Mom," he said in a dismal voice. "How was your day?"

He never asked her how her day had been, and had never cared. She didn't think he cared now. "Mark, what's wrong?"

He looked offended. "Why do you think something's wrong?"

"Because you're sweeping. You asked me how my day was."

"You act like I'm lazy and don't care about anybody but myself." He threw the broom against the house, as if giving up. "I just thought somebody needed to sweep."

"Uh-huh," she said skeptically. "Thank you. Now what's wrong? Come on, Mark. You have to tell me sooner or later."

He sighed and headed into the house, and she followed, dreading whatever was going to be thrown at her next. He grabbed his backpack from the floor and jerked out an envelope.

"From the principal?" she asked.

"No," he said. "It's my stupid report card."

Now it all made sense. She opened the envelope and watched as Mark went to the refrigerator and stood perusing the contents. She had a feeling that he didn't have an appetite, despite his feigned interest. She probably wouldn't have one, either, by the time this was all over. She unfolded the card and looked down at the grades lined up on the right side. The blood drained from her face. "F, F, D . . ." Her voice got louder with each letter . . . "D, F, C." She looked up at her son's back. He seemed very interested in a shriveled orange that should have been thrown away weeks ago. "Mark, what in the world . . . ?"

He swung around. "I'm sorry, Mom, okay? I thought I was doing better than that . . ."

"You've never had an F in your life. None of you have. Even D's . . ."

"Don't overreact, okay? I mean, they're just grades. Some states don't even have them anymore, and I think that's a good idea, because it's not right to judge people like that. Some kids get messed up for life because their grades make them feel so bad about theirselves. Besides, I did good in PE, and it wasn't easy because we had to run two miles . . ."

She gaped back down at the report card. "Your C was in *PE?*"

"Well, I forgot to study for a couple of tests about nutrition and muscles and stuff. If not for that I would have had an A."

A million reactions filed through her mind as she stared helplessly at the report card. Some were illegal. Others were controversial. All were justifiable.

"Now, Mom, I knew you were gonna blow a fuse, but if you'll just calm down and think about this . . ."

She closed her eyes and held up a hand to stem further conversation, and he stopped midsentence. "I think you'd do best," she whispered, "just to go upstairs . . . and keep a low profile for, say . . . a year or two . . . until I decide what to do with you."

"Yes, ma'am." He was gone before she opened her eyes.

She was shaking, almost as badly as she'd been when she found out about the marijuana. She sat down and covered her face with both hands.

The door flew open, and Rick stepped in, dropped his backpack on the floor, and headed for the refrigerator. Annie flew in behind him. "Mom, I made honor roll! Check out this report card."

Cathy took it numbly, wondering what the joke was going to be, and saw the letters lined up down the side of the computer printout. "Great, honey. This is great."

Annie frowned. "You don't look like you think it's great. What's the matter with you, anyway? You look kinda pale."

"No, really," Cathy said. "Great report card. You've come a long way."

"Do I deserve something for that? Like those new shoes I want? Mom, you know how hard I worked for those grades, and those shoes are all I'll want between now and Christmas, I promise, and you always punish us when we have bad grades, so doesn't it stand to reason that you should reward us when we have good ones?"

"Yes, maybe," she said, still thinking about all those F's. "You do deserve a reward. What about you, Rick?"

Rick turned around, as if he hadn't noticed his mother was in the room until she called his name. "Oh, yeah. In the backpack."

"Do I have to dig it out?"

He sighed as if he didn't have time to be bothered. "Guess not." He pulled the report card out and thrust it at her. "Now, before you say anything, that one C was in calculus, and it was really hard, and ninety-five percent of the class made a C or below . . ."

She studied the grades and saw that most of them were A's. One B. Not a single D or F. She wanted to fall to her knees and thank God for his mercy. "This is good, Rick," she said. "Really good."

"Really?" he asked, shrugging. "Cool." He saw Mark's report card folded in her hand. "Boy, Mark's must be really bad."

"What makes you say that?"

"Well, you usually go ballistic over C's. What did he have?" He grabbed at the report card, and she tried to snatch it back. But he had it open before she could stop him. "F's? I can't believe it! Look at this, Annie! F's, all over the place. The kid is flunking out of seventh grade."

Before her eyes, Rick and Annie became best friends as they shared a laugh over their brother's plight. It was probably the first time they'd spoken cordially to each other in days. "Man, is he in trouble!"

"What are you gonna do to him, Mom? First pot-smoking, now this? He's just asking for it, man!"

"*Shut up!*" Mark cried from upstairs.

Annie and Rick let out a howl of laughter, and Cathy jerked the report card back. She wondered if God had been thinking of teenagers when he said that every intent of man's heart was only evil continually. "Upstairs, everybody," she said. "To your rooms."

"Why?" Rick blurted. "What did we do?"

"We're the good ones, remember?" Annie cried.

"You have Scripture to learn. James 3:6. Tell your brother to memorize it, too."

"Mom, you're kidding!" Annie said. "I don't have time for this. I have a date tonight."

"Not unless you've memorized that Scripture." She handed them her Bible.

Rick took it, and angrily turned to James. "This is ridiculous, Mom. We got good grades for this?"

"What's it say?" Annie asked. "Is it the one about provoking your children to anger?"

Rick shot his mother a look and began to read. "'The tongue also is a fire, a world of evil among the parts of the body. It corrupts the whole person, sets the whole course of his life on fire, and is itself set on fire by hell.' Oh, great, Mom. This is real uplifting."

"Upstairs!" she yelled.

"What about the shoes?" Annie ventured before she went.

Cathy shot her a seething look. "Bad timing, Annie."

"Well, can we talk about it after I memorize about my evil tongue?"

But the phone rang before she could respond, and the children scattered to answer it. Cathy pulled her feet up on the couch and covered her head with both hands. She wasn't strong enough for this, she thought. This was the kind of thing for which she needed help. She wished she could have walked in and yelled, "Wait until your father gets home." It took two parents to raise teenagers. One just didn't cut it.

But their father wouldn't give Mark's grades any thought at all.

No, she was going to have to act on her own. She just wasn't sure what to do. All she knew for sure was that her son was in the wrong crowd, that they were leading him down the wrong path, that he wasn't learning and he wasn't behaving while he was at school.

Her instinct was to jerk him out and homeschool him, like Brenda used to do. But she had to make a living, and besides, her kids never listened to her. What made her think that Mark would learn anything at all from her?

Private school, she thought. That was his only hope. She would take him out of his school, remove him from the friends who were changing his life for the worse, and put him into a new school.

Then she could *pay* to see him flunk out.

She crumpled into tears.

She went into the dining room which she used as a computer room, and turned on the computer with tears rolling down her face. She pulled up her e-mail program, and with rapid-fire keystrokes, began composing a letter to Sylvia. She wished she could get her sound Christian wisdom now.

She wrote out the letter, explaining her dilemma to her friend who had much worse problems. Then she closed it by saying, "Advice welcome, and prayers needed, if you have any extra time. Love, Cathy."

She pressed her thumbs to her tear ducts and cried like a baby as the e-mail program sent the letter flying across cyberspace.

Later that evening, Brenda was pushing the "send" button on her own e-mail program, which she'd accessed on her office computer during her break. She'd been battling depression all day after the medical bills that had come in. Fortunately, she had managed to pay most of them, thanks to her income from this job. But each night in this huge, noisy room had become worse than the one before it.

Her boss was hostile, to say the least. He verbally attacked anyone who fell short of their quota, monitored calls as if he was guarding national security, and had pet names for the employees, like "Bozo" and "Airhead." He called Brenda "Grandma" because, at thirty-six, she was one of the oldest employees. The name was designed to rankle her, but Brenda had made it her business to smile right through any abuse he threw at her.

The people she called with her sales pitch ran the gamut from being rude to downright vile. She burst into tears several times a night, longing for the days when she could put her kids to bed and spend time unwinding with David. She was tired all the time, and had started to become irritable with Joseph, so much that she knew that homeschooling her other three children would be a bad idea right now. It seemed that she never caught up on her sleep, and the cycle of sleep deprivation night after night added up to her being as close to depression as she'd ever been in her life. She didn't want her kids to be trapped at home with a cranky mother, when they could be at school with a teacher who slept at night and had time to think.

But her kids' report cards had indicated that they were bored with school. Their grades were less than stellar, despite the fact that they'd already covered most of this material two years earlier. Every single day, they begged her to resume their home-schooling.

For one of the first times in her life, she didn't quite know what to do.

She wished cyberspace was as immediate as the phone, but it wasn't. She would have to wait for an answer, she thought. She felt like Tory felt last night, missing Sylvia and wishing with all her heart that she was here. She hadn't realized how valuable her prayer partner was until she was gone.

Quickly, she choked down the sandwich she had brought from home, then got back to work, praying that Sylvia would have time to e-mail her back before she got off tonight.

CHAPTER
Twenty-Eight

The sound of a mother's anguish ripped across the corridors of the Missionary Children's Home. Sylvia heard it from the room where she played with some of the smaller children, using cardboard toilet paper rolls as instruments and sticks for percussion. The children were laughing as they made the sounds, but over the voices came the woman's cries.

Sylvia picked Carly up and stepped out into the hall. She looked up toward the door, and saw the woman who was wailing. Julie Anderson was trying to calm her.

"What is it?" Sylvia asked, hurrying toward them.

"She came here looking for her children," Julie said. "But they're not here."

Sylvia's heart burst. "Oh, the poor woman. Are you sure?"

"Yes," Julie said. "Hers were eight, ten, eleven, and thirteen."

"Not even one of them?" Sylvia asked.

Julie shook her head. The woman's pain was unquenchable, and Sylvia adjusted Carly on her hip, and touched the woman's back, trying to comfort her.

"How did they get separated?" Sylvia asked.

"They were with their father. She found him dead, but the children weren't with him. They're not in the hospitals, so she was told to come here."

"Maybe they're still alive," Sylvia said. "Let's take her somewhere and pray with her."

Julie looked as if she hadn't thought of that. "Yes," she said. She looked down at the woman, and told her in Spanish what they were going to do. "In here," she said, and led the woman to one of the few empty rooms.

Carly sat on Sylvia's lap, sucking her thumb, as the three women began to pray together. The Nicaraguan woman's crying ceased as they prayed, and though she could not understand their language, the words comforted her. Sylvia knew that the Spirit of God was offering comfort that Sylvia and Julie did not have to give.

When they had sent the woman on her way, Sylvia went back to working with the children. God had provided several Nicaraguan women to come and help with the children. One of them was a woman who had lost her two children in the flooding. She had spent the first days grieving, but then had turned her despair into hard work for these kids. More came to help each day. It made it possible for Sylvia to do some of the public relations necessary to get the word out about the home, and the fact that parents might be able to find their children here. A steady stream of parents had come since she'd first put the posters out, and some of the children had been reunited with their parents. But in the last few days, the number of children had grown. More were being brought in than were being taken out.

She didn't take Carly and return home until after dark that evening, and she rocked her quietly and savored the feel of the little girl relaxing in the comfort of her arms. She was getting attached to the child, she knew. Too attached. In the last couple of days, she hadn't tried very hard to locate Carly's mother. She told herself that she had already done everything she could, but every time a mother came to the school looking for her child, her heart tightened into a fist, until she knew it wasn't Carly she wanted.

When Carly was asleep, she laid her down in the basket-bed she had made her, and smiled at the sweet expression on the child's face, as if she had no idea that she had been left alone in the midst of a disaster, and that she had no family.

"I'll be her family, Lord," Sylvia whispered as tears filled her eyes. "Let me raise her."

She knew the prayer was almost a betrayal of the child, for she should be praying for her family to come. She forced herself to utter that prayer, but she knew the Lord knew what she wanted most.

She heard Harry coming, and got up, afraid to let him see her doting too much over the child. Already he was worried about her. She went into the kitchen and began to make him a tamale, knowing he probably hadn't eaten all day.

"Sylvia!" he called from the doorway.

She went running to tell him that Carly was sleeping, but stopped cold when she saw the young, dark woman with him. She was no more than eighteen or nineteen, and had big, black eyes and a bruise on one side of her jaw. "Hello," she said, forgetting to use Spanish.

"Sylvia, this young woman is named Lupe. She's looking for her baby."

Sylvia's heart crashed. Her instinct was to pray that she wasn't the mother, that she wasn't going to take Carly away. But she knew better. Carly needed her real mother, not some American imitation. She swallowed. "Have you taken her to the school?"

"No," Harry said. "Honey, she has an eighteen-month-old girl."

"I see." She touched the woman's arm, inviting her in, and motioned toward the basket on the floor. "Carly's sleeping. She was exhausted from all the noise at the home, and drifted right off when I got her home . . ."

But already the woman was approaching the basket, slowly, as if she feared that the child there might not be her own. Sylvia froze, and Harry put his arm protectively around her.

The woman knelt over the basket, and leaned over the child. She began to cry, and brought her bandaged hand to her mouth.

Sylvia wasn't sure if she was crying for joy, or despair. She approached the woman and knelt down beside her. She picked the sleeping baby up, and turned her so that the young woman could see her.

But the woman only turned away.

"She's not hers," Sylvia said. She tried to hide the relief flooding over her. "Harry, she's not hers." She clutched the baby to her chest, and the child kept sleeping. Harry got the young woman to her feet and walked her outside.

Sylvia got up and took the baby to the rocking chair, and began to rock her again as tears flowed down her face. She hadn't lost her, she thought. God had let her keep the baby a little while longer.

When Harry came back in, he saw Sylvia's tears and sat down next to her. "Crying for the mother?" he asked softly.

"Half of me," she said. "But the other half is crying because I was so afraid she was going to take Carly away."

"Don't you want her to have her mother?"

"Of course. But Harry, it's been occurring to me lately that . . . maybe God gave her to us. Maybe he wants us to raise her."

Harry let out a heavy sigh. "Oh, Sylvia. You can't believe that."

"Why not?" she asked. "He knows how I've missed being a mother. Why wouldn't he have given me a second chance to do that?"

"Because we have other work to do here. You're needed in the school, Sylvia. You're needed for my patients. If we do all the things God has given us to do, we won't have time to raise another child."

"But I can do all those things with Carly," she whispered. "I can, Harry. Haven't I been doing them?"

"Yes, but Sylvia, she's not yours. Even if her mother is dead, she probably has a father, a grandmother, aunts and uncles. They'll come for her eventually."

"What if they don't?" Sylvia asked. "Are we going to put her in the home when she's old enough?"

"Well, I don't know. We'll just have to pray about that and see what God leads us to do. You know, some of these families who've lost children might want to adopt her."

Sylvia closed her eyes, as if she couldn't stand the thought of such a thing. "We'll see," she whispered, pressing her cheek against the baby's crown. "We'll just pray about it and see."

Later that night, when Harry and the baby were asleep, Sylvia read her e-mails from home. She sent the same response to Tory, Brenda, and Cathy, asking them all to pray that she would do the right thing for Carly. She confessed to them how she wanted to raise this baby, and how she believed in her heart that God had sent her directly to Sylvia for a reason.

Then, when she had finished pouring out her heart, she addressed their own problems one by one. It was clear that they were keeping too many things from each other. Cathy didn't want the others to know the trouble she was having with Mark. The only reason she told Sylvia, she suspected, was that she was so far away, and it was safe. Brenda didn't want anyone to know that her job was pure torture, but how necessary it was for her to keep it to pay their bills. Tory had finally started sharing, but she didn't know either of her two neighbors' problems. So Sylvia chided them all, hoping they would listen.

Brenda, I've been praying for you and the kids and for Joseph, and I never forget to pray that David will come to a saving knowledge of Christ. I'm also remembering your finances. I thought hard before writing that out so clearly, because I'm writing this to all three of you, and don't want to betray confidences. But girls, I have to tell you, this is not the time for keeping things to yourselves. You need each other. And I have an idea.

Cathy, I've been praying for you and your kids, too, especially Mark, who's turning corners in his life that will take him to dangerous places. And I was thinking about your problem with Mark in school, the kids with whom he's yoking himself, the lack of interest in his grades. And Brenda desperately wants to homeschool again, but here she is working at a place she hates at night, not getting enough rest, and still barely making ends meet.

You girls aren't sharing, and you hold each other's solutions in your hands. Why don't you two put these problems together, and solve one for each other? Brenda, think about quitting that job, go back to homeschooling your kids, but also start homeschooling Mark. Cathy could pay you what she was considering paying a private school. Then Mark would get the personal attention he needs, and be removed from the influence of the kids he's following. And Brenda, we know you can do it.

It's just an idea, and if I were there in person, I probably wouldn't say it straight out like this. I'd take you aside one at a time. But I don't have a lot of time to be tactful right now. Forgive me if I've stuck my nose in where it doesn't belong.

And dear Tory, don't be afraid. I know there's a lot of uncertainty right now. I know you worry about this less-than-perfect child you're carrying. What will she look like, how disruptive will she be, will you be up to the challenge? I can only tell you that you are. And when you hold her for the first time, I believe all your fears will vanish. That child is a gift from God, exactly as he made her. Sometimes we have to look at the events in our lives that look like crises, and realize that God doesn't always send sunshine. He sends showers, too, hurricanes sometimes, mud slides and floods. And out of those, sometimes, come little rewards like Carly, beautiful blessings like children's homes committed to raising godly children, salvation for thousands who would never have heard if they had not come to the point of desperation.

Your showers are going to yield blessings, too, Tory. Hang in there, honey. You're not alone. But Barry might be right now. Go easy on him, and show him mercy. Don't tell the kids about the pregnancy just to force him into accepting the baby. Give him time and space, and when you tell them, tell them together, with great joy. Trust me, it will come. I wish I could be there to share it with you.

When she hit "send," she was weeping, and wishing she could hug each one of her neighbors now. Oh, how she missed them.

But then she went back to Carly in the little basket-bed, and stroked her back, and realized that God took things and people away, but he also brought new ones into our lives. His compassions never failed. They were new every morning.

Even during the stormy season.

CHAPTER
Twenty-Nine

When the kids had left for school the next morning, Cathy saw Brenda out watering her garden. She got up her nerve and bounced across the street. "Did you read Sylvia's e-mail?" she asked bluntly.

"I sure did." Brenda turned off the water. "Cathy, why didn't you tell me about Mark?"

"Why didn't you tell *me* how much you hated your job, and that you were having more money problems?"

"Because you've all done so much to raise money to pay our bills. I don't mind working. It's not your problem."

"But I'm your friend. I could have at least listened."

"And so could I. What's going on with Mark, Cathy? Daniel told me he'd gotten in trouble at school, but that's about all I could get out of him."

"He probably didn't want to tell you for fear that you'd never let him cross that street again." She looked down at her feet. "Mark got suspended for smoking marijuana in the bathroom."

Brenda caught her breath, and Cathy knew this was probably one of the worst things Brenda could imagine. A surge of unexpected resentment shot through her. Brenda's kids would never do anything that rebellious, because Brenda was the perfect mother. Quickly, she shook that bitter feeling away, and told herself it could happen to anyone's kids. "Then he went back to school, and got his report card. He's failing most of his classes."

Brenda nodded this time, as if she could relate to that. "I wasn't thrilled about my kids' report cards, either. Their grades weren't bad—they just weren't great. I think it's because they're bored."

"Yeah, that's it," Cathy spouted in a sarcastic voice. "Mark's bored. Fat chance. He just isn't studying, isn't doing homework..."

"But maybe that really is because he's bored. Maybe if they made it more fun ..."

"That's a little easier for a homeschooling mom than an overworked, underpaid teacher with thirty kids in each of seven class periods. Besides, *life* isn't always going to be fun. They have to learn to sweat their way through hard things." She lowered herself to Brenda's porch steps. "Sylvia's idea was a good one, Brenda. I can't homeschool Mark myself. It would be disastrous for me. My kids won't even listen to me about putting their napkins in their laps. I could just see me trying to teach calculus. They'd grow up to be a bunch of ignorant, illiterate adults who hated me because I didn't make them go to school."

Brenda laughed at her image. "Like you could undo everything they've already learned?"

"Well, yeah. I know it sounds stupid, but they'd unlearn it just for spite. I know they would."

Brenda laughed and sat down beside her. "Well, I'd like nothing better than to go back to homeschooling," she said.

"You see?" Cathy asked. "That's why Sylvia's idea is genius. You start homeschooling again, and I pay you everything I would have paid a private school ... or I'd match what you're making in your job. Whichever is more. You'd get to do what you really want to do. I know taking on Mark would make things a little different, but you could do wonders with him, Brenda, and I think he would behave for you. He wouldn't want to be the only kid acting up."

She could see that Brenda was warming to the thought. "Are you sure you'd want to pay me that much?"

"Yes," she said. "It would solve so many problems for me, and it just might save my son's life. Brenda, please say yes."

"What about Mark?" Brenda asked. "How will he feel about all this?"

"I'm not sure," Cathy said. "But he doesn't have a choice. Something has to be done right away. And as far as I'm concerned, it's either you or private school. And he can refuse to do homework in private school just as easily as he can in public school. Besides, I hate to make him the new kid halfway through the year. If he was with you, he wouldn't be."

The smile inching across Brenda's face spoke volumes. "I'd be willing to try it, Cathy."

Cathy restrained herself from shouting and turning a cartwheel. She didn't want to frighten Brenda off. "Brenda, if you can't handle him, then you can quit. No hard feelings."

"Oh, I can handle Mark. He's a good kid," Brenda said. "Maybe he's got some bad influences, but once we remove those, he'll be fine. He's smart as a whip."

Cathy got tears in her eyes and threw her arms around Brenda. "That's what I love about you, Brenda. Your optimism. And I would just love to have someone like you influencing my son."

"All right, you've buttered me up," Brenda said, jumping up and doing a little jig. "I'll quit my job tonight! We can tell the kids today when they get home."

"Yahoo!" They both turned and saw that Joseph had been listening from the side of the house, and he was jumping up and down in celebration. "Now things can get back to normal again!"

"Honey," Cathy said with a laugh, "with one of my kids around, *normal* is the last thing it will be."

CHAPTER

Thirty

"*Mom,* don't you think you're overreacting?" Mark yelled when Cathy broke the news to him. "I get in trouble one time and get one bad report card, and the next thing I know you're jerking me out of school? You worked me like a dog at the clinic. Haven't I been punished enough?"

"This isn't punishment, Mark. This is help. I'm trying to put you into a situation where you'll learn, and where you aren't influenced by kids who are headed the wrong direction."

"Maybe I *am* one of them, Mom, d'you ever think of that? Maybe they're the ones following *me.*"

"Oh, well, that helps," she quipped. "Then of course you can stay in school. I didn't realize they were teaching you such leadership skills."

"That's not what I mean."

She touched her forehead and told herself to calm down. "Mark, I choose to believe that you are a good kid, and that you would never have done any of the things you've done lately, including letting your grades fall, if it weren't for some outside influences. Can you look me in the eye and tell me I'm wrong about that?"

"My only other choice is to convince you I'm evil, which I'm not, Mom. Only my tongue is, according to James 3:6."

Cathy couldn't help grinning. Maybe Brenda could do a better job with the Scripture lessons, too. She sat down with him, facing him across the table. "Mark, I know this all feels terrible to you, but believe it or not, I'm doing it to help you, not hurt you. I wouldn't make this big a change in your life just to punish you. I really think it will be good for you."

He looked pained, and stared down at the table. "Can I still see my friends?"

"Not the ones who were smoking dope in the bathroom with you. No way."

"Well, can I at least keep playing basketball and baseball?"

"Yes," she said. "We'll get you on the church team since you can't play at school anymore."

He propped his chin on his hand and stared at her miserably. She could see that he wanted to cry, but he wouldn't let himself.

"I want to go live with Dad," he said.

She had anticipated that. Whenever things got hot around here, the kids threw that up at her. "Well, I'm sorry, kiddo, but that's not an option."

"Why not? He wouldn't freak out every time my grades slipped."

"I think you're wrong about that," she said, though she knew he was absolutely right. "Neither one of your parents is willing to give up on you, Mark. I have high hopes for you. Big plans. You have so much potential. I'm not going to let you destroy it."

"Well, can I sleep late?"

"Of course not. You know the Dodds always get up early to start school."

"But they have all those chores they have to do before they get started. I could just go after the chores are done, and then I could sleep an hour later."

"Come to think of it, I think we'll have some chores for you to do around here. That way you won't feel left out."

"Mom, why can't I just sleep late?"

"Because you're going to become a disciplined young man, if it kills you!" Cathy said.

"Great. I'll be the only disciplined one in the whole house. How come Annie and Rick don't have to do this?"

"They aren't flunking out, and they don't take drugs."

"Not that you know of."

Beautiful, she thought. She loved it when her kids planted explosive seeds like that. "Mark, so help me, if you have something to say about Rick or Annie, say it."

"I'm just saying I'm not the only one in this house who messes up sometimes."

"No kidding. My angels?" Disgusted at her own sarcasm, she got up and went into the kitchen.

"So when do I have to quit school?"

"I think I'll let you go a few more days, just to say good-bye to everybody and give you time to get used to the idea. That's what Brenda's doing with her kids. Then you can all start in a week or so."

When Mark looked as if she'd just ended his childhood, she came back to the table. Her heart was overcome with love for the boy who realized just how much his irresponsibility had cost him. She hoped it would be enough to change his behavior. "Mark, I do love you. I want what's best for you. You know I do."

"It's not best," he said. "I'm *not* gonna do better. I'm gonna hate it and do terrible."

"Don't make up your mind to do that, Mark. Make up your mind to excel."

"I might as well just get a job, if I could find anybody who'd hire a twelve-year-old," he muttered, getting up and heading for the stairs. "My education is over. So is my social life."

"It won't be that bad, Mark."

But as he shuffled up the stairs, she knew he wasn't buying it. It would be every bit as bad as he thought, until Brenda could prove differently.

She just hoped Brenda had more success than the school system had.

CHAPTER
Thirty-One

Barry had finished his work for the day, but he dreaded going home and facing Tory's coldness. So he sat in his office, staring out the window as the sun went down and cast dark shadows on his walls.

His door opened, and Linda Holland, the woman from marketing, stuck her head in. "Barry! I thought you'd gone home."

He shrugged. "No, too much work to do." He shuffled some papers around on his desk, as if he'd been in the middle of something.

"Barry, you were staring out the window." She came in and dropped the files in her arms on his desk. "Are you all right? I know it's none of my business, but this is the second time I've caught you like this. What's wrong?"

He leaned his head back in his chair. Again, her clothes looked rumpled, as if she'd overslept and had to grab something off the floor. He had seen her cubicle and knew she was sloppy and unorganized. But she did good work. "Nothing's wrong," he said. "Everything's fine."

She plopped down on a chair, making it clear that she wasn't going to take that for an answer. It wasn't until she crossed her legs that he realized she wasn't wearing shoes again. She had a slight run in the toe of her stockings. "Barry, come on. You can tell me."

He rubbed his lip with a finger. It irritated him that she thought they were good enough friends to be confidants. Sure, he bantered with her sometimes in the break room, laughed and teased her. But he didn't go around spilling his guts to office acquaintances. "Actually, I don't want to talk about it."

She seemed a little taken aback. "Well, if that's not a conversation ender, I don't know what is." She got back to her stocking feet, and he could see that she was trying not to appear hurt. "Your loss, because I'm a great listener."

There was something little-girlish and vulnerable about her. She was entirely unself-conscious. He couldn't imagine her taking the pains with her looks that Tory took, when she couldn't even manage to keep shoes on her feet. And he was sure that any life-altering decision she made would be based on her heart alone, and not on what people thought.

As she closed the door behind her, Barry leaned back in his chair again. Maybe he was being too hard on Tory. Maybe her desire to keep the baby really didn't have anything to do with what people thought. Maybe it was truly a matter of conscience.

But he had a conscience, too, and she wasn't willing to listen to his. Yes, he had been pro-life, had written letters and even held an occasional picket sign. He had grieved for all the babies that were needlessly sacrificed in abortion clinics each year. But this was different. Why couldn't she see that?

He dropped his face into his hands at his desk, and wiped away the tears that had been sneaking up on him so often lately. He felt more alone than he'd ever felt in his life. Even more alone than he'd felt as an eleven-year-old boy, when Nathan had gotten pneumonia and had to be hospitalized for a week. His parents had spent every waking moment at the hospital, fighting for the life of the child that may not have even wanted to live. And he had stayed at home alone, eating TV dinners and watching television, until his father rolled in around ten and told him to go to bed. He had lain awake those nights, staring at the ceiling and knowing he should pray for Nathan. But somehow he couldn't.

Like now, there had been no one in the world to talk to, no one to whom he could confess the traitorous thoughts in his heart. Not even God.

Now, like then, he found himself unable to pray. He knew he should be praying for the child Tory was carrying, but instead, he wanted to pray that God would take it from her, make the decision for them, end this suffering.

But he knew in his heart the damage had been done. Even if Tory did have a natural miscarriage, the two of them might never be able to get over this difference of opinion.

He got up and went to the window. He didn't have a pretty view. No one in the building did, for there was too much machinery around the building, too many practical structures surrounding him. At night, the ugliness was not as apparent, so he gazed out through the glass, seeing his own reflection. The man standing there with the loosened tie and white dress shirt looked unfamiliar to him.

He pressed his forehead against the glass and began to wish that he had confided in Linda. She was safe. Someone he could talk to without fear of condemnation. Linda didn't seem to have any stringent standards that she expected those around her to uphold. She was human, and she accepted that others were as well.

He was suddenly very sorry that he might have hurt her.

When someone knocked, he swung around as if he had been caught in those thoughts. "Yeah?" he called.

Linda stuck her head back in. "I finished one more file you might need." She hesitated a moment, then crossed the office to put it on his desk.

She wasn't fooling anyone, Barry thought. There was no reason he was going to need that file tonight. She could have easily waited until morning. But it was obvious she was worried about him, and something about that warmed him.

"Linda, do you have a minute?"

She shrugged. "Sure."

He went back to his chair, and she plopped into the one across from his desk and pulled her feet under her.

Barry dropped his hands on his desk and leaned forward. "I'm sorry I was rude to you before. I lied. I really do need to talk."

She nodded, as if she had known that all along. "It's okay. What is it, Barry?"

"My wife . . . she's pregnant."

She looked a little disappointed. "Oh, how nice. You don't seem very happy about it."

"Well, I was. Ecstatic, really. I love kids."

"So you were ecstatic, until . . ."

She was prompting him, trying to get it out of him. "Until we found out . . . the baby has Down's Syndrome."

"Oh, Barry!" She dropped her feet and leaned forward. "Oh, how awful. You must be devastated."

He studied his hands. "Linda, are you a Christian?"

She looked startled and slightly offended by the question. "Of course I am. What do I look like? A heathen?"

Her answer didn't sound like a testimony to God's grace, but he accepted it, nonetheless. "I just wondered because . . . Christians sometimes have strong ideas about . . . abortion in cases like this."

"Oh. Well, I would think that all that pro-life stuff doesn't apply to medical abortions, does it?"

"What's a medical abortion?"

"One that's done for medical reasons. The health of the baby or the health of the mother."

"Medical abortion," he repeated, testing the word in his mouth. "Sounds like it could cure the baby. At least make it better."

"Well, in a way it does. It's all in how you think about it."

"No matter how my wife thinks about it, it's just plain murder to her."

"Oh, I see," she said, bringing her fingertips to her mouth again. Her polish was chipped. "Is that it? Tory doesn't want to do anything about the baby?"

Again, her choice of words surprised him. "She wants to have it. Down's Syndrome and all."

"But it won't be normal! It'll have a terrible life, and be miserable, and your family will never be the same . . . if you even keep it. Putting it in an institution seems so cruel . . ."

Vindicated, he leaned back in his chair. "I know. I've told her all that. She won't listen."

"I hope you don't mind my saying so, Barry, but those pro-lifers always just blow my mind." Quickly, she held up her hands to stem any protest. "I'm sorry if you're one of them. I mean, I know some of them mean well and all. But they're so sure they're right, and that they stand for God's side, but when it's them or their kids who are pregnant, they take the easy way out, just like everybody else. And that's okay. Nothing is black or white, Barry. There's a lot that's gray in this life."

He felt his heart sinking, for he wasn't sure he agreed with her. He'd always thought that certain things really were black or white. Sin was sin. Wrong was wrong.

Still, she made sense, and he had been thinking the same things often over the last few days. "I just know that God is a God of mercy. That he loves that baby, too, and that he loves me and my kids and my wife . . . Would he really hold it against us if we did this for the sake of our family?"

"Of course he wouldn't." She leaned up on the desk. "Barry, if you don't mind my saying so, maybe Tory is too hormonal to think clearly. Maybe this is just a decision that you're gonna have to make."

"I've thought of that," he said. "She is hormonal. She's upset and moody, and wants very little to do with me, mainly because of what I want her to do."

"That's what I thought," Linda said. "Barry, this could all be over in just a few hours." She waved an arm dramatically, as if wiping the slate clean. "And then you could all go on with your lives. Have another baby, if you want. But not this one."

He stared down at his desk. "She won't listen to reason. She's a mother protecting her cub. She's made me feel like Hitler. Like I'm condoning some kind of ethnic cleansing."

"Barry, sometimes there's a cost for doing the right thing. When her body is back to normal, and the stress is gone, and she's thinking clearly again, she'll thank you."

"Still, I can't force her. I can only pray that she'll make the right decision."

"I'll pray for you, too," Linda said.

He smiled, the first time he had smiled in a very long time. "Thanks," he said. "I appreciate that." He met her eyes, and realized they were a startling green color. He'd never noticed that before.

She got up and extended her hands in an exaggerated *ta da* pose. "So . . . you want me to order us a pizza? You have to eat."

He swallowed and looked at his watch. As tempting as it was, he knew it wasn't a good idea. "No, uh . . . I guess I'd better get on home. There's a can of Spaghettios with my name on it."

"Yuck. Are you sure?"

He thought about it for a moment, then realized that sharing a pizza would worsen his problems with Tory . . . even if she didn't know about it. "No, I really need to go."

"Okay." She started to the door, and turned back as he got his coat and shrugged it on. "Barry, if you ever need to talk, don't hesitate to come to me, okay? I really do understand. And . . . I'm usually here at night. I get here so late in the morning sometimes, that I always have to work late to stay caught up. But I'm always willing to listen."

He nodded. "Thanks."

And as he headed out to his car, he felt reinforced, refreshed . . . and angrier at his wife. It was good to know that someone else saw things as clearly as he did.

CHAPTER
Thirty-Two

The phone calls, letters, and signs from the ladies of Cedar Circle made the clothing drive a great success. Truckloads of clothing were left at Cathy's clinic—the main drop-off place—and needed to be sorted. Steve had helped her transport them to her garage, where they would be sorted before they sent them to Sylvia. Saturday morning, Cathy, Tory, and Brenda met to finish the work.

Tory took great pains with her appearance that morning, overcompensating for her emotional low. Already, her pants were beginning to grow tight around her stomach, and she realized that she would have to go up one size at the very least, and possibly graduate into maternity wear sometime in the next couple of weeks. Ordinarily, that would have been fine with her. She had always enjoyed maternity clothes, and liked for people to know that she was pregnant. But this pregnancy was different.

Instead of the glow of joy, she felt the overshadowing of despair. She didn't want people to see that she was pregnant, then look into her eyes and see the sorrow there. She decided to leave her shirttail out today, hoping to cover the little pooch she wore like a sign in front of her. She took pains with her hair and makeup, as if they could distract anyone's eyes from her stomach.

Cathy and Brenda were already in Cathy's garage when Tory got there. They had a huge stack of clothes on a table and were sorting them into sizes.

Cathy gave Tory an amazed look as she came into the garage. "Tory, I wish I could look as good as you on my best days. If I didn't know you couldn't keep food down, I wouldn't be quite as impressed."

"Don't be impressed." Tory grabbed some clothes and started looking for the sizes. "I'm just tired of looking frumpy. Besides, if you remember my last pregnancy, I looked like I just rolled off my death bed for seven of the nine months."

"I don't remember you looking like that at all . . . ever," Brenda said. She hugged her. "Everything okay at home?"

"Sure." Tory's voice was dull, flat. "As long as Barry and I don't talk to each other, we're doing great." Tears burst into her eyes as she said those words, and she hated herself. She didn't want pity from her friends, yet she couldn't seem to say anything positive. She swallowed back her emotion. "So where are we on this clothing drive?"

Cathy couldn't seem to switch gears so easily, but she followed Tory's lead. "Well, I've run off some more posters to put all over town," she said slowly. "Steve and I are going to go out to do it this afternoon. And then we're planning to get flyers and go to soccer fields, and do what we did when we were raising money for Joseph and getting word out about the school board meeting."

"So that's how you did it," Brenda said with a grin.

"Yeah, and that's how she and Steve fell in love," Tory said. "If they didn't have a cause, they'd probably fall apart." It was a cruel thing to say, completely unwarranted, but she couldn't seem to stop the bitterness spilling out of her.

Cathy looked hurt, but quickly changed the subject. "Did I tell you Steve has found us a pilot?" she asked. "In fact, he's one of his best friends, and he has his own plane, and he's a Christian."

"Yeah?" Tory asked, looking up.

"He's agreed to fly the clothes to León. I've e-mailed Sylvia to find out where they can land, and as soon as we get a planeload, he'll take them on down."

"Really?"

"Really," Cathy said. "And he's paying the expenses himself. He considers it a donation, something he can do for the people down there."

"Pays to know people, doesn't it?" Tory asked. "So can you handle the drop-offs at the clinic?"

"Yeah, it's working out okay," Cathy said. "It's a public place, and somebody's there most of the time. They drop them in a big bin in the parking lot. I think I can handle it."

"I've put out the word at church," Brenda said, looking up at Tory. "You weren't there Sunday, but Pastor made an announcement during the worship service. People are gonna bring clothes Wednesday night, and I'll just bring them home in David's truck."

Cathy was getting excited. "When I told my church they were for Sylvia's work, people just started cleaning out their closets. I think we'll have a planeload in just a week or so, at this rate."

"And we haven't even really gotten started," Tory said. "I haven't had time to send out the letters I was going to send to the churches in the area."

They heard a horn honking, and all three turned to see Steve in his pickup truck, turning into the cul-de-sac. He was wearing that smile he always wore, that down-to-earth, everyone's-a-friend smile, that had made Tory like him from the first time she'd met him. He got out of the car and walked up the driveway.

Cathy was glowing. "Came just in time," she said. "We have plenty for you to do."

He chuckled. "Put me to work anywhere you need me," he said. "But I thought you might want to know there's a soccer game going on down at the field right now. Must be a hundred cars in that parking lot."

Cathy caught her breath. "Really?"

"Yep. We can stick flyers on the windshields. Worked for the school board meeting, and for Joseph."

Brenda waved Cathy along. "Go on with him. We'll finish up here and close the garage."

"Well, the kids are inside. They're still asleep, but if you need anything, you can probably rouse one of them."

"We've got it under control," Tory said.

Cathy bopped out to the truck with Steve and got in. Brenda grinned as she waved at them driving off. "They make a cute couple, don't they?"

Tory watched them until they disappeared. "Yeah, it must be great to be at that falling-in-love stage again."

"Tory, you're not envying Cathy again, are you? *She* envies *you*, you know. You have a husband who loves you and takes care of you so you can stay home and raise your children. You and I really have it made."

"Oh, I know," Tory said. "The luck's just been dripping off of me lately." She sighed. "Sometimes I wish I could turn my life back to before I got married and had kids, when things were so simple. All I did was go to work and accomplish things, and come home and kick my shoes off and make plans for the night. Back then, I thought working was stressful, and before that, I just knew that college was the hardest part of my life." Her voice broke off. "But all that was a breeze compared to this. No life-or-death decisions, no parenting mistakes that could change the course of your life, no choice that could make you forget why you got married—"

Brenda dropped her hanger and pulled Tory into a hug. She held her, and Tory began to cry again. "Honey, I wish there was something I could do to help you."

"There's not a thing," Tory said in a high-pitched voice. "Not a thing in the world. And really, there's nothing to decide. I'm going to have the baby. I just have to make up my mind to be happy about it. I just feel so guilty."

"Guilty? What do you feel guilty about?"

"I feel guilty that I'm not overjoyed about this new baby. I'm really no better than Barry. He's a little more blatant with it. He just doesn't want her to be born, whereas I just sit around all the time, wondering if she's gonna be hideous, if people are going to point and stare, how embarrassed I'll be." She choked on her words. "I can't believe this is me thinking these things."

"But you're still committed to having the baby," Brenda said. "You'll work through all that, and by the time she comes, you'll love her."

"Just like my other kids?" Tory asked. "Because I did have reservations when I was pregnant with them, too, worried that I wouldn't be able to love them like I should, that I'd be selfish, that I wouldn't want to spend time with them. And in large part, that turned out to be true, until I watched you and Joseph." She drew in a deep breath and let it out roughly. "Oh, Brenda, I wish I was more like you."

"More like me?" Brenda asked, astounded. "Why in the world would you say that?"

She wiped her eyes and wished she had a box of tissues. "Because you're so positive and so patient, and when Joseph was in the hospital dying, you were still looking up to God, asking for his will."

"Oh, you make me sound too good to be true," Brenda said. "You know how much I grieved. How I begged God to stop it, to keep Joseph from dying."

"I know," Tory cried. "But you were so strong, and so sweet, and it changed me. Honestly, Brenda, I don't know if I would have made the same choice about the baby a year ago. I don't know if I'd have been strong enough."

"Well, you're strong enough now. God's timing is always perfect."

"I'm strong enough to make the decision. But I don't know if I'm strong enough to carry it out. Strong enough to do what it's going to take."

"Right now, all you have to do is be pregnant one day at a time, until that baby comes, and then you can be her mother, one day at a time, just like you do with your kids now."

"I might wind up being a single mother," she said. "Then Cathy and I really will have something in common. And the two of us will sit around and envy *you* for having a husband." She tried to laugh, but it quickly faded. "Oh, Brenda, I don't want that."

"Then don't let it happen," Brenda said. "It doesn't have to. Don't forget the power of prayer. Sometimes that's all you can do. I've been praying for David for years."

Tory knew she had. She had prayed for David, as well. Seeing him come to Christ was the biggest desire in Brenda's heart. Tory had never dreamed that Barry's heart would grow hard, that he would put up a barricade between himself and God, that he would claim that the Lord was leading him to do something that he knew was wrong. "At least David would never want to abort one of his children. Never in a million years."

"You can't say what anyone would do until they've been through it," Brenda said.

"Yes, I can. If they really believe what they say they believe . . . it's predictable every time. You just can't tell what people really believe."

"I guess it's the age-old problem," Brenda said.

"Maybe it's better that David is honest about his beliefs. He doesn't fake it, or do a 180-degree turn when things get hard. If Barry had been an unbeliever, had never taken a stand on abortion, then I wouldn't be so . . . so . . . miserably disappointed in him."

"But he is a believer," Brenda said. "And I know he isn't faking. He's just confused. He's depressed. If it came right down to it, if you agreed to get an abortion, I bet he couldn't go through with it."

"Well, we'll never find out for sure, will we? At this point, even if he changes his mind, I'm not sure things will ever be the same. He's different, to me. And I'm different now. Not better, not stronger. Just different."

"Don't give up on your marriage, Tory," Brenda said. "I know it seems like the right thing to do, but it isn't. I've been disappointed in David. I know what it's like not to have your prayers answered for your husband's heart to change. I've mourned over David's soul, and grieved over the fact that I go to church alone, and teach my kids their faith alone. It can get really lonely sometimes."

Tory watched her as she went back to sorting the clothes as she spoke, and realized that Brenda was right. She did know some of what Tory was going through. "So how do you do it? How do you hang on, when deep in your heart you want a godly husband and father?"

"I hang on to what he is, not what he isn't. He loves me, and he loves the kids. And he's a good provider and a faithful companion. I'm happy with him, even though things aren't perfect. And I trust God to answer that prayer one day."

"I don't have as much time as you have. This baby will be born in a few months, and I don't know what that's going to mean to my marriage."

"I'm just asking you not to give up," Brenda said. "Pray hard, and expect God to work. I can't help believing that he will, for both of us. Maybe he'll work faster for you than he has for me, since there's a life at stake. But he will work, Tory. You'll see."

Tory let out a deep, ragged sigh. "I hope you're right, Brenda. I hope you're right."

CHAPTER
Thirty-Three

Later, when Cathy and Steve had passed out all the flyers they had at the soccer fields, and had spoken to dozens of people about helping with the Nicaraguan clothing drive, Steve passed the street that would have taken them up Survey Mountain to Cedar Circle. "Where are we going?" Cathy asked him.

"It's just a beautiful day," he said. "I thought we'd drive up Bright Mountain to the Point. I hear it has a great view. We can just sit in the truck and look down on Breezewood."

An uneasy, uncomfortable memory shot through her, of one of her misguided dates trying to take her to the Point on their first and only date. "Isn't that where all the teenagers go when their parents think they're at movies?"

He grinned. "It's broad daylight. I have exactly an hour and a half until I have to pick up Tracy at her friend's slumber party. I just want to sit with you and hold your hand. Is that okay?"

She couldn't help laughing softly. Steve was the last person she should fear. He was a godly man, much godlier than she, and had already led her into daily Bible studies and prayer that had deepened her relationship with Christ. She knew he wasn't going to take advantage of her in any way.

But some part of her resisted the thought of any intimacy at all with him, for she couldn't help the niggling fear in the back of her mind that this was only temporary. Soon, he would see the chaos of her life for what it was, and he would retreat. Either he'd get tired of three kids who expressed themselves at the top of their lungs, or he would realize that her own spiritual education was much more deficient than he thought. He would judge her parenting, flee from her kids, or simply find a younger, less complicated woman to take her place, like her husband had done.

It was just a matter of time.

He pulled up to the Point, and even in daylight she could see why this was such a popular place for the kids. The view of the hills surrounding Breezewood was breathtaking. She imagined it was even more beautiful at night. He backed into a parking space, so that the gate of the truck was facing the view below. He opened his truck door. "Come on."

"Come on where?"

"Let's get out," he said. "It's a beautiful day. We can sit on the tailgate and listen to the breeze."

It couldn't have been more right if he'd brought along her own personal throne from which to view her city. In fact, she preferred tailgates to thrones, any day. She got out and shut her door. Steve opened the tailgate and sat down, and patted the place next to him. "We have a beautiful town, don't we?"

She smiled. "Yeah, we really do."

He took her hand and held it in both of his, content to just look into the breeze and over the skyline of the small town below them, and the mountains jutting in the distance. "So tell me about Mark. How's he doing in school? Any more bathroom episodes?"

She sighed. "Well, I wasn't going to tell you, but since you're being so nice and holding my hand and everything . . ." She gave him a lopsided grin, and he returned it. "He came home with the worst report card ever, in the history of report cards, I think. He's flunking out." She swallowed and shook her head. "I'm really so embarrassed to tell you."

"Why should you be embarrassed?" he asked. "You know, he has two parents. It's a lot of burden to be the only one trying to educate him. His dad ought to be involved in this somehow."

"His dad's not really involved in much of anything," she said. "Oh, he has him every other weekend, but I don't even think he's home most of that time. From what I hear, he plays golf all day Saturday, and he and his wife usually go out at night and leave the kids there by themselves, or let them run wild."

"His loss," Steve said, and Cathy looked up at him, amazed that he could see through the tough, smart-aleck veneer of her kids to the treasure that their father was missing. "So who gets them for Thanksgiving?"

"I do. Which, of course, means that I don't get them for Christmas."

"There's got to be a better way," he said. "But since you get them for Thanksgiving, what would you say to spending it with Tracy and me?"

Her eyes narrowed with suspicion. "You would really ask me that when I just told you that I'll have my kids?"

He grinned. "What's that supposed to mean? I only invite you places when you're alone?"

She shrugged. "Well, yeah, basically."

He looked wounded. "I just thought it might be a good chance for all of us to get to know each other. My parents will be there, and my mom's doing most of the cooking, and she likes a big group to cook for. She's wanted to meet you, anyway."

Cathy tried to imagine the possibilities, and wasn't sure if it was a good idea. "Oh, I don't know, Steve. I would really like to make a good impression the first time I meet your parents."

"Well, why wouldn't you?"

"Because of the kids," she said. "I'm not sure how that would be. Remember the first time—and the last time—you took us all to lunch? It was disastrous. Annie kept wanting to leave to meet her boyfriend, and when I said she couldn't, she got up and left anyway. The boys were bickering and arguing with me . . ."

"But we know each other a little better now," he said.

"And you like me anyway?" she asked.

He shoved her playfully. "Come on, it'll be fun. Wouldn't you welcome the opportunity not to have to cook Thanksgiving dinner?"

"Oh, but I would cook something. I couldn't let your mother do it all herself."

"I'll be doing some, too," he said. "But that's the deal. My mother's very offended when other people bring things."

She shot him another suspicious look. "You told her about my cooking, didn't you?"

He threw his head back and laughed. She thought it was the best sound she'd heard in a long time. "No, I didn't tell her anything. She really just wants to do it."

"Well, as long as you know what you're getting into."

He tightened his hold on her hand, and met her eyes in a lingering gaze. "I do," he said.

She could only hold that gaze for a moment, before those fears of his fleeing assaulted her again. She looked away.

Several pleasant moments of quiet passed, and finally, he put his arm around her and pulled her closer. As she leaned into him, he rested his chin on the top of her head. It felt so natural that it brought tears to her eyes. She tried to blink them back. How would she explain tears?

"So what are you going to do about Mark and school?"

She thought that over for a moment. "Being the third child doesn't really play in his favor. I've already discovered what doesn't work on my other two. Threatening to ground him for life doesn't quite do it, and I can't take away the phone or the computer, because he doesn't care much about either one right now. So I've decided on something that he thinks is pretty drastic, but it just might work."

"What?"

"I've decided to homeschool him."

He let go of her. "Are you kidding me? How are you going to do that and work, too?"

"I'm not doing the homeschooling, Brenda is. I'm paying her to teach Mark at home. That way, he'll be supervised all day and he'll learn a lot. I respect Brenda tremendously, and I know she can do it."

Steve gaped at her with amazed amusement in his eyes. "You know, that's a great idea."

"It sure is. Sylvia gave it to me." She shook her head. "I don't know what we'd do without her. Even from so far away, she's still dispensing her wisdom and getting us through these spots."

"So when does he start?"

"Monday."

"*Monday?* As in day-after-tomorrow?"

She nodded. "I gave him this past week to say good-bye to his friends. But frankly, I didn't want him around those dope-smoking kids any more than he had to be. Brenda's kids are celebrating. Even Daniel, who seemed to really love school. Their last day was Friday, too."

His smile faded. "You've made all these decisions, and you never mentioned a thing? Cathy, you're shutting me out again."

"I just don't want to burden you with my dirty laundry. I didn't even tell Brenda and Tory, until Sylvia blurted it all over cyberspace. But I'm glad she did, because it gave me a solution."

"You know, we're not supposed to be loners, we Christians. We're supposed to support each other, share things. How can we help if we don't know what's going on? People can't even pray for you if you haven't told them you need it."

"I gave that unspoken prayer request in Sunday school last week."

He groaned. "Give me a break. In biblical times, do you think people had unspoken prayer requests? No. They all lived together, grandparents and aunts and uncles and cousins, and they knew everything that was going on with everybody. It gave them accountability, but it also gave them relief. How heavy could a burden be when there were others to help you carry it?

Today, we lock ourselves away and put on that happy face, and hide our secrets even from our Christian friends. And then we wonder why our burdens are so heavy."

The words didn't sound like a rebuke, but an encouragement. "I know. I should have shared. It's pride that kept me from it."

"That's understandable," he said. "But I want to help you. I really can't stand the thought of you struggling with this alone all week." He tightened his hold on her, and laid his jaw against her hair again. She marveled at the comfort he gave her, the feeling of being protected, the thought that God had given him all of the things she needed, things that he was so free to share. She wondered if she had anything to give him.

"But for what it's worth, I'm proud of you," he said. "I think you're doing the right thing. It's a drastic step, but this calls for drastic measures, and you haven't wimped out. You're willing to take a stand to help your child. I think that's great."

It had been a long time since she'd felt affirmed as a parent. In fact, there hadn't been many times in her life that she had. The tears returned to her eyes.

He reached down and hooked a finger under her chin, pulled her face up to his. She couldn't hide the tears as he smiled down at her. "You're really pretty, you know that?"

She breathed a laugh and looked away. "You're crazy."

"Nope. I know what I see." He pulled her face back to his and wiped away the first tear as it fell. "Don't cry," he whispered.

But he didn't ask why she cried. Cathy knew he understood that the affirmation of her motherhood had seeped like long-needed sustenance into her soul. God had sent him to quench her thirst, and the realization of that sent another tear rolling down her face.

He wiped it away, too, then pulled her closer. His kiss was sweet, undemanding, unhurried. His rough, work-worn hand stroked gently across her cheekbone, and lingered there when the kiss broke. Looking up at him, Cathy felt as vulnerable as she'd ever felt in her life. She knew he could see right into her.

"Well, I'd better get you home," he whispered.

She smiled. "Yeah, it's almost noon. The kids are probably almost awake by now, and if I don't hurry home, they'll all scurry out before I can get them to do anything."

"The birthday party is probably almost over," he said, looking down at his watch. "I'll need to be picking Tracy up pretty soon."

But he didn't hurry to get off the tailgate. "I enjoyed sitting up here with you."

She smiled. "Without an agenda. So you think you and I really do have something in common, even when we're not working for a cause?"

"Is that what you thought?"

She shrugged. "Tory mentioned it."

"You tell Tory that what we have in common is a real intense affection for each other."

Intense affection. It said so much, yet she longed to hear—to say—a little bit more. Still, she basked in that "intense affection" as he took her back to Cedar Circle.

CHAPTER
Thirty-Four

Tory didn't know why she had chosen to do her grocery shopping on Saturday, when it was so crowded. She wished she had waited until Barry got home so she could have left the kids at home. The grocery store was like Toys-R-Us to them, for they could find the desires of their hearts—or stomachs—on every aisle, in every section, on every shelf.

At the moment, Spencer was begging for a pack of bean sprouts, which he'd never tasted in his life. He didn't know what they were for, but he liked them because they looked like worms. He was willing to fight for them.

"Spencer, I want you to quit asking me for things. I told you, we just came here to get things we need. We don't need bean sprouts."

"But look at them, Mommy. Please, can't I have them? I promise I won't scare Britty with them."

"Shut up, Spencer," Brittany said from the bottom of the basket. "You're gonna get her all mad before we even get to the candy aisle."

"She's got a point," Tory said.

Sighing miserably, Spencer put the bean sprouts back. That was when Tory spotted the boy with Down's Syndrome, bending over the produce and picking up the carrots, feeling the stalks, then moving to the cucumbers and the kiwi. He picked up each one there, ran his fingers over it, then grabbed a ball of lettuce and spread both hands around it.

His mother must have seen her staring. "Phillip? Come on, honey, let's go."

He didn't turn around and come right away. Instead, he pushed his high-magnification glasses up on his nose and moved faster down the produce aisle, feeling things more quickly.

"How old is your son?" Tory asked the woman.

She looked surprised at Tory's interest. "He's fifteen."

Tory's eyes followed him. "What's he doing? Stroking the vegetables?"

The mother grinned. "I can never come through the grocery store without him feeling every single one. We have a garden in the backyard, and he likes to help tend it. There's something about the texture and shape of all the different things that interests him."

A sweet smile fell across Tory's lips, but at the same time, her eyes misted over.

"Excuse me," the boy's mother said. "Is something wrong?"

Tory shook her head. "Uh, no." She looked from Spencer to Brittany to see if they were listening. They were both preoccupied with scanning the shelves for anything they might have missed. She turned back to the woman. "It's just that, I'm carrying . . ." She didn't want to say the word "baby" yet because she hadn't told the children, but she patted the little paunch below her waist. "Down's Syndrome," she said.

The woman's eyes filled with compassion. "I'm sorry," she said.

Tory looked at the boy again, unable to say more.

The woman followed Tory's gaze. "My little vegetable-feeler over there is about the best thing that ever happened to our family," she said. She reached into her purse and pulled out a piece of paper, jotted a phone number down. "Look, my name's Marlene. If you ever need to talk to anyone about this, or if you have questions . . . please give me a call."

Tory took the phone number gratefully. "Thank you. I appreciate that." She watched the boy as he felt the zucchini and the squash. "Does he go to school or anything?"

"Oh, sure he does," she said. "He goes part of the day to the public school and the rest of the day he goes to a school for kids with Down's Syndrome. He absolutely loves it. You know, you really ought to stop by there sometime. It might put some of your fears to rest."

"I'd like that," she said. "Where is it?"

"Down on Brandon Street, behind the old post office. Listen, why don't you call me this afternoon? There's a lot I can tell you to make you feel better."

"Thank you," Tory said. "I will, as soon as I get my kids down for a nap."

The woman patiently waited until the boy had gotten to the end of the produce aisle, then she took his hand and pulled him along beside her. He went willingly, babbling in words Tory couldn't understand about the produce that he had just examined. She couldn't wait to finish shopping so she could get home and talk to that mother.

That afternoon, when she'd gotten the kids down for their nap, Marlene gave her the name of the school Phillip attended, as well as the number to several other resources that Tory could call on for help and answers. With great trepidation, she waited for Monday morning, so that she could visit the school and see if there was any hope for her child.

CHAPTER
Thirty-Five

Monday morning, all four of Brenda's children popped up earlier than usual, excited about resuming their homeschooling routine. She made French toast and scrambled eggs, and they all laughed and chattered as the family ate breakfast together.

But when eight o'clock came, Mark wasn't there. Cathy had warned Brenda that she had to get to the clinic at 7:30, so she wouldn't be able to stay with Mark until he crossed the street. Brenda feared that Mark had gone back to bed after his mother left for work.

She sent Daniel over at 8:20, and he banged on the door until Mark finally answered it. He confirmed her suspicions when he showed up in his wrinkled T-shirt and gym shorts. She suspected that was what he'd slept in. He hadn't brushed his hair or his teeth, and his eyes were barely open. He carried his sneakers in his hand.

Because she liked for her homeschool situation to be as structured as possible, she had divided up areas in the room they used for class. She showed Mark where he would be seated with Daniel, since they shared the same curriculum.

Mark compliantly took his seat, then laid his head down on his desk. She got Joseph, Leah, and Rachel started on their assignments, then came back to Mark and Daniel.

Mark's head was still down.

"He's sound asleep, Mama," Daniel whispered.

Brenda stayed calm. She had known Mark would test her today. This was no surprise. "Mark!" She shook him, and he sat up and squinted sleepily at her. "Mark, this is school! I expect you to sit up with your feet on the floor and listen to what I say."

"You were talking to them," he said.

"Some of what I say applies to all of you." She pulled her chair up to their table and took in a deep breath. "Now, we just got off to a bad start, but I know that things are going to turn around." She smiled and patted his hand. "I'm so excited about teaching you, Mark. Daniel needed somebody to challenge him and you're so bright, I knew you'd be the perfect person."

Mark rolled his eyes and propped his chin on his hand. "Give me a break. The only reason I'm here is because I was flunking out of school and my mom overreacted."

She wasn't used to being spoken to that way by a child, but she quickly rallied. "Mark, the way we do things here is that we do a lot of reading on our own. I'm familiar with all the material because I'm a little bit ahead of you. But then we discuss it and we do activities around it. And sometimes we take field trips that have something to do with what we're all studying. We try to be flexible. We try to be spontaneous if we can, but there are a few things I expect from you in return."

"Here it comes," he said, looking at Daniel. Daniel began to snicker. Brenda shot her son a warning look.

"Mark, I expect you to show respect for me and for Mr. David when you see him. We're going to be spending a lot of time together and that's not very much to ask. I also expect you to listen and do your assignments. My goal is to make learning fun for you and to make you learn even more than you would have if you were at school, so that at the end of the year when you take the test—"

"Test?" Mark cut in, horrified. "We have tests?"

"Of course we have tests," she said. "I give tests all the time, don't I, Daniel?"

"All the time," Daniel said with a groan, mirroring Mark's bored posture.

"That's how I can tell your progress. I give grades just like every other teacher does, and I expect you to try as hard as you can."

Mark looked down at the circle between his arms. "I don't want to be here."

She smiled, because she had no intentions of getting angry. Leaning forward, she got close to Mark's face. "Mark, why do you think my kids are so excited about doing this?"

"Because they're lazy and they don't want to get up and go to school every day."

She only stared at him for a moment, as several different emotions clashed like competitors through her mind. "No," she said, keeping her voice level. "It's actually because we have a lot of fun doing this. They like learning. Even Joseph is going to be studying, and he has a good excuse not to. He's studied all through his recovery, because he loves it. It can be the same for you, too, Mark."

"But I didn't do anything wrong. I just had one bad report card. If I could go back to school, I know I could pull my grades up."

Leah, Rachel, and Joseph stopped working and waited for her reaction. This was a test, she thought. And she could pass it. "You don't have that option, Mark. You're here. Now why don't you try to learn something?"

Mark brooded, and finally, she got up and reached for the books she kept on the shelf. "Now, we're starting with Bible study. That's always our first subject of the day." She knew he hadn't brought a Bible, or anything else, so she got one of hers off of the shelf. She handed it to Mark. "We've been continuing to study the Bible even while they were in public school, and we're up to the captivity in Babylon . . ."

Mark came to attention. "You gotta be kidding," he said. "Does that mean I have to read all of this?"

"Not all at once," she said. "But you'll love this, Mark. You'll just soak this up, like my kids do. You have the potential to learn a lot more than you've learned, Mark. And you'll like it when you start doing word studies and cross-referencing. Daniel's already been through the Bible once."

"Can't I just watch the movie? Don't they have *The Ten Commandments* on video?"

Daniel snickered again, and she began to sense the possibility that Mark could have more influence on Daniel than Daniel had on him. The other children could adopt his bad habits as well. She made a decision to nip that in the bud.

"You know what? I thought it would be nice if you and Daniel shared a table, since you'll be doing similar material, but now I see that it's probably better if you work alone. So Mark, let's get your books and move you over to this table." She began to move his things over to the table where she usually sat to check the children's work.

Mark just sat there. "Anyway, isn't Bible study against the law?"

Yes, she thought. It was a test. "It is not against the law to teach the Bible," Brenda said, making a Herculean effort to keep her voice calm. "I can teach anything I want to at home as long as I also teach you the basic skills. So there's no point in contacting the ACLU just yet." She walked him to his new station, and plastered that smile back on. "Now open your Bibles."

"But I didn't do anything wrong yet," he argued. "Why do I have to read the Bible? It's like you're expecting me to mess up!"

The test was getting harder. Her smile fell off again. "What do you mean, you haven't done anything wrong? This is not a punishment."

"Sure it is," he said. "My mother only makes us memorize Scripture when we're in trouble."

Brenda wilted. She would have to talk to Cathy about this. "Well, that's not the case, not here. We do it every day. It's part of our curriculum. Today we're going to be studying King Cyrus and how God used him to bring the Israelites back from Babylon."

"King who?" he asked, looking thoroughly frustrated.

She almost felt sorry for him. "Just read the passage I wrote on the board."

"Board?" he asked. "What board?"

"The dry erase board on the door, Mark." She tried not to let him get to her, and went to the front of the room. "Kids, I want you to read the passage that I wrote on the board. Then look in your concordances and find other places where Cyrus was mentioned. And I'll give you a hint what we're looking for. There's a very important prophecy that was given hundreds of years before King Cyrus was around, that told in advance that God was going to use him in this way."

Her kids got to work quickly, anxious to be the first to find the prophecy, but Mark stared at her as if she had asked him to detonate a nuclear bomb. "Mark, do you know how to use a concordance?"

"I don't even know what that is!"

She pulled out the concordance at his table. "Here it is. You can look up any word, and it will tell you where in the Bible that word appears. Let's look up Cyrus. The first one is in Second Chronicles."

He looked as if he was in genuine pain. "Where is Second Chronicles?"

As irritation rose inside her, she realized that she was taking the wrong approach. Before she could expect stellar work from him, she was going to have to help him catch up.

She thought that over for a moment and looked around at her children. How could she keep them progressing and still help Mark? If she went back to the beginning, to the books of the Bible and the creation itself, it wouldn't hurt her children. They could always use review. It might teach them responsibility to have them help Mark memorize the books. She could always assign Daniel more advanced word studies, and Leah and Rachel could do a study on all the other biblical references about the creation. Even Joseph could dig a little deeper than he had before. But Mark *had* to start at the beginning.

"You know, let's just forget about Cyrus," she said to the kids. "Turn to Genesis 1. We're going to start back over with the creation."

"But we've already done that," Joseph protested gently.

"It never hurts to start over," she said in a bright voice. "It'd be nice to be able to dig a little deeper."

"You're only doing this for me, aren't you?" Mark asked. Her children turned to look at him.

"Of course not. I want all of the kids to know the Bible. I just thought it'd be nice if we could start over. Since we last studied Genesis, I've learned some new things."

"You think I don't know anything about the Bible," Mark said. "You think I'm some kind of heathen, don't you?"

"Of course I don't," she said. "But your mother asked me to teach you for a reason, and I think the number-one thing we should learn is the Bible. To me, that's first in importance. In the morning we study the Old Testament, then we do history and English and then math and science. And then in the afternoon we do New Testament."

"So when do we have electives?" he asked.

"Oh, we work art and music in throughout the day," she said, "but we concentrate on academics."

He looked as if he was going to cry. "This is a nightmare!"

"Mark, it's not a nightmare. It's going to be fine. You'll see. My kids love learning this way."

"But you're starting completely over with the Bible just because of me, and everybody already knows this stuff. Even Joseph. It's humiliating."

"So, they'll help you, they'll challenge you."

"I don't like to be challenged," he said. "That's just a nice word for slave driving."

She was getting her first headache in weeks. "Mark, open the Bible to Genesis 1."

She knew he hadn't brought a pencil with him, so she dug through a box for one, then found him a notebook. She hoped tomorrow he would come more prepared, but she blamed herself that he hadn't. Cathy had been so busy with the clothing drive and her work at the clinic that she knew school supplies hadn't really crossed Cathy's mind. Besides that, she had probably assumed he would bring his backpack. She'd have to set Cathy straight on that tomorrow.

Meanwhile, she was determined to teach Mark *something* before she sent him home for the day.

CHAPTER
Thirty-Six

The parking lot of Breezewood Development Center was the last place on earth that Tory wanted to be. She sat in her car staring at the front door, trying to get the courage to go in alone. She had asked Brenda to go with her, but it was her first day to resume homeschooling, so she'd had to stay home. She hadn't mentioned it to Barry, for she knew this was the last place he would ever want to go.

She got out of the car, straightened her dress, and looked cautiously at the building, feeling a lot like a little kid on her first day of kindergarten. The mystery of what lay beyond the doors was almost more than she could bear. She needed someone to hold her hand and cross the pavement beside her. That was Barry's job. The bitter thought brought tears to her eyes. But Barry wasn't here, so she was forced to walk in alone. She wondered how much more of this journey she would walk alone.

As she walked in, the sounds that came from the classrooms were much like those from any other school. She heard laughter and chattering, teachers talking in calm, gentle voices, music playing. She found the office, and was surprised to see two adults with Down's Syndrome working behind the counter.

"May I help you?" one of them asked her in a slurred voice.

"Yes." She cleared her throat and tried to hide her shaking hands. "I was wondering if you let people observe the classes."

Without answering, the clerk disappeared into an office, and after a moment, a woman came out of the back room. "Hi. Can I help you?"

Tory cleared her throat. "Yes . . . uh . . . I was wondering. . . . Do you let people . . . parents . . . observe the classes?"

"Yes, of course. Do you have a special needs child?"

Tory patted her stomach, and the corners of her mouth trembled. "I'm carrying one. Down's Syndrome. I just wanted to see."

The woman seemed to understand completely, and her face filled with compassion. "You're very welcome to come and observe any of the classrooms here." She handed the stack of papers she held to the girl who had initially helped Tory. "Honey, would you punch holes in those pages for me so I can put them in my binder?"

"Yes, ma'am," the girl said, and hurried away to do her task.

The woman came around the counter. "I'm Phyllis Martin. I'm the director here."

"Tory Sullivan," she said. As they shook hands, she knew the woman could feel her trembling. "I'm . . . a little nervous."

"Parents often are, until they see that there's nothing to be nervous about."

As they walked out into the corridor, Tory glanced back at the girl punching holes in the pages. "You have paid staff who have Down's Syndrome?"

"Sure," she said. "We try to help the kids get jobs as they get old enough to graduate. Some of the best ones we keep for ourselves. We get real attached to these kids. When are you expecting?"

Tory hadn't thought much about her due date. It seemed so far away. She had a lifetime of problems to solve before then. "Next May."

"When did you find out?"

She shrugged. "About a month ago."

The woman reached a classroom and paused, and Tory looked through the window. The children seemed about five years old, and were walking around in a circle with grins on their faces as the teacher played a game with them.

"They're all different, you know," the woman said. "Children with Down's Syndrome have different degrees of difficulty. Most of them can walk at this age, but their muscle tone is very weak, so we take them early, even as infants, and do physical therapy to help them develop. As they get older, we help them with their speech. Some of them learn to speak very clearly."

The woman opened the door. Tory stepped back. "Oh, no, I don't want to go in. I don't want to disturb anybody."

"Oh, it's no problem at all," Phyllis said. "Come on. You can come in and watch as long as you want, and then if you want to go to an older or younger class, you're welcome to do that. You might especially be interested in our classes for mothers and infants."

"Mothers?" Tory asked. "Mothers are involved?"

"Sure. We help them learn how to stimulate their children so that they can develop to their utmost potential. By the time they get to this class, most of the children are able to learn games and songs and follow some instructions. We've educated most of the parents right along with them."

One of the teacher's aides came to the door, and Phyllis quietly introduced Tory. Slowly, Tory followed the aide into the room. The teacher started a tape of children singing, and the kids held hands and walked around in a circle. They sang with sounds that bore little resemblance to the song, but the smiles on some of their faces made up for it. Tory took a seat at the back of the class and watched with awe as the woman gently worked with the children.

"Tell you what," Phyllis whispered. "I'll come back in about twenty minutes. We have a mom and baby class starting about then and you can come in and watch."

Tory watched, astounded, fighting the urge to burst into tears at the sight of the class full of children with so many disabilities. But there was hope here, she realized. This was not an ugly, dismal place. It was uplifting and encouraging, and every child was made to feel special.

Three of the children were in wheelchairs. Half of them wore glasses. Some had braces on their legs. But they all smiled and giggled like any other children. And they could color and clap their hands and play ring-around-the-rosie.

Later, she felt much more hopeful as she followed Phyllis up the hall to the class of moms and babies. "This class is for babies as young as you want to bring them, on up to about three years old," the woman said. "Then we start working with the children in groups without the parents."

Tory's face grew serious again as she stepped into the room. Awestruck, she looked around at all the mothers talking like old friends, holding their babies on their hips, or holding their hands and trying to walk with them across the floor. They had become a community of people with problems, a circle of friends bound by common struggles.

Phyllis introduced her, and several of the mothers expressed compassion for what Tory was going through. Three of them exchanged phone numbers with her.

But what struck her the most was not the camaraderie of the women who had made the same choice that she was making, but the beauty in the babies themselves. There was nothing ugly or hideous about them, as she had expected. She began to wonder what her own baby would look like, whether she would have Brittany's hair color or Spencer's, her eyes or Barry's. Would she let Tory put bows and barrettes in her hair? Would she smile a lot? Would she need glasses?

When she finally left the school and headed to the mother's day out program to pick up Spencer, she was feeling much better about her baby's plight. She made her run by Brittany's school to pick her up, then as the kids napped, she went through the box of maternity clothes that Barry had brought down from the attic weeks ago, before they'd known their baby wasn't perfect.

Her heart lifted at the sight of the clothes she had worn during her last two pregnancies. She decided to wash them all and iron them so that they would be ready to wear when it was time. For the first time since she'd learned about the Down's Syndrome, she was able to think of this child without the fearful weight of dread crushing down on her.

CHAPTER
Thirty-Seven

Noon came in the nick of time, just when Brenda felt she was about to lose Mark altogether. She gathered all the kids into the kitchen and enlisted them in helping make lunch. She had chosen tacos, one of her family's favorites, which Daniel declared were much better than the tacos they'd been eating at school. They added a chair to their dinner table for Mark. David came in and washed up, and shared the lunch hour with them.

The kids all had their chores for cleanup after the meal, and she gave Mark the task of wiping the table. Since it had already been cleared off, she doubted that would be too much of a drain for him. But when she saw him wandering from the room, she checked his work. Crumbled meat and spilt sauce still dotted the table.

"Mark, you didn't finish your job," she said. "It was just a little job. Please come back and do it."

He shot her a look as if she had wounded him. "I thought this was supposed to be just like school. We don't have to wipe our own tables at school."

"It's not a lot to ask," she said, trying to keep her voice calm. "Come on, Mark. Everybody else is doing their job."

Angry, he jerked up the wet rag and began scrubbing the table, knocking the crumbs onto the floor. "Is that why you want us here?" he muttered. "So you can get us to do your work for you?"

She tried to remember that he had helped raise money for Joseph's heart, that he had come to the hospital with his mom and waited all night, as nervous and worried as the rest of them. She reminded herself that he could be a sweet kid when he wasn't in one of his moods, that he was going through puberty just like her own son, and didn't yet know where he fit into this world.

But she wasn't going to let him get away with disrespect, any more than she allowed her own children. "Mark, if you don't do what I say, you're not going to get the privileges that everybody else gets."

"My mom's paying you," he said. "You *have* to give me the same privileges."

"She's not paying me to baby you, Mark. She's paying me to teach you, and part of what I'm trying to teach you is responsibility."

"I'm not responsible for your kitchen table."

She couldn't believe she was embroiled in this argument in front of her children. All four of them turned and watched her with wide eyes and open mouths. Though her own kids were not perfect, none of them had ever defied her this blatantly.

"You know, Mark, you're right. My kitchen table is not your responsibility. So I tell you what. Why don't you go out to the workshop with Mr. David and get in the elective that you've been so concerned about?"

"Elective?" he asked. "What elective?"

"Carpentry," she said. She shot David a look. He was gaping at her as if to say, "Why me?"

"David, you must have a job that Mark can do out there."

He shot Mark a skeptical look. "I can think of something for him to do."

"Am I being punished?" he demanded.

Over his head, David grinned and mouthed, "Am *I?*"

She tried not to grin. "Mark, the word *disciple* means 'to teach,' and that's what I do here when I homeschool. I try to disciple my kids. I teach them. But there's another word that comes from that. The word *discipline*, and discipline is not punishment. It's an action also designed to teach. I'm trying to teach you something today."

"What?" he asked defiantly.

"I'm trying to teach you that if you don't live up to your responsibilities as I give them to you, just like all the other kids in this house have to do, then you won't get the privileges that they get."

"What privilege are they going to get, anyway?" he asked. "The privilege to read some boring chapter on history?"

"Right now they get to go outside and play for a little while, or they can stay in and play on the computer, or they can read. They don't have to do schoolwork for a little while after lunch. You, on the other hand, will be out in the workshop listening to the buzz saw and sanding furniture."

He rolled his eyes and leaned back hard against the wall. David wiped his hands. "Come on, kiddo," he said. "Let's go."

"This is not fair," Mark whined. "My mother is not paying for me to come here and work."

"Well, if you want me to talk to your mother about this, Mark, I'll be glad to do it right now." She headed for the phone.

Mark stopped her. "No! I don't want her to be bothered at work. She's already in a bad enough mood when she comes home every day. I'll just go."

Mark took off out of the house and headed to the workshop as David shot her a grin that said, "I'll get you back."

Brenda stood at the door and let out a huge sigh. It was no wonder Cathy spent so much time yelling. In the space of a few hours, Brenda was close to resorting to it herself.

Later, when free time was over, Brenda invited Mark back into the house, confident that his attitude had changed since he'd spent the past hour sanding.

But she hadn't won yet. As the other kids worked on the science assignments she gave them, Mark sat doodling on his paper. She told herself that she wasn't going to hover over him, and she wasn't going to let him draw her into another argument. He had to learn that there were consequences for failing to get his work done.

She sat at the computer and sent an SOS e-mail to Sylvia, telling her how this first day was turning out. But before she sent it, she erased it. She didn't need to say negative things about a child who had been placed in her care. She wouldn't want Cathy talking about Daniel behind her back. She was above this, she thought. She could handle a little aggravation, and concentrate on the positives. Joseph was slowly returning to health, her other kids were able to get their education at home, and she had money coming in without having to work at night. Mark was worth the trouble.

After a while, she got up and went around to check her children's work. When she got to Mark, she saw that he had done absolutely nothing. She pulled out a chair and sat down at his table, getting face-to-face with him. "Mark, what have you been doing this whole time?" she asked.

He shrugged. "Nothing."

"Well, I asked you to do this assignment." Her voice was calm, unperturbed. She could do this, she told herself. She would not let her children see him get under her skin. "Can you tell me why you didn't do it?"

"I didn't understand it," he said.

"What's to understand? I very clearly told you to read that chapter and answer the questions at the end of it."

"But it didn't make any sense to me. Why can't we go on a field trip or something? Mom told me that was why homeschooling was so cool, that instead of reading books we did things."

"We do go on field trips. We go on them all the time," she said, "but right now we've got to get a basis for what we're learning, because field trips don't do any good if you don't know what you're seeing." Her voice was rising and she checked herself.

This boy was no different from Daniel, she thought. He was just a little misguided, a little less disciplined, but he had a long way to go before she would give up hope.

"Look, Mark, why don't you and Daniel work together?" She winked at Daniel as he looked up at her. "Daniel, maybe you can help Mark understand exactly what he's supposed to do. Show him how you take notes when you read."

"Sure, Mama." Daniel came to sit beside Mark, and the two boys grinned conspiratorially. She got a sinking feeling in her stomach again.

She sent them to a table in the corner of the room while she went around and checked Leah and Rachel and Joseph's work. She was standing over Joseph explaining rock formations and the crust of the earth when she heard something crash. She swung around and saw Daniel and Mark horsing around, giggling and pretending to fight.

"Daniel!" she shouted. Daniel let Mark go and backed away. He looked up at her with a startled look on his face. "Yes, ma'am?"

"I will not tolerate this!" Her voice was getting loud. "Now if you can't behave, then you can go back to school."

"I'll behave," Daniel said quickly. "I'm sorry, Mama."

Mark shot Daniel a look that said he was crazy. "Man, if I had the chance to go back to school, I'd do it in a second. In a heartbeat. Why do you want to be here?"

Brenda wanted to grab Mark and throttle him. "Mark, so help me, you're testing my patience, and I've been told I have more than most people." Her eyes stung, and she began to tremble. She didn't think her children had ever seen her lose control, but Mark was pushing her to the edge of her ability to endure.

She counted to ten in her mind, tried to take a few deep breaths, closed her eyes. A few moments of explosive silence ticked by as her children waited to see what she would do. She opened her eyes and saw that Mark was the only one who wasn't concerned with her reaction.

What was it she always tried to do in cases like this? Oh, yes, positive reinforcement. There hadn't been many negatives in her repertoire . . . at least not until today.

"All right, kids," she said. "I'll tell you what. If you'll get your science work done in the next half hour, then I'll take us all on a field trip tomorrow. It'll be sort of a back-to-homeschool party and we'll go to the park at Lake Brianne. I know it doesn't have much to do with what we're studying right now, but somehow we'll figure out a way to tie it in." She forced a grin, and the kids began to smile.

Mark was the only one who seemed unimpressed.

"Mark, if you get your work done, you'll get to go to the park with us." She looked around at the other kids, knowing they would all have their work done. "But anyone who doesn't have it done will have to stay behind."

"Stay behind?" Mark asked. "And do *what?*"

"Help Mr. David in his workshop," she said. "You won't be alone and you'll still be learning, but you won't get the privilege everybody else gets unless you do your work."

She drew in a deep breath and checked her watch. "I'm giving you thirty more minutes. Everybody get busy." With that, she left the room and hurried out to David's workshop.

David was busy with his power drill when she stepped inside his workshop. It was sweet refuge, and she shut the door hard behind her. David looked up and pulled off his goggles. "What is it?"

She slid onto a stool. "I don't know how much more I can take."

A slow grin traveled across David's face. "My Brenda doesn't know how much more she can take? Brenda, you've been through heart disease with Joseph. I think you can take a lot."

"I don't know if I can take Mark," she said. "I'm about to pull my hair out. I think maybe I've made a terrible mistake. Maybe telemarketing wasn't really so bad."

His smile faded, as he realized she was serious. "Brenda, you don't mean that."

"I do mean it," she said, "but I can't get out of this now because I've committed. Cathy's counting on me."

"So what are you going to do? Break him, like a wild horse?"

She shook her head. "I don't want to break him. I just want to redirect him a little. He's such an angry kid. And he has a way of making the adults around him just as angry."

"Well, maybe that has to do with growing up in a house without a father."

"But he *has* a relationship with his father," she said.

"Every other weekend?" David asked. "Come on. That's not a relationship."

"Well, whatever the reason, he can't go on like this. Not if I'm going to teach him. And you're probably going to hate me. But I need your help again, David. Remember, I'm doing this to help supplement our income."

He grinned and looked up at the ceiling, as if he could find some patience there. "What do I have to do this time?"

"I've given him an ultimatum," she said. "If he doesn't get his work done in the next thirty minutes, he's not going on the field trip with us tomorrow."

"Field trip?" David asked. "You just started school!"

"I know, but it just hit me that maybe I could give him some positive incentive, maybe something to look forward to and work toward."

"Do you think he'll do it?"

She clutched the roots of her hair. "I hope so. But I don't know, and if he doesn't, I can't let him catch me in a bluff. I'm going to have to leave him here with you."

He moaned. "Brenda, I can't get any work done when he's here. He spends the whole time roaming around picking up machinery that could cut his hand off."

"Well, maybe you could teach him what everything does so he won't do that."

"Or maybe he'll get his work done," he said, putting his goggles back on.

She sighed. "Maybe."

He started drilling again, his face grim. "If I could just get more work done, I'd make more money and you wouldn't have to do stuff like this," he shouted over the noise of the drill.

She felt even worse. Reaching over, she tapped him, and he shut off the drill. "David, this is not a big deal. I can do it, okay? Don't start feeling bad about yourself. We just have some financial obstacles right now, but it's not our fault. We couldn't have anticipated all these medical bills."

"Yeah, but if I had a better job with insurance . . ."

"David, this is what we chose." She grabbed his hand, pulled him close. He grinned like a little boy and took the goggles off again. "I like having you here," she said. "I need your help. I like the flexibility. I like that you're your own boss."

"It's a good thing I am." He leaned over and kissed her, then pressing his forehead against hers, said, "Well, I guess we're in this homeschooling thing together, aren't we? Sure, you can leave him with me if you have to."

She hugged him, so thankful that they could work as a team in this. It would do Mark good to be around a man who wielded a certain amount of authority.

Brenda braced herself as she went back in. She checked Joseph's work and saw that he had done everything he was supposed to do and more, just as he always did. She kissed his forehead and told him she was proud of him.

She checked Leah's and Rachel's papers, saw that they, too, had gone beyond the call of duty. They loved to learn and knew that the more they learned this first run-through, the more they could do when their mother started working with them on projects and examples.

Then she made it over to Daniel, who still sat beside Mark. Daniel was just finishing the last problem. She knew he would have been finished fifteen minutes ago if Mark hadn't slowed him. She glanced down at Mark's paper. He had written one sentence but had failed to do any of the rest of the work. She wondered how he had passed the time while she was gone. Her heart rate sped up, and her palms began to sweat. She swallowed and commanded herself to stay calm. "Mark, why didn't you do what I told you?"

"Well, I read it. I've got it up here," he said, tapping his head. "I didn't need to write any of it down."

She narrowed her eyes. "So you're telling me that you did the assignment in your head, but that I don't need to see it on paper?"

"Yeah, something like that."

She gave an exaggerated sigh. "Well, it's going to be a fun trip to the park tomorrow," she said, turning back to the other children. "I was thinking maybe we could stop by Kentucky Fried Chicken and pick up a bucket of chicken and have a picnic." Leah and Rachel and Joseph all began to cheer. Daniel was more reticent, though, as he looked up at his mother, as though wondering what she was up to. "Joseph, we'll take a wheelchair in case you get tired, but you don't have to use it unless you want to."

"Okay," he said.

"We'll ride the train that goes around the lake, and maybe we can do some fishing." Joseph hadn't been away from home in a while, except to go to church. His round face beamed with excitement.

She turned back to Mark. "Mark, I'm sure Mr. David will be able to keep you busy all day."

His expression crashed. "What?"

"You'll be helping him tomorrow," she said. "You should learn a lot from him."

His mouth dropped open. "You're leaving me here?"

"Well, sure," she said. "I told you how it was going to be and you didn't do your work so . . ."

"I'm telling my mom," he spouted. "She's paying you good money."

"She's paying me to teach you," Brenda said, "and I'm trying to." She looked at her watch and realized the school day was over. Cathy had told her to send Mark home when it got to be three o'clock. "Mark, you're welcome to go home now. I'm not going to give you any homework today, but I would like for you to finish that science assignment tonight."

"If I do, do I get to go to the park?" he asked.

"No," she said. "I warned you about that and you made your choice, but if you do your science assignment tonight and turn it in tomorrow morning, when we start back on our studies Wednesday, you'll be able to help on the project we're going to do. And if you have any trouble doing it tonight," she said, "I could certainly explain everything to your mother."

"No," he said, "she'll go ballistic."

"She might," Brenda said. "I'd really like for her to have a good feeling about the way today went."

He stood up and got his books together, and shot her a look that said he couldn't believe he was being treated this way. Then without saying good-bye to any of them, he headed out the door and across the street.

CHAPTER
Thirty-Eight

For the first time in weeks, Tory couldn't wait for Barry to get home so she could tell him about the school and what she had seen, and plead with him to go back there with her. If he could see these babies, understand the hope for them, the potential, the joy they could bring to their families' lives, she knew it would change his heart.

She cooked a big meal and tried to make their home comfortable with scented candles and a fire in the fireplace, but when suppertime came, Barry was still not home.

"Where's Daddy?" Brittany asked. "Is he working late again?"

"He's not coming," Spencer said. "Let's eat without him."

Tory realized that Spencer was probably right. Disappointed, she started to set the table.

"He's always in a bad mood," Spencer said. "He comes home and he doesn't want to talk or play. What's he so mad about, anyway?"

Tory searched her brain for an explanation her children could understand. "He's got a lot of stress at work, honey."

"Well, he should get glad in the same pants he got mad in," Spencer said.

Tory's mouth fell open. "Spencer, where did you hear that?"

"School," he said, reaching around her for a roll. "Teacher says it."

They should teach four-year-olds calculus, she thought. They retained everything.

"You don't have school," Brittany chided. "That's Mommy's Morning Out."

"Is too school," Spencer threw back. "Huh, Mommy?"

"We can call it that. But Spencer, please don't say that glad-mad-pants thing again. It's not very respectful. Besides, Daddy's not mad at you."

"Is he mad at you?" Brittany asked.

"Maybe a little," Tory admitted. "I've been kind of grouchy lately."

"Just because of all that puking," Spencer said.

"Well, when Daddy gets home tonight, how about if we all try to be really good? I won't be grouchy, and you two won't beg him to read you books. We'll just let him relax, okay?"

Brittany gave her a long, pensive look. "You promise you won't throw up?"

"I can promise to try. I'm feeling okay right now."

"You're prob'ly well," Spencer said. "Thank goodness." He took a big drink of milk, then wiped his mouth with the back of his hand. "You could call Daddy at work and tell him we're waitin' for him to eat."

"So could you," Tory said, not quite ready to take that big a step. "How about I dial the number and you talk to him?"

"Okay," Spencer said. She dialed and handed Spencer the phone.

"Daddy, this is Spencer," he said, as if Barry wouldn't recognize his own child. "We're waiting for you. Mommy made a good supper." He paused. Tory wished she had put him on the speaker phone so she could hear. "Why not? Well, when will you? Well, why do you have to stay there?" His tone deteriorated into a whine. "You're never here. I know, but . . . Will you come after? Will you bring us ice cream? All right," he said. "Okay, bye."

He hung up and flashed a victory sign to his sister. "Yes! He's bringing ice cream."

Tory tried not to look too anxious. "When?"

"Later. He said to eat. He has work to do."

Tory tried not to betray her fierce disappointment as she finished setting the table. She was quiet as the children chattered about what kind of ice cream he might bring. As they argued about the merits of chocolate over strawberry, she mentally rehearsed the speech she would make when Barry got home. There wasn't time for anger. She had to make him understand about the school, about the hope they could have for their child, about the mothers she had met.

It was eight o'clock before Barry got home, carrying a bag of Blizzards for all of them.

As the children took theirs out to the picnic table to avoid a mess, she and Barry sat down on the patio. She could see the stress and fatigue in his body, and in the lines on his face. He had nothing to say to her, and expected nothing in return. She watched him lean forward and set his elbows on his knees as he gazed out at the children.

"Barry, Saturday, at the grocery store, I met someone," she said.

He looked over at her. She knew it surprised him that she had initiated a conversation, when she'd spent weeks avoiding him. "Oh, yeah? Who?"

"A woman who had a child with Down's Syndrome."

He turned his head away then, as if he didn't want to engage in this conversation.

"Her child was a teenager, and he was really sweet. He was feeling all the produce."

He set his jaw and said nothing.

"She gave me the name of her son's school and . . . I went by there today."

He didn't look at her, and she knew he didn't want to hear.

"It just showed me how much potential these kids have. They're not invalids; they're not helpless. They even had a couple of them working in the office. Paid employees."

He started shaking his head before she had even finished her sentence. "You can't tell me anything about the education of retarded children, Tory. I have Nathan, remember?"

"I know," she said, "but Nathan's autistic. Our baby will have different needs and different potential."

"That school is something that tries to make the best of a bad situation," he said. "There are better ways to do it."

She knew he was talking about abortion again, and all her promises to herself not to get angry fled. "Not better ways, Barry. Your ways are not better."

He was growing cold, callused, she thought. "You know, you're not only abandoning the baby," she told Barry, "but you're abandoning Brittany and Spencer, too. They asked me tonight why you're always so mad when you get home."

"Mad?" he asked. "I'm not mad."

"They think you are. Abandon me if you have to, Barry, but don't abandon them."

He shook his head as if he couldn't believe she'd uttered those words. "You've got a lot of nerve. You take an important decision like our family completely out of my hands, and you have the gall to tell me that I need to treat my children better? I come home to this house and I have no control over anything that goes on here. You're in there, heaving in the bathroom while the kids are bouncing off the walls, and I'm sleeping down in the basement because the chill in our room is just too much."

"Barry, I'm trying to tell you that we don't have to abort this baby. There's hope. She can have a life that's fairly normal."

"Best case," he said, looking back at her, "but worst case is that she's an invalid, that she can't do anything, that she can't talk, that she'll never be able to walk, or that she'll be sick all the time and hate her life and die young."

Her eyes filled with tears at the picture he had of their child. She shook her head hard. "Oh, no, that's not the worst case, Barry," she said.

He got up, set his hands on his hips. "What is, then?"

"The worst case," she said, "is that her father would want to abort her before she ever has a chance to try."

Barry went in and slammed the door behind him. The children both looked up from the picnic table, but neither of them asked what was wrong. Their parents were fighting again. It was getting to be a habit.

Tory got them to bed early that night, then retreated to the bedroom and cried herself to sleep.

CHAPTER
Thirty-Nine

Since the field trip to the park took place on Tuesday, Brenda invited Tory and Spencer. She hoped it would cheer Tory up and distract her from her troubles. She couldn't help chuckling as they pulled the van out of the driveway and waved back at Mark, who stood next to David with a stricken look on his face. It was clear that he couldn't believe they were leaving him.

"Are you sure you're not going to turn around and go back to get him?" Tory asked Brenda.

"Not on your life," Brenda said. "Mark will be fine. He just needs a little tweaking before we can really get things off the ground."

Tory gazed out the window. "You know, I haven't been around Cathy's kids all that much, but all three of them strike me as smart alecks. I don't know why you'd ever commit to teaching Mark."

"I knew I could help him," Brenda said. "Like I said, he's going to be fine. David plans to work his little fingers to the bone today, and then tomorrow when I tell him to get his work done, maybe he'll take me more seriously." She looked over at the big shirt Tory wore over her khakis, and she could see that her stomach was rounding out slightly. "So how are you feeling?" she asked softly, keeping her voice down so the kids—chattering in the back—wouldn't hear.

"Feeling good today," Tory said. "No nausea."

"Isn't that something new?" Brenda asked.

Tory smiled. "Yeah, it's new, all right. I'm fifteen weeks now. Maybe I'm getting past it."

"So what about Barry? Has anything changed?"

Tory shook her head. "Still sleeping in the basement." The rims of her eyes reddened and she laid her head back on the seat. Brenda knew they couldn't go into this in any more detail with the children in the back of the van. Besides, she wanted this to be a day of fun, not conversations that dragged them all down.

It wasn't until a few hours later, when the children were involved in throwing bread crust to the ducks over the little bridge at the duck pond, that Brenda and Tory were able to sit down in the shade and pick up their conversation.

"So what are you going to do about Barry?" Brenda asked Tory.

She shook her head. "I don't know." She watched a mother pushing her baby past the kids in a stroller, and Spencer leaned over and made a face at the child. The baby giggled.

"Mommy, look!" he said.

Tory grinned. "He loves babies."

"Almost all children do."

"I've been thinking about telling him and Brittany."

Brenda gave her a glance. "Well, you're not going to be able to hide it a lot longer, but do you think it's a good idea to do that when Barry is still so confused?"

"He's not confused, Brenda. He knows exactly what he wants."

"But Tory . . . I know Barry too well. He's not the kind of man who could easily abort a child. There's got to be something going through this mind, something he's got to work through."

"Well, there is, of course," Tory said. "His autistic brother, Nathan. Barry thinks he's never contributed anything in his life. He thinks he's miserable. But I don't think he is. I think he just sits there as content as anybody on earth. And his mother loves him."

"But you can at least understand where Barry is coming from."

"Well, I can understand it," she said. "I just don't agree with it."

Brenda shifted on the bench and propped her elbow on the back of it. "Tory, I've been praying really hard for you, and so has Sylvia. She reminds me in every e-mail to remember to pray for you."

"I appreciate that."

Brenda wondered if Tory had been getting enough sleep. "I think your marriage is going to be all right, and I think Barry is going to get used to the idea of the baby and come around. Just give him some time."

"I don't want to give him time," she said wearily. "I want to take all control of this from his hands because he's not thinking clearly. If I were to tell Spencer and Brittany and they got all excited about my pregnancy, then he'd have to stop talking about abortion; he wouldn't have any choice."

"That's one way to change his mind," Brenda said, "but are you sure it's the right way? It could just alienate Barry more at a time when you really need him."

"I'm not worried about being alienated by him," Tory said. "I'm worried about saving my child's life."

"Well, it's not like he's stalking you, ready to take the baby. He's not breathing down your neck and demanding that you do it, is he?"

Tory crossed her arms and stared after the children. "Oh, no, he's just giving me the silent treatment, sleeping in the basement, coming home late at night."

"Still, I don't think you should tell the kids. I think you need to give him another couple of weeks, maybe a month. Then when you absolutely can't hide it anymore, go ahead and tell them, but only after you've warned him."

Tory didn't want to hear any of that.

"Promise me you'll pray about it," Brenda said.

Tory nodded, but Brenda knew the commitment was shallow. "I've *been* praying about it. And I keep thinking that with all this prayer, God could still heal my baby."

"Sure, he could," Brenda said.

"I mean, just because the lab test showed a chromosome problem doesn't mean that it's going to stay that way. God has raised people from the dead. He's made the blind to see. He can fix a stupid little chromosome."

"He certainly can," Brenda said, "and you know me. I sure believe in miracles."

But it was clear that Tory wasn't so sure. Her eyes filled with tears and she looked away. Brenda squeezed her hand. "You're going to be all right, Tory. You're going to love this baby and you're going to take care of her, and your family is going to be fine."

"There you go again," Tory said. "That incredible optimism."

"Well, what's there to be pessimistic about?" she asked. "God is totally in control, and he's not going to let anything happen to you that he didn't plan."

"Are you sure?" Tory asked, meeting her eyes. "Are you sure that Satan is not involved in these things sometimes, giving us children who are deformed or retarded or have heart disease?"

"Satan is not more powerful than God. Nothing happens without God's permission. Everything is for a reason."

"Barry mentioned that God isn't supposed to give us more than we can endure, but if God knows me at all, he knows this is not the kind of thing that I can handle." She breathed a bitter laugh. "I have to have everything perfect, neat, and organized. I've spent years taking care of my looks because perfection is such a big thing with me, and now he gives me an imperfect child. Some irony, huh?"

"Maybe," Brenda said. "Maybe not. Maybe this is how God is going to show you that perfection isn't the important thing."

"Couldn't he just send me a letter, or a video? Or even do something to me, instead of my child?"

"This is how it's supposed to happen. And you know what? Barry is part of God's plan, too. Somehow he's going to use Barry in this. I have a lot of faith in your husband."

"Why?" Tory asked.

"Because I know him to be a believer," she said. "It hasn't been that long since Barry came to the hospital to talk to David about his faith. He tried to lead David to Christ, but David just wasn't interested. That took a lot of guts, and whenever I see Barry now, I get these warm thoughts, because I know he cared enough about my husband to tell him the truth."

"Yeah, we've come a long way since that," Tory said. "Who would have thought he would go from sharing his faith with David to demanding an abortion of his own child?"

"Who would have ever predicted any of what's happened lately?" Brenda asked. "Who would have thought you'd be pregnant? Who would have thought I'd be homeschooling Mark? Who would have thought Sylvia would find a little girl and keep her?"

Tory stared out into the breeze with vacant, pensive eyes. "Do you ever feel like life is just one series of crises after another?"

"No," Brenda said without hesitation. "Actually, I feel like it's one series of blessings after another. It's like Sylvia said. God sends the showers *and* the sunshine."

"So that's what you think this is? A shower?"

Brenda smiled. "A shower of blessings, maybe," she said. "You just never know. I bet the parents of all those children in that Down's Syndrome school think their children are blessings. Soon, you'll be one of them," she said.

Tory was pensive as the kids came back down from the bridge, ready to move on to their next activity.

CHAPTER

When they got home that afternoon, Brenda went around the house to the workshop. Through the window, she saw Mark working hard to cut out a shelf. David stood over him, encouraging and supervising, and Mark seemed to be listening. He looked so industrious with his goggles and gloves on that she almost hated to disturb him.

She opened the door, and Mark looked up. Suddenly, that look of concentration on his face changed to an angry scowl. "So how are you two doing back here?" she asked.

David gave her a wink. "Mark's been a real big help today."

Mark pulled off his gloves and slammed them down. "Can I go home now, or do you want me to dig a ditch or something?"

Brenda started to remember the hostility she'd felt earlier. She'd had peace today without Mark, but her problem obviously was not solved.

"You go ahead home," she said. "I just saw your mom drive up. Steve's with her. He had a truckload of clothes they're sorting through in the garage. Maybe you can help them."

"After working all day in here? I'm not helping nobody do nothing."

Brenda decided to let Cathy handle that. Mark pushed out past her, and she turned back to David.

"That kid needs a lot of help," he said as he went back to what he was doing.

⁓

Across the street, Cathy grabbed an armload of clothes from Steve's truck and went to drop them on the table she had set up in her garage. She saw Mark coming with a grim look on his face, and hopeful that he'd have a better attitude than yesterday, she abandoned the clothes and met him halfway. "So how was your second day of homeschooling?" she asked, her voice dripping with enthusiasm.

"Mom, you should never pay her," Mark snapped. "She's just using me, that's all. She's not trying to teach me anything. This is all just a trick."

Cathy shot Steve a look. He was grinning and trying to look busy with the clothes. "So what did she do? Make you work?"

"They went on a field trip, Mom. She made me stay and work with Mr. David all day in his stupid workshop."

Cathy's own smile faded. "Mark, what did you do to get punished?"

"Nothing," he said. "I just didn't understand my work. She goes around and gives us assignments without teaching us anything, and then she disappears so you can't ask questions. We're supposed to be mind readers, I guess. I waited till she got back so I could ask her, and the next thing I know, she's telling me I didn't get to go on the field trip 'cause I didn't get my work done."

Cathy was still skeptical. "Mark, I know Brenda. She wouldn't punish you over a misunderstanding. Why is it that her kids could figure out the assignment, but you couldn't?"

"Because she explained it better to them. She treats me like the wicked stepchild. Like I'm just getting on her nerves if I ask her one thing. I can't help it if her kids are smarter than me!"

That did it. Until now, Cathy had reserved her judgment until she could talk to Brenda, but she hated it when Mark thought he was dumb. His older brother and sister had told him that for twelve years. He'd embraced that lie in school. She didn't want Brenda perpetuating it. "They are *not* smarter than you. They just listen better."

"I'm telling you, Mom, she just didn't want me with her. She took off with her own kids and left me here."

Cathy glanced across the street. Brenda wasn't out. "So where did they go?" she asked weakly.

"They went to the park at Lake Brianne, spent all day there. I had to stay in that stupid workshop breathing sawdust and varnish and listening to a buzz saw all day long."

Cathy was getting aggravated. "Mark, there's got to be more to this."

"There's not, Mom! It's not the last time she's gonna do it. She's gonna take advantage of me every chance she gets. She hates me. She's only doing this so she won't have to work a real job. Mom, she's nothing like you think."

Cathy was getting angry. "Well, maybe I need to have a talk with Brenda," she said. "Mark, you go on in and put your stuff away."

"Mom, I'm telling you. You don't want to keep paying her. Let me just go on back to school. It's not too late."

"Go in the house, Mark," she said. "I've got to go talk to Brenda."

When the door closed behind Mark, Cathy swung around and started down the driveway.

"Now hold on there," Steve said, stopping her. "You don't want to go off half-cocked and start yelling at your friend. Keep in mind, this is Mark we're talking about."

She glared up at him. "And what is that supposed to mean? He's my son!"

"I know, but I'm just telling you kids have a way of exaggerating things. It's probably nothing like he said."

"Are you calling my son a liar?"

536

Steve closed his eyes. "No, Cathy, I'm not calling Mark a liar. I'm just telling you that when things are filtered through a child's eyes, they don't come out exactly right. You know that as well as I do."

"Well, I don't care. I'm going to talk to Brenda and get to the bottom of this. Do you want to come with me?"

Steve seemed to consider getting back in his truck, but then he glanced toward Brenda's house. "Yeah, I'll come. Maybe I can keep you from ruining a friendship."

"Fine." Cathy started across the street, and marched around Brenda's house where she had seen her go before Mark came home. She found Brenda in the backyard, encouraging Leah as she jumped to a hundred on her jump rope. Tory was with them, sitting on the swing next to Brittany. Tory waved at Cathy, but Cathy barely noticed.

"Brenda, I need to talk to you."

"Ninety-nine, one hundred. Oh, hi, Cathy. Hey, Steve. Leah just passed the hundred mark." When Cathy didn't respond, she looked up at her and saw the anger on her face. "Uh-oh. What did he tell you?"

Cathy sat down. "He says that you went on a field trip today and left him behind to work for David."

Brenda nodded. "That's right."

"He says it was because he didn't finish his work."

"Right again."

"Well, maybe he needed a little more explanation about the assignment."

"It was easy, Cathy. He just refused to do it."

Tory got up. "Listen, I've got to get home."

Brenda nodded and Cathy didn't say anything. But Tory couldn't leave until she found Spencer, and at the moment, he wasn't anywhere in sight.

Brenda tried again. "Cathy, I probably should have talked to you yesterday, but I didn't want you to get a bad feeling about the first day. You obviously didn't get the whole story from Mark. "

"How do you know what I got?" Cathy asked. "I didn't tell you everything he said."

"If he told you that I took the kids on a field trip and left him to work for David, that's only part of the story."

"That's enough," Cathy said too loudly. "Brenda, I'm paying you to teach my son. Not to apprentice him in carpentry."

"Calm down, Cathy," Steve said quietly.

She turned on him. "Calm down? Would you calm down if this was Tracy?"

"Cathy, please," Brenda said. "Just sit down for a minute, would you?"

Cathy didn't want to sit down, but when Brenda did, Steve pulled her down. He sat down next to her with his arm around her.

"Tell us what's going on, Brenda," Steve said calmly.

Brenda met Cathy's eyes without any anger. "Yesterday I had a terrible time with Mark. Cathy, he didn't want to do anything. He went back to bed after you left for work, then Daniel had to go get him, and he came over barely awake. He kept laying his head down trying to sleep. Every time I gave him an assignment, he refused to do it, and he was disruptive and disrespectful all day long."

Cathy's face fell by degrees. "Oh, no."

"By the end of the day I was very frustrated with him," Brenda went on, "and I gave him an ultimatum. I told him that if he didn't finish his science assignment within thirty minutes, that he wouldn't be going with us on the field trip today." She leaned forward, locking in to Cathy's eyes. "I only dreamed up this field trip as incentive to make him finish. I thought I'd give him something positive to work toward, instead of a threat of punishment. I *wanted* him to go with us." She reached across the picnic table and took Cathy's hand. "Cathy, I love you, and I love Mark, but I've got to teach him that I mean business, and he called my bluff. I really wanted to take him to the lake. But when he refused to do his work, I had no choice but to follow through."

Cathy covered her face. Steve began to stroke her back, trying to calm her down.

After a moment, she looked up at Brenda over her finger-tips. "Brenda, I'm so sorry. I should have known."

"I know you've been busy and I thought I could handle it. I thought if I could just teach Mark this lesson today, that tomorrow he'd come back and he'd know that when I said to do something, he had to do it, that there were consequences if he didn't. He's going to have to learn that sometime."

Cathy felt attacked. "I guess that implies that I haven't taught him consequences. I know I've done an awful job, but I've tried . . ."

"I know you have," Brenda cut in quickly, "but you're just one person. He just needs some authority. Some discipline."

Cathy groaned. "So what happens now? Are you going to keep teaching him?"

"Of course I am," she said. "Mark's going to be fine. Probably by tomorrow, if you'll just go home and reinforce what I've done today. Let him know that he's not going to get away with treating David or me with disrespect, that horsing around with Daniel in the classroom is not going to be tolerated, that he's not going to smart off to me, that when I tell him to do his work, he needs to do it. I need your help with that."

Cathy realized that Tory was standing back, still waiting for Spencer and pretending not to listen to the whole scene. Cathy was embarrassed, humiliated, and wanted to do worse to Mark than make him learn carpentry. "I could just die," she whispered.

Steve touched her hair. "Cathy, don't. You knew Mark was having problems. That's why you made this move. This isn't new. You're doing fine."

"Steve's right," Brenda said. "And the bright side is that he made a really nice bookcase today."

Steve began to chuckle and Cathy shot him an unappreciative look. "It's not funny," she said.

He quickly wiped the smile off of his face. "Sorry."

Cathy moaned. "All right, Brenda. You did the right thing. I'm sorry I jumped on you. I'm just so sensitive about my kids." She wiped the wetness under her eyes. "I'll do my best to reinforce what you've done, and he'll be back bright and early tomorrow. And, trust me, he'll be wide awake and ready to work."

Brenda nodded as if she knew that would be the case. "One more thing," she said. "Try not to teach him Scripture when you're mad at him."

Cathy met Steve's eyes. She really didn't want him to hear this, but the damage had already been done. "What do you mean?" she asked in a weak voice.

"I mean every time I try to teach him Scripture, he thinks he's being punished," Brenda said. "He says you only make him memorize it when you're mad."

Cathy's head was beginning to throb. "I guess that's true. Whenever they smart off to me or get me flustered, I start to remember how much catch-up I need to do in their spiritual education."

"But the Bible isn't something that's negative and angry," Brenda told her. "It needs to be treated like it's critical information, pertinent to their lives. They need to be shown how it applies, and if you only do it when you're mad, they won't ever want to learn it at all."

"She's right," Steve said.

Cathy covered her face again. "But when do I do it, then? I only seem to have power over them when I'm mad at them."

"You have a lot more power than you think," Steve said carefully.

Looking defeated, she got up. "Well," she said, "I guess I'd better get home and take care of this."

Brenda came around the table and gave her a tentative hug. Cathy was stiff as she returned it. "I do appreciate what you're doing, Brenda. It's just going to take a little adjustment."

"I know," Brenda said, "and I'm willing to do whatever I can. I'm a pretty patient person, you know."

"That's why I picked you."

As she and Steve crossed the street again, Cathy was thankful for his silence. She hated the fact that he had witnessed this whole thing. Now he knew just how bad things were. She wondered if she would ever get Mark through this stage.

Rick and Annie were pulling into the driveway just as they reached the house. "I need to go in and talk to Mark," she said.

"No problem," he said, grabbing a bunch of hangers out of a box. "I'll just work on these clothes."

Cathy went in and stormed up the stairs, and found Mark sitting on his unmade bed with dirty laundry all around him, eating a bag of potato chips and watching his television.

She leaned in his doorway with her arms crossed. "Mark, I got the real story of what happened today, and Brenda was absolutely right to make you stay home."

"Oh, right. I should have known you'd take her side."

"Not only am I going to take her side, but as of this moment, you are grounded from the computer *and* the television until further notice."

"Mom!" he cried.

"When Miss Brenda tells me that you're behaving properly at her house, then I'll consider giving you back your privileges."

"This is just plain child abuse!" he screamed. "I can't believe you're doing this to me! I haven't done anything wrong! I smoke one stupid joint in the bathroom and you rearrange the rest of my life!"

"Mark, stop raising your voice to me right now!"

"I *have* to raise my voice to you!" he screamed. "I have to yell to be heard over you!"

She knew that Steve could probably hear from the garage. Part of her knew that she should close the door and do this quietly, but the other part of her needed for Steve to know that she was taking care of this, that she did crack down on her son when he needed to be cracked down on, that she did have some measure of authority over his life.

Mark was the only one who didn't realize it.

She pulled the plug on the television and marched down the stairs as Annie and Rick came in.

"What's going on up there?" Rick asked.

"What did Mark do now?" Annie piped in, grinning with delight. "Has he already been thrown out of the Dodds' home-school?

"No, he hasn't been thrown out," Cathy bit out, "and please pick up your backpacks and take them to your rooms."

"Well, hello and welcome home to you, too," Annie said.

Cathy saw Steve through the open door, shaking his head. He had heard everything, and he did not seem amused.

"Don't talk to me that way, Annie," she bit out. "Just do what I say."

Rick was at the refrigerator perusing the contents. "There's nothing in this house to eat. There's never anything."

"Then you're welcome to go to the grocery store for me," Cathy said.

"Well, if you weren't always so busy with that clothing drive."

"Excuse me?" Cathy yelled. "Are you seriously telling me that I'm wasting my time collecting clothes for people who've lost everything they own?"

Rick shrugged. "No, all I'm trying to tell you is that there's nothing to eat in this house."

Cathy fought the urge to sit down and cry like a baby, but she knew that wasn't going to accomplish anything. "Rick, take your things upstairs now. You, too, Annie."

Annie got her backpack and slid the strap over her shoulder. "You know, Mom, I think it's great that you're doing this to help the Nicaraguans."

She wondered what Annie was buttering her up for, and braced herself for the extended curfew question or an advance on her allowance. "Annie, I don't know what you're up to, but if you're smart, you won't pick now to ask for boots, clothes, later curfews, or money."

As if the garage provided refuge from the madness inside, Cathy went back to the clothing table, letting the screen door bounce shut behind her.

Steve appeared to be lost in deep thought as he sorted the clothes by size.

"What?" Cathy asked, finally. "Just go ahead and say it."

He turned to her, his eyes serious. "You've got to get a handle on those kids."

She bit her lip and furiously hung a dress on a hanger.

"Now you're mad at me," he said.

"I'm not mad. I'm just a little worn down."

"Well, I don't blame you," he said. "I'd be worn down, too."

She started pushing the hangers furiously, one by one. "Look, I appreciate your concern, but I'm doing the very best that I can. I know that's hard to believe from your position with only one child. Tracy doesn't have a disappointing relationship with another parent every other weekend, where she has no authority and no discipline at all. From your perspective it looks like I'm just being dragged along by a runaway train." Her voice broke off and she choked back tears. "But let me tell you something. It's not easy with three kids and no father to help. You don't have any right to judge me."

"Judge you?" Steve dropped the clothes he was folding. "Who's judging you?"

"Everybody, okay? Brenda and Tory and you ... and even my kids." She covered her eyes with her hands and tried to stop crying. "Oh, great! This is about the worst dating rule I can break. Start crying because there's not a father in the home, and then the date thinks that you're building a case for marriage, as if he can come in like the knight in shining armor and fix all the problems!" She stopped, stunned that she had uttered the M word at all. "Well, I'm *not* looking for marriage, okay, Steve?" she lied. "This is not a buildup for any kind of relationship. I'm just telling you how I feel."

His face had softened. "I know that, Cathy."

"Because marriage is the last thing I'm looking for, you know. It's completely out of the question. It wouldn't last two months, not with my kids in the house and some guy who wanted authority in the home, especially if he had raised his differently. Hypothetically, I mean."

Again, he nodded. "I know."

"Do you?" she asked. "Well, how do you know, because I probably look like some wimpy little single mom who's constantly on the prowl for somebody to rescue her. Well, I don't need rescuing."

"Of course you don't."

"And my kids don't need rescuing. I can lay down consequences just like I'm supposed to. I can take care of them. I can
change things."

"Sure, you can."

She was sobbing now, and her lips curled in an emotional
sneer. "I don't need any help from their father or from you or
from anybody."

The pronouncement seemed to shake him, and for a
moment, he just stood staring down at her, as if he didn't know
whether to pull her into his arms or run for his life. She turned
away from him, hating herself for losing control like this.

This was probably the end of them, she thought dismally. He'd
never want to speak to her again. What was wrong with her?
Didn't she know better than to throw fits in front of Steve? To snap
and scream and yell, then act like a dysfunctional, heartbroken
dishrag?

"You haven't broken any dating rules," he whispered, stepping up behind her and setting his hands on her shoulders.
"You're just having a bad day. It's okay. I understand."

She drew in a deep breath and wiped her face with both
hands. She didn't want him to see her like this. "I need to go in,"
she said. "I'll just work on the clothes later. The pilot doesn't
need them loaded until tomorrow. I'll get them ready."

She hated dismissing him that way, but he accepted it and
dropped his hands.

"So, when can I see you again?"

She breathed out a laugh and turned to look at him. "You
have got to be kidding."

"No, I'm not," he said. "Are you still coming for Thanksgiving?"

She almost laughed. "Are you crazy? You really want me to
bring my kids to your house to be with your mom and dad for
Thanksgiving?"

"Yes," he said, "I told you I did."

"Still, after all this?"

"Yes," he said. "They're looking forward to it. *I'm* looking forward to it."

She wiped her face with her fingertips. "Well, I guess so then. Might as well hammer a few more nails in my coffin."

He grinned slightly. "Cathy, you and I are okay. Okay?" He bent down and pulled her into a hug, and she sucked in a sob. "It's going to be all right," he whispered.

The words warmed her, but they seemed like a wobbly promise built on nothing more than sand. She wondered if things ever really could be all right again. Suddenly, she wanted to drive to Knoxville to lash out at her ex-husband, beat her fists against his chest and kick him in the shin and tell him how destructive his actions had been in their family, how torn her children were, how his absence in the home had turned them into different children than they might have been. She wanted to tell him that no one else would ever be able to take his place in their eyes, not in a real way, not even if Steve stepped in. But he wasn't here, and he didn't really care, anyway.

But Steve was, holding her and whispering that it was going to be all right. And she wanted to believe it. He kissed her forehead, then bent down and kissed her lips. Warm comfort seeped through her anxious, angry heart.

"I'll call you tomorrow," he said, then went to his truck.

As he drove off, she stood staring after him, perplexed that he would even give her the time of day when things were so complicated. She couldn't imagine that their relationship was worth it to him.

Sooner or later, he would see things as they really were. And then they would be history.

CHAPTER
Forty-One

Barry was late for supper again. Though it didn't surprise Tory, it made her angry. She told herself she was angry for the children, who missed their dad and didn't understand why he was behaving this way. She paced the kitchen back and forth, back and forth, ready to lambaste him the minute he came in. When she finally gave up, she fed the kids, and fought the headache bearing down on her.

After supper, she got Brittany and Spencer busy making Thanksgiving turkeys out of construction paper, and set about to clean the dishes. As she scrubbed spaghetti off of the plates and table, a vengeful thought came to her mind. The children had a right to know about their little sister. They had a right to understand why their mother's stomach was getting bigger, and they had a right to pray for the sibling who needed their prayers.

She stopped scrubbing and regarded the two children at the kitchen counter, elbow deep in glue. Spencer had made fangs for his turkey, and Brittany was trying to convince him that turkeys had no teeth. They were innocent, she thought. Completely innocent of the fact that children were born imperfect, that there were "options" in the world, that parents ever stopped loving each other. Should she burden them with this?

And how much longer could she keep it from them? She knew Brittany's teacher would start questioning her about her growing stomach soon. She hadn't forgotten the comment she'd made to her about being pregnant just a few weeks ago. She was sure the teacher hadn't forgotten, either. She didn't want her children to overhear teachers or neighbors talking about her condition.

No, they had a right to know. And since Barry wasn't here to consult, she had to go with her own feelings. Both Sylvia and Brenda had warned her not to tell them without Barry's blessing, but they both had husbands who came home for supper, who slept next to them in bed, who loved all of their children like fathers should.

"You can't put a hat on a turkey!" Spencer was saying. "Turkeys don't wear hats."

"That's a pilgrim hat," Brittany threw back. "Thanksgiving turkeys wear pilgrim hats."

"They do not. Do they, Mommy?"

"Hey, if yours can have teeth," Brittany said, "then mine can wear a hat."

Tory bit her lip as tears pushed into her eyes. How should she say it? Should she sit them down and break it like important news, or just throw it out with matter-of-fact nonchalance? Should she tell them there was something wrong with this baby?

No, she thought. That was more than a mother could break to her children alone. Tonight she could only tell them there was going to *be* a baby.

"Mommy!" Spencer insisted, and she turned to look at him. "They don't wear hats, *do* they?"

She tried to smile. "We can pretend they do. Britty, why don't you help Spencer make an Indian headdress to put on his?"

"Okay," Brittany said, grabbing more construction paper.

"No," Spencer said. "I don't want an Indian. I want it to be a Titan. I want it to be a football helmet."

"*Mommy!*" Brittany cried, indignant. "Turkeys can't wear football helmets! I'm not gonna help him with that."

"All right," Tory said. "Then make another turkey with the Indian headdress, and Spencer can do the football helmet himself. Can't you, Spencer?"

"That's gonna be the stupidest looking turkey anybody ever saw," Brittany declared.

But Tory's idea seemed to please Spencer as he got the scissors and began cutting. "I like stupid turkeys. I *want* mine to be stupid. I'm gonna make a whole herd of 'em."

Tory wiped her hands on a dish towel, got a bar stool, and pulled it around the counter. She sat down, facing her children. "I've got to talk to you guys."

Spencer couldn't look up from his cutting. "Wait a minute. I have to do my helmet."

"No, I can't wait." She touched Spencer's hand, stopping him. "Just look up at me for a minute and listen. I need to tell you something. Both of you." They both stopped what they were doing and looked up at her. Brittany had Elmer's glue on her chin, and Spencer had it drying on his hands.

"Have you noticed that Mommy's getting a little tummy?" she asked them both.

Spencer grinned and started cutting again. "Yeah, you're as big as a cow."

She would have been hurt if she didn't know that Spencer's teacher muttered that every time she looked into the mirror.

"You're not fat, Mommy," Brittany said. "My teacher thinks you have a eating-us-order. I heard her tell Sarah's mom that."

Heat rushed to Tory's face. Had her child's teacher been gossiping that she had an eating disorder? She would have to have a talk with her tomorrow.

"I am getting a little bit of a tummy," she said, standing up so the children could see. She pressed her shirt against her stomach to show her belly. "But there's a reason for that. There's something *in* my tummy. Do you know what it is?"

Spencer's hand flew up. "Bucket chicken from the park!" he cried, without being called on.

Tory grinned. "No, Spence. Something a lot more exciting."

Brittany's eyes got big. "Kevin Holiday's mom has a baby in her tummy." She caught her breath and lowered her voice to a whisper. "Do you have a baby?" she asked in a reverent voice.

Tory smiled. "Yep, a little baby."

The children's eyebrows shot up, and Spencer dropped the scissors.

"What do you think about that?" she asked, her eyes twinkling with moisture.

"Can we get it out now?" Spencer asked.

Tory laughed. "No, honey, it's going to be a few more months. It's not ready yet. Mommy's going to need a lot of help from you. You're going to be the big sister, okay, Britty? And, Spence, you're going to be the big brother. This is why I've been sick so much."

"Does Daddy know?" Brittany asked.

Tory hesitated. "Yeah, he knows."

She heard the garage door opening, and realized she couldn't have timed this worse if she'd tried. Barry was home, and the children were full of the news of the pregnancy. They would attack him with it before he even got in the door. He would be livid.

She was almost sorry for what she had done.

"Daddy's home!" Spencer said, jumping down from his stool. Spencer turned a bad cartwheel and came to his feet with his arms in the air. "Daddy's home and we're gonna have a baby," he sang.

"Not right now, dummy," Brittany said. Spencer turned another lopsided cartwheel. "Soon, though, huh, Mommy?"

"In a few months," she said again. "Spencer, don't do cartwheels in the house."

The door opened and Barry stepped inside. "Daddy! Daddy!" Brittany cried. "Mommy told us!"

"We're gonna have a baby!" Spencer cried. "Not now, but in a few months."

Tory turned back to the sink. She didn't want to see Barry's face. She heard the silence, and that was enough. He dropped his briefcase loudly on a chair.

She made herself look up at him. He was gaping at her, furious, while the children pulled on him and danced around him. "Daddy, see Mommy's tummy? It's a baby!"

He ignored the children and glowered at Tory. "You didn't."

"They had a right to know."

"I had a right to be consulted," he flung back.

"I would have consulted you," she returned, "but you're never here. And it's starting to get obvious."

He jerked his jacket off and stormed back to the bedroom.

The children were suddenly silent. "Is Daddy mad?" Brittany whispered.

"No, honey."

"He acts mad," Spencer said, climbing back up on his stool. "Maybe he doesn't like babies."

"He loves babies," she said. "He loved you when you were a baby."

They both got very quiet and looked in the direction their dad had gone, then brought their big, pensive eyes back to her stomach. Tory fought the urge to cry. For the first time since she'd considered telling them, she realized that she may have hurt them more than she'd helped them. Now they were aware that their father was angry about the baby. There were no explanations she could give them, nothing that would make sense to them. She had made matters worse.

In moments, Barry came back out of the bedroom wearing jeans and sneakers and an untucked golf shirt. He moved swiftly toward the door.

"Where are you going?" she asked.

"Out."

"Out? When will you be home?"

"When you're in bed," he said.

"Barry, we need to talk!"

"I have nothing to say to you," he said through his teeth. "You defied me in front of my children. You've gotten them involved and it's only going to hurt them, Tory. I have nothing more to say to you tonight." Grabbing his keys, he slammed out of the house.

Tory only looked down at the stunned children, wishing with all her heart that she could protect them from this madness.

CHAPTER
Forty-Two

Barry pulled up to the window at the fast-food restaurant and paid for the burrito he'd ordered. As he drove, he choked it down, then wished he hadn't. He thought of heading back to the office, but he'd finished all of his work for the day and was sick of the place. He needed someone to talk to, he thought, but he hadn't disclosed his problem to anyone except Linda Holland. Even now he wasn't sure why he had shared such a personal thing with her. He supposed it was nothing more than her being in the right place at the right time.

The secret had bonded them in a way he hadn't expected. She had started bringing him cups of coffee that he hadn't asked for. She consulted him on more than she needed to, as if it was an excuse to check on him and boost his spirits. Almost daily, she asked him if he'd like to have lunch with her and talk. He always gave her some excuse not to. Occasionally she asked him if Tory had come to her senses yet. It vindicated him, to some extent, to have someone understand his position.

He didn't know where else to go, so he drove to the Point at the top of Bright Mountain. It had been dark for more than an hour, but was still too early for the teenagers to gather just yet. He pulled into a space and looked out over the lights of Breezewood below. He rolled the windows down, and the cool autumn breeze whispered through the car.

Maybe he needed counseling, he thought. Just someone who would listen objectively and not judge him for doing what was best for his family. But if he suggested it, Tory would want to counsel with their pastor. Barry didn't know him well, since they'd only started attending his church a couple of months ago. He didn't relish the idea of telling him what he had in mind. No one could understand this unless they had lived through it themselves.

He stared down at the cellular phone, and wondered how hard it would be to find Linda's number. Feeling bold, he called information and asked for Linda Holland, and in seconds, he had her number. Would it be misconstrued, he asked himself, if he called her just to talk? Would she think it meant more than it did? Or would she understand that he just needed a friend?

Before he had made the decision entirely, he was dialing the number.

"Hello." Her voice was clear and upbeat over the line, and it took him a moment to respond.

"Linda?"

"Yes?"

"It's Barry. Barry Sullivan."

There was a pause, then, "Hi, Barry! Where are you?"

"In my car," he said. Guilt surged through him, for he knew she really wanted to know where Tory was. "Look, uh, I just needed to talk. I hope I'm not bothering you."

"Not at all!" she said, too enthusiastically. "Things were pretty quiet around here tonight and I was kind of glad to hear that phone ring."

He had never thought of her as a lonely woman. She always seemed to be too busy, too distracted to have mundane feelings.

"Is everything okay with Tory?" she asked.

He shook his head as if she could see him through the phone. "Actually, no."

Linda was quiet for a moment. "Do you want to meet somewhere? Talk face-to-face?"

"No," he said quickly. "That's not necessary. The telephone is fine."

"But that cell phone bill could get pretty high, and Tory might wonder about it."

He hadn't thought of that, and wasn't sure if he cared.

She sighed. "You sure you don't need a shoulder to cry on?"

He stared down at the steering wheel with dull eyes. "It's just that when I came home tonight the kids came running out to me tell me we were having a baby."

"She didn't," Linda said.

"Oh, yeah, she did. Told them everything. Told them and got them all excited. They were bouncing up and down, turning flips."

"Did she tell them about the Down's Syndrome?"

"Not as far as I could tell, but I have to admit I didn't stick around very long to find out."

"Oh, Barry, I'm so sorry. You poor thing."

He closed his eyes. It was good to be understood.

"This is so awful," she said. "I wish I could do something. Do you want me to call Tory and tell her what a stupid move that was?"

He laughed sarcastically. "Yeah, I'm sure that would improve things a lot."

"Just an observation from an impartial bystander," she said. A moment of silence followed. "Come on, why don't you meet me out for a cup of coffee? It'll cheer you up."

"No, I'd better not."

"Just a stinking cup of coffee. We can meet in a perfectly public well-lit place. I have absolutely nothing else to do tonight, Barry, and you don't either, so we might as well at least have a piece of pie and a cup of coffee and a little friendly conversation. You know the alternative is that you're going to go back to the office and work yourself into oblivion."

He knew it was true. She really did understand. "All right," he said, finally. "Meet me at Shoney's on Torrence Boulevard."

"Will do," she said. "I'll be there in fifteen minutes."

He breathed a deep sigh as he hung up. They were just two friends having coffee, he told himself. Tory wouldn't like it if she knew, but Tory didn't like much of anything he did lately. He started his car and headed back down the mountain. Something in the back of his mind told him he was treading on thin ice, and once he fell through, there may be no way to get back to the surface again.

But when Linda arrived, he was waiting for her in the parking lot. She brought laughter into the restaurant with them, and made him feel better before he'd even touched his coffee.

CHAPTER
Forty-Three

Tory was waiting up when Barry finally got home. Since putting the kids to bed, she had cleaned all of her baseboards and ridden her stationary bike five miles. She was drenched with perspiration and her face glowed with anger.

But Barry's expression mirrored hers as he came in and dropped his keys loudly on the table. "Tory, I don't want to get into this with you right now."

She snatched the keys up and hung them on their hook. "I don't want to get into it with you either, Barry," she said. "That's not why I waited up. I didn't do anything wrong, and I don't intend to apologize."

"Didn't do anything wrong?" he asked. "The fact that you told the children when I hadn't given you permission—"

"I don't *need* your permission to tell my children they have a baby sister on the way!"

"Fine." He threw open the basement door and started down the stairs.

"Your mother called tonight," Tory said. Barry stopped and looked up at her. "She wants to know if we're spending Thanksgiving with her."

"Tell her no."

"No?" Tory repeated through her teeth. "Why not? We spend every Thanksgiving with her. She looks forward to it."

"Well, *I'm* not looking forward to it," he said. "Did you tell her, too?"

"No, of course not!"

"Well, don't sound so surprised at me for asking," he said. "I didn't think you'd tell the kids, but you did!" He came back up the steps and stood in the doorway. "I don't want my mother to know you're pregnant. I don't want her to have to deal with this. And I don't think the kids can keep from telling her now if we go."

"No one would have to tell her!" she said. "She would look at me and know."

"One more reason not to go!" he said, going to the cabinet and getting a glass. He swung back to her. "I can't believe you told the children."

"And I can't believe what you've been demanding of me."

"I *haven't* demanded it," he said. "If I'd demanded it, it would have happened."

"No, it wouldn't," she bit out. "Not as long as I have breath in my body."

He slammed the glass down. "You just told them to spite me," he said. "It had nothing to do with the baby or the kids."

"I'm *showing*, Barry! Open your eyes. I can't hide this much longer."

"I'm not asking you to hide it," he said. "I'm asking you to do something merciful about it before time runs out."

"Abortion is not merciful no matter how you look at it," she cried. She burst into tears and shook her head frantically. "I can't even believe this is *you!* The man I married never would have condoned this. You sit in church and worship just like you believe ..."

He crossed the room and leaned over her, his body trembling with restrained fury. "You could never in a million years understand. A year from now, you'll be devastated and asking, 'Why me?' You'll wonder what could have made you put this life sentence on a child who never asked to be born."

"You're wrong. Those children I saw at the school were not enduring a hard life. They were happy and content."

"Well, were their parents content?"

"Your mother is!"

"She has no choice!"

"If your mother knew what you wanted for our baby, she would be just as disappointed in you as I am."

"Maybe so," he said. "That's why we're not going for Thanksgiving. I have enough trouble knowing that my wife despises me. I'm doing the best I can. I can't do more than that, Tory."

She had heard Cathy utter those words today, and they flitted through her mind like autumn leaves blowing across the yard. That phrase usually came from someone who was doing all the wrong things.

"So what *are* you doing, Barry?" she asked. "I'm the one carrying this baby. I'm the one getting to know it. I'm the one who's been throwing up and feeling my body change and hiding my stomach. What exactly *have* you been doing other than coming home late and sleeping in the basement?"

"I've been thinking and praying about it a lot."

"Well, isn't that wonderful?" she snapped. "Seems that your thoughts are outweighing your prayers, because God would never tell you to do what you're suggesting."

"You don't have a *clue* what God would tell me!"

"Well, since *I'm* the parent who's carrying the child, he's going to have to tell *me*," she cried, "and I don't think he has."

"You wouldn't hear it if you did hear it."

She wanted to break something. "God does not condone murder. He's a big enough God to change things himself if he wants them changed."

"All of a sudden, you're the theologian," he said. "You're the one who spent the first few years of your children's lives wishing you didn't have them around so you could write a stupid novel."

"Oh, that's constructive." Her face twisted. "I've done better in the last few months, Barry, and you know it. That was a low blow."

He turned away and rubbed the back of his neck.

She felt as if the top of her head would blow right off, or her heartbeats would blend into one long, fatal grip. She got up to leave the room, but stopped at the door. "So if we don't go to your mother's, what are we going to do for Thanksgiving?"

"We can stay here," he said.

"Oh, great." She threw up her hands. "I'm supposed to hustle around and cook an entire Thanksgiving dinner for only four people, one of whom is not speaking to me?"

"I don't care whether we have Thanksgiving dinner or not," he said. "I don't feel real thankful right now."

"No kidding!" She said the words with disgust. But as she padded back to the bedroom, she had to admit that *she* didn't see much to be thankful about, either.

CHAPTER
Forty-Four

Thanksgiving morning, Cathy woke her children up at seven o'clock, intent on training them in proper table manners before they got to Steve's house just before lunch. She figured the four hours she would have to go over things with them would just about do it.

They came to the table too sleepy-eyed to be combative, and she fed them a big breakfast, then sat down with them as they all began to wake up. "Now, kids," she said, "I don't know how to emphasize to you enough how important today is for me. When we get to Steve's, I don't intend to be embarrassed or humiliated."

"Even if I do embarrass you, there's not really anything you can do to me," Mark said as he picked at a strip of bacon. "You've already taken away the computer and the television, and ruined my social and educational life. I can act any way I want to and you can't do anything about it."

She stared at him for a moment, no emotion passing over her face as she turned his words over in her mind. "You know, you're wrong about that, Mark," she said in a calm, controlled voice. She looked at Rick. "Rick, would you please go upstairs and remove the television from Mark's room?"

Mark looked up at her. "Remove it? Why?"

"Because the tone of your voice tells me that temporary grounding from it isn't going to do it. We need to remove it from your room altogether. And if you continue to talk to me the way you do, you'll lose all of your other possessions, one by one."

"But my dad gave me that TV," he said. "You can't take it away if he gave it to me."

"Then I'll return it to him," she said. She looked at her older son. "Rick?"

Rick looked as if he was considering objecting, but then he seemed to think better of it. She imagined him taking inventory of his own possessions, and realizing he could be next. "I'm going," he said. He went upstairs and came back a few minutes later, holding the television in his hands. "What do you want me to do with it?"

"Just put it on the floor in the dining room," she said. "You can take it with you to your dad's this weekend."

"That's it," Mark said, throwing the bacon strip down. "I've had it. I'm going to live with Dad."

She knew that her ex-husband wasn't interested in full-time fatherhood. Every time this had come up before, he found some way of talking the kids out of it. She hated seeing their hearts broken, even when she was so angry.

"No, Mark, you're not going to live with him," she said. "You're going to stay right here and you're going to learn how to behave."

Rick returned to the kitchen and den area, and plopped into the recliner in front of the television. "Rick, come back over here."

Groaning, he got up.

"Now, we're going to go over a few things that will make me very happy," Cathy said.

"Are we going to learn Scripture?" Annie asked, propping her face on her hand.

Cathy remembered what Brenda had warned her about teaching the kids Scripture when she was angry. Then it occurred to her that she was always angry at her kids. When could she teach them Scripture if it wasn't when she was mad?

"No, we aren't about to learn Scripture. We're going to learn manners." She drew in a deep breath. "Now, when we get to Steve's, we're going to go into the house, and I want each of you to say, 'Hi, Steve. How are you?'"

"I'm not gonna say that," Rick argued. "That's cheesy."

Cathy shot him a threatening look. "Rick, so help me, you'd better say it."

"So you want us all to walk in one by one and repeat exactly what the one before us says?"

She couldn't believe they were making this so hard. "You don't have to repeat it exactly, as long as you get the same effect."

"'Cause I was thinking about saying, 'Hey, Steve, how's it going?'"

She thought that over for a moment. "I guess that would be all right, as long as you shake his hand."

Mark sat straighter. "Can I say, 'Hey, Steve, whassup?'"

She looked at her watch, glad she had gotten them up four hours early. It was going to take every minute. "Why don't you just go in and shake his hand and say, 'Thank you for inviting us over'?"

"You've got to be kidding, Mom. I can't say that."

She wasn't sure, but she thought smoke was beginning to waft out of her ears. "Then just say hello."

"What about me?" Annie asked. "Do you want me to curtsy?"

Cathy offered a saccharine smile. "No, thank you, Annie. You can just flash him one of your beautiful smiles and tell him the food smells good."

"Yeah," Annie said, "that's a good one. It smells good. I like that. What are we having, anyway?"

"Don't ask him that," Cathy said. "That's rude." She looked from one child to the others. "So let's go over this again. We walk into the house, and instead of groaning or plopping on the couch, you each say your piece."

"'Hello there, Steve. How is it going?'" Rick said, like a bad actor. Mark grinned.

"No," Cathy said, "that won't do."

He feigned exaggerated politeness and reached out to shake his mom's hand. "Hello, Mr. Bennett. How-do-you-do?"

He sounded like Ernest T. Bass on the "Andy Griffith Show." She tried not to smile, and turned to her daughter. "Your turn, Annie."

"The house looks great, Steve!" Annie said with an overly bright smile. "Something smells great, and whatever it is, I know we'll eat every tasty bite."

Laughter pushed into Cathy's throat, but she knew that if her children saw that she was amused, she wouldn't be able to teach them another thing. "Okay, that's good," she managed to say. The mirth was taking over, and she couldn't fight it. "Real . . . real good." She covered her face and began to laugh.

The kids all burst out laughing, too.

After a moment, Cathy tried to get serious again. "Okay, we've got the greeting down. I don't suppose you could all promise not to say another word until we leave?"

Fresh gales of laughter blew over them.

After a moment, she tried to get control again. "Guys, I'm serious. Sometimes you do tend to pull my strings when we're with other people. I really want to make a good impression."

"Why, Mom?" Annie asked, more seriously. "Are you gonna marry him?"

"We haven't talked about marriage. I just don't want you to embarrass me. And let's face it. You know it's your favorite pastime."

They looked at each other with amused, guilty eyes.

"Okay, so every time they address you, you say yes, ma'am or yes, sir."

"Yes, ma'am," Rick said with a grin.

"And when they offer you something to eat, you say 'thank you' or 'no thank you.'"

"Mom, we already know this. We weren't raised in a barn."

"And when we're at the table, you don't start demanding to leave the moment you put the last bite of pie in your mouth."

"What kind of pie?" Annie asked.

"I don't know."

"So how long do we have to stay?" Mark asked.

"Until we finish visiting and it seems like the right time to go."

"What if it seems like the right time to go as soon as we put the last bite of pie in our mouths?" Rick asked.

They all grinned again.

"I'll decide when it's the right time to go," Cathy said. "Annie, I'd appreciate it if you'd spend some time with Tracy. She really likes you."

"I like her, too. She's a good kid. Sure, I'll play with her hair, and paint her nails. She likes that."

"Do we have to sit there like little statues?" Mark asked. "Or can we watch TV and play with his computer ... Because I shouldn't be grounded on a holiday, you know."

Cathy smiled. "I guess it's okay for just the length of time we're at his house," she said, "but as soon as we come home you're grounded again."

"Cool," he said. "I can watch the football game."

"No way," Annie spouted. "We're watching the soaps."

"Annie, you're not watching the soaps. You'll all watch whatever is on when we get there."

"What if he doesn't care what we watch?"

"Just promise me you won't fight over the television."

"We won't, Mom," Rick said. "Come on, we're not going to embarrass you." He started to get up from the table. She grabbed his hand and pulled him back down.

"We have to go over our table manners," she said. "Does anybody know what the small fork is for?" They all moaned, but Cathy didn't let it stop her.

CHAPTER
Forty-Five

Tory considered having hot dogs for Thanksgiving dinner to vent her anger toward Barry, but she realized that her children didn't deserve that. They deserved the whole works, turkey and cranberry sauce, dressing and pumpkin pie. She decided she was going to do exactly what her mother would have done on Thanksgiving Day, whether she was speaking to her husband or not.

Barry spent most of the day outside washing the car and cleaning out the garage. He enlisted Brittany and Spencer to help him, which thankfully kept them busy while Tory cooked.

Just before noon, his mother called to wish them a happy Thanksgiving. Tory could hear the pain in her voice. It was the first year since they'd been married that they hadn't shared Thanksgiving with her, and Tory knew she must be lonely. It was impossible to explain why they hadn't come—without setting Barry off again—and even harder to explain why they hadn't invited her over. As Tory tried to make polite conversation with her mother-in-law, she found herself wanting desperately to tell her the truth. When Betty finally blurted her concerns out, Tory began to struggle with her guilt.

"Is Barry mad at me, Tory?" her mother-in-law asked. "Did I do something?"

"No, of course not," Tory said. "He's just been under a lot of stress at work. He's been a little depressed. I think he didn't want to be around you because he was afraid you'd sense it."

"Sense what?" his mother asked. "All I wanted to do was feed him Thanksgiving dinner."

Tory blinked back the tears in her eyes and looked out at her family in the wet driveway. "All I can say is pray for him, Betty."

"Was it something I said when he dropped by a few weeks ago?"

Tory frowned. "He came by?"

"He didn't tell you? He said he was in the area, and stopped in for lunch. I made him a sandwich, but he didn't eat it. He was sitting with Nathan, and then all of a sudden he seemed to get emotional, and he ran out. What's wrong with him? Tory, are you two having problems?"

She sighed. She knew that he didn't want her to tell his mother anything that might upset her. But all her speculation was upsetting her, anyway. "Things are a little tense," she evaded. "He's been really busy at work, and I've been busy with the kids ..."

"I miss my grandkids," she said. "Will you at least be here for Christmas?"

"If I have to come without him, we will," she said. "In fact, I considered coming without him today, but I didn't think that would go over too well."

Betty was quiet again. "Something's going on, Tory. I sure wish you'd tell me what it is. I hate to think you've just decided to quit celebrating with me. Nathan and I sure do look forward to the holidays because we get to see you."

Tory knew that wasn't true. Nathan never looked forward to anything. "No, of course we haven't quit. This is a one-time thing, Betty." She rubbed her face. "All I can say right now is there's a reason, okay? When we finally tell you, you'll understand completely and you'll know it didn't have anything to do with you. Just know for right now that Barry needs your prayers, and so do I."

She called Barry to the phone, and listened to his polite, but distant conversation as she moved around the kitchen. As she did, she silently prayed that God would touch him through his mother's pain, and lead him into confessing the truth to her. His mother was the last person on earth who would want him to abort a retarded child. Tory knew that Betty could return Barry to his senses.

But he didn't break down and tell her. When Barry was off the phone and back outside, Tory went to her computer. While the last few items for their meal baked, she e-mailed Sylvia and asked her what she thought about enlisting the help of Barry's mother. Should she defy him a second time and tell her, or should she respect his wishes to keep the pregnancy quiet for now?

She sent the e-mail, then went back into the kitchen and checked the oven.

Not an hour later, her computer made the sing-song noise that told her she had mail. She hurried back into the laundry room and sat down in front of the screen.

Sylvia had written back.

Don't do it, Tory, don't tell his mother. He's losing your respect. He doesn't need to lose hers as well. I know what you're thinking, honey. You're thinking that if you force his hand by telling his mother, that he won't be able to demand this awful thing. But it also might drive him away. I don't want to see you wind up single and struggling to raise kids on your own. For the sake of your children, all three of them, you need to try to keep your marriage together. Barry will tell his mother when it's time, just like he would have told the children. But right now you've got to give him more time. Please, Tory. I know you're not listening to everything I say. You never do. You didn't listen about telling the children, but trust me on this one.

Tory wiped her eyes and wished that Sylvia could be here to help her through this time. Brenda was wise and Cathy was refreshing, but only Sylvia had the maternal touch that Tory needed right now, especially when she couldn't even share the pregnancy with her mother-in-law.

The smell of turkey wafting in the air, the rolls baking in the oven, the pumpkin pie, all reminded her of her childhood when things seemed so simple and her mother was still here. She longed for those days again. With all her heart, she missed her mother.

She heard the door closing and quickly tried to dry her eyes. She heard footsteps, then glanced behind her to see Barry standing in the doorway of the laundry room. Their eyes connected, and for a moment she saw less anger and more compassion as he took in her tears. She saw him swallow.

"Is dinner about ready?"

"Yeah," she said. "Just another five or ten minutes. As soon as I get the table set."

"I'll do it," he said. "The kids are washing up with the hose. They'll probably be soaking wet when they come in, but at least they won't have dirt all over them."

"It's okay," she said. "I'm glad they're having fun with you."

He nodded and kept standing at the door, watching her as if he wanted to say something about the tears, or about the pain that seemed to radiate between them. Finally, she looked up at him. "I sure would like to tell your mother about this," Tory said, wiping her eyes and carefully avoiding the word *baby*. "She's the only mother I've got, and the only person close to me who's ever been through this. I need to talk to her."

His face hardened again. "Don't do it," he said. "Tory, don't you do it."

She started to cry again and turned away. "I wish Sylvia was here."

He nodded. "I wish it, too."

"Why?" she asked. "She wouldn't take your side, you know."

"I know," he said. He breathed in a deep breath as if he didn't know what else to say. Finally, he turned and went to the kitchen, and started getting out the plates. She followed him, checking the oven and deciding the turkey was done. She pulled the big roasted bird out of the oven. This was absurd, she thought, to go to all this trouble for a four- and five-year-old. But she wanted them to have the memories of Thanksgiving scents and tastes and feelings. This might be the last year—for a long time—that she would have the time to do it. She hoped they wouldn't grow up feeling the pervading sense of heaviness over the day, remembering the time that their mom was pregnant with their little sister, and their dad moped around as if he'd lost his best friend.

Somehow they got through the meal without Tory or Barry having to exchange too many words. They focused on the children as they ate their Thanksgiving meal, and avoided the subject of gratitude as they did.

CHAPTER
Forty-Six

On what was Thanksgiving Day back in the States, Sylvia managed to put out the clothes that her friends from Cedar Circle had sent her. Though she and Harry hadn't been able to take time off to celebrate, she felt that the gratitude among these people was appropriate to help her remember the day.

She was grateful that Tory, Brenda, and Cathy had put the clothes on hangers and stacked them by size, so that she wouldn't have to take valuable time to do it, and so the poor victims of Hurricane Norris wouldn't have to dig through mounds of clothing to find something they could use.

She carried little Carly on her back, in a backpack with the holes cut out for her legs. It was the best way to care for her and still have the use of her hands. Now and then, Carly got fussy and wanted to get loose. Then she would hold her for a while, or put her down and let her practice walking, clinging to both of Sylvia's hands. It amazed Sylvia that she never got tired of taking care of the baby.

Harry came out of his clinic with his stethoscope around his neck, and crossed the compound. He rubbed noses with Carly, then kissed Sylvia on the cheek.

"The clothes are almost all taken," Harry said. "What are you gonna do when you run out?"

"The girls will send more," she said. "We can count on them." She turned her back to Harry. "Will you get Carly out for me?" she asked.

He picked the baby out, carefully pulling her legs from the holes. She giggled as he buried his face in her stomach and tickled her with his nose. "You know, you could let Julie and her people at the home watch her just for today," he said.

She shook her head. "No, I want to take care of her. God gave her to me."

His smile faded, and he handed the child to Sylvia. "Sylvia, God didn't give her to you. She has a family somewhere."

"I didn't mean to say that," she said. "I just meant that I feel responsible for her, and I like that feeling."

"You like it too much," he said. As she put Carly on her hip and bounced her, Harry touched her face. "Sylvia, don't make me watch you get your heart broken. Her mother could still come."

"I don't think she's going to," Sylvia said. "I think Carly's an orphan."

"But you can't count on that, Sylvia. God didn't bring us to Nicaragua so that we could start raising another child."

"How do you know?" she asked. "How do you know that isn't exactly why he brought us here?"

"Because there's too much work to do," he said. "Look at all these people."

"You can take care of them," Sylvia said. "And I can take care of her. She doesn't take away from our ministry. And who's to say that she's not our most important ministry?"

Harry looked as if he didn't know how to answer that. Distraught, he just stared at her.

"Excuse me, Señor Bryan?" one of the Nicaraguan ladies who was helping Sylvia with the clothes said. "Thees man, he talk to you."

Harry saw the man next to her, standing with his arms full of clothes for his family. He had tears running down his face, and when he saw Harry and Sylvia, he crossed through the people and approached them.

"My name ... Carlos Sanchez," he said, his voice wobbling with emotion. "Want to say ... *gracias* ... for clothes." He was struggling with the right words, and he stopped for a moment and tried to get his voice under control. "You ... how-I-say ... remind me ... that he love me." He pointed to the sky, and nodded as if they would understand. "Your Jesus ... he send you."

Tears came to Sylvia's eyes, and she touched his shoulder and smiled. "He loves you more than an armload of clothes," she said. She set Carly down on the ground at her feet, and straightened back up. "His arms extend even wider than that." She opened her arms and straightened them out. "Wide enough that they nailed him to a cross."

The man began to weep, and Harry put his arm around him. "Do you know our Jesus?"

"Priest tell me of him ... but you show me."

That day, they led that man, his wife, and his six kids to Christ. He brought them all to their meeting that night, where Jim, their pastor, baptized them.

That night, as she and Harry fell, exhausted, into bed, he pointed out that her hands had needed to be empty to show that man Jesus' love.

"They were empty," she said. "I put Carly down, and he heard what I was saying."

"But there are many more families like that one," Harry said. "God sent us here for them. Not for one little girl."

"Then he'll have to prove that to me," Sylvia said. "He'll have to bring her mother to us, because if he doesn't, I want to raise her, Harry. I want to be her mother."

Harry got very quiet beside her, but she didn't want to entertain his doubts. Instead, she lay on her side and watched the child sleeping in her basket next to their bed.

CHAPTER
Forty-Seven

Steve's house was full of Thanksgiving scents, turkey and cranberry sauce, dressing and gravy, fresh rolls baking in the oven, pecan pie cooling on a trivet. His mother, Lorraine, chattered nonstop with Cathy, talking about everything from home decorations to the dogs they used to raise. She told stories about when Steve was a boy, and tales of Tracy, the cherished grandchild.

Steve had pulled Cathy aside once when his mother left the room. "This relationship has to work out now," he whispered with a grin, "because I don't intend to break my mother's heart."

His dad sat in a rocking chair in the kitchen listening contentedly to the conversation between the two women. The kids gathered in the den watching television. Cathy was amazed at how quiet they had been. Mark was playing on the computer that Steve had just bought and set up the day before, and like a kid with a new toy, he tried out all the new functions that he didn't have on his own computer. Everyone seemed to be enjoying the day.

But then she heard Steve's irritated voice in the other room. "I had a code on that. You're not even supposed to be able to get that."

What had her kids done now? Cathy grabbed a dish towel and wiped her hands. Lorraine gave her an uncomfortable look. "Excuse me," Cathy said. "I think there might be a problem in there." She headed through the swinging door between the kitchen and the den, and saw Steve standing in front of the television with the remote control.

"Steve, what's wrong?" she asked.

He glanced up at her. "I had a code on this. They're not supposed to get MTV. I don't want my daughter watching it."

"Why, Daddy?" Tracy asked. "It's just music."

Cathy looked down at the screen and saw a half-dressed woman moving suggestively with unholy rhythm. She swung around to her children. "What have you done?"

"Nothing!" Rick said.

"He broke the code," Tracy told her with a giggle. "He's been trying all afternoon. He finally figured it out."

Annie had a guilty grin as she flipped through a magazine. "I had nothing to do with this," she said.

"Right," Rick threw back. "Like you weren't tossing out as many guesses as I was."

Cathy closed her eyes. Breaking the television's remote control code was not something they had gone over this morning. It had never occurred to her. Now she realized it was critical. She suddenly knew why God had spelled out Levitical law so specifically. Nothing could be left to common sense.

"Rick, I can't believe you did that."

"I just *told* you Annie helped."

"Both of you," she said through her teeth. "You've just lost your television privileges at home for a week. It's going to be real quiet around our house this week."

"Mom!" they both yelled.

"I didn't have anything to do with it," Mark said from the computer.

Cathy wasn't certain she believed him. Instead, she turned to Steve. "Steve, I'm so sorry. I thought they were awfully quiet in here, but I didn't know."

"It's okay," he said. She had never seen his face look quite so tense. "The damage has been done. You can't undo it." He had tried hard to protect his daughter from the kind of sexual imagery that MTV offered. She wondered how long they had been watching.

She was about to ask, when the computer beeped an alarm. Both of them turned to see what Mark was doing. "This computer's a piece of junk," Mark said. "It doesn't do anything right."

She could see that Steve's patience was reaching its limit. He turned off the television and put the remote control in his back pocket, then went to the computer. "What is it, Mark?"

"It keeps saying it's performed an illegal operation."

Steve studied the error message, then punched a few keys, trying to figure out what had happened. Cathy recognized the problem immediately. Mark considered himself a computer guru, and had probably changed most of Steve's settings.

"Mark, did you readjust his settings?"

Steve looked up at Mark.

"Just a few," Mark said. "I was just trying to make it work better."

Cathy wanted to jerk him out of the chair. "But I've told you before, you don't give it a *chance* to work better. You just start randomly changing things without knowing what you're doing. You can't do that, Mark. You've messed his whole computer up now."

"I'll fix it," Mark said. He moved Steve's hand away from the keyboard and began typing. It beeped again.

Cathy realized that today's pleasant hours had come with a price. "Steve, is there any way to restore the defaults?"

Steve's jaw muscles were popping. She had never seen him do that before. "I don't know."

She grabbed Mark's arm. "Mark, get off the computer."

"I can fix it," he said, still punching. "I promise. Look." It beeped again.

"Now!" Cathy said, too loudly. "Get off the computer *now!*"

Mark swiveled around in the chair at Steve's desk. "Well, what am I supposed to do? You won't let us watch TV."

"Just sit on the couch next to your brother and sister and don't say a word until we go to the table."

"Great!" Mark jerked himself up from the chair and plopped down between his sister and brother on the couch. "Some Thanksgiving. I should have gone to Dad's."

Cathy locked glowering eyes on him and pointed her finger in his face. "Don't you say that to me again. So help me, if you do, you're going to be sorry."

Steve didn't wait to hear his response. He just pushed through the swinging door back into the kitchen. Cathy gave her children another threatening glare, then followed Steve.

His mother was humming a Tom Jones song and his father was rocking back and forth to the rhythm. She wondered if the woman had ever been depressed in her life. She reminded her a little of Brenda.

"Steve, I don't know what to say."

"It's okay," he said, counting out the silverware and dropping them on the counter a little too hard. "No harm done. Somehow we'll get everything put back together."

The swinging door opened into the kitchen, and Cathy turned to see Rick in the doorway. "Is it going to be long before we eat, 'cause it's really boring just sitting in there staring at the wall."

"They're restless, poor things," Lorraine said. "They need to be outside playing touch football like Steve and his brothers used to do on Thanksgiving. The whole neighborhood would come over, and we parents would sit out on our porches and watch."

"Boy, we've come a long way since then," Cathy muttered. "Kids don't do much of anything outside anymore."

"Well, Steve, you have a football, don't you?"

Cathy knew he was still smarting. "Somewhere," he muttered.

"Well, why don't you go get it and give it to Mark and Rick?" his mother asked. "Even the girls would probably like to play. Steve, you'd like to get out there, wouldn't you?"

"Maybe after lunch."

"Sure," his mother said, "it's getting too close to lunchtime now anyway." His mother continued to chatter as if nothing had ever gone wrong, and Cathy marveled at the patience in the woman. Did she really not notice how rude her children had been to crack the code of the television and mess up the computer settings? Was she of the "kids will be kids" school, or was she simply in denial?

Because of his mother's efforts, Steve's heavy mood lifted as it got closer to time to eat, and they piled the table full of food. Cathy went back into the living room before calling her kids to the table.

"Tracy, your dad wants you to go wash your hands," she said.

Tracy got up. "Come on, Annie."

Cathy stopped her daughter before she followed the child. "No, Tracy, I need to talk to Annie for a minute."

Tracy left Cathy alone with her children. They all looked up at her with dull, what-now eyes.

"Rick, Annie, Mark, I'm telling you for the last time," she said. "I expect you to behave at that table. I expect you to be polite. Say please and thank you. Yes, ma'am and yes, sir. Do it for me. Consider it a Thanksgiving Day present."

"Yes, ma'am," Rick said. She didn't take the time to examine whether there was sarcasm in his voice. She didn't care whether there was or not. She was just happy to hear him say the words.

"Now go wash your hands. You won't believe all the food they've got. And please, don't break anything."

The children groaned, but thankfully kept their comments to themselves as they headed for the bathroom sink.

After lunch Cathy, Steve, and the kids went to the front yard to play football while his parents sat in the swing watching the activity with glee. The football game had been a good idea, Cathy thought. The kids' hostility and restlessness worked itself out in the game, and for a while, she didn't have to worry about them destroying any more electronic items in Steve's house.

They played boys against girls, and she, Annie, and Tracy held their own. When the men won, Cathy and Annie and Tracy made it look as if they'd thrown the game. The men never knew for sure.

The children managed to thank Steve's mom for the wonderful meal before they headed home in Rick's car after the game. Steve took Cathy home some time later.

"I'm sorry again about MTV and the computer," she said as he pulled into her driveway. "I could just die."

"It's okay," he said. "Nothing a couple of hours with technical support can't work out." He chuckled. "Actually, it wasn't so bad."

"Don't lie."

He laughed. "Your kids have a lot of potential," he said. "I see great strengths in them."

Her eyebrows shot up suspiciously. "Really?"

"Sure. Mark has a natural curiosity, and I think that once he gets used to homeschooling with Brenda, he's going to blossom. He's got a very determined nature."

Cathy gaped at him, amazed that he could see the good in the boy. "Some people call that stubbornness."

He smiled. "And Annie has that innate nurturing ability that women are supposed to have. Watching her with Tracy makes me think she'll be a great mom someday. And she has that sharp wit that could take her far in life."

"Sharp wit, huh? Not to be confused with smart mouth?"

"*Often* confused with that." They both laughed. "And then there's Rick, and I see in him a keen mind and a lot of strong leadership skills."

"Not manipulation?" she asked.

"It's all in how you look at it," he said.

She regarded him quietly for a moment. "Well, thank you for looking at it the way you do," she said quietly. "I see the problems in them, but when I think back to when their father left, and all the stuff they went through . . ." Her voice cracked, and she swallowed. Her own emotion when she talked about the divorce often surprised her. So many times, she had given her bitterness to God and asked him to heal her. But whenever she saw the effect it had had on her kids, that bitterness took hold of her again. "Annie was devastated," she said. "She had been a Daddy's girl, and then he was gone. She cried all the time. Rick couldn't talk about it at all. Just held it all in. For a while there, I hardly ever heard a word out of him. And Mark got angry and broke a lot of things, and did just about anything it took to get attention from his father. I think it really only pushed Jerry farther away. He didn't want to be bothered with kids who were in emotional turmoil, especially if it brought any guilt on him."

"Did you talk to him about it? Tell him what it was doing to the kids?"

"Sure, I did," she said. "He got defensive. One time he said, 'How do you think it makes me feel when you tell me these things?' As far as he was concerned, it was all about him."

Steve turned the car off and sat there quietly for a moment, turning it all over in his mind. He took her hand. "I can't say I know how you feel, Cathy, since I haven't been divorced. When a spouse dies, at least we're able to have good feelings about them. It's not like they're still around, constantly reminding us of past failures. But, you know, the problems in your children's past don't have to dictate how they're going to turn out. That's up to you."

"Yeah," she said with a sigh. "I know too well that it's all up to me."

"I didn't mean you, alone. You're *not* alone, you know. God is a parent to your children, too, and he's teaching them stronger lessons than you could ever dream up. Your mistakes aren't going to thwart God's plan for their lives."

"So I'm off the hook?" she asked facetiously.

"No, not off the hook, but out of the hot seat, maybe. I think the Lord shows special mercies to single moms and their families. It's critical that you keep your focus on him."

She couldn't help thinking that he was the wisest, most wonderful man she had ever met. "Steve, how do I teach them the Bible when I've waited so long to start? How do I catch up on all the values and the morals, and all the things they need to know and understand, when it took me this long in my life to realize it? I can't start over. I can't change everything. But I want so much for them to have what I missed."

"You pray a lot," Steve said, "and I'll pray for you. And then you just look for opportunities in everything. Don't try to make them memorize passages. Just read to them from Scripture. Pick out some of the most fascinating stories. Get them tied up emotionally in what's happening in them."

She let her gaze drift out the window. "I'm just so insecure with my own knowledge of the Bible."

"Then start it together," he said. "You told me that Brenda was teaching Mark Genesis and the gospel of Matthew. Why don't you start with the same things and reinforce it at home?"

"Mark will just get mad and think I'm forcing him to do more homework than he has to."

"Maybe at first, but after a while the kids will start asking you for it. If you miss one day, they'll remind you. You'll see."

"I can just see it now. They'll probably go blind rolling their eyes at me."

"Cathy, God promised that his Word would never return void. If you believe that, then you'll just go with it anyway and not worry about the eye-rolling. They'll realize that the worst thing that can happen is that they have to sit with you for twenty minutes. From where I sit, that would be a major perk." He winked at her, and she returned a wistful smile.

"I appreciate your advice, Steve. I consider you one of the best parents I know."

"Don't," he said, bringing her hand to his lips and kissing the knuckle. "That wouldn't be very fair. I only have one to take care of, and she doesn't have rejection and abandonment issues in her life. Her mom died, but she knew she loved her before she did, and she was real involved in her life until then. She has good memories, even though she still cries over her loss sometimes."

Cathy's heart broke. "Really? I thought maybe she was past that now, since she was so young when her mother died."

"It's tough. A little girl needs her mom."

Cathy saw the pain on his face, and knew that he still missed his wife, as well. There were grief and loss in both their lives, and the lives of all their children. Could anything good ever spring from that loss? she wondered. Could anything whole come from broken lives?

As Steve brought her hand against his jaw and held it there, she thought it just might be possible. Maybe God had a plan to put all the pieces of these two families together. Maybe there was hope, after all.

CHAPTER
Forty-Eight

Like the happy family they'd once been, the Sullivans went to their church's Thanksgiving service that night. Brenda and her kids were already there in one of the front pews. Barry hung near the back of the sanctuary, his face grim and his eyes vacant, as if he wasn't sure he belonged here anymore.

The pastor greeted them at the pew before they had the chance to sit down. "So what's new with your family?" he asked Brittany and Spencer.

Brittany spouted out, "My mommy's gonna have a baby!"

The pastor spun around, delighted. "Tory, I didn't know. Congratulations!"

Stunned that Brittany had made the announcement without warning, she shot Barry a look. He was staring coldly at the floor. "Thank you," she told the pastor. "It was supposed to be a secret."

"Oops!" he said, patting Brittany's head. "Did she know that?"

Tory tried to laugh, but knew it seemed fake. A few families around them who had heard Brittany congratulated her. She tried to accept it with the kind of smile she might have had if things weren't so twisted.

She sat down, and Barry slipped into the pew next to her. She could feel the chill radiating from him, and knew there would be a fight when they got home.

Tory didn't say a word as the service started. She was not going to apologize. The praise team began to lead the congregation in worship, but she found it difficult to join in. Beside her, Barry was also silent. He stood still, his hands at his sides, not participating at all. Tory closed her eyes and began to pray for her husband's heart to be changed.

That night, after they got the children to bed, she and Barry found themselves alone. He hadn't spoken a word to her since they'd left the service, but now he had plenty to say. "I told you the kids couldn't keep this secret," he said. "I told you that, as soon as they knew, things would get out of hand. You had no right to tell anybody about this. No right at all. Not until I was ready."

"You weren't *ever* going to be ready," Tory said. "You wanted me to get rid of this pregnancy, end it like it never happened."

"You're not objective," he said. "You can't make the right decision."

"How can *you* be objective?" she asked. "You're this baby's father!" She tried to lower her voice, get it back under control. "I watched you sit there like a statue tonight, not praising God, not thanking him, not even acknowledging him, and it was so unlike you, Barry. And I realized how much you've changed in the last few weeks. Or maybe that's exactly how you always were and I just didn't see it."

"You're changing the subject," he said. "We're talking about the baby, not my spiritual life."

"It's all tied in together," she said. "I'm disappointed in you." Her voice cracked as tears filled her eyes. "I feel like my best friend has died, and that he's never coming back. You've taken his place, and I don't know who you are."

His eyes flashed. "I've never done *anything* to hurt this family! I've only protected it. That's what I'm still doing. I'm still your husband and the father of your children."

"All three of them," she threw back. The tears overcame her, and she sucked in a sob. "I'm sorry that I went over your head to tell the children. I told myself that night that the children needed to know, but the truth was, there was a lot of revenge in my timing. I wanted to get back at you for not being there for me."

"Well, I hope you're happy. It worked."

"I really am sorry," she said. "I should have waited until you said we could tell them. But it's too late now. And they were happy about it. They don't know any better. And *I'm* starting to be happy about it, too, Barry. I want this baby."

He just stood there staring at her, so obviously broken, but unable to cry.

She took a step toward him. "Barry, please come to the Developmental Center with me. Please come and see these children. Then you won't be so depressed. You'll see that they have hope, they have potential, they can learn."

"There is nothing you can show me that I don't know," he said. "Nothing. I don't want this for my family."

She threw up her chin. "Then I'm prepared to go through this without you. But I need to know. What are you going to do when I have this baby?" she asked. "Are you going to leave? Are you going to abandon your whole family because you're worried about what a retarded child is going to do to disrupt things? I'll tell you what's going to disrupt us, Barry. The father just ripping himself out of this home. *That's* disruptive. I need to know your plans, Barry."

He shook his head. "I don't know, Tory. If you insist on going through with this, I don't know what I'll do."

Her face twisted as more tears rolled down her face. "Just an hour at the school. If you could just come with me and see."

"I won't do it," he said through his teeth. "I can go sit with Nathan. I can watch my brother who does nothing all day. He just exists, waiting for his days to be over, one at a time."

"But this baby won't be that bad."

"Maybe not," he said, "but maybe she will. Would you still feel the same way about our child, about her life being so valuable, if you knew she was as bad as Nathan, or worse?"

She only had to think about that for a second. "Yes," she said, "because she's mine, and God gave her to me, and she has a soul, no matter what her body is like."

"You've never believed Nathan had value. You've avoided him like the plague. You haven't ever been comfortable with him."

"Then I'm going to have to change," she said.

He stepped toward her. "Tory, time is running out. Soon that option won't be available to us. It won't just be a fetus. It will be a baby."

"It's a baby already!" she shouted. "Barry, *why* can't you think of it that way?"

"Because I don't want to," he whispered harshly.

"That's clear," she agreed. "But she *is* a little baby girl. Soon she'll have a ribbon in her hair and the smell of baby powder in her clothes. Don't you realize our family is at stake? Not just the baby."

"That depends on you," he said.

"No! It depends on *you!* Because if you keep going this way, I'm never going to be able to trust you again. I used to admire you ... look up to you. But now ..."

He turned to the basement door, putting his back to her.

"Barry, it's not too late to love this baby. It's not too late to turn things around."

But Barry started down the basement steps, ending the conversation.

CHAPTER
Forty-Nine

Tracy went home with her grandparents for the week-end, and Cathy's kids headed to their dad's in Knoxville. Steve surprised her and rented two horses, and they spent the afternoon riding in the pastureland behind Sylvia's house.

"I've been thinking about your kids," he told her once as their horses walked side by side.

"Oh, no," she said. "Here it comes."

"Here what comes?"

She grinned. "The point where you tell me that you really like me, but you don't think we're meant for each other."

He laughed out loud. "What would make you think that?"

"My kids," she said. "You've been thinking about them, and you've realized what a handful they are—"

"No," he cut in. "Nothing like that at all. Just the opposite. I want to take your boys on a camping trip."

She stopped her horse and turned to face him. "You want to take my boys out into the woods? Alone?"

"Yeah, I was thinking next weekend. They will be with you next weekend, won't they?"

"Well, yeah, but . . ."

"I have a lot of camping gear, and I thought we could go into the mountains and spend the night, do a little fishing."

"With *my* boys?" she asked again. "Steve, why would you want to do that?"

He seemed to think his words over carefully. "I just got to thinking about them, about their need for a male role model. I just thought it might be a nice way to bond with them."

Cathy was still stunned. He wanted to bond with them? "I don't even know if they'd go."

"Sure they'd go," he said. "Every boy wants to go camping."

"But I can't guarantee how they'll behave. You could have a migraine and gray hair by the time you come back."

"We'll be fine," he said. "Trust me."

"You're not going to take them out in the wilderness and beat sense into them, are you?"

His eyes twinkled. "Not a bad idea." He laughed at the look on her face. "No, I thought we'd just have fun. And I was thinking that maybe you could take this opportunity to bond with Tracy a little bit."

Her eyes widened and she started to see the pattern here. Instead of pulling away because of her children, Steve was actually thinking in terms of a future together. Was there no end to God's goodness?

"I think that would be great," she said. "She and Annie and I can go shopping. I can teach her how to bake my famous cheesecake."

"She'll love it."

"I will, too. But you're getting the short end of the stick. Are you sure you're up to this?"

"Just try me," he said with a grin. He patted her horse's rump, and the animal started along the path again.

"I'll race you home!" he said.

Cathy didn't answer. She just gave her horse a kick and sent it galloping off ahead of him.

CHAPTER *Fifty*

Almost a week after Thanksgiving, which Sylvia and Harry hadn't had time to celebrate, Harry brought home news that had the same devastating effect of the mud slides burying the countryside. The baby's mother had been found.

Sylvia rocked back and forth, back and forth in the rocking chair, holding the little sleeping girl in her arms. She knew this was good news for the child. But her heart was crushed. How could she let her go? Tears rolled down her face as she stared up at Harry.

"I'm sorry, honey," he said. "I know how much she means to you."

"Are you sure it's her mother?" she whispered.

"Positive," he said. "She has a picture. She's been in the hospital and just heard about the Andersons' children's home. She sent someone to look for the baby."

Sylvia closed her eyes, but the tears kept coming. How could she be so selfish? She should be celebrating for the baby. "Why did it take her so long to look for her?" she asked.

"She was unconscious from a head injury when they took her to the hospital. She's been in a coma since the hurricane. She didn't even know where the baby was. But they said she's been awake for three days and she's been begging and pleading that someone go find her baby."

Sylvia dropped her face to the sleeping child's and kissed her cheek. There was still a chance that Carly was the wrong child, she thought. Then she quickly chastised herself for wishing such a thing.

"Honey, the baby's name is Selena."

Sylvia forced a smile. "Selena. That's nice. It fits her." Her face twisted with pain, and she wiped away more tears. "I'm sorry, Harry. I'm happy for her. Really, I am. It's so silly. I just thought . . . that God had brought her to me. A gift."

"She wasn't a gift," he whispered. "Just a loan. She needs her mother."

"Where's her father? Where is everybody else, if she's so loved?"

"Her father was killed when the house fell on them," he said quietly. "The relatives came as soon as they could."

Sylvia swallowed back her pain. "Well . . . Guess we'd better go."

Harry kissed her forehead. "I'll go with you."

The baby stirred as Sylvia got up. Her cheeks were pink from sleep, and her hair stuck up on one side where she had been pressed against Sylvia. "We're going to see your mama," Sylvia told her, knowing she didn't understand. She wiped her face. "She'll be so glad to see you." Her voice broke.

Harry touched her shoulders. His strong hands were gentle, comforting. "Honey, God has work for you to do. Important work. This community needs you, just like little Carly—or Selena— needed you. He sent you to care for her until her mother could, just like he sent you to this community to help them through this devastation. This isn't the end. He isn't finished with you."

She brought the baby's blanket to her face and sobbed into it, then pulled herself together and wrapped it around the child. "Let's go," she whispered. "We have a family to reunite."

CHAPTER
Fifty-One

The temperature had dropped considerably during the week following Thanksgiving, and Friday morning, Tory bundled her children into sweaters before piling them into the car for school. She saw Cathy walking Mark across the street to personally deliver him to Brenda, who stood on her porch. She waved at them both, then turned back to her children's seat belts.

She felt the fluttering in the lower part of her abdomen, and brought her hand to her stomach. Then it came harder, that unmistakable feeling of a foot against her uterine wall. She froze with her hand over the baby, waiting for it to happen again.

From Brenda's porch, Cathy called, "Tory, are you all right?"

She straightened, smiling. "I felt her move!" she called.

Cathy leaped off the porch and crossed the yard. Brenda followed behind her.

"This early?" Cathy asked as she reached Tory. "What are you, three months pregnant?"

"Seventeen weeks," she said. "I felt Spencer at twelve."

"Oh, yeah," Brenda said. "When I was pregnant with my last three, I felt it really early."

Both women touched Tory's stomach, feeling for any sign.

"I want to feel, Mommy!" Spencer said, unhooking his belt and sliding out of the van.

"Okay, honey. Just a minute."

"Me, too, Mommy!" Brittany cried.

Brenda placed Brittany's and Spencer's hands over their mother's stomach, and they all waited in silence. They looked ridiculous, Tory thought. She didn't have enough stomach for all of the waiting hands. Then she felt it again—the slightest flutter. "That's it!" she cried.

"I felt it," Spencer said.

"I didn't," Brittany whined. "Do it again, Mommy."

"We have to wait, honey. I'm not sure you can feel it as much as I can. It's not much. Just a little flutter."

"Like butterfly wings?" Brittany asked.

"A little stronger than that. Just two little feet or hands . . . maybe an elbow."

Brenda leaned over the children to hug her. "Tory, this is the perfect opportunity," she whispered. "Go to the office and share this with Barry."

Tory just looked at Brenda. "Okay, kids, back in the car. We're gonna be late."

"She's right," Cathy said. "This could build a bridge. Just go and let him feel his daughter."

Tory sighed as she buckled the seat belts again. "But what if it doesn't do it again?"

"It's going to do it from now on out," Cathy said. "Introduce him to his child, Tory. Once he sees that it's a live person and not just a concept, he'll come around. I know he will."

Tory closed the door to the van and lowered her voice. "But we're not really even speaking to each other right now," she said. "Thanksgiving was awful."

"Then start fresh today," Brenda told her. "Come on, Tory. You need to do this."

Tory didn't want to. She didn't want Barry dousing her excitement. "Well, I was going to write today."

"Tory, what's more important?"

Her face twisted, and she closed her eyes. "I know what's more important. I'm just so tired of the fighting."

"But it could be a step that would end the fighting," Brenda said. "Take that step."

The baby moved again, and she looked down at her hand over her stomach. There was a little girl in there, one who would smile and hug and have idiosyncrasies of her own. She might delight in the feel of produce, or whistle songs in perfect pitch. Her father needed to know her.

"I know what Sylvia would say," Cathy told her. "She'd say get in that car and head over to the office. Do not pass *Go*. Do not collect two hundred dollars."

"All right, I'll do it," Tory said. "But what if I get there and he doesn't even want to feel it?"

"Just give him the chance."

"Okay," she said with a sigh, "after I get the kids to school. I'll let you know how it turns out."

Brenda gave her a hug, then turned to go. "I have to go teach the kids."

"And I have to get to the clinic," Cathy said.

Tory felt as if they were abandoning her as she watched them head across the cul-de-sac.

CHAPTER
Fifty-Two

Barry's secretary was not in her cubicle, but the door to his office was open. With a lump of emotion in her throat, Tory went to the doorway, knocked softly, then leaned inside. Barry wasn't at his desk.

She couldn't decide if she was disappointed or relieved. Part of her wanted to turn and run back to the elevator and pretend she had never taken this vulnerable step. The other part of her wanted him to know she had tried.

She stepped into his office and scanned his desk for a notepad. His desk was too clean, and she didn't see one. She glanced back through the door toward his secretary's desk. Surely, she had one. She went to his secretary's cubicle and found a notepad lying there with a pen next to it. She sat down in the older woman's chair, wondering if she was out sick today. Quickly, she jotted a note to Barry, telling him she had been there, that she'd wanted to share something with him, but that she would just see him at home.

That was when she heard the voices in the cubicle next door.

"We were at church the other night and the kids told everybody that she was pregnant."

Her hand froze on the notepad, and she sat up, listening. She had no doubt that it was Barry's voice she heard.

Then she heard a woman's voice. "It was unreasonable to tell the kids. But how could she be reasonable, with all those hormones raging through her?"

Tory stood frozen, unable to move to the right or to the left, unable to flee or confront.

"I think you need to give her an ultimatum," the woman said. "Just tell her how it's got to be."

"Ultimatums don't work on her," Barry said. "She's made up her mind and she's not going to change it."

"Well, maybe you just don't need to make it easy for her."

"I've already been sleeping in the basement," he said. "I don't know what more I can do other than leave."

"Well, leave then," she said. "Maybe that's the best thing. You don't have to get saddled with this, Barry. Especially if it's not your choice. I don't know why women think they're the only ones allowed to have choices. You know, that word applies to you men, too."

Tory was dumbfounded, unable to believe that her husband was sharing such an intimate secret with someone she didn't even know—a woman, no less—when he didn't even want to discuss the baby with their children. She had never felt such rage. Blood rushed through her head like waves crashing against the shore. She thought for a moment that she might faint, but the thought of doing it here . . . now . . . was more than she could bear. No, she wouldn't faint, she told herself. And she wouldn't run and pretend she hadn't heard.

Slowly, she went around the cubicle and stepped into the doorway. The woman looked up at her.

Barry turned around. "Tory!"

"Surprised you, didn't I?" she asked through stiff lips. "I came by to tell you that I felt the baby move. I thought it might make a difference, but I didn't know the two of you had already settled our baby's future."

It was only then that she turned and fled to the elevator. She was on her way down before Barry could even react.

CHAPTER
Fifty-Three

Tory flew home, sobbing all the way. Her tires skidded to a halt in her driveway, and she got out and bolted into the house. She headed for the closet where they kept their suitcases, jerked one off of a shelf, and ran into the bedroom.

She heard the door close at the other end of the house, and Barry yelled, "Tory! Tory! Where are you?"

She threw the suitcase on the bed and unzipped it so hard that she feared she might tear it.

Barry was at the door in an instant. "Tory, I don't know what you think you heard but—"

"What I *think* I heard?" She went to Barry's drawer and pulled it out, almost dropping it on the floor. With both arms she picked up a pile of his clothes and thrust them into the suitcase. "I *think* I heard you telling some of our most private secrets to a woman I don't even know! I *think* I heard you telling her what our sleeping arrangements are! I *think* I heard her advising you to give me an ultimatum about our baby's life!"

She went back to the dresser and slid another drawer open, took another armload of clothes to the suitcase, and dropped them in.

"What are you doing?" he demanded.

"I'm packing your suitcase! I don't want you here."

She pulled out another drawer, but he stopped her. "Tory, I know you're hurt. Maybe I shouldn't have been talking to anybody about us, but—"

She jerked away from him. "Who is she, Barry? Who is this woman who's making judgments about my baby?"

"Her name is Linda Holland. She works in marketing. We've gotten to be friends. It's no big deal."

"It's a big deal to me!" she shouted. She went to the closet and grabbed some things, threw them on the bed.

"Stop it! I'm not going anywhere."

"Oh, yes, you are," she said. "So help me, you're out of here."

"And what is that going to solve?" he asked.

"I can have peace during my pregnancy!" she sobbed. "I won't have to walk around trying to pretend I have a marriage when I don't. I won't have to know that my husband is sharing my most intimate secrets with some other woman. You won't *know* my intimate secrets," she said. "You won't know when the baby moves, or when my water breaks, or when I go into labor. And neither will she. Those choices she was telling you about? You've made yours, Barry. *I* thought our only problem was that our daughter has Down's Syndrome. But there's a lot more than that going on here."

"You're wrong about that," Barry said. "I am not having an affair with her."

"I don't know what you're having with her," she said, "but whatever it is, I feel betrayed and violated."

She zipped up the suitcase and slid it across the bed, unable to pick it up. "Here. Take it. Go."

He refused to touch it. "I'm not going anywhere."

"Oh, yes, you are. Either you're going or the kids and I are going, and since I'm pregnant and those two children need a place to sleep, I suggest you let us stay here."

His eyes began to redden. "Tory, I don't have anyplace to go."

"Go to your mother's," she said. "Tell her what you're doing. See how she likes it."

"I'm not going to my mother's." He jerked the suitcase off the bed. "I'll check into the Holiday Inn until you cool down."

"You do that. And go on back to the office and tell Linda that your wife's hormones ran amuck today. Tell her you didn't have to give me that ultimatum after all. I gave *you* one."

She left the bedroom and bolted up the hall.

Barry followed her with the suitcase. "What are you going to tell the kids?"

"Maybe nothing," she said. "Isn't that the way you like it? Or maybe I'll tell them that their father won't talk to their mother but he'll talk to some woman who thinks she's got all the answers."

She slammed herself into the bathroom and locked it behind her. She wanted to break something, wanted to smash her fist through the glass.

Instead, she threw up.

She heard Barry outside the door, and she wondered why he hadn't taken the suitcase and gone. She sat on the floor, weeping into the circle of her arms, listening for him to leave. Finally, she heard his footsteps move, heard him walking through the kitchen, heard the door close.

As she realized her husband was gone, the baby fluttered again. She set her hand over her stomach and leaned back against the wall, wondering what she was going to do now.

CHAPTER
Fifty-Four

The hospital in León was filthy and unsanitary, nothing like the clinic where Harry and the medical missionaries practiced medicine. Though the American clinic was poorly equipped for serious surgeries, it was sanitary.

Now, as Sylvia walked through the halls and heard people moaning in the rooms, babies crying and nurses shouting, she wondered what was going to become of the baby. Would she have to leave her here with her mother, or would a relative take her home? Would little Carly miss her?

With dreadful reluctance, Sylvia followed Harry to the room at the end of the hall and watched him knock on the door. She held back, not wanting to reach the door, not wanting to walk through it and hand that baby over. She started to cry again and pressed her forehead against the child's. The baby looked up at her and touched the tears with one extended finger.

"You're not going to forget me, are you, Carly?" she asked. Those big black eyes just searched her wet face.

"Sylvia, honey." Harry prompted her to come on, get this over with. Sylvia stepped into the doorway, feeling as if that threshold would take her to something terrible and out of her control.

A young, pretty woman lay on the bed, one side of her face bruised and scarred. A row of poorly done stitches zipped across her cheekbone. Sylvia saw Carly in the woman's mouth, in the shape of her nose, in her eyes as she sat up and beheld the child in Sylvia's arms.

She let out a cry. *"Mi bebe!"*

It was only then that the baby, surprised by the voice of her mother, turned and saw the woman lying on the bed. She started to cry as if the sight had frightened her, and Sylvia bounced her and tried to calm her down.

But then the baby reached. With both arms extended, she leaned away from Sylvia, toward her mother. Sylvia had no choice but to surrender the child, and the woman closed her bruised, bandaged arms around the baby and began to sob with joy.

Sylvia smiled through her tears. This young, injured woman loved her child the way Sylvia had loved her own babies.

Harry stepped up behind her and put his arms around her. "Are you okay?"

She nodded, unable to speak.

When the woman had calmed down, she told Sylvia in a burst of Spanish how the hurricane had leveled their house. A wall had fallen on her. She'd had a head injury, and by the time her consciousness returned, no one knew where her baby was. Grieving over her dead husband, she had almost decided her child was dead, too. No one had any word on where she was. Everyone who had walked through the door had heard her grief-stricken pleas, and along with her hope, she had almost given up her will to live.

The woman took Sylvia's hand and squeezed it hard. *"Gracias,"* she wept. "You are an angel of God."

Sylvia barely understood the Spanish, and she moved questioning eyes to Harry. "Did she call me an angel of God?"

"Yes, she did."

Sylvia turned back to the woman, frowned, and shook her head. "No, not me."

"*Angel*," the woman repeated in Spanish. "He sent you to protect my Selena." The child had relaxed on her mother's breast. She was home. "God loved us enough to send you."

The words stunned Sylvia. She had believed the child was a gift from God—a reward, perhaps, for coming here on faith. She had counted Carly as part of her work.

Maybe she hadn't been wrong. Maybe she had been sent to care for the lost child of a desperate mother. Instead of Carly being Sylvia's provision, maybe it was the other way around. Maybe it wasn't over yet.

"What will you do with the child tonight?" Sylvia asked, her Spanish halting and broken.

"I don't know," the woman said.

Sylvia thought of offering to keep the baby one more night, but she knew she couldn't wrench her away now. But the woman was in no shape to even sit up.

Sylvia bucked up the strength that she would need to get through this and turned to her husband. "Harry, I need to stay here overnight."

"Stay here? Why?" he asked.

"Because she needs help tending to Carly . . . I mean, Selena. I can't separate them tonight, so I'll stay. Tomorrow, I'll take her home and keep her until her mother gets out of the hospital."

Just then an older woman bolted through the door. She took one look at the baby and let out a yell. She threw herself over the bed rail, kissing the baby and the mother and weeping as she chattered in Spanish.

Sylvia knew the woman was the baby's grandmother, or some other close relative who loved her.

Harry pulled Sylvia from the room. "I can't go yet!" she said. "Harry, I didn't say good-bye!"

"We need to go," he said, "before it gets harder. She's in good hands, Sylvia. Her mother's, her grandmother's . . . and God's.

You have to trust that." He held her as she wept out her heart. Finally, she allowed Harry to walk her down the corridor.

He took her home in silence, walked her into the house, then held her on the couch as she wept against his shirt.

CHAPTER
Fifty-Five

While Leah and Rachel helped Joseph memorize his multiplication tables, Brenda took Mark and Daniel outside to do an experiment to show them what color flame different compounds would produce. She had gotten compounds from an advanced chemistry set with strict instructions on what not to do.

Mark had given her little trouble today, since the science project interested him. She had found that he needed almost constant stimulation, but if she could get him interested in what they were doing, he forgot to be a smart aleck.

They had only gotten as far as Noah in the Old Testament, and John the Baptist in the New, but on their test this morning, Mark had named Shem, Ham, and Japheth. She considered that a divine victory.

The experiment captured his imagination, so when she asked Mark to memorize the results of burning each compound, he seemed anxious to comply. When they had finished, she took the supplies to David's workshop and set them on a shelf.

"David, the kids are all working on assignments. Would you keep an eye on them while I run over to check on Tory?"

"Sure," he said. "I'll just take a break."

Brenda had seen Tory screeching into the driveway earlier, and a few minutes later, Barry had driven up. She hoped things had gone well at Barry's office, but from the looks of things, they hadn't.

Barry had slammed out of the house and screeched out of Cedar Circle, and when Tory drove by to pick up the kids sometime later, her eyes had looked red and swollen. Brenda crossed the lot between their homes and knocked on Tory's door. When she didn't answer, Brenda tried the knob. It was unlocked, so she opened it and stepped inside.

"Tory?" After a few seconds, she heard a voice responding from the back. She headed for the bedrooms. She saw the children napping as she passed their rooms, and was careful not to wake them. Quietly, she started back to Tory's room.

But Tory was on her way out. Her eyes were red, and she had a Kleenex pressed under her nose. She looked as if she had been crying all morning.

"Tory, honey, what's wrong?"

Tory led her into the living room so the kids wouldn't wake up. "I did what you said," she told her, dropping onto the couch. "I went up there to let him feel the baby move, only he was sitting in this cubicle with a woman."

"What?"

"He was telling her how he's been sleeping in the basement, how our marriage is falling apart, that he can't reason with me, that I'm too hormonal."

"He was saying all that to a woman?"

"Yes, and she told him he should give me an ultimatum, that he had choices, too." She tried to find a dry place on the tissue and dabbed at her eyes.

"Oh, honey. What did you do?"

"I let them know I was there," Tory said, lifting her chin. "You know me. I can't keep my mouth shut. Maybe I should have just gone on home and confronted him tonight, but I didn't."

"Did the two of you get to talk?"

"Oh, yeah. He came home and I packed his suitcase so he could leave again."

"You didn't."

She wiped her face and breathed in a sob. "I did. I packed all of his clothes in that suitcase, threw it at him, and he's gone. He's checked in at the Holiday Inn."

"He'll be back."

"No, he won't," she said through tight lips. "I won't let him in. I'm thinking about having the locks changed."

"Tory, that would be ridiculous." She touched Tory's shoulder, helpless to know what to do for her. "Did you tell him about the baby moving?"

"Yeah, somewhere in all the screaming and yelling I did. Not that he cares. This baby has had an execution verdict from Day One."

Brenda closed her eyes.

"Can you believe this?" Tory asked. "He's sharing our marriage problems with another woman. She knows more about what he's thinking than I do!"

"What did he say about her?"

"He swore that it was nothing. But it is, Brenda. I know it is. That's what all this is about. It's not just about the baby. I should have known." She blew her nose. "All this time, I've thought this was about Down's Syndrome. But it may really be about an affair."

"Maybe not. Maybe it really is nothing."

"It's something, all right. I don't know how much more I can take."

Brenda pulled her into a hug, and she felt Tory relaxing in despair against her shirt. She wished she knew what to say, but no special words of wisdom came to her mind.

Suddenly, the front door flew open. "Mama!" Leah cried. "There's a fire! Mark and Daniel!"

Brenda let Tory go and dashed outside. Smoke filled the air, and she saw flames dancing from the picnic table next to her house.

Mark and Daniel stood off to the side as David tried to drown it with the hose. She heard a siren coming from around the corner and realized someone had called the fire department.

She ran to Joseph, standing on the side of the yard. "Honey, you have to get out of this smoke." She turned around and saw that Tory was behind her. "Tory, will you take him into your house? Leah and Rachel, too?"

"Sure," Tory said, wiping her nose again. "Come on, guys. I'll see if I have any Popsicles."

Brenda watched her children leave, then looked across the fire to the older two boys. Daniel was crying. He knew he was in trouble. Mark, however, just held his chin up defiantly, as if he dared anyone to confront him.

As the firemen talked to David and doused the flames, Brenda approached the boys. "What happened?" she demanded.

"I told him not to do it," Daniel cried. "We were working on our assignments and I told him just to do what you said. But he had to try that experiment again, and he went into Dad's workshop while Dad was in the house, and he got the compounds back out. This time he didn't get it right and it caught fire."

Her eyes flashed as she grabbed Mark's hands and looked them over. "You could have been burned."

"But I wasn't," he said.

"Mark, do you understand how dangerous this could have been?"

"We were outside," he said. "It's just a stupid picnic table."

"You could have burned my house down!"

"Well, it's not like I meant to do it."

For the first time in her life, Brenda thought she had the capacity to hurt a child. "Can you just say you're sorry?"

"For what? All I did was a stupid experiment. I'm trying to learn like you keep telling me."

"I told you to do your assignment." Her voice was rising. "Why couldn't you just follow orders?"

"Why can't you just calm down?" he asked. "You sound like my mom."

She felt her scalp tingling as the fury built up inside her. "Mark, you deliberately disobeyed me . . . *again*."

The firemen were busy dousing the grass in case any live sparks remained. David came up behind her and put his arm around Brenda's shoulders. "No harm done," he said. "This time. I can rebuild the picnic table."

"See?" Mark told Daniel. "No harm done."

"No thanks to you," David said. "How about a little more remorse and a little less attitude?"

"Attitude? The experiment was her idea. She showed us how to do it."

David shot Brenda a look that said no amount of money was worth this.

"Mark, you're really testing my patience." Brenda's hands trembled.

"What?" he asked. "Now everybody's mad at me. I was just trying to do my work."

"You were *not* trying to do your work!" Brenda bellowed. "You were doing exactly what I told you not to do, and it could have hurt or killed somebody."

"But since it didn't, can we just move on? The picnic table was old, anyway. You needed a new one."

Brenda grabbed Mark's arm and glared into his face. "I've tried to work with you, Mark. I've tried to help you. But I can't stand this anymore. I don't know what to do for you."

He jerked away from her. "Then just let me go home."

"No, I'm not going to let you go home, because your mother's not there, and you might burn *her* house down."

"So what do I have to do?"

"You have to go into the living room and sit there by your-self until your mother gets home."

"The *living* room? There's nothing in there, not even a TV."

"You don't *need* anything to do. You just need to sit there and think."

"Think about what?"

"About what you did wrong today. What you need to apologize for."

"I haven't done anything wrong," he insisted.

"Just go into the living room," she demanded. "Now!"

Finally, Mark obeyed and started into the house.

Brenda turned back to Daniel. "Go get your brother and sisters from Miss Tory's," she said. "I want everybody back to the school books, now."

Daniel wiped his face and looked up at her. "I'm sorry, Mama. I should have stopped him."

"Next time, tell me or your father *before* he blows something up." She saw the deep contrition on her son's face, and pulled him into a hug. "Oh, honey, I'm so glad you're all right. And I'm sorry you had to see me lose my cool. I thought I was above that."

She tried to hold back her tears, but failed. Daniel hugged her back, then headed to Tory's house to get his siblings. She wanted to go with him, to tell Tory how sorry she was that their talk had been interrupted. Tory needed her, but she couldn't leave Mark in there alone. There was no telling what he might do.

"You okay?" David asked.

"No," she said, "I'm not okay."

He turned her around to face him. "Mark's getting to you, isn't he?"

Her face was getting hot with emotion. "He's driving me crazy, David. I don't know if I can take this."

"Maybe you just need to have another talk with Cathy."

"David, if I don't keep teaching him, what are we going to do? We need this money."

"Maybe I can get a job at night. We'll work something out."

"No. I can do this. I know I can. I've just got to figure out how to get through to him. I thought I was making progress. He seemed so interested today, and he did really well on his test this morning. But this . . ."

"You know, you don't have to finish school today," he said. "You could just take the rest of the day off."

"No," she said. "It's like getting back on a horse after falling off. I've got to keep going or I'll give it all up entirely."

That afternoon, when Mark went home from school, he told his mother that Brenda made him sit in the living room alone all afternoon with nothing to do.

"All right, Mark," Cathy said. "Give it to me straight, because you know I'll find out from Brenda. What did you do?"

"I had an accident doing a science experiment. It caught fire and almost killed me. The fire department came and everything."

Cathy's mouth fell open, and she looked out the front window and saw the charred picnic table and the black spot on the Dodds' lawn. "A fire?" she asked, turning back to him. "Mark, were you hurt?"

"Of course I was hurt," he said. "It knocked me off my bench. But she was over at Tory's house, so there was nobody but Daniel there to help me."

"Wait." The story wasn't adding up. Brenda had left Mark alone while he did a potentially dangerous science experiment? "Just ... I'm going to talk to Brenda, okay? I'm going to get to the bottom of this."

"Fine," he said. "You'll see. I'm supposed to psychically know chemistry and get the experiment right."

"So she really left you *alone* to do it? Just you and Daniel?"

"That's right. While she hung out with Tory."

This time when Cathy stormed over to demand an explanation, she found Brenda more agitated than she was.

"Hold it!" Brenda said at the door. "If you came to lambaste me about keeping him in the living room all afternoon, you'd better get the real story first."

Cathy had never seen Brenda angry. She responded with maternal defensiveness. "He said you were at Tory's while he was doing a dangerous experiment. He said he almost got blown up!"

"Of *course* he said that!" Brenda almost shouted. "Cathy, either you trust me or you don't."

"Well, *were* you at Tory's?"

"Yes! Because I saw her screech home and run in crying, and then Barry screeched home, and left with a suitcase. They've separated, and I was trying to comfort her."

"Separated?" Cathy asked. "Oh, my gosh."

"And *since* Mark is thirteen years old I thought he could be trusted without adult supervision for fifteen minutes!"

"Well, yeah, but not with dangerous chemical compounds."

"He didn't *have* dangerous compounds, Cathy. They were on a shelf in David's workshop. But Mark can't be trusted on the same *block* with dangerous compounds!"

"Now, wait a minute," Cathy said. "He's never blown up anything before. It was an accident!"

Brenda closed her front door behind her and came out onto her porch. She dropped onto her swing. She looked as if she was close to bursting into tears. "They call me Homier-than-thou, you know."

Cathy crossed her arms, still fuming. "Who does?"

"The other homeschooling moms. They call me that behind my back, because I'm usually so organized and structured. 'Don't compare yourself to Brenda Dodd because nobody can have that tight a schedule.' They're all more flexible and relaxed, which works for them. But they don't understand that I *have* to be structured to keep five kids progressing. But look at me today! I want to pull my hair out."

Cathy suddenly felt sorry for her. The anger drained out of her. She sighed and sank into a rocker. "Mark did this to you, didn't he? He ruined your disposition and your way of life."

Brenda breathed a laugh. "Let's not go that far. I'm just having a bad day. But he almost burned my house down, Cathy," Brenda said. "He destroyed the picnic table. Did he tell you the fire department was here?"

"Yes. But if it wasn't a science experiment . . ."

"He had an unauthorized run-in with a Bunsen burner, after we had done the experiment and put everything away. Thankfully, no one was hurt. My blood pressure may never be the same . . ." She rubbed her eyes. "I had put the compounds in David's workshop. Mark went in there and got them while David was in the house. He knew better."

Cathy buried her face in her hands. "I don't get it. By now, I thought he would have settled in. That he'd be learning . . ."

"He's learning," Brenda admitted, calming down. "Really, this morning, he did so well on his test that I thought I'd be praising him all day. I was feeling really good about his progress, until . . ."

"Until he tried to nuke your house."

Neither of them saw humor in that.

"Is he going to give you a nervous breakdown?" Cathy asked.

"No," Brenda said. "I won't let him."

"So does that mean you're not going to teach him anymore?"

Brenda smiled. "Cathy, I committed to do it, and I will."

"But if you're going to start hating and avoiding me, and he's going to refuse to learn another thing for the rest of his life . . . I'll let you off the hook, Brenda."

Brenda seemed to be thinking it over. Suddenly, she got up. "Wait here a minute." She went in to her desk, got Mark's test paper, and brought it back to Cathy. "Here. See? He is learning."

Cathy looked down at it and saw that he had correctly answered questions about Noah's family, about the Tower of Babel, about the seven days of Creation. She wiped her eyes. There *was* hope. "You're a miracle worker," she said. "This is amazing."

"Cathy, this is not a big deal. You've been going over the same material. Maybe he learned it from you. But he's doing really well in math, too."

"Math? You're kidding me."

"No. He even picks it up faster than Daniel. See? There's hope."

Cathy's expression softened. "Brenda, I promise I'll buy you a new picnic table."

"I don't want another picnic table," she said. "That's not it. I just want him to listen to me, to show remorse when he does something wrong. I want his attitude to improve."

"Well, since those things seem about as likely as peace in the Middle East, you'd better think this quitting thing over again," Cathy said. "I'll make other arrangements if I need to."

"Not yet." Brenda sighed. "I'll give it a little more time. But I can't promise anything. I can't stand this kind of turmoil in my life. It's not good for my own kids. Even if it does make me less homier-than-thou."

"I'll do what I can to straighten him out," Cathy said.

When Cathy had gone home, Brenda went back into the bedroom and dropped down on the bed, her hand over her forehead to dull the throbbing.

Joseph came into the room and leaned on the side of her bed. "Mama, are you okay?"

"Yeah, honey," she said. "I'll be fine."

"Can I lay down with you?"

"Lie," she said. "Can you lie down with me."

Joseph grinned. "That, too."

She scooted over and he climbed up next to her. For several moments, they lay side by side, staring quietly at the ceiling.

"Mama, I feel kind of sorry for Mark." He turned over on his side and looked at her.

She looked into her little boy's eyes. "Why, Joseph?"

"The way he's always horsing around trying to get us to laugh, instead of doing his work. I think it's kind of a cover-up."

"A cover-up for what?"

"I think *he* thinks he's stupid and he thinks he doesn't want to learn, but he seems really proud when he does."

"That's the thing about trying to do the right thing for somebody," she said, stroking the cowlick in Joseph's red hair. "You know it will make them happy in the long run. But when they put up such a fight, it's almost not worth it."

"We're supposed to love the ones who make it hard, too. Right, Mama?"

She smiled at her son, and touched a cheek that was rounded from the use of steroids. "Thank you, Joseph. I needed to be reminded of that today."

"You're the one who taught me," he said. He slipped off the bed, twisting his shirt, and she caught a glimpse of the scar that cut through his little chest. He was recovering so well, and the pink in his skin was more than she had ever hoped to see again. Yet, here he was, able to lie with her on the bed and impart wisdom about their neighbors. She gave him a tight hug.

"Don't crush me," he said with a giggle, and she let him go.

As he left the room, Brenda wilted back onto the bed and began to pray that God would help her to do the right thing.

❧

That night, Brenda went back over to Cathy's house and renewed her commitment to teach Mark. She told her not to worry about her giving up, that Joseph had shown her that God had ordained this.

Relieved beyond words, Cathy marched Mark down the stairs and made him apologize to Brenda for burning up her picnic table and for disregarding her rules. He seemed genuinely sorry as he got the words out.

When Mark had returned to his room, she and Brenda sat on the couch. "Bad day," Cathy said.

"Yeah. Sounds like it was for everybody. Have you talked to Tory?"

"A little while ago," she said. "She's pretty upset." She thought that over for a moment. "You know what I'd really like to do?"

"What?" Brenda asked.

"I'd like to call Sylvia."

A slow smile crept across Brenda's face. "That's a great idea. Let's get Tory, and we can all talk to her. That'll cheer all of us up."

CHAPTER
Fifty-Six

The grief in Sylvia's heart clung more tightly than Harry's arms. It seemed bigger than the blessings he whispered in her ear, more mighty than the joys she had come to León to proclaim. It was slanderous, self-pitying, systematic grief that disassembled her, piece by piece. She didn't know how she would ever overcome it.

Harry didn't let her go until the telephone rang, and reluctantly, he got up to answer it. She blew her nose as he muttered in the other room. He probably had an emergency, she thought. Someone who needed him more than she did. He would have to go to the clinic and leave her alone.

It was probably just as well. There was little he could do for her here.

But when he came back into the room, he didn't have that look of apology she'd expected on his face. Instead, he was smiling. "Sylvia, it's long distance from Tennessee. Brenda, Tory, and Cathy."

She sat up straighter. "All of them?"

"All three," he said.

"But how did they know?"

"God knew," he said, taking her hand and pulling her to her feet. "Come talk to them."

She went to the telephone in the other room. A smile tickled across her face as she answered. "Hello?"

"Sylvia." All three of them spoke at once. The sound was like Mozart after fingernails on a chalkboard.

"Oh, boy, are you three a godsend!" She started to cry again. She sucked in a breath, and tried to control her voice. "Whose house are you calling from? I just want to picture where you are."

"We're at Tory's," Cathy said, "all on different extensions."

"What's wrong?" Brenda asked Sylvia. "You sound stopped up. Are you sick?"

Sylvia drew a deep breath, and thought of lying to keep from bringing them down. But she didn't have the energy to keep it to herself. "We found the baby's mother," she said. There was silence on the other end for a long moment. It was clear that her neighbors didn't know whether to rejoice for the child or grieve for Sylvia. "I ought to be happy," she admitted. "I mean, she needs her mom, doesn't she, instead of some silly old woman who wants to be a mother again?"

"You're only fifty years old," Cathy said. "For heaven's sake, that's not old."

"It feels old." She swallowed hard and dabbed at her eyes again. "I thought God was letting me have another crack at motherhood, but instead, he was just letting me baby-sit."

"Oh, Sylvia . . ."

She pursed her lips and waved a hand in the air, as if they could see it. "Never mind that. Carly's fine. That's the important thing. Now, what's going on with all of you?"

They were all hesitant to blurt it out. Finally, Cathy spoke up. "Looks like it's a banner day for all of us. Tory, you go first."

"What is it, honey?" Sylvia asked.

Tory's voice was hoarse. Sylvia knew she had been crying, too. "Barry moved out today," she said. "We had a terrible fight after I caught him confiding in another woman about our marriage."

"Oh, no. Where is he?"

"He's at the Holiday Inn."

Sylvia suddenly forgot her own grief. "Oh, Tory, you've got to get him back."

"Sylvia, this woman works with him. Every night, he works late. He was telling her about our sleeping arrangements!"

"Did you see them together? Were they touching?"

"No, not right there in the office, but—"

"Okay," Sylvia said, still hopeful. "It wasn't right for him to confide in her, but that's not enough to end a marriage over."

"Sylvia, he's listening to her about aborting our child."

Sylvia closed her eyes. She wished she could have five minutes alone with Barry and straighten him out. "Okay, that's it. I'm going to stop feeling sorry for myself right this minute. I wish I could do something for you."

"Thank you, Sylvia," Tory said. "There's really nothing."

"Don't give up on him, Tory. He's still a good man."

"It's hard." Her brevity spoke volumes. Tory usually waxed eloquent about her problems. Now she could hardly speak at all.

"I know, honey. But I still believe he's going to come around. So Cathy and Brenda, are you two helping Tory?"

"We're trying," Cathy said, "but like I said, it's been a banner day for all of us."

"There's more?" Sylvia asked. "What is it?"

"Mark again," Cathy said. "Brenda just about lost it today when he caught her picnic table on fire. Mark's very gifted, I guess. If he can send Brenda over the edge, he can send anybody."

"Brenda, you aren't going to quit, are you?" Sylvia asked.

"No," Brenda said quietly. "I'll keep going. There's got to be an answer somewhere."

"I just don't know what it is," Cathy added.

"All boys are hard at this age," Sylvia told them. "You should have seen Jeff when he was twelve. I thought I would lose my mind. One time he was doing an experiment on electricity and blew out the wiring in our whole garage. Thank goodness it was on a separate circuit breaker, or it would have lit up the whole house."

"Really?" Cathy asked. "Your Jeff did that?"

"Sure did. And I probably never told you that he had to go to summer school after his seventh grade year, because he failed algebra *and* English."

"Sylvia, I never knew that," Cathy said. "I thought Jeff was the perfect child."

"Heavens, who gave you that idea? He turned out fine. He's happy and has a good job . . . and his mother misses him terribly. But there were some trials in raising him." She shifted her thoughts to Brenda, who quietly let the others talk. "What about Joseph, Brenda? Is he okay?"

"He's doing great. Hasn't shown any sign of rejecting the heart. And I think he gets wiser every day."

"Talk about answered prayers," Sylvia said. "If we ever forget that God is watching over us, we should think of Joseph." She pressed her eyes as remorse filled her. She had been so blind to God's goodness. All she had seen was the impact things had on her. But God was still there, working quietly in all their lives. "Oh, I wish I could give you all a really big hug, and we could stand around in a circle and cry our hearts out together, until we could each remember how blessed we are!"

She knew they were all crying, unable to speak, so she took the lead again. "You know, someday we're going to laugh about all of these things. I've always said that in every crisis there's a blessing. It's not so easy to see when it's *my* crisis, but it's there whether I see it or not."

"I'm sorry, Sylvia," Tory said, her voice cracked. "I usually buy what you tell me, but that one's really hard to swallow."

"But it's true. You just watch. Look back at what we went through with Joseph. Brenda's stronger for it. We all are. You'll be stronger for this, honey."

"For having a retarded child," Tory asked, "or for losing my marriage in the process?"

"Whatever God lays out for you, Tory, you'll be able to stand it. You'll see. He'll equip you. His grace is sufficient."

"Is it sufficient for you?" Tory asked. "Giving up the baby when you were so sure that God had given her to you?"

Sylvia was silent for a moment as she turned Tory's painful question over in her mind. "I'm just now beginning to realize that God did give her to me," Sylvia said. "Even though I couldn't keep her, she was a precious, wonderful little gift, and I'm glad I got that time with her. I wish you could have met her."

"Maybe someday," Brenda said.

"I doubt it," Sylvia said. "I may never see her again. She'll grow up and not even remember the lady who took care of her after the hurricane. I guess that's how it's supposed to be. I've already raised my kids. I'm not supposed to be a mother again."

"I can't imagine that," Cathy said. "I can't imagine looking back and knowing I've raised my kids successfully. What peace there must be in that."

"I know," Tory said, "and I keep looking back to when my marriage was happy, and my kids were bouncy, and the only problem I ever had was that I didn't have a long enough stretch of time to write a novel. I didn't have a clue what real problems were."

Brenda agreed. "And I look back to when teaching my kids was my biggest objective, and I had never had a sick child or a neighbor who was mad at me."

"I'm not mad at you," Cathy insisted.

"Well, not anymore."

"Brenda, I overreacted, but I didn't mean it."

"Guard the friendship," Sylvia cut in. "I hear tension in both of your voices. Don't let this come between you. I need you too much. All three of you. We're going to be all right, all of us. We'll get through these storms. One of these days, I'll even stop feeling like a fool."

"If you feel like a fool," Brenda said, "then you're missing the best part of the blessing."

"Missing it?" Sylvia asked. "What do you mean?"

"I mean that Carly needed somebody who could love her until her mom was on her feet. That somebody turned out to be you. I don't think it was all some divine joke, or a misunderstanding, or an accident. I think God picked you, Sylvia. Right out of all the people in León, he chose you to take care of little Carly. I would count that a high honor."

She found herself dissolving into tears again. "You're right, Brenda. That is a high honor. Maybe it's as high as God choosing Tory to take care of her special little baby."

She heard Tory weeping on the other end of the line. Sniffs came from both of the other women, as well. "Girls, let's pray together. We haven't done that in a long time."

As they started to pray, Sylvia felt the peace of God falling like a warm, cleansing shower over them.

CHAPTER
Fifty-Seven

After the week she'd had with Mark, Cathy had serious reservations about letting Steve take either of the boys camping Saturday morning. She offered them each twenty dollars if they behaved for him. If it provided the incentive they needed to cooperate, it would be forty dollars well spent.

Steve didn't take the boys far, since he knew a long car ride might ruin the trip before it even got started. He took them to a wooded area just outside of Breezewood, and got Rick and Mark to help him unload his truck. He heard Mark muttering under his breath as he did, but he cheerfully ignored it.

When they had set up the tent, he tossed them each a fishing pole. "Come on. Let's get down to the lake and see what's biting. Mark, grab that box."

Mark picked up the box he pointed to and opened it. "Stinks," he said. "What is it?"

"Bait," Steve told him. "Crickets."

Mark's eyebrows shot up. "Did you catch them?"

"No, I bought them."

"They sell these things?"

Steve grinned. "Mark, have you ever been fishing before?"

"I don't know. I don't remember."

"He hasn't," Rick said. "But I did a long time ago."

"When?" Mark asked, as if he'd been slighted.

"When you were a baby or something. Dad and I went."

"Oh." Mark studied the crickets again, then put the top back on. "I didn't know Dad liked to fish."

Steve had spent the last week praying that the Lord would help him to have compassion for the boys, and that he would see into their hearts, the way their mother tried to do. Now he saw that his prayers were being answered. "The question is, will you like it? Come on. Let's go see."

A little later they sat on the edge of the lake looking across the Smoky Mountains, fishing as the autumn breeze chilled them. Mark couldn't take his eyes from his white cork ball bobbing on the water.

"When I was a kid," Steve said in a quiet voice, "my parents had a lot of land. We had a little lake on the back of the property, and I would go there to fish. Sometimes I would just sit there for hours. Of course, I was never alone. I had three male labs that we bred, and they would follow me. They'd sit next to me and just look out over the lake as we fished. It was a great place to think."

"Why are you doing this?" Mark's question cut through the moment.

Steve looked over at him, bracing himself. "Doing what?"

"Taking us camping. Fishing with us."

Rick shoved him. "Mark, shut up."

"I just asked him a question!" Mark said.

"It's okay," Steve interrupted, pulling his line in and checking his bait. "What reason do you think I had for bringing you here?"

"'Cause you want to score points with our mom," Mark said.

Steve laughed. "There's some truth to that."

Both boys looked up at him, surprised by the honesty.

"But I also wanted to get to know you guys a little better. Tracy doesn't like to touch the crickets. It's fun to fish with guys sometimes."

Mark wasn't buying. "You thought we needed a male influence," he said belligerently. "But we don't. We have a dad. If we wanted to go fishing, he'd take us fishing."

"Mark, stop it!" Rick said.

"It's okay," Steve said. "I'm not trying to horn in on your dad. I just thought it would be a pleasant way to spend a couple of days."

There was silence for a moment, and Steve steeled himself for another accusation. How would he get past the suspicions and make friends with the boys? He breathed a silent prayer for help.

Then to all their surprise, Mark got a bite. He got to his feet and started jumping around. "I got one! I got one!"

Steve laughed out loud as he grabbed the line and helped him pull it in. The trout was an admirable size, big enough to keep, and Mark glowed with pride.

Rick was next to catch one, then Mark caught another. By noon, they had enough for lunch. Steve taught Mark and Rick how to clean the fish and cook them. Mark kept a marker on the fish he had caught, and refused to let anyone else touch them. He told them it was the best thing he'd ever tasted.

After lunch, they piled into the truck and went to rent mud bikes. They spent the rest of the day getting filthy and making a lot of noise.

"I gotta get myself one of those," Rick said, as they headed back to the camp. "I'm gonna start saving my money now."

"Where will you ride it?" Steve asked.

"I don't know. Maybe the land behind the Bryans' house. That new Gonzales family is nice and they're never home. They probably won't mind."

"It might tear up the property," Steve said. "Besides, if you can do it anytime, it gets old. Maybe you ought to just rent them once in a while."

"Maybe," Rick said, "but it sure was a blast."

Mark looked down at his mud-caked clothes. "So how are we gonna bathe?" he asked. "I don't think I can sleep like this."

"We'll bathe in the lake," Steve said.

They both looked at him like he was crazy. "Are you kidding?" Rick asked. "It's cold in there."

"Not that cold. You don't have to, if you don't want to."

When they reached the camp, he took his clothes off down to his shorts, then ran and plopped into the lake. "Come on in," he said, teeth chattering. "It's nice and warm."

The boys laughed. "It is *not* warm," Rick said.

"Your lips are turning blue," Mark accused.

"That's just from treading water," Steve told him. "The aerobic exercise is pumping the blood through my lips."

Rick guffawed harder. "That's the lamest thing I've ever heard!"

Mark grinned and pulled off his mud-caked shirt. "I'm gonna get in." Leaving his jeans on, he dove into the water. He came up and flung the water out of his hair. "Nice and warm, Rick. Come on!"

Suddenly, Steve and Mark were allies, trying to coax Rick in. Not one to be outdone, he pulled off his shirt and did a cannonball right between them. Steve and Mark attacked him as soon as he came up.

They laughed and screamed and splashed and ducked each other until they couldn't stand the cold anymore. Then they all got out, shivering and running to find towels and dry clothes. Steve had a new fire started before Mark had managed to get his wet jeans off.

Things were going just as he'd hoped, he thought. Cathy would be pleased.

CHAPTER
Fifty-Eight

While Steve was getting to know her boys around a campfire, Cathy spent the day shopping with Annie and Tracy. Steve had left her his credit card and told her that Tracy needed a couple of new dresses and some school clothes. He told her to buy Tracy anything else she saw that she might need. He trusted her to use good judgment.

She had never had such a peaceful day shopping for school clothes. Normally, she and Annie fought from store to store as Annie begged for things that were either inappropriate or too expensive. But today Annie delighted in choosing things for the little girl. Tracy liked everything the teenaged girl suggested.

That morning, Cathy had french-braided Tracy's hair. Annie had taken her upstairs and applied a little makeup, which Cathy had promptly made her remove. They had eaten out in a nice restaurant, and with Tracy watching with adoration, Annie acted like a perfect lady.

That afternoon, she had taken Tracy to the clinic and let her play with two puppies and a litter of kittens she was boarding for the weekend. She managed to get a precious picture of Tracy with a kitten against her face. She hoped it would come out well enough to blow it up for Steve.

That evening, they rented the movie *Babe* and laughed as the little pig ventured through the plot. When it was over, Tracy leaned against Cathy, watching with sleepy eyes as the credits rolled across the television screen.

"Are you ready to go to bed, Tracy?" Cathy asked.

Tracy's peaceful expression suddenly changed. "Where am I gonna sleep?"

"I was thinking you could sleep in Rick's room," she said. "I made him clean it up before he left."

"By myself?" Tracy asked.

Annie, who had been getting ready for an eight-thirty date, sat down next to them. "Mom, she can sleep with me if she wants to."

"But you're going out. I don't want her to stay up late. She's worn out." Cathy looked down at the frightened little face. "Tell you what, Tracy. You can sleep with me. I'm worn out, myself."

Tracy's worried expression faded. "Okay." The three went upstairs to Cathy's room, and Cathy began to take Tracy's french braid down. When Annie had been this young, she had loved brushing her hair and arranging it with bows and barrettes. Annie hadn't allowed her to touch her hair in years.

A soft smile came to her face as she remembered those times, and she caught Tracy's eyes in the mirror. The child was smiling and watching her with pensive eyes.

"Are you going to marry my daddy?" she asked.

The question startled Cathy, and she stopped brushing. "You know, I have a real bad feeling that when your dad gets home from the camping trip, he won't even want to date me anymore."

Annie began to laugh, but Tracy looked disappointed.

When she had gotten Tracy into bed, Annie plopped down next to them. "Let's say prayers," Cathy said as she pulled the covers up over the child. Tracy closed her eyes and folded her hands, and Annie bowed her head.

Cathy prayed for her boys and for Steve out "in the wild," for their attitudes and their dispositions, and that they were still speaking to each other by the next morning. Then she thanked God for the blessing of the day spent with Tracy.

When they whispered "Amen," she smiled down at the child. "It's been fun spending time with you girls today."

"We could do that all the time, Mom," Annie said, "if you'd just take me shopping and act right."

Tracy giggled, and Cathy rolled her eyes.

"I wish Annie was my sister," the child said. "We'd have fun."

"Nah," Annie said. "We'd probably get tired of each other and fight like my brothers and I do." She grinned down at Tracy. "On the other hand, it might be pretty cool to have a sister."

"Now don't get carried away," Cathy said, sliding under the covers next to the child. "This is just one night. Steve and I are just friends."

"Yeah, Mom, just friends. Like Danny Botcho and I are just friends." She looked down at Tracy. "You should see him, Tracy. He's got eyes to die for."

"My daddy has eyes to die for," Tracy said, and giggled.

Cathy grinned. "No comment."

As Annie left the room and Tracy began to fall asleep, Cathy lay in bed, wondering if there really could be a future for the two families, or if it would all come to a crashing halt this very weekend.

CHAPTER
Fifty-Nine

By the time darkness settled over the area, Steve and the boys were exhausted. "You know something, guys?" Steve asked, leaning back against a stump and carving on a piece of wood. "I had fun today."

"It was pretty cool," Rick said.

Mark couldn't be so generous. "It made Mom happy."

Steve accepted that. "I like making her happy. I think your mom is about the coolest person I've ever met."

Rick chuckled. "Yeah, she's pretty cool, all right."

Steve grinned. He knew Cathy would love to have heard him say that. "You know, when I was a kid, I didn't appreciate my mom half as much as I do now. I used to think she was about the dumbest person in the world, and I would smart off to her with this scathing sarcasm, almost every time I opened my mouth."

"You?" Mark asked.

"Yep, and my mom would sometimes get tears in her eyes and fuss back at me and tell me that I didn't need to talk to her that way. And I would think, 'Who cares if I talk to her that way? She's my mom. That's what she's for.'"

In the firelight, he saw Rick and Mark shoot each other grins.

He kept carving, shaving away pieces of wood just for the sake of keeping his hands busy. "But then I had a roommate in college, and he didn't have a mom, hadn't had one since he was eight years old. She had died in a car accident, and his dad had raised him. At Thanksgiving and Christmas, I'd sometimes take him home with me, and he seemed so moved by the fact that I had a mother there cooking in the kitchen, making everything warm and nice, feeding us and pampering us. And I started to realize that my mom wasn't just this person put there to drive me crazy, or embarrass me, or wait on me hand and foot. I realized she was really a pretty neat person. What a blessing to have her."

There was silence for a moment. Finally, Rick said, "You know, Mom's a screamer and a yeller."

Steve grinned. "I know."

"You know she doesn't take a lot of guff from anybody," Mark said.

"Nobody but you."

"I don't give her that much guff."

"Buddy, you give her plenty."

Mark was quiet for a moment. "So what are you going to do? Marry her?"

"I don't know," Steve said, looking down at the piece of wood in his hand. "Maybe in time." He looked up at both boys. "What would you think about that?"

Rick didn't look too happy. "It sure would mess up the dynamics of our household."

Steve burst out laughing. "The dynamics of your household? What do you mean? Would I stop the yelling, the sarcasm, the volume?"

"You'd come in and start trying to change us," Rick said. "That's what always happens. I've seen it a million times." He sounded like a wise and bitter old man. "The mom gets married and the husband comes in and starts ordering people around."

"Do you see me ordering Tracy around?"

"No, but she's easy."

"Besides," Mark said, "we don't have room for two more people in our house, and you don't have room for four more in yours."

"You're right," Steve said, looking up at the dark sky. "Bad idea." For a moment, they were quiet, and he wondered if they were buying it. When he looked at them, they all started grinning.

Finally, he got serious. "I'm not going anywhere, guys. I hope you'll try to get used to me."

"How do you know she's the right person?" Rick asked. "Maybe there's somebody else out there who doesn't have kids who would love to be Tracy's mom. Somebody who could just move right into your house and there'd be no big deal and no adjustments."

"Sounds like a nice scenario." He shook his head and looked off into the night. "But there's something about your mom."

"Oh, brother." Mark stretched out on his stomach and kicked his feet in the air. "Where's your ex-wife, anyway?"

Steve's face sobered, and he went back to carving. "I'm not divorced. My wife died of cancer," he said, "a few years ago. Tracy's another one of those kids who's growing up without a mom."

The boys were both quiet for a moment. "So is that why you want to marry mine?" Mark asked. "So Tracy will have one?"

Steve grinned. "If that was the case, I'd just hire a good baby-sitter. I wouldn't pick a working mom with three teenaged kids. The thing is, your mom and I, we hit it off right away."

The boys were both quiet.

"But like I said, I'm not gonna do it until everybody's okay with it."

"So is that why you brought us out here, to start working on us?"

"Nope," he said. "Honestly, I just wanted to go camping. It's been a long time since I've had any guys to go mud biking with, and I don't think I've ever caught that many fish. It's a good time, guys. I'm glad you came."

Mark shrugged. "It wasn't terrible or anything."

That night, as Steve lay in his sleeping bag looking at the stars, he thanked God for the blessings of the day. Despite Mark's underwhelming comments about the day, Steve knew it had been a success.

CHAPTER
Sixty

Tory lay awake for most of Saturday night, which caused her to oversleep the next morning. The doorbell woke her up, and Brittany yelled from the living room, "Mommy, somebody's at the door!"

Tory sprang out of bed and saw that it was ten o'clock. It was too late to make it to church, she thought dismally. She pulled on her robe and stumbled to the front door, looking for Spencer all the way through the house.

Brittany had a box of cornflakes, and had laid the cereal out in rows on the coffee table.

"Britty, what are you doing?"

"Counting the cornflakes."

Tory moaned and grabbed the box away from her. "Where's your brother?"

"I don't know."

"What do you mean, you don't know? Where is he, Brittany?"

The doorbell rang again. "Maybe that's him," Brittany said.

Tory bolted for the door. "Spencer!" she shouted as she opened it.

"See? I told you she was asleep." Spencer was standing at the door next to David Dodd, Brenda's husband. The child was still in his Superman pajamas, complete with the cape.

"You looking for him?" David asked with a wry grin.

"Spencer!" She pushed her tousled hair back from her face and pulled the boy in. "David, where was he?"

"I found him climbing through the window into my work-shop," David said. "Fortunately, I happened to be in there at the time. He said he just wanted—"

"I just wanted to play with the tools," Spencer said. "That buzz saw is cool."

"The buzz saw? Spencer!" She jerked him. "You could have cut off an arm!"

"I'd still have another one," Spencer said.

She turned mortified eyes to her neighbor. "David, I am so sorry."

"Don't worry about it," he said. "If I hadn't been in there, he'd have never gotten in. I've started locking everything since the Mark incident."

"But the buzz saw? Oh, Spencer! What were you thinking?" But Spencer scooted past her and went to help Brittany count cornflakes.

She leaned against the door. "Thank you for bringing him back," she said. "I didn't sleep well last night. I finally got to sleep about five, and I guess I just didn't wake up."

He was quiet for a moment. "Brenda told me what's going on, Tory. Are you sure you're all right?"

"Yeah, I'm fine." Again, she finger-combed her hair. "I don't know what's gotten into me. I've got to do better."

"Don't beat yourself up," he said. "I'd oversleep, too, if I didn't get to sleep until five." He glanced back at his house, then turned back to her. "You know, Tory, I might be out of line here, but I wouldn't be against going to visit Barry if you thought it was a good idea."

Tory couldn't think. "I don't think there's anything anybody can say to him to reason with him. He just feels the way he does, and nobody's going to change that."

He shrugged. "Well, okay."

"Look, I appreciate you bringing him home. I'm sorry to be so negligent."

"Don't even think about it," David said. "No problem at all." He yelled past her into the house, "Spencer, you mind your mother, okay? You got me to answer to if you don't."

Spencer stood up and peered at him over the back of the couch. "Yes, sir."

Tory closed the door as David started back down the steps.

CHAPTER
Sixty-One

Barry lay on the made-up hotel bed, staring at the ceiling. Daylight flooded through the sheer curtains, making the room look even more dismal.

He hadn't slept last night. He had tossed and turned in the big bed, and several times had picked up the phone to call Tory. But anger always stopped him.

It was Sunday morning, and he missed being in church with his family. He missed the madness of trying to keep Spencer clean long enough to get him to his classroom, and the frenzy of finding just the right bow for Brittany's hair. He missed the hurried breakfast and the last-minute dash for something they forgot as they were pulling out of the driveway.

Was that all behind him?

His eyes filled with tears, and he wiped them away with his wrist. He didn't want to be a father without his children. He didn't want Tory to be like Cathy, a single mom doing the best she could. He didn't want to be like Cathy's ex-husband, letting time and distance dull the feelings he had for his children. He didn't want to call them once a week and have them sum up their lives in the word *fine*.

He got up and looked at that phone again, wondering if Tory was home or if she had gone on to church without him. He wondered what he would say if he called her. He couldn't apologize for talking to Linda Holland. He had done nothing wrong. And he couldn't suddenly make himself happy about the baby. He wasn't ready to let Tory call the shots on that.

Frustration overwhelmed him, and he fell back down. He couldn't call. The ball was in her court. She would have to do it.

When his pager began to beep, his heart jolted. Maybe it was Tory, he thought. Maybe she wanted to talk to him. He got up and grabbed the pager off of the dresser, and saw that the number wasn't one he recognized. Maybe Tory was in trouble, he thought. Maybe she was calling from another location. Maybe she was in the hospital . . .

Quickly, he dialed the number.

"Hello?"

It was a woman's voice, and it took him a moment to realize it was Linda. "Linda? Is that you?"

"Barry, you got my page."

"Yes. I thought it must be Tory."

"I just wanted to see if everything's all right. I know Tory overheard what we were saying the other day. She overreacted, didn't she?"

He dropped back on the bed. "You could say that."

"So what happened?"

He knew he shouldn't be telling her any of it. "Well, I'm in the Holiday Inn as we speak."

"Oh, no. She threw you out? Because of me?"

"Because of a lot of things." He didn't want to talk about it.

"Well, I'm coming over right now. I'll take you to lunch," she said.

"No." His voice was firm. "Don't come, Linda. I've already eaten." It was a lie, but he knew her presence would only complicate things.

"Well, okay. But Barry, I feel terrible about this. I want you to know that if you want to talk, I'm here."

He closed his eyes. "I appreciate it."

There was a long pause. "Are you mad at me, Barry?"

He frowned. "Mad at you? No, why?"

"Because I feel this tension in your voice. Like you're blaming me for this somehow."

"No," he said again. "I'm blaming Tory . . . and myself. Not you."

"Good," she said. "Because I really care about what you're going through."

He didn't know what to say to that. It felt good to know that someone cared, when he was lying here alone in a dark hotel room on a Sunday morning.

"Look, you call me if you decide you want to talk," she said softly. "I'll be right here, by the phone all day."

"Okay," he said.

"And can I call later? Just to check on you? Maybe we could have dinner."

"Sure, you can call," he said.

"All right."

When she had hung up, he dropped the phone back in its cradle and stared at it for a long moment. If he did have dinner with her, it would be because Tory had driven him to it, he thought. She couldn't expect him to stay in solitary confinement. He knew she wasn't.

He took a shower and got something out of a vending machine for lunch, and considered Linda's request to have dinner with him.

Then he kicked himself for even thinking about it. What was he doing? Tory had thrown him out because of her, and now he was considering having dinner with her? No, he thought. He couldn't. He would say no, and nip this in the bud. Then he realized that it was something he needed to do face-to-face. Maybe he should have dinner with her to tell her that he wasn't going to have any more intimate conversations with her. If his marriage was ruined, he didn't want it to be because of another woman.

By the time she called that afternoon, he'd had his fill of Nascar racing and ice skating on television, and had rehearsed his speech to Linda at least a dozen times in his mind. Then he went down to the lobby to meet her, so she wouldn't come up to his room.

As he waited, he couldn't help realizing that he was looking forward to a meal and some benign conversation. Even if he was ending things before they'd ever begun, it felt good to have someone to share a meal with today.

CHAPTER
Sixty-Two

David didn't know what had gotten into him as he stepped into the hotel. It wasn't like him to get involved in a family squabble. But this was Tory and Barry, and they had both done a lot to help when Joseph was in the hospital. As painful as this was going to be, he felt he owed it to them to take one shot at saving their marriage.

Besides, Spencer and Brittany needed their dad. Tory needed her husband. When he'd seen her at the door today, looking troubled and weary, he had known something had to be done.

Barry had paid him a visit in the hospital, to talk to him about another serious matter—David's faith, or lack of it. He had known that Barry had done it out of concern for him, and though it hadn't changed his mind, David hadn't held it against him. He hoped Barry would receive this visit in the same spirit.

He got off the elevator on the third floor and found 311, knocked on the door. To his disappointment, Barry wasn't there.

He checked his watch and wondered if Barry was down in the restaurant having dinner. His heart surged with pity for the man who had alienated himself from his own home. But then he remembered what Brenda had said about the other woman Barry had confided in and the late hours he'd been keeping. David started to get angry again.

He rode the elevator back down and walked across the lobby, found the restaurant, and peered in. He scanned the patrons. He didn't see Barry, and started to leave. But just before he did, he glimpsed a couple in the back corner of the restaurant, partially hidden behind a plant.

"Just one in your party, sir?" the hostess asked.

"No," he said, "I just came to meet somebody. I think I see him now."

The woman let him go on back, and David stepped between two tables to get a better view. It was, indeed, Barry, sitting at the table with an attractive woman who was leaning toward him in quiet conversation. David felt the heat coloring his face. For a moment, he considered turning around and going home. This was none of his business, after all, and he didn't want to be the one to catch Barry with the other woman. That was not what he had come here for.

Then he changed his mind and realized that Barry's family rested on this moment. Maybe the shame of being caught would turn things around.

Dreading this with all his heart, David slowly approached the table. Barry looked up. "David!"

The woman turned around.

"I thought I might find you here," David said quietly. "I took a chance."

Barry looked suddenly embarrassed. "Linda, this is my next-door neighbor, David Dodd. David, Linda Holland. She's one of my colleagues at work. She came to bring me some papers."

"On Sunday?" David asked.

Barry's ears began to redden, and the color flushed across his face. "We work hard," he said. "We have some projects that are going on and we had to get them done."

"I see," David said, but he didn't really see at all. There were no papers on the table.

The woman quickly got to her feet. "Well, since I don't have anything else," she said, "I guess I'll be getting on back now."

"Yeah," Barry said. "Thanks for coming."

"No problem," she said. "If you need anything else . . ."

Barry shot David a look that made him feel like an intruder. But he told himself that he wasn't. The woman was the intruder, and Barry was like a stray animal trying to find a place to rest.

As the woman hurried away, Barry pulled some cash out of his wallet and left it next to the check on the table. "Why don't we go back to my room?" he asked.

David nodded. "Yeah, that might be a good idea. I just want to talk to you."

Looking as if he'd rather be run over by a freight train, Barry led him up to his room.

David was relieved to find there was no evidence of Linda Holland in Barry's room. Maybe this hadn't gone too far yet. Maybe he had come just in time.

"So what do you want to talk about?" Barry asked.

David sat down on a chair facing Barry's bed and settled his elbows on his knees. Clasping his hands together, he looked down at the carpet. "What do you think I wanted to talk about?"

"Well, my marriage, obviously," Barry said, sitting down on the edge of the bed. "No offense, David, but this is really nobody's business. We've been having some problems for a while, and I've just had enough."

"Your wife is pregnant," David said.

Barry breathed a laugh. "You think I don't know that?"

David kept his eyes locked on Barry. "Earlier today I rescued your son from a buzz saw. He was crawling through the window of my workshop."

Barry looked stricken.

"Tory had a rough night, so she overslept and Spencer got away."

Barry swallowed. "Was he hurt?"

"Of course he wasn't hurt," David said. "Somebody would have contacted you if he had been. I would have called you. But the point is, he *could* have been. Your wife is not feeling well, and she's depressed, and you're not helping matters any."

"Hey, I'm feeling pretty down, myself."

David met his eyes. "So why are you sitting in a hotel huddled over a table with another woman?"

He breathed an exaggerated sigh. "You make it sound like we're involved with each other," he said. "I haven't done anything with her. I've just been *talking* to her. Sometimes a person *needs* somebody to talk to."

"I don't think I have to tell you that it's not appropriate for you to talk to another woman about problems with your wife."

Barry gave him a disbelieving look. "David, I don't need *you* lecturing to me about morality."

David's temper flashed. "If you want to talk immorality, who's the one closest to it here, Barry? I'm just minding my own business at home, rescuing your child from buzz saws while your wife tries to get through this pregnancy, and you're here in a hotel with another woman."

"I didn't have some kind of secret rendezvous with her," Barry said. "I went down there to meet her because I knew it wasn't right to have her in my room!"

"How do you think these things start?" David asked.

Barry threw up his hands. "I don't know. Why don't you tell me? You seem to be real experienced."

David got up and slid his hands in his pockets, as if to keep them from swinging at Barry. "For the record, I'm *not* speaking from experience. But I've seen it happen before. They start out with friendship, with sharing their problems, and before you know it, you're telling her things that are none of her business. When Brenda told me last night what was going on with the two of you, that Tory had caught you with another woman, and that you wanted to abort your own child—"

"Wait a minute!" Barry shouted. "Stop right there! Tory had no business telling Brenda any of that stuff, either. It's no different than my confiding in Linda."

"It's a lot different," David threw back. "Tory confided in a close friend and neighbor who happened to be of the same sex. You confided in a woman who Tory considers a threat."

"I have not done anything wrong," Barry said.

"Well, then, are you going to tell Tory that you had dinner with this woman tonight?"

"I don't see any reason to tell Tory anything. She's not real interested in what I do right now."

"Did you know that your baby had moved? Did you know that was why she came to the office the other day? She was hoping you'd want to feel the baby kick, and that you'd understand it's a real human being she's carrying."

"You don't have a clue what you're talking about," Barry said through his teeth. "Have you ever had to make these decisions that I'm having to make? Have you ever had a retarded child? I don't want to trap my child in a life that will make her miserable. A human being needs to be able to contribute something. There's nothing worse in this world than a child who grows up trapped because her life is worthless."

"Whose life is worthless?" David asked. "I can't imagine a child *anywhere* whose life is worthless."

"I have a brother!" Barry bit out.

"I know all about your brother," David said. "I know how he sits there staring into space day after day. But our value doesn't come from being good or productive or leaving something behind. You ought to know that." He stepped across the room and met Barry face-to-face. "I can't believe I just fought tooth and nail for my own child's life, and now you're willing to give yours up just because you can't imagine that in twenty years she might contribute something. What about all the babies who die at three and four months old? They don't contribute anything, but they're precious to their parents. Life is a gift, man! It has nothing to do with what we can give back. It's just a gift, Barry. You've got to see it as that."

"I don't need this lecture from you," Barry said. "Talking to me about gifts when you don't even believe in the God who *gives* the gifts."

"Well, apparently neither do you!"

Barry stared at him with fire in his eyes. "You've got a lot of nerve coming here." He headed to the door and opened it. "I think you should go."

David slid his hands into his pockets and nodded. Quietly, he left the room and headed to the elevator. The room door closed hard behind him, but in a second, it opened again.

"David!"

David turned back, and Barry stepped out into the hall. "Are you going to tell Tory that Linda was here?"

The elevator door opened, and David caught the door and held it for a moment. "No," he said finally. "You are."

Barry slammed his fist into his other hand. "I don't have anything to tell her."

David shrugged. "Just tell her you're sorry, that you're coming home, that you're ready to be a father to all three of your children. It's easy, man. All it takes is a little bit of courage. You remember how to be a man, don't you?" Then he got on the elevator and let the doors close behind him.

CHAPTER
Sixty-Three

Barry went back into his room and locked the door behind him. He went to the window and sat down in the chair beside it, and stared out into the parking lot below. He couldn't remember ever feeling as low as he felt right now. Having an unbeliever come to him preaching morality was more than he could stand. He couldn't believe he had given David reason to do that.

You must be so disgusted with me, Lord.

He opened the drawer on the telephone table and found the Bible the Gideons had put there. As if it held the salve he needed for his chafed conscience, he opened it. As always, it fell open to the Psalms, and he began to read, without any delusion that the passage had opened there for him . . . until he came to a passage in Psalm 103 that crushed his heart.

"He will not always accuse, nor will he harbor his anger forever; he does not treat us as our sins deserve or repay us according to our iniquities. For as high as the heavens are above the earth, so great is his love for those who fear him; as far as the east is from the west, so far has he removed our transgressions from us. As a father has compassion on his children, so the LORD has compassion on those who fear him; for he knows how we are formed, he remembers that we are dust."

The reality that God knew him—knew his failings and short-comings, his temptations and his mistakes—brought Barry to tears. Maybe God had sent David to set him straight. Maybe it was because Barry *was* an unbeliever that God had sent him. Maybe he knew how vital his message would be, the message Barry should have believed, when brought by someone who had no faith.

He closed his eyes and thought back over David's words about the baby.

Life is a gift, man! It has nothing to do with what we can give back.

That was exactly the message of grace, the message that Jesus Christ's death on the cross had preached, that no one on earth was worthy of the gifts that God gave. But he had loved us enough to give them anyway.

Barry had almost forgotten, and now, here he was, letting someone who didn't have a clue about the grace of Jesus Christ preach to him about grace in his own baby's life.

His eyes filled with tears. He leaned his head back on the chair and thought of Nathan sitting in the backyard, whistling a tune over and over and over until he heard something new.

But he loved his brother. And when he tried to picture life without Nathan, he couldn't. He knew many, many things would have been different in his life without Nathan. Some would have been better, but some worse. Nathan had always been an anchor in his life, a stable, constant, never-changing element that kept his family what it was.

He wiped the tears from his eyes and remembered back to when he was six years old and his mother had met him in the front yard as he walked home from the first day of school. She'd had tears in her eyes when he approached, carrying his new Flintstone lunch box and a Bullwinkle satchel.

"What's the matter, Mama?" he had asked.

She had laughed then, and wiped her tears away as she leaned down to hug him. "I was just thinking what a great gift it was watching you walk home from school today."

He had been confused. "It's no big deal, Mama. Everybody does it."

She shook her head. "No, honey, not everybody. Never forget that."

That had drifted deep into his subconscious where it had nested and flourished, and he knew that much of his life had been formed around that thought, that not everyone had the gifts he had. The lack of those simple gifts was an undeserved curse. Or was it? Was the whistling a gift? Or the consistency in Nathan's life? Had those been Nathan's offering?

It was hard to imagine that those things constituted a contribution to the world, yet he knew David was right. If God measured him against mathematicians and child prodigies, where would he wind up in the ranking? Maybe he'd be even more different from them than Nathan was from him. Maybe that's what God wanted him to know.

As a father has compassion on his children, so the LORD *has compassion on those who fear him; for he knows how we are formed, he remembers that we are dust.*

Had he been uncompassionate toward his own child? Had he turned his back on her, as Tory claimed? If God could look upon Barry without disgust, how could Barry hold such a high standard for his baby? God knew what this baby was like, how she was formed, what she was made of. God knew why.

Overcome with remorse, Barry got out of his chair and fell to his knees beside the window, and wept and prayed for forgiveness, for letting his life get so turned around and his focus get ripped off of Christ. He had abandoned Tory when she needed him most. He had betrayed her verbally and emotionally, and if she hadn't brought this to a crisis, had probably been heading toward physical betrayal as well.

He dropped his head on the bed, unable to believe he had drifted so far from being the strong family man that he had been just a few months earlier, so far that an unbeliever had come to straighten him out.

He wept out his broken heart to God, pleading and begging for forgiveness for the sin of giving up, of turning away, of directing his own path.

By the time he'd finished praying, he'd resolved to accept the baby that Tory was carrying, though he couldn't yet make himself feel good about it. God had a long way to go with him, he thought, but at least he was pointed in the right direction now. Still feeling the heaviness of the grief driving him, he packed his suitcase with all the things Tory had so angrily thrown in, then checked out of the hotel and headed home.

CHAPTER
Sixty-Four

Tory had gotten the kids to bed early and lay on her own bed, staring at the ceiling. It was too early to go to bed herself, but she couldn't manage to do anything else. She wondered what Barry was doing, if he was eating right and getting enough sleep in his hotel room. She wondered if Linda Holland was keeping him company. She started to cry again.

When she heard the door to the house close, she jumped upright. Someone was in her house!

She got off the bed and grabbed a vase from her bed table, then backed into the closet and tried to see up the hall. She heard footsteps coming and realized that whoever was in the house could go for the children first. Terrified, she forced herself to leave the closet, the vase held high over her head.

Barry was walking toward her. She caught her breath and dropped the vase. It crashed on the hardwood floor.

Barry froze. "Don't move," he said. "You're barefoot."

She stood in place, looking at the broken glass around her. "You scared me," she sobbed.

"I know," he told her. "I should have called or something. Here. Don't move." He swept the glass away with his shoe, then picked her up like a bride and carried her to the bed.

She wept from relief in the wake of panic. "Just stay here," he said, "and I'll clean it up in case the kids wake up." He hurried to the laundry room and got a broom and dustpan. In seconds, he was back, sweeping up the broken glass.

She sat up, wiping her face and wondering why he was home. "What are you doing here?" she asked.

Barry sat down next to her on the edge of the bed. "I had a visit from David tonight."

"Really?"

"Yeah," he said. "He seems to think I have some things to apologize for."

Tory thought of giving him a list, just in case he wasn't sure, but she decided to let him talk. He looked down at her stomach with pain on his face, then reached out and laid his hand on it. The touch spoke volumes.

"David had a message for me today," he said quietly. "It was about how life is precious and it doesn't have anything at all to do with what we contribute. He reminded me of Joseph and how hard everybody was fighting for his life just a few weeks ago."

A tear rolled down her face.

"And then I had a good prayer time," he said, "and I realized that he was right. His message was Jesus, even though he didn't know it, and Jesus doesn't look at people according to how smart or how perfect they are. Thank goodness." His mouth twitched at the corners as he tried to keep his voice level.

"And there was another thing that David told me."

"What?" Tory asked.

"It was about Linda." Tory felt her defenses rising again. She didn't want to hear what she was about to hear. She closed her eyes and dropped back to her pillow.

"Tory, look at me." She met his eyes, afraid of what she might see. "I can promise you that nothing ever happened with Linda. Nothing like you think, anyway. She showed up at the hotel tonight, but I didn't let her come to my room. I met her in the restaurant, and David found us there."

She closed her eyes and began to sob harder, and turned to her side, away from him.

"It was wrong, Tory. I was wrong to confide in her like I did. I don't have any business sharing confidences like that with another woman."

"Why'd you do it?" she demanded.

"I don't know. She was there, it seemed like, from the very beginning. She was noticing my moods, showing up when I was down. She didn't have an agenda. Just wanted to listen." Tory shot him a disbelieving look over her shoulder. "At least, that's what I thought. But then today, I think I realized that she had other plans."

"Oh, Barry!" She sucked in a sob, and he turned her back over to face him.

"Tory, she never meant anything to me. And I can promise you that it won't happen again."

"What are you going to do about it?" she asked. "She works there with you every day."

"We don't work that closely together," he said. "Only once in a while do we even cross paths. I'll just tell her that I can't have any more heartfelt conversations, that my wife and I have worked things out. I'll ask to work with a different marketing team." He touched her face and gently urged her to look at him again. "Please, trust me. Forgive me."

For a moment, Tory lay there, searching her mind for an answer. How could she forgive him for all that had happened? All the disappointment, the betrayal, the heartache? She didn't have that in her.

But I have it, she felt God's Spirit say. *Let me do it.* Slowly, Tory sat up, and pulled Barry's hand back to her stomach. "You're not going to pressure me to get an abortion anymore?"

"No," he said. "I won't."

Her words came out on an uncertain whisper. "Barry, are you serious?"

For a moment he only looked at her, and she saw a million emotions pass over his face. "I don't want a retarded child," he said. "I can't stand the thought. It just breaks my heart that one of our children will have to suffer that way. I don't know when or if I'll ever be able to be happy about this, Tory. Maybe by the time the baby comes. I don't know. But just be patient with me. I need some time."

It was exactly what Sylvia had told her, exactly the wisdom that she had avoided. Time was always the last thing she had to give. But she realized now that she had no more choice than Barry had about the baby being born into this family.

"You need to know that I'm going to keep praying for a miracle," Barry said, "that maybe there was a mistake, that the lab tests were wrong. I have to keep praying for that miracle."

Suddenly, the baby fluttered. Barry caught his breath. "Was that . . . ?"

"Yes," she said, finally able to smile again. "It was the baby saying, 'Hello, Daddy.'"

He frowned and looked down at his hand covering her stomach, concentrating. The baby fluttered again. Tears began to roll down his face. "Seems perfectly normal, doesn't she?"

She reached up and wiped his tears. "Kicks just like any other baby. Please smile about her," she whispered. "She deserves so much more than tears and anger."

"I'm trying," Barry said. "I really am." His voice broke off, and he swallowed. "I know I've destroyed a lot in you in the last few weeks, a lot of your respect and admiration and everything else. Maybe that's part of why I was talking to Linda, because she was looking at me like you used to, admiring me."

Tory didn't know how to answer that. "Be patient with me, too," she said. "A lot of damage has been done. I forgive you and I'm glad you're home, but I just need some time, too."

He nodded. "Do you want me to sleep in the basement?"

"No. The bed's too big for just one person."

He lowered his ear to her stomach, his eyes closed. He kept his ear pressed against the roundness, as if he could hear his baby's voice. She thought of stroking his hair, offering him comfort, but she couldn't make herself do it.

Finally, he raised up. "I'll go get my suitcase."

As he headed back out to the car, Tory fell back on the bed, so thankful that he was home. But she wished with all her heart that he had been able to bring a salve to heal her wounded heart and restore the respect she had lost along the way.

CHAPTER
Sixty-Five

Barry managed to put off telling his mother about the pregnancy until Christmas Day. She had invited them to come for Christmas dinner after the children opened their presents. Tory knew that he would have put the announcement off indefinitely, if she hadn't insisted on going. At first, it had disturbed and angered her again, but then she realized he was trying to protect his mother from any grief. She would hurt to learn that Tory and Barry were facing the same heartache she had once faced, and her son wanted to spare her.

It was difficult for her to hide her protruding belly when she went through the door, but she managed to cover up with her children's coats. The kids ran into the house and threw their arms around their grandma, then hurried to the playroom she kept set up just for them. It was full of the toys that Barry had as a child and new things Betty had picked up along the way.

Betty hugged her son as if she hadn't seen him in years. "It's good to see you two," she said. "You're just such strangers."

"Mom, I'm sorry about Thanksgiving."

"You've already apologized for that," she said, waving him off. "We got over it." She always spoke in the plural, as if Nathan shared her feelings.

Tory looked at Barry as Betty reached out to hug her. They had agreed to tell her the moment they arrived, so that Tory wouldn't have to keep hiding her stomach. They hadn't even been sure that the children wouldn't shout out the news as soon as they came inside.

Barry caught her look, and drew in a deep breath. "Mom, we need to talk to you. Would you mind sitting down?"

"Well, sure." She sat down in a chair and let Barry and Tory have the couch. "What is it?"

Tory looked at Barry, offering him a chance to go on. "Mom, we've had a rough couple of months, and that's why we didn't come Thanksgiving. The truth is, Tory and I weren't getting along real well."

She looked from Barry to Tory, then back again. "Well, I hope everything's all right now," she said.

"It's better." Barry looked down at the floor. "There's something that we've kind of been holding back from you."

"I knew it," she said. "What is it?"

He couldn't look up at her. "Tory and I are going to have another baby."

A smile stole across her face, and she threw her hand over her mouth. "Well, for heaven's sake. Why didn't you tell me? What's the big secret? I had terrible thoughts going through my mind." She saw their serious expressions, and her joy floated down.

"It's . . . the baby," Tory said.

Betty's face fell. She had been through this herself. She knew the shock and the grief and the anger and despair. She and her husband had probably gone through many of the same things Tory and Barry had.

"Mom, there's something wrong with the baby."

Her eyebrows came up. "What is it?"

"Down's Syndrome," Tory said.

She nodded as her eyes began to mist over. "When did you find out?"

"A few weeks ago," Tory said. "Barry didn't want to tell you."

She shot a stricken look to her son. "Why not, Barry?"

He cleared his throat and looked down at his hands. "Because I didn't know how to take it, Mom. The truth is, I wasn't sure about the wisdom of bringing a baby into the world in this condition."

Her eyes softened at once. "I wish you'd told me," she said. She got up and went across the room to her son, sat next to him on the couch, and hugged him with all her might. He clung to her as his own eyes filled with tears. "I'm so sorry. I can't *tell* you how sorry I am." Then she moved over to Tory and embraced her with all her might. "Oh, you poor thing. Your heart must have broken."

"It did, but I'm okay now."

"You *should* be okay," his mother said, pulling back. "Children with Down's Syndrome can usually walk. Most of them can talk. They can learn things. They can smile. Compared to my Nathan, your baby will be incredibly gifted."

Tory realized that everything was relative.

"Have you called the American Association for Retarded Children?" Betty asked. "Has anybody given you the number for their support group?"

"A support group? Well, no."

"I didn't know you belonged to a support group," Barry said.

His mother smiled and used her apron to dab at her tears. "Well, I haven't needed them in a number of years, but it helped me a lot when I first had Nathan. Sometimes I thought I was going to die from my broken heart. We didn't know ahead of time, you know, didn't know until Nathan was several months old that things weren't right with him. And then I found other parents who had children like him, and it helped so much. It's what got me through."

Barry's brows drew together. "Mom, I thought you'd always accepted it. It always seemed like a joy to you, and I've been feeling so guilty because I haven't been able to feel that."

"It'll come in time," she said. "Trust me. It will. What a blessing to know in advance. By the time the baby comes, you'll have gotten over the shock."

Tory moved the coats aside and showed her mother-in-law her stomach. "It's a girl," she said with a smile.

"A girl!" Betty touched her stomach, and tears came to her eyes again. "A new grand-baby. Oh, I can hardly wait!"

After they had shared Christmas dinner and exchanged gifts, the children begged to look at the scrapbooks of Barry when he was a little boy, something they always did when they came to visit his mother. Tory knew where Betty kept the scrapbooks, and she got them out and sat between the children on the couch. Barry had disappeared into the garden, and she assumed he was sitting with Nathan, probably contemplating his wasted life. She hoped that Nathan's subconscious wasn't picking up on the condemnation from his brother.

"I found some more pictures," Betty said, coming out of the bedroom. "The other day I was going through some of Stanley's things and I ran across this scrapbook that Barry kept when he was a boy."

Tory looked up, surprised. She'd thought she'd seen everything of Barry's, but now she felt as if she'd stumbled on a new treasure. She set down the photo album they had seen so many times, and took the new scrapbook. It was crumbling at the edges, and some of the Scotch tape he had used for the pictures had come loose. Pictures lay loose between the pages.

She opened it and saw a picture of Barry in a children's orchestra, holding his violin. She didn't know he had ever played. "That's Daddy," she said.

"Who's that?" Spencer asked, pointing to one of the kids beside Barry.

"I don't know," Tory said. "Probably just a boy in his class."

"Who's that?" Brittany asked, pointing to a girl.

"Just a girl in his class, Brittany. I don't know these people."

"Is this Daddy?" Brittany asked, pulling a picture out.

Tory studied it. "Yeah, Daddy and Nathan." She saw the much younger-looking Nathan sitting in his wheelchair as Barry horsed around next to him. She turned the page and saw a picture of Barry jumping from the high dive at the YMCA, and another one of him coming up out of the water. She saw a baptismal certificate and his first Bible memorization ribbon. She kept turning, fascinated at the memorabilia from Barry's past, at all the signs and clues that he had once been a child, though it was hard for her to imagine.

She came to several pages folded up and stashed between pictures and opened them up. "What's this?" she asked his mother. "Looks like a report or a paper."

"Yep, he wrote that in the seventh grade," Betty said. "You should read it. It's about Nathan."

Tory surrendered the scrapbook to her children and their grandmother, and sat back quietly to read the story that her husband had written about his brother.

It was crudely written, by no means a work of art, but it was the story of a boy named James who had a retarded brother. The work had a touch of science fiction. It started with a newspaper report, claiming that technology had been invented whereby parts of other people's brains could be transferred to retarded children. James, the character, decided that he would give half of his brain to his brother. But the doctor pointed out that, in order to do this and make his brother normal, he would lose half of his own intelligence. The doctor told him to think it over.

She followed the story as the boy walked home, thinking over his plight, trying to decide if it was worth it for him to stop making straight A's in school, to stop being one of the smartest kids in the class, to stop outshining his brother in so many ways. Instead, he tried to picture what it would be like if his brother was more like him . . . and he was more like his brother . . . If there was some kind of middle ground between the two. Finally, he made the decision. He would gladly give up his intellect to make his brother normal.

It was not meant to be a tear-jerking story, or even one that gripped the emotions. It was written matter-of-factly by a boy who desperately wanted his brother to have a better life. But she found herself crying at the end, realizing that this came from a child who loved his brother, not one who rued the day he had been born.

CHAPTER
Sixty-Six

While Tory and the children were poring over his scrapbook and his old pictures, Barry went outside to sit with Nathan. It was getting cool, and his mother had put a sweater on his brother. She had buttoned it all the way to the neck, and Barry realized that it might be too tight at his throat.

"She's got you bundled up here, doesn't she, Nathan?" He unbuttoned the top two buttons, giving Nathan some relief. "So did you get everything you wanted for Christmas?"

Nathan was whistling "Silver Bells," the last song playing on the tape his mother had put on during dinner. He had sat at the table with them, his wheelchair pulled up to a plate, complete with a place setting she knew he wouldn't use. He had stared at a place on the wall and whistled along with the tape.

Now, Barry pulled a chair up next to his brother and sat down. He patted his arm. "It's good to see you, man." He realized the peace he felt when he was sitting next to his brother.

There was no pressure, no need to be clever or funny. With Nathan, he had always been able to be himself, exactly as he was. Nothing more, nothing less.

"Remember how we used to play?" Barry asked. He pictured his brother answering. He always had, though Nathan just stared straight ahead. Instead of reminding Nathan of the game they used to play, he started whistling the tune to "Away in a Manger." In just a couple of beats, Nathan had changed tunes and was whistling along with him. They whistled several verses of the same song, and finally Barry changed the tune to "We Three Kings." Nathan switched gears again.

He could hear the energy and the vibrancy in Nathan's whistle, could almost sense an invisible smile carrying out over the notes as Barry whistled with him. It was the only thing the two brothers had ever been able to do together, yet there had been times when it had been enough.

He changed the tune to "Chestnuts Roasting on an Open Fire," and Nathan picked up the tune again. Barry's eyes grinned as he whistled with his brother in perfect unison.

When Tory finished reading the story, she went looking for her husband. She found him in the prayer garden with Nathan. Through the window, she saw them sitting side by side, and wondered why Barry had been out there so long.

Quietly she opened the back door and stepped out onto the patio. She wasn't surprised to hear the whistling, but this time it wasn't just Nathan. Barry was whistling, too, in perfect unison with his brother, so precisely and perfectly, that one might have thought they had rehearsed for many years.

Stricken, she realized they probably had.

She stood just outside the door, not willing to disturb them, listening to the moving sound as tears came to her eyes. Then Barry turned and winked at her as he whistled, and nodded for her to come closer.

She stepped slowly up to him, and he quickly changed the tune to "Jingle Bells." Nathan was quick to follow.

Barry started laughing at the look on her face, and finally stopped whistling. Nathan kept going. "It's a game we used to play," he said. "No matter what I ever changed the tune to, Nathan could whistle it all the way through."

"He'd whistle with you?" she asked.

"Sure," Barry said. "In perfect rhythm. If I slow the tempo, he slows down, too. It's the only way I've ever been able to communicate with him."

She studied her brother-in-law. "Fascinating," she whispered.

"There's a lot about Nathan that's fascinating. When I get to heaven, the first questions I'm going to ask will have to do with Nathan."

"Maybe you won't have to ask," she said with a smile. "If he beats you there, he can tell you everything himself."

Barry leaned forward, looking his brother in the face. The whistled tune of "Jingle Bells" sounded as festive as any tape she'd heard that day. "Maybe that's what it's about," he said, his face sobering.

"What?" she asked.

"Heaven," he said. "Maybe even if there isn't a contribution here, maybe there's something later. Maybe life on this earth is nothing more than a blip in God's eternity. Maybe in heaven we'll hardly even remember that Nathan wasn't perfect here. Maybe he'll have a special job, and contribute more than you and I ever dreamed."

She thought that over as Barry got up and got her a chair. Barry started whistling "Silent Night," and Nathan changed songs.

Tory sat down. "I found this," she said, handing Barry the short story. "It was in an old scrapbook."

He took it from her hands and unfolded it. He began to laugh. "Oh, no, that awful story I wrote about switching brains."

"You gave him half of yours," she said. "Half your intelligence so he could be normal."

He chuckled. "It was a nice thought," he said. "Too bad there's never been the technology."

She looked down at the yellowed pages, and more than she'd ever known anything in her life, she knew that if the technology *had* been developed, Barry would have easily given his brain to his brother. Like the whistling, this knowledge changed things somehow.

She watched as he moved his chair in front of Nathan and pressed his forehead against his, trying to get him to look him in the eye. Nathan still seemed vacant, but he kept whistling. Barry started "Oh, Holy Night," and Nathan switched again.

As the two men whistled, face-to-face, Tory thought it was the most beautiful sound she had ever heard. She felt that admiration, that lost respect, seeping back into her heart, and she began to understand a little of what Barry had experienced earlier. Could it be that it hadn't been a lack of love for his child that had prompted his decisions? Could it be that his ideas, though misguided, were really prompted by lifelong grief over his own brother's plight?

Later that night when the children had fallen asleep on the floor in front of the television, the adults went back out to the prayer garden. Betty sat on the swing facing them. "Now that the shock is gone," she said, "and I've gotten used to seeing Tory pregnant today, why don't we talk about this some more?"

Barry sobered and looked out across the lawn. "Mom, I love you and I love Nathan, and I don't want to hurt you for anything in the world. And I know it's wrong. But I've had a real hard time picturing us having a baby who would never contribute anything."

"Oh, but everybody contributes something," Betty said.

"What could Nathan possibly contribute?" he asked. "I mean, I know that I feel good when I'm around him. And I know that he's been an anchor for you, and I know that you've loved him and cared for him all these years. But I can't help thinking that he's trapped in there somewhere, and he can't get out. And he can't do any of the things he might have had the potential to do, if something hadn't gone terribly wrong."

His mother got to her feet slowly, dusted off the back of her pants, and reached for her son's hand. "Come with me, Barry. There's somebody I want you to meet."

"Who, Mom?" he asked, getting up.

She looked down at Tory. "Would you keep an eye on Nathan for me, Tory? Barry and I are going to go next door for a second."

"Next door?" he asked. "Why?"

"I told you," she said. "There's somebody over there I want you to meet."

She walked him out the front door, then hooked her arm through his and led him to the front door of the neighbor next door. The house was lit up and the porch light was on, almost as if they were expected. His mother knocked on the door. "Millie, are you there?"

A little, decrepit old woman came to the door in her robe. She opened it and peered out with kind eyes. "Come in! Come in! What a joy! Merry Christmas."

"Merry Christmas to you," Betty said, hugging the woman. "Millie, I want you to meet my son, Barry."

"What a wonderful young man," the woman said, shaking his hand. "I've been out on my patio listening to you and your brother whistle."

He lifted his eyebrows. "You could hear us over here?"

"Of course," she said. "It's one of my favorite things. I listen to Nathan all the time. Whenever I'm lonely I go sit out on my back patio. It's been a real treat hearing all those Christmas tunes."

Barry looked at his mother. "I had no idea anyone else could hear. I'm really sorry."

"No, no. Don't apologize. Please sit down," she said, and she pulled them in and led them to an old Victorian couch in a parlor like something right out of the twenties.

Betty sat next to the old woman. "Millie, I want you to do me a favor and tell Barry how you came to know the Lord."

The woman threw her arthritic hands into the air. "What a wonderful story," she said. "Your mother hasn't told you?"

He glanced at his mother, wondering what she was up to. "I haven't seen her much in the last few months," he said.

"He hasn't heard," Betty told her.

Millie's eyes glowed with joy, and he could tell that whatever the story was, it meant a lot to her. "Well, you may not know this, but my dear husband of sixty years passed away last July. I thought I would just die."

Barry leaned forward. "I'm so sorry. Then this was your first Christmas without him?"

The woman nodded, but the look on her face was anything but grief-stricken. "I had a very hard time. Mourned for months, and one night I just got to the point that I wanted to die. I had some sleeping pills that had belonged to Samuel, and I gathered them all up and figured out that it was probably enough to end it all peacefully."

His mouth came open. "You were going to kill yourself?"

Tears came to her big eyes. "And I decided that I didn't want my children to find me in the house, because I wanted them to feel free to come live here if they ever wanted, and I didn't want it to have that stigma. So I took the pills and I got a big glass of iced tea and I went out back on the patio. I started rocking and drinking my tea and considering those pills."

Barry was riveted. He kept his eyes locked on the woman.

"And then I heard the whistling."

"Nathan's whistling?"

"Yes. It was a Sunday, and your mother had taken him to church earlier. He was whistling 'In the Garden.'" She smiled and looked at Betty, her bright eyes dancing. Then she began to sing. "And he walks with me and he talks with me, and he tells me I am his own. And the joy we share, as we tarry there, none other has ever known." She smiled. "I knew the song when I was a little girl, but I had forgotten. You see, I hadn't been to church in a very long time, and as Nathan whistled that song, I started thinking that before I took those pills, I should try just once going back to church, to see if I could get rid of that miserable loneliness. That night was the first time I went back to church in twenty years."

Barry's eyes widened. "You're kidding me."

"Oh, no. I wouldn't kid about a thing like this." She clapped her gnarled hands together. "And I found such warmth there. There were people my age and they invited me to sing in the senior adult choir, and they made me a soloist." She threw her hands over her heart in a flourish. "Can you imagine? They showed me true, genuine love. Within a week, I had accepted Christ, and my whole life changed." Beaming, she clapped her hands as if she couldn't believe her fortune. "And then we started traveling and we went to Branson, and oh, I just had a glorious time. And my life has been full and busy ever since. Why, even today, this first Christmas without Samuel, I was too busy to get down. Some of us worked at the soup kitchen downtown, and we gave out food to the poor. It was just such a blessing."

"You see," Betty said to Barry, "you think your brother hasn't contributed anything, that he doesn't have a purpose. But you're wrong."

"I led three people to Christ today at that soup kitchen," the woman said. "Now don't you see that that's Nathan's fruit, too? If God hadn't used his whistling to draw my heart to him, then I could have never led anyone else's heart."

Barry was stunned. In Nathan's seemingly unproductive life, he had probably borne more fruit than Barry ever had. It was just what he needed to hear, the best Christmas present he could have had. He thanked Millie and hugged her.

When he had finished crying with his mother and thanking her for what she had shown him, he walked back out into the prayer garden where Tory was sitting in the rocking chair, soaking in the same peace that Nathan had given him all those years. Tory needed it, he thought. She'd had a rough few months. She hadn't had much time to rest her emotions or her fears, but now she was leaning back, her eyes closed, as she rocked next to Nathan's wheelchair. As he got closer, he saw that her hand was on Nathan's arm. He didn't think he had ever seen her touch him before.

Tory opened her eyes as Barry sat down on the other side of Nathan, pulled his chair up, and leaned in, pressing his forehead against his brother's face. He wondered if, on some level, Nathan could tell he'd been crying. "You're quite a guy, aren't you, Nathan? You have secrets."

Nathan just kept whistling. Barry began to sing. "And he walks with me and he talks with me." Nathan changed his tune and picked up "In the Garden."

He felt Tory watching him cry with his head pressed against his brother's forehead. "Tory, he's probably responsible— directly or indirectly—for more people coming to Christ than I've ever been. Haven't you, Nathan? We're going to get to heaven and you'll have those crowns lined up, and I'll have some shrunken little baseball cap."

He laughed softly through his tears, and started singing along with his brother again.

CHAPTER
Sixty-Seven

On the way home, as the children slept in the backseat, Barry reached across the seat to hold Tory's hand. She unhooked her seat belt and scooted across to the middle of the seat. The gesture moved him to tears. It had been so long since she had been affectionate with him. He grabbed the middle belt, hooked it over her lap, then pulled her closer. She rested her head on his shoulder. It felt like old times, when she had admired and respected and loved him, when she had looked up to him as her protector. Now he felt like her protector again.

His tears rolled freely with the thought of the grace even she had given him, and unable to see through his tears, he pulled over to the side of the road. She looked expectantly up at him. He put his hand on her stomach again and felt the baby move, and realized that all through the day she had been feeling that evidence of the live baby inside of her, moving and bucking and flipping, reminding her that even though she wasn't whole or perfect, she was still a child.

He pressed his head against hers, as he had done with Nathan, and she wiped his tears. "Can you ever forgive me for the last few months?" he asked.

"I've forgiven you. And the baby forgives you. You were wrong, but I think I understand why you were wrong."

He pulled her into his arms. "Thank you for being the kind of mother who would fight to protect your baby," he whispered. "I'm proud of you. Very, very proud. A year ago, I don't know if you would have fought this hard, but I guess that's God's timing, isn't it?"

She nodded, unable to speak.

"And if it takes the rest of my life, I'm going to restore your faith and respect in me."

"It's not going to take that long," she whispered.

"How long, then?"

She smiled. "It happened a couple of hours ago," she said, "when I read that story you had written. When I heard you and Nathan whistling. When I watched you talking to him."

He tried to stop his tears. "I want the very best for our baby," he said, "just like I wanted it for Nathan. I can't stand not to have the best for them."

"But we have to let God decide what's best."

"I know," he said. "And tonight, he showed me that I can trust him with my child. He has things under control."

CHAPTER
Sixty-Eight

Back on Cedar Circle, Cathy and Steve finally found themselves alone after a hectic Christmas Day with all four children, since their father had given up his time with them so he could go skiing for the holidays. Annie had gone out with her boyfriend, and Rick had agreed to work a holiday shift at the grocery store. Tracy had gone to stay with her maternal grandparents.

That had left only Mark at home, until Brenda had come over and invited him to spend the night with Daniel.

"Yeah," Mark said on a laugh. "Like you really want to spend extra time with me."

Brenda and Mark hadn't had any major incidents since the fire, and Cathy cautiously suspected that things had improved.

"Well, I haven't seen you in a week," Brenda said. "I don't want your brain to stagnate during the holidays."

"So what are we gonna do? Read poetry?"

"No, I rented your favorite movie about that kid with the BB gun."

"*A Christmas Story?* Oh, Mom, can I? I love that flick, and I haven't gotten to watch TV in weeks."

Cathy knew the invitation was designed to give Steve and her time alone. "Brenda, are you sure?"

"Yes," she insisted. "Daniel got a new computer game he wants to show him, too."

"You promise you won't make me do history or anything?" Mark asked, pulling his shoes on.

"On Christmas?" Cathy asked. "Come on, Mark."

"Hey, Mom, she's tricky. She had us at the grocery store figuring out price-per-ounce in our heads the other day while we were getting stuff to make gingerbread houses. It took me and Daniel three aisles to figure out it was school."

"Daniel and me," Brenda corrected. "I won't trick you into anything tonight. I promise."

Cathy packed Mark an overnight bag, then tried to blink back her emotion as he and Brenda left the house together. Cathy watched through the screen door as they crossed the street.

Steve put his arms around her. "Hey, why the tears?"

"Did you see that?" she asked. "They like each other now. They're voluntarily spending extra time together."

"It's all those prayers," he said. He pulled her to her couch and sat down, still holding her. She felt a greater sense of well-being than she had felt in years.

"So are you finally ready to exchange presents now that all the chaos is behind us?" she asked him.

"I guess so," he said. "Yeah, I think it's time."

She got up, leaned behind the Christmas tree, and grabbed the big, flat present she had wrapped for him. "Be careful," she said, "it's fragile."

He tore into the paper and saw the beautiful portrait she'd taken of Tracy, sitting in Cathy's office with a kitten to her cheek. She'd had it set in an elaborate gold frame and matted with colors that matched his living room.

He was amazed. "When did you take this?"

"When you were camping with the boys," she said. "I just thought she looked so precious that I wanted you to have it."

The rims of his eyes reddened, and he leaned it back against the post. "Well, that just reinforces it."

"Reinforces what?"

He patted the space next to him. "Come sit down."

She plopped down on the couch.

"Now it's my turn," he said.

She closed her eyes. "I'll sit here patiently while you go to get it."

He shook his head. "You don't have to. I've been carrying it with me all day."

Her grin faded, and she opened her eyes. "Carrying what with you?" she asked.

He reached into his jeans pocket and closed his fist around it. "Now, if you don't want this, promise me you won't run screaming. Promise you'll still hang around with me, no hard feelings."

She couldn't imagine what it was. "Okay. I promise."

He opened his hand, revealing a diamond engagement ring. It took her breath away. Her face went slack. "Steve . . ."

"Cathy, I know it's not going to be easy with the kids and everything, and maybe we need a long engagement just to prepare everybody . . . but don't say no just yet."

She could feel the blood draining out of her face. "I wasn't going to say no. I was going to ask you if you were crazy."

He smiled. "I could say something hokey like, 'Crazy in love.' It would be the truth."

Her eyes sparkled. "Steve . . ." This time the word came on a rush of awe.

He kept talking, as if to prevent her from turning him down. "Plus I promised the boys that I wouldn't marry you until they were okay with it . . . but I never thought I'd feel like this again."

She swallowed the lump in her throat and blinked back the tears. "I never thought I would, either," she whispered.

His mouth trembled at the corners. "I love you, Cathy, and I want you to marry me. I realize we need to take it slow. There's a lot to work out. A lot to get ready for. A lot to prepare the kids for."

"You have no idea how much." She put her hand over her mouth and began to laugh softly. "You'd be getting the short end of the stick," she said. "You'd get all my kids, and you'd have to give so much more."

"And you'd get Tracy," he said, "and me. I'm as bad as three kids, at least."

She laughed, but then her expression melted into worry. "But are you sure it's not just the emotion of Christmas? The festive feeling? The sense of peace on earth and goodwill toward men? Turkey does have that chemical that gives you a sense of tranquility. Maybe it caused minor brain damage. Are you sure you want to commit right now?"

He laughed as if he couldn't believe she would suggest such a thing. "So I must be brain damaged if I want to marry you?"

"Well, yeah. I mean, this can't be real."

"Cathy, I've known you were the right one for me since last summer when we were going around putting out flyers on windows for Joseph. I want to marry you. I want to take you on with all your problems and all your kids. Will you even consider it?"

"Will I consider it?" She almost screamed with laughter. "Of course I'll consider it. Let's see." She tapped her face, pretending to consider it. "Okay, I've considered it. Yes!"

They both laughed as he slid the ring on. "Look at this ring!" she whispered. "It's so beautiful."

He pulled her into his arms and kissed her, and she found herself still chuckling as he did. It wasn't funny, not at all. But crying didn't seem right, and her emotions were overflowing. He was grinning, too, as they broke the kiss. They both crumbled into joyful laughter as they basked in the awareness of what they had just done.

CHAPTER
Sixty-Nine

In León, Sylvia was beginning to feel better about her time with the baby. God had brought her into her life for a reason, and maybe it had nothing to do with her. Maybe it *was* for the child, who needed someone to care for her while her mother was recovering. She knew she had been an instrument, and she had begun to feel thankful. But the depression didn't lift entirely until she got the phone call from her daughter in North Dakota.

"Mom, you're going to be a grandma."

"What?" she asked. "Sarah! You don't mean—"

"No, not yet," her daughter said. "I'm not pregnant yet. But we're ready to start a family. I wanted you to pray for us."

Her heart shot to the sky, and she realized that even though motherhood wasn't in her future, grandmotherhood might be, and that was an even better prospect.

"Harry!" she bellowed across the house. "Harry, come quick!"

Harry came running from the other room. "What?" he asked. "What's going on? What is it?"

"It's Sarah on the phone!"

"Is she hurt? Is everything okay?"

She was crying and laughing at the same time. "Oh, Harry, they want to start a family."

He began to laugh with relief that they weren't in a crisis. "See?" he said. "It's not over for us yet. God may have babies in our future."

Together, they hugged and laughed, and Sylvia felt energy and purpose seeping back into her body.

CHAPTER *Seventy*

The birth pangs began coming sooner than they were supposed to, in March instead of May. Tory prayed that they would stop, that the baby would have more time to grow and develop. But the contractions kept coming. She had been having the preparatory Braxton-Hicks contractions for the last two months, but these were different. Hard contractions racked her every ten minutes, ripping through Tory's back and cutting through her abdomen.

"We've got to get you to the hospital," Barry said.

"No, it's impossible! I'm not due for another two months. It's too soon."

"But Tory, you can't just hold it back. If you're in labor, the baby is going to come whether you want it to or not."

"I'm not going," she cried. "The baby is not ready."

But then her water broke and the contractions got closer together, and she knew there was nothing she could do to stop it. She heard Barry on the phone, talking to the doctor in a panicked voice.

He came running back through the house. Tory was in the clutches of a contraction.

"Honey, the doctor says you need to get in right away. He said that babies with Down's Syndrome are often premature."

"Not *this* early!" she shouted.

"Honey, there's a big danger of infection, since your water's broken. But if there's any hope of stopping the contractions, they can do it at the hospital, not here."

She grabbed his shirt. "Do you think they can stop them?"

"I don't know. But our baby's best chance is there. We have to go."

Finally she agreed to get up. She was drenched with perspiration. "What about the kids?" she asked.

"I already called Cathy," he said. "She and Annie are coming over to watch them."

She heard the door open and heard Cathy calling out. Tory made her way into the living room before she was kicked with another contraction. She leaned against the wall, her eyes squeezed shut.

"I've got to get her into the car," Barry said. "Help me, Cathy."

Cathy put one arm around her shoulders and Barry took the other and they carried Tory to the car. Annie stood back, watching, horrified. "That's it," the teenager said. "I am, like, never having children."

"Honey, you're going to be all right," Cathy told Tory. "Just hang in there. I'll call Brenda and she and I will be at the hospital soon. I'll let Annie take care of the kids."

Tory couldn't answer. Barry ran around the car and got in the driver's seat.

"Be careful, Barry," Cathy said. "Drive carefully."

He was anything but careful as he pulled out of the driveway, spinning his tires and burning rubber as he headed to the hospital.

It was a long night. Tory fought the pain for hours, begging and pleading with the doctors to stop the labor so the baby wouldn't be born too soon and die. She knew the baby already had too many battles to fight. She didn't want this to be one of them. Her lungs probably weren't fully developed, and her other major organs might be too weak to make it through.

But in her heart, she knew that the baby's time had come. Her water had broken, and the delivery was imminent.

Barry didn't leave her side. He stayed with her, sitting on the edge of the bed, mopping her face and helping her through the contractions. She drifted into a light sleep between pains, but on the edge of her consciousness she heard her husband praying over her.

"Lord, save the baby," he whispered. "Please don't let anything happen to it. I know I deserve it because of all the things I've said and all the things I've wanted. But if you'll let her pull through, I'll love her just like I love my other two. We'll fight all these battles together. Please, Lord, let the baby be born alive."

The prayer gave Tory the energy to fight and the peace to accept whatever was to come. She didn't know what God had in mind for them, whether it was something easy or terribly hard, whether it would take a lifetime of struggling or just the next few hours. She had no idea, but she gave it up to God as the contractions grew closer and closer together.

Concerned by something on the baby's heart monitor, the doctors decided to do a cesarean. She protested, afraid the anesthesia might hurt the child, but the doctors assured her it would be much easier on the baby than a normal delivery. When she finally consented, they wheeled Tory into the delivery room with Barry by her side. As the anesthesia began to take effect, Barry held her hand.

"What if God is going to punish me for what I've done?" he asked her. "What if he's going to give me what I wanted? What I was praying for? How could I have wanted my baby to die? Can he forget that?"

"If I can, he can," Tory said. "I don't have any forgiveness in me, except for what he gave me. And I've forgiven you." She took his hand and squeezed hard. "But the truth is, he'll have to forgive me, too. I've had so many awful thoughts go through my mind. Thoughts about what she'll look like, how embarrassed we'll be to take her in public . . ." Her voice broke off, and she sucked in a sob. "Oh, Lord, if you let her live, I won't be ashamed of her. I'll love her and treat her the way you treat me. Like a precious, beloved child who belongs to me."

"Me, too, Lord," Barry whispered, too overcome with emotion to get the words out clearly. "Oh, I'll teach her things and be patient with her, and I'll protect her like you protect me. I'll protect her from others . . . and from herself. I'll be a parent like you. Just please give me the chance."

Barry stayed beside her as they began to do the surgery, and when the baby was pulled free, Tory relaxed back into her pillow, holding her breath and listening for some sign that her baby was alive.

A team of doctors, nurses, and technicians surrounded the baby, and they hurried her across the room and began to work on her.

For several moments, there was silence, and Tory lay helpless on the table, clutching Barry's hand.

"Barry, is she alive?" she asked, looking up at him. He was straining to see between the people surrounding the child.

"I think so," he said. "She's blue, though."

She sat up and saw them working on her child, then suddenly a little fist punched up at the air, and the baby began to cry. Barry started to laugh, and Tory joined in, so overwhelmed with love that she couldn't believe there had ever been any question that this baby would be wanted.

He let go of her hand and went to the table where his little daughter lay. Tory saw the awe on his face as he beheld the child.

She heard the team discussing the baby's color, her sluggishness, her respiratory effort, her heart rate. As they worked on the baby, she realized that she had problems. She wasn't home free just yet. The doctors around Tory got between the child and her as they finished her sutures. Frustration climbed in her heart.

Barry came back to her side and bent over her. "Her heart rate is good," he said, taking her hand. "But she's having a hard time breathing, so they're giving her oxygen." He wiped the tear rolling down her temple.

The doctor moved, and she saw them putting the C-pap on the baby's tiny face. Quickly, they laid her in an incubator, while one of the nurses took her vital signs.

"Why are you putting her in there?" Tory asked. "Can't I hold her first?"

"No," the doctor said. "We need to get her under the radiant warmer. The box is a portable transport isolette. It's made of Plexiglas and has the warmer in it."

She watched as one of the nurses stuck an IV in the baby's umbilical cord while another held the bag. They closed the cover of the incubator. One nurse had her hands in the holes on the side and was listening to her heart rate as they wheeled the isolette out.

"Where are they taking her?"

"ICU," a nurse told her.

"But is she gonna be all right?" Barry asked. "Is this just routine, or is she in trouble?"

"It's not routine," the doctor said. "She's got some problems. Her lungs aren't quite developed. We'll have to evaluate her more before we know what else she needs."

Hours passed before they were allowed to see their baby, and Tory began to wonder if she would die before she had even gotten the chance to look into her face. When they finally brought Tory a wheelchair to take Barry and her to see the baby, they were both overcome with emotion. She weighed only three pounds, and lay limply on her back. A nurse explained the EKG leads were stuck to her chest, monitoring her heart. A saturation probe was attached to her foot, monitoring the oxygen concentration in her blood. The little two-prong Hudson C-Pap assisted with her breathing. A feeding tube threaded into her throat, keeping gas out. The sounds of bubbling and humming surrounded the isolette.

But through the machinery, Tory looked down at the baby she had expected to be ugly. Her ears were a little smaller than normal, a little lower, but she was the most beautiful baby she had ever seen. She reached through the hole and touched her daughter's little face.

An alarm bonged, startling Tory and Barry. The nurse began to adjust the machinery. "Too much stimulation causes an increase in her oxygen levels," she said. "It's best not to touch her until she's more stable."

Tory wept as they pulled her away to make room for the other nurses. She looked up at Barry and saw that he was weeping, too. He bent over and held her close. "She's so little," he cried. "How will she survive?"

Tory didn't know the answer, but she gave the problem to God, even as her heart broke over her child. But God knew about suffering children. He understood about a parent's grief. Back in the room, they prayed together some more, knowing that only God could help their little girl now.

When Barry was able, he went into the waiting room to tell Brenda and Cathy about his daughter. He let them go in to be with Tory for a while.

"I need to call David and tell him," Brenda said quietly. "He was really worried about that baby."

Barry stopped her. "I'll call him."

Brenda shot him a look, wondering if he meant it. "Really?"

"Yeah, really. Go on in."

When they were in the room, Barry went to a pay phone and dialed the number. David answered on the first ring. "Hello?"

"David, it's me, Barry."

"Barry, how are things going?"

"We're not sure," he said. "The baby's here. She's got some problems from coming so early. She's hooked up to every kind of gadget you can imagine."

"Like Joseph was."

"Yeah. Like Joseph." His voice broke off. "I thought I knew how you felt then, man. But I didn't have a clue."

"Is she . . . gonna make it? Are they giving any hope?"

"We're counting on it," he said. "She's beautiful, David. Down's Syndrome and all."

"I'm glad to hear that."

Barry swallowed and forced himself to go on. "Hey, David, I've been meaning to thank you."

"For what?"

"For shooting straight with me a few months ago," Barry said. "For being a friend."

Again, silence. "I'm a little surprised to hear you say that," he said finally. "In fact, I was surprised you called. I didn't think you and I would ever have a pleasant conversation again."

"Well, it just so happens that you were right that night. I should have told you months ago. You know, the message you gave me was the message of grace. It was a uniquely Christian message." He looked down at the buttons on the phone. "I know you still don't believe in Christ, and when you have examples of Christians like me running around, well, I can't say that I blame you. But I thought you should know that you've already got the basic concepts down. At this point, conversion would be a piece of cake."

David laughed softly. "Well, it's not like I don't have the background, but you know how it is. Faith is a hard thing for some people to grasp."

"I know it is," he said, "just like my faith that this baby was going to bring any good into our lives. But she made me a believer."

"Good for you," David said.

Later that day, Barry went home and got Brittany and Spencer, and took them to the hospital to see the baby. He found Tory in ICU next to the isolette, trying not to do anything that would set off an alarm.

Barry saw the look of awe in Brittany's and Spencer's faces, and wondered how he ever could have believed this baby had no value. Already he could see the impact on her older sister and brother.

"Isn't she beautiful?" Tory asked the children.

"She looks like a doll," Brittany said. "Can she move with all that stuff on her?"

"She moves her hands and feet," she said. "She can't cry with the feeding tube and oxygen, though."

"Can we get her some clothes?" Spencer asked.

"As soon as it's okay for her to wear them," Barry said.

"I can't wait to hold her," Brittany whispered with wonder.

Barry's eyes seemed to continually fill with mist these days, and he sat down and pulled Spencer onto his lap and Brittany against his side.

"This baby is very special," he told them. "She's not like other babies."

"Why not?" Spencer asked.

"She's just a little more delicate," Barry said. "She's going to need a lot of extra care and a lot of extra attention. She may not be quite as smart as you, or quite as big, or quite as healthy, but we're going to love her just like she is, and we're going to help her every day of her life."

"Is she gonna be like Uncle Nathan?" Brittany asked.

Barry was quiet for a moment. "Not quite like Uncle Nathan. She may be able to walk, and laugh and smile and talk. She just won't be able to do it as well as we do."

The children stared down at the baby as if trying to imagine what she might be like when she grew older. Then came the question.

"Why?" Spencer asked. "Why is she that way? Why did God send us a baby like that?"

Tory's eyes filled with tears, and she touched the baby's tiny hand. She swallowed the tears gathering in her throat. "God let us have a baby like this because he trusted us," she whispered. "He knew we were a family that could take care of her."

That made sense to Spencer, and he smiled and puffed out his little chest. "I can take care of her," he said. "I'm her big brother. Don't worry, Mommy. We won't let anything happen to her."

Brittany's ponytail bobbed as she nodded agreement. "That's right, Mommy. She'll be fine with us."

And Barry knew that it was true, that those words had come from the mouth of God, because their family was still intact. They were going to be all right.

CHAPTER
Seventy-One

Their home had never felt so empty as it did the day they brought Tory home without the baby. Barry had set the bassinet up in the corner of the master bedroom. Already he had begun getting estimates to add a new room onto their house. By the time the baby was old enough to have her own room, it would be ready. But right now, the family seemed to have a hole in it, because one of them wasn't home.

That night as they went to bed, he lay awake looking at the bassinet in the corner of the bedroom. "It feels strange without her," he whispered.

"Funny how a little tiny thing like that can wriggle her way into the family." Tory looked up at him with sad eyes. "Do you think she's going to make it?"

"She has to," Barry said. "She just has to."

He held Tory until she fell asleep. As she slept in his arms, he cried into the pillow and prayed again that God would forgive the choice he almost made. More than anything in his life, he wanted the baby to live.

They named the baby Hannah, after Tory's mother, and with each passing day, she grew strong enough to be weaned from another machine. The first time she held her, Tory's heart almost burst with the fierce love that overwhelmed her. Barry was so emotional that, when she handed Hannah to him, he almost fell apart. She didn't know if he would ever forgive himself for wanting to abort the baby.

When they finally brought her home after twelve weeks, it seemed as if the family was finally complete again. The neighbors of Cedar Circle set up a huge banner that said, "Welcome Home, Hannah!" That night, the children were happier than they'd been in weeks as Barry read them a story and put them to bed.

Then he went back to the bedroom where Tory had been feeding the baby. Hannah was asleep as Tory rocked back and forth, back and forth, the circles under her eyes dark from the hours she had been keeping.

He bent down and took the baby from her. "You need to get some sleep," he said. "Here, I'll take over for a while."

"You can lay her down," Tory said. "She'll sleep."

"No, I want to hold her," he said. "Go ahead. Get in bed."

She surrendered the baby and the rocker and climbed into bed, turned on her side, and watched her husband rock their new child. Her eyelids were heavy, and a sense of peace greater than she had ever known flooded through her. She had just about dozed off when she heard Barry singing.

"And he walks with me, and he talks with me, and he tells me I am his own . . ,"

She smiled as she remembered the story he had finally shared with her about the woman whose life Nathan had saved. Then, in a soft, soothing voice, he whispered to the baby, "You need to know about your Uncle Nathan and the lady who knows the Lord because of him."

And as the baby's eyes drifted closed, Barry softly began to tell her about his own brother who sat in his wheelchair, whistling tunes and touching lives without even knowing it.

"Some people think Nathan has a cursed life," Barry whispered to the baby, "but it just depends on whose eyes you're looking from, God's or man's."

He looked up at Tory, and saw her smiling at him from the bed. "You were right, you know."

"About what?" she asked.

"About the crisis being the miracle."

She looked down at the baby, knowing it was true. As imperfect as this baby was, she was perfect for their family, for this time in their lives.

As Tory drifted off to sleep to the tune of "In the Garden," she had the sweet, spiritual sense that they had, indeed, gotten the miracle they had prayed for.

Share Your Thoughts

With the Author: Your comments will be forwarded to the author when you send them to *zauthor@zondervan.com*.

With Zondervan: Submit your review of this book by writing to *zreview@zondervan.com*.

Free Online Resources at

www.zondervan.com

Zondervan AuthorTracker: Be notified whenever your favorite authors publish new books, go on tour, or post an update about what's happening in their lives at www.zondervan.com/authortracker.

Daily Bible Verses and Devotions: Enrich your life with daily Bible verses or devotions that help you start every morning focused on God. Visit www.zondervan.com/newsletters.

Free Email Publications: Sign up for newsletters on Christian living, academic resources, church ministry, fiction, children's resources, and more. Visit www.zondervan.com/newsletters.

Zondervan Bible Search: Find and compare Bible passages in a variety of translations at www.zondervanbiblesearch.com.

Other Benefits: Register yourself to receive online benefits like coupons and special offers, or to participate in research.

ZONDERVAN®

ZONDERVAN.com/
AUTHORTRACKER
follow your favorite authors